Dream Dancer

A Novel of Two Lands

By

S.J. Schwaidelson

In loving memory of
STEVE SIEGFRIED

CONTENTS

ACKNOWLEDGEMENTS

No book is created in a vacuum, and this one is no different. I have had support and encouragement from so many people along the way that listing them would be a second book. There are, however, some people who I need to thank aloud for their stalwart belief that this book would see the light of day.

First, Darin Murphy of CAA; he got the ball rolling so long ago, and for that I am forever grateful. Tracey Berse Simon, Joel Baskin, and Laurie N. Smith, are the unsung heroes of this process. I could not have finished this without their cheerleading.

Thanks go to Joan Naidish for riding to the rescue with a final editing markup, catching what these tired eyes could not longer see. Our mothers would be so happy.

The cover is the work of Sean Murphy of SMM Photography, St. Paul, Mn. A true renaissance man, Sean was the voice of *yes, you can! Yes, you can!* in my head. Every time I wanted to throw in the towel, he gave me a dozen reasons why he was not going to allow that to happen.

Eric Pasternack's determination to get this book up and out the door has been invaluable. He's the one who said "yeah, we can do this"…and he has. He's editor, critic, formatter-in-chief, mining expert, and general factotum. There is not a kinder person on the planet.

Last, but certainly not least, I must acknowledge the patience of two guys who lived through the creative process all the while humoring their mother who had conversations with characters. Misha and David, you are the best sons a writer could have.

WINTER IN PERU
SUMMER IN THE STATES
1988

CHAPTER 1

Leah stopped singing **Every Breath You Take** when she reached the fork in the path. Glancing up into the trees, she saw nothing unusual, but wondered who was watching out for her today. She pushed up her Twins cap and swiped her forehead with the back of her arm. Her t-shirt stuck to her skin, soaked through with perspiration. Rivulets trickled down her back; she squirmed against a growing pool of sweat at the waistband of her shorts. With a deep breath of hot, humid forest air, she reminded herself that had she been, at that very moment, back in Minnesota, she would most likely be freezing; instead of trotting through the forest, she would be stomping snow off her boots. *This,* she thought with a grin, *is certainly preferable to that.*

She peered down one path, then the other; her eyes could follow the trails only so far before they disappeared into the thick growth. Somewhere in the distance, she caught the low rumble of a big cat, probably the jaguar. *The* jaguar. The same one she always heard when she traversed this part of the forest. Over the months she had been there, Leah learned to differentiate between sounds. This sound was, in an odd way, comfortingly familiar. Hector told her about the cat: he belonged to the Mamacuna, was very well fed, and for all intents and purposes, rather tame. Although she had never seen him, she heard his deep, rumbly voice with great regularity. Leah suspected he kept his eye on her much the way the villagers kept their collective eye on her. She couldn't always see who was watching her movements through the forest, but she knew she was always watched. She didn't mind. "Okay, Hector," Leah said out loud, "where are the steles?" She looked down the path to the left, then checked the map again. "That's gotta be it," she muttered as she readjusted her pack.

എ ⊖ ൙

A chain of accidents, beginning almost twenty years earlier, brought Leah to this peaceful world. Dr. Hector Morales stumbled onto the people when he fled Trujillo after the great earthquake. He was permitted to stay because he convinced their high priestess he would not reveal where he found them. He remained there for three months before he felt ready to return to what was left of his home. There, he resumed his research on epidemiology, but every chance he had, he ran back to the forest.

In time, Hector found he could no longer divide his time between Trujillo and the people he had come to love. He closed up his laboratory, resigned from the hospital, and found the perfect place to perch a small clinic. From there, he could tend the people while keeping one foot in the modern world. He devoted his days to the clinic, but at night he worked in his little lab and wrote long papers on the transmission of tropical diseases. Despite his remote location, his reputation was growing almost as fast as his love of his work.

Hector was the only link between the people and the outside world. His clinic, an abandoned sheep ranch, sat on a ridge at the edge of the forest. The residents of the modern hamlet closest to the clinic knew some of what lay behind the curtain of green, but they wanted no part of that ghost world. Whatever the doctor did out there in the forest made them think he had spent too much time in the hot sun around his little house. Even the local padre had given up trying to convince Hector to keep out of the forest.

And that was fine with Hector. "Let them think what they want," he told those few who knew the truth, "all the more reason for them to stay out." Still, Hector knew the days of people staying out of this corner of the world were numbered. There were mining expeditions much too close for comfort as well drug cartels looking for prime coca growing land. Eventually they would find their way to this eyebrow of the world and his people would lose their home. It was simply a matter of time despite his trips to the capital to plead for the absolute conservation of the land. The outsiders would come.

Leah Fine was an outsider, but she was the kind of outsider he needed. As a doctoral candidate in anthropology, she would be able to record the people's world before it disappeared. She had written to him from the University of Minnesota after she read a brief article he'd written on folk medicine in an anthropological journal. From the moment she stepped from Paolo's silver bird onto the little landing strip near his house, he knew had made the right decision. She was everything he wanted her to be, and then some. She came speaking the language well enough to make the transition to the old dialect an easy one; she had an air of calm about her, of confidence and ease. He liked her from her letters, but he loved her in person. He had no hesitations at all when he walked her into the forest to the village where she would live for the next year. Leah had not disappointed him. Willingly, he gave her new keys to the kingdom every time she set a foot on his doorsill.

❧ ⊖ ❧

On Hector's advice, Leah was using this trip back to her ayllu for a little side research. Convinced that his charge understood the rain forest thoroughly, Hector offered Leah a chance to see something quite unusual and, as he expected, she jumped at the opportunity. Hidden deep within the forest were nine *huacas*, shrines, dedicated to *Mamaquilla*, the Moon Goddess who shared the Supreme Throne with her male counterpart, *Inti*, the Sun God, joining together to become Viracocha, the Great Faceless Deity.

"I've never made the pilgrimage myself since I am a man and it would be inappropriate," explained Hector when he gave her the map, "but you, a woman, can make the pilgrimage without desecrating the huacas."

Leah had heard about the huacas, but no one had offered to show them to her. All she knew was that they were hidden along the edge of the forest along the line where the forest gave way to the first foothills of the Andes. "I figured eventually I would ask Saba about them."

"Before you can ask, niña, you have to know what questions to ask. Saba didn't ask you to join her at the summer solstice, did she?"

Leah admitted she had not, much to her disappointment. She knew about *Janajpachallacta*, the Village of the Sky, where the Mamacuna and her council of sages lived apart from the ayllus. The major religious ceremonies were held there, including the two solstice ceremonies so central to the people's spiritual consciousness. Although she had hinted she wanted to go, Leah was told she could not even enter the stone village nestled in the mountain without an invitation from the Mamacuna herself.

"That was because you haven't made a pilgrimage," laughed Hector. "It's a sort of Catch-22, if you don't mind the reference. One cannot ask; it must be done in secret. Once you have made pilgrimage to the huacas, Saba will have no reason not to ask the *Qewa Ñawi* to the winter solstice, the big *Situa*, in June."`

Leah smiled at the use of her local nickname. Whenever he wanted to remind her she was still a guest of the people, he referred to her as *Grass Eyes.* "Okay, *janpeq*," she countered using his own nickname, "how long will it take?"

"Not long. If you leave here early tomorrow morning, you should reach your ayllu in three days, instead of the usual two."

Her smile lit up the darkest corners of his house. "Hector, you're on. Tell me what I have to know."

Suddenly, Leah spied the steles, almost completely overgrown by forest brush. The first marker on Hector's map, they stood between the path and a long deserted shrine to San Francisco de Assisi, left by monks of the last century. Three neglected, yet carefully mounded stone graves, probably belonging to the members of the order who perished in the forest, sat a few feet behind the weatherworn statue of Saint Francis. Leah paused long enough to take a swig from her canteen before she followed the path which the map indicated would lead to an arroyo.

❧ ⊖ ❧

The swiftness of the waters, coupled with the greenish color, told Leah this was no little creek, but rather a deep stream. She found a footpath on the rise above it, and followed the track for a couple of kilometers. The next marker was easy to spot: two carved monuments, far more ancient than the first set and clearly Chimu in design. Pulling the little Leica from her pocket, she photographed the pillars from all sides and then sketched the fine details in her black notebook. According to Hector, this was the gateway to the pilgrims' path.

The actual path ran between the steles and deeper into the forest. Leah stood quietly for a moment, studying the map and the position of the sun. Once beneath the green canopy, the sun would be obscured and she would be unable to judge the amount of remaining daylight. Her watch was helpful, but Leah knew just how quickly the forest became dark once the sun dipped behind the mountains. She estimated approximately four more hours of light before she should make camp for the night. Checking the map, she figured she could make it to the second huaca, where a secluded pool and waterfall would provide a safe campsite. With a quick tug on her pack, she was off.

❧ ⊖ ❧

Leah almost missed the first huaca. The small monument, cut from stone similar to that of the steles, was tucked several yards away from the footpath. It was a tiny break in the brush that caught her eye, for no actual marker was visible. Leah turned off the well-traveled track to follow the narrower one which soon became littered with the remains of recent offerings to Mamaquilla. Bright parrot feathers fastened together with colored threads, bowls of seed pods, and a few baskets of tiny eggs sat on either side of the path; Leah recognized them as the type of offerings new brides left for the Goddess to ensure quick conception. At the end, a small, intricate carving of a man and a woman standing side by side but not touching stood beside a mound of perfectly smooth stones. Leah photographed the huaca from all sides and sketched the things she knew her camera's eye would miss, careful not to touch any of the offerings. That would have been an act of sacrilege, and even if she thought she was alone, chances were, she was not.

Satisfied with her examination, Leah was about to leave, when suddenly something inside her prevented her from moving. She recalled one of the women in her ayllu told her a girl who believed she was being passed over for marriage could come to the Goddess and ask for help. If she left something precious to her at the huaca, Mamaquilla would intervene and a mate would appear.

If she listened to her mother, Leah was too long unmarried. Her parents were hopeful that the man she had been seeing in Minnesota would be the one to place a ring on her finger, but Leah put the relationship on hold before leaving for Peru. A romantic at heart, Leah decided to leave something for Mamaquilla, a token of her faith in the concept of God and God's power to answer prayer, whether it be from one of the people or from a nice Jewish girl so far from the nearest synagogue. As if on their own accord, Leah's fingers went to the flap of her breast pocket on which she wore a pair of silver birds, given to her by her Grandma Sophie for good luck. "Wear them every day," ordered Grandma, "and they will remind you your love for your family flies to them from wherever you are." She chose the one with the emerald eye, leaving its mate with the tiny sapphire eye in place.

Leah's step was lighter as she made her way from the first huaca toward the second. According to the map, it was only about three kilometers, an easy walk now that the path had widened significantly. She made good time, moving briskly as she listened to the sounds of the rain forest. The monkeys' chatter syncopated against constant birdcall created a natural symphony, always changing, never played the same way twice. Leah had come to love the music, appreciating the variety, always expecting the unexpected sound.

The light was fading when Leah caught the first whisper of rushing water. Its constant noise, not unlike that of an airplane far overhead, grew louder as she followed the footpath. As the map promised, there was a split in the trail. One led deeper into the forest, but the other, smaller path moved to the west, toward higher ground. Leah followed the western fork and soon, the dense brush gave way to an unexpected clearing bounded by the high cliff. The shrine sat at the precise place the forest abruptly stopped, but beyond that, at the end of a sheer rock wall, was a pool with the waterfall at the far end. It was too late to examine the huaca built at the end of the path; she would look at it in the morning. Skirting the sandy edge of the pool, Leah found a grassy spot in which to make camp for the night. A ring of blackened stone suggested someone else had done the same before her. She shucked her pack, took a few pictures, then decided there was more than enough time for a swim before settling in for the night. Quickly shedding all her clothes, she ran to the edge of the pool and dove in.

A dip was just what she needed and Leah emerged from the water refreshed and ready to set up camp. Because animals would come to the water to drink, she positioned herself closer to the waterfall, between the rock wall and the high grass but where she had a clear view of the pond. She spread her bedroll on the ground, and set about preparing something to eat from the supplies Hector had kindly provided.

Suddenly, Leah sensed she was not alone. Her eyes scanned the ridge above the pool, searching out what had disturbed her solitude. In the dusk, she almost missed him standing on a rocky ledge high above the pool. She watched as he stretched his arms forward, then brought them above his head in a slow, sweeping motion before he dove into the waters below. He reappeared in a moment, shaking the water from his dark hair, and swam toward where Leah was sitting behind the tall grass. At first, she thought she had been spotted, but he seemed not to notice her when he emerged. Leah could see him clearly in the last light of the day. His skin was burnished bronze. With high cheekbones, an aquiline nose, and eyes not as narrow as most, he was easily the tallest and most handsome man she had seen in the forest. His dark hair, wet and held back by a thin *llautu*, fell in soft waves, not perfectly straight like others of the people. Completely nude, his body was lean, yet powerfully built; the ridges of his muscles were visible as he moved. He stopped at the center of the sandy strip and faced the sheer rock wall across the pool. He stood there in perfect stillness, his face turned upward.

Leah, afraid to move, kept her eyes on his broad back. The last ray of sunlight disappeared, yet the man remained motionless. Her stomach rumbled, loud to her ears, and for a moment, she thought he might hear her. She crouched deeper in the grass, but kept her eyes on him. The full moon rose in the sky, bathing the pool and its visitor in pale, eerie light. Leah's legs were cramping and she was growing increasingly weary. She considered stretching out and just going to sleep right there in grass, but she dared not.

Then the woman appeared. Coming from the huaca, the woman approached the man. She wore a long cape that swayed gently as she took slow, rhythmic steps toward him. Her arms were extended forward and she carried a basket. When she had almost reached him, the man turned to face the woman.

The woman, her head bowed as though she were afraid to look upon him, dropped to her knees. Without looking up she placed the basket beside her. The cloak slipped from her shoulders as she raised her arms to the sides. Slowly, the man knelt in front of her, their knees almost touching, his arms extended to mirror hers. Their bodies came together and although Leah could not hear the words, she saw his lips moving near the woman's ear. The woman moved sinuously to unheard music and again, the man matched her, move for move. Gently he maneuvered her backward into the sand. His hands touched her flesh as he began to arouse her. He stroked her breasts, her belly and her thighs with great tenderness. Leah clearly heard a moan at the moment the man entered her.

Riveted, Leah watched with wide eyes as the man thrust deep into the woman. There was something, though, which struck Leah as odd about the act. At no time did his mouth take possession of the woman's; he never kissed her as a lover would. There was passion, yet no passion in their intercourse; it was as though it was a performance of some kind. Leah saw the woman arch against the man as she was brought near to her climax, yet her arms never clutched his body. Her hands never touched him; they remained in tight fisted balls at her side. The man's buttocks rose up and down with a pace obviously set to excite his partner; he seemed to be aware of what gave great pleasure. In silhouette, his throat stretched taut as he kept his face to the sky.

There was no denying her own arousal as she watched them from her hiding place. Far from being a dispassionate observer, Leah could feel her breath come in short gasps as the two on the sand raced toward climax. Heat infused her body; moisture seemed to seep down from within her and she could almost smell her own musk. Grasping at sharp bladed grasses beside her, she willed herself to be calm.

The man did not cry out at the moment of his release, but the birds in the surrounding trees knew. There were startled shrieks as the birds took flight. Leah's eyes flew upward and saw, amidst the flash of colored feathers, a single condor circling over the pool. Once, twice, three times the condor passed over the man and woman before it disappeared over the cliff. When she turned back to the man and woman on the sand, she saw the man roll off his mate, then kneel, arms outstretched toward the moon. Quickly, the woman rose and replaced the basket directly behind the man before she picked up her cape. She bowed low to him although his back was to her, then backed away from him, her fingers repeatedly touching her lips in the traditional sign of respect. At the edge of the sand, the woman swung her cape over her shoulders and fled.

Her rapid footfall soon faded and silence returned. Slowly, the man reached behind him and took the basket. Filling his hands with its contents, he stood and with jaguar grace, walked to the edge of the water. He called to Mamaquilla as he flung what looked like flower petals onto the surface of the pool. The man raised his arms to embrace the moon, paused, then dove head first into the dark water. Leah did not know where he went, but he did not reappear in the pool.

☙ ⊖ ❧

Unable to move, she sat for what seemed an eternity. Only when the forest was completely quiet again did she rise stiffly and walk back to the fire ring. With shaking hands, Leah managed to build a fire. She lit the tinder and sat back to watch the small flame tongues grow until they ignited the larger branches she had stacked. Too exhausted to eat, she slid into her bedroll.

Her night was filled with strange dreams of the man and the woman coupling on the sand. When the first rays of morning sun brushed her eyes, Leah was all too glad to awaken and leave the troubling images behind. The air was already heavy with the promise of another hot day, so once the fire was buried and her pack ready, she took advantage of the pool. The water was still cool, but the refreshing feeling of the place was gone. She did not linger in the water; instead she came out quickly, slipped on her shirt, and sat down to braid her long, dark hair. She was almost done when she realized she was no longer alone; she could sense the man's presence all around her. Afraid, she measured her breathing to keep the creeping sense of panic at bay while she continued to twine the tresses. She could not see him, but she could feel his eyes. Without excess of motion, she reached for her trousers and yelped when a hand shot out of the long grass to capture hers.

He pulled her to her feet and stood face to face with the grass-eyed woman, her wrist still trapped in his powerful fingers. The man was much taller than Leah realized; he towered over her. His broad chest was bare, but around his waist he wore a breechclout; a llama skin carry pouch hung from a colorful sash woven in intricate designs, the kind she had only seen on the most important of the people's leaders. Unlike some of the high-ranking men, this one wore no gold or other adornments, as though his body was enough without additional decoration. When he spoke, Leah could see white, even teeth behind finely sculpted full lips. His free hand gently raised her chin and his deep brown eyes probed her widened green ones. Leah could feel his breath on her face and felt heat growing from her belly. Suddenly embarrassed by her lack of clothing, she averted her eyes.

"Do you seek me, Qewa Ñawi?" he asked in the local dialect. His voice was low, soft in the cadence of the forest, making shivers run up and down her spine.

Leah was puzzled by the question. "Would I have reason to seek you?" she whispered in the same language, hoping her nerves were not betrayed by her quivering voice as she kept her eyes on her feet.

His laughter was a warm caress. "Are you in need of a baby to fill your arms?" he asked, hooking an elegant finger beneath her chin to draw back to him.

Leah's eyes flew open. She knew, in that one moment, he was the one who served Mamaquilla apart from all others. Any woman near this huaca would be seeking his help. Indeed, that was what she had witnessed the night before. "No!" she said sharply, instinctively trying to pull away. "I am bound to no man and I do not want a baby!"

"But you are alone and you have made an offering to Mamaquilla. She heard your prayer and sent you here... to me." With a small smile, he lifted her hand and turned it over. The man dropped the small silver bird with the emerald eye into her open palm. "Is this not yours?"

Leah stared at the pin. "This is mine," she murmured, "but it was meant for a time in the future, not now."

The man stared into her eyes until she turned away. "Is this the way of your people? To make prayers for days to come instead of this day?"

"Yes, this is the way of my people."

He considered her words for a silent moment. "You are not of our people, yet you speak with ease. Are you one of them?"

This time, Leah smiled; she understood his reference to "them," the missionaries with the strange god for whom the people had no use. They were not hated, but rather dismissed as fools with no understanding of the ways of the people. "I am not one of them, I am simply a seeker of knowledge. A *mulkan*."

When he released her hand, it was almost reluctantly. "Go on your way, Qewa Ñawi; no harm will come to you." As swiftly as he had appeared, he disappeared into the forest, leaving Leah breathless and shaken.

With trembling fingers, Leah managed to put on her trousers and boots. She could barely tie the laces and finally sat down in an attempt to regain her composure. If the man was unsettling, the gnawing sensation in the pit of her stomach was worse. His touch was flame, hot and frightening, arousing a part of Leah she had no wish to arouse. None of the stories about the *Aclla* had prepared her for the raw sensuality she experienced on meeting him face to face. With an indelicate snort, she told herself she knew why he had been chosen. The man exuded eroticism and it was no

wonder women sought him out. Her nerves steadied, Leah re-pinned the
little silver bird next to its mate on her pocket flap, hoisted her pack onto
her shoulders and marched, eyes forward, to the huaca close to the pool.

Ꮗ ◯ Ꮗ

This huaca was similar to the first, but the offerings left to Mamaquilla
were subtly different. Had she not been living in her ayllu for as long as
she had, she might not have recognized the nature of the offerings. On the
altar, a stone woman knelt, a bowl in her hands. In the bowl and around
the base, were a variety of foods, the traditional ones given to a woman who
had skipped a menstrual period, the first indication of incipient pregnancy.
Herbs used for tea to ease the nausea floated in clear water, as they would
when given to the hopeful woman. Leah was impressed with the eloquence
of the huaca and the offerings, touching her tenderly with its simplicity.

She took her pictures quickly, not wanting to linger where the Aclla
had been. Following the map, she progressed to the third huaca, keeping
one eye on the path, the other on the forest around her, convinced that he
was somewhere near.

From one huaca to the next, Leah moved at a good pace. Each huaca
was slightly different from the one preceding it, the offerings indicative of
each month of a pregnancy. At the third, around the base of an elegantly
carved woman with a slightly rounded belly, neatly folded packets of leaves
and moss, the type used at the time of menses, were scattered about, a
happy sign that they were, at least for the time being, of no use. When
a woman knew for certain she was with child, she would leave similar
packets in the doorway of her hut to tell her husband the joyous news.
On each new moon of the pregnancy, a woman would eat special foods
prepared by the local collahuaya, and each huaca reflected those changes.

Leah recorded what she saw, photographing and sketching at every
shrine. She lingered at some of the more complex sites, studying the elegant
simplicity with which the people addressed Mamaquilla. In all her mean-
dering, Leah did not see another soul. This was not unexpected; pilgrimage
was a private affair, not one to be shared, especially with a stranger. Since

the pilgrim was usually a woman whose prayers for a child had not been answered, there was a certain poignancy to the offerings.

By the time she reached the ninth huaca, Leah knew she would not make it back to her village by darkness. She did not really mind, for this was the largest of the huacas, with a stone building a few yards from the huaca itself. There was much to examine here and she was glad to have the rest of the afternoon in which to do it. The clearing surrounding the shrine showed evidence of others having camped there; Leah chose a spot to the side with a small fire ring and thick, tufted grasses on which to lay her bedroll. Shucking her pack, she wandered over to the shrine and its little house.

Leah smiled at the kinds of offerings left at the huaca. Beneath a stone statue of a woman holding a newborn infant at her breast, garlands of fragrant forest flowers about her neck, were small, simply fashioned toys, and tiny, delicate garments made from softened leather and finely woven alpaca wool, the type a newborn would be given for extra protection from the cool breezes of winter in the foothills. She longed to examine more closely the profusion of offerings, but good sense kept her from touching anything on or around the huaca.

The rough-hewn stone building beckoned to Leah. Inside, the walls had been made smooth with mud carried from the stream running nearby. Despite the heat outside, the room was cool, making Leah shiver when she first entered. Light filtered in from the door and several openings in the upper walls that served as windows. Leah took a sharp intake of breath once her eyes adjusted to the dimness and could see the drawings covering the walls. Endless pictures of rounded bellies and tiny figures filled the space, each with its own unique style. Pulling a penlight from her pocket, she studied each drawing, amazed at the finesse of the work unlike anything she had even encountered in the villages. There was an exquisite poignancy to the art, a capturing of joy and hope, longing and fulfillment. Yet in one corner, apart from the others, was the most tragic of all drawings. A clearly female form was drawn sitting against a stele, her arms upraised, a lifeless child laying across her lap. Leah felt tears sting her eyes as she leaned closer to study the picture. There was an element of universal sadness in the upturned face, yet it was the pain that only one who had lost a child could fully comprehend.

Light was quickly fading in the tiny temple. Going outside, Leah felt the first cool breeze she had felt in weeks as she went to her campsite to build a fire before eating the last of her provisions. With a grin, she thought how happy Rina would be when she returned to the ayllu the next day with a ravenous appetite. It was almost dark when she removed her boots and crawled between her covers. For a few minutes she tossed and turned, finally deciding she was not quite ready for sleep. Reaching over to her pack, she pulled out a spy novel Hector had lent her back at the clinic. "Nothing like a good book to put you to sleep," she said aloud although there was no one to hear. The fire provided just enough light and with her head on her pack, she read until she drifted off, the paperback still in her hand.

Leah slept soundly, but her dreams were filled with the man at the pool. He danced *taqui*, the slow ceremonial dance, around her as she stood near the pool. When he stopped, his dark eyes bore into hers; she felt his breath on her face, the scent of him as sweet as the forest flowers around the huaca. In the dream, he did not hold her, but kissed her eyes, the tip of her nose, and finally her mouth. His hand caressed her breast, causing a fire to ignite in the pit of her belly. Stirring, Leah moaned, only to hear low, gentle laughter traverse the span of her dream. For a moment, her eyes fluttered open, only to be met by dark brown ones, inches from her face, the glowing embers of her campfire reflected in their depths. She tried to open her mouth, but his finger sealed her lips. The specter brushed a kiss against her cheek, then dissipated. In the frail light of dawn, Leah reassured herself it had been nothing but a dream and drifted back to sleep.

When she awoke, the birds were noisy in the trees and the sun was already high. Jumping up, Leah quickly stamped out the last of the dying embers and rolled her gear. She checked her campsite for any debris she might have left, and spotted her pen light on the ground beside her pack. As she slipped it into her pocket, her hand froze. One of the silver birds was missing. Certain it had been there the night before, she searched the grass around where she had slept to no avail. Leah pulled on the pocket flap until she could see it and noticed the one that was missing was the one she had left at the huaca, the one with the tiny emerald eye. She told herself it must have fallen off, but somehow, she didn't quite believe it. Something inside told her the dream was not completely a dream.

ↄ ⊖ ∾

The hike to the ayllu took Leah through areas she knew fairly well. When she stopped to drink from her canteen, she caught sight of two faces peering down at her from the branches of a tree. "*Yau!* I see you!" called Leah, happy to be within playing distance of her ayllu. The little boys giggled and tumbled from their hiding place with shouts of glee to welcome her back. With her two young escorts, the rest of the way seemed short and Leah caught herself thinking, *it's great to be home.*

They arrived in time for the midday meal. Women were already gathered at the central fire preparing food for those who were working in the fields. This ayllu was not large, with only twenty or so families living a co-operative, pastoral life. A peaceful people, they kept to themselves and as far away from civilization as they could, preferring to live as their ancestors had lived. There was the occasional raid by another tribe from the east, and infrequent visitation from stouthearted missionaries who tripped across their location by chance, but generally, they existed within the larger framework of their isolated tribe, sharing ceremonies and events with the other ayllus like their own scattered throughout that remote corner of the rain forest.

Warm shouts of *Yau! Allinllanchu!* greeted Leah as she walked into the tiny village. They were used to her now; the questions she asked were answered with good-natured teasing. They included her in most aspects of tribal life and kept an eye on her when she insisted on wandering about the forests. They called her by name and some even managed to say anthropologist, although it was usually accompanied with gales of laughter at the strangeness of the word. The children loved her stories, eager to hear tales far removed from those their parents told. On cool winter nights when they would gather around the central fire, Leah would take her turn at storytelling. She told grand tales about noble ladies who slept for a hundred years only to be awakened by the kiss of a handsome warrior. Once, in an unguarded moment, Leah had complained that she missed having a desk and chair. There was no word in their dialect to describe exactly what a desk was, but when pressed, she drew a picture in the dirt. When she had returned from a trip into the forest, she found a crudely made, but perfectly functional desk and stool in her hut. Touched by the gesture, Leah invited all interested parties to try sitting at the desk. Most thought it a bit strange, but it would not have been polite to mention it. Since then, she had lashed together a frame bed and a nightstand under the watchful eye of the village craftsmen who judiciously nodded when she wrapped the vines right.

Leah went directly to her hut; she wanted to shuck the pack and change into cooler, more comfortable clothing before going to see Saba, the *collahuaya*, to tell her about her pilgrimage. Although she often wished she could walk about in the same similar state of undress as the local women, her inbred sense of modesty won out. She settled for a clean pair of shorts and a polo shirt, and replaced her hiking boots with leather sneakers. No sooner had she tied the laces when the light coming in from the door was blocked. A woman stood there, arms akimbo, waiting to be invited all the way in. Leah noticed the downward turn of the mouth and figured she was in trouble for something. "Come in and sit down, Rina," she offered brightly, hoping to diffuse Rina's anger, as she often could, with a smile.

"We would have worried more had the janpeq not sent a chasqui for you, Li-ah."

"A chasqui?" echoed Leah. She had left Hector only two days before; it was most unusual to send a runner so soon. Unless, of course, it was an emergency. "Where is he now?"

"Sleeping. He arrived late last night and told us you were making pilgrimage." There was an element of disbelief in Rina's voice. "Is this true?"

Leah nodded. "I made pilgrimage to learn how Mamaquilla was served by those in need." She hoped she had not offended her friend by visiting the huacas without first asking permission. For a moment, she considered asking her about the man at the pool, but she quickly dismissed the idea. Instead, she asked, "Did the chasqui leave a packet?"

Rina pointed to a leather pouch on the bed. "He says he will wait for an answer to take to the janpeq."

Unnoticed when she came in, Leah now opened the bag and withdrew a single sheet of paper. She read it quickly, paled, and sat down with a thump. The older woman immediately sat down beside Leah and waited until she put the paper aside to speak. "The janpeq has sent bad news, Li-ah?"

She didn't answer right away; she just stared at the paper. Finally, she remembered Rina was standing there. "Sad news, but not unexpected," she sighed. "My grandmother died on the night of the last full moon."

Rina was puzzled. Leah's people were many, many days away, but the last full moon was but three days ago. How could she have gotten the news so fast? There were things about this woman she did not understand and how she knew of events in the outside world was one of them.

Leah guessed what the Indian woman was thinking. "The janpeq talked on the talking box to my father the night of the day I left him." Rina, she was certain, had heard tales of the talking box Hector kept in his house. She read the message aloud, slowly translating the painful words. "Your father called tonight, Sunday, twelve January, to tell you of the passing of Grandma Sophie. She died peacefully, in her sleep, while at the home of your Aunt Esther. Funeral set for Monday, thirteen January. He says: 'We wish you could be with us, but we understand. Grandma was very proud of you and your work.' He sends love from your mother, brother and sister and rest of family." Leah paused, smiling sadly at Rina. "My grandmother was not well."

"Was she very aged?"

"Yes, very," replied Leah. "She had seen one and ninety summers, Rina, and that is very, very old, even by our counting.

Impressed, Rina remained silent for a moment. "Was she a happy woman?" she asked quietly.

Since a woman's happiness was measured by the number of descendants, Leah quickly recounted her grandmother's progeny for Rina's benefit. "She had ten grandchildren, of which I am the youngest, fifteen great-grandchildren, and two great-great grandchildren."

"A very happy woman, I think," offered Rina. Few of their tribe lived more than sixty summers and to have great-great grandchildren seemed an impossible feat. "What will you do to mark her death?" Rina asked gently.

"The laws of my people have no rules for grandchildren, but I will say prayers for her. I will remember her in my heart every day." She was not up to explaining all the laws and customs that would seem so strange to Rina. Hector had closed his note to Leah with a promise to forward any message she had for her family. She explained this to Rina and when her friend left, Leah sat at her desk and wrote out the words Hector would relay to her grieving family in New York. This was just one more time she was thankful Hector spoke fluent English.

Leah moved through the rest of the day quietly, staying close to her hut instead of involving herself in routine village chores. Everyone now knew about her loss and several of the women stopped by to offer their condolences. When Hector's runner awoke, she gave him the courier pouch and sent him on his way. Returning to her hut, she told herself she had notes to assemble; work on her ethnography was behind schedule and needed attention. Never before had Leah felt so isolated from her family. In her mind's eyes she envisioned them gathered at the cemetery, then at her aunt's house where seven days of mourning were taking place at that very moment. She could see her brother and sister sitting together on Aunt Esther's blue chintz sofa, speaking in hushed tones, her cousins and their children standing around in small groups. She yearned to be there, sharing the grief her mother most surely felt.

As she sat there making feeble attempts to work, more women stopped by to express their sympathy and remind their pale friend that her grandmother had been amply blessed. After all, they told Leah, the old woman had seen many generations and this was a mark of great favor from Mamaquilla. It was all right to grieve, but Li-ah must also celebrate the good fortune of having sprung from this great woman's womb in a line of daughters. In keeping with mourning tradition, Rina brought the evening meal to Leah before the others in the village ate. One in mourning was excused from the communal meal, but later, when the sun had disappeared from the sky, she would be escorted to the central fire, seated in a place of honor, and there, she would be obligated to recount the triumphs of her grandmother's life. Leah was touched by their desire to count her amongst their own by calling a mourner's circle for her, and graciously accepted the offer. Rina brought her a tunic of grey vicuña wool, the one she had worn when her own mother had died, telling Leah she could choose to wear it in the circle as a sign of mourning.

∝ ⊖ ⌒

When the fire was ready and the villagers gathered, the women came to Leah's hut. They sang songs of praise for a good woman as they walked to the fire, then took their places with their own families only when Leah was seated. Saba, their collahuaya, intoned prayers of swift passage for the woman So-Fi, and then spoke of the natural cycle of birth, family and death. When she finished, Rina's own little girls, Pia and Hua presented Leah with a basket of cooked eggs, symbolic of life's constant renewal. She accepted the eggs, understanding it was her cue to speak.

"In the tradition of my people," began Leah, her voice quivering with emotion, "eggs are given to mourners just as they are given here. Even though we are from very different places, some things are shared by all people. My grandmother was very important in my life; she was the cord that bound us all together. When I went to study far from my home, she encouraged me. When I wanted to come here to live with you, I was afraid to tell her for I thought she would not understand why I wanted to come, but I was wrong. She hugged me and kissed me and told me to do the things I wanted to do..." Leah grinned, then added, "and then come home, get married, and have babies." Her audience laughed with her, understanding all mothers say the same things to their daughters. "My grandmother had great strength, great patience, and was a great cook. She made things for us to eat that only she could make." Thus Leah began to recount the nature of her grandmother's life. She told them of the pogroms in Russia, how Sophie had left her own country to travel over great water to settle in the place from which Leah had come; how she worked to help support her family when times were hard, how she had four children who grew to be good, happy people. Although she had spoken of life in America before, this was the first time Leah provided a detailed description of her own family. Some of the things were so far removed from the life in the ayllu, the listeners could scarcely believe her words. Others, they knew to be true, for the relationships between people are basically the same wherever one lives. Long into the night Leah spoke, until the last log on the fire fell, causing sparks to fly up into the blackened sky, signaling the end of the mourner's circle. Leah completed her tale, then sat quietly as one by one, the villagers filed past her murmuring words of condolence. When it was over, the women led Leah back to her hut and bid her goodnight.

Lying on the makeshift bed, Leah could not sleep. She was not in the mood to work, nor was she able to just lie there in the dark. Suddenly, she remembered the novel Hector had given her and decided to read. She fumbled for matches in the dark, found them and lit the wick of her camping lantern. The book was not on her desk, so she checked the front pocket of her pack. It was not there. Leah searched the folds of her sleeping bag, thinking perhaps she had rolled it inside that morning, but it was nowhere to be found. Annoyed with herself for having lost it, Leah blew out the lantern and crawled back into bed. She lay there for a long while, listening to the sounds of the forest. Closing her eyes, she tried to hear her grandmother's voice. She would miss that thick, accented English, the odd way she constructed a sentence, the distinctive laugh. There would be no one who would say to her "Don' do dat!" when she licked the tip of a knife. Grandma wouldn't be there to cry, "Dot's vhat you tink?" when she provided a silly answer to a serious question. She would miss the way Grandma's eyebrows shot up when she was surprised, and she would miss that cool hand on her arm whenever they crossed a street together. Leah didn't feel the tears on her cheeks as much as she felt the aching, vacant space in her heart.

CHAPTER 2

S trange dreams chased Leah from one end of the netherworld to the other.

She stood with her grandmother at the corner of Fifth Avenue and Fifty-Ninth Street, waiting for the light to change. Leah was little, wearing the navy blue coat and matching hat Grandma Sophie picked out for her at Macy's, and white cotton gloves. On the other side of the street, in front of the Plaza Hotel, she could see her mother and father. Although she waved to them, they did not see her.

"You study hard," instructed Grandma Sophie, "Dis is vhat's important. You study hard."

"I want to go to Mommy and Daddy, Grandma. Can we go there?"

The corner was crowded with pedestrians. The light changed; Grandma Sophie, holding Leah's hand, marched into the crosswalk. In the middle of the street, with car horns honking all around, Grandma faded away. Leah stood alone in the street.

"Don't go away, Grandma! Don't leave me here! I'm scared! I'm scared!"

No one took notice of the little girl in the blue coat; they just streamed past her. The tidal wave of people pushed Leah forward to the curb.

"Mommy! Mommy!" Leah tried to find their faces in the crowd in front of the hotel, but they, too, were gone and the Plaza was fast disappearing into the mist. "Mommy! Mommy!" she cried, and still, no one stopped to help the little girl.

She was jostled and spun around. She caught her reflection in Berg-dorf Goodman's window. Gone was the little girl in the blue coat, re-placed by Leah as she was in college: taller, slender, blue jeaned, and serious. Her sweatshirt had emblazoned across the front. In her hands, she carried an old, yellowed notebook. A page fell to the sidewalk. Leah looked at spidery Yiddish script, but she could not make out the words. She bent to pick it up, but a gust of wind carried the page aloft. Her eyes followed the sheaf.

The page floated above the fountain toward what should have been Central Park, but the park was gone. Dense jungle replaced the familiar path to the zoo. The ordinary sounds of New York City faded from her ears and she heard the chattering of monkeys and the sharp cry of a condor.

The throng of pedestrians still moved just as they always did in Manhattan, purposefully, without taking notice of anything. Leah began to ask strangers if they noticed that Central Park had disap-peared. They looked at her as though she were mad, but did not answer. A man emerged from the dense growth and moved swiftly in her direc-tion. Leah bolted, but he was too fast for her. He caught her before she reached the Fifty-Eighth Street. He captured her in strong arms and pinned her against his chest before covering her face with soft, butterfly kisses. When she protested, he laughed. She sighed and sagged against him, powerless to stop this assault; he whispered words she did not un-derstand into the shell of her ear. A moan escaped her lips; he laughed again as he kissed her ear and the smooth column of her throat. Leah tried to twist away, to see who did this to her, but she could not glimpse his face. She struggled, he laughed once more before he, too, faded away. A bright blue feather fluttered to the ground at her feet.

Leah bolted upright in her bed, her body drenched with sweat. Her heart was pounding; the images had been so vivid, so real. Frightened, she got out of bed and lit the lantern. Familiar shadows on the thatched walls helped to calm her nerves, reassuring her everything was as it should be. Unwilling to go back to bed, Leah decided to work for a while. She was about to sit at her desk when she stopped short. In the middle of the rough-hewn surface, atop her black notebook, sat the novel Hector had given her. Tucked into the pages was a single, bright blue parrot feather.

Leah removed the feather and cradled it in her palm. The dream, she understood, was not completely a dream. The feeling of fear dissipated, leaving her with an odd sense of security and protection. Only one person could have done this; only one person would have found the book. For whatever reasons, the Aclla had come to her.

With the morning came the resumption of normal life for Leah in the ayllu. She had promised Saba she would read aloud from an article Hector brought the last time he visited the village. Since her arrival, he had used her as an educational tool, sending information he would not have been able to take the time to translate so Leah could read it to the local *janpeqs*. Saba, the village's priestess cum healer, was not opposed to learning better ways so long as they did not interfere with the traditions. Leah treasured her time with Saba; she was an open woman, eager to teach the traditional ways to someone with an honest interest and no desire to change them.

The collahuaya sat outside her hut waiting for Leah. Set apart from the others, Saba's hut was a larger, more formal structure as befitting her status. Only the hut of Mayta, their headman, was bigger, but his included the council room where the elders met. Saba's extra room provided space for the shelves holding her many supplies. Leah loved the way Hector's bottles and boxes sat companionably on the shelves with Saba's clay jars of leaves, herbs, roots, and medicinal mud.

On the ground beside her, Saba had laid out a sitting mat for Leah as well as a pot of special herb refresher tea she had prepared for the occasion. She considered herself very lucky to have a reader amongst her people, if only for a short time. This meant she could learn things without the pressure of the janpeq's busy schedule.

"The day is half gone, lazy woman!" called Saba as her guest approached. "We have many leaves to learn and I have many questions for you today!"

"And I have many questions for you, too, Mama Saba!" replied Leah with a smile. She would, when the time was right, ask about the altars and the Aclla. Settling herself on the mat, Leah began translating the text into a language Saba could understand.

∾ ⊖ ∾

At midday, Leah and Saba took a break to eat lunch. As was the custom, two children brought the meal to the collahuaya, with more than enough for her to share with her guest. Saba thanked them, rewarding the little bearers with tiny bananas she produced from the pouch tied at her waist. The older woman took what she wanted from the grass basket, and passed it to Leah. She watched carefully as Leah chose a modest selection of cooked potatoes and fruit. Long ago she had learned there was no point in complaining about Leah's appetite; she was worse than some of the children in her pickiness, but the Qewa Ñawi had not wasted away as she had predicted and, according to the janpeq, she had only grown more beautiful by outside standards. Still, the slight clucking of her tongue was not lost on her guest who acknowledged the gentle chide.

Leah politely waited for Saba to pick the topic of friendly conversation. As an old woman, not to mention religious expert, it was Saba's right to initiate conversation. She could only imagine what the collahuaya would choose on this day. Sometimes she asked about the world beyond the mountains, other times she lectured Leah on the customs and history of the people. It would have been bad manners for the younger woman to speak first.

"Did you pass an easy night?" asked Saba gently.

"I had strange dreams," Leah answered honestly.

"That is to be expected on the night of mourning, Li-Ah. Those dreams are messages to you from your grandmother."

"If those were messages from Grandma," Leah snorted, "I'm worried."

Saba studied her young friend for a moment. "Now that the woman So-Fi is on the other side, she will be able to guide you with knowledge she did not have before. She will see more and tell you more."

"You think so?" asked Leah honestly.

Saba nodded slowly. "You honored her with your words, Li-Ah. Any mother would have been made proud by your recounting." She paused for a moment. "You did well last night, Li-ah. We learned much about your people, things you have never spoken of and thoughts you have never shared. You are always the one to ask the questions, but last night, you answered many questions we had about you." Saba waited for Leah's response; she knew she had surprised her.

And Leah was surprised. It was a very personal comment from Saba, the kind the people never made outside their own families. "Thank you for your words of praise, Mama Saba," said Leah modestly. "Perhaps now people will be more comfortable talking to me now that I have shown something from inside."

"Ai!" cackled the old woman. "You are sharper than I thought. For two seasons I have watched you amongst our people and I have wondered if you would catch on. We are not so secretive as you once thought, are we, Li-ah? We are merely cautious in the ways we share."

Some of those ways were indeed a mystery to Leah even after her months in the ayllu. There were protocols in conversation, dining, and even sitting. The final word always rested with the collahuaya and the headman; often they conferred before they concurred. In other villages, Leah heard the leaders could be stuffy and difficult, but in their village, Saba and Mayta were easygoing and definitely more interested in the welfare of their people than personal gain. Mayta had taken a good deal of flak from other local *capacs* about the pale lady living in their midst, but he dismissed their criticism with a shrug; they had benefited from Leah's sojourn. Since Saba had broached the subject of secrecy, Leah felt she had the opening she desired to ask the questions.

"You honor me with your candor, Mama Saba," said Leah with a smile. "I hope, since you understand my thirst for your wisdom, you would teach me more of your ways."

Saba considered the request, chewing on the end of a root as she watched Leah's eyes. "Ask your questions, Li-ah, and I will decide if I shall answer them."

With a deep breath, Leah launched into the topic of fertility rites. She recounted to Saba what she already knew about the public rites before asking about the ceremonies performed in privacy at the solstice gathering to which Leah had not been invited.

"You ask about the most sacred of all ceremonies, huahuan," replied the priestess. "No one from outside the people is permitted to know those secrets."

"Am I wrong to ask?"

Saba cackled, her smile splitting her nut-brown face. "No, you are never wrong to ask, Li-ah, especially since you have already made pilgrimage to the huacas of the Mamaquilla." She already knew in her heart Leah had encountered the Aclla at the pool; it would serve no use to hide the truth from her. "I will tell you, however, that you are not asking the questions in your heart, Li-ah; you are dancing taqui around a false fire." Leah's knitted brows spoke volumes to the old woman. "The things you wish to know have less to do with the rites of child bearing; you wish to know about those women who cannot conceive."

Leah bowed her head, hoping Saba would not detect the creeping redness on her cheeks. "This is a true thing, Mama Saba," she stammered. "If you choose not to tell me, I will ask no more."

Taking the young adventurer's hand into her own, Saba patted it kindly. "You have seen the one who would not be seen; you have spoken to the one who will not speak. Do not be ashamed, Li-ah, for he has chosen you to see and hear him." She could see the confusion in the grass green eyes. "The aclla comes to be in a way shrouded in mystery and ancient rites. Long ago, when the Inca Capacs ruled over us, maidens were called to serve Inti...and sometimes the Inca himself," she added with a meaningful glance. "In the old way, a girl chosen to serve would be called an aclla. But, *huahuan*, those days are long gone and with them the ways of the Inca." There was no small measure of disgust in Saba's voice each time she mentioned the old ruling class. "When the people left to return to our old ways, the Mamacuna Rahua, may her name be recalled with joy, said the ways of the Inca were an abomination. She taught us the way to honor Viracocha was to honor Mamaquilla and Inti. We chose the path of Mamaquilla and this path kept us safe. In the days of the Mamacuna Tocto, may her name be recalled with wisdom, we were taught an aclla was called to serve Mamaquilla because of purity of heart. Mamaquilla does not see male nor female; Mamaquilla only sees what is here, inside." She thumped the center of her chest for emphasis. "But in the days of the Mamacuna Cahua, may her name be recalled with devotion, it came to pass that there was barrenness amongst the women. The Mamacuna prayed and fasted and offered endless sacrifices to Mamaquilla. It was only when she read the *jonchi* on the night of the *Huayara*, did she understand that one youth could find favor with Mamaquilla and open closed wombs. The one who is the one is chosen by Mamaquilla Herself, and he is declared Aclla."

"Is there always an aclla?" asked Leah.

"No. We have gone for many cycles of the sun without an aclla amongst us. Each time an aclla leaves his *mita* to return to the world, the search for one favored by Mamaquilla begins anew."

"How are they chosen, Mama Saba?"

Saba leaned against the wall of her hut and smiled. No one outside of the people had been told the ways of the *Rimoc*, but Li-ah, she was certain, would not abuse the knowledge she was about to receive. "When there is no aclla, the Rimoc observe boys on the edge of manhood. They watch the youths and as the time approaches for the manhood ceremony in the month of Capac Raimi, a single youth is tapped by the Mamacuna's own chasqui. Because he is apart to prepare for his manhood ceremony, he leaves his meditations unnoticed and goes to the Janajllacta. It happens when one least expects it, Li-ah. At the *situa*, the young man and *chinan* of good reputation represent the Earth and the Sky. This you already know." She related in great detail how they are treated as a king and his queen, like those of olden times, living for a time in the Janajllacta, on the mountainside where the Rimoc, the mystics of the people, lived apart from the other villages. "On the night of the solstice," explained Saba in hushed tones, "they lie together but do not couple beneath the stars. We believe that if the Goddess is pleased with her symbols on Earth, the year will be plentiful for us."

"How can you tell if Mamaquilla is pleased, Mama Saba?" asked Leah, so enthralled by the tale she had long ceased taking notes.

"There are many signs, if you know what to look for. The first, and most obvious, is the color of the sunrise. If it is grey and misty, the rains will be plentiful, maybe too much, and the people prepare for this. If the sky is pink with rows of clouds, it means the fields shall flourish. If the clouds are in many puffs scattered in the sky, there will be many children. If there is rain and the sun cannot be seen, it means there will be trouble for the people. But if, when the sun rises, there is a halo with the points of a star, an event of great importance will occur. We do not know what the event shall be, but it shall be of concern to all of us."

"But how does the youth become the Aclla?" Leah pressed, her curiosity piqued.

Saba smiled, her face radiant at the thought. "The youth is sent to the huaca by the pool to spend his time in meditation. Within the space of the next full moon, a barren woman seeks him out, and, should she be with child after he intercedes on her behalf, he is given the mantle of *kuntar* and is hailed as Aclla." Saba leaned back, letting the impact of her words fall on Leah. "What you saw at the pool was a barren woman seeking to open her womb, may Mamaquilla have compassion on her."

Leah's mind raced with questions; she tried to put them in an order which Saba could answer logically for her. This Aclla, the old woman said, was extremely powerful. He was known to have visions that the current Mamacuna viewed as most important. He saw things in the sacred smoke others did not see, and when he spoke, even the eldest of the Rimoc listened carefully to his words. But what made him powerful was his ability to speak with Mamaquilla and have his prayers answered. Many babies were born because, believed Saba fiercely, he had asked Mamaquilla to make them born. While he served as Aclla, the man lived alone, away from the routine demands of living in an ayllu. His thoughts and prayers must be untouched by the mundane activities of village life. The people saw to it offerings of food were left for him and in return, he appeared at Janajllacta whenever he was summoned.

"If he is permitted no contact with others," asked Leah, "how does she send for him?"

""You must ask her, Li-Ah," laughed Saba.

"How can I ask the Mamacuna if I am not permitted entry to Janajllacta?" Leah smiled slowly. "Or is it now that I know the questions I will be given permission?"

"Good, good, Li-ah, you divine the things I do not tell you!" cackled Saba with glee. "You have answered your own question, huahuan."

Leah felt inordinately pleased with herself; she knew Saba would answer at least some of her questions. "What about the children, Mama Saba? Are they sacred?"

"If there are children given by Mamaquilla, they must serve their mita in the Janajllacta for one year when they reach the coming of age," she answered, "and when the time comes for them to marry, the choice of a mate is most carefully made. But we can go for years and years without an aclla amongst us. In fact," she whispered as she leaned forward, "until this one, there had been no Aclla since I was a young girl."

"What happens to the Aclla...I mean, does he spend his entire life away from all others?" asked Leah, inexplicably concerned about the fate of the man at the pool.

"Oh, no!" chortled Saba, "at some point, like any young man, he sees a girl who interests him and, when the time is right, he may declare for her. Assuming her parents approve the match, they are made as one as any young couple. "

"And they just settle down in an ayllu somewhere and no one is any the wiser?"

Saba nodded gravely. "Never is it mentioned that he was the one, but when the time comes for the children of that union to find a mate, there are, obviously, some restrictions; there can be no chance that his children are permitted to marry with the children who were given to us by Mamaquilla. That would be bad fortune. The sons and daughters of one who was Aclla are encouraged to match early with suitable mates. You know," teased the old woman, "how *that* is done."

Leah knew well how a young woman was courted; for a fleeting moment she wondered if the Aclla's nocturnal visits had been his first attempts at courting her. The thought made her shiver despite the heat of the afternoon.

Saba saw the far-away look in Leah's eyes and she did not have to be told what the young woman was thinking. "Did you see him?" she probed gently. "Did he see you?"

Leah nodded.

"This would explain your strange dreams, Li-Ah," she said in a most matter-of-fact tone. "Do not worry about this; in time you will come to understand what you need to understand. And what you do not understand will be of no importance." She paused to let her words be considered. "Enough of this," grinned Saba, bringing her young friend back to the moment. "We have work to do. Read to me the papers the janpeq has sent."

The rest of the afternoon passed quickly for Leah as she lost herself in her translating for the aging priestess. By the time the aroma of the evening meal reached them, both Saba and Leah were ready to quit for the day.

CHAPTER 3

The Aclla waited at the edge of the forest until Hector bid his last patient of the day farewell. The sun had already disappeared behind the cordillera and the cool air felt good after the unbearable heat of the long afternoon. He saw the janpeq go into his stone house and when the glow of a lamp shone through the window, the Aclla approached.

Hector was not surprised when his unexpected guest materialized in the doorway. He smiled and waited until the young man took the chair opposite him at the table. Without being asked, the doctor filled a cup with homemade beer and slid it across the table. The Aclla raised the cup and drank its contents before returning the doctor's smile. Only then did Hector ask, "What brings you to my humble house tonight?"

"Questions, Hector," he replied easily in Spanish.

Hector laughed and filled his own cup. "Always the same. What questions have you today, my potent young friend?"

"Tell me about the woman."

Sitting up straight, the doctor felt his mouth open and shut of its own accord. "*You* are asking me about a woman? Have you taken up comedy, Tan?"

He did not laugh. "Not any woman, Hector; the pale one. The one who comes to you from the ayllu near the fork in the river."

Hector shrugged. He had wondered why it had taken Tan so long to notice the young American, and how the man would react when he saw her. A connoisseur of beauty, Tan would have seen Leah; little escaped the man who knew the jungles as well as he knew the lines on his mother's face. "What do you want to know?"

"Everything."

"She is from across many miles...."

Tan cut him off sharply. "Don't feed me a child's pablum, Hector. She is not a Spaniard; her language is different from yours."

Hector's curiosity was piqued. "And how would you know that?"

"She carries a book I cannot read."

"Of course you can't read it; it's in English." Hector stopped, a frown crossing his face. "What on earth were you doing poking about her things?"

Tan toyed with the cup before him and shrugged his broad shoulders. "The yunka is a lonely place, Hector. I cannot seek company in the open, so I find it in other ways." He glanced toward the window. "You know, I was sorry to see the two stranger women leave before the rains came. Their methods of teaching were crude, but I learned from them."

Hector's laughter echoed off the stone walls of his tiny house. The stranger women were two nuns who had come to run a school for the children of lumberjacks temporarily working in the area. Once or twice they had mentioned someone had been hovering near the makeshift schoolroom, but no prowler was ever caught. "So it was you who made them feel like fish trapped in a pool!"

"Their clothing was ridiculous, Hector, but their lumpy bodies were best hidden." Tan allowed himself a smile at the small joke.

Morales straightened in his chair, a feeble attempt to hide his embarrassment at realizing Tan must have seen the holy sisters in some state of undress. "What did you learn from them?" he asked, changing the direction of the conversation.

"I learned that their god likes those who do not question sacred mysteries; that an answer is an answer even if you do not understand its nature. Or the question, for that matter. Beyond that," he added smugly, "I learned to spell better than you do."

Hector snorted; he knew from his years with Tan that the young man was more than just bright; he was quicker than anyone he had ever met. He taught Tan to speak Spanish in a few short weeks when, in Tan's first year

as aclla, he had sliced open his leg and the wound had become badly in-
fected. Summoned by the Mamacuna, Hector insisted that the young man
be brought to the clinic where he could be properly medicated. Hector
often wondered what the world would have held for Tan had he been born
where a real education was available. Now, as he studied the smooth face,
he realized it was time to talk about the world beyond the mountains. "So,
my friend, you want to know about Leah, for that's her name. I will start
by telling you she is like no one you know. She is not one of them," he said,
knowing full well Tan would understand the reference to the Catholic missionaries.

"She said she was a mulkan, Hector. What does she seek?"

This was one more surprise for the doctor; Tan did not have idle conversations with strangers. In fact, he did not have conversations at all! "She
is a student, Tan, the way the children were students in the little school
house," he explained. "Only, she studies in a great institution."

"A university?" sneered Tan, allowing the word to hang in the air
between them.

"Yes, a university. Where did you learn such a word? Do you know
what it means?"

Tan's smile was slow, almost cynical. "Hector," he drawled, "I read your
magazines when you think that they are safely tucked away in your desk
at night."

"What is it that you seek, Tan?" asked the doctor, believing there was
more to this conversation than he was being allowed to read in the bronze
face.

Tan jumped up, knocking over the chair as he slammed his broad hand
on the table. "I want to know, Hector!" he shouted. "I want to know what
is beyond the edge of the forest, beyond the tops of the mountains! I want
to know what you know and I want to know it all! You studied in this
America; I will go there, too!"

The thin whistle which came from Hector's lips broke the tension. He
knew the thirst burning inside Tan; he had had it himself as a boy living
in a rural town not all that far from where he sat now. It was the thirst for
knowledge that drove the priests mad until they agreed to send him to the

capital to study in a formal preparatory school, with real books and teachers. From there, it was true; he had gone to medical school in America and stayed until he finished his residency. He recognized in Tan the passion he knew so well. "Do you know what you are asking, Tan?"

"Yes."

"Do you know these things you want will take you far from this place, so far that you may never return?"

"You returned; so will I."

"You are a person of great importance to the people; are you willing to give that away so that you may seek knowledge?"

"The importance I hold is not forever. What will I be left with when my time is finished?" His eyes burned into the doctor's. "Already I am different. I will never be able to take a woman and live in an ayllu without wanting to know what is beyond the mountains. Will you help me, Hector?"

Falling back against his chair, the doctor studied Tan's face. There was more to his difference than just knowing how to read. Tan was taller than any Indio he had ever encountered in the district. His face was less angular, his eyes rounder, his hair was not bone straight like the others of the people. Hector knew Tan's grandfather had been an *illaq*, a traveler, from the north, from Mexico he surmised. The grandfather had filled the grandson's head with stories; it was no surprise that Tan wanted to know more. And in the end, Hector knew Tan was capable of mastering anything set before him. "I will teach you, my friend, but I will not begin until you have had time to consider my words carefully." Hector waited while Tan righted his chair and sat down with a thump. When he spoke, it was slowly, measuring each word's weight before it was spoken. "If you want to leave here to study in a great house of learning, it can be arranged. But before that, you will study with me for the next moon cycle, after which time I will decide whether you are able to survive in the world beyond the mountains. During this time, no one must know of what we do; it will frighten the people if they think you are leaving. You will come to me when you can, beneath Mamaquilla's eye, and learn what I tell you to learn. If, at any time, you find that you cannot eat the fruit of our learning, you must tell me. Do you understand, Tan?"

"Yes, I understand."

"Good." Hector rose from his seat and went to the young man's side. "Return to me in three days and we will talk again."

The Aclla left the little house as silently as he came. In the morning, when Hector went to his desk, he noticed the three magazines which had come from Piura with Paolo had disappeared.

Only two weeks were necessary before Hector accepted the depth of Tan's desires. More than just a bright kid, Tan had a spark of what he suspected was a real genius for mathematics. Tan knew arithmetic backward and forward like any young man of the people, but he swallowed whole the theory and concepts of advanced mathematics put before him like so much quinoa, devouring with relish the principles of algebra, geometry, and trigonometry. He had no trouble mastering the use of a pencil for his calculations, switching to the more practical method instead of using a *quipu*, a counting string, and within a matter of days, Tan was filling the notebooks he took from Hector with pages of problems solved as fast as they were given. Language, too, came easily. Once the rules of spelling and punctuation were more clearly defined, Tan began to write about the things he saw about him. In one small notebook, he recorded the poetry he had in his heart as he performed his duties to Mamaquilla.

The nights were spent huddled over Hector's table, books spread before them, Tan soaking up learning like a dry sponge dropped into a bowl of water. For his role as teacher, Hector made a special trip to Piura to raid bookstores in search of textbooks and anything else he thought he could use with Tan.

On the afternoon Leah walked into his clinic for her monthly touch with western civilization, Hector was out at an ayllu. He left a note stuck to the door, instructing Leah to make herself comfortable until he returned. On his desk, she found her mail packet exactly where he always left it. In his ancient refrigerator where vials of vaccine were kept chilled by the grace of the makeshift generator, Leah found several bottles of Mexican beer and helped herself to one. She settled herself in an overstuffed armchair, popped the cap, and began reading the letters from home, but not before toasting her absent host. Cool inside the stone house, and very comfortable in the chair, Leah barely made it through the third letter from her mother and most of the beer before she drifted off to sleep.

Long shadows danced on the wall when Leah opened her eyes. With a yawn, she stretched her legs, arching her back to diminish the slightly cramped feeling. It was unusual for Hector to be so late in returning from a house call, but Leah did not worry. Reaching over, she flicked on the lamp beside her, relishing that little touch of modernity. When her eyes were drawn to a quick movement in the corner near the back door, Leah almost leapt out of the chair. Tan was sitting at the table, his long legs casually crossed at the ankle, his fist supporting his face. A slow smile curved upward; he was amused at her reaction. "Buenas noches, señorita," he drawled, his voice soft and caressing.

Leah righted herself and, instead of averting her eyes as she had at the pool, she stared at the Aclla. "What are you doing here?" she asked in Quechua, not fully realizing he had addressed her in Spanish.

He ignored the question and asked one of his own. "What language are you reading?" he asked in Spanish, pointing to the letters in her lap.

"*Inglés*," Leah replied, switching to the other language. "It is the language we speak in my country."

"Ah, America. Is it a difficult tongue to learn?"

Leah shrugged. "They say it is because there are more exceptions to the rules than not." She studied his face intently, trying to decipher what he wanted, but the mask he wore was impenetrable.

His eyes bore into hers, giving nothing away. He wanted to kiss her, but kept himself in check. His adult life has been spent tending to the needs of women he did not want and now that he saw one he wanted, he was not permitted to have her. The growing fire in his loins made him shift position, hoping she would be unable to detect his discomfort. It was one thing to come to her under the cloak of night, to brush a hand across her breast, to feel the warmth of her lips in a stolen kiss, but it was something else completely to face her grass-eyed gaze. To come to her in the light would be to declare himself and that he could not do. It was folly to have remained once he saw her asleep in Hector's chair and now it was too late to flee, too late to disappear into the forest.

Leah spoke again. "Why are you here?"

"Like you, I visit Hector on occasion."

"Oh."

They lapsed into uneasy silence and remained that way until Hector arrived, tired and dirty, from the trek through the forest. His eyes popped when he saw Tan at the table and Leah in the easy chair. "¡*Madre de Diós!*" he cried, squelching a laugh, "What have we here?" Neither guest uttered a word. Leah busied her hands with her mail while the Aclla thumbed the pages of his notebook. "My two favorite people are sitting in my house, both fine conversationalists, and there is nothing but silence! How can this be?"

Leah and the Aclla exchanged glances, but it was he who broke the silence. "I am not accustomed to common conversation with women," he announced in Quechua.

Hector's laughter echoed through the stone house. "Common conversation, indeed! Tan, you amaze me." He went to the sink and let the water run for a moment. "You two have much to learn from each other, but I see you are too foolish to talk. Tan, this is Leah; Leah, this is Tan. So much for the formalities," he laughed as he washed away the dirt of the forest. "Leah, you are planning to stay the night, I hope."

"I have no choice, Hector. It's too late to start back. Do you mind?"

He shook his head. "It's just as well. I need you to take a small detour on your way back with medication for one of the ayllus near yours. Besides, in case you have forgotten, today is a Tuesday." On Tuesdays, the Fines would be home in case Leah could call.

Leah's smile lit up the room. "Oh Hector! I'd completely lost track of the days! Do you think I can get through?" Connections were not always as reliable with a satellite phone.

"I don't see why not." Hector walked over to the cabinet where he kept his telephone hidden and pulled it out. "You don't mind waiting a few moments, do you?" he asked his other guest.

Tan shook his head, settling back to watch Hector punch in the first of several strings of digits. He had seen him use the telephone before, but he was curious as to why Leah would. From the corner of his eye, he saw Leah quickly going through the papers in her lap, reading their contents with an occasional chuckle.

As soon as Hector finished with the Peruvian operator, he motioned for Leah to come over. He handed her the phone and waited beside her until the final connection was made.

"Hi, Dad!" she cried, happy to hear him so clearly. The room faded behind her as she savored the precious contact with her family.

At the table, Hector took the chair beside Tan. "It's always a pleasure to hear her on the telephone with her family," he said softly. "She misses them and this is the best way to ease her homesickness." He noted the puzzled look in Tan's eyes and explained the word.

"You have been to America, Hector. What is it like?" asked Tan, wishing he could understand the strange sounds flowing so rapidly from Leah's mouth.

Hector laughed quietly. "The mountains are made of metal and stone... built by men. The air is dirty, the people...well, the people are not like people here." He paused to consider his description and added "but it is the cities I describe. Much of America is open and wild. There are no rain forests like we have yet there are great expanses of land that seem to touch the very edge of the universe. And the farms go on for miles and miles."

Tan thought for a moment. "They have a university there?"

"Many, many universities, Tan. And libraries the size of Macchu Pichu, filled from floor to ceiling with books."

"I would like to go there."

Hector smiled at his friend. "You would do well to go to Lima or Quito. You would be more comfortable in those cities."

"They speak English in America, yes?"

"Yes."

"Then you will teach me English."

The sharpness of Hector's sudden laughter made Leah turn around. Seeing nothing amiss, she resumed her conversation, missing the anger in Tan's eyes. "Why on earth do you want to learn English?" whispered Hector, stifling any further outburst.

Tan's voice, dangerously low, was flint hard. "I cannot learn what I need to learn here," he growled, "I want to go to America."

All traces of amusement left the doctor's face. Tan was serious, deadly serious. He could not understand why Tan would want to go to America, but he had obviously made up his mind. Stroking his stubbly chin, Hector considered whether such a thing could even be arranged. It would take a great deal of work to get Tan ready for such an adventure and even then, there were no guarantees that the man from the wilds of the yunka could manage in the wilds of western civilization. When Tan had talked of leaving, Hector naturally assumed he would go to Quito or Lima; never had he dreamt that the young man would want to leave South America completely. "I do not say that is impossible," replied the doctor, his voice grave, "but I will tell you that it will take time to see if such a thing can be arranged."

"Find the answer and I will respect what you discover. But know this: I will go to this place with or without your help." Tan gathered up his notebooks. "I will leave you with your guest."

"Tan, that's ridiculous. At least stay and listen to our conversation. You need the practice."

"I do not indulge in idle conversation with women," he repeated.

"Your arrogance will be your downfall, Tan," chided Hector, hoping to delay Tan's departure.

"Here, in this place, I am what I am, Hector. When I am a stranger someplace else, I will be less arrogant." Tan strode out of the little house without even a glance at Leah who still sat at the desk, absorbed in her conversation.

ை ⊖ ௸

When she asked about Tan, Hector told Leah very little. Sensing that whatever transpired between them was private, she let it go and instead filled Hector in on the news from America. Since newspapers and magazines were invariably out of date, there was a lot to talk about. There was a war in the Middle East, another earthquake in the Pacific, and New York City was heading for bankruptcy once again. "My mother is still aggravating over the Shining Path," clucked Leah; "she worries there are still terrorists here."

"Did you reassure her no one in their right mind would bother with this place?" laughed Hector. It wasn't exactly true, but the guerillas had not infiltrated his corner of the forest.

"It doesn't help; I told her to quit believing everything she reads in the Times."

Late into the night, Leah and Hector talked about the world around them and the world at large. Hector had not realized until that night how much he enjoyed having Leah around. She was bright, astute and a pleasure to behold. Unlike others who had attempted to reach the people, she had managed to become, in so many ways, one of them. She was well liked amongst the villagers; her work, according to the letters he had gotten from Dr. Muñoz, well received. He understood why a pre-doc had been allowed to tackle a project of this magnitude and hoped that, once she had her degree and could choose a course of postdoctoral study it would bring her back to his corner of the world. After Leah had turned in for the night, gladly accepting his offer of the tiny guesthouse beside the clinic, Hector could not fall asleep. He chided himself for feeling like an adolescent, but he had to admit that it had been too long since he had thought about a woman the way he was beginning to think about Leah. It would do no good, he reminded himself; he was almost old enough to be her father.

Over breakfast, Hector sensed there was something Leah wanted to discuss but held back. Gently, he prodded her until she threw up her hands to cover her reddening face.

"It's the aclla, Hector. Ever since I saw him at the pool near the second huaca, he has been with me. He comes to my hut in the dead of night, leaving me flowers or small carvings, sometimes taking things, only to bring them back a few days later."

Hector opened his mouth to speak, then closed it again. This explained a great deal about Tan's behavior, more than he wanted to know. A swift pang of jealousy nipped at his heart; he dismissed it as quickly as it had come. Leah had been with the people long enough to recognize a courtship ritual, yet she seemed not to understand this. On his last visit to the ayllu closest to Janajpachallacta, rumors were circulating that the aclla was court-ing a woman, and that he might very well declare for her, but no one knew the identity of that lucky maiden. Was it possible that Leah was the woman he was courting? It was beginning to seem likely. Still, Hector needed to ask questions lest she become suspicious. "You are certain it is Tan?"

Leah nodded and pointed to the single bird on her shirt pocket. "You see this? This is one of a pair. I left one at the first huaca...as an offering," she admitted a little sheepishly, "and he returned it to me at the second. That same night, he took it back. Now, they come and go, never two together; first one, then the other."

"And this bothers you?"

"Wouldn't this bother you?" countered Leah, frustrated.

Frowning, Hector toyed with the egg on his plate. "You know the rituals of the people, Leah. What does all this tell you?"

There was a long sigh. "That I am being courted?"

"Does *this* bother you?"

"Yes!"

"Does it bother you because it occurs, or because you are committed to another?" He had never questioned her about her love life back home, but there had never been a reason to before.

"There is no one in my life at the moment, Hector. Before I came here, I broke off with the guy I'd been seeing for the last year." She raised an elegant, if not sarcastic, eyebrow, "There isn't anyone waiting breathlessly for my return."

He was relieved to see her humor back in place. "So it bothers you because it is happening."

"Yes, but it's more than that," Leah sighed again. "If anyone in my ayllu knew he was courting me, all hell would break loose. They'd start wanting to braid up my hair with beads and smear me with flower attar. Rina would throw petals around my hut and Saba would start making love potions to insure a successful mating. It's no small thing to be courted by the aclla!"

"So why not sit back and enjoy it?"

Leah looked at him as though he were crazy. "I have to leave here eventually. As much as I love the people and the forest and the smells and the sounds, I want to go back to the States." Her own vehemence made her laugh. "Look, Hector, I'm a nice Jewish girl from a nice Jewish family who would like nice Jewish grandchildren living someplace where there are working telephones and pastrami sandwiches!"

"Ah, you can take the girl out of America, but you can't take America out of the girl."

"Something like that." She turned those luminous green eyes on him. "You seem to know him well, or at least he seems to be perfectly comfortable in your house. Can't you talk to him?"

Hector waved hands up in protest. "No way!" he cried. "There is no way I am going to say anything about this. Besides, it would be a terrible breach of protocol."

"Please, Hector," she wheedled.

"You are asking a lot, Leah."

"I know, but who else could I ask?"

"I'll have to think about it."

Not totally satisfied with the answer, Leah knew it was the best she could get out of Hector for the moment. "Come on, Hector;" she said, changing the subject, "let's do the dishes."

The doctor watched Leah carry the plates to the sink as he considered her request. Wistfully he regretted he was not young enough to give Tan a run for his quipu.

∽ ⊖ ∾

Alone in his clinic, Hector went about the routine business of checking his supplies. Paolo would be coming at week's end and tonight would be his last chance to add anything to his shopping list before the pilot stopped at the hospital to pick up his order. A sudden rap on the doorframe startled him.

"*Buenos días,* Hector," said Vincente Lubrano.

"What do you want?" replied the doctor with a frown.

"Merely a social call. I came to see how you and your clinic are surviving these days." Lubrano stepped into the room and glanced at the closet where Hector stood. "I see you are low on supplies. Hasn't your pilot been here lately?"

"My clinic is just fine, my supplies are coming and you do not make social calls. Why are you here, Señor Lubrano?"

"I was in the area," he shrugged. "It would be rude not to stop."

"No, it wouldn't. In fact, I would prefer if you didn't."

Lubrano laughed. "Have you considered our last conversation, Hector?"

"I told you then and I will tell you now: the land is not negotiable."

"You do not own the land, Hector; for all intents and purposes, no one owns the land. The government would not mind a new revenue base in the north."

"The government is not the issue, Lubrano and you know it."

"Ah, but it is. The congress is interested in opening several northern areas to mining...and you know as well as I do that bauxite is important."

"And you know as well as I do that there isn't enough bauxite here to mine. I know what you want and you won't get it."

"As far as the congress is concerned, any taxable income is good income."

"Congress will not pass legislation that will insure the rape of the land. You can whistle all the little tunes you want, Lubrano; they will not open the district to mining. They're not stupid in Lima. They know who pays you."

"You cannot stop progress, Hector."

"That isn't progress, this is deliberate rape of the land," Hector turned back to his closet.

"Perhaps." Lubrano strolled toward the door. "If it is a choice between a few migratory ayllus and millions of dollars coming into Peru, which do you think the government will choose?"

Hector faced Lubrano. "It depends, Señor Lubrano, on whether the dollars are coming into the country's coffers or into a few deep, well lined pockets. I think you will find the people of Peru are growing tired of supporting your lifestyle at the expense of their land."

Lubrano's laugh was unpleasantly sharp. "I think, Hector, you will find you are very wrong."

∽ ⊖ ∾

The first letters Hector sent off on Tan's behalf were to colleagues in Lima, Quito and Minnesota. He painstakingly described the progress his student had made over the relatively short period of three months and asked them all for advice. It would take a while for the responses to reach him, but Hector was confident someone would tell him what path would be best. In the meanwhile, Tan began his study of English and, much to Hector's amazement, the language came almost as easily as Spanish had. His accent was thick but manageable, his ability to retain vocabulary, astounding. Hector made another quick trip to Piura where American magazines were aged but available, and books he had ordered were waiting to be picked up. He had tried to broach the subject of Leah, but Tan cut him off, making it perfectly clear it was none of his business. Dutifully, he reported this to Leah, who sighed and admitted the nocturnal visits continued but with less frequency. Hector refrained; however, from telling her what Tan was doing.

The winter rains began in earnest in early May, making Leah's trips to Hector's clinic fewer and farther between. Holed up in her ayllu, she worked hard on the last sections of her ethnography, knowing that her time with the people was rapidly drawing to a close. She spent endless hours with Saba, recording the old woman's tales and customs, studying her collection of herbs and their uses. Because of her devotion and the respect she had shown, Saba decided to take Leah to Janajpachallacta, where the local priestesses would gather for the winter solstice. Excited, Leah prepared according to Saba's direction, fully aware that should the Rimoc forbid it, Leah would be unable to cross the narrow bridge linking the village to the sacred gathering place.

They set off at first sun five days before the ceremony. From all across the district, collahuayas and chinan, the girls chosen to serve the collahuayas, were making their way to Janajpachallacta in order to gather before the full moon. As they neared the foothills, their little band met other travelers, joining with them until they were a somewhat noisy caravan carving a path through the thick jungle. Leah recognized many of her fellow travelers, and they accepted her presence as Saba's assistant without question. A few wanted to explore her clothing, fascinated by her multitudinous pockets.

Hard as she could, Leah pressed Saba for information about the gathering, but the old woman would simply cackle at her and say, "You'll see, you'll see."

All the way to Janajpachallacta, Leah listened to the chatter of the others, hoping for some stray piece of intelligence to reach her ears, but no one talked about the gathering, only the events of the past year. Several women mentioned they had heard the Aclla was courting a maid, but no one knew who she was. A young collahuaya was certain it was one of the girls of her ayllu, but the others dismissed the notion, saying she was too inexperienced to know anything of the kind.

"Do not listen to her," instructed Saba when she could pull Leah to one side. "She is a good collahuaya, but she has a flapping tongue. The aclla is from an ayllu near hers, but he does not go there."

Leah started to say something, but clamped her mouth shut. She wondered how Saba would know where the aclla went at night. She was not, however, about to ask.

Soon enough they began their ascent out of the forest. Unlike the other ayllus, Janajpachallacta was really a small city of stone buildings hewn from the walls of the mountain above the forest. Leah spotted scouts perched in trees along the route, each one sending a signal to the next in line announcing their arrival. Those already there began to stream down the path in welcome. Like any other reunion, this one was filled with shouts of greeting and plentiful hands to relieve the trekkers of their burdens. Saba took great pride in introducing Leah to her colleagues, impressing them with the stranger's command of their tongue.

Once within the boundaries of the village, one of the residents, an old friend of Saba's, led them to the house carved into the mountain which would be their home for the next few days. Saba left Leah to unpack their belongings while she went across the bridge to where the Mamacuna was already receiving guests. It would be with her permission that Leah would be allowed to attend the ceremonies.

While she waited, several women stopped to visit with Leah. The ones she already knew from her visits to ayllus near her own brought their friends to meet the stranger who spoke like them. Most of the women were older than Leah but closer to her in age than Saba and her friends. They were anxious to hear what she had to say, eager to hear about the way she had come to their land. All had seen, at one time or another, a great silver bird in the sky, but it was hard for them to believe that ordinary people rode within its belly. Leah was sitting outside her house, surrounded by the women when Saba returned. The old woman shooed them away before leading Leah back inside.

"Someone has already spoken about you, Li-ah," pronounced Saba, a slightly miffed tone in her voice. "But no matter, they have agreed to your presence at the ceremonies, but ask to meet you first. " She stopped talking long enough to knit her eyebrows. You must change your clothes. They are dirty and your leggings would be bothersome to the old biddies." As much as she respected the Mamacuna and her court, Saba thought they were getting too old.

Digging into her pack, Leah pulled out the woolen tunic Rina had helped her make for the occasion. As she stripped off her pants and shirt, Saba clucked her tongue at Leah and said "You are far too pale, my ususi; you will never live a long life with such a terrible skin condition. One day you'll be old enough to understand why you must expose yourself to the elements; you need toughening."

"Yes, Mama Saba," sighed Leah, knowing no amount of explanation would ever convince the collahuaya that this was her natural color. She slipped the tunic over her head and went to work on her hair, brushing it hard to remove the last vestiges of travel dirt before twining it into two long braids similar to the ones Saba wore. Saba handed her a broad leaf with which to wipe her face and, after a quick inspection, declared Leah fit to be seen by the Mamacuna.

⟿ ⊖ ⟾

The Mamacuna and her Rimoc held court in the shade of a grove, eating from wide wooden bowls piled high with fruit offerings brought by the residents of the village. Saba took her place to the left of the Mamacuna leaving Leah to sit in the spot one of the other women indicated. The Mamacuna, an ancient looking woman with dark, leathery skin and probing black eyes, sat on a rough-hewn stone chair. From beneath a heavily embroidered mantle, two snow white braids hung almost to her lap. Her aged fingers of her right hand flew deftly over the knots of the longest, most complicated quipu Leah had ever seen while her left hand rested on the head of a large, black jaguar who seemed perfectly content to sit beside the old woman. Cocking her head to one side, the Mamacuna listened to Saba, and then nodded. Leah could not make out what was said, but the others seemed to agree with it.

"Tell us what you want from us, Qewa Ñawi," asked the Mamacuna at last, her voice clear despite her advanced age.

Leah composed her answer carefully, knowing that what she said now would determine how she was treated during her stay. "I am a seeker of knowledge, *Coya,* a woman who would learn wisdom from you and the people to carry back to my own land."

"What can we teach a woman," scoffed the old woman, "who flies in the belly of a silver bird?"

"We know only things different from the ones you know; my knowledge would be incomplete without your wisdom." Looking surreptitiously through her lashes, Leah could see the small smile on Saba's lips; it was a good sign.

"Mama Saba tells us you are not one of them." The last word was spit with distaste, an attitude Leah had encountered before.

"I am not one of them," replied Leah. "I do not believe the way they do, nor do I seek to change your ways. I seek only to learn from you."

The interview lasted more than an hour, with questions asked by almost everyone gathered. Leah's nervousness gave way to comfort as they chuckled at some of her answers. By and large, the court was as interested in her as she was in them. Curiosity, the universal equalizer, allowed for an easy exchange of ideas as the Mamacuna gently corrected and added to Leah's understanding of the people and their ways. At the end, when the Mamacuna seemed satisfied that Leah posed no threat, she handed a string of shells to the woman on her right, who in turn, presented them to Leah. "We accept Li-ah's presence at the gathering," she announced to the company. "Li-ah will serve with the other *chinan* and you, Saba, shall be her *mama'amuata.*"

Saba beamed; it was more than she had dared to hope. If Leah was allowed to attend, she was certain it would be in the role of an observer, not as a participant; to be named mama'amuata to Leah meant that the old woman had found her teaching to be complete and without fault. Saba had not asked for this unusual honor, she had merely asked that Leah be allowed to watch. With a somber nod, she accepted the silent accolades of her peers.

As the group drifted away, the Mamacuna placed a restraining hand on Saba, preventing her from joining Leah where she waited with some of the other women. "You have done well, Saba," said her leader when the others had left them alone. "I thought you were losing your good sense when I received your request to bring the Qewa Ñawi to us, but now that I have met her, I understand. The janpeq was correct in his thoughts that she was one to be welcomed and not denied. The woman Li-ah can do great good for us in the outside world."

The words puzzled Saba, who gave little thought to how the outside world viewed the people so long as they stayed away. "How can she help us, Coya?" she asked.

"By writing our words and telling a true story, they will be less likely to come looking for us. If the strangers think there is no great mystery here, they will pick some other people to bother." Her smile was broad, her chuckle deep with amusement. "The strangers only come when they think we have something to give. If the woman Li-ah tells them we are a simple people who live quietly with no secret riches, they will not come. The woman understands this." The Mamacuna removed a string of gold beads from around her neck and placed it in Saba's hand. "I hear you have had visions, Saba," she murmured.

Saba, for all her years, blushed furiously. "One or two," she answered modestly, "but they have come to pass."

"I am getting old, and the time is coming for me to find my own hua'amuata. I spoke for you so many years ago when you first came to the gathering with your own Mama'amuata. You served me well then and you have served me well since then. Besides the woman Li-ah, have you a *hua'amuata in* your village?"

Saba shook her head no. "There is a youngster whom I watch, one who in the next cycle of the sun I will begin to train if she proves to be less flighty than she is right now. She is young, but has promise."

"You will bring her to me at the Capac Raimi. Until then, I want you to consider coming to Janajpachallacta after the next gathering."

Swallowing hard, Saba agreed to think about it. To take her away from her ayllu might leave them without a properly trained collahuaya unless one could be convinced to take her place. Never had she thought herself worthy of joining the Rimoc on the mountain, but the Mamacuna did not invite one without good reason. The thought was both frightening and flattering at the same time; she would give it serious consideration.

No one would dare ask what words had passed between the Mamacuna and Saba, but Saba knew there were whispers around her as they made their way across the bridge. Not until they were alone did Saba tell Leah about the Mamacuna's request. "Say nothing to anyone, no matter how hard they might press you, Li-ah," instructed the old woman, her face still bright. "I tell you only because I am your mama'amuata now and everything must be open between us."

Impulsively, Leah hugged her. "I am so happy for you, Mama Saba! This is a great honor, even if you choose not to go. Mamaquilla must be pleased with you!"

Saba took Leah's hand in hers and squeezed it. "Come with me, Li-ah, and we shall make pilgrimage to the huaca on the mountain. If we go now, we can be back in time for the evening meal."

They walked back across the bridge, but this time, instead of going to the gathering place, they climbed higher on the mountain. Through a series of complicated turns on the path, Saba led them to a ridge overlooking the endless sea of green fanning out to the east. The high, rock wall held several natural alcoves and caves, all of which they passed without stopping. Finally, they came to a large grotto from which trickled a thin stream. Tucked into the wall was an altar stone. A small basin cut from rock sat atop it, blackened by years of fires lit in honor of Mamaquilla. The remains of offerings surrounded the base of the altar, evidence that the shrine was still in use. Opening her pouch, Saba removed a leaf packet and emptied its contents into the basin. Deftly, she struck her firestones until a spark ignited the powder, sending a plume of scarlet smoke into the air. Saba handed a second packet to Leah and instructed her to add it to the basin. A sweet aroma filled the niche where they stood, making Leah think of the lilac bushes growing in her backyard at home. Saba covered her eyes with her hands, intoning a prayer to Mamaquilla, a request for good sense and the ability to serve Her with a true heart.

When the smoke had drifted away and the embers still smoldered, Saba turned to the younger woman. "I have had visions in the past, but never like the visions I have had in this last cycle of the moon. They are curious to me and you must hear them."

The sharing of visions was a sacred task, one that was not done without good reason. Averting her eyes in proper respect and touching her fingers to her lips, Leah gave the appropriate response. "If you share your visions with me, I shall be bound to hold them in my heart." She knelt at Saba's feet, as was custom.

Saba allowed a small smile of approval at the correctness of Leah's reply. This woman would have been her own choice for spirit daughter had she been one of the people. Now that the choice had been made for her, Saba was not unhappy, even if it were to be only temporary. Turning away from the altar, Saba stretched her arms wide, as if to embrace the rain forest below. "Thanks to Mamaquilla who allows us to see where there is no light. Thanks to Mamaquilla who allows us to hear where there is no sound. Thanks to Mamaquilla who gives us children of the heart." She faced Leah again, sucked in her breath, and recounted her vision.

"In my heart, I saw you at the pool of the second huaca to the Mamaquilla," began Saba. "The Aclla approached you and there were words I could not hear. A bird, a condor, flew above you both, circled three times and vanished, and then the Aclla vanished. You were alone but not alone. The Aclla was with you, is with you always. You have captured his heart. When I see you in the vision, the condor circles above you in silence." She paused and placed her hands on Leah's bowed head. "The Aclla will leave us to follow you. I saw him standing in *Ruti-Suyu*, a place of great cold with mountain white on the ground, but it was no mountain. Wherever you go, he will seek you. The condor circles endlessly above you, leading him to you." At that moment, a condor appeared in the sky and circled over them before disappearing. "Ai!" cried Saba, her hands flying to cover her eyes.

Leah was shaking uncontrollably; she was afraid. She had not seen the condor, but felt its presence as acutely as if it had landed on her head. God or Goddess, it did not matter; she had never felt as close to the Divine as she did at that moment. From deep within her, she experienced what her own grandmother had called *kavanah*, that moment when you are certain God hears your prayers. Finding her voice, Leah spoke the words she had not the heart to speak before. "Your vision is true, Mother; the Aclla came to me at the huaca and he has come to me many times since, in the dark of night when I sleep. He takes things and returns them. It frightens me."

"Do not let it frighten you, Li-ah. For whatever reasons Mamaquilla has, She has caused this to happen," said Saba, honestly believing there would be good from all this. "Let Mamaquilla guide you in what needs to be done; She will tell you as She tells us what is right and good for the people."

꙳ ⊖ ꙳

They returned late, but in time to eat the evening meal with the others. Saba made light of their visit to the shrine, without letting on what had occurred there. "There is much to teach this grass-eyed woman if she is to act properly at the ceremony!" announced Saba to her friends. Everyone had a turn, tossing their own advice to the newcomer who had not the benefit of growing up amongst the people. They thought the way she scribbled odd lines in her little book was positively silly, refusing to believe the marks could actually mean something. As the shadows lengthened, the women drifted back to their lodgings to prepare for the long day ahead.

Leah sat with Saba at the door of their house talking about the ceremonies that would commence in the morning. At that time, the collahua-ya would cross the bridge once more to join with her spiritual sisters in worship. Leah would go with the chinan who served the other collahuayas; they would be sequestered in an area not far from the convocation, where they would be taught the things they needed to know. Leah was too excited to sleep despite the complete exhaustion she felt after the long journey. She lay on her pallet of llama skins tossing and turning, unable to close her eyes for more than a moment. When Saba's gentle snoring became too much to bear, she took her alpaca cloak from its peg on the wall and walked out into the night.

The air was much cooler in Janajpachallacta than in her own ayllu. A breeze wafted through the deserted streets; the scent of the central fire lingered familiarly. Leah wandered toward the precipice spanned by the bridge and stood there, looking at the other side. The faint sound of voices could be heard, the Rimoc, she knew, chanting their songs to the Mamaquilla as they would all through this night. Holding the cloak close about her, Leah listened as best she could, wondering what prayers were being offered, what visions were shared, what secrets were revealed? Down below, in the recesses of the cliff face, she spotted a small dot of light, a fire she decided, belonging to one of the watchers who, for the next few days, would keep vigil in their stony nests as they had done since the beginning of time, when other tribes might try to raid the people as they gathered.

As she was about to return to the stone house where Saba slept soundly, something touched Leah's bare foot, making her jump. Spinning around, she saw no one. She shivered beneath the cape and took a step when she realized something was beneath her foot. Bending down, she picked up a single, perfect condor feather. It was all she could do to stifle a cry as she ran back to the safety of her lodgings.

CHAPTER 4

The Aclla stood in the center of the circle, a mantle of condor feathers covering his entire body. His headdress, a helmet of upright tail feathers, added to his height; he towered above the Rimoc. He remained completely still as the men seated around him tossed perfectly rounded pebbles at his feet, symbols of the never ending cycle of life. With each pebble, an elder spoke the name of a child born in his ayllu that year. When each had spoken, the eldest Rimoc tallied the numbers and there were murmurs of approval. Their ceremony complete, the elders rose, leaving the aclla alone in the circle.

He remained alone until the moon reached its zenith and the Rimoc returned to the circle. The Aclla knelt on the ground facing the Mamacuna. When all were settled, she stood and addressed him.

"There are many pebbles at your feet, how many pebbles are yours?"

"Six."

"How many sought you out?" asked the Priestess.

"Two for each huaca to Mamaquilla."

"How many did you turn away?"

"There were eleven who were not ready."

The Mamacuna was impressed. "You are certain of this, Opener of Sealed Wombs?"

"Yes; and there is one who has not yet brought forth." The question always rankled him; the answer was easily verified and would be at the solstice ceremony. Still, custom demanded the Mamacuna ask and that he answer. But this would not be the difficult part of the night; that would come when the Rimoc revealed their visions and he had never known them to be wrong. He told no one of his desire to leave the people, to travel to the land of America, yet he was certain that someone in the circle already knew. This he could feel and it took every ounce of his strength not to squirm.

Two young chinan approached the circle, each bearing a vessel. They set them before the Mamacuna and withdrew; they were not permitted to witness the revelations to follow. Once they were gone, the High Priestess prepared elements of the sacred *jonchi*. How the smoke dissipated coupled with the length of time it took to float toward the clouds were signs for the Rimoc to read. With a pop and a flash, pure white smoke rose from the basin toward the heavens. No one spoke; all eyes intent on the column ascending upward. When the last wisp of smoke disappeared from view, the Mamacuna rose and slowly walked toward the Aclla. She placed her aged hands on his bowed head.

"You have greatly pleased Mamaquilla, my son," she said, her voice filled with emotion. "My heart tells me of your devotion to her." She paused, letting the impact of her words reach the others. "But it is my vision which tells me you are no longer happy in your mita to Her. Is this true, churi?"

"My life belongs to Mamaquilla, the Giver of Life. I serve the Mamaquilla with my whole heart."

"An answer that is not an answer," sighed the Mamacuna, "is a hole in the heart through which Mamaquilla can see, my son." She kept her hands on the Aclla; she could feel him tremble beneath his mantle. She cleared her throat and spoke to the congregation. "The jonchi rises straight, with no bends nor billows to mar its perfection. This is a powerful sign from Mamaquilla. She has accepted our gifts of this last cycle of the sun and waits with pleasure that which will come. She is happy with Her people and tomorrow, when we gather to offer our prayers we must thank Her for Her bounty with the fullest measure of our hearts. As for our visions, we will speak the things we have seen, and then we will keep vigil in our dwellings where each of us must search our hearts for that which we hold most precious."

One of the oldest mystics, a woman from a distant ayllu, rose and held out her hands. "I have seen the Aclla in a place far from this place. A white place." She stopped speaking and resumed her seat.

"I have seen the condor circling above the head of a maiden new to our company," said another.

One by one, the others rose to relate their visions. Not all of them concerned the Aclla directly, but each added one more twist to the struggle the man waged within himself. When it was over, the Aclla felt hot tears course down his face to splash silently onto the ground. Not a word was said, but he knew they had seen. In silence, the Rimoc left the circle. The Mamacuna departed with them, but her jaguar did not follow. The large cat approached the kneeling Aclla and lay down beside him.

Alone in the darkness, the fire faded to glowing embers, the aclla remained on his knees, his eyes downcast. Thus he stayed for what seemed like hours compressed into a fleeting speck of time. Only when the Mamacuna approached him, did he look up.

She had returned to the circle to speak privately with him, her right as Mamacuna. She alone had the power to release him from his vows and she had never doubted that one day she would. At any time, an aclla could be released from his mita, for he could not perform his duties if his heart was not whole. Yet, it was unusual for an aclla to leave his mita without declaring for a woman and there was no real evidence that he was courting a maid. What disturbed the Mamacuna most was the repeated visions of him in a white place not in their mountains. She, too, had seen it, yet it was no place she could name. And with it, she had seen eyes, many eyes, but the most prominent ones had been green; green like the grass that flourished around hidden forest pools.

With gentle fingers, she lifted the feathered helmet from his head and stroked his thick, dark hair. Like the hair of his grandfather whom she remembered well, it was softer than that of the rest of the people, with an odd way of curling rather than falling straight past his shoulders. When she looked into his eyes, she saw the pain and confusion he felt, the desire to serve both his people and his own needs. There had not been an aclla of this power since before her own birth, and that aclla, too, legend said, left the people when his time was done. There was something draining about serving Mamaquilla, something that ate at the marrow of one's bones all the days of one's life. There were times even she had felt the need to escape, to flee the never-ending responsibility to her people. Unlike others, she had wandered far from the mountains when she made her spirit journey before joining the Rimoc. She had been a young woman then, curious and brave, and she had walked far to see how the strangers who came to their land lived in their own villages. What she saw both frightened and disgusted her; hard roads, wasted foods, fetid odors hanging in the air like displaced rain clouds. Yet, the sounds of music and laughter, the variety in the marketplaces, all made her wonder if, perhaps, there were good things to be gained by contact with the strangers. She learned to speak their language, but she never felt their words were honest. Then the visions came, the ones making it clear her place was with the people, guiding them, protecting them from outsiders, seeking to bring only the best from the outer world into their villages. Hector Morales was one of the best. She had never doubted her wisdom in seeking him out when he first traveled through the district. The janpeq had proven to be a good friend to them all, a man who, like her, wanted to see the people remain the people and not be dragged into what he called *modernidad*, the word he used to describe life outside their world. In the same breath, however, it was the healer who had told her the aclla was exceptional, that he thirsted for greater knowledge.

Once again, she chose her words carefully before speaking them to the man at her feet. "The janpeq tells me you seek something you cannot find here, my child. Is it your desire to leave us to seek this elusive feather?"

"No, Coya, it is not my desire, but the heart within my heart tells me this is the path I must follow."

"Ai, the inner chamber is strong in you; this is a good thing. It will keep you close to us even when you are far away. Do you know what it is that you seek, churi?"

The Aclla shook his head. "I know only that I do not know and must come to know. There is knowledge beyond the mountains that touches us without touching us, knowledge we can use to make ourselves stronger than we are. I want to bring that wisdom back so we may use it. "

Mamacuna touched the smooth skin of his cheek. "And the Qewa Ñawi has nothing to do with this?"

He looked away from her probing eyes. To lie would be useless, she already knew the truth from her visions. "I think I am bound to the woman with grass eyes, but not the way a man is bound with a woman in body. I see her in my own visions, but I see more. I, too, see the white place with stone mountains made by man's own hand. It is a strange place Mamaquilla shows me and I know that is the place I must find. She tells me it is where I will discover the things I need to bring to the people."

"I have loved you as a son for many, many sun cycles past," she sighed. "And I have known for a long time you would leave us...that the Qewa Ñawi would herald your departure from our midst. It was only a matter of time before she appeared." She hooked a thin finger beneath his chin and lifted his face toward hers. "Her power is strong, Na-Tan Manco, and I believe it is good. "

She called him by his name, the first time since he had become the Aclla and the importance was not lost on him. Again, his eyes burned with tears. "A piece of me is broken, Coya, and I feel great pain," he said, a part of him hoping she would forbid him to leave the people but knowing she would not.

"A piece of us will be broken when you leave," replied the Mamacuna sadly, "but you will go. And with the help of Mamaquilla, you will return." She smiled to ease his pain, although she could not bear to tell him that he would never return to live amongst the people. "Do you know when you will leave us, churi?"

"Not before the Capac Raimi. I need time to finish the work which has been given to me." He did not say whether it was the work of Mamaquilla or work the janpeq had laid out for him.

"Then it is settled. Go now and prepare yourself for tomorrow. Tell no one of this, for it would serve no purpose. They will be told only when the time is right."

The Aclla took her hands and held them to his brow. Strength coursed through her into him, and comforting warmth flowed into his chilled body.

Leah slept restlessly, tossing and turning beneath the thick llama wool blanket. Her dreams were again filled with strange images: snow and slush, books and condor feathers. And the Aclla. He was there, haunting her every step, his dark eyes following her movements. In her dream, he danced taqui around her, his hand barely touching hers, his lips brushing against her lips. She moaned, wanting more, yet frightened by what she felt. Again, his lips touched hers, and this time, she reached for him, her own hand stroked his warm, smooth cheek. His hand reached for hers and they joined, fingers intertwined, palm against palm. Sleepily, Leah's eyes opened, met by his deep brown ones. Another moan escaped her as he turned her palm upwards and kissed its center, then placed it against his breast. "Your heart is in my heart, " he whispered.

"Your heart is in my heart," echoed Leah.

The Aclla released her hand and disappeared into the darkness.

Leah's eyes fluttered and closed, and she slept a deep, dreamless sleep.

The sun was barely visible when Saba roused her hua'amuata. "Come, Liah! Wash the sleep from your eyes and get dressed! You have much to learn while I am with the old ones."

Sleepily, Leah rubbed her eyes and smiled at the old woman. Never had she seen the placid Saba so excited. She sat up and laughed, feeling refreshed and ready to face her newest challenge. "It must be the mountain air, Mama Saba," she called to the bustling woman, "I feel wonderful." Leah was about to stand up when she noticed that instead of one condor feather sitting on her notebook, there were now two perfectly formed tail feathers. Her dream had been no dream.

If Saba noticed the feathers, she made no mention of it. Already dressed, she helped Leah into the vicuña tunic and braided her long hair, using shells and beads in strategic spots to indicate Leah's new rank as *hua'amuata*, her spirit daughter She helped the newest acolyte to wrap the woven girdle about her waist and attached Leah's leather carry pouch on the right side. Saba pulled a colorful quipu from her own pouch and tucked it into Leah's. "This is for you, my hua'amuata. Use it well."

Leah blushed; the quipu she had made for herself when she first came to the people was nowhere near as elegant as this one. "I shall keep it with me always, Mama Saba," she said solemnly. She glanced at it and realized it was tied in the same pattern as the one she had tied for herself. She saw Saba's knowing grin and returned it.

Out of nowhere, Saba produced a chinan's red felt hat, and proudly placed it on Leah's head. With a tug and a pull, she adjusted it to just the right angle, then stepped back to admire her handiwork. "If it were not for your eyes, ususi, you would look like one of us!" she announced proudly. "Now, go to the foot of the bridge and join the others." She escorted Leah to the door and watched her walk up the cobbled path, calling after her "And be sure not to shame me with any frivolous questions!" Accompanying laughter confirmed the teasing nature of her words.

∞ ⊖ ∞

The girls were already gathered near the bridge when Leah arrived. They giggled at her apologies and complimented her hat and alpaca cape, an honest effort to make her feel less awkward, even if she was much older than they. After all, it had been the Mamacuna who had named her as a hua'amuata instead of merely confirming a priestess's choice. Surely this woman had powers the Mamacuna thought important enough to cultivate! Some of them already knew Leah from her wanderings in the rain forest. Now that they were all gathered, they made their way across the bridge. Silently, hands beneath their capes, they moved in single file toward the place where they would learn from the Rimoc.

The day began with a lecture on rules for proper decorum at the gathering to be convened at sunset. Each hua'amuata would have a specific role at the ceremony. This year, it was a most auspicious occasion, since the full moon coincided with the solstice. Not only would the Aclla choose a chinan to be his consort for the duration of the gathering, the lucky girl would be personal assistant to the High Priestess until the next *situa* instead of just being with her for one moon cycle. It was an honor every one of them wanted, but when the selection was made, they knew it would be Mamaquilla Herself who guided the Aclla's hand.

Listening intently, Leah made copious notes on what was being said. The teacher explained patiently the preparations needing to be complete before Inti disappeared behind the mountaintops. Nocturnal worship of Mamaquilla was only one part of the rite; there were sacrifices to be made in full view of her husband-partner in Viracocha, Inti. One at a time, the maids recited the rules as delineated by the knots on their quipus. When Leah's turn came, the aged Rimac halted the progression: the Mamacuna herself had arrived. The old woman took her seat before she spoke.

"You come to us from another people, Li-ah. You have not learned the litany of your quipu for your mama'amuata has given it to you on this day," said the old woman without rancor, "therefore, you must find the words in your heart."

Leah was, at first puzzled, but then she understood. Moving to stand directly before the Mamacuna, she held her quipu in one hand while the other touched the first knot. "This is the counting of my moons with the people," said Leah tentatively; a nod from the old woman reassured her. "In the first moon I came as a newly born babe, without understanding, only respect for the people who took me in and taught me. The second moon brought strength in being and in knowledge, and I could walk amongst the people with ease. The third moon was my moon of growing, I found a place where I could sow my questions and watch the answers spring from the ground like shoots of tender grass." Leah's voice stopped trembling and grew in strength and confidence; she knew what she said was correct. She told of the months she spent walking through the forest, visiting other villages and learning their ancient ways, describing to their amusement some of the oddities she had encountered. " The sixth moon was the moon of the pilgrimage, when I found my way to the shrines of Mamaquilla. It also brought sadness and loss to me when I learned of the passing of my own grandmother, a woman rich in blessings and wisdom." She paused to accept the sympathetic clucks and sighs of her listeners. "And now, this is the tenth moon, an auspicious one for now I am no longer an illaq sojourning with the people, I am hua'amuata to Saba and I shall serve her and the people as I am instructed." Leah sat down to the approving murmurs of the others.

"You have learned well, Li-Ah," said the Mamacuna, "and Saba is honored to have you as hua'amuata." She stood up. "You did not come to us by chance; you have come to us because Mamaquilla wills this to be. Mamaquilla does not decree events frivolously; She sees in your heart your desire to be of our people. Therefore, because your time with us is short and this may be the only gathering you will ever attend, you will carry the sacred fire into the gathering." As silently as she arrived, the Mamacuna left the circle of chinan. As she left, the jaguar stopped before Leah and sniffed her for a long moment before he padded after his mistress.

The girls closest to Leah gave her affectionate squeezes; there was no animosity at her being given the honor of carrying the large, golden bowl, an honor much coveted by the chinan. With proper humility, Leah bowed her head, but the blush creeping across her cheeks was noticed causing everyone around her to giggle.

Clapping her hands, the teaching Rimac called the girls to order and brought them back to the subject at hand. With the telling of the quipus completed, she had the acolytes walk through the ceremony so that each of them knew exactly where to be and when. Once she was satisfied with the drill, the old mystic left and a meal was served.

The other chinan clustered about Leah congratulating her. Each had a little story to tell about other gatherings. As they ate and talked, Leah felt the last of her apprehension drain away. She was ready to face anything that Mamaquilla could possibly throw at her now.

After the meal, each acolyte was to find a quiet place in which to meditate on the bounties of Mamaquilla and to pray for continued favor in Her eyes. In silence, the girls went off toward the mountain, careful to bypass the circle where the Mamacuna and the Rimoc were holding council. Leah followed the path she had taken the day before with Saba, hoping no one else would go to the grotto huaca.

She was right; the grotto was deserted. Leah stood before the huaca and for a moment, reflected on everything that had happened to her since she left home to come to the people in the Andes. It seemed that indeed there was a grand scheme, a sort of destiny, which had made her jump at the chance to record an isolated people. She found a nurse at University Hospital who came from a town not far from the clinic, willing to teach her the dialect spoken in the area. Her parents had thought she was crazy when she announced she would be spending a year in the mountains of northern Peru, but it was Grandma Sophie who had calmed their fears. At the very last minute, a sudden panic gripped her heart as she sat at the airport and she almost backed out. She managed to get on the plane, but not without great trepidation. By the grace of God, Hector Morales had been at home when she arrived in the little courier plane, instead of wandering about the forest with his knapsack of magic antibiotics. He welcomed Leah with open arms, leading her into his little house where a hot meal waited and she asked the first of a thousand questions. Now, as she stood at the huaca tucked into the wall, Leah wished her days in the mountains were not numbered as few as they were.

But there were tasks to be accomplished before the sun touched the top of the mountain and it would be time to return to the gathering. Leah spread her alpaca cloak on the ground and sat on it at an angle so she could see both the huaca and the gorge below. Leah fingered her quipu, thinking about the things which were important to the ceremony, things like unity with Viracocha, honesty in one's heart, and belief in destiny, each concept counted by a newly tied knot on her quipu. The longer she sat, the more images floated before her mind's eye. Grandma Sophie, her parents, the cold streets of Minneapolis in winter covered in snow giving way to faces of the people, and then the eyes that penetrated her dreams. Turning her face upward, she pleaded with God to give her a sense of peace, of direction, for the thought of leaving the people was, if possible, more frightening than the thought of coming had been. There was no answer save the rustle of leaves against the steep rock walls of the canyon. On impulse, Leah opened her carry pouch and pulled out a small, well-worn book. Although she always carried it with her, like the bird pin now attached to her tunic, she had not looked at her prayer book in several weeks.

The book had been purchased in Jerusalem when she was sixteen. All in Hebrew, she easily found the page she was seeking, one she had read over and over whenever she was unsure. Quietly, but certain the God of the people and the God of Abraham were one and the same, she began to softly sing the *Hallel*, a collection of verses from the book of Psalms. The tunes were the tunes of her childhood, the lullabies her grandmother sang when, on special occasions, Leah slept at the Brooklyn apartment. They were comforting, familiar sounds. Closing her eyes, her finger on the place, Leah swayed gently as she sang, her voice rising above the rock walls and floating upward to the heavens.

◦ ⊖ ◦

The Aclla knelt on the ridge directly above the place where Leah sat on her cloak. He had been perched there for several hours, contemplating the ceremony to come. With all his might he prayed to Mamaquilla, begging Her to show him a sign that the path he had chosen was the right path. He turned his face to the sun, letting the warmth cascade over him. Tonight, when the assembly convened, he would perform the duties that were as much a part of him as his own right hand. For seven cycles of the sun he had served Mamaquilla. Never had he questioned the wisdom of Mamaquilla, or the Rimoc for that matter.

His mind wandered back to a simpler time, when he sat at the fire with Iztak, his grandfather from over the mountains. Iztak had come to the people when he was a young man, an illaq who wandered into the ayllu one hot, rainy day and never left. He fell in love with the first girl he saw, a tall, slender beauty named Aima, in whose parents' house he took shelter. She bore him three sons, the eldest of whom was Tan's father. Manco did not grow as tall as his father, but he had the straight nose and soft, wavy hair of his father's people. When it came time for his manhood ceremony, Manco was summoned to Janajpachallacta. Much relieved when he was not declared aclla, he retuned to his village to declare himself to Cura, his childhood sweetheart. One year later, on the night of the summer solstice, a brief, violent thunderstorm shook the mountains and the yunka as Cura gave birth to a baby boy who cried lustily the moment his face appeared in the firelight.

Named Na-Tan Manco, the boy grew tall under the watchful eye of his parents, but it was clear to everyone in the ayllu the child was completely devoted to Iztak. Together they tilled the potato fields, laughed at private jokes, and shared great secrets. Everywhere the old man went, the little boy was there, two strides for Iztak's one, his little arms swinging in imitation of the bigger ones beside him. At night, Tan would snuggle into Iztak's lap to listen to tales of people and places the boy could barely imagine.

And then, one afternoon as they sat fishing on the bank of the arroyo near the ayllu, Iztak slumped over. Tan tried to rouse his grandfather, but he had seen death before and knew in his heart his grandfather had gone to join his ancestors. He took the fishingpole from Iztak's hands and laid it beside the old man. For a long time he just sat there; it would be the last time he had his grandfather to himself.

Tan grew taller than the other children; always the leader, he was forever plotting new adventures for his friends. As he approached his own manhood ceremony, the mothers of the ayllu made sure their daughters looked particularly lovely when he was around. Handsome and strong, his name was whispered in the circles of young ladies as they spun llama wool into thread. Tan began to notice the way the girls smiled at him from beneath lowered lashes before they disappeared, giggling, into the forest, teasing him to follow, yet no one girl caught his attention and held it for more than a fleeting moment.

On the night before he was to go into the jungle to prepare for the ceremony, his father took him aside to speak with him about the coming ceremonies. "Already you are taller than me," said Manco with great pride, "and your strength is spoken of in other ayllus."

"This makes me feel strange, *Taitai*," confessed the boy, his long fingers playing with the strands of his quipu. "I sometimes feel different from the other boys, as if I do not belong with them."

Manco put his arm around his son. "You are different. You are different from your brothers, too." It was hard to explain what he himself did not understand. Sucking in his breath, he began "There is no aclla, churi. When you go into the jungle tomorrow, do not be surprised if a chasqui from the Mamacuna taps your shoulder."

The boy's eyes widened and he shook his head. "No, Taitai, I do not want to go to Janajpachallacta. I do not want to be sent away from my ayllu!"

"What you want is not always the right path, Na-Tan Manco. If you are summoned, you must go." He held him close. "My father left his people and if Mamaquilla demands it, you will leave yours." Silently, he wondered if perhaps his son would succeed where he had once failed.

On that morning, when he bid farewell to his grandmother, the old woman pressed a small object into his hand. "Take this with you, beloved churi of my churi. Had your grandfather lived, he would have been the one to have given it." Na-Tan Manco opened his hand and saw a small, golden conopa in the shape of a star. Aima closed the slender fingers over the object. "Iztak made this for you when you were born. He knew then what you will soon know." She pressed her fingers to his lips. "Now is not the time for questions," she whispered.

Tan kissed his grandmother's soft cheek and sprinted into the dense jungle. Her words frightened him, but the feel of the golden conopa still clutched in his hand gave him strength. When the chasqui found him deep in meditation at the huaca near the river, Tan was prepared to go to Janajpachallacta and face the tests. In the morning after the ceremony, the sun rose with a radiant halo. Within the first moon, the barren woman conceived and he was declared Aclla. His name was no longer spoken aloud outside his parents' house. And it was only under the cover of darkness on nights when Mamaquilla did not show Her face, did he visit his ayllu to sit for a few hours with his parents and grandmother, only to be gone before first light.

For the full cycle of the sun he lived in the forest, alone and apart, with no constant company save Inka, the Mamacuna's jaguar. The women who came to him were forbidden to speak more than the prescribed words, leaving him with an empty, lonely craving deep within him. In the first year, when he injured his leg, he had not cared when the cut festered. If his body were imperfect, he would be released from his mita. But the Mamacuna cared. She summoned the white skinned janpeq to ask for his magic salve to save the life of this most potent aclla. Hector obliged, insisting that the boy be brought to the clinic and during his stay, their friendship took root. Tan began to visit the healer with great regularity, asking questions about anything and everything he encountered. Hector suspected this was more than just a way to pass the time. The gift Mamaquilla had bestowed on him was not the one everyone thought it was. The precious gift was the burning, driving thirst to know more. Tan was certain Iztak knew this and in the time they had together, he had tried to prepare his grandson for the life of a mulkan.

Into his musings came a strange, yet beautiful sound. The Aclla listened to the voice, unable to understand the words. They were not words of Quechua, certainly not Spanish, although the melody sounded like ones he had heard at Hector's. Listening closely, he decided it was not English, for he had enough knowledge of the language to be able to make out its sound in a song. Still, there was a warm familiarity about it, as though he had heard these songs before. He knew the only person on the mountain who could be singing had to be the woman Li-ah. The Aclla crept along the edge of the ridge until he could see into the grotto below.

The Qewa Ñawi swayed gently as she sang her haunting melodies. She could not see him, nor did he want her to. In her lap she held a small book, the one he knew she always kept in her pouch, the one which, when he stole a look at its pages, had markings unlike anything he had ever seen. She looked so beautiful sitting on the ledge below, her long, dark hair in twin braids falling down her back. He was glad she had taken off the hat; it would have obscured his view. Her face, bathed in the light of the late afternoon sun, reflected the golden color. He could only imagine the green of her eyes, green as the grass near the edge of water. He had even seen them grow dark when she was angry, as she had been that night at Hector's. Still, he wanted to lose himself in those eyes; from the moment he saw her at the pool, he knew she had been sent by Mamaquilla Herself. The sight of the slender, agile body rising from the water aroused him in a way no other woman had. Had the barren woman not sought him out at that moment, he would have fled into the forest far away from what he feared: that this was the one who would take him away from his world.

Gradually, the strange melody faded. The sun had reached the very tip of the mountain. Tan watched as she swung her cape onto her shoulders and replaced the hat to become the prefect image of a chinan preparing for the ceremony. He could not take his eyes from her as she delicately picked her way down the rocky path toward the gathering place.

CHAPTER 5

The chinan gathered at the foot of the bridge. Leah found her place at the end of the line and joined in the excited whispers as the girls who had served Mamacuna at the last ceremony tried to calm the newcomers. The newcomers, in turn, asked nervous questions, seeking reassurance that the way they had learned their part in the ritual was indeed proper and correct.

All chatter ceased with the appearance of the procession coming from the center of the village. Leah saw Saba go by with the other village collahuayas; her mama'amuata seemed perfectly focused on the chant as they moved in a single line across the rope bridge. She wondered if Saba knew her spirit hua'amuata was to carry the sacred fire to the Mamacuna. Leah did not have time to dwell on it; the teaching Rimac was calling each acolyte forward to receive her object.

The large, beaten gold basin was warm in Leah's hands. Inside, in carefully created designs, were the powders, the *uchapa,* which would be lit to create the Jonchi of Vision. Centered in the design was a small stone, its own center hollowed out, containing embers of the sacred fire that burned in the Mamacuna's private huaca. When the procession began, Leah would be last in line immediately followed by Mamacuna flanked by the two Rimoc most empowered with visionary skill.

Final instructions faded away when two Rimoc approached; now only the birdcalls and the faint rustle of leaves were heard. The sky was now completely black save for thousands of twinkling stars and the low, rising moon. In perfect silence they awaited the hymns that would summon them across the bridge.

With the first notes of reed flutes, the chinan started to walk. As they crossed the narrow chasm, Leah could hear the sonorous chanting of the collahuayas. No one was behind her, yet she felt the presence of Mamacuna close by. Slowly they approached the opening left for the procession and as soon as Leah could make out the shapes of the collahuayas in the darkness, she felt a warm hand on her shoulder. Without turning, she heard the deep purr of the jaguar and knew the Mamacuna walked immediately behind her. Keeping her eyes forward, Leah willed her hands to stop trembling lest her shaking disturb the delicate patterns in the bowl.

The chinan walked around the inner circle. The Mamacuna, when the line passed the seat of honor, stepped out to take her place on the stone chair. The chinan circled again, this time, as they passed Mamacuna, each delivered her object into the waiting hands. When Leah's turn arrived, she moved toward the Mamacuna with eyes downcast and placed the golden bowl on the stone altar directly in front of Mamacuna. Lifting her eyes for a moment, she caught sight of Saba, her own eyes shimmering with tears. Feeling satisfied with her performance, Leah backed away, touching her fingers to her lips repeatedly as a sign of respect.

The ceremony began with the bringing of gifts from each of the ayllus. Baskets of fruits and flowers were placed near the stone altar. Offerings of fine tunics of alpaca wool, llama skins and other skillfully crafted objects were set on the altar. One collahuaya presented an enormous jaguar pelt, the skin of an animal that had long terrorized several ayllus. This gift was received with personal thanks from the Mamacuna who did not usually look kindly on the killing of the large cats sacred to Viracocha.

The offerings were followed by the arrival of the children, six in all, each with a garland of jungle flowers around their necks, ranging in age from almost a full year old to a tiny but very loud newborn. Leah was not prepared to see so many children reputed to be fathered by the Aclla. Each child was carried by a woman of that ayllu, but not by the mother. The babes were brought to the Mamacuna who, in turn, wound a quipu about their tiny fingers. On behalf of the Mamaquilla and Her people, the Mamacuna welcomed them into this world, instructing them to grow strong so that they may one day serve She-Who-Had-Given-Them-Life. As the nursemaids carried their little charges to one side, a woman stepped into the circle carrying a sapling. The tree was placed in the center and the woman announced that a woman of her ayllu was with child after a long period of barrenness. Leah already knew the sapling would be planted in a grove behind the Mamacuna's house, where many such saplings had been planted over the years. This was done to acknowledge the coming bounty of Mamaquilla and to pray for the safe delivery of this child.

The Mamacuna rose and approached the altar. Intoning words in a language Leah did not fully understand, she summoned the spirits who served the Goddess directly. As she moved her hands over the golden basin, she asked Mamaquilla to open her eyes behind her eyes, those which would allow her to see into the future of the people. There was a sudden flash and a column of smoke ascended into the sky.

All eyes followed the column. Unlike the night before, when the jonchi rose up in a perfectly straight line, the top of the column caught a small breeze and fanned out, a celestial palm tree floating in the air. To one side, the fronds seemed to flutter, and a wisp of smoke separated; a bird had left the tree and soared toward the circle of the moon. Slowly, the smoke dissipated; the congregation turned their eyes to the Mamacuna. Her eyes followed the last, lingering hint of sacred smoke, looking for any other sign the Goddess might reveal at the last moment. If the tree represented the people, she was certain the bird was their beloved aclla.

They awaited her words; she was required to speak but she measured the way she would tell of the coming departure. Raising her hands to embrace the moon, she kept her face turned upward. "The people will be strong, we will flourish," the Mamacuna announced in a clear voice, "but one of the people will leave our home to seek destiny elsewhere. It will be a great loss to us, but we will survive this loss with great strength." She paused, letting her eyes scan the circle, then took her seat.

The moon, now high, cast an eerie light on the circle. The children and their nursemaids were led away, leaving only the collahuayas and chinan with the Rimoc and the Mamacuna. From somewhere in the ranks, a high voice began the chant beseeching the bounties of Mamaquilla for the people in the coming cycle of the sun. Others joined in the chant that continued for almost an hour, when the moon had, at last, reached its zenith. Silence again fell over the congregation as the chinan knelt to await the coming of the Aclla. He entered the circle alone, his mantle of condor feathers covering his body, his helmet worn low on his forehead so that only his eyes were visible. With slow, measured steps, he approached Mamacuna until he stood before her. Sinking to one knee, he bowed his head and awaited her words.

"Your prayers have brought life and joy to our people, Aclla of New Life!" announced Mamacuna proudly. "Mamaquilla has favored you with Her blessings and you have served Her well. What do you ask in exchange for this, Aclla?"

There was a tense moment of quiet. Without lifting his head, he replied, "I ask for the good fortune Viracocha can bestow upon the people. This and nothing more."

A ripple ran through the congregation. Most had expected him to ask to be released from his mita. Had he asked for release, the prophecy in the smoke would have been instantly fulfilled. Mamacuna smiled slightly and raised her hands over his bowed head. "Arise, and choose amongst the chinan for your consort."

The Aclla rose and took a garland of flowers from the hands of the Rimac standing nearest to Mamacuna. Slowly, he walked toward the kneeling maidens, their eyes on the ground so that all he saw of them was a row of wide-brimmed felt hats. Leah froze when brown toes stopped in front of her. She longed to pick up her head, to look at him, but she dared not; it would have been a terrible breach of protocol. Instead, she willed herself to be still. A single petal dropped to the ground, skirting her knees before it came to rest directly in her line of sight. Then the feet moved on. In a moment it was over. The Aclla and his consort had left the circle and the singing began again. With a deft move, Leah scooped up the fallen flower and tucked it into her pouch before rising with the others.

The rest of the ceremony passed too quickly for Leah. She sang the songs she knew, listened to the ones she didn't, and danced taqui until her feet ached. At the first sign of lightening sky, Mamacuna brought the rituals to a close, giving each participant a token for having served at the winter solstice. Too tired to thoroughly examine the delicate carving the Mamacuna had placed in her hand, Leah allowed Saba to lead her across the bridge and back to their lodgings where she could sleep as long as she liked.

∾ ∅ ∾

The Aclla slept beside his consort on a pallet of soft llama skins, an alpaca coverlet over them both. The dreams that had tortured him for months continued to haunt him: the white covered land, the man built mountains, the crowds of strangers. He knew this to be his destiny. In the dream he was searching, hunting for the grass-green eyes he was bound to follow. As soon as he saw them, coming toward him over a strange bridge, the aclla awoke with a start, only to find his consort breathing quietly beside him. He would sleep beside her for the remainder of the gathering, but they were not permitted to couple. Studying the supple form outlined by the blanket, he wondered why, at the last moment, when the petal dropped from his hands, Mamaquilla had steered his choice to this woman. Mamaquilla knew best; She knew it was not the time for Her chosen one to lie beside the Qewa Ñawi. He wanted her more than he had ever wanted any woman, but Mamaquilla spoke loudly to him: *this is neither the time nor the place.*

∾ ∅ ∾

The afternoon gathering of the priestess and the chinan was a more re-laxed, less awesome event. Leah, refreshed after several hours of deep sleep, took her place in the circle, this time with Saba sitting directly behind her, the older woman's strong hands resting lightly in her shoulders. The Aclla and his consort sat beneath a thatched awning near the Mamacuna. Each collahuaya presented her hua'amuata, reciting what special qualities had brought them together. When Saba's turn arrived, she rose, and addressed the gathering.

"My hua'amuata comes from far away; she will not stay with us. I will not be able to teach her all the things a hua'amuata must know, but she is smart." Saba allowed herself a wide smile. "Already she has learned many of our ways, and she had made pilgrimage to the huacas."

From beneath modestly lowered lashes, Leah caught the aclla's steady gaze in her direction. His dark eyes bore into her, directly into her heart where he implanted the message that he would be with her always. Leah, never one to put much stock in telepathy, suddenly felt a link of communication open between them. Turning her eyes back to the quipu in her hands, she told him she understood. A warm feeling flooded through her, one she could neither describe nor completely understand. Her cheeks were flush beneath the wide brim on her hat, and she was glad that no one could see. Focusing her attention on Saba, she listened to what her ma-ma'amuata was saying. She did not see the eyes of the Mamacuna suddenly turn in her direction.

As Saba recounted for her audience the things she had taught Leah, the other priestess nodded and clucked, impressed on how much the foreigner had learned in her time with the people. But it was when Saba began to describe the things Leah had taught her, that all eyes were riveted on the pair. "The markings on paper, like those of the janpeq, she tells to me and I learn how to heal my people better. She has shown me how to count the medicines the janpeq gives us, so I can give the proper amount to a sick child. My hua'amuata gives me time to think about the things the janpeq tells me, and helps to answer my questions so I can teach others." Saba paused for effect, assuring herself she had their complete, undivided attention. "My hua'amuata is a gift from Mamaquilla. Mamaquilla tells me there are things to be learned from the outsiders, things that can help us grow stronger. I will cherish my gift for as long as I have it."

Leah was touched by the old woman's words. She felt herself to be cherished, more than just comfortable amongst the people. It would be hard to leave when the time came and that time was coming soon. Fingering the knots on her quipu, Leah let the love coming though Saba's fingers comfort her.

∾ ⊖ ∾

The rest of the week at Janajpachallacta flew all too quickly for Leah. Ceremonies and offerings were separated by lectures and hands-on demonstrations taught by the collahuayas and the Rimoc. The mystics taught the proper way to receive a waking vision, how to decipher a dream vision, what to do when the vision required action on the part of the recipient. The collahuayas showed them how to recognize medicinal herbs and roots as well as how to prepare and administer them. Leah marveled at how the other chinan were able remember everything they were told without writing it down; she was the only one taking notes. When they weren't pressing Leah to read to them from her scratching, the other girls happily told Leah about their ayllus and their lives, their hopes and their dreams for the future. Many of the girls already had a boy in mind, some were even betrothed, but their marriages would not take place until the training was complete. Most had been in training for several years while others were, like Leah, newcomers.

On the last night of the gathering, two of the chinan were to be elevated to the full position of collahuaya, filling the places of two who had died during the past year. In a moving ceremony, the two girls were stripped of their rough woven tunics and dressed in finely woven sheaths of the softest alpaca wool dyed deep crimson. The collahuayas who served as their Mama'amuata wound colorful woven belts about their waists, placing longer, more intricate quipus in pouches hanging at the right hip. Their old hats were taken away, replaced by broader brimmed ones with a thin line of beaten gold thread at the base of the crown and a *paicha*, a thick tassel of multicolored vicuña threads attached on the right side. Thus adorned, the new collahuayas were escorted around the circle of women until they came to the Mamacuna who welcomed them to her ranks with a warm embrace. In turn, she presented them to the Aclla who sat on his own stone bench; his consort was seated on the ground beside him. As the new collahuayas knelt, he removed two condor feathers from his mantle and inserted one in each hatband.

Leah took the opportunity to study the Aclla openly, since all eyes were on him. When he stood, he towered over the others around him. The feathered mantle did little to conceal the straight line of his shoulders or the broadness of his chest. His arms were sinewy and powerful. The Aclla's face was a series of chiseled planes, bronzed by the sun, and smooth. His nose was straight, almost hawk-like, and lacked the flattened bridge so common to the people. But it was the way he carried himself that struck Leah most: erect, proud, and gracefully fluid. The solemnity of the presentation of feathers was relieved when he smiled at each new collahuaya, revealing a row of even, startlingly white teeth. There was something indescribable about him, a quality that Leah thought bordered on regal. She attributed it to the adulation to which he was accustomed, to the adoration by the women who cherished his unique gift.

The dancing began and Leah was swept away with the other chinan, moving in the measured steps of the taqui around the newly appointed collahuayas. With eyes on her feet, Leah imitated the complex series of steps and turns until she felt she knew them. Arms linked, they moved in rhythm to the drums and reed flutes played by the older women until their hats had slipped from their heads and bobbed on their backs, held by woolen cords. Leah laughed gaily with the others, enjoying the sense of sisterhood, taking no notice of anything but the brightly turning colors around her.

Micay, the Aclla's consort glanced up. Following his eyes, she saw that they were trained on the pale one. Obviously, some magic worked between them for she could feel the power of his gaze on the woman Li-ah. How she wished it were her he looked at with such interest! To become the declared of an aclla, most especially this one, was something all chinan dreamed of and she was no different. Sighing just a little, she settled herself so that her shoulder touched his thigh. As if without thinking, the aclla raised his hand and set it casually on her shoulder. The girl sighed again, pleased that in some small way, he knew she was alive. Right now, she would have to comfort herself with that; after all, she was the one who slept beside him in the night and, perhaps, after the pale woman was gone, perhaps he would be the one to take her maidenhead after declaring himself to her.

The gesture was intentional; the Aclla hoped the Qewa Ñawi noticed.

 e~ ⊖ ~e

The sun shone brightly but the air was crisp on the morning of the departure from Janajpachallacta. Dressed in clothing appropriate to her new
station as a chinan, Leah walked alongside Saba as they sang the farewell
hymn, a song whose lyrics told those waiting at the bottom of the mountain the gathering had gone well. In small bands, they made their way into
the rain forest, groups heading in the same direction walking together.
When the song had ended and they were deep in the jungle, Saba encouraged Leah to walk with the other chinan in their party while she stayed
with her own friends.

The girl who had been the Aclla's consort was with them and for a
time, Micay avoided all contact with Leah. When they made camp the first
night out, she found herself assigned to gathering firewood with the foreign
woman. Micay refused to talk to Leah until they came to a small stele
almost completely buried by undergrowth. Without a word, she backed
away from the marker and led Leah in the opposite direction.

"I don't understand what that was, Micay," said Leah when they were
a safe distance away.

"It's a *machai,* a burial marker. Have you never seen one before?" she
sneered, as though Leah were some sort of idiot.

"No, not one like that," replied Leah, a little annoyed with Micay's
hostility. "Who does it belong to?"

"A very powerful *sinchi,* a capac of the first order!" Her tone implied
that Leah's knowledge of the people was not what it was cracked up to be.

Leah wanted to go back to examine the stele, but refrained, knowing
it would offend Micay. Still, she wanted to know more about it. When
she asked her companion, Micay merely looked down her nose and began
picking up pieces of dead wood. Leah could not ignore her attitude. "I
think you don't care for me, Micay," said Leah, filling her own sling.

"Oh?" Micay tried to sound as if she didn't care, but the flush on her
face said something else entirely.

"You have no reason to treat me unkindly, Micay," said Leah softly. "I
carried the fire because this will be my only situa. You are the lucky girl,

not me. The Aclla chose you to be his consort. Perhaps this is the first step before he courts you."

"Do you think so?" answered Micay sharply. "Everyone saw he had eyes only for you when you were dancing taqui last night!"

"I think you read too much into a glance, Micay."

"And I think you have bewitched the Aclla. It would be better for us all if you went back the way you came and left us alone. You bring bad luck, Qewa Ñawi. You are not of our people nor will you ever be; you will bring the strangers to our land with your endless scribbles."

Leah felt her cheeks grow hot. "That is not my intent..."

"Whatever your intent is, Qewa Ñawi," spat Micay with venom, "it will not help to keep the strangers away. The Mamacuna may believe your stories, but it is clear to me that you wish to take the Aclla from us and with him the blessings of Mamaquilla."

She knew anything she said would be useless in changing Micay's mind. "Think what you want, Micay," Leah said with a shrug, walking away to rejoin the others.

⬳ ⊖ ⬲

The Aclla was summoned to Mamacuna as he prepared to leave Jana-jpachallacta. As soon as he entered her presence, he sensed the old woman's concern for him. She did not waste time with social pleasantries, cutting immediately to the reason for the summons.

"Before you leave us, churi, you must complete a cycle of pilgrimage to your huacas," she instructed, referring to the nine fertility shrines in the rain forest. "At each huaca, you must leave something of yourself, to mark the time you have served Mamaquilla."

In the past, he had always been especially careful not to leave any sign, for it might distract those who come to pray. Now, she was requiring him to do the opposite of that which he was taught. "I leave a piece of my heart here," he said quietly; "will that not be enough?"

The Mamacuna shook her head. "No, churi, you must give something back to Her.... something only She will know you value." He said nothing, so she went on. "Mamaquilla knows what is in your heart; She knows that which you will take with you and that which you will leave behind. You must ask Her permission to leave as you make an ending to your service to Her."

"Does She approve of my desire?" he asked, his voice so soft his words seemed to dissipate with the rustle of the leaves around the sacred circle. "Or am I not listening to her with my inner heart?"

The Mamacuna took his hand in hers. "She knows your heart, churi." She told him of the vision she had seen in the sacred smoke the night before, when she had made her private offering to Mamaquilla. "Like the night of the solstice, the smoke rose like a palm tree, with wide leaves floating above me. Again, a smoke bird flew from the tree, but this time, a second smoke bird appeared and flew after the first. I believe the first bird is the woman Li-ah. As I knew this day would come, I did not understand that it would be a woman who would cause you to go, churi. She is bound to you as you are to her and you must follow the will of Mamaquilla."

The Aclla bowed his head; Mamacuna merely confirmed what he already knew in his heart. With her blessings in his ears, he left Janajpachallacta, promising to come again in time for the Situa Raimi, the vernal equinox.

CHAPTER 6

Her time in the forest was dwindling. Leah worked furiously to finish recording the people's religious and mythological hierarchy, spending endless hours listening to stories and Saba's litany of rituals and customs. Even a few of the men agreed to talk of their nuts and bolts approach to the mysticism central to their beliefs. Visions were for the womenfolk, they told her again and again; their job was to feed the people of the ayllu, not dabble in things they did not care to understand. Instead, they took her with them to the potato fields and allowed her to participate in the ritual selection of sites for the coming year. She stood with Saba as the soil was examined and the decisions made. She learned which signs were favorable and which indicated the spirits of the land were not yet ready to be displaced by neat rows of tubers.

At the situa, Leah had been invited to visit several of the other collahuayas. Welcomed as a long lost friend, each lady wanted to impart her special knowledge to the Qewa Ñawi. Leah found herself spending more time traversing the distance between her ayllu and other, more remote villages. She quickly learned new paths and discovered that no matter where she went, there was an ayllu at which she could stop for a meal or even for the night if necessary. Periodically, she ran into Hector on his rounds. The doctor unabashedly displayed his delight in the way she got around as if she had been born there.

"You should stop at the old burial ground," he suggested one afternoon when they met on a path between ayllus.

"I've been to the one for our quarter, but not to any of the others. Where is it?"

"Up in the foothills. This is an old fashioned burial ground...they do things up there the ancient way. It's quite a site, Leah; don't miss it."

"Wanna come with me?" she asked, hoping to have his company for a little while longer. She hadn't had time to get to the clinic as often as she liked and she found she missed Hector.

He shook his head. "I wish I could, but I have three more ayllus to visit before I get back to the clinic tomorrow. I suppose you heard Sinchi Camor speared himself in the foot."

Leah tried not to laugh, but she did. "I heard. Mayta said he was too old to be out spear fishing with the boys and got what he deserved."

"I wouldn't argue about that, but the wound still needs tending. I gave him a tetanus shot two days ago on my way out, but I want to check on him before I head back." He slung a fatherly arm around her shoulders. "But I'll walk with you 'til the fork splits the path. Then you're on your own. I'll stop at your ayllu and tell Mama Saba you'll be late getting back."

"What a pal you are, Hector!" she teased.

Hector smiled, but behind the smile was an ocean of worry. It was all right for her to be tramping around the jungle alone now, but he did not know how much longer it would be safe. Paolo had reported seeing heavy land moving equipment parked on the mesa directly south of the clinic. The implied threat was rapidly becoming real.

They walked together until the path forked. One track led toward the river, but the other ran due west into the foothills. Hector made her promise not to stay too long in the foothills before he headed toward his next house call. "Saba will be waiting!" he called just before Leah disappeared around the bend in the trail.

"¡Sí, Papa!" laughed Leah with a last wave of her hand.

The yunka gave way to the rockier walls of the mountains and Leah felt unexpectedly exposed by the lack of green cover. She kept her eyes darting between the ledges on the west and forest on the east. Nothing seemed to live on this narrow boundary between the world of the people and the mountains. Every noise caused her to startle. When she reached the markers of the burial ground, Leah stopped.

The silence was deafening. Her own breathing reverberated against the rock walls. For a long moment, she stood at the base of the path to the burial ground while she debated whether or not to follow the narrow path into a crevice of the rock. The sun was already sliding into the mountains and the shadows were growing longer by the minute. She knew she had underestimated the time it would take her to see the burial ground and make it to her ayllu in time for the evening meal. The thought of sleeping so close to the cemetery disturbed her, but not nearly as much as the thought of sleeping out in the open. Still, this would be her last chance to see the ancient site. "Is there a choice here?" she asked aloud, and then laughed when she heard her words come back to her on the wind. "I guess not," she whispered before she started up the path.

The burial ground was like nothing she had seen before. She had seen death in her own ayllu and knew the people wrapped the corpses into a curled, upright position. However, to see the canyon ledges dotted with these mummies caused her to suck in her breath sharply. Some of the figures looked as if they were part of the landscape; others looked as though they had just been delivered to the final resting place. They all looked as though they were about to get up and stretch away the cramped feeling from having been left in so uncomfortable a position. Without venturing onto the burial ground itself, Leah took note of the baskets around the figures as well as the garlands of flowers left draped about their throats. She found she could identify the sinchis and the collahuayas by the red stripes on their shrouds although there was nothing else to mark any kind of rank. If the old mamacunas were there, they were not identifiable as anyone more important than a collahuaya. The mummies seemed to be grouped by ayllu; at the foot of each path leading up the canyon walls, there were steles denoting the different communities. Leah smiled to herself; it reminded her of the cemetery where her own family was buried. There, arches carried the names of Russian shtetls from which the groups had come. It was an oddly comforting observation; people wanted to be with their own. One of the more recent additions on the ledge closest to her was that of a collahuaya and instinctively she knew it was Rahua collahuaya from the ayllu at the bend in the river, a woman she had gone to see several times early in her sojourn. The recognition made her shiver; these were not simply subjects of a study; these were people she knew.

The shadows were growing longer by the minute, but Leah paused to pick up a stone as she passed between the markers. Gently, she placed it atop one of the steles. Had she been to visit Grandma Sophie's grave, she would have done the same thing.

As soon as she was on the path in the forest, Leah realized it was too dark to make it back to the ayllu without getting lost. She listened for the sound of rushing water and kept walking towards it until she found a safe place to make camp for the night. On a small rise above the river, she found a fire-ring, the sign of a wayfarer's stop. She built a small fire and unrolled her blankets. Although she was convinced she could manage to catch a fish as Mayta had shown her, Leah decided she was too tired to do anything more than light a fire and eat the cooked potatoes she had been given at the ayllu she'd visited that afternoon. With her camp pot in hand, she went down to the river for water, and set it in the fire to boil.

Sitting on the rise, Leah watched the shore for any wildlife. Although she knew the fire would keep most anything away, she did not want to go to sleep until after dark, when most of the animals around her would do the same. For some reason unbeknownst to her, she had long ago stopped worrying about the big cats in the forest; they seemed to simply stay away from people and the water was too fast at this spot to afford good fishing for those who would venture out. Finally, she went back to her blankets and crawled between them.

She had barely closed her eyes when she heard the unmistakable rumble of cat. It wasn't close, but she knew it wasn't too far away. With the least amount of movement, she pulled her knife from her pocket and opened the blade. Tense and ready, she waited. The rumble drew closer; Leah held her breath. Looking through half-closed eyes, she spotted a movement in the undergrowth. She waited, not daring to move.

"Shhhhhhhhhhhhh."

It was not an animal sound. Leah's fingers tightened around the knife handle.

"Inka, down!" hissed a very human voice in the local dialect.

The cat stretched out before the fire and began to groom itself like any other cat she had ever seen. As it turned its head, she spied its collar. Her grip relaxed and slowly, careful not to make any sudden moves, she sat up.

"You're not sleeping," said the aclla as he sat down beside the cat.

"No, I am not."

"Did I frighten you?"

"No."

He grinned at her. "You are a terrible liar. I think you were frightened or you would not have opened your knife."

Leah glanced down at the open knife in her hand. She closed it with a snap and slipped it back into her pocket. She regarded him for a moment. "I thought you were unaccustomed to idle conversation with women."

"I am."

She thought she saw his face redden in the firelight. "Yet, you are talking to me."

"I am not certain you are simply a woman."

"Oh? If I am not simply a woman, what am I?"

He shrugged his broad shoulders. "I do not know...but I would find out."

Leah snorted and the jaguar ceased his grooming to stare at her with wide, yellow eyes.

"Why do you find this funny?" he asked, suddenly serious.

"Because I wonder if you are simply a man!" she blurted out.

He crossed the distance between them in a single motion. He took her hand in his and held it against his chest. "I am flesh and blood. My heart beats as any other man's heart beats. My eyes see and my ears hear. My lips move and my teeth chew. But," he moved her hand to his temple, "it is my mind which is hungry. As hungry as yours." He released her hand and stood. "Sleep well, Qewa Ñawi; you will be safe in the night." He held his hand out, palm down, to the jaguar, then disappeared into the jungle. The cat, however, did not follow.

Leah watched him go. For a long time she stared into the brush and wondered why he had come to her. She had more questions than answers and she knew there were no answers for the questions she had. She looked at dark animal looking at her. "Inka, huh," she said aloud and the cat gave her what she thought might be a smile. "I suppose you're the reason I can sleep well?" Inka yawned.

Sighing, Leah lay down and drifted off to sleep, the sound of Inka's constant purring in her ear.

In the morning, the cat was gone. Instinctively, Leah's hand went to the flap of her shirt pocket. The emerald-eyed bird was gone; the one with the sapphire was in its place.

℘ ⊖ ℘

As her departure time grew near, Leah began sending her belongings to the clinic with Hector's chasquis. Sadness crept over Leah each time she packed another parcel, as though she were dismantling a piece of her life. Even the letters from home which the runners brought, filled with her parents' excitement at her impending homecoming, left her with a sense of regret that she would soon be leaving the people.

A week before she was scheduled to walk out of the jungle for the last time, a chasqui arrived carrying a thick Federal Express envelope. Hector had attached a note: *Thought this looked too important to sit on my desk. See you soon.* The postmark was Minneapolis, and Leah knew what the envelope contained.

With a definite lack of enthusiasm, she broke the seal and let the contents spill onto her lap. One by one, she read the documents. Professor Muñoz had wrangled a single at the dormitory she requested. Her old office was currently in use, but he arranged for a bigger one closer to his own. She was scheduled to teach one section of freshman anthropology, one section of upper level cultural anthropological field methodology, and assist in a seminar on Andean mythology and folklore in conjunction with the Hispanics department. In addition, Muñoz unofficially registered Leah for several classes including the dissertation seminar he taught. Instead of the usual excitement she experienced whenever one of these packets reached her, Leah felt empty. It was not that she disliked teaching; actually, she loved it, but, as the papers slid onto her makeshift bed, the reality of her impending departure crashed down around her.

The chasqui was waiting for any response that would have to be mailed immediately. Taking a pen from her desk, Leah hastily scribbled a note to her professor, filled in a few forms, and stuck them into the envelope he had, understanding her circumstances, kindly provided. She gave the packet to the runner, thanked him again, and watched as he disappeared into the jungle.

$$\approx \ominus \infty$$

The people of the ayllu threw a farewell feast on the night before Leah was to begin the long journey home. Mayta spoke long and eloquently about the sun cycle she lived with them. At her turn, Saba recounted the honors the Qewa Ñawi had received at the situa. As she was presented with gifts, Leah gave gifts in return. To Saba, her Mama'amuata, she gave her gold bracelet, the one she always wore. To Mayta, she gave her Swiss Army knife. The children got her colored pencils and some paper, along with a promise that the janpeq would send her their creations. If an object was not necessary to her trip, Leah gave it away so that each of her friends had a memento. In honor of their sister, the women of the village danced a taqui, drawing Leah into their line as they circled the central fire. There were generous amounts of laughter and tears, ending only when the women escorted Leah to her hut, showering her with flower petals as they would a bride on the eve of her wedding.

Leah awoke in the morning to find more garlands heaped on her bed. Sadly, she dressed in the fine vicuña tunic she had been given at Jana-jpachallacta, packing her bush clothes for when she arrived at Hector's. Other than her makeshift furnishings and her backpack, now filled with the gifts given to her last night, the hut was stripped of her belongings. Her desk and nightstand would be carried to Saba's hut after she left. A message from the Mamacuna herself arrived, delivered by one of her chasquis, instructing Leah to make a last pilgrimage to the nine fertility huacas before she left the people. The garlands were to be her offerings and Leah draped them around her neck before she went to fasten her one remaining bird pin to her tunic. When she noticed that the one with the emerald eye had replaced the sapphire-eyed silver bird, Leah was not surprised; she had expected this switch to take place in the night. With a last look around the place she called home, Leah went out to meet the villagers who would walk with her as far as the edge of their fields.

ଏ∽ ⊖ ∾ୠ

Leah made her pilgrimage backwards, beginning at the last huaca to Mamaquilla. She laid a garland of flowers at the foot of the huaca and offered a Quechua prayer for safe journey. She did not linger at the huaca, knowing there were time constraints if she were to arrive at Hector's in time for Paolo to fly her to Piura.

One by one, she visited the shrines, leaving a garland at each. The offerings had changed since she was last there, but in essence, they were the same. Fruits, flowers, children's toys and clothing graced each of the huacas, gentle reminders to Mamaquilla that without Her help, the people would not survive. At each huaca, Leah felt her strength building, as though the backward pilgrimage had been especially designed to help ease her pain at leaving the people and places she loved.

Leah made camp at the pool where she had first seen the aclla. Night was falling and she barely had time to build a small fire before the darkness enveloped her completely. Spreading her bedroll on the ground, she ate the potato flour cakes Rina had prepared, savoring what would be her last taste of village food. As was the custom when making pilgrimage, she would not eat again until the next nightfall, when Hector would probably make her eggs filched from his precious chickens. Snuggling beneath her warm blankets, Leah swiftly fell into a deep sleep.

ଏ∽ ⊖ ∾ୠ

From his perch on the cliff overlooking the pool, the Aclla watched the Qewa Ñawi. In her tunic and long braids, he mused as he chewed a blade of sweet grass, she looked like one of the people. He waited until she stopped moving beneath her blankets and then some; he wanted to be certain she was completely asleep before he approached this time.

With jaguar stealth, he made his way toward the Qewa Ñawi. He squatted beside her, marveling at the lustrous quality of her skin in the fire-light. He wanted to touch her face, but refrained, afraid she would awaken. With a sigh, Leah shifted position, causing the aclla to hold his breath for a moment. When her eyes did not open, he stretched out, his body fitting neatly against hers. As gently as he could, he wrapped his arms about the woman and joined her in the land of dreams.

Some time between darkness and the thin edge of grey velvet morning, when a fine mist rained gently down upon her, Leah awoke. The aclla's arms still cradled her, his breath soft and sweet against her face. In the soft light, she studied his face: its defenselessness in slumber, the way his thick black lashes rested against his finely sculpted cheekbones, the unexpected curl of dark hair on his forehead so uncharacteristic of the people. As sleep overtook her once more, she snuggled against him, but not before she was certain she had memorized every plane of that face.

The birds were already skimming the water hunting for their breakfast when Leah opened her eyes and found herself alone. There was no sign of the aclla, yet she knew she had not dreamt his arms about her in the night. She went about the business of smothering the last embers of her fire and rolling her bed. With her last two garlands back in place, she untied her pack to put in her small, llama fur pillow. Inside was his parting gift to her: a tiny golden aclla, complete with minutely carved condor feathers in the headdress. With trembling fingers, Leah slipped the little conopa into her pocket.

She needed to leave him a gift in return. It wasn't enough he had the silver bird; he had taken that himself. Whatever she decided on, it had to be something of value to her alone. Leah walked the short distance to the huaca and stood before the altar, silently asking Mamaquilla for advice. As she lifted a garland from her neck, the flowers caught on the Star of David she wore. With a smile, Leah extricated the flowers, set them at the base of the huaca, and then, unfastened the chain bearing the star. She re-hooked the clasp, then placed it in the hands of the stone image standing beside the shrine. By not putting it on the piled stones of the huaca itself, she knew the aclla would know it was meant for him.

∾ ⊖ ∾

Leah reached the clinic as the sun was just slipping behind the mountains. Hector welcomed her with a warm embrace and a cold beer, taking her pack as she slumped, exhausted, in his best easy chair. With a sympathetic ear, the good doctor listened to Leah's account of her last days with the people, understanding well her pain at having to leave. As promised, Hector fixed his guest a cheese omelet, and sat with her as she gobbled it down.

"Get a good night's rest, niña," he ordered, seeing her to the guesthouse. Paolo will be coming early tomorrow and stay only long enough to board you and your gear. Everything is already in the shack out on the landing strip." He handed her a packet containing the airline tickets she had left with him long ago. On impulse, Hector brushed a light kiss on her forehead. "Buenas noches, Qewa Ñawi."

It didn't take long for her to fall asleep, and it seemed she had slept only a few minutes when Hector was gently shaking her awake. "Time to get going, niña," he said. "Paolo will be here in less than an hour."

Leah pulled her khaki trousers and boots from her pack. Reluctantly, she folded her tunic and carefully tucked it into the carry-on she had left at the clinic with her one real suitcase a little more than a year ago. It seemed strange to be putting things in such an orderly fashion and she wondered how strange it would feel walk back into civilization after so long away. Leah barely had time to eat the biscuits and eggs Hector had prepared when the steady drone of a propeller filled the air. Out at the strip, they stood beside her small collection of boxes, all clearly labeled with her flight numbers and New York address. It was only a matter of hours before she would be sitting at her parents' kitchen table.

"Is there anything I can send you from the States?" Leah asked her friend.

"Oh, perhaps a can of tuna or a jar of peanut butter," he laughed. But the smile faded and his face grew serious. "What you can do is to tell whoever will listen that we are in greater danger than ever before, niña. The mining companies want in. The drug cartels are coming closer. The people are threatened, but you knew that was why you were given permission to come here in the first place. Tell them of us without telling."

Leah was aware of the environmental threats; you couldn't live in the district and not be aware of the little groups of surveyors sneaking around the mountains and the edges of the jungle. Bauxite, silver, even the small quantities of emeralds were enough to lure the treasure seekers to so remote a northern corner of the Andes. But the coming of the cocaine growers presented a more immediate threat. They knew the people grew the coca they used in their ceremonies and that the land was good for the crop. If the drug growers came into the district, the safety of the people would be more than threatened; it would be destroyed. "I will do what I can to keep the people where they are, janpeq," said Leah.

Hector slipped his arm about Leah's shoulder and hugged her. "It's all we can ask, Qewa Ñawi."

ɚ ⊖ ᴔ

Leah made the early connection from Piura to Lima with only minutes to spare. She handed her passport and visa to the customs inspector who barely glanced at her suitcase, but seemed fascinated with the contents of her three boxes. An antiquities inspector was summoned to determine whether or not she was carrying national treasures out of the country, but the bureaucrat confirmed her collection of gifts were merely crude native trinkets. By the grace of Mamaquilla, he did not ask to examine the contents of her pockets. Had he seen the golden aclla, surely she would have been arrested.

On the tarmac at Lima, the American Airlines 747 seemed bigger than anything Leah had ever seen, a shimmering behemoth waiting to carry her away from her beloved jungle. As in Piura, there was little time to spend wandering about the airport, but Leah did manage to purchase some magazines and a newspaper. The flight was called; Leah boarded, and was amazed when the attendant directed her to the first class cabin. "There must be a mistake," said Leah anxiously. "I have a coach ticket."

The attendant took her folder and removed the contents. She studied the ticket carefully, and then a folded piece of paper stapled on the inside. She smiled as she handed it back to Leah. "Read the note, I think you will then understand, señorita."

Leah smiled as she read the note from Hector. *My parting gift to you, Qewa Ñawi. Fly north in the belly of the bird in comfort.* It was a touching gesture, one that took her by surprise. Settling back in the wide seat, Leah silently toasted her friend with the complimentary champagne provided.

∞ ⊖ ∞

Hector sat in his easy chair, ostensibly reading a medical journal while his pupil sat at the table struggling with an essay in English. The doctor was honestly impressed at the progress Tan made working day and night to master the things he needed to know in order to follow the grass-eyed woman. Now that she was gone, he knew the aclla would want to quickly shed his mantle of condor feathers and fly in the belly of the silver bird himself.

Initially, Hector was disappointed with the responses to his queries concerning Tan's education. None of his colleagues in Lima or Quito expressed any interest in the young man. They merely dismissed him as another Indian trying to get out, but the answer from Minnesota, the place Tan wanted most to go, was optimistic. His medical school classmate and close friend, Arne Halstaad was ecstatic at the prospect of hosting Hector's protégé. As chairman of the epidemiology department at the university's School of Public Health, he called in a few odd favors and was ready to slide Tan into the U of M as a special student. He suggested the candidate complete a series of standardized tests, enclosing the ones he was able to obtain, and told Hector how to get the others through the university at Lima. Following a syllabus Arne also sent along, Hector began to finesse Tan's studies. While he had glanced at the exams, Hector knew to tailor his teaching to the tests would do Tan a disservice; he needed to learn what he could and answer the questions as best he could. That way, should he be accepted, they would know how to guide him.

In response, Tan had fortified his little home hidden deep in the forest.

There, he kept the lantern Hector lent him, and built crude shelves against the wall on which to keep the books he borrowed. Each day brought another challenge: stories to read, formulae to learn, maps to memorize. Long into the night he sat on a pile of vicuña skins, devouring everything he was given. In order for him to leave immediately following the summer solstice, Tan had to take the tests no later than the moon he now called October. There were only four weeks left to master the things he had been taught. When the work became oppressive, he took to running along the mesa above Mamaquilla's sacred pool to work off his frustration. When his temper ran short, Hector would take away his books and send him to the Mamacuna for the night. She would listen to his new litany of history, geography and science, and if she did not understand it all, she understood his need to speak these things aloud. As aclla, he continued to perform his duties to Mamaquilla, but with every hymn he added a prayer of his own for Her blessings on his quest.

At night, when his eyes could no longer stay open, Tan would touch the golden rope holding not one, but now two stars around his neck: the one made by Iztak, his grandfather and the one the Qewa Ñawi left for him at the huaca. He would fall asleep imagining grass green eyes looking into his. He knew where she was, that she would be in the place called Minnesota, but he had no assurances that she was the final reason Mamaquilla was permitting him this journey. He only knew something was driving him and that Mamaquilla looked kindly upon him.

AUTUMN IN THE STATES
SPRING IN PERU
1988

CHAPTER 7

Three days of her mother's cooking was hardly enough to fortify Leah before her return to Minneapolis, but it would have to do. Her parents drove her to LaGuardia to catch the noon flight, sad to see her leave so soon, but somewhat mollified by her promise to come home for Thanksgiving. Airborne again, Leah finally looked forward to going back to school.

When she stepped out of the jetway into Minneapolis-Saint Paul International Airport, she was halted by a mass of moving flowers. Laughing, she parted the bouquet to find Jay's grinning face.

"Welcome back to civilization!" he cried, thrusting the oversized offering into her hands. "No doubt they pale by comparison to the ravishing jungle flowers you're used to, but hey, what the heck!"

Leah gave him a quick hug and thanked him. "I guess I'm glad to be back, but..."

"But what? Don't tell me! You're going to go back to the wilds of Peru as soon as you finish your degree!" His voice sounded a little hurt, but Leah couldn't tell if he was putting her on.

"Well," she drawled, making a joke out of it, "I kinda liked living someplace without locks on the door."

"Locks, shmocks...but can you get a fresh bagel there?"

Leah laughed, letting him slide a friendly arm around her. "Speaking of bagels, I have a dozen in my suitcase. Mother insisted." As soon as the words were out of her mouth, she knew why her mother had insisted on bringing the bagels to Minnesota. "Speaking of my mother," she said casually, "am I to assume you were in touch with her and that's how you knew when I was arriving?"

Jay held up his one free hand in mock protest. "Me? Talk to *your* mother? Why on earth would I do that?"

Leah shot him a sidelong glance and let it go. Her parents approved of Jay Weiss and his incipient medical career. What was not to like? He was a nice Jewish boy from a nice Jewish family; he obviously loved her, they shared a wealth of common interests and, as her mother pointed out so pointedly last year, religion. He was tall, handsome, and kind, all the things a mother would want for her daughter. Leah allowed herself a private smile; even Mama Saba would approve of Jay. He was just that kind of guy. But he was also the kind of guy who wanted a wife whose career would take second place to his, and she was not that kind of girl. They had that conversation two weeks before she left for Peru.

They collected the baggage and hauled it out to Jay's illegally parked car. The airport patrol lady, on the verge writing a ticket, lectured Jay on the evils of law scoffing and let him off with a stern warning. Sitting in the front seat, Leah barely listened as Jay rattled on about what she had missed during the last year while she stared, unblinking, at the familiar Minnesota landscape.

"Let's drop your bags and go have a pizza at Old City," Jay said as he pulled up in front of the dorm.

"Thanks, but I'm really tired. Can I take a rain check?"

"Come on, Lee; I'll bet you haven't had pizza in over a year."

"True, I haven't, but..."

"But nothing. You'll at least have one decent meal before you're forced to face dorm food."

"Look, Jay, it's not that I don't want a pizza..."

"You just don't want to have pizza with me."

"I didn't say that." Leah leaned back in the seat and sighed. "I thought all this was settled before I left."

"We agreed to take a year off and see how we felt. Well, the year is up and my feelings haven't changed, Lee." He took her hand. "Have yours?"

She disengaged her hand from his. "I really don't want to have this discussion right now, Jay."

⊘

Although the narrow room on the eleventh floor of Middlebrook Hall overlooked the Mississippi River, Leah longed for the relatively spacious comfort of her thatched jungle home. Her clothes hung in the closet like strangers; she hardly recognized the skirts and dresses, the sweaters and jeans. They all seemed so foreign and uncomfortable looking. Even dressed in shorts she had worn in the jungle a scant week ago, Leah felt out of synch. When she opened her eyes in the morning, it took her a full minute to realize she was not at her ayllu...or even at Hector's.

Slowly, almost methodically, she started to put some order back into her world. She spent as little time in her room as possible, but enough time to get used to living there. She slept late in the mornings, but once she was up and moving, she would grab her pack and head across the bridge to her office on the east bank of the campus.

The muggy September afternoons, reminiscent of the steamy summer days in the rain forest, made Leah a little less homesick for her ayllu. As she strolled across the Washington Avenue bridge, Leah paused to look out over the river. Dark, muddy, steadily flowing, the Mississippi was hardly mighty. Here, it wasn't even a half-mile wide, with minimal barge traffic and little hint of its ultimate majesty to the south. Leah thought standing above the Mississippi to be slightly bizarre.

Ford Hall was cool, almost dank, behind the thick walls. The first moment she walked back through its doors, Leah noticed the smell: that musty academic aroma she always associated with the place. And she noticed the absence of activity. Summer school was over but the rush before fall quarter had not quite begun. She poked her head in the department office, but it, like the rest of the building, was deserted except for a lone secretary with a phone against her ear. She waved Leah in, but did not stop her conversation. Leah checked the wall of pigeonholes for one with her name and found it crammed full. Sticking purposefully out, however, was a white envelope with her name written in Dr. Muñoz's elegant scrawl and inside were the keys to her new office on the second floor.

The lock stuck and Leah had to jiggle the key to turn the old bolt. When it finally opened, the smell of must was close to overpowering, indicative of the fact no one had been in there all summer. She pushed open the window and was relieved to feel a faint breeze. The desk had been cleaned out; only the bare basics of office supplies remained in the top drawer. Leah dumped the mail and her book bag on its pitted surface and sat down. The chair, an old wooden swivel variety with squeaky wheels, was not uncomfortable, but a cushion was definitely in order.

There were infinite forms to be completed. One by one, Leah examined them all, filling out the easy ones, putting the tougher ones into a separate pile to take back to the dorm. She glanced at the journals and magazines, separating the ones that contained something of interest. There were several letters from colleagues, a welcome back note from her friend Mary, and assorted junk mail. But it was the envelope at the bottom of the endless pile that caught her eye. It had a Piura postmark and had been sent, of all things, by Federal Express. Leah tore it open and the contents spilled out on her desk.

"A chasqui from your ayllu arrived right after you left," Hector had scrawled; "Saba forgot to give you this. She thought it only proper that you have it with you, but instructs me to tell you that you may not attach it to your hat until you return to us here. *Tu estimado amigo,* Hector."

Leah fingered the thick paicha; the very feel of the vicuña threads made her feel a little less detached. Holding it to her nose, she tried to smell the rain forest and indeed, the scent lingered in the fibers. Leah found a pushpin the desk drawer and hung the tassel on the bulletin board in front of her.

෧ ⊖ ෧

The demands of academia sucked Leah back into her old patterns of class-library-eat-sleep before she could protest. Class took up most of her time, but instead of the writing papers and cramming for the tests, she was grading the endless student submissions. Although she was in the dorm where food service was provided, she managed to eat just as badly as when she had to cook for herself. She tried to remember when meals were served in the cafeteria, but too often she was on the wrong side of the river to make it back to the dorm in time. Out of desperation, she rented a little square refrigerator and kept it full of yogurt. Jay made sure she had at least one decent meal each week and encouraged their mutual friends to bug her until she agreed to meet people for lunch or dinner.

The Jewish holidays fell early in the quarter. Had Leah been in her own place, she would have hosted Rosh Ha'Shanah dinner at her own table, but this year, she accepted invitations to other people's houses. The first night of Rosh Ha'Shanah, Leah and Jay attended services at the Hillel House before walking home with the Rabbi Mark Steinberg, his young son, Avi, and a small army of other students needing a place for the holiday. As was the tradition, anyone without a place to be was welcome at the Steinberg's. This year, according to Mark, it was a small crowd for first night: only twenty-three.

"I can't believe you haven't seen the kids in over a year," commented Mark Steinberg as they strolled toward his house near campus. "You won't recognize Elisheva; she's a walking opinion."

"When I left she was barely talking!"

"Well, now she never stops talking," grumbled Avi as he kicked a small stone down the sidewalk. He nudged Jay and the two of them took off after the rock.

"She won't even remember me, Mark."

"Oh, she remembers you. I think every other sentence out of Tova's mouth this last year has started with 'when Leah gets home....'"

"And what exactly am I supposed to do when I get home?"

"I think it's something about braiding hair." The rabbi's eyes followed Avi and Jay as they detoured into a small park. "What are you going to do about him, Lee?"

"Him as in Avi or him as in Jay?"

"You know what I mean. He's been gyrating since you left a year ago; I thought he'd go nuts before you got back. He must've spent half of the shabboses moping around our house. In fact, we almost cancelled our trip to Chicago last summer because Mindy was afraid to leave him alone."

"No way!" cried Leah.

"Well, we talked about taking him with us," laughed Mark; "he was so lonely, so miserable without you."

"Do you mean to tell me he didn't have a single date all year? I mean, come on, Mark; he's a med student. A prize catch. Someone didn't corner him?"

"It wasn't from lack of trying, Leah. Mindy introduced him to at least five nice girls.........as per your instructions."

"She wrote me about a couple of them."

"But Jay didn't take the bait. I know you were hoping he would meet someone and then you'd be off the hook...no pun intended, but he didn't and methinks you're not."

"Definitely not," sighed Leah.

"Which brings me back to my first question: what are you going to do about him?"

"Frankly, I haven't decided."

"He's perennially optimistic, you know."

"I know," sighed Leah, "but I'm not so sure I believe in the same happy ending he does." Leah glanced around; there was a small parade walking with them. She had no wish to share her situation with strangers. "Do me a favor, Mark; change the subject."

∞ ⊖ ∞

With so many people for dinner, Leah was pressed into kitchen detail as soon as she arrived. With a quick hug and a promise to sit with the girls, Leah fell right into Mindy's serving pattern. Once everyone was seated, the blessings made, and the apple slices dipped in honey, Mindy was up and prepping the soup. Leah remained at the table until people were done with the first course before she began picking up empty plates. Wonderfully efficient, they worked in tandem throughout the meal. There was precious little time to talk while the meal was being served, but once the main course was cleared and everyone took a breather before dessert, Mindy and Leah had a few moments alone in the kitchen.

"I was surprised when Mark said you were coming *with* Jay," said Mindy as she handed Leah a wet platter.

"As opposed to coming alone even though we both knew we were going to the same place?"

"You know what I mean."

"I do, Mindy."

"And?"

"And what?"

Mindy shot her look that made Leah laugh.

"Okay, here's the scoop: he wants us to pick up where we left off. And, I'm not so sure I want to do that."

"Leah, Jay's a wonderful guy. You two do so well together. You've got so much in common that I can't believe you'd walk away from him." Mindy handed Leah the last platter, then picked up a sponge.

"It's very complicated, Mind."

"I know from complicated and you and Jay are not...we did a lot of talking while you were gone and I think Jay has come a long way in understanding your need to have a career that is not second place to his. That was, according to him, the biggest issue."

"But it goes beyond that," sighed Leah. "There are some things which are just ingrained into a person's psyche and Jay's got a second banana thing about women and careers. Ask him if he's planning to take a paternity leave when his wife has kids. When Paul Goodman's wife gave birth, he took six weeks off and Jay was astounded. He thought that was positively loony."

"Would you want him around for the first six weeks after birth?" asked Mindy. "I would've killed Mark if he hung around the house."

"That's not the point. The point is that he doesn't see sharing household responsibility as a way of life. His attitude is very old fashioned. He was doing it before I left......at the apartment. I would make dinner and he would do nothing. I would say, 'come help me with the dishes,' and he would bring over a plate. Our worst fights were about this stuff. At least Mark pitches in."

"Ah, but he didn't always. I had to train him.......with rewards." Mindy stopped wiping the counter and stared at Leah for a long moment. "What happened in Peru, Lee? Something radical happened down there and I don't mean the usual life in the jungle something. I mean something happened to *you*. I can see it in your eyes and I can hear it in your voice."

Leah laughed unexpectedly. "You sure know how to ask all the wrong questions, Mindy."

"They're only wrong because you don't want to answer them. That doesn't change the fact that you still need to answer them, even if only for yourself." She tossed the sponge at Leah. "Has it turned out that the jungle doctor is a factor in all this? Did you and he...?"

"Hector?" cried Leah. "Oh, God, Mindy! What a thought. No, heavens no!"

"I just thought I'd better ask."

"Oh, I'll have to write to Hector and tell him you asked if we were carrying on. I think he'll laugh 'til his sides split."

ꝏ ⊖ ꝏ

Autumn collided with winter earlier than usual. The first measurable snowfall came in late October, right before Halloween, covering the campus in a thick, white blanket. Wistfully, Leah thought about spring in the Andes as she trudged to class wrapped in a down coat, her feet tucked snugly into Sorrel boots. Each day, when she arrived in her office, she would finger the tassel hanging on the bulletin board, think about how hot it was in her little corner of the world, and hope that someone was remembering her.

Slowly, she worked her life back into some normal patterns. She started going out more, seeing old friends, and spending more time with the Steinbergs. Mindy occasionally pressed her to talk about what really happened in the jungle, but Leah managed to skirt around that one issue with ease. Unwilling to talk about the aclla or his nocturnal visits to her, Leah instead told her endless tales of the Mamacuna and her court, hoping that the mystical side of her experiences would keep Mindy away from that one delicate area.

Jay tried to provide pleasant diversions. Despite her protestations, he kept alive the hope that she would see the error of her ways and come back to him. Determined to convince her to change her mind, he saw her whenever they could manage a free evening together and he kept everything light and unpressured. Theatre tickets, concert tickets, Sunday walks around the lake were all designed by Jay to keep his arm around her.

On a cold November night, he was waiting for her in the lobby of the dorm. "Let me take you away from all this, my dear lady!" he sang, sweeping her grandly into his arms.

"What is going on?" demanded Leah. "You said you had clinic every night this week."

"My dear young anthropologist, you are talking to the latest recipient of the prestigious Castleberry Fellowship in pediatrics."

Leah's mouth fell open. "Oh, Jay, that's wonderful! Congratulations!"

"Not enough, Señorita Fine. How 'bout celebrating my promising future with dinner at Luci's?"

With more papers to grade than she could bear to think about, the prospect of dinner at her favorite Italian restaurant was tempting. "Do you think we can get in on short notice?" she asked, suspecting the reservations were already made.

"Assolutamenté. I'll pick you up at seven."

Something inside told her there was more to this than he was letting on, but Leah agreed anyway. "I'll meet you down here at seven sharp."

Small was not the word to describe Luci's. Minuscule, cramped, a postage stamp all would have been far more accurate, yet despite its size, the food was the best Italian in either of the twin cities of Minneapolis and Saint Paul. Jay discovered Luci's right after they opened, and after that, all special occasions had been celebrated at the restaurant. As they sat awaiting *insalata caprese* with roasted red peppers, Jay told her about the fellowship. It meant he could do his residency in Minnesota, where he wanted to be, rather than having to apply to hospitals all over the country in hopes he could get into a good program. He wanted either Minneapolis or Saint Paul Children's Hospital and now he'd have his choice. It also meant he could buy a small house, something he dearly wanted.

"And I suppose you'll plant tomatoes in the back yard," teased Leah when he admitted he had already started looking for a house.

"And radishes and green peppers and anything else you want in your salad."

"What about broccoli?"

Jay made a face. "If you want broccoli, sweetheart, you'll have to grow it yourself."

"Not this girl," laughed Leah. "Ask our ayllu's sinchi: Mayta will tell you I have a black thumb."

Jay picked up her hand and carefully studied the extended digit. "Looks okay to me, but there is clearly something wrong with one of the other fingers."

"Oh? And what's that?"

He separated her ring finger from the others. "This one lacks an appropriate piece of jewelry."

She yanked her hand away. "Oh, no it doesn't. It looks just fine the way it is."

"I know," said Jay reaching across the table to retrieve her hand, "we agreed that we'd just be friends, but the truth of the matter, Lee, is that I love you. I want to spend the rest of my life with you. I figured this out while you were gone, but I didn't want to tell you in a letter. I wanted to wait until we could sit face to face and discuss it."

Leah felt herself redden under his steady gaze. All things considered, it was quite a declaration from the carefree, no strings Jay she had been seeing of late. "Jay, the reason I broke it off in the first place was because you felt that your career would always come first. I wasn't then and I'm not now prepared to limit my options."

"I'm not asking you to, Lee. You've got at least another two years here before you get your PhD. That'll be most of my residency. After that, we can go wherever you want."

"I have no idea what I'll want to do in two years, Jay!" cried Leah. "I may want to go back to Peru for a while. I may want to spend a year on Jupiter! I don't have a clue!"

"You don't have to make any decisions now," he said softly. "I just want you to think about it."

"Think about what, Jay? Giving up everything I ever wanted?"

"No. Think about sharing it with me when we're married."

Leah looked across the table into a pair of anxious blue eyes. She suspected he had been coached on appropriate answers by one Mindy Steinberg. "I don't know what to say." Her voice was a mixture of exasperation and sympathy.

"Then don't say anything," replied Jay. "Let's take this one step at a time. I won't pressure you, Lee; I learned my lesson all too well. I don't want to change you, because I'm in love with the woman you are."

Leah smiled weakly at him, wanting to say something reassuring, but not quite ready to say she loved him. "I need time, Jay; time to figure out what I'm going to do when I finish my degree. I do care for you," she admitted, the smile fading slightly, "but I'm not prepared to make a commitment."

"I'm not asking you to, sweetheart. I am only asking your permission to see you...to court you. Like a date, not a friend."

The mozzarella arrived and, for the moment, the conversation ceased in favor of the savory cheese. Throughout the dinner, Leah and Jay talked about a wide variety of things, but their relationship was not one of them.

Instead of a chaste kiss in the dorm lobby, Jay took Leah into his arms and held her close. He made no move to kiss her. "I love you, Leah," he whispered into her ear. "As a friend, and as more. However you want to handle this, I'll go along."

❧ ⊖ ❧

Riding up alone in the elevator, Leah considered her situation and wished she had Saba handy for a long talk. Somehow, the old woman was always able to put puzzles into perspective.

A couple of girls were standing in the vestibule when the elevator doors opened. They invited Leah to join them for popcorn, but she declined; she was tired and still had papers to grade for the morning's intro class. It would have been nice to sit around and chat, but duty called louder than the enticing smell of popping corn.

Snow had started to fall again, making a little mountain range on the ledge outside Leah's window. She changed her clothes in favor of an old flannel nightgown and stretched out on the bed, the stack of quizzes beside her. Reaching over, she flicked on her stereo; haunting Andean flute melodies drifted from the speakers, tunes similar to the ones the people played in her ayllu. For a moment, she was transported, but the pile of papers could not be ignored, so with an exaggerated sigh, Leah began to read freshmen essays on the development of agriculture in the southwestern United States.

> Leah was at the last huaca, standing before the stone house. She could see inside, where the aclla, on his knees, prayed to Mamaquilla. She opened her mouth to call to him, but no words came out. He turned, then rose, moving toward her, dancing the slow steps of a taqui, his sinewy arms spread wide to encircle her, yet not touching her. He was warmth around her, his strength flowed from him into her. "Your heart is in my heart," he told her, "as I am in yours. You are bound to me forever."
>
> "I am bound to you forever," she echoed.
>
> "I will come to you," said the aclla as he disappeared into the mist.
>
> There was a moment of panic when he faded away, leaving her alone at the huaca.

Early morning light streamed in Leah's window, awakening her. She opened her eyes and groaned at the profusion of test papers scattered on the floor. Sometime during the night, she must have rolled over to wrap herself in her alpaca blanket; the same blanket under which she had slept in Peru. For a moment, she remembered the dream and shivered. The aclla was, as always, still with her, and she was beginning to believe the dreams were sent to her by him, just as Saba had said he could do. She wished she had dreamt of Jay but that had not happened. The aclla, his brown eyes boring into hers, had once again invaded her sleep, reminding her of what she had left behind.

Leah did not believe for one New York minute that she was in love with him; he was merely a memory, serving Mamaquilla, giving hope to women who might not have any without him. Yes, he was handsome. Yes, he elicited from her a definite sexual response, but no, she did not pine for him. Almost angry at the queasy feelings she experienced after these episodes, Leah jumped off the bed and headed for the bathroom. A long, hot shower was what she needed before she tackled the rest of the papers.

CHAPTER 8

Preparations for the summer solstice took the aclla away from his departure preparations, leaving Hector to make the final arrangements. The Rimoc had been preparing for the aclla's request to be released from his mita since the Mamacuna officially informed them following the gathering at the spring equinox. Discreet chasquis had been sent from Janajpachallacta to search out new candidates for the ceremony; those chosen were tapped on the shoulder by a chasqui while they prepared for the manhood ceremony in solitude. Only the local collahuaya would know when a young man had been tapped and would not immediately return to his ayllu after his initiation into manhood. When the candidates were assembled, the Mamacuna would consult the Rimoc and ultimately choose the youth who would sleep beneath the watchful eye of Mamaquilla. And unlike Micay, who had been chosen by the aclla himself, this time the lucky chinan would be selected by the Mamacuna.

In spite of all the secrecy, rumors flew about the jungle as swiftly as brightly colored parrots. The girls who would be going to the situa spent extra time working on their tunics and their adornments, hoping that the exquisite designs might catch the eye of the Mamacuna. Boys preparing for manhood ceremonies were on edge, keeping an extra sharp eye while in the forest in case a chasqui should appear from nowhere.

As the solstice approached, the aclla went up to Janajpachallacta to prepare for his release. For three days, he fasted and prayed at the huaca in the grotto, the same one the Qewa Ñawi had used for her own meditations.

Somehow, it made him feel closer to her. A condor circled continually overhead, reassuring the aclla that his decision was indeed favored by Mamaquilla. On the last night of his vigil, the Mamacuna came to him at the huaca. The aclla knelt before her, but she asked him to sit beside her on the crude stone bench outside the grotto.

"Have you taken leave of your parents?" she asked him.

"I asked for and received their permission and their blessings for my journey before I came."

"And Aima?" she asked.

"That was hardest of all, Coya. I think I will not see my grandmother again in this world."

"Your grandmother understands, for she understood Iztak well. Your mother is sad, but happy to know her son will be free of his mita. She worries that the time alone has broken your heart."

He gave her a wry smile. "My mother worries too much."

"All mothers worry too much, churi. It is what we do best." She left him alone to resume his meditation.

The aclla appeared before the Mamacuna and the Rimoc on the night before the gathering was to commence. Standing in the center of the circle wrapped in his mantle of condor feathers, his helmet set straight upon his brow, he recounted the number of babies born to those who sought him out. At the end of the recitation, he knelt at the feet of the Mamacuna, his head bowed. "The time has come for me to ask for release from my mita, Coya," he said aloud, a little surprised when his voice trembled as he spoke the words. "I have served with my heart and my seed, giving to our people the gifts given to me by Mamaquilla."

"You have served well, churi. Proof of Mamaquilla's love for you can be seen in the faces of those who have received Her blessings through you."

"My feet are on a path away from the people, Coya, but my heart will remain here."

The Mamacuna sighed and smiled sadly. Na-Tan Manco had been a fine aclla, accepting his responsibility with grace and dignity, never complaining about the long loneliness that accompanied service to Mamaquilla. She would have preferred to see him declare himself to a woman of the people; there were many girls who would have gladly welcomed him into their huts. But Mamaquilla had spoken to her about his destiny through visions and dreams, and she knew what he sought was meant for him. "You will be missed greatly by our people, and we shall all pray to Mamaquilla for your safe return." She did not have the heart to tell him he would never return to them as one of the people. Standing, Mamacuna held out her hand and commanded him to rise.

As he stood, the Rimoc came forward, circling around the aclla nine times...once for each of the fertility shrines in the jungle. The *Apu-Rimac*, the Mamacuna's male counterpart, approached the aclla. Reaching up, he removed the helmet of feathers from the aclla's head and brought it to the Mamacuna. Two of the Rimoc removed the mantle from the aclla's shoulders and brought that, too, to the old woman. The aclla now stood almost naked in the center of the circle, the only adornment on his body the golden chain with its two stars.

The Mamacuna allowed herself to study the man standing before her. "Your body has grown strong in the service of Mamaquilla," she said softly. "There will come a time when you will truly bind your heart to a woman's heart." She raised her hands upward in supplication to the Goddess. "May she be worthy for you are sacred to Mamaquilla." No one had to tell her who the woman would be; she already knew. Far to the north, in the Ru-ti-Suyu, that woman was walking between two man-built mountains, her arms laden with the things the janpeq called books, her grass green eyes were narrowed against a cold wind. She washed the vision from her mind's eye and spoke to the man. "You were aclla, now you are once again Na-Tan Manco Ba-Arro, but you shall be known as Villac-Quilla, He Who Serves the Goddess. Go in peace." She waited until Tan prostrated himself before her and then, along with the Rimoc, she was gone.

How long he lay on the ground Tan did not know. But when he rose, he felt the burdens of his duties lifted from his shoulders, he was free as a condor to soar through the skies. He found a tunic laid out for him, as well his carry pouch. Dressing quickly, he took a last look at the center of his former life and descended from the mountain.

The moon had risen and set before he reached the compound. Hector left a lamp burning for him and Tan was glad. Bone tired, he stretched out on the worn sofa and fell into a dreamless sleep.

In the morning, the aroma of food awakened him. Sitting up, he saw Hector standing at his stove, a towel tucked into his trousers, tending to breakfast. "Good morning," he called in English, the language they now exclusively spoke.

"Good morning to you!" He waved a spatula at his guest. "Go wash and we'll eat. Paolo is coming before noon and we have to be ready to go."

Tan's smile was bright enough to light a moonless sky. He would soon take his first flight in the belly of a silver bird and he could not wait. Like a silly child, he bounded from the sofa.

The table was set with forks, knives and spoons. When Hector put a dish of scrambled eggs and fried bananas before him, Tan automatically picked up his napkin and placed it in his lap. "Do I have to tip you?" he teased, referring to the lessons on restaurant deportment Hector had painstakingly reviewed.

"*Cállate y come*," growled the doctor. He was nervous about the whole expedition, yet almost as excited as Tan. "There are a few things to go over before we leave, Mr. Villac-Quilla."

Tan liked the sound of his new name. At the last equinox, he had shyly approached the Mamacuna about a surname, explaining that he needed one in order to go to America. She had thought about it and then provided one, but not before making him promise to tell no one except the janpeq until she announced it at the solstice gathering.

Tan swallowed the last of his eggs and asked Hector what was on his mind.

"It's about money, Tan," he said, hating to have to discuss something so delicate at the table.

"Dollar, half-dollar, quarter, dime, nickel, penny. One hundred pennies to a dollar. What else do I need to know?"

It was Hector's turn to laugh. "Not that kind of money. I'm talking about real money. Big bucks. Tuition. Living expenses, that sort of thing."

"Ah, we have not discussed that." Every time he asked how he would pay for his education, Hector changed the subject. Opening his carry pouch, Tan removed a smaller pouch tied tight with a strip of leather. He deftly unknotted the thong and poured the contents onto Hector's table. "Will these be of use to pay for my education?"

Hector gasped at the array of emeralds scattered on the worn wood. "¡Ai, Mama!" he cried. "Where did you get these?"

"From the mountains. The Coya said they are valuable."

A single rough hewn stone would have more than paid for Tan's education with enough left over to pay for a new car, a house and anything else which might catch a young man's fancy. Hector blew a long whistle then one by one replaced the stones in the bag, keeping only two modestly sized stones on the table. "We will take these to the assaying office in Piura and have them tested, Tan. If they are worth what I suspect they are worth, we'll sell them and put the money in the account I have already opened for you in Piura. The money will be there if you need it, but understand this: your education is already paid in full. As for the others, we'll put them in a safe deposit box at the bank and you can claim them when you return."

Hector was not rich, but he was not exactly poor either. He had no use for significant amounts of cash in the jungle, choosing instead to take the government stipend received for his services and put it into the clinic. When he sold his house in Trujillo, he bought a couple of acres on the Peruvian coast, thinking that one day it would be a nice place to build a little beach house when the jungle had sapped the strength from him. A beautiful spot, it did not take long before land developers in Lima decided it was a great place for a resort. Since he had no emotional tie to the land, Hector negotiated an incredible price and sold it off. He could, he decided, well afford to buy a condo there if he was ever ready to call it quits. Having money sit in a bank did no one any good; he decided his next investment would be Na-Tan Manco Villac-Quilla.

In addition, Arne Halstaad had arranged a grant for Tan through a group of private benefactors who sponsored foreign students at the university. That would cover part of his tuition and academic expenses. "But I don't want you to feel pressed for money, Tan," he said in earnest. "I want you to concentrate on your studies, to find an area you wish to master, but at the same time I want you to have some fun."

Tan's brows knitted over his dark eyes. "Fun?" he asked. "I am going to America to learn, not to play games."

"I know you are going to learn," Hector sighed, "but Tan, everyone needs to have fun. You will want to go to movies and concerts and restaurants. You will not be alone like you have been here. You'll meet women and may want to take some of them out." He dared not mention Leah; every time he uttered her name, a mask dropped over his pupil's face. He waited for comment, but when there was none forthcoming, he continued. "For now, you will live at the home of Dr. Halstaad. It's near the campus and you will be able to walk to classes. As soon as you are ready, he will help you find a place of your own."

"An apartment?" The word rolled lovingly off his tongue.

"Yes," laughed Hector, "an apartment; a place to call home." Hector went into his bedroom and returned carrying some clothing. "Here, Tan. Put these on. They won't be a good fit, but they will have to do until we get to Piura. You can't very well go in your natural state of undress."

Tan smiled and accepted the outfit. He removed his tunic and slipped on the pants, tying his own sash around his waist. Looking down, he thought he looked ridiculous, but the healer was right; he needed to be wearing pants. They were far too short for him, but it did not matter. He pulled the shirt over his head, then tried to tuck it in the way Hector wore his own shirts. Laughing, he let the doctor to assist him. "Will Mamaquilla recognize me so covered up?" he asked.

"Mamaquilla would recognize you if you wore a bag over your head, my friend. As soon as we get to Piura, we will go shopping. There is much you need if you are to survive in the Ruti-Suyu called Minnesota." Hector stopped for a moment, and then asked quietly "Have you been to see your parents, Tan?"

"Yes. I said good-bye before the gathering."

Hector waited to see if he said more, but the face was impassive. It could not have been easy for him to say farewell to his parents, let alone his grandmother who was aging rapidly. "I will look in on them and write you about it each time," he said; it was a promise he meant to keep.

ତ୍ତ ⊖ ୧୭

In the bag Hector provided, Tan packed the things he would be taking with him, the little things he had been bringing to the clinic for over a month. There were books the doctor had given him, dictionaries and other references Tan felt he could not be without, as well as his notebooks and a well-worn copy of Tom Sawyer, the first novel he had read in English. Hector had encouraged him to take some things that would remind him of home, and Tan had chosen the alpaca blanket his mother had woven for him as well as several conopas given to him by the Mamacuna. Closing the bag, he placed it beside Hector's at the door.

Tan stared into the polished glass mirror only to see a stranger with his own face. He smiled at himself, but even that, too, looked different from his reflection in the waters of the pool. Reaching for his carry pouch, he took the small silver bird and fastened it to his borrowed shirt. It was his talisman now, a totem to bring him luck on his travels away from the people. "I am ready, Hector," he said quietly, for the first time believing that he was actually leaving his world.

ତ୍ତ ⊖ ୧୭

Tan clutched the armrest for the entire flight to Piura. He stared out the window, searching for familiar landmarks as the little plane roared over the rain forest, then the foothills, and finally the high peaks of the Andes. Frightened yet exhilarated, he kept quiet as his world gave way to the mountains and then to the desert coastal plain. When they landed, it was on shaky legs that Tan descended the stairs to the ground, ignoring Hector's bemused smile.

Hector found a taxi to take them to the hotel. The car ride was, to Tan, almost as frightening as the plane, yet his face remained impassive, as though he had been doing this all his life. They checked in and left their bags before setting off to attend to their business at the bank and then to shop.

From store to store, Hector led Tan through the maze of supplies necessary for the trip north. Everything from underwear to a winter coat needed to be purchased and the shopkeepers were more than happy to help Hector spend his money. At the end of the day, laden with bags and bundles, they returned to the hotel for dinner. Dressed in his new clothes, Tan looked like any other prosperous member of Piura's society, except for his hair.

"I want a haircut," announced Tan over coffee.

Hector's head shot up. "A haircut? You are going to cut off your hair? Are you serious?"

"Yes," said Tan, fingering the longer than shoulder length tresses. "Look around us, Hector. No man wears hair this long. I look strange to them; wild."

The doctor was tempted to tell him that in America some men indeed wore hair that long, but they were not the kind of men with whom Tan would probably associate. He knew a haircut would forever change the countenance of his friend. "In the morning," he sighed.

As promised, Hector took Tan to a barber. An Indian himself, he tried desperately to talk Tan out of a haircut, but the stubborn man refused to listen. In a matter of minutes, it was over. The barber handed Tan a mirror and stepped back.

The face was his own, but not his own. Instead of the long straight line across his brow, there were soft waves, almost curls, unlike anything he had ever seen. His ears, he thought, were huge and a much paler than the rest of his skin, for they had been hidden from the sun since he was a child. Suddenly, Tan smiled, and his teeth seeming broader and whiter without the curtain of hair around his face. "I like it," he announced. "It feels strange, but I think I shall get used to it. This is good."

They set out again to hit the shops. Shoes were the hardest to find, for Tan's feet were wide from having walked barefoot for a lifetime. After that came luggage; he needed sturdier baggage than the battered suitcase

Hector lent him. Their last stop was at the haberdashery they had visited the day before. Several items required quick alterations and they had to pick them up. Ties and shirts were also waiting.

"I think you own more clothing than I do," commented the doctor dryly when they returned to the hotel.

"I will need more clothing than you," Tan shot back with a grin. "I am going to Ruti-Suyu, remember?"

A trip to the government office was necessary to pick up the passport and visa for Tan. Hector had filed the papers for a U.S. student visa as soon as the Mamacuna decided on a surname, but there was the matter of the passport photo. With a few pulled strings, the agent agreed to wait until Tan came to Piura before officially issuing the document. They found a photographer who took instant passport pictures and Tan waited anxiously to see the results. He laughed at the solemn face in the photo; it appealed to his sense of the ridiculous. Immediately, they walked the picture to the government office and waited while the agent inspected Tan's visa. Satisfied all was in order, he affixed the photo to the passport and wordlessly handed the booklet to its owner.

Hector took a long look at Tan. He was amazed at the change that had occurred literally overnight. Gone was the boy, replaced by a rather elegant, well attired young man. Hector knew the trousers must feel strange against his skin, yet Tan gave the impression he had always worn western clothing. The haircut, however, was indeed the crowning glory. Tan could go anywhere and do anything without giving the slightest hint that he had spent his entire life running virtually naked through the jungle. "You know, Tan," Hector said with chuckle, "when you get to Minnesota, make it a point to read Tarzan Of the Apes, by Edgar Rice Burroughs. I think you will find it amusing." Almost as amusing was the way Tan pulled a small notebook from his breast pocket and immediately inscribed title and author.

∽ ⊖ ∾

Late in the afternoon, they caught the flight to Lima. Hector insisted on going that far with his protégé, just in case at the last moment he suffered an attack of cold feet. Tan looked with suspicion on the jet waiting to take them to the capital, a 737 gleaming in the sun. "You are sure this one will fly?" asked Tan, less than convinced something this big could actually become airborne.

"This is nothing; wait until you see the one that will take you to America!" the doctor laughed. "Now, that's a big jet!" As with Leah, Hector booked first class; on the few trips he made, he refused to be jammed into coach.

Tan marveled at the interior of the plane before he investigated the contents of the seat pocket with relish. He listened attentively to the attendant as she described emergency procedures, giving Hector a silent look asking for the probability of needing a flotation cushion. The doctor patted his hand reassuringly and kept his sarcastic comments to himself. There was no point in scaring the man any more than he was already scared.

Coy glances from the flight attendant in Tan's direction were not lost on either traveler; Tan was the one to comment about it. "Are all women like this?" he asked with a raised eyebrow.

"Most, if I recall correctly…especially when the man in question is good-looking."

Involuntarily, Tan blushed. It was not the sort of thing one man usually said to another, but he understood why Hector had; it was a well-couched warning. "Women in America, will they be as brazen?" he asked in Quechua, hoping no one else would understand the question.

Hector nodded. "Probably worse. But don't worry, you'll get used to it."

The flight to Lima was short, just a little more than an hour. Once inside the terminal, they walked to the ticket counter where Tan selected his seat for the next leg of the journey, then they went off to rent a car. The doctor planned to visit a colleague for a couple of days and had decided wheels were in order.

"Will I learn to drive a car in America?" he asked, a little anxious about such a thing.

"In time, I suppose, but not until you are ready. I'm sure someone will teach you should you decide to learn." It was just one more thing he knew Tan would eventually list amongst his worldly accomplishments.

The car taken care of, they went in search of a place to sit down. It would be a couple hours before the flight to Miami would board. In a small bar, Hector ordered a couple of Cokes, deciding it was time to introduce Tan to the finer things in American life. "The thing I miss most in the forest," Hector told the man who had once eaten only sacred food, "is an ice cold Coca-Cola."

"Coca?" Tan's eyebrows shot up. Many of the people chewed coca, but it dulled the senses and Tan, as aclla, had only used it when the Mamacuna provided it at the Renewal Ceremony at the equinox.

Hector had mentioned about drug use to Tan, but realized it had to be further discussed, albeit briefly. Quickly, he told him about the origins of the drink, and then explained about controlled substances. "If anyone... anyone at all offers you coca, called cocaine, or even marijuana, decline. Under no circumstances are you to take their drugs. They are different from ours and dangerous. This is not something to be tried," he warned sternly, "this is not an option. It is against everything we believe." His words were strong and Tan gave them great importance. "You will try their alcohol," continued Hector, "and you may or may not like it. Their beer is not unlike the chicha you drink at home and you know it can do to you what the coca does. If you are smart, you will drink in moderation, stopping before the senses are dulled."

"I think I will not drink their alcohol at all!" replied Tan. "I cannot afford to have difficulty in concentration in America."

"Good," Hector agreed, "just keep it that way."

A pleasant female voice over the loud speaker announced the American Airlines flight to Miami. They gathered up their things and slowly walked toward the gate, neither man quite able to speak. Silently, they passed through security, joining the streams of people heading toward destinations all over the world.

Tan presented his ticket and passport to the gentleman at the gate who examined them carefully. "Seat number 6-A, Señor Villac-Quilla. Have a pleasant flight."

Turning, he opened his arms to embrace the Healer. "I will write often," he promised, suddenly feeling overwhelmed.

"You will make me proud, Tan, I am certain," he said in Quechua. "I will miss your company." Hector fought back the tears. "Go in peace and return to us in peace, Tan."

"We will meet again soon, janpeq." Tan hoisted his carry-on bag onto his shoulder and walked into the jetway. He was on his own.

WINTER IN THE STATES
SUMMER IN PERU
1988-1989

CHAPTER 9

India Halstaad sat in her father's car, her well-tended fingertips tapping impatiently against the steering wheel. She was annoyed at having to drive him to the airport, thoroughly annoyed at having to wait outside while he went in search of his latest charity project, and definitely annoyed at the large snowflakes she could see falling beyond the overhang beneath which she was parked. She had better things to do than serve as a welcoming committee to some jungle escapee coming to freeload at her parents' house while he pretended to attend classes at the U. She'd been this route before, the last time with a disgusting, pimply boy from Chile who ogled her at every turn. Glancing at her watch, India wondered how much longer this was going to take; she had a date at seven and it was already five-thirty. There would barely be enough time to wash her hair if they didn't hurry.

Finally, she spotted her father through the plate glass window, with him a tall man carrying a tote bag on his shoulder and a suitcase in each hand. The electric doors opened and they stepped out into the frigid air. She smiled when the tall man shuddered at the sudden blast of Arctic cold. As they approached, however, India's mouth slid open. Instead of a disgusting native type, this one was gorgeous. His face lit up with a smile at something her father said, and she could feel herself growing warm just at the sight of that even row of white teeth. Catching herself, India took a deep breath and waited while her father put the bags in the trunk.

"India!" he called jovially, "this is Tan Villac-Quilla. Tan, I'd like you to meet my daughter, India."

"How do you do?" Tan asked gravely, extending a bronze hand.

She took it and his natural warmth flowed into her. "Welcome to the frozen northland, Señor Villac-Quilla."

Tan climbed into the back seat and, upon seeing the seatbelt, immediately fastened it. India noticed the motion in the rear-view mirror and wondered if what her father had said about him never having been out of the jungle was actually true. Easing into traffic, she kept one eye on the road and the other on the newcomer.

⇛ ◌ ⇚

The Halstaad family lived in a rambling old house on an elm-lined street in the area locally known as Dinkytown. Ingrid Halstaad greeted them at the door, warmly welcoming Tan to his new home. Still in its Christmas finery, the lower level of the large Victorian house was festooned with fragrant pine boughs and red ribbons. An enormous blue spruce dominated the living room, gaily colored ornaments hanging from every branch. Dr. Halstaad showed Tan his room upstairs, then led him back to the cheery yellow kitchen where his wife had prepared a simple but hearty dinner for them.

The first part of the conversation centered on an explanation as to why the Halstaads had a tree inside their house. Hector had mentioned something about Christmas traditions, but had not quite prepared Tan for this. Sitting at the table, Tan found himself drawn out by the charming mistress of the house; her blue eyes sparkled as she shared her customs while at the same time she coaxed Tan to talk about his.

India hated to leave the kitchen, but her date would soon arrive. Suddenly the prospect of spending the entire month of January at home seemed infinitely more intriguing than she ever could've anticipated. The man positively exuded sensuality; every movement was fluid, almost catlike in its grace. His regal bearing bordered on the arrogant, and paired with the way he bored into one's eyes when he talked, made India think of a king. There was just something about him. At the first opportunity, she quizzed her father about the man sleeping in the guest room. Halstaad told her what he knew about Tan from Hector's letters, but it merely served to whet her appetite.

ം ⊖ ൭

The Halstaads were planning a New Year's Eve dinner and Tan was expected to attend. "It will be a small gathering," explained Ingrid as they sat at
the breakfast table the next morning. "Eight other couples, all university
people. I think you will find them an interesting mix."

Tan liked the woman Mrs. Halstaad. Her blonde hair matched her
daughter's but that was where the similarity ended. Ingrid Halstaad was a
petite woman with a gentle laugh that reminded Tan of his own mother.
She appeared to be in complete control of her household, reigning like a
queen, but not above doing things herself. He liked the way she handled
the frying pan when she cooked eggs for him long after everyone else had
gone off for the day. Although she chided him for sleeping so late, it was
the gentleness of her teasing that gave him reason to smile. As he ate, she
sat opposite him, asking him his preferences in food so that she might
prepare things he would eat. The gesture was more than kind, it was sincere
and Tan found himself relaxing. When she told him about the party, his
only question concerned appropriate attire.

"A coat and tie, if you prefer, but a sweater would be perfectly acceptable." She caught the uneasiness in his eyes and continued, "If you'd like,
I can look at what you've brought to help you decide." As almost an after
thought, she added: "And should you have any other questions, I'll be
happy to help you find the answers."

Tan thanked her and accepted the offer. He would need women's advice
if he were to learn what is and is not correct in Ruti-Suyu.

ം ⊖ ൭

India was waiting for Tan to finish in the bathroom. She had seen the door
close, and then heard the shower running. He could not possibly take long,
she thought, sitting on her bed thumbing through a magazine. Soon the
water stopped and she stuck her head into the hallway. The bathroom door
was ajar. With a quick adjustment to her robe, she went down the hall
and pushed the door open. Tan was standing at the sink, a towel wrapped

around his waist, his hair still damp. He looked up as he carefully replaced his toothbrush in its case. Through the mirror, his eyes met hers.

"Sorry, Tan," she cooed, "the door was open and I thought you were done." When he did not answer, but began to gather his things, India stepped into the steamy room. Around his neck, she noticed the gold chain and, hanging from it, what were clearly two Jewish stars. Reaching out, her nails raked his bare chest as she lifted the ornaments. "My father said you had never been out of the jungle until four days ago. How did you come by these?"

He firmly, but gently, removed her hand. "They were gifts," replied Tan, keeping his voice even.

A woman friend, no doubt, decided India. "Tell me, Tan, is it true girls in your tribe can sleep with whoever they want before they get married?" Her voice dripped with honey meant to attract him with her boldness.

It accomplished just the opposite. The woman India did not arouse him; instead, she left him quite cold. "No, it is not true." He chose not to explain further. "If you will excuse me, I must dress now." He left her standing alone in the bathroom.

His clothes were laid out on the bed. With great deliberation, Tan worked the buttons of the blue oxford shirt, making sure each round disk was inserted into the correct hole. He slipped the tie around his neck and stared intently into the mirror as he slowly counted the steps as Hector had instructed. It looked all right, but not as nearly as flat as Hector's had been. He untied the knot and prepared to begin anew when there was a sharp rap at the door. Before he could answer, the door opened and India breezed in.

"Here, let me do that," she said, smoothing the silk. "I'm very good at ties."

"Thank you," replied Tan, keeping his body perfectly still as she deftly worked the fabric into a proper Windsor knot.

"There now, that's better." India stepped back to admire her work, her eyes quickly taking in the complete picture. She tried to imagine him running bare-ass through the jungle but it was hard to see him as anything but this incredibly smart looking preppy. Whoever picked his clothes ob-viously knew what he...or she was doing. "My father would like to see you before the guests arrive," she told him, reaching out to pick an imaginary piece of lint off his shoulder. "And do wear the yellow sweater, Tan, it goes well with your coloring." She had just enough time to see his face redden before leaving the room.

∾ ⊖ ∾

Dr. Halstaad was sitting in the study when Tan rapped on the open door. "Come in, and sit down." He nodded his approval at Tan's attire. "You look nice, Tan." Pulling a large manila envelope from the drawer, he opened it and spread out the contents. "These are for you. Our friend Hector has done a very thorough job in getting you set up for life in the United States." He slid a slim, leather folder across the table.

Tan examined the folder and looked up. He was surprised to see his name and the Halstaad's address on the papers inside. "What is this, Doctor?"

"Your checkbook. When you need money, you can go to this bank, write out the amount you need, and they will give it to you."

"Ah, Hector told me about a checkbook. This one looks different from his. Hector said there would be money deposited into the account on a monthly cycle, enough money for me to purchase books."

"And other things you might need," chuckled Dr. Halstaad. He slid a small green card towards Tan. "This also works as money, only at the end of each month, you will be sent a bill. In turn, you will send them a check to cover the amount of the bill."

"American Express, yes?"

"Yes."

"Don't leave home without it?"

Dr. Halstaad laughed aloud. "I see you have already been indoctrinated into the finer points of American culture."

"I like to hear advertisements on the radio." He fingered the card, examining the numbers carefully. "My English was improved once we were able to pick up American radio on Hector's short-wave."

"Your command of English is extraordinary, Tan," said the doctor seriously, "which brings me to the next topic. Wednesday morning, we go to the registrar's office. I've picked a number of classes which might interest you and you need to decide which ones you want to take."

Tan took a sheet of paper from Dr. Halstaad and studied the list carefully. It was a well considered plan, with classes in math, English, Spanish and Western philosophy. "What do you recommend?" asked Tan seriously.

Dr. Halstaad studied his copy of the list. "Math, and English as a Second Language, of course; the Spanish is a mid-level language class which will help you with your grammar and writing skills. This will be important should you decide to pursue advanced studies in Peru. As for the philosophy class, Hector thought you would enjoy it."

"When do classes begin?"

"Next Monday. We'll spend tomorrow walking around campus so you can learn your way around. The day after, you'll sit for an exam in English in order to determine class placement. This is a requirement of the University but should not present any major problems for you, Tan. Hector assures me your written skills are as excellent as your speech." The host paused, and when he spoke, it was in more serious tones. "You are welcome to stay with us as long as you want, Tan; we are very happy to have you." He waved his hand, encompassing the endless shelves of books. "Read what you'd like from here, ask when you have questions; discover for yourself what it is you'd like to learn. You've been given a great opportunity, so use it wisely."

Tan thanked Dr. Halstaad, but the older man dismissed his words with a smile. "Think of me as a father type, Tan. There's no question you cannot ask, nothing that cannot be explored. Mrs. Halstaad and I are so pleased you have come, we cannot possibly put it in words."

"In the place I call home," said Tan slowly, "a young man seeks a teacher who will share with him a skill needed to survive. I was unable to seek a teacher from my ayllu; my teachers were the Rimoc until Hector took an interest in me. I can never repay the debt I owe him, but if I succeed in my studies, I will at least make a start. If you would be my teacher here, then I will, too, be forever in your debt."

Dr. Halstaad considered the importance of Tan's request; it was not to be taken lightly. "It is done," he replied gravely. "Now, let's join my wife and see if she needs any help."

The dinner party was an interesting introduction to American social customs. To some degree, Tan was the center of attention. Standing in the living room, a glass of plain soda in his hand, Tan answered their questions, providing insights into the condition of the natives of South America.

He didn't understand all the jokes, but it didn't matter. Tan quietly observed the way the friends interacted, deciding that it was not so very different from the way people at home behaved. He was a little surprised at the way the women conversed with men not their relatives; there was no deferential behavior, and, in essence, no sense of modesty in the way the ladies met the eyes of the men. Tan did not know why he was surprised by this; he simply was.

They rang in the New Year with icy champagne, a taste Tan thought interesting at best, but certainly nothing to be excited about. There were no religious observances, no ceremonies, only a chaste kiss here and there, and lots of good wishes. Later, when the guests were gone, Tan offered his assistance in the kitchen where Mrs. Halstaad was loading the dishwasher.

"Tell me what you thought," she asked, taking the glasses he carried. "Did you enjoy yourself?"

"A most pleasant evening, ma'am." He replied politely, trying to put words to his thoughts.

Ingrid Halstaad suppressed a smile. She liked the way her called her ma'am, and her husband, sir. It was an old fashioned touch she knew came directly from the very old fashioned Hector Morales. "To be perfectly honest, Tan, I think you were a big hit. Everyone commented on how well you spoke English and how well you expressed yourself. When I told Mrs. Jackson you'd been speaking English less than a year, she could hardly believe it!"

"I did not shame you?" asked Tan, his dark brows knit in concern above his eyes.

"No, Tan, you did not shame me. You were wonderful." She leaned over and pecked his cheek. "Your mother must be very proud of her son."

He blushed, and took a moment to compose his answer. "My mother does not understand why I have left my home to travel to a land of snow. She thinks I am bewitched by the spirits of the mountains."

"Mothers do not always understand their children, dear. You can only hope that she will come to understand in time."

Their conversation was cut short by the arrival of India, who breezed into the kitchen, coat in her hand. "Happy New Year!" she called brightly.

Her mother responded in kind, then added, "Well, I think I'm done here," said Ingrid, flicking on the dishwasher. "I'm going to bed, and Tan, you might consider doing the same. Arne likes to get an early start and I know he wants to be back from campus in time for the football games." She wished them good night and left Tan alone in the kitchen with India.

"Let's have some champagne," said India as soon as her mother was gone.

"No, thank you. I think I will do as your mother says and go to my bed." The way she was looking at him made Tan fidget.

India would not be put off. "There is an old custom in our country, one you might like," she began, edging toward him. "In order to insure good luck in the coming year, we kiss."

"I do not know this custom," replied Tan, not quite believing her.

Running a hand up his chest, she drew him close. "Here, let me show you how." Her lips tasted of champagne. With firm pressure, she moved her mouth against his, hoping to prod him into a warm response. There was none. "Surely you can do better than that," she pouted.

Tan met her eyes, staring into their crystalline blue depths. No woman had ever touched him like this, and this was a clear violation of his body. To rebuke her might anger her, and this he did not want to do. "I say to you good night, Miss Halstaad." He left the kitchen and went directly to his room.

∾ ◯ ∾

Fortified with a hot breakfast of farina and coffee, Tan was ready to face the bitter cold with Dr. Halstaad. Upon seeing his soft boots, Mrs. Halstaad insisted on digging out an extra pair of Arne's Sorrel boots, along with a knit stocking cap and a scarf. "These things will have to do until we can get you your own, Tan," she told him as she helped adjust his stocking cap. "There, you look like one of us," she laughed, taking in the bundled up young man. Hector had done well to find Tan a mountain parka and shearling gloves in Piura, but he was obviously unaware of the extreme cold of Minnesota in winter. As they went out the door, Ingrid reminded her husband that not everyone found the frigid air invigorating. "Don't you bring him back with frostbite, Arne!" she called after them.

The East Bank campus of the University of Minnesota was only a few blocks from the house. Tan listened to the scrunch of snow beneath his feet, marveling at the most unexpected sound it made. As they walked, Dr. Halstaad pointed out places of interest, places Tan would eventually know well. There were shops and restaurants, most of which, explained Dr. Halstaad, were closed because of the holiday.

They entered campus through the main gate and walked toward the mall. This building and that hall.... Tan tried to memorize what he was being told. When they stopped directly in front of Northrop Auditorium, the mall laid out ahead, Tan laughingly told Dr. Halstaad he thought the jungle less confusing. "All these buildings look the same to me!" he cried, throwing his hands up in frustration.

"Don't feel too bad, fella, they all looked alike to me when I first arrived and I grew up in Minneapolis. Don't worry, you'll get used to it." Going on, they headed toward the West Bank. As they crossed the river, they stopped long enough for the older man to give Tan a brief history of the state.

This small river could not possibly be the Mississippi of Huck Finn and Tom Sawyer. "I thought the Mississippi would be much wider," commented Tan as he looked at the frozen ribbon beneath them.

"It is, once you get past Iowa, the state south of Minnesota," replied Dr. Halstaad, launching into a description of the river's progress to New Orleans.

They began walking again. As they neared the end of the bridge, Tan stopped short. Coming toward him was a familiar form. Head down to the wind, her hands deep in her pockets, a woman wearing a bright blue jacket was walking with another woman, listening intently to what was being said. She picked her head up and laughed, and it was the sound of her laughter, which pierced his soul. She did not notice the two men standing close to the rail. He closed his eyes and for a moment, let his heart reach out to her.

"What is it, Tan?" asked Dr. Halstaad as he followed Tan's gaze to the women.

The younger man shook his head. "Nothing. Her laughter reminded me of someone I knew."

The rest of the day passed in a blur for Tan. She was here, and he knew he would be able to find her again.

CHAPTER 10

No sooner had she passed the two men standing on the bridge than Leah felt uncommonly warm inside her jacket. Unbidden, the words *You are in my heart* raced through her mind, and she turned to see whom she had passed. Neither looked to be anyone she recognized, but the sensation of just having been invaded was unshakable.

"Are you quite all right?" Mary asked, following Leah's glance.

"Yeah, fine." The words were not at all convincing. Straightening around, she laughed, "Whose bright idea was this anyway, Cavanaugh?"

"Yours, bozo. You were the one who said 'Let's go for a walk.' Wanna go back?"

Leah shook her head. "No, I'd rather be out here than sitting in a deserted dorm pretending to be working on my thesis."

"Have it your way, but I warn you, I've kinda gotten used to having ten toes and ten fingers."

Leah said nothing, but burrowed deeper into her jacket. The warm feeling now flowed through all of her body. She felt Tan's presence in the very depths of her soul and instead of being afraid, she was calmed by the sensation. Every night, as she slept, she knew his thoughts touched hers. If the messages were not always clear, there was no denying that they were there, yet, there had always been distance between them.

Now, however, something had changed. From the moment she set foot on the bridge, Leah sensed he was physically near. She turned again and saw the two men turn to go down the steps to the West Bank mall, and for a fleeting moment she was certain one of them was, impossibly, Tan.

ତ୍ତ ⊖ ∾

Winter quarter began none too soon. Leah's dissertation topic was unofficially accepted by the committee now that her masters' thesis was close to
completion. Her class load eased slightly, but her teaching load increased
dramatically. Instead of assisting in Intro to Cultural Anthropology, she
would be doing it on her own for the first half of the quarter while the instructor was on emergency leave, with only an undergrad assistant to help
with the paperwork. She was also assisting Dr. Muñoz for an upper level
seminar on Myth and Religion and for fun she was going to do the cultural
half of a class on Andean archeology with Mary.

Classes resumed the Monday morning after New Year's. Leah was ready
for the Intro group, most of whom had been in the first class during fall
quarter. Eighty-five students were registered, about half of whom were
there because they wanted to be; the others because they had to be in order
to meet one requirement or another. By the end of the first week, Leah had
settled into a comfortable routine. The weather remained bitter cold, but it
did not slow her daily march across the bridge to the East Bank. A part of
her kept an eye open for something she could not quite define, something
that could account for the strange warmth she suddenly felt on New Year's
Day. The surge had reoccurred several times since, but with no discernible
regularity. It had happened in her office, in class, in her car, and even while
eating dinner in the dorm. It was spooky, as though someone were watching her, but each time she looked, she saw no one looking at her.

ତ୍ତ ⊖ ∾

Leah was sitting in her office reading notes when Mary stuck her head in
the door. "Are you available for lunch, Lee?" she asked.

"No, not really; I have to finish this stuff for Muñoz," she replied, "I'm
meeting Jay for dinner, so I think skipping lunch is in order."

Without being invited, Mary flopped down on the other chair. "Have
you noticed the guy hanging around the back of your intro class?" Mary
had been in and out of the lecture lately, doing special presentations on the

uses of archeology in anthropological fieldwork.

Leah thought for a minute; she had no idea what Mary was talking about and said as much. "I know almost everyone in that class, if not by name, by sight. Nope, I haven't noticed anyone new. Who is he?"

Mary's eyes opened wide in disbelief. "He is the talk of the back half of the room, Lee. About six-two, dark eyes, dark hair, and a definite prep palate. A real hunk." She studied her fingernails for a minute. "I was hoping you'd know who he was so you could introduce me."

"I'll keep an eye out for him. If I can, I'll get his phone number and you can call him yourself." Leah liked teasing Mary. She talked a good game, but her shyness around men was legendary.

When she next walked into the lecture, Leah scanned the back for the unknown student. Silently, she matched the faces in the seats to the names in her grade book and deciding there were no extra bodies present, she launched into her lecture on male and female godhead relationships.

For forty minutes, Leah discoursed on cultures with a male and female divine partnership, using a variety of multi-cultural references to explain the nature of dual supremacy. Since the class was an introductory survey, she avoided going too deeply into the exceptions, concentrating instead on where the rules applied. As she spoke about Mamaquilla and Viracocha, she experienced that strange warmth coursing through her body. It was, this time, a welcome sensation, reminding her of her own closeness to the people in the rain forest. At the end of her lecture, she opened the floor to questions.

She saw a hand rise in the back row. Half hidden behind a post, she could not quite see his face. "You, in the back," she called out. "What can I do for you?"

From out of the shadows, the soft, familiar slur of a jungle accent called back to her. "Do you believe native populations of the Andes to be foolish in their beliefs?"

Leah gripped the edge of the podium until her knuckles turned white. She could barely collect her thoughts, and when she answered, she stammered. "N...n...no, I do not." Swallowing hard, she willed herself calm. "The major difference between Western religion and their own lies in the worship of an equal male and female deity.

"To serve Mamaquilla is as great a calling to one of the people as, say, that of a priest, rabbi or imam. There is no reason to think anything less of it. There is no place for judgment here." She waited to see if he said anything else, but there was no sound from the back of the hall. "Read chapter 6 for next time and be prepared for a quiz," announced Leah, her eyes still on the place where her questioner had been.

She tried to get to the back of the hall before he left, but could not. Knees shaking, she hurried to her office, telling herself she must have been mistaken; the voice belonged to someone else; it could not be his voice.

☙ ⊖ ❧

Leah returned to the dorm to find a message from Jay canceling dinner due to an emergency at the hospital. Relieved, Leah picked up her mail and headed directly to the cafeteria. She had, after all, skipped lunch, and was ravenously hungry.

A group of girls from her floor waved her over. Leah joined them, but her mind was not on their conversation, nor was it on the food. She pushed more food around than she ate; finally she gave up in favor of another cup of strong, bitter coffee.

They went up to the eleventh floor together, heading to their rooms once the elevator deposited them in the vestibule. Coat over her book-laden arms, Leah walked to her room alone. She was about to put the key in the lock, when she froze. Attached to the knob, hanging straight down, was a quipu. Slowly, she lifted the knotted strands and counted the series of knots. Instinctively, she understood the pattern. On the first strand, there were nine: one for each huaca. The second strand had four all together: one for each solstice, followed by one for each equinox. The third strand held seven knots. She did not know for certain what the number signified, but she guessed it was the number of sun cycles the aclla had performed his mita. Each of the next six strands were patterned in clusters of double and triple knots; it wasn't hard for Leah to recognize the patterns of the ayllus along the six major paths through the rainforest. The last strand contained two knots separated only by a small gold bead. When her finger touched the metal, it was warm and she could sense the presence of its maker. Gently, Leah removed the quipu from the doorknob and took it inside where she laid it on her desk, the strands fanned out to reveal the knots. Closing her eyes, she sent him a message: *I know you are near.*

The dreams increased in intensity. Night after night she saw him at the huaca by the waterfall until one night, Leah bolted upright in the bed, her flannel gown drenched with sweat and sticking to her most uncomfortably. Struggling to untangle herself from the sheets, she pulled the offending garment off and tossed it on the floor. "This is ridiculous," she said aloud as she slid back beneath the covers. "Go to sleep!" The words seemed to echo in the empty room. No sooner had she closed her eyes again then the dark eyes of the aclla appeared before her.

"*Your heart is in my heart,*" declared a warm, caressing voice, "*you are bound to me forever.*"

"Go to sleep!" she whispered and for a moment, she thought she heard him laugh.

e⟶ ⊖ ⟵o

The harsh jangle of the telephone penetrated the netherworld, awakening Leah unkindly. Since it refused to stop ringing, Leah was forced to get out of the bed and answer it. "Hello?" she mumbled, still half asleep.

"You were supposed to meet me for breakfast a half an hour ago, Lee," Mary groused. "Why are you still asleep?"

"What time is it?"

"Ten o'clock, you slug. Wake up and get your butt over to Ford Hall now, we have a departmental meeting in twenty minutes and you are first on the agenda." There was a momentary pause. "Does any of this sound familiar, Lee?"

"Oh my God! I completely forgot!" Phone still in hand, she ran into her closet and began pulling out clothes. "Hold down the fort 'til I get there and tell Muñoz I'm sorry I overslept."

"Don't kill yourself, Lee, but do get a move on."

Leah dressed in jeans and a heavy chamois shirt. Racing into the communal bathroom, she washed and brushed her teeth with unholy haste. Back at the dresser mirror, she brushed her hair back and plaited a single braid, then clipped the whole thing to the back of her head. A dab of mascara, a touch of lip-gloss to ward off chapping was more than enough to satisfy her vanity. Two little gold balls would do for earrings, and then she picked up the remaining silver bird from the little crystal dish where she always put it at night. Eyes on the mirror, she fastened it to her collar and stopped, fingers in mid-air. The pin she had in her hand was the one with the emerald eye, not the sapphire eyed bird she had worn yesterday, the one that had ultimately come back with her. Her hands dropped lamely to her side as she stared at the bird, unable to decide what exactly she was feeling at that particular moment. She ruled out panic and scared; those were definitely not the right words. But there was no time to stand around and worry about it. Safe was what she had felt in the jungle and for some inexplicable reason, safe was the word closest to what she felt now. With a deep breath, Leah grabbed her jacket, stuffed her feet into her boots and left, securely locking the door behind her.

In the lobby, Leah flew right past Tan. He watched the bright blue jacket shoot out the doors and for a moment, considered sprinting after her. No, he decided, it was not the time, although he knew she noticed the switch. He felt it the minute her hands touched the bird. That her door was open and her room empty had been Mamaquilla's way of telling him to remain silent. Smiling to himself, he ambled out of the dorm.

⥀ ⊖ ⥁

At the meeting, Leah forced herself to listen attentively to the list of proposed research grants for the following year. There was nothing on the list that jumped out at her, nothing that really piqued her interest. Finally, the chairman of the department turned the floor over to Dr. Muñoz.

"There is one more possible grant to be mentioned," he began, shuffling his notes to the right place. "This one is from the Peruvian Ministry of Indigenous Culture. They want to establish an exchange program with us, to facilitate the recording and publication of current cultural trends of the mountain people." He looked at Leah and grinned when her mouth opened in shock, exactly what he expected. "They were most impressed with the paper Ms. Fine submitted last quarter and they're convinced that her initial research bears further investigation.

"The core of the grant is to record the cultural world of the indigenous population, and to use it as a defense as they fight for a national protection policy. Unlike some of the other countries, a great number of Peruvian officials are already taking up the fight for ethnic preservation. In response to their request, I will be writing the grant on behalf of the University in conjunction with representatives of the Peruvian Embassy. There will be one half-time position to be filled by a graduate student, and one quarter time clerical position to be filled by a candidate pulled from student employment."

No one had to guess who the graduate student would be. When the meeting adjourned, Professor Muñoz escorted Leah to his office to look at the documents that had arrived the day before. "I wanted to be certain about the embassy's role before I talked with you about it," said Muñoz, clapping Leah on the back. "They called this morning; had you been here on time, I would have mentioned it," he chided, "Besides, it was a good surprise, was it not?"

Leah had to agree with him; it was a wonderful surprise, one which might very well take her back to the Andes sooner than she had dared to hope. The ramifications of such a project raced around Leah's brain. If the grant went through, she could become a major player in Andean anthropology. She would have her choice of positions, instead of sweating out academic whimsy in faculty appointments. The opportunity was staggering. "When do we start?" she asked, her face aglow.

"Now." Muñoz handed her a thick envelope. "Take this home and plow through it. For our regular meeting next week, try to have an outline for the application. I know this is a lot to ask on top of your teaching load, but I think you will find it will go quickly; most of this will come from your research. For spring quarter, we will exchange part of your teaching load for this one."

Clutching the package, Leah thanked him profusely and left. It was too good to be true; she knew a multitude of things could go wrong before the grant was submitted, much less accepted. Still, it was worth pursuing in the event they could pull it off.

∞ ⊖ ∞

In his office, Dr. Muñoz put his feet up on the windowsill and looked out over the campus. The grant was, to be sure, an exciting proposition, but he was concerned about one aspect. He hadn't told Leah shortly after the call from the embassy he had had two other calls. The first was from a good friend in Washington, a fellow South American well wired into the international ecological community. "Be aware," he warned Muñoz, "there are those who would use the information you gather to force changes in the Andes which some of us believe would be detrimental." He told his colleague of lumber and mining companies wanting greater access to the resource rich lands, and in order to obtain those rights, they would remove the native population at whatever cost necessary. Unmentioned, however, was the growing drug trade. Muñoz wondered how much of the study would be funded by those behind the scenes with an eye to the profit that could be derived from well-hidden coca fields.

The second call had proved even more disturbing. Vincente Lubrano of the Peruvian Consulate was anxious to meet with him and "the lovely girl" who had recently finished her fieldwork in the district. Specifically, he was interested in what data she had gathered in the area of local agricultural and migratory patterns. Despite his protestations that Señorita Fine's work had not been in that area, Lubrano was persistent. The only conclusion Muñoz could reach was that the first caller had been right: the drug cartels were looking for a way in.

∞ ⊖ ∞

Hector hated Lima. He hated the city, the air, and most of all, the government. To him, the purpose of the government was to stick its long nose in where it was not wanted and this foray to the capital did nothing to alter that impression. He had waited two hours for his appointment with the deputy minister of cultural affairs and now, as he sat cooling his heels in a hallway, his temper was growing increasingly sour. They were the ones who dragged him to Lima, yet they could not manage to keep a nine o'clock appointment. He glanced at his watch for the hundredth time; if he was not admitted by eleven, he was leaving.

Finally, the door opened. "Señor Morales," said the deputy minister, "please forgive the delay."

Hector rose from his chair, but he did not shake the extended hand. He wanted to blast the officious little man, but kept his mouth closed. He had no idea why he was there and suspected yelling at the deputy minister was a useless exercise. Instead, he asked, "Why am I here?"

He opened a folder, then passed a piece of paper to Hector. "Your clinic, Doctor Morales, is situated on a parcel of land whose ownership is currently under dispute."

"I own the land outright."

"I'm afraid there is a question about the property lines."

Hector stared at the deputy minister. "I bought the land from José Roderigo himself. There was no question at the time of the deed transfer."

"But that does not preclude the possibility that the deed was in error."

"We had the proper surveyor's report. Granted, it's a remote, inaccessible place, but it was surveyed by the Department of Piura when Roderigo staked the original claim, and again when I bought it."

The under-minister shrugged. "The fact remains, there is another claim on the parcel which we must consider."

"May I ask who claims they own my clinic?"

"La Plata Mining and Lumber."

Hector's eyes rolled backward. "This is a joke, yes?"

"No, Doctor Morales, this is no joke. They have a valid claim to the land and to be honest, that is the claim the courts will support."

"How much is this going to cost me?" asked Hector, his eyes narrowing.

"You do not have enough money to do it, doctor."

"So there is some money changing hands here."

"I did not say that. I simply point out that the legal process is expensive. Very expensive."

Anger was creeping up in Hector like the red line of a thermometer. "And I am supposed to simply pick up and move?"

"You may not have a choice... unless you contract independently with La Plata."

"Not an option," spat Hector.

"But do understand, doctor, it is not just the clinic we're talking about; it's all the land...from the clinic to the northern edge of the plateau and east to the Marañon is owned by La Plata.

"Are you insane?" Hector's voice was rising quickly.

"Not at all. You and your friends would be wise to seek other...arrangements."

Hector jumped out of his seat and slammed his hands down on the deputy minister's desk. "You paper-pushing bribe-taking pissant bureaucrat!" shouted Hector. "You'll have to kill us all before you drive us off our land."

"It's your choice, doctor."

Hector leaned over the desk until his nose was inches away from the deputy minister's. "I will not roll over and die quietly. I will make sure everyone in Peru knows who you are and what you are doing in here. Remember, Señor Minister, we used to cut live, beating hearts from our enemies before we offered them to Viracocha!"

ↄ ⊖ ᴄ

Outside on the street, Hector doubled over gasping for air. His heart pounded and his eyes were hot with anger. He was not so naive to believe the government actually cared about what happened to the people of the forest, but he did not want to believe they would sacrifice them to the ultimately short-term interests of the mining companies. He clutched his sides and willed himself not to vomit.

Suddenly, a hand touched his shoulder. Hector snapped upright and glared at the offender staring at him. "What are you? Another fat, balding pencil pusher?"

The little man momentarily looked hurt before a deep, rumbly chuckle seemed to come from his portly belly. "Heaven's no, Dr. Morales! No, not at all. Oh, no, not a pencil pusher at all. I'm a man of action...or so they tell me. Yes, that's me...a man of action." He stopped laughing as suddenly as he began. "Are you ill, Dr. Morales?" he asked, but before Hector could answer, he prattled on, "I hope not. It wouldn't serve at all if you were ill. You certainly can't afford to be sick right now, what with so much to do and so much at stake. Oh, no, no, no, you must not be unwell. You're needed...far too important a fellow to suffer from a malaise of any kind. And without the Mamacuna to send you herb packets here in Lima! Why, you would have to go to a hospital and they would probably slap you right into a bed and......"

"Enough!" roared Hector. "Who are you and what do you want?"

"Me? Want something from you? Oh, no, quite the opposite, Dr. Morales; you want something from me. Yes, yes, that's certainly the case. You...." The chatter ceased and the little man cocked his head to one side. "Oh, dear, I suppose you have no idea who I am, do you?" Hector shook his head. "Oh, my most sincere apologies, Dr. Morales. Truly, I am so sorry. I should have caught you before you went into to talk to that stone-skull bureaucrat, but we only learned you were here an hour ago. My fault, I assure you; my fault completely." He latched onto Hector's elbow and began steering him across the street toward a small park. "Let's find a nice tree under which we may sit and I'll tell you everything you need to know."

"Before I go one more step," growled Hector, halting their progress, "you will tell me who you are."

"When we are sitting and you've had a moment to catch your breath," grinned the man. "I promise I'll answer all your questions and even some you haven't thought of yet. It is a silly thing to say to so important a gentleman as yourself, Doctor, but you should trust me. Yes, that's quite so. Once we've had our little talk, you'll understand."

Hector realized he was going to sit in the park with the portly little man and hear him out whether or not he wanted to. "Let's go; you've got five minutes and then I'm leaving."

Five minutes turned into two hours and when Hector left Antonio de Leon, his frustration had given way to hope.

CHAPTER 11

"*I left the woods,*" Tan read aloud slowly, "*for as good a reason as I went there. Perhaps it seemed to me that I had several more lives to live, and could not spare any more time for that one. It is remarkable how easily we fall into a particular route, and make a beaten track for ourselves. I had not lived there a week before my feet wore a path from my door to the pondside; and though it is five or six years since I trod it, it is still quite distinct.*" He paused, his finger at his place, and looked up at Ingrid. "This is something I understand!" he grinned. "I know how fast my feet make a path. And I know the feeling to have several more lives to live. This Thoreau was a very wise man."

"I'm not surprised you like him, Tan," said Ingrid over sound of running water, "he lived alone in the woods.... much like you did."

"But he went there after he had lived much of his life with people. I was separated from my family before I could enjoy..." he searched for the word, then grinned, "solitude. And, he had visitors."

"True," she laughed, "although he did not always like having them. How do you like having people around all the time?" Since coming to live with them, the most obvious challenge for Tan had simply been to be around people. She and Arne were aware of his living arrangements before he arrived; in fact, Hector had mentioned his protégé may lack certain social graces because he had spent his days alone. But instead of holing up in his room, Tan spent much of his time either in the kitchen with her or in the study with her husband.

"The sound of voices is a good thing, ma'am," he told her. "And to speak to others when I wish to speak is a very good thing. I did not know I would enjoy this, but I do."

"I'm glad to hear it, Tan, because we enjoy hearing you."

Without being asked, he joined her at the sink and began to help with the salad she was making. "Food was always left for me. Until I found Hector, I never helped to prepare a meal. In my ayllu, a man never helped with the cooking, but Hector said this was a good thing to know."

"It will be a very good thing to know if you want your own apartment. You should be able to feed yourself."

"Am I not learning from you?" Tan cried with mock horror. "Can I not fix the coffee in the coffee maker?"

"Only when you remember to turn in on, Tan." She laughed lightly when she saw his face fall. "But you make excellent coffee when you do. Before you know it, you'll be able to boil an egg."

Tan was about to say something about that when India breezed into the kitchen. She had taken to coming home on weekends, something which Tan found puzzling; he did not understand how she could spend so much time driving up and down from her college in Northfield.

"Oh, good, someone else to make the salad; I hate making salad," she grinned as she tossed her coat on a chair. "I would ask if you need any help, Mom, but it looks like you have an extra pair of hands already."

"I am happy to help," Tan said gravely, "your mother does much for me, so this is something I can do for her."

"It's nice to have a *willing* pair of extra hands, India," Ingrid chided her daughter. "As long as you're here, why don't you set the table?"

"Sure, but first I have a question for Tan." She turned her blue eyes on him. "I happen to have a couple of tickets to **PYGMALION** at the Guthrie and I was wondering if you wanted to go."

Tan stopped tearing lettuce. "The Guthrie...a place for plays, yes?"

"Yes, Tan, a theatre," said Ingrid. "And the play is by George Bernard Shaw, a very important English playwright."

"English...British?"

"Yes. It would be a good experience for you, in fact, you might find the story somewhat close to your heart." Ingrid gave him an enigmatic smile. "Yes, Tan, I think it's something you should see."

ℯ⌒⊖⌒ℴ

Tan was dazzled by the theatre. "So many people are waiting. Will we all stand for the play?" he asked as they waited to check their coats.

"It's like a lecture hall," India explained, "but the lights will go out before the stage is lit; like at the movies."

He followed India to the entrance and was surprised a moment later when a woman handed him a program before pointing out the location of the seats. "Do I read this before the play? Will I have time?" he whispered.

India opened her program and showed Tan the list of actors and their parts. "You can read the articles about Shaw and about the play before the lights go down. But afterward, you take this home. It's like a souvenir."

"Souvenir?" he repeated carefully.

"Memento...something to remind you of the event." She slipped her hand into the crook of his arm. "Relax, Tan; you're supposed to be having fun."

Tan glanced at her manicured fingers and wondered how he could have fun if she insisted on leaving her hand on his arm.

At the first intermission, India had to pry him out of his seat. "It'll still be here when we get back, but I need something to drink. Come on, we can talk in the lobby."

"The play is over?"

"No, silly," she giggled, "this is an intermission, a break so we can stretch our legs."

He was thankful for that. He had been sitting riveted to the edge of his seat and he was definitely cramped. Once again, he was following India someplace.

In the lobby, they waited in line at one of the little refreshment bars. India ordered a white wine, but Tan opted for plain soda water. He barely listened to her as she prattled on about something; he was too busy looking at the throngs milling about, drinks in hand. He tried not to stare at the people around him, but it was difficult. From the clothing they wore to the snatches of conversations he heard, Tan could neither listen nor look enough to satisfy his curiosity. He paid particular attention to the interactions between men and women; the way the women listened then spoke, the way everyone seemed to need to do something with one's hands. He saw men engrossed in conversation with women, something which did not occur in public in his world. As best he could, he followed India's train of thought as she discreetly pointed out this thing or that person. It was an assault to his senses; he could barely respond to India's comments, much less form the words to express his own. He was, however, terribly aware of her arm intertwined with his as she propelled him through the crowd toward a vacant table.

"See the guy in the blazer with the red striped tie?" asked India, momentarily pointing her bright red fingernail toward a man standing near the wide wall of glass. "That's the president of the University...and the guy with him...the one on his left, used to be the mayor of St. Paul."

Tan followed her finger and saw the two gentlemen. He was about to ask her what a mayor was, but something caught his eye. It was the flick of a long mane of dark hair right behind the mayor's elbow.

The noise and the crowd faded from his consciousness and silently, he willed the woman to turn although he did not need her to turn. He knew what he would see: a pair of grass green eyes. And then, as if on cue, he saw her shoulders shudder ever so slightly, as if a cool breeze had touched her, and she turned. For a fleeting second, she scanned the room in his direction, but she seemed not to see him. She turned again; as Tan watched, a tall, red haired man slipped his arm around her waist and drew her close as he said something to her. Leah shook her head "no," but he did not remove his arm. Tan's lips formed a tight line.

"See someone you know?" asked India, breaking his concentration.

In imitation of the stranger, Tan disengaged his arm from India's and slid it around her waist. "No."

India glanced up at him, puzzled, yet inordinately pleased. A trumpet sounded through the loudspeakers. "Ah, the five minute warning; let's go back to our seats."

◦◦ ⊖ ◦◦

At the second intermission, Tan looked for, but did not see Leah, nor did he see her as they walked to the car after the play.

◦◦ ⊖ ◦◦

The house was dark when they got home. Tan used his key to let them in, then helped India off with her coat. "Thank you for this evening," he said formally as he closed the closet door. "This play was a good thing to see."

"Do you think of yourself as Eliza Doolittle?"

"A little," he confessed, "although Hector does not dress as neatly as Professor Higgins."

"Hector thinks he's well dressed when he remembers to tuck in his shirt," said India. "I simply adore Hector, Tan, but he's been in the jungle too long. I don't know how you got to be such a fashion plate if he was doing the shopping."

Tan looked down at his own clothing. Based on the others he had seen at the theatre, he thought his grey pants, white shirt, dotted tie, and blazer were more than appropriate. "Do I look like a dish?" he asked seriously.

"Dish? Oh, yeah, no question about it. You're a feast for the eyes," she giggled.

"Should I have dressed in something else?"

India stopped laughing. She shook her head. "That was an expression, Tan. Fashion plate means like a picture in a magazine and dish, well, it's a thing you eat from, like a plate, but it can also mean handsome. Very handsome." Unexpectedly, she reached up and loosened the knot of his tie. "Y'know, I liked it when you put your arm around me during the inter-mission." He remained silent. "I liked it very much." Standing on tiptoe, she pressed her lips to his, then let her tongue touch the soft skin for a moment. When he did not respond, she pulled back slightly. "Don't you want to kiss me?"

"You are very beautiful, India, but no, I do not wish to kiss you."

India stared up into his dark eyes. "More's the pity, Tan. You don't know what you're missing." She left him standing in the foyer as she went up the stairs.

⌀ ⊖ ⌀

The next morning, Tan was fidgety as he sat in the kitchen drinking coffee.

They had discussed the play over breakfast, but Ingrid sensed there was something on his mind. She wasn't about to pry, but she made certain there were plenty of openings for Tan to start the conversation. Judging by the way he kept spinning the mug in his broad hands, Ingrid figured there was another social observation coming. Finally, she sat down opposite him and pulled the mug from his grip. "Okay, Mr. Villac-Quilla, something happened last night. What's on your mind?"

He looked up at her and smiled. "I think you know me well, ma'am."

"Well enough to know you've got something buzzing around up there. Come on, Tan. Spill." She saw the puzzled look on his face and said, "That means you should just tell me what you're thinking without worrying about how it comes out."

"Do all men touch women who are not their wives?"

"Oh, that," said Ingrid reaching out to pat his hand. "It depends...it's a complicated thing, you know."

"On what does it depend?"

"Well, it depends on the relationship between the man and the woman. If they are friends, like we are, it's quite all right for me to touch your hand, or even your arm when we are talking. You probably wouldn't put your arm around me, but you might put your arm around a girl closer to your age.... especially if she is someone special. If you are walking with a woman, it is very proper to offer her your elbow so that she might put her arm through it."

"India always puts her arm through mine."

"Yes, I've noticed," she said somewhat dryly. "Does that make you uncomfortable?"

"It did, but I see that done often. I think it is all right."

"Only if you are comfortable with it. If not, she shouldn't."

"And kissing?"

Ingrid's eyebrow shot up, but she quickly lowered it. "A man kisses a woman on the cheek when they are friends...good friends. A kiss on the lips, a romantic kiss, happens only between a man and a woman when there is a different kind of relationship. I think you know what I mean."

"Then it is not a duty to kiss a woman?"

" Heavens, no! You shouldn't have to kiss anyone you don't wish to kiss." She wondered if India had kissed him, but she bit back the question; it was not one she felt comfortable asking. She did, however, wish to ease his concern. "Although our customs differ from yours, Tan, there is nothing which requires you to do anything which makes you uncomfortable."

"Except for one thing," he said gravely.

"Which is?"

"Sitting for long hours in class." He flashed her a grin, then reached over and patted her hand.

ॐ ⊖ ॐ

At Dr. Halstaad's insistence, Tan paid a call on the International Student Association. Through them, he met several other Peruvians, including another Quechua speaker, a pleasant fellow named Luís Quevedo from a village near Cajamarca. A student in the medical school, Luís was happy to have a friend who spoke his own language. Together, they explored the Twin Cities, eating strange foods and laughing about the complexities of life in America. The Halstaads were delighted that Tan was beginning to get out a little more, and often insisted that Luís dine with them. Luís introduced Tan to the University's gym and pool. Twice a week they met to work out and swim, and, in the process, they joined a volleyball league. Tan proved to be a strong competitor and was soon looking forward to practices and the intramural matches that came with it.

After practice one evening, Tan invited Luís to come in for coffee. Sitting in leather wing chairs while the stereo played Andean flute music Tan had found at a local music shop, they spoke of their homes and how they had come to be in Ruti-Suyu. The subject had never really come up before; to speak of one's past life would, at home, be considered women's gossip. In the comfort of Dr. Halstaad's study, it seemed appropriate.

Luís blamed his education on the local nuns. "Sister María José thought I was too smart to leave running barefoot through mountains," he laughed, "so she sent me down to Trujillo, to the Jesuits, who civilized me and turned me into a science fiend. I did my bachelor's at the University in Lima, and one of my professors got me the scholarship which brought me here." He paused and studied his friend's placid face. "What about you, Tan? Did the Jesuits get you, too?"

"No, I had no contact with the missionaries. I came because I wanted more than our janpeq could teach me."

"This cannot be your first school?" cried Luís.

Tan shrugged, "There was no school where I lived."

"Then how on earth did you end up here? I mean, you told me Dr. Halstaad arranged your entry, but you never mentioned you had not gone to at least a village school. How did you learn English ...or Spanish for that matter?"

"Hector. He was my teacher."

"But Minnesota?"

Tan shrugged again. "They said they would take me. So I am here."

"Amazing. I am truly impressed. So what did you do back home? Did you have a craft?"

"No. Not really." Tan was reluctant to discuss his past; he was unsure how Luís viewed the ancient religion.

But Luís was more aware than he anticipated. "Is that why you have the name Villac-Quilla? Were you...or rather, are you a rimac?" He asked the question hesitatingly; one did not usually talk about these things outside of one's own ayllu. But up in the mountain ayllus, away from the coast, some villages still practiced the old ways combined with the ritual of the Catholic Church.

Tan's face remained impassive as he considered his answer. "No," he said quietly, "I am not, although had I stayed, eventually I might have eventually joined them."

"You are not a Jew, yet you wear a Jewish star. You carry a quipu with red strands. You do not have a craft. What exactly are you, Tan Villac-Quilla?"

The word formed in his mouth, yet he hesitated. Obviously, Luís knew something about the old ways, but admitting he was what he was, that was something else.

The silence spoke loudly to the medical student. In a hushed voice, he said, "Your name says much, perhaps too much." Luís paused, weighing carefully what he would say next. Grandmothers told tales of men who once lived alone in the yunka, men whose mita was devoted solely to Mamaquilla. Until this moment, they were nothing but stories to be told on long, winter nights. "Are you...?"

Tan nodded.

Silence hung above them like the canopy of the rain forest. The haunting strains of the music faded until nothing was left. Luís stroked his chin, composing his thoughts, his eyes averted from those of the aclla who sat stone-like in the chair. Even in his village, no one ever spoke with those who lived in the sacred mountains; it was forbidden. All the taboos and mores drummed into a child were no longer abstracts to Luís; they were, at that moment, reality. Already, he had broken the law by asking Tan the first question. "Perhaps I should go," he offered, not knowing what else to say.

"No, it is not necessary. I was released from my mita by our Mamacuna before I left; I could not have left without her permission." He smiled, breaking the tension between them. "I need your friendship here, Luís," admitted Tan; "I would be more lonely than I ever was in the jungle without a voice from home."

"I accept your offer of friendship, Tan Villac-Quilla."

"Thank you, for I have a question for you."

"If I know the answer, I shall give it."

Tan got up and refilled their cups. Returning to his seat, Tan pulled the chain from beneath his shirt. "You said these are Jewish stars," he said in English. "I have heard it called the Star of David. What do you know about this?"

"Are you asking what I know about Jews?" replied Luís, somewhat surprised by the question. Tan nodded, so he went on. "You know about the Middle East, don't you?"

"I read the newspapers and listen to the news on television."

"Israel and Jerusalem?"

"A country and a city."

"And a great deal more. The Christian God, the one called Jesus, was born a Jew in the city of Bethlehem, near Jerusalem. Jews have been around for thousands of years...like your people. They believe in one God, the Faceless One." He searched for a quick way to explain it. "Have you ever read the Bible?" he asked, switching into English.

"No, but I have heard of it."

Luís scanned the shelves behind the desk until he saw what he knew would be there. Jumping up, he pulled the thick volume from its place and handed it to Tan. "This is a Bible. You should read this. The first half is a history of Jews and their laws. The second half is a history of Jesus and his followers. Interesting reading, if you can wade through the statistics," he said with a grin.

"I shall begin it tonight."

"Don't let the language throw you; it's supposed to be a little stiff. Why do you want to know about Jews, anyway?"

"Curiosity. Is this wrong?" The question was an honest one.

"No. Just be careful, though. Jews tend to stick to their own kind. Like you do at home. They have a long history of persecution, the worst of which happened only fifty years ago, in Germany."

"Nazis?" The word felt strange on his tongue.

"Yeah, as a matter of fact. You've learned about World War Two?"

"A little."

"It's gruesome stuff; makes the Caribs look like nice, friendly fellows. You might ask Dr. Halstaad about it."

The conversation drifted to less monumental topics, taking the momentary edge off Tan's revelation. When the hour grew late, Tan walked his guest to the door. In an unusual gesture, he extended his hand to Luís. "I hope the things you know about me do not get in the way of our friendship," he said seriously. "We can be of great help to each other."

Luís accepted the gesture, but added his own: he touched his fingers to his lips several times. "What you have told me will remain with me. Our ways are not their ways, and they would not understand the paths of our people."

Later, alone in his room, Tan gave thanks to Mamaquilla for sending him a friend of his own kind.

◦❖◦

At the beginning of February, midterms loomed ahead of Tan as enormous storm clouds on the horizon. His work was on schedule, his assignments complete, yet he could not shake the fear which gripped him each time he glanced at the calendar, those fast approaching dates circled in red. The Halstaads hid amused smiles as Tan constantly reviewed material. When he sat in the kitchen reading aloud, Mrs. Halstaad refrained from reminding him he had all but memorized the textbooks. His dogged determination to master the intricacies of Western philosophy in a matter of weeks impressed Dr. Halstaad to no end, causing him to send relentlessly funny letters to Hector describing Tan's quest for perfection. Hector, in turn, wrote to his protégé about the perils of burnout, instructing him to lighten up and have some fun.

The boiling point was reached on the Wednesday before exams began. Feeling trapped as a caged jaguar, Tan paced the study as he recited the declinations of the verb "to be" for Mrs. Halstaad who sat quietly working on her needlepoint. "This is absurd!" Tan suddenly shouted, making her miss a stitch. "If I can speak the language, and I know how to use the word, why must I memorize such trivial things!"

She put her canvas in her lap and beckoned Tan to take the chair beside her. "Because if you had studied English as a child, you would know these are necessary. What your teacher is asking you to do is to understand how this irregular verb is irregular. It is simply an exercise, Tan, and a rather easy one for you, if you would relax."

"How can I relax, ma'am? These are important examinations and I must ace them all!"

The intensity in his voice and the fire in his eyes made Ingrid Halstaad reach for his hand and take it in her own. "Tan, midterm exams serve two purposes. One is to see where you are in relation to the rest of the class, measuring how well you have learned the material being taught. The other part is really an examination of the teacher. If the entire class does poorly on a portion of the test, the teacher must review how the lesson was presented. In either case, the exam is merely a measuring tool for both student and teacher."

Tan knitted his dark brows as he gave her words serious consideration. "If this is so, ma'am, why is so much importance given to these exams?"

"Because this is the way it is." She gave him a reassuring squeeze and suggested that he take a break from studying. "It's a beautiful night, Tan, why not take a brisk walk and when you come back, I'll have some hot chocolate ready for you in the kitchen."

She was right; he needed to get outside and walk, much the way he would walk in the jungle whenever things weren't going well. Bundled against the biting cold, he left the house and headed toward campus.

It was early evening; people were still out and about in Dinkytown where the bars stayed open until one in the morning. The cold, fresh air felt good in his lungs, clearing out the must of academic endeavor. Alone, but not lonely, Tan strolled past the shops and cafes, pausing every so often to glance in a window to marvel at the array of goods one could buy with paper rectangles and metal disks, not to mention plastic. When he reached University Avenue, traffic was still heavy, so instead of trying to cross, he turned east.

A group of students stood outside a low grey building. They were a merry crowd, laughing and talking; a few sang songs with words he did not understand. As he worked his way through the crowd, he noticed a sign taped to the front window in strange letters, beneath it, the words **HAPPY PURIM** in English. He wondered what *Purim* was, mentally memorizing the spelling so he could look it up later. Someone bumped Tan from behind, and he turned to see a pair of grass green eyes looking right at him.

"Sorry, buddy," said the tall man standing with his arm around her shoulder. The woman Li-ah said nothing, but her eyes widened when they met Tan's.

"No problem," muttered Tan, still staring.

The man addressed the woman. "Come on, sweetheart, Mindy and the kids are waiting." He steered her around Tan and together they disappeared into the building.

For a moment, Tan stood there, unable to move. Whatever this place was, it had something to do with the Qewa Ñawi and he needed to know more.

Ꙅ ⊖ Ꙅ

In the morning, Tan left the house earlier than usual. He went back to the grey building and was relieved to discover the doors unlocked. Going inside, he heard voices coming from a room on the side and he peeked in. About a dozen people were there, wearing strange cloaks, bands of leather wrapped around their arms and little black boxes fastened to their heads. He wondered what kind of ritual this was, for certainly, from the way they were singing, they were deep in prayer. Looking about, he spotted a place where he could sit until they were finished.

He did not have to wait long. Soon the people were filing out of the room, chatting amongst themselves, unaware of the stranger in their midst. In a matter of minutes, the lobby was empty. Tan rose and went back to the room where they had been. A robust, dark haired man remained, folding a white cloak as he hummed to himself. He looked up and smiled at Tan.

"Can I help you?" he asked in a cheery voice.

"Perhaps. I have questions," said Tan, more than a little unsure of what he was doing there.

"Ask away."

"This is a place for Jews?"

"Yep. This is called Hillel House. It's a place where Jewish students can meet to pray or study or just hang out. You Jewish?"

Tan shook his head as he chewed on his lower lip, thinking about how to ask the next question. "Can you tell me about these?" He pulled the stars out so the man could see them.

The tall man tucked the white square in a small velvet bag and came toward Tan. "I'm Rabbi Steinberg," he said, extending his hand. "Let's go to my office where we can talk."

CHAPTER 12

"*You know that guy?" Jay had asked Leah.*

Leah was unwilling to believe what she had seen. It didn't matter that she knew he was near; to see him standing so close to her, looking so different yet so familiar was a shock. She couldn't possibly tell Jay who he was and what, if anything, he meant to her. As it was, things were not all that terrific between them. Try as he might, Jay could not hide the disappointment he felt when she told him about the possibility of a grant from the Peruvian government. They saw each other regularly, but something had changed; the distance was already growing between them. One part of Leah wanted to tell him she would marry him in a minute, while another part knew that commitment would mean the end of her research.

Purim eve was supposed to be a jolly affair, a celebration of the first order that Leah had loved since childhood; but like everything else in her world these days, this night was different. She had barely listened to the reading of the Book of Esther; she hardly remembered to rattle her noise-maker at the mention of Haman's name. She tried to focus her attention on Avi, Tova and Elisha sitting with them, but all she could see was a pair of dark brown eyes staring at her from out of the darkness. She did not have to be in her bed to know the dreams of the jungle would interrupt her sleep.

For the next few days, Leah walked about campus with one eye over her shoulder. The empty seat in the back of the lecture hall remained empty, and there were no more strange offerings tied to her doorknob. The emerald-eyed bird remained emerald-eyed. With midterms to occupy her, Leah threw herself into her work, correcting exams, writing and editing her own papers, and setting her priorities in some semblance of order. Muñoz kept after Leah on the subject of the grant, reviewing the materials she collected, making suggestions and additions as they worked together to compile the necessary documentation.

"You seem distracted, Leah," commented Dr. Muñoz one morning as they sat in his office. "Is all this getting to you at last?"

Leah laughed at the implication; her advisor always warned her that one day the fun would be over and the grunt work would begin in earnest. "No, I'm still enjoying myself, but I'll be the first to admit I'm not getting nearly enough sleep these days."

"Perhaps you are seeing too much of your doctor friend."

"Not according to him. He's complaining that I'm too busy to even meet for a cup of coffee!"

Dr. Muñoz leaned back in his cracked leather chair, his hands his in lap, and studied his best student. "It's more than that, Lee. There is an unusual degree of tiredness around your eyes that I am not accustomed to seeing. Perhaps you should take the weekend and go off somewhere with your friend. If you would like the use of my cabin...."

"That's awfully kind, Dr. Muñoz, but really not necessary," Leah protested.

The professor waved a slender hand. "Do not say no, just say you will consider the offer." He smiled a little sheepishly and added, "It was my wife's idea, Leah. She said I was working you too hard and a few days off in the snow would do you a great good."

It did not surprise Leah in the least that the offer came from Ysabel Muñoz. A most observant and considerate woman, she was well aware of how hard her husband worked his assistant. "Tell *la señora* that I will think seriously about it. And tell her thanks."

They finished the portion of the document scheduled for typing and Leah gathered up her papers. As she was about to leave, Dr. Muñoz called her back. "I have been withholding information from you, Leah."

"Oh?"

"There is an element of the grant which we need to consider carefully before we agree to our end." Dr. Muñoz, in great detail, told Leah of his conversations with his contact in Washington as well as a call from Vincente Lubrano. "It's Lubrano whom I do not trust. He says he is from the consulate, not the embassy, which means his connections are, conceivably, tied to industry. His interest may not be in the best interests of your people."

Leah let a thin whistle escape from her pursed lips. "Whoa, Dr. Muñoz, how much of this is fact and how much of this is conjecture?'

"Seventy-five, twenty-five," he answered quickly. "I've done a little digging around. Lubrano is rich. His father and elder brother run a conglomerate of mining companies. Like any good second son, he is in government service. But there is something about him I do not trust. He has, maybe, too much mouth for one in government service. I have made inquiries to a variety of sources and the answers will help us to decide."

Astounded by the revelation, Leah let the impact of his words settle in before she spoke. *Too much mouth* meant he was too cocky and that could only mean one thing: cocaine. "Please keep me posted, but I will defer to your judgment, Dr. Muñoz."

In an effort to brighten her gloomy face, Muñoz changed the subject. "Do you have anyone in any of your classes that you might like to use for the quarter time position?" he asked, referring to the opening, which would occur at the start of spring quarter. "It's clerical, but if we have a work-study candidate from our own department, we can make a specific request."

Leah didn't have to think; she already had someone in mind. "As a matter of fact, there is a girl in my 1-102 class who turns in exceptional work and I know she is looking for a job. I'll talk to her as soon as I can."

"She must be trustworthy and exceedingly clever. The information she will be handling will be sensitive," said Dr. Muñoz.

If she was anything at all, Sarah Perkal was exceedingly clever. An excellent student, Leah had found Sarah to be a good sounding board whenever she thought her classes were lacking in pizzazz. They had spent some time together during fall quarter when Leah needed a hand in pulling material for reading assignments.

"Then I shall leave this to you, Leah. After all, you'll be the one to work most closely with her."

e~ ⊖ ~e

At the end of her lecture, Leah reviewed the readings assigned for the coming week and then announced the students who needed to make appointments with her. "Please use the sign-up sheet on my office door and then remember to keep your appointments," she chided the class. "Your grade may depend upon it."

By the time she got back to her office later in the day, the sign up sheet was almost completely full. *Amazing what a little thing like a grade could do to motivate people,* she thought with a grin. She unlocked the door and went in, closing it behind her to discourage unscheduled interruption. On her desk, the neat piles beckoned, each one belonging to another part of her tightly organized life. Eschewing the tedious ones, Leah started with her mail, specifically with the fat envelope with a Peruvian postmark. Hector's letters were always welcome diversions and this one was no different. He wrote enthusiastically about her possible return to Peru and relayed a most excited message from Saba who demanded that Leah add a new string to her quipu to count the moons until she could return. Enclosed in the envelope were strands of white and black vicuña wool of the proper length to make such an addition. Leah could almost hear Hector's gentle laughter as he stuffed the thread inside his letter.

"On a more serious note, Qewa Ñawi," wrote Hector, "I was summoned to Janajpachallacta. I was afraid the old lady was failing, but this was not the case. In fact, she looks more robust than ever. We had a very pleasant visit, but near the end of the evening, she sent everyone away so we might speak alone. The lady wanted to send a message to you; she said she was worried about relying on your good senses (her words). I am writing the message as she said it. I'm not sure I understand it, and even less sure that I want to, but here are the words she asked me to write to you:

Daughter in Ruti-Suyu, your heart sings with great strength. This I know. You have told me this yourself. You speak well and often and we hear you. I cannot answer the questions you ask with answers you can touch, but in your heart you have the answers you seek. Open your heart and do not be afraid of the dreams you are sent. You are safe within the heart of the people. This will protect you. Mamaquilla Herself has ordained this. Do not run from that which you know will embrace you. Your heart is in our heart; you are bound to us forever.

"I hope you know what she is talking about, niña. I got the clear impression that the lady knows something I do not, or at least something you have not told me. If you would care to comment, I would not object." The letter continued on a less curious plane and ended with Hector's usual declaration of undying devotion. "As always, I will tell you I miss your company and can only hope you will come back soon armed with an enormous number of bad jokes. *Tu estimado amigo*, Hector."

There was no denying the Mamacuna knew what was happening to her and, moreover, she knew why. Leah wished she could write directly to the Coya, and receive a private response, but there was no way to bypass Hector. In all her letters to Hector, she had resisted telling him about the strange feelings and the more bizarre events, like the switching of the pins in her dorm room. Obviously, Hector knew he was here, but he had never once mentioned the man in his letters. *Why not?* wondered Leah. More than once, Leah reconstructed the night he had been at Hector's, so obviously at home, as though he spent a great deal of time there. *And* he seemed to know something about America, *and* he spoke fluent Spanish, something the others did not. She refused to believe Hector would be setting her up. "A flaming jigsaw puzzle," she mused aloud, letting the words drift over her. "Then why don't the pieces just plain fit?"

A knock on the door startled Leah and the letter in her hands slid to the floor. "Come in," she called, recovering herself.

A frizzy blonde head popped in. "Excuse me, Lee, but I didn't want to wait for my appointment, " sighed Sarah Perkal, "I was too nervous to wait until Thursday."

"Come on in, Sarah" Leah grinned, almost relieved not to have to think about Hector's letter for a moment. "There's nothing to worry about; your work is fine, better than fine, actually." She paused, waiting for the girl to sit down on the extra chair. "Your exam was an 'A,' not that I would have expected anything less from you. And your paper, or should I say *drash*, was exceptional."

The girl blushed bright red at the use of the Hebrew word; she knew exactly what Leah meant. "I guess it was a little pedantic," she confessed, her eyebrows drawn together.

"You attacked the topic like a Talmud scholar, Sarah, ripping it to shreds before putting it back together in an order more to your liking. It was an artful piece of work," exclaimed the teacher, relishing the moment, "but I will admit I've never seen anyone attack Frazer quite like that."

Sarah brightened considerably at the compliment. "I worked really hard on the paper; I really want to do well in this class."

"And that's why I wanted to see you; I want to offer you a job. One that actually pays real money." Leah explained what was required of the clerical aide. "It'll be a boatload of typing and grunt work, so if you don't think you want to do it, please be honest and tell me. I won't think any less of you if you say no."

"Are you kidding?" cried Sarah, nearly jumping up from the chair. "I want this job; it'll be great. I'd love to do it! God, this is great!"

Her enthusiasm was refreshing. Leah had visions of a crestfallen student when she described the kind of work entailed. Still, she had to be certain. "I know from reading your papers last quarter and this, that your interests lie in Semitic studies. In the questionnaire I had everyone fill out at the beginning of the term you said you were taking both Arabic and advanced Hebrew, in addition to Biblical literature. This is the opposite side of the world, y'know."

"I understand that, but..." she paused to carefully construct her next thought. "You may be working on South American culture, but the areas of ritual and mythology align closely to what I want to study. There are like no hidden cultures left in the Middle East, but I am most interested in the religions which preceded...ours," she added with a smile.

Leah knew it was that very reason which caused her to stray from her original plans of studying in Israel, landing her in South America instead.

It was the lure of the possibility that she could record something which had never been recorded before which drew her to the Andes. "I spent a year in Israel," she sighed, "poking around looking for a clue that we did not spring fully formed from the head of Moses. It was a frustrating time for me."

"I know that feeling," laughed Sarah. "I've read a lot of stuff published on Andean mythology. There's a great sense of the magic in it all. I love the way it all sorta fits together. And you make it sound so reasonable! I never get bored in your lectures even if they're kinda simplified for the people who are in there because they have to be. I mean, just because I read this stuff when I'm on vacation doesn't mean everyone else does."

"You mean they don't?" cried Leah with mock horror.

"Frankly, I don't think most of the kids in that class read much more than the funnies in the newspaper. But then again, some of them do.... I mean I see some of them in the library on occasion, but sometimes I think I'm the only one who really likes this stuff."

Leah was curious. "Anyone else in that class you can point to as having a serious interest?"

"Well, kinda. There's this guy who sometimes sits in the back," said Sarah thoughtfully. "I don't think he's registered for the class, though. He looks Chicano, but his accent is really different. You know who I mean."

"No," Leah said quietly, "I don't."

"Oh, you do. He's the guy who asked you about whether or not the religion in the Andes was bogus." She looked at Leah who kept an impassive face. "He's the one who wears a bird pin on his shirt just like yours. We just thought he was a friend of yours."

It took great effort for Leah to keep from screaming. Keeping her voice as even as she could, she asked Sarah what she knew about the drop-in.

"Not much; he doesn't really talk to anyone. But I'll tell you, it isn't because no one talks to him. I think every girl in the class has tried to get his attention." She blushed prettily. "He is incredible looking. I can't believe you don't know him." Then she added, "I think his name is Dan or something like that. Do you want me to find out about him?"

Something told Leah that Sarah could discover anything she set her mind to. "No, that's okay; I was just curious."

"Well, if I find out anything, I'll let you know."

When Sarah was gone, Leah slumped in her chair. There was no longer a question about it; the man in the back of the room was exactly who she knew he was.

CHAPTER 13

"If I was able to teach India to drive," declared Ingrid, "I can certainly teach you, Tan." The subject had come up over the dinner celebrating Tan's successful completion of midterms. Arne suggested the time was right for him to learn, and Ingrid was more than willing to take on the task. "It's the perfect time, what with snow and ice still on the ground. That's an important factor in learning to drive in Minnesota," she told him. "If you wait until spring, the first snowfall you encounter will terrify you."

Tan was hesitant. He wanted to drive, but the act of controlling a mechanical being such as a car was something he had not seriously considered doing, at least not for a while. After some persuading, he agreed. "If I get a license," he asked, "will I be able to get a car?"

Dr. Halstaad laughed aloud, catching Tan off guard. "Not only will you be able to get a car, Hector has already instructed me to arrange for insurance. All you need to do is pass the test and it is done." Hector had, in his own thorough way, left no eventuality uncovered.

"Then it's settled," Ingrid announced with a broad smile, "we will begin on tomorrow afternoon with a trip to the DMV to get the book, a learner's permit. Then, we'll sign you up for classroom training."

Driving, as it turned out, was not nearly as difficult as Tan had anticipated. As soon as he had his permit, Ingrid took him to a large, empty parking lot behind a high school. She patiently explained how to start the ignition and move the transmission lever from park to drive. In seconds, he was slowly creeping forward, but exhilarated by the sheer magic of the moment. For two hours he circled the parking lot, practicing turning, reversing, and stopping. When darkness began to fall, he switched on the lights, and prepared to change places her with her, but she insisted that he drive home.

"There's still plenty of light, Tan," she told him, "and no reason why you can't get us safely home on the city streets. We'll leave the freeways alone until you are more comfortable."

Feeling every inch a king, Tan slowly maneuvered the car onto the street and drove carefully back to the house, never once missing a stop sign. He maneuvered smoothly into a space, scraping the curb only once.

At the dinner table, Tan regaled them with the wonders of driving. Still flushed with success, he described the amazement he felt at being able to steer the metal beast without hitting anything in its path. "And traffic! How respectful everyone is of each other!" he cried. "It is all so neatly done!"

No one had the heart to tell him not all drivers were as respectful as the ones he first encountered; there would be plenty of time for him to learn that lesson. Then the telephone rang; the sudden sound still made Tan jump, but he was gradually getting used to it. Ingrid answered the phone in the kitchen and spoke to the caller for a few moments before she emerged smiling. "It's for you, Tan." She glanced at her husband and winked.

Although he used the telephone to call Luís, Tan rarely received calls. He went into the kitchen and picked up the receiver. "Hello?"

"*Yau! Allinllanchu, churi?*" asked a familiar voice.

"Janpeq!" The joy in Tan's voice was unmistakable. Sliding comfortably into Quechua, he immediately asked Hector if anything was wrong.

"No, nothing is wrong; I was a little lonely tonight and thought I would see if Mamaquilla would let the telephone company work in our favor. I missed your sound, churi. How is school?"

Tan launched into a long stream of words, few of which the Halstaads understood, but they did not care. It was the most, if not the fastest, they had ever heard him speak, and his excitement was undeniable. Ingrid turned to her husband. "And how did you manage this, dear?"

"Oh, in my last letter I just mentioned that I thought Tan was a bit homesick and suggested Hector pick up the telephone. I figured it would do Tan good to hear Hector's voice, that's all." He glanced into the kitchen and smiled. "And I do believe I am right."

Tan was perched on a stool, his elbows resting on the counter, still spouting at a fantastic pace. Obviously there was much to be said, and the Halstaads decided to leave well enough alone as they resumed their dinner.

"Your grades are excellent," Hector reassured his protégé. "The papers you send are good; your style improves with each one."

"I am working harder than I ever thought possible, Hector. And I love it. I cannot get enough. For each thing I learn, there are ten more I want to learn. Every day is an adventure!"

"That is how it is supposed to be. But what of the other things; are you having fun?" While sounding light, the question was serious.

"Fun?" asked Tan. "I am not a child, Hector."

The doctor clucked his disapproval. "Surely you are not spending all your time in the library, Tan. What are you doing to keep yourself fit?"

Tan told him about Luís and the volleyball team, about going out with classmates after class, and finally, with great pride, about his driving lesson. "Dr. Halstaad tells me I may have a car when I am ready. Is this so?"

"This is so, and I will arrange for money for a car when you tell me you are ready. I trust your judgment in this, but I want Arne to go with you to pick one out."

"Of course, Hector, that is not a question. I will leave the ultimate decision to him."

Hector broached the subject of Leah, albeit with certain trepidation. "You have made no mention of Leah in your letters, Tan. Have you seen her?

There was a hesitation before he answered, "Yes."

Hector could almost see the mask drop over Tan's face, but he continued anyway. "You have not spoken to her, though, have you?"

"No."

Hector sighed, a sound that could be felt over two thousand miles. "Tan, you are, I think, speaking to her in the ways of a Rimac. Do you think this is fair to her?"

He did not have to ask Hector how he knew. "She writes to you."

"Of course she writes to me, Tan!" exploded Hector. "But never about you. The Mamacuna, however, called me to Janajpachallacta to relay a message to Leah. Obviously, there is some other form of communication going on around you three!"

"What did the Coya tell you?"

"The Coya, may Mamaquilla protect her forever, dictated a rather amazing message, Tan. She *knew*. She knew exactly what is happening to Leah and the words she sent applied directly to you, although I'm not sure she thought I understood. Tan, if you want to talk to her, talk to her! Pick up the telephone! But for God's sake, don't ruin her sleep!"

Tan couldn't help but chuckle and was relieved when Hector, too, laughed. "I did not mean to be so distracting to her," he admitted rather sheepishly.

"Oh yes, you did. I know you too well, and I know why you wanted to be in America, and I know too well that you will continue to pester her in the sacred ways. It's not as though you are a thousand miles apart; you *can* just as easily pick up the phone. Like you are doing now. Here is her phone number." He rattled off the digits. "This is a much more efficient way of talking to someone, Tan, than monkeying about in their dreams." He stopped, realizing he was shouting. "The Mamacuna had a message for you, too, Tan. She says, and I quote 'Tell my churi to follow his heart as well as he follows his head. He will understand.' Do you understand?"

He could be on the moon and still the Mamacuna would know what was in his heart. "I understand, Hector, and I will do what I must do."

The conversation turned to less pressing matters, and Hector knew he had made the right decision sending Tan to the United States. The young man did not disappoint him; in fact, he seemed to be feasting at the banquet of education. He made no mention of his trip to Lima, nor of anything which might cause Tan to worry. There was no point; there was nothing Tan could do. At the end of their talk, Hector asked to speak to Arne.

Dr. Halstaad went into the study and closed the door, knowing what would be said between them would need to be private. "Any hope of your coming north, my friend?" he asked Hector as soon as Tan hung up the extension.

"Not quite yet, Arne; perhaps next year some time," chuckled Hector, wishing it were otherwise. "Tell me, how is your house guest?"

"A paragon of virtue, Hector. If I did not know he had lived in the jungle his entire life, I would never suspect."

"Then he is well civilized?"

"Disgustingly polite and proper. Ingrid thinks he's a marvel and wishes our own boys were more like Tan."

Hector remembered the Halstaad boys as very young children and could sympathize. They were a rough and tumble lot, although all three were now married and living settled lives. But it was not the boys who concerned him. "What about India?" he asked, "how does she get on with Tan?"

There was a long, parental sigh. "Not nearly as well as she would like to, I'm afraid. It seems our not so little girl is precariously close to throwing herself on that poor, unsuspecting boy."

Hector's laugh was hearty. "Hardly an unsuspecting boy, Arne! Tan is merely maintaining virtuous decorum. So I take it he is not chasing after her like the young pups of her high school days."

"More like running in the opposite direction."

For a moment, Hector considered telling Arne about Leah, but decided against it; this was Tan's business alone and not to be spoken of without his permission.

It was Arne who brought up the subject of cars and for the rest of the time that was discussed. They agreed a late model used car would be in order, perhaps something a little sporty.

When he returned to the table, Dr. Halstaad found Tan and Ingrid deep in discussion about the merits of American versus foreign cars. "I see you have discovered her passion," he joked, taking his place at the table. "My wife is one of the few women I know who has an intrinsic understanding of mechanics. Come the summer, she likes to do her own oil changes."

"Perhaps you will teach me how?" asked Tan.

"If you would like, but I'll warn you, it's a dirty business." She liked the way he wanted to experience everything, that nothing was too mundane for his examination.

Over coffee, Dr. Halstaad asked Tan how he felt after speaking with Hector. "A little less homesick, but a little more at the same time. It was good to hear his voice so clearly."

"He is pleased with your progress, Tan, but feels you are, perhaps, working too hard."

Tan smiled, shaking his head, "There is no such thing as working too hard, Dr. Halstaad. I am years behind the others and have much to do if I want to begin real work toward a degree." There was no way to explain that his unquenchable thirst would more than make up for the lack of formal education. Glancing at his watch, Tan jumped up, almost overturning his chair. "Ai, Mama!" he cried, hastily folding his napkin, "I am to meet Luís at eight, and it is already ten to! Please excuse me, ma'am, sir..."

"Wait and I'll drive you over," offered Dr. Halstaad.

"Thanks, but no. It's only a few blocks," he grinned, "and I like to run."

When he had gone, Halstaad leaned back in her chair and commented, "Thank God he's starting to sound like a normal guy."

"And behave like one, too, Arne," she laughed. "He actually left a pair of boxers in the bathroom."

🙠 ⊖ 🙣

The cold air pierced his lungs, but Tan relished the sensation. Running at a quick pace, his backpack on his shoulder, he easily traversed the distance to the gym in a matter of minutes. Luís was already in the locker room when he arrived.

"I thought you had forgotten," he said, speaking Quechua. "It's not like you to be late."

"Hector telephoned; it's the first time we've spoken."

"All is well at home?"

Tan paused and thought about the question. "Hector said everyone was well, but I think he does not tell me everything." He saw Luís raise a questioning brow. "I cannot put a name to it, but something has changed there." He shook off the feeling. "If there was something wrong, I think he would tell me, so I think I am only homesick....Just a little." Re-dressed for the gym, Tan felt good wearing shorts and no shirt; he missed the constant exposure to the elements and longed for warmer weather when he could wear less clothing.

The gym was not crowded, but several men were busy at work on the weight machines. A small group gathered around a series of mats on the floor where they wrestled, more for the physical exercise than for competition. Setting himself up on a Nautilus, Tan started slowly, building up weight and resistance as his body warmed to the work. It was a poor substitute for what he did at home, but it would have to do. Between the weights and swimming laps, at least he felt his body wasn't growing soft.

Luís was finished with his routine and was sitting nearby when three of the wrestlers approached. All the weight machines were in use, requiring that they wait their turn, something which obviously did not appeal to them.

"Come on, man, hurry it up," said one to Tan as he went into his last series of exercises. "We don't have all night."

He told them he'd be done shortly. "Go swim," he called to Luís, reverting to his native language. "I'll be done soon."

"Hey, Paco, whaddja call me?" snarled the wrestler closest to Tan.

"I was not speaking to you," he replied as he continued to work the machine.

"I heard you. Don't give me any bullshit, Paco." His smile was most unfriendly.

Tan completed the routine and leaned back, taking full measure of his antagonist. "My name is not Paco, and I said nothing of offense either to you or about you." He stood, but his path was blocked by the wrestler. "Now, if you will excuse me." He started to walk around him, but the other man would not let him pass.

"Whatsa matter, Paco, Mexico isn't good enough for you?"

Tan side-stepped him and moved away but he could feel eyes on his back. No one had to tell him the wrestler was following him. Quickly, he calculated his options.

"Hey, Latino boy, I'm talkin' to you!"

Tan continued ambling toward the entrance to the pool, aware that all eyes in the gym were on him. He reached the mats, and paused.

"I hope you know what you are doing," called Luís, having no doubts that the skills Tan learned in the rain forest would serve him well here.

"I can handle it," he replied without turning, waiting for the assault.

"Whadja call me, Paco?" persisted the wrestler. There was no response. "Whatsa matter, you scared?"

This time, Tan faced his opponent. "I called you a sorry excuse for your mother's afterbirth."

That was enough to set the wrestler into a charge. He came at Tan, his arms extended, prepared to throw the foreigner to the mat, but he was not prepared for the reaction. With terrific speed, Tan caught his assailant and with a single twist, brought him down hard, quickly pinning the wrestler beneath him, rendering the assailant helpless. "I could break your neck, you know," he growled. "Do not fuck with me." He measured the terror in the wrestler's eyes and added "In my country, men do not bother fighting with men; it is no challenge. We fight with cats...," his voice took on a low, menacing hiss, "big cats." With a graceful turn, he was on his feet, looking down at the wrestler. "Get up, and act like a man; childishness does not become someone of your size."

As they left the gym, both Peruvians suppressed the urge to laugh. "Did you really fight cats at home?" asked Luís.

"Of course; didn't you?"

"Well....once," admitted Luís sheepishly, "and I have the scars to prove it."

Tan smiled at his friend. "It's a manhood thing in my ayllu. Something everyone does until they are old enough to know better."

"Did you realize you could get killed doing it?"

"Yes, but that's what made it...fun." Tan dropped his towel near the wall and walked to the edge of the pool. Reaching his arms straight out, he murmured something, then raised them above his head before bringing them slowly to his sides. Only then, did he dive into the water.

Luís did not have to hear what he said to know what it was; he had seen others do the same things before swimming at home. Surely, Mamaquilla was pleased with him.

CHAPTER 14

"I know it's short notice, but the department is throwing a cocktail party tomorrow night in honor of some guy up from Chile," explained Jay when he finally reached her at her office, "here to teach a seminar on research he's been doing in pediatric nutrition in Third World countries. A bunch of people are going to be there from the Hispanics department and I think Muñoz is invited. Anyway, I thought you might like to go."

Leah glanced quickly at her calendar. Wednesday nights were traditionally lecture prep nights, but she was in already in good shape for Thursday's class. In truth, it sounded like a nice change from her routine and she accepted. "What's the dress code?" she asked, mentally going through her closet for an appropriate outfit.

"How should I know? I'll wear a coat and tie. Why don't you wear that slinky grey thing?"

Leah snickered at the description. "Oh, all right, I'll wear the grey for your benefit." A tap on the door post made her look up and she waved Mary in. "Gotta go, Jay; Mary's here. I'll see you tomorrow at seven, if I don't talk to you before then." She knew she would; it was habit.

"Nice of you to show up," said Mary, hanging Leah's coat on the hook beside the door. "We were beginning to think you went back to Peru."

"Can't a person spend the morning in the library? Geez!" She frowned and then smiled in spite of herself. "What did I miss?"

"Nothing. Absolutely nothing. Nothing is going on in this place except everyone's bitching about the weather. Ran into Mark Steinberg at the copy shop this morning; he's looking for you. Says to tell you he found the article you were looking for. You can pick it up from him either today or tomorrow. Whatever."

Leah brightened considerably. "Great! I'll go over to Hillel before I go back to the dorm. What about you?"

Mary assured her that she was hanging in as best she could. "My orals are set for the first week in April, if I live that long. Beyond that, I cannot see. You, however, still look tired. I thought you were going to take Muñoz up on his offer of the cabin for a weekend."

"I am. A week from Friday I am leaving here at nine in the morning for a wonderfully quiet weekend alone in beautiful Somerset, Wisconsin."

Mary gasped. "Isn't the ever devoted Dr. Weiss accompanying you?"

"Nope. I'd rather go alone, thank you very much. All I want to do is eat, sleep, and read smutty romance novels."

"Sounds great. Can I come?"

"No way! This is going to be a one-woman weekend. No phones, no papers, no notes."

Mary stood up and ambled to the door. "Have it your way, but beware, I am green with envy." There was no ill will in her voice, only a touch of wistfulness. "By the way, how would you like your old apartment back?"

Leah almost choked. "What?" Her apartment, a cozy one bedroom affair just a few blocks from campus had been leased to another graduate student before she went to Peru. She hated to give it up, but there was no way to sublet it while she was gone. "Don't tell me Rob is moving out!"

"As a matter of fact, he just got a job teaching at UW Stout for spring quarter and he was wondering if you would like to take over the lease... starting right after finals. Oh, and he's not coming back, either."

It was too good an opportunity to pass up. "Tell him to give me twenty-four hours to find out if I can get out of my dorm contract," she told Mary. "I think I can because I have a single."

"No problem, Lee. See you later."

"Thanks, Mary," called Leah as she closed the door. Elated, Leah set to work on the crisis pile.

ల⊖ల

The last student left at a quarter to four, not too late for Leah to catch the rabbi before he left for the day. Snow was drifting down again, making it five consecutive days that enough had fallen to declare the city a snow emergency. She walked as quickly as she dared along the ice-encrusted sidewalk.

Mark was sitting on the edge of his secretary's desk when she barreled up the stairs and together they went to his office. "Since when are you interested in Kabbalist stories?"

Leah explained it was teleportation that she was really after. There were legends galore about great mystic rabbis appearing and disappearing. "Some of the stories are similar to what the Spanish heard when they first landed in Peru. I figured it was worth a look. It's funny the way people all over the globe have the same tales."

"I figured it had something to do with Peru," he laughed; he knew her far too well to believe it was idle curiosity.

"Not that I think there's any connection; it's just for comparison," she told him. "You are an absolute sweetheart for digging this up for me." She kissed his cheek. "Thank you. Oh, and tell Mindy Friday night is fine for dinner, but Jay can't make it. Well, I gotta run." Leah slung her backpack onto her shoulders. "Thanks again, Mark." As she went out the door, she ran into a body. "Oh, sorry!" she said. Looking up, she froze.

"The fault is mine," answered a too familiar voice. Tan backed out of the doorway to let her pass.

She brushed by him, then stopped, turning back to face him. "What are you doing here?" she demanded, slipping into Quechua without thinking.

"Seeking knowledge," replied Tan. His lips curved upward ever so slightly.

Leah clenched her jaw until the muscles twitched. When she finally spoke, it was quiet, almost inaudible. "You are invading my nights," she accused in his own language, shaking her forefinger at him. "You dance taqui in my dreams; you are chasqui I cannot answer. You abuse your abilities until I cannot sleep!"

As she talked, Tan moved slowly toward Leah, forcing her to step backward until her back was pinned against the wall. She poked him on his hard chest, her finger pounding out the point she was trying desperately trying to make. "Stop doing this to me; stop coming to me! Stop..."

His lips came gently down on hers, silencing her words, drawing the essence of her soul into him. Leah's eyes closed, the pressure of his mouth against hers, sweet yet unyielding. When he released her lips, he placed his hand on her forehead, at the place where hair was parted, then drew his thumb down the curve of her cheek until it rested beneath her chin. Lifting her face, he put his mouth to her ear and whispered, "My heart is in your heart, as your heart is in mine."

Her green eyes opened to look into his brown ones. "*You frighten me,*" she told him without words that she knew he heard. Willing herself to be calm, she stalked down the stairs and out the door.

Mark stood in the doorway, having witnessed the scene with a slack jaw and a puzzled frown. "What the hell was that?" he asked Tan once Leah was gone.

"That, Rabbi, was the reason I have come to Ruti-Suyu."

∞ ⊖ ∞

Leah had no recollection of how she got home. Foregoing dinner, she went straight to her room, needing time alone to sort out what had just happened. When his lips touched hers, it was as natural as breathing. His hand on her face was warm; she could still feel his finger on her chin. Everything about it was frightening; yet so reassuring it was as if she were wrapped in a snug cocoon. Taking the golden aclla from its place in her top dresser drawer, it was uncommonly warm to the touch. Leah held it tightly in her palm as she lay atop her bed and fell into a deep, dreamless sleep, the first in too many nights.

When her eyes opened again, the red numbers of the clock glowed 1:47. The little golden conopa was still wedged in her palm; she stared at it, wondering why she was holding it in the first place. Outside the snow was still falling, though heavily now, and the windowsill was already a miniature range of peaks and valleys. Leah stood there, gazing out over the Mississippi, the shadows of the east bank campus barely visible through the barrage of snowflakes. Her thoughts drifted southward, to the ayllu where everyone would be asleep in their huts, except perhaps for Saba who, even at this hour, might be sitting beside her small fire grinding herbs for the poultices she used daily. Closing her eyes, Leah concentrated on Saba, telling the old woman how she needed her advice in this most delicate of times. "Hear me, Mama'amuata," she whispered into the night, "tell me what I do not know. I am afraid of not knowing."

∽ ⊖ ∾

Far away, Saba's meditations were interrupted by a vision of her hua'amuata standing in Ruti-Suyu, snows dancing around her, yet she was warm and dry. The old woman struggled to sit upright, the need to allow the vision full reign clear in her mind. Her small fire glowed red, still alive although at the end of its burning time. Saba took her carry pouch from its peg on the wall and removed a leaf packet. With a quick word to Mamaquilla, she sprinkled the powdery contents onto the embers and watched the smoke rise as it filled the air with a sweet fragrance. She studied the shapes floating above her as they floated slowly into the still, night sky. Closing her eyes, a small smile on her lips, Saba answered the call of her hua'amuata, sending a message of her own to Ruti-Suyu.

∽ ⊖ ∾

Leah did not turn on the lights when she traded her jeans for a warm, flannel nightgown. She did not want to go to bed, nor did she want to work. Sitting at her desk in the darkness, Leah could make out the shape of the golden aclla she had dropped on her pillow. In her hands, she held the quipu that had been tied to her doorknob, her fingers slowing counting the series of knots over and over. Eight times she recalled each huaca in the series, remembering details she thought she had forgotten. On the ninth counting of the ninth knot, Saba's gap-toothed grin floated into her mind and her own heart pounded within her breast. "Face what you fear, but do not run toward it," spoke a voice from within. "What you fear most will come to you as a good thing, like the jaguar sent by Mamaquilla as a sign of prosperity. Do not be afraid."

The voice dissipated into the night and Leah's heart stopped racing. A strange calm settled over her and she set aside the quipu. Climbing into her bed, she slipped the golden aclla beneath her pillow and did not have too long to wait until sleep slid over her.

❧ ⊖ ☙

In the morning, Leah stopped at the dorm office to ask whether or not there was a current waiting list for space. Told that there was, she informed the secretary of her plans to move out. Feeling better than she had in weeks, Leah practically skated across the icy bridge to her east bank office. The rest of the day moved at a good clip, keeping Leah's mind off the Aclla and the uneasy suspicion that she did not have complete control over her own life these days.

Sarah Perkal stopped in to drop off a short paper. "It's not where I'd like it to be," she admitted with a frown, "but it's okay."

"Not great, huh," teased the teacher. "I'm sure you answered the ques-tion adequately." Leah knew adequate was not enough for Sarah; she was certain the paper would be "A" quality work.

"Oh," said Sarah, plopping into the spare chair, "I've been meaning to tell you about the guy in the back of Intro."

Leah's head snapped up. "Oh, do tell."

"Tan's from Peru, alright. He's here as a special under the aegis of Arne Halstaad from Public Health. He lives with them. I think his last name is Villac or something like that...wait, I remember, Villac-Quilla. He says he thinks he's going to major in math."

"You talked to him?"

Sarah gave Leah a wide smile. "Yep, I sure did. He is really something else. Speaks English really well, and has already placed out of first ESL. He comes to your class because he says he interested in your lectures about his neighborhood."

Leah cut her off. "Neighborhood? He said neighborhood."

"Yep, neighborhood. He said you had a really good understanding of Andean religion and he liked listening to you talk."

"Oh, for God's sake!"

Sarah shrugged. "Every girl in that class has her eye on him, although he doesn't come as often as he used to. They wiggle their butts at him, too, but he doesn't seem to notice. I'll tell you one thing, 'though, you should talk to him.... he seems to know an awful lot about your area."

Leah sat back with a groan and closed her eyes. She didn't want to know why Sarah said that, but she had a feeling she was going to find out.

"And, he's a devoted follower of Mamaquilla."

Leah asked Sarah how she managed to get all this out of a guy who didn't seem to talk to anyone before. "I'll admit, I'm curious," added Leah.

"It was easy. I saw him on campus and I followed him to the student union. I just happened to bump into him at the vending machines. Said I, 'oooh, aren't you in Anthro 1-102?' Says he, 'no, not really. I am a drop-in.'" Her imitation of his accent was wonderfully perfect. "So we sat there and talked for a while. He's got a great smile with these little dimples that you can see when he laughs..."

"I can't believe it!" cried Leah. "I can't believe he talked to you!"

"Why not?" Sarah giggled, "I'm no dog, y'know."

"That's not what I meant. I meant..." she stopped short of saying he doesn't usually talk to strange women, but then she would have to explain how she knew that.

Sarah repeated the gist of her conversation with Tan. "He likes Minnesota, but he was wondering if the trees ever get leaves or if they stay bare all year 'round. I assured him he'd regret asking in July when it gets seriously hot." Knowing she had done well, Sarah sat back and wiggled her eyebrows. "Anything else you want me to find out?" She was more than willing to accost him again. "I know how to find him."

"No, that's okay. You've told me more than enough." Leah tried to sound casual, but her voice was tight. "Thanks, Sarah," she called as the girl bounded energetically from the office.

Cutting her afternoon hours short, Leah met Rob at the apartment to work out the details of the transfer. "Any day during spring break is fine with me," she said, looking around the familiar room. She waited while he called the landlord to tell him the news, then handed Leah the phone to make the final arrangements.

Happy, she caught the bus back to the west bank and went home to change her clothes. By a stroke of luck, her bathroom was vacant and she quickly turned on the shower, a signal that it was about to be occupied. On impulse, she took her keys with her, locking her own room before going in for her bath.

୧୦ ⊖ ୧୦

Dried and dusted with perfumed powder, Leah pulled the heather grey jersey from her tiny closet and slipped it over her head. A simple sheath with a turtleneck and long, tapered sleeves, it clung to her curves, accentuating Leah's high breasts, narrow waist and slim, almost boyish, hips. She brushed out her hair, separating it into three tresses for a braid, but a glance in the mirror changed her mind. Letting it go, Leah decided to leave her hair free, with only two small clips to keep it from falling into her face. She applied little make-up, only a dab of olive green shadow before brushing on some mascara, and a little red lip gloss. Satisfied with the effect, she removed the bird pin from her shirt and fastened it onto her dress at the left shoulder, where it seemed ready to take flight. Still, the dress lacked something, thought Leah. She thought for a moment, then pulled out the ceremonial sash Saba had made. It added a subtle touch of color without being obvious. Pleased with the effect, Leah slipped her feet into a pair of soft black boots just as the telephone rang. "On my way down," she informed Jay who waited in the lobby. Grabbing her alpaca cloak, she ran to meet her date.

Before going up to his room to change, Tan dropped his pack on the stairs and stopped in the kitchen, in hopes there would be a few cookies left over from Mrs. Halstaad's luncheon party. Instead of the cookies, he found India wrapped in a short terry robe, drinking a glass of milk. "Well," she sniffed, "you don't look very pleased to see me, Tan."

"I am always pleased to see you," he replied with as much sincerity as he could muster.

India sashayed over to him, her scent filling his nostrils. "Dad told me about the shindig for Teodoro García and I just thought you'd enjoy having a woman on your arm. Do you mind?"

"It would be an honor to escort you," he managed; the last thing he wanted to do was spend an evening with India.

Reaching up, she caressed his face. "Then it would be in your best interest to get dressed, don't you think?"

Tan plucked her hand from his cheek. "If you will excuse me?" He left her standing in the kitchen, the cookies forgotten.

⁓ ⊖ ⁓

Nattily dressed in a blue oxford shirt, striped tie and a blue blazer, Tan checked the crease on his grey wool trousers, idly wondering why people would voluntarily wear such uncomfortable, restrictive clothing.

Ingrid rapped on the open door and smiled at the sight of him. "You look terribly handsome, Tan. I must remember to compliment Hector on his taste in clothing." Her good-natured jibe was answered with smile from the man standing before the mirror blushing. "Come down whenever you're ready."

During the short ride to the hotel, India sat in the back seat, her hand carelessly resting against Tan's knee. He politely helped her from the car, allowing her to slide her arm though his as they walked through the lobby. When India slipped off her coat, Tan involuntarily sucked in his breath. She was wearing a black dress which ended somewhere in the middle of her slender thighs. Tan had never seen anyone dressed in similar fashion; the looks she received from men around her did not go unnoticed by him.

As discreetly as possible, Tan scanned the room. He was new to these situations and the best way to learn was to carefully observe. This was not so different from the lobby of the theatre, he decided as he watched the interaction. He noticed the spaces between people, the way the hands were used, the smiles and the laughter. He saw some people shake hands while others, upon arrival, brushed kisses on each other's cheek. It was easy to spot the guest of honor standing in the center of the room; there was a growing cluster of people surrounding him...including the Qewa Ñawi and the red-haired man.

$$\backsim \ominus \backsim$$

Señora Muñoz spotted Leah and Jay in the crowd. "Why didn't Diego tell me you were coming?" she asked after she kissed Leah European style. "I would have asked you to join us for dinner this evening. Teodoro is staying with us."

"That's very kind, Señora Muñoz," Jay answered with a smile, "but between the two of us, we are lucky if we get a cup of coffee together."

They stood about chatting, catching up on common interests, until Dr. García was free. Dr. Muñoz made the introductions, making sure to mention Jay's interest in pediatrics.

But it was to Leah he turned first. "I understand you are the woman who lived in the mountains," he said firmly grasping her hand. "Diego told me you were present at a real Intip Raimi. Tell me, is it as mystical an experience as I have been told?"

She was about to answer when Leah felt a sudden warmth. She did not have to look to know whom she would see across the room. There was an aura, an indescribable ripple in her subconscious that told her he was physically near. Her heart pounded furiously inside her chest; she surreptitiously checked to see if it was visible through her dress. She willed herself to concentrate on what Dr. García was asking, but it was almost impossible. Focusing her eyes on the guest of honor, she began to explain the ceremony she had witnessed.

The Halstaads approached the cluster of people listening to the woman in the grey dress. Dr. García noticed their approach and paused, mid-question, to welcome them. "Good to see you again, Arne." The two men shook hands. "You know Diego Muñoz, of course, and his wife, Ysabel."

"Yes, we've met before." Dr. Halstaad introduced his wife and daughter. "And allow me to introduce Tan Villac-Quilla, the student my friend, Hector Morales, sent us from Peru."

Both Jay and Muñoz looked at Leah, but it was Jay who spoke first. "That's the name of the doctor near your village, Lee."

"Yes," she replied, keeping her eyes shielded from Tan's gaze.

"Perhaps you have met, then?" Muñoz asked, noticing the red creeping over his pupil's cheeks.

Tan came to her rescue. "I am sure I would remember." His well-tempered English made Leah look up, only to see his wide, teasing smile and the dimples Sarah had mentioned. "How do you do...?" He paused as though he did not know her name.

"Allow me to present a student of your culture, Tan," said Muñoz, his pride in her evident. "This is Leah Fine, and this is Jay Weiss, a student in our medical school."

Dr. García, however, was anxious to get back to the topic he had been discussing with Leah. "I am curious to know how you managed to be welcomed by the Mamacuna," he said, drawing her attention to him. "We've all heard the remote tribes are hostile to outsiders."

With one eye on Dr. García and the other on Tan, Leah attempted to answer the question. "I think it was easier because I made it a point not to interfere with life in the ayllu. In the beginning, I kept my questions to a minimum, learning their customs through limited participation while establishing a relationship with the medicine woman." Leah glanced at Tan, swallowed hard and went on. "She was the one who took me to Mamacuna at the winter solstice."

"I have often found," interjected García, "those who are completely isolated and remain faithful to the old ways, tend to be more healthy than those who try to keep one foot in each world. But tell me, what was it like, attending a solstice ceremony?"

"There's great power and wisdom in the way the oracle of the smoke is interpreted," she said gravely. "The Mamacuna and her Rimoc consider their visions gifts from Mamaquilla. The visions may include both good and evil omens, but generally, they are reminders to maintain the status quo."

"I would not presume to disagree, Miss Fine," Tan interrupted, "but the Rimoc also make certain predictions which have an uncanny way of coming to pass. Have you not found it so?"

When she looked at him, Leah noticed the mate to her pin fastened to Tan's shirt collar. "I have found that to be true, but wouldn't you agree that those occasions are somewhat rare?"

"Not as rare as you might think, Miss Fine."

It was the way he drawled her name that made Leah shiver. When his eyes met hers, they bored into the bottom of her soul, making her shift slightly in order to slip her free arm through Jay's.

The silence which followed was broken by India Halstaad. "Oh, look, Tan; there's Luís!" With a sweet smile and a gentle tug, she made their apologies and guided Tan away.

"I'm surprised you've never met him, Miss Fine," said Dr. Halstaad. "Hector Morales was Tan's teacher."

Leah knew her face was red. "Hector is many things to many, many people, Doctor. You can't imagine the size of the district he services, let alone the number of people he knows!" Leah's laugh was brittle as she added, "I think Hector tends to forget just how many people count him as a good friend."

Neither the blush nor the forced quality of her laughter was lost on Ingrid Halstaad. Something happened to Tan as soon as he was in close proximity to this woman, and there was no doubt in her mind that Leah was well acquainted with him. There was gentleness in his manner, a kind of caressing quality to the way he spoke to her. For whatever reason she had, Leah Fine was not telling the truth about Tan Villac-Quilla. And, she definitely noticed the bird.

ᏽ ⊖ ᏽ

"She's very lovely," snipped India as they made their way across the room.

Tan raised an eyebrow at her, annoyed at her tone. "Yes, Señora Muñoz is a handsome woman."

"Don't be funny, Tan. I meant the one in the grey dress."

"I did not notice."

"Yeah, right."

Tan stopped walking and turned India to face him. His voice was taut when he said, "You have no knowledge of either what pleases or displeases me. Do not guess, India; it is unbecoming."

A pout formed on India's lips; she did not like to be rebuked, especially by him. Still, with no witty reply readily available, she settled for a doe-eyed glance at her escort.

ഇ ⊖ ೧

Until someone came to whisk Dr. García away for more introductions, the conversation about Peru continued. After he was gone, Dr. Halstaad took the opportunity to ask about Hector. Leah reassured him that the good doctor was quietly going about the business of protecting his part of the rain forest while running through the district tending to the needs of the people.

"I wish he could come north for a visit," sighed Mrs. Halstaad. "It's been far too long since we've seen him."

"He mentioned something about coming up next year," Dr. Halstaad told them. "He wants to attend an immunology conference in Atlanta and if he does, you can bet Minnesota will be on his itinerary."

Leah, unable to stand there any longer, excused herself and went in search of a ladies' room. She needed a moment alone to compose herself. Seeing him was unsettling enough; hearing him speak directly to her was positively unnerving. At the sink, she splashed some water on her face and repaired her lipstick. The face in the mirror still seemed too red, too flushed, but there was nothing she could do about it. She left the lounge and returned to the reception, but not before she headed to the bar for a glass of wine. Halfway there, Tan appeared from out of nowhere, sans the blonde. Touching her elbow, he laughed when she startled.

"Must you always sneak up on me?" she hissed. "Don't touch me!"

"Does my touch burn?" he asked mockingly in English, dropping his hand. He laughed softly as Leah's face went from pink to red.

"Your touch is a violation of my chastity," she replied in Quechua.

"I think not, Qewa Ñawi." Although he called her Grass-Eyes, he continued in English. "We are not in the jungle now. Here, you do not serve Mamaquilla. You have no mita in America."

"And neither do you?"

"I have been released from my mita." Tan saw Jay approaching. Quickly, he switched into Quechua. "What Mamacuna saw in the jonchi is the same as what you know in your heart," said Tan, his eyes narrowing. "You are not born of the people, but Mamaquilla has favored you with Her blessings and this you know in your heart as well." He stopped speaking when Jay arrived, but Leah went on.

"What is it you want from me?" she persisted in Quechua but at the same time keeping her face from displaying the anger she felt. It was obvious to Tan that the other man did not know anything nor did she want him to. "You haunt me like a ghost, ever present, yet invisible. You speak of devotion to Mamaquilla, yet you have cut your hair. You say you are a mulkan, but what is it you really seek?"

Her sharp words cut into him until the muscles of his jaw twitched. In a forced, even tone, he spoke again, directly addressing her accusations. "I did not ask to be bound to you, yet our *unachai* is knotted together like a quipu. You have visions, this you cannot deny, for you dance taqui in my sleep as I dance in yours. In my world, you said you were the mulkan; in your world, I am the one. One soul seeks the other. Whether or not you admit this, it is so."

She knew he spoke a truth they shared, the difference between them being his ability to accept it without question. "Why?" Leah blurted, letting the questions ask more questions through a single word.

Tan shook his head. "I do not know, Qewa Ñawi." He felt her anguish in his heart before he allowed words to form on his lips. "I would take you here, in the middle of a room full of people, if I thought that would answer the question for us both." He paused again, as India suddenly appeared at his side, her hand going immediately to the crook of his arm. Tan did nothing to ward her off, but caught a fleeting look of confusion in Leah's eyes. "You are deep in my heart, Qewa Ñawi, as deeply as I am embedded in yours. Deny it, if you will; you know I speak only the truth." He allowed the sudden pain he felt to subside, then smiled coldly at Jay. "Your woman is very beautiful," he said in well measured English," but you must feed her more. She is quite...skinny. Now, if you would excuse us?" He melted into the crowd, India still attached at the elbow.

"What the hell was that all about?" asked Jay as soon as they were out of earshot.

Leah merely shrugged. "He was telling me about his village."

"He looked awfully intense for someone talking about his hometown. That is one tightly wrapped dude. I'm not so sure I like him." Jay grinned at Leah, "But he's right, y'know, you're getting down-right anorexic."

Leah sighed and let her head rest against Jay's shoulder. "It's the food in the dorm. Once I move back into the apartment, I promise I'll eat more."

"Why wait? Let's blow this pop stand and go get something to eat."

While Jay went to get the car, Leah waited in the lobby of the hotel. She saw the Halstaads retrieving their coats. Tan went with Dr. Halstaad, leaving India and her mother a few yards from where she was standing. Surprisingly, India strolled over.

"I just love it when Tan speaks in his native tongue," she cooed, "I find it positively erotic."

"Quechua does have a lovely tonality," agreed Leah, forcing herself to be pleasant.

India leaned a little closer in order to whisper conspiratorially "Frankly, I find Tan positively erotic. Don't you?" She watched, amused, as Leah turned bright red.

The comment annoyed Leah, but she managed a polite smile. "I see my friend waiting for me outside. It was so nice to have met you, Ms. Halstaad."

⁋⊖∞

"Who is she to you?" India asked Tan after her parents had gone upstairs.

"Who is who, India?" Tan casually remarked, hanging his coat in the closet.

"Damn it, Tan, don't play games with me; you cannot possibly win. I'm talking about Leah what's-her-name. The one with the *other* silver bird." She allowed herself a smug grin when his eyes flared dangerously, only to be reigned into control again.

He refused to acknowledge the last remark. "She is a student who spent last year in my district. Beyond that, I cannot tell you very much." He allowed a small smile in her direction. "If you are so curious, why don't you call her and have lunch or do whatever women in America do when they want to pry into another's business?"

India flounced up the stairs, refusing to comment. Only when he heard her door slam, did Tan go to his room.

Tan stripped off his clothes and sat, wearing nothing but his shorts, staring at the screen of the computer. India's old Mac had been easy to master once he got past the strangeness of seeing his words appear in front of him like magic. The text of his English assignment glowed on the screen, the only other light coming from the small lamp on his desk. He knew he should be working on his paper, yet he could not concentrate on the words. His thoughts drifted southward to the huaca by the pool, warming his insides as he recalled the first time he saw Leah swimming gracefully in the blue water. He had had visions before then, visions of snow and grey skies, places he could not name, and the green eyes so foreign to his world. Lying awake on his pallet, he would pray to Mamaquilla for answers to his questions, some sign that his fate was in the jungles and not away from his people. But as the visions increased, he knew She was sending him away. Rather than surreptitiously watch the young women of the ayllus around him, he refused to look at their lovely faces, afraid he might become attached to someone when he knew in his heart he could not declare. It was when he saw the Qewa Ñawi hiding in the grass that he knew Mamaquilla had heard his prayers. Her answer, however, was not the one he hoped for.

A noise brought him back to the present. India stood at the doorway. "May I come in?"

Tan could easily read the smoldering cornflower blue eyes. His body responded in a way he did not anticipate. He was afraid if he stood up, she would see what he could not hide beneath the thin cotton of his shorts. "I am studying, India, and must not be interrupted," he said, keeping his voice low. He noticed she wore nothing but her nightgown. "This is not ...appropriate."

She came in any way, closing the door behind her. "In America, if a man wants a woman, and the woman is equally willing, there is no taboo," she said coming to stand behind his chair. Her hands were warm as they touched his bare skin.

"And if the man does not want the woman?"

India glanced down into his lap. "I think that is not the case."

When he stood, Tan towered over the diminutive India. His finger touched the long ribbon. "A woman comes to me with no barrier, India."

The intent of his words was not beyond her comprehension. She shrugged, and the gown swirled into a satin pool at her feet. "There is no barrier," she murmured, lifting her face to his. Her body was indeed lovely. Dark pink roses tipped her full breasts, a contrast to the pale pink of her skin. She lifted his hand and placed it over her heart, moaning at his touch. "I want you," she breathed, her blue eyes staring boldly into his.

Tan hesitated. To take her would run the risk of conception, yet, she seemed determined to have him. There was no denying he was more than able to pleasure the woman. And amongst the young men at home, this would have been viewed as something natural. It would have been easy, too easy, to carry her to the bed and make love to the lush, curvaceous India, yet, he knew it was wrong. In a swift motion, he slid the gown up over her, replacing it gently on her pale shoulders. "I cannot give you what you want, India; my heart is bound to someone else."

"I wish," she whispered, "I was the one who has captured your heart."

Tan watched her go and for a brief moment, regretted that what he said was true.

CHAPTER 15

The breakfast table was set for two when Tan stumbled sleepily into the kitchen the next morning. "You slept late, Tan. Did you stay up working after we came home?" Ingrid asked as she filled his coffee cup.

"More or less." He was almost afraid to meet her eyes for fear she might guess what had transpired in his room.

"India left quite early to go back to Northfield. She was unusually quiet, so I can assume you two had it out last night." She raised a pale eyebrow in his direction. When Tan said nothing, she continued as gently as she could. "I know my daughter, Tan; I'm not blind to the way she behaves around you. I also know you better than you realize, and I'm sure you handled yourself in a considerate manner."

"She's very beautiful, ma'am, but very determined in her ways."

"And she usually gets what she wants. But not to worry, she's also pretty resilient." Ingrid smiled at him, then paused for a long moment before she said, "Tan, there is something else, though. Something of a rather personal nature I must ask you."

Tan stared into his cup, guilt washing over him like the waterfall at the huaca. If she asked, he would tell her the truth about last night, even if it meant leaving the Halstaad house in disgrace. "There is no question you might ask that I would not answer, ma'am," he quietly said.

Ingrid pulled up the chair next to his and sat down. She covered his hand with hers, making him look at her. "Before she left, India told me what happened. She was rather remorseful about it, and embarrassed, too. But she said something else. She said that you are bound to someone else. Am I right in thinking the woman in question is the one we met last night at the reception, the one who wears a silver bird to match the one on your collar?"

"We are not in love, as you say in English, yet I am bound to her."

"Does she know this?"

"Yes."

"Does she understand this?"

"In some ways, she does, ma'am. But the ways of Mamaquilla are not always as clear as they could be. We both struggle with what we know, but we have not come together on a single path." The pain inside reflected in the darkest part of his eyes.

As a mother, Ingrid felt for this son of another mother. Had it been one of her own sitting across the table, she could not have felt any more deeply than she did now. She wished she knew what his own mother would tell him, what his people would do in such circumstances, but she did not. "I've no great words of wisdom for you, Tan, only to let you know that I'm here if you need me. If there's anything I can do..."

"Thank you," he said simply when she could not finish. "I am honored to have you speak to me this way. What will be will be no matter what, and I accept what Mamaquilla has provided for me. If the woman is to be bound to me, then it will be so. If not, Mamaquilla has brought me here to learn things I will bring back to my people." When he smiled, it was a warm and honest expression. "Besides, I have Hector to think of; I cannot return to him without having honored his wishes that I learn everything that I can."

Ingrid squeezed the hand beneath hers. "You're a good man, Tan Villac-Quilla, and we are proud to have you under our roof for as long as you wish. And when the time comes that you do leave us, know that you'll always have a place in our home." She gave him a last, motherly pat. "Now, eat your breakfast and be on your way or you'll be late to class!"

Tan did as he was told, relieved not to have been thrown out, but unsure of why he wasn't. Still, he appreciated her frankness and wondered if her husband would be of the same mind. Obviously, she had no delusions about her daughter's virtue and was unwilling to take him to task for what she had been told by India herself. Although he had not coupled with the daughter, the father might consider the rejection of his daughter the greater insult.

Midterms behind him, Tan relaxed. With his advisor's reassurance his command of English had improved dramatically, he planned to apply for admission into the College of Liberal Arts during spring quarter. He spent his days running between classes and the library, a smile usually on his face and a feeling of tremendous freedom in his heart. Neither the snow nor the cold that lingered into March could dampen his spirit. Whenever he could manage the time, he went to concerts and lectures in the evenings, at first with the Halstaads, later on his own. He liked meeting his classmates at these events and often found himself sitting with his new friends who, once they learned he had come from a backwater, insisted that he join them on Saturday nights. The phone at the Halstaads began to ring with more frequency, much to their relief, and soon Tan was as busy as any other college student. His studies came first, but it did not stop him from exploring his new world. Occasionally, he saw Leah walking on campus, but he did not approach her again. The time had not yet come and he was in no rush. He did, however, learn that she spent her Saturday mornings at the Hillel House.

Coming around the corner, Tan spotted Rabbi Steinberg walking just ahead of him. "Mark!" he called, waving at the other man. He jogged to catch up.

"What's happenin', Tan?" he asked with a smile.

"I finished that book. When can we talk? I have a thousand questions!"

The rabbi thought for a minute, then brightened. "Are you free for dinner tonight? It would be an interesting experience for you."

Tan was delighted to be invited to the Rabbi's house. Mark had regaled him with tales of his three kids and Tan wanted very much to see how American children lived. "I would be pleased to come," he replied, then added, "and thank you for inviting me."

Mark suppressed a laugh. He loved the formal way Tan spoke when he had to reply to any sort of request. "Done. I'll tell my wife to set an extra place. Besides, she's dying to meet you."

ల⟶ ⊖ ⟵ల

Leah had her coat on and was about to leave her office when the telephone rang. For a moment, she considered not answering, but her curiosity got the better of her.

"I'm making a pot roast, so you can't say no," said Mindy as soon as Leah picked up. "And besides, the kids are complaining that you haven't been here in ages."

"Oh, I guess this is a dinner invitation," Leah laughed. "All things considered, it sounds like a pretty good idea. In fact, it sounds like a great idea...except for one thing."

"And that is?"

"Jay's coming over tonight after his rounds."

"So, call him and tell him to come here instead."

"I doubt if he'd do that, Mindy. He never gets out of the hospital until after ten...if he's lucky." But the thought of pot roast was overwhelming. "Tell you what. I'll call over there and leave a message for him telling him where I'll be. If he gets off early, he can join us."

"Sounds like a plan to me, so come on over whenever you can."

ల⟶ ⊖ ⟵ల

Leah walked the short distance to the Steinberg's. Fresh snow covered the slush of the day with a fluffy coverlet shimmering in the fading light, making winter dreary Dinkytown sparkle like crushed diamonds. Despite the snow, the air was not cold, but rather pleasantly brisk. Her cheeks were bright pink, as bright as her eyes, when she rang the doorbell.

"Leah! Leah! Leah!" cried four-year-old Tova, barreling down the narrow hallway from the kitchen to throw herself into a pair of open arms. "You smell good," announced the little girl, snuggling into the softness of Leah's alpaca cloak.

Mindy appeared, wiping her hands on her apron. "Good Shabbos, Lee. You've arrived not a moment too soon; I was getting ready to roast *them* for dinner."

The little girl giggled, her head of wild black curls bobbing in Leah's face. "Let me hang up my cloak," Leah pleaded, "and I'll tell everyone a story. Okay!"

Two more urchins danced out of the living room shouting "Hooray!" In a matter of seconds, they were pulling Leah toward the stairs and up to Avi's room where a secret fort had been constructed.

"Holler if you need me!" she called as she went.

"No, you holler if *you* need me, you poor, unsuspecting woman!" laughed the rebbetzin.

For the next hour, Leah spun tales for the children. Using lots of voices, she enthralled her little listeners. Just as she reached the end of the story of Deborah, the judge-general of ancient Israel, a great, booming voice was heard outside the tent.

"Fee, fie, fo, fum!" it roared, "I smell the blood of hungry little children waiting for their dinner!"

With shouts of "Abba," the children scrambled out of the tent to attack their best giant. Leah crawled out last of all, laughing at the sight of Mark on the bed covered with squirming legs and arms.

The rabbi looked surprised when he saw Leah. "What are you doing here?" he asked as he struggled out from under the children.

"Mindy caught me as I was walking out the door and asked me to come. She bribed me with pot roast."

"That's some bribe," agreed Mark. He suddenly remembered whom he'd brought with him. "Uh, Leah, I...uh...invited someone also tonight. I...uh...hadn't mentioned who to Mindy, but I think I should tell you."

Judging by the look on his face, Leah didn't have to ask who was downstairs; even if he hadn't mentioned it, she would have guessed Tan was someplace near. She felt him. "Not to worry, Mark. I won't run away."

The rabbi looked sheepish, when he said, "Sorry.... I think." Then he grabbed Avi and hoisted the little boy up in the air. "Everyone get washed up for dinner and come downstairs. The other guests are here," he told them, his eyes merry with pride at his brood. "If you are very nice, maybe, just maybe, Leah will make braids for the ladies."

"Oh, would you?" breathed Tova, fingering her wild hair.

Leah acquiesced and marched the two little girls into the bathroom, while Avi went into his room to put on a clean shirt.

∽ ⊖ ∾

She came down the stairs laughing, a little girl riding on each hip and Avi clinging to her back. About halfway down, Leah stopped, frozen on the tread. Looking up at her, his dark eyes smiling, was Tan.

"Who's that?" whispered Tova, staring at the bronze colored man she had never seen before.

"Who that?" Elisheva echoed, clinging just a little tighter to Leah's waist. She was wary of strangers.

Leah simply said "Hello."

Mark appeared at the archway to the living room to see what Tan was staring at. "You look good like that, Lee," he chuckled, "what with a couple of kids hanging off you." He glanced from Leah to Tan. "I guess you two know each other."

"We do." Tan could not take his eyes from hers, boring into her green ones with great intensity. Mark's casual comment stirred him deeply, the fire in his soul growing stronger merely at the sight of her surrounded by children.

The moment strained until Mark cleared this throat. "Well, come on down, guys, dinner is waiting."

∽ ⊖ ∾

At the table, Leah positioned herself near Mindy, with Tova on one side and Avi on the other. Tan sat directly opposite and she found it strange to be sitting at the table with him, a yarmulke perched precariously on his thick, black hair. When Mark chanted the blessings over the wine, she noticed Tan barely sipped his; she drained her glass. The ewer and bowl were passed for the ritual washing of hands, and Leah busied herself helping the children, but watched through lowered lashes as Tan performed the ritual as though he had been doing it every day of his life. The only thing missing was the way others moved their lips, silently reciting the blessing. Tan carefully copied the way Mark dipped his bread in salt when a piece was given to him. As the platters of aromatic foods were passed, she noticed he eschewed the meat dishes, a small, but to her, significant sign, that he was in some way still bound to his mita. When she took a slice of roast from the platter, she did not miss the way one eyebrow rose in her direction.

Feeling compelled to comment, Leah turned to Mindy. "It's so nice to be able to eat meat once in a while," she said lightly. "While I was in Peru, I ate strictly vegetarian, as I do in the dorm now."

"What? No kosher meat in the jungle, Lee?" laughed Mark, but he noticed Tan looked puzzled. "I've told you about kashrut, Tan. Observant Jews only eat meat that has been slaughtered according to a strict set of laws. Lee, here, for all her wanderings, has always managed to survive on roots and berries."

"Which would explain," he said slowly, a grin twitching at the corners of his mouth, "why she is so skinny." The smile broadened as she turned bright red.

"I don't think you're skinny," whispered Avi, "I think you're just fine."

"Spoken like a true gentleman, Avraham," intoned the rabbi with gravity.

Mindy steered the topic of conversation away from Leah and towards other things. She was acutely aware of the looks passing over her table between the two, more because they were so intense than because Mark had duly reported the incident at Hillel House. Leah had been her friend since they arrived in Minnesota, and had since then become a regular at their Sabbath gatherings. In the same breath, she also liked Jay a great deal and hoped those two would finally get theirs lives arranged together. Now, however, looking at the newcomer, she suspected her husband was correct when he said there was something special between those two.

Leah found Tan's scrutiny throughout the meal vaguely discomforting, but she was unwilling to let him get the better of her. She noticed the bird on the edge of his collar and wondered if anyone noticed it matched hers. As the conversation turned toward religion, Leah watched Tan as he listened, asking an occasional question, but mostly ingesting everything he heard.

"How different are your beliefs?" asked Mindy. "Are you Catholic?"

"No," replied Tan, "I am not. I continue in the ways of my ancestors, but in many respects, they are not so different from your own." He glanced at Leah, whose face remained impassive. Mindy urged him to go on. "Our God, Viracocha, has no face; He is inscrutable, just as you believe. Yet, we worship Him in two ways that do have faces. One is the Inti-Illa, the face of the Sun God who brings light to our world, and the other, Mamaquilla, the Moon Goddess who gives us fertility and sustenance."

"A trilogy, like the Christians?"

Tan shook his head. "Not really; two halves to make one. I suppose it might be close to your concept of God and..." he paused to look at Leah, "and the Shechinah, the feminine side of God. They are, in the end, all parts of the same whole. Different groups of my people also have other faces of Viracocha whom they worship as God, like Pachamama, the Earth Goddess or Illapa-Illi, the Thunder God."

"It sounds so complex," admitted Mindy, enthralled by the various aspects of a new, unknown religion.

Tan's laughter was light when he admitted "To you, perhaps, but to me, it is as simple as the washing of hands, something you learn early in life, but do every day."

Mark sat back, a Cheshire cat grin on his face. His eyes met Leah's questioning ones, as if to say, *pretty impressive, huh?* Mark noticed Tova leaning sleepily against Leah's shoulder. "And on that note, let us begin *z'mirot* before the children fall asleep in their plates."

Leah lost herself in the Sabbath songs, letting them wrap around her like another kind of cloak. Peace had settled over her, making her calm despite the constant pounding of her heart against her breast. Closing her eyes, she allowed the melodies to warm her, oblivious to the glances she was getting from both Steinbergs.

Tan watched her, too, delighting in the way her face glowed as her lips moved in unison with the others at the table. Unlike when she stood in the

Mamacuna's circle, here she was no stranger to the ritual. With the child against her, she was as serene as Mamaquilla Herself, and he longed to take her in his arms. The beauty of the songs matched the beauty of her face, arousing in him a new, deeper sense of passion, a kind never before had he experienced.

The *z'mirot* moved gracefully into the grace after the meal; Mark paused only to tell Tan that it was one thing to thank God for food briefly before one ate, but an art to sing praises when one was sated and ready for a nap. Leah barely glanced at the booklet set before her as she sang the traditional Hebrew words from memory, words she knew as well as her own name. Acutely aware of the brown eyes watching her, she glanced across the table to him, and smiled, only to receive a warm smile in return. *You are in my world now, Aclla,* she told him with her eyes, and *here, I am as one with my people.*

As you are one with me, was the clear, inaudible reply.

~ ⊖ ~

Leah helped Mindy get the little ones to bed. Avi let her unbutton his shirt and help him out of it, but made her turn around while he pulled on his pajamas.

"Do you like Tan?" Avi asked as she tucked him into bed. When she didn't answer, he went on. "He's really cool and he knows all about Indians. Abba said so."

"Tan," the name seemed strange on her lips, "knows about Indians from South America, not about the Ojibwe and the Sioux."

"Then I guess I hafta teach him." Avi let her give him a kiss before he rolled over.

Downstairs, Mindy asked Leah to help her with the last of the dishes, more to have a little private moment with her than because she needed a hand. Although Mark had warned her about saying anything unless Leah brought it up first, Mindy had to tell her she didn't know Tan was coming. "I swear, Lee, all he said was set an extra place. He never told me who was coming."

'I believe you only because he was surprised to see me. Don't worry about it. It's no big deal."

"Mark told me what happened at Hillel."

"I figured he would." Leah took a platter from Mindy's wet hands and began to dry it. "I know you must have a dozen questions, Min, but do me a favor. Don't ask me tonight."

"Are you sure?"

"Positive. If I was okay talking about it, I would, but I'm not, so let's not. Okay?"

In all the time Mindy had known Leah, she had never heard her say something like that. "Just promise me that if you need to talk to someone, you won't hesitate to call me. Promise?"

"Oh, all right," sighed Leah, "I promise...just as long as you promise not to bug me until I do." She glanced at the clock on the wall. "And I guess Jay isn't going to make it."

"Did you drive?"

Leah shook her head. "I walked."

"Then stay here tonight. You can't walk home in this weather."

"You're right; I just may have to," she laughed.

ᔆ ⊖ ᔆ

When the last dish rinsed, the women joined Mark and Tan in the living room. The conversation had turned to the development of rabbinic Judaism, and Mark was explaining how the lack of central organization had caused sects to develop independently.

"Not unlike your people," interjected Leah. "Those who remained in the highlands and the rain forests, away from the Incas and then the Spanish, adapted the ancient traditions of the ancestors to suit their needs. And the people made it very clear to those few westerners who braved the wilds, that you weren't interested in what they had to offer."

"What they had to offer," countered Tan, his eyes intent on hers, "was a world of brutality which was against everything we believe. The missionaries may have had our souls in minds, but those who came with them were more interested in enslaving us."

"No one takes issue with that, but you see, it was not so different for us. There were those who sought to destroy us because of what we believed and often, slavery was not enough for them; death was the only solution. The Spanish had something for us, too, something called the Inquisition. They gave us the choice between conversion or death."

"And yet your people survived."

"And yet we survived, but we did it in their world. Your world, so isolated from outsiders, has had its advantages." Leah averted her eyes for a moment, breaking the hold he had on her.

"But it has kept us from reaping the benefits of civilization at the same time it has protected us as a people. There are few who would spend their time in the jungle and the mountains to bring medicines and improved nutrition to us." Tan smiled lazily, for her benefit. "Yet, they are more than happy to come into our world and carry out our customs to satisfy academic curiosity."

Leah's face burned, angry at the accusation yet knowing at least some of it was indeed the truth. She shifted uncomfortably on the couch, refusing to look at him, instead, turning her face toward Mark as if to ask him to bail her out.

"You can't fault academic curiosity, Tan," said the rabbi, taking up Leah's invisible banner. "Without it, you would not be here, for you would not have known about coming here. It's not like she was there to steal magic secrets.... or coca leaves!"

Tan's laughter surprised both Mark and Leah. "I think you are right. Perhaps I will write an ethnography on the people of Minnesota to publish as an oddity of civilization when I return to my people."

A sharp rap on the door caught everyone's attention. With a puzzled look, Mark went to open it. "Look who's here, Lee!" he called from the foyer. "A white knight here to fetch his lady home!"

A snow covered Jay poked his head around the corner. "Anything left to eat?" he asked in a jolly voice. "I am home from the wars and demand sustenance!" He pounded his chest for effect.

Both Mindy and Leah jumped up at the same time, but it was Leah who scolded him. "Some nerve you have, Jacob Weiss, marching in here at the stroke of midnight demanding food!"

"And shake yourself off before you set one more foot in this house, mister," called Mindy as she bustled into the kitchen, "otherwise, I'll be forced to hand you a mop before you get a single slice of pot roast."

Leah strolled over to him, letting him give her a peck, as much for her benefit as for Tan's. "How was your night, dear?" she asked in a syrupy voice.

"Terrible, or I would not have been so compelled to fight the snow to find you." He let her lift his sodden muffler from around his neck and carry it to the radiator. "I'm sorry I'm so late; being here would have been infinitely preferable to what I was doing at the hospital."

Leah patted his cold cheek and clucked sympathetically. As she turned to carry his coat into the kitchen, she caught Tan's eyes simply smoldering beneath half closed lids. The ever creeping blush rose again. Quickening her pace, she fled into the kitchen.

Jay sat at the dining room table bantering with the rabbi between mouthfuls; Leah sat rigidly beside him. He noticed the way Tan's eyes bored into Leah and how she kept hers averted. Conversation between them was strained and he had the sense this guy was deliberately pushing Leah's buttons.

"If you do not believe in destiny," Tan said with his eyes on Leah, "how would you account for the moments when we do unexpected actions?"

"We develop a sense of right and wrong as children;" explained Mark. "We automatically rely on that sense when making decisions. If we choose to do something extraordinary, it's because somewhere inside, the foundation for that choice is already there."

"Sometimes, it's what we don't do that is the strange decision." Jay glanced pointedly at Leah.

Tan pressed forward, and directed the next salvo at Leah. "So, you make decisions based on what *you* know and what *you* feel. Do you not take into account the wants and feelings of others?"

"I do.... or at least I try to; I can't speak for everyone here." Leah narrowed her eyes at him. "And I suppose you are more aware of what people want and don't want?" Leah abruptly stood up, took Jay's plate and swept into the kitchen. Mindy practically ran after her.

There was a tense moment of silence before Jay said to Tan, "I didn't know you knew Mark and Mindy."

"You would have no reason to know," he answered.

In the little Leah told Jay about Tan, she never mentioned that she ran into him at Hillel. In fact, when he tried to get her to talk about him after the cocktail party, Leah refused with such vehemence, he figured she'd run into this guy before...and whatever happened couldn't have been good. "I didn't figure you to be Jewish."

"I am not. Does that matter?"

Mark jumped in, sensing the tension between them. "Tan's been over to my office several times; he is curious about Judaism and I've been giving him some books to read."

"Why doesn't this surprise me?" There was a singular lack of amusement in the question.

Tan's jaw tightened. "I don't see why it is of any importance to you."

Jay refused to be put off by the other man's seeming nonchalance. "It becomes my business when you become a pain in the ass."

"Jay, settle down," said Mark softly. "I'm the one who invited Tan to join us this evening."

From the kitchen, Mindy and Leah monitored the exchange. "Uh oh, it sounds like they are fighting over you," she grinned.

Leah's response was less than amused. "It isn't funny," she said through clenched teeth. "It isn't funny at all!"

"Where's your sense of humor, Lee? I'd be flattered to death if two gorgeous men were battling it out for my favors."

⁊ ⊖ ⁌

"Pain in the ass?" repeated Tan. "I think you speak without cause."

"On the contrary, bud. I think you're one big pain in the ass when it comes to Lee and she's too much of a lady to tell you that to your face."

"Jay!" warned the rabbi sharply.

Jay did not back down. "You got a lotta nerve following her to Minnesota. You couldn't take no for an answer in the jungle?"

"Did she tell you she said no to me?" asked Tan, leaning back.

"She didn't have to tell me anything. I've known Lee a helluva lot longer than you have, fella. And I know a helluva lot more about her than you'll ever know."

"Mark," said Tan with a slow grin, "was it not the Roman, Publilius Syrus, who said *Familiarity breeds contempt*?"

"That was definitely a hit," Mindy whispered to Leah. "Two points for Tan."

"Mindy!" groaned Leah.

"Sshhhh, Jay's gonna launch."

"Oh, that's good," sneered Jay. "I bet you read a lotta Latin while you were running buck naked through the jungle."

Tan wondered how much Leah had told the red-haired man, but he sensed it wasn't very much. He took a calculated risk with his next shot. "At least when I was running buck naked through the jungle I did not worry about whether or not I could keep my woman."

"She is not your woman!" Jay's voice rose dangerously.

"Nor is she yours," stated Tan. He felt his muscles coiling in readiness.

The rabbi saw hands clenching into fists. "Knock it off, both of you!" Mark bellowed. "There will be no fighting in my house!"

Leah stormed out of the kitchen. "I've heard about enough! I don't belong to either of you!" she nearly shouted at the two combatants. All three men looked at her, two of them clearly ready to do battle. "Screw you both!" Leah spun on her heel, grabbed her cloak from the closet, and bolted out of the house before anyone could move to stop her.

Leah ran until she thought her lungs would burst. She did not care if anyone followed her, she only knew she had to get away from them. Torn in two, she struggled against the wind, stinging tears turning to icicles on her cheek. Part of her wanted to smack them both, the arrogant prigs, while the other part wanted to run away and hide. In either case, she had no desire to see either of them ever again.

Leah knew if she went back to the dorm, Jay would be there, waiting in the lobby with a hangdog look. On impulse, she cut across the empty mall and headed to her office.

༄ ⊖ ༄

She sat at her desk and stared at the tassel hanging on her bulletin board, tempted to rip it down and stomp on it, as though that might alleviate her rage. There was nothing she could do, no way to escape the oppressive feeling in her heart. Anger, she reminded herself, was a useless emotion; it left her impotent and frustrated. Grabbing a book from the pile on the desk, she slammed it open and began reading; anything to take her mind off her two problems.

It was almost two-thirty before Leah thought it safe enough to return to the dorm. By now, Jay would have either called the police or decided she went to crash at Mary's; she hoped for the latter conclusion. Putting her cloak back on, she left Ford Hall.

Snow was still falling as Leah made her way over the Mississippi, but the wind had died down, making the journey almost pleasant. No one was out, but Leah didn't mind; she usually enjoyed the solitude, much the way she had enjoyed the jungle. She stopped in the middle of the bridge to look out over the frozen river. She wished she could, just this once, skate along its rough surface until she reached open water, then swim to its end. She sighed aloud at the foolishness of it, especially when she heard the faint booming of the ice below, that indescribable herald of the coming spring, when the ice would melt and the river would once again run its course unfettered. Pulling her long hair from inside her cloak, Leah removed the restraining elastic and let the gentle breeze blow through it.

"Your hair falls across your face, Qewa Ñawi, but it does not hide your pain," spoke a voice so quiet she was not certain she heard it, yet the sound of his Quechua musical and unexpectedly calming.

Leah leaned against the rail, too tired to fight. "My pain is not your concern any longer. Go away."

"I feel your pain in my heart as if it were my own."

She wanted to tell him that it was only because he caused it, but she bit back the words. "Go away."

"I cannot."

Another sigh, this one from the very bottom of her soul, passed her lips. "There is no mita here. You are free to go."

"I cannot," he repeated, stepping closer to Leah. "Your heart is in my heart, as my heart is in yours. We are bound together, Qewa Ñawi, and I cannot go."

That was just about enough for Leah. She turned on him, her eyes blazing green fire as she shouted in English, her words echoing against the walls of the bridge shelter behind her. "Stop with that, already! Please! You cannot...you cannot...*I* cannot bear it any longer! You scare me! You haunt me! This is not the way of Mamaquilla or any other god, do you understand me?" She stumbled, falling against his chest and her hands pummeled him.

He put his arms about her and let her strike him, understanding her in a way she did not yet understand. "Like a jaguar caught in a net, you fight, but soon you will grow tired and sleep in my arms."

Leah's tears spilled out onto his jacket, her sobs muffled by the thick layer of his down parka. "I'm so tired already," she cried, "I'm just so very, very tired."

His ungloved hand caressed her face, smoothing away the torrent of tears streaming down her cheeks. The scent of her filled his nostrils, the ache in his soul growing more acute with each moment he held her. Lifting her chin, he searched for her soul thought the green windows of her eyes. "My heart is filled with your tears," he murmured, "I will cause you no more pain. Only when the moment is right will we come together again." Tan's mouth came down on hers, searing it with his heat, drinking her in as a dying man would take his last taste of water.

She clung to him in that moment, answering his need with her own until her knees buckled beneath her. Gathering up what was left of her strength, she pulled away from him with an anguished groan and fled, leaving him alone on the bridge, the taste of her lingering on his lips.

CHAPTER 16

Jay was dozing on a bench when Leah marched into the dorm lobby. She stopped long enough to shake him awake. "Go home, Jay," she growled as he rubbed his eyes.

"Lee, we have to talk."

"Oh, no we don't. I have nothing to say to you."

"Lee, I love you!" he cried.

"Love me? You love me?" She stared down at him. "What exactly is it about me that you love, Jay? Is it my mind? My body? My choice of a career? No, that can't be it; you hate what I do. Hate is a little strong. Okay, how about tolerate? And while we're on the subject, Jacob Weiss, I seem to remember breaking off the romance with you a while back. If anyone is following me around, it's you, not him. You got that?"

"But, Lee..."

"Don't you but me, Jay. I saw what went on tonight. You were ready to whip out your club and beat someone over the head with it. It didn't matter who it was, did it? Do you think beating up on him was gonna make me swoon in your arms? Are you that stupid?"

"But, Lee..."

"And arrogant?.... Let's not forget narcissistic. What are you, God's gift to women?" She stopped suddenly and laughed, but it was a cynical sound. "No, excuse me, I had the wrong combatant.... that's Tan...he's the Goddess's gift to women. Which makes you God's gift to the healing arts... right? Oh, sometimes it's so hard for us mere mortals to keep God's gifts straight in our feeble little minds." The elevator bell dinged and Leah ran to catch the lift.

Jay stumbled off the bench and tried to follow her. The night manager, watching the exchange from behind his desk, moved faster and cut him off at the elevators. "Why don't you go home, buddy. You can call her in the morning."

"You don't know Lee, do you? She'll hang up on me."

"Yeah, well, better than getting your fingers slammed in the door. Those things are damn heavy."

❧ ⊖ ❧

In her room, Leah threw her cloak on the chair, her boots in the closet and herself on the bed. No sooner had she hit the pillow then she was asleep and when she opened her eyes again, the midday sun was streaming in the window. Leah groaned and sat up, but only long enough to pull off her skirt and sweater before she dove beneath the covers.

The phone was ringing. "Shut up," mumbled Leah, wishing the noise would stop. It didn't. With a grunt, she got up and went to the wall, grabbing the receiver. "Hello, this is Leah Fine and I am sleeping, so at the sound of the tone, please leave your message." Finished, she hung up. The phone rang again as soon as she reached the bed. Growling, she picked it up again. "Hello, this is Leah Fine...."

"You don't have a machine," shouted Jay, "so don't try it again. You hear me, Lee?"

"At the sound of the beep, take your message and stick it in your ear!" She slammed the receiver down and counted to five. The phone rang. "I'm not talking to you, so piss off, Jay!" The receiver hit the wall where she threw it, then dangled helplessly, bouncing on the coiled cord. She could still hear him yelling.

"Listen to me, Leah, I'm trying to apologize and you won't let me! I know you're there, so pick up the goddamn phone." For some unknown reason, Leah began to giggle; he could hear her. "If you don't pick up this phone, I'm coming over there to break down the door!"

She was still laughing when she put the receiver to her ear. "Stop shouting, I'm here. Say what you want to say and get off my phone, you bully!" The mirth abruptly ceased.

"I called to tell you how sorry I am about last night. I was frantic when you didn't come straight back to the dorm, honey."

"Don't honey me, buster, I'm not in the mood."

"I wanna know what the hell was going on, Lee, that's all. Who is this Tan guy and what does he want from you?" He was talking rapidly, afraid she would hang up on him again.

Leah gritted her teeth. *If I knew the answers*, she thought, *I'd tell you.* "In the order of the questions: one, I haven't the foggiest notion, two, he's a guy from Peru, and three, I don't know that either. Okay?"

"Lee, I love you."

"I've heard that before."

"This is unfair, Leah."

All her resolve crumbled. "Jay, we've been over this already. I know that it stinks, but it's the best I can do. I wouldn't blame you if you never called me again. But until I straighten my own life out, I cannot give you a better answer."

There was a long, painful silence. "And I can't accept that, Lee. I won't accept that. I'll give you all the time you need 'cause in the end, I believe we'll be together. But for right now, I think it's best if you call me when you are ready to talk. You know I love you, and...." he stopped talking.

Leah knew he was on the brink of tears and she hated herself for it. "I'm going up to the Muñoz's cabin on Friday. I promise I will call you when I get back on Sunday night. Will that be okay?"

"I guess so. Did you want to take my Jeep instead of the Saab?"

"No, but thanks." Leah sighed, a long painful sound. "Please, Jay, I'm doing the best I can."

"I know, sweetheart. Drive carefully and if you need me, just holler."

"I will, I promise." This time, when she hung up the phone, it was done gently.

∾ ⊖ ∾

Somehow, Leah managed to get through the week. She performed admirably in both the classes she taught and the classes she took, pulling herself together one hour at a time. What she noticed most, however, were her dreams, or rather the strangeness of them. Every night, she would fall asleep, determined not to dream of the rain forest, but she would see herself standing at the pool, alone, as if she were waiting for something. She would walk to the water's edge, scan the rocks rising above it, searching for something, some sign that she was not alone. And then the dream would fade into blackness and she would sleep a dreamless, restless sleep.

And in the morning, she would awaken quickly, always surprised to find herself in her little room, still alone. By Thursday, she was almost willing to admit she missed the piercing brown eyes, the sight of the Aclla's well formed body floating in slow motion from his perch on the wall, slicing into the calm waters below. No, she repeatedly told herself, she would not invite him back into her dreams. She knew she could summon him, but she flat refused.

On Friday morning, Leah stuffed the few things she would need into her bag and threw it in the back of the car. She drove to the parking ramp nearest her office and hurried to her only class. Barely able to concentrate, she sat there watching the clock on the wall, counting the minutes until she would pick up the keys from Dr. Muñoz.

ஒ ⊖ ஒ

The cabin was a testament to la señora's love of Native American artifacts. The furnishings were all rustic bent wood, with lots of Menomonie and Ojibewe blankets and rugs scattered in strategic locations. On the walls, in perfect order, were hung the accouterments of cabin life: fishing poles on one side, snow shoes on the other. In the corner, on little shelves of varying height sat several pairs of cross-country ski boots; the skis themselves stood in a rack beside them. She found the thermostat and adjusted the dial before running out to the car to bring in her stuff.

Leah built a fire in the stone hearth and settled down to eat her dinner of vegetable soup and fresh rolls. From the stack of books, she selected the one with the most gold embossing on the cover and plopped it in her lap. With an Indian blanket across her legs, Leah opened the book, armed herself with a spoon, and sighed. This was just too good to be true, she giggled to herself. In minutes, she was lost in an adventure, oblivious to the wind howling outside the cabin, happy to be alone and far away from where anyone could find her.

She fell asleep on the couch, the pungent scent of burning pinewood mingled with the warming soup making her snug and warm beneath the colorful blanket. Leah slept soundly, no dreams worth remembering, nothing to haunt her night. And when she awoke, her book on the floor beside her, she stretched languorously, relishing the lingering aroma that hung delicately in the morning air. She rose and made a pot of coffee, then went to change her rumpled clothing. Digging a pair of long underwear from her bag, she dressed to explore the woods.

After a quick breakfast of croissant and coffee, Leah bundled herself up and went for a long walk along the edge of the frozen lake. The area seemed completely devoid of other humans, but animal life was active around her. Winter birds called to each other and flew from tree to tree. She spotted a couple of deer strolling along the water's edge, searching for a place where the ice was thin and could be broken with a single hoof to reveal a little fresh water. There were other tracks along the virgin snow as well; small footprints that Leah decided belonged to a fox.

In the woods, Leah did not feel the same prevailing safety she used to feel in the jungle; there were no children secreted in trees looking out for the Qewa Ñawi. Still, she sensed no danger here, nothing to frighten her. Her thoughts traveled back to the first time she had ever gone wilderness camping, when she was twelve, back in the Adirondacks of New York. She was a Girl Scout then, and her first night in the woods filled her with both wonderment and fear. Every noise scared her, every rustle of a leaf or the hoot of an owl kept her from closing her eyes. How tired she was when she returned to the safety of her parents' home! How they hid their smiles when she told them all the scary things she had heard! It was her father who told her she would one day overcome those fears and come to love the woods and the noises.

She returned to the cabin only when her stomach began to growl. Unlike her time in the rain forest, she had brought with her kosher frozen foods that she could easily heat up in the oven. She picked out a beef potpie and parked herself on the couch again with her book to wait until the buzzer sounded.

Another walk in the opposite direction followed lunch, and then a hot shower and a change into a cozy flannel gown. One book led to another as she sat before the fire, periodically helping herself to a handful of crackers, a little cheese or a sip of the wine she had bought just for this occasion. Warm and drowsy, unable to keep her eyes open any longer, Leah moved into the master bedroom, where a smaller fireplace just cried out for use. Tucked into the big bed, her wine glass on the night stand, Leah read until she fell asleep, the flames casting flickering shadows on the walls.

Leah was standing at the foot of the waterfall, wearing her vicuña tunic and a pair of leather sandals. Her ceremonial sash was tied around her waist; her hair was plaited into two long braids and held in place with a llautu decorated with tiny beads of the kind Rina liked to make on long, rainy winter nights. Touching her neckline, Leah felt not one, but two bird pins, and suddenly she was cold. She ran to the huaca, but no one was there. Going back to the pool, she scanned the rock wall, seeing nothing up there. The jungle was screamingly silent, the most frightening element of all. She cried out, but no one answered her cry. Her heart was thumping; it seemed to reverberate against the rocks. Panic-stricken, Leah fled the pool, slashing her way thought the jungle with her bare hands until they bled. Paths that were familiar were now darkly strange, with no landmarks to guide her way. She ran for what seemed forever, calling for Saba to rescue her from her terror. When she came to the clearing where her ayllu had stood, it was empty, no sign of the people to be found in the undergrowth. Once again she started running through the forest, looking for something she could not name.

The jungle gave way to the highlands, the highlands to the mountains. Leah seemed to travel five days worth in a matter of minutes, climbing the rocky path, which led to the Janajpachallacta. Panting, she crossed the bridge to where the Rimoc would gather. She could hear their chants as the sky grew dark and the moon appeared on the horizon. As she approached the circle, the Mamacuna halted the singing and stepped into the circle, facing Leah, her arms open, her face glowing. Leah ran to the Mamacuna, but as she reached her, the High Priestess vanished.

Drenched in sweat, Leah snapped awake and struggled to control her breathing. Fighting back the terror, she tried to recall every detail of the dream, as if it were a warning that she must heed. Nowhere in the dream did the aclla appear, although she could feel his constant presence. Saba had been standing with the Rimoc, but it was Mamacuna who had opened her arms to her. Looking about the room, Leah tried to remember where she was, and it took a more than a few seconds to figure out she was still at the cabin.

A thin trail of grey light fell to the floor through a break in the curtains. Getting up, she wrapped herself in her robe and went hesitatingly into the kitchen, half expecting to find Tan sitting at the table. The room was empty. With shaking fingers, Leah managed to start a pot of coffee. When it was finally ready, she poured herself a cup and pulled a chair over to the picture window overlooking the water. Eventually, her heartbeat slowed, and she pulled herself together. If something catastrophic had happened in Peru, there was nothing she could do about it from here. She would have to wait until she returned to the cities.

The drive back to campus was slowed by a light, but hazardous snowfall. Crawling along the freeway, Leah kept the radio tuned to an all news station, anxiously awaiting word of the disaster she was certain had occurred in Peru. There was nothing on the radio, but she remained convinced something had happened. She arrived at the dorm in time for dinner, but she went straight to her room. After a quick call to Jay, assuring him she was safely returned and promising him they would meet for dinner during the week, Leah tried Hector's phone number and prayed she could get through.

❧ ⊖ ❧

She could not get a line through to the region. Between attempts, she paced the room for fifteen minutes before she would begin pressing the long string of numbers. Finally, after three hours of pacing and pressing, a phone was ringing on the other end.

At first there was no response from the mountain clinic. Leah nearly broke down in tears, fearing that whatever happened had taken Hector with it. Then, just as she was ready to hang up, a familiar voice said, "¡Hola!"

"Hector!" she almost shouted, "it's Leah!"

"Is it really you, niña?"

"Yes, it's me, Hector. Tell me, are you all right?"

"What could be wrong? The weather is beautiful, everyone is healthy, there isn't a broken bone for miles, and I am on the verge of terminal boredom. What could possibly be wrong?"

In an effort not to sound foolish, Leah began to explain her dream. "I'm not one for visions, Hector, but this one was terrifying. Have you been to Janajpachallacta lately?" The line crackled a little, then there was the tiniest buzzing sound, but Leah had the creeping sensation that was not the reason for the long pause. "Hector? Are you there?"

"I am here," he said in very formal Spanish, "I was there two days ago, and everything was in order."

In order. The words struck Leah as odd. "Hector, I've been having strange dreams. Scary dreams. Is the Mamacuna still alive?"

"Yes."

"Is it possible she is sending me messages?"

There was another silence, then came an answer Leah could just not believe. "Leah, don't be absurd. You know better than to believe in ghosts and goblins. You are being foolish, niña. Use your head."

Leah was dumbfounded. "I see," she choked before she fell silent. Then the light went on; he was using *usted* in place of the familiar *tú.* Someone was listening. "Hector, you're absolutely right. I am being foolish. It must be all the work I'm doing on their religion. Forgive me, my friend. I'm glad to hear everything is all right."

"All is well with you?" he asked.

He used *usted* again. "As well as can be expected. I'm working very hard."

Hector's laugh sounded genuine when he said, "You are supposed to work hard, Leah."

Leah wanted to ask him about Tan, but she refrained. The creepy feeling she was getting from the conversation warned her off. "I'll write soon, Hector. I promise."

"I shall look forward to your letter. Take care of yourself, Leah. It was good to hear your voice." The line went dead.

Leah stared at the telephone in her hand. She was certain someone was either listening in on the conversation or sitting in the living room with Hector. In either case, it left her shaking.

In his clinic, Hector turned back to the man waiting impatiently at his table.

"How fortuitous that she called while I was here," Hector's guest said with a cold smile.

"As I told you before, she did no geo-political work while she was here. She simply recorded cultural and religious life. As for the call.... she was inquiring only after my health and the well being of the people."

"And the ghosts and goblins?"

Hector waved his hand in the air. "Dreams; no more, no less. Haven't you ever had a bad dream, Señor Lubrano?"

SPRING IN THE STATES
AUTUMN IN PERU
1989

CHAPTER 17

Riding high on a victory wave, Tan's volleyball team prepared for the first round of intramural play-offs. Luís had all but rearranged the hospital's schedule in order to work in extra practices for the guys, and, as their captain, he worked them harder than ever. Tan thoroughly enjoyed both the practices and the games and stopped at the gym whenever he had a free hour if to do nothing but bounce serves off a wall. Although a newcomer to the sport, he was counted as the strong man for the Aliens, their tongue-in-cheek team name, and a force to be reckoned with on the court.

They rolled over their first two opponents with ease, battering the Frontiersmen and Psychobabble into the ground. From the side, they watched the Medics trounce the Middleclassics despite the dorm team's powerful international contingent. With finals exams a week away, scheduled matches ran long into the night in an effort to have the tournament over in time for hard core booking.

"Watch out for the tall redhead in the middle row," said Luís, pointing to a thin guy in a black t-shirt, his back to the net. "He's got height and a lot of power at the net."

Tan followed Luís's finger and swore under his breath. They had played the Medics earlier in the season, but he had not known the identity of the red haired man before last week. Now, it was a different story. Leaning against the wall, Tan studied the way he played, looking for the mistakes, the vulnerable spot which would bring him down. "You know him?" he asked Luís.

"Sure, he's in some of my clinics. Smart guy." Tan grunted. He did not bother to tell Luís why he asked.

There was a short break to give the Medics time enough to catch their breath and get ready for the next round. The Aliens took the court for a quick warm-up, Tan in the server's position.

The referee's shrill whistle sounded and the Medics returned with Jay in the back row, ball in hand, ready to play. He spotted Tan and smiled coldly, as if to tell him there was more at stake here than just a trophy.

They volleyed for the serve; the Aliens took it easily from the Medics. Luís took the ball, then tossed it to Tan. "Whenever you're ready!"

He lined up his first serve and aimed carefully for the guy positioned middle right. He was the weakest player on the team, the one most likely to short-shoot. With a resounding slap, the game began.

The Aliens took the first three points quickly. Then, after one of their men dropped the white ball, the service changed. Back and forth, the ball sailed across the net, deftly handled and returned with increasing force. When Tan rotated into the front row, he found himself staring at Jay through the net, and it was his turn to smile. It was at that moment Jay Weiss noticed the gold chain resting against Tan's bare chest, a chain from which two gold stars dangled, plastered against sweat dampened skin. He recognized the smaller of the two stars and for a moment, his eyes widened, only to be filled with white-hot anger at seeing it there.

Slam! Jay spiked the ball at Tan, only to have it returned in kind. Slam! The ball, aimed at Tan's head, was narrowly deflected by a rapid movement by Luís from behind, who passed it to Tan, who then sent it flying over the net. The ball passed to Jay, who deftly aimed it at Tan with tremendous force.

The game was drawing a crowd. It was evident to those on the sidelines there was a grudge match going on and it wasn't necessarily between the two teams. No matter where they stood in the rotation, the same two men seemed to have it in for each other. Sweat poured off their bodies until the floor beneath their feet was slippery wet. The ref, at one point, called a halt to play so that the floor could be wiped, but when play resumed, the grudge match continued.

Tan lost track of the score; the only thing that interested him now was pounding the ball into Jay's head. His muscles strained until the cords stood out on his arms; the heat of competition coupled with raw, seething anger colored his every move. Twice, Luís ordered him to settle down and play the game, but Tan was oblivious to his warnings. It wasn't until Tan stood again in the server's position and the ref called game point, that he stopped, less to catch his breath than to aim a last, devastating shot directly into Jay.

Holding the ball at arm's length, Tan prepared his serve. Jay was ready for him, crouching in the back row, ready for anything the Peruvian could dish out. With a resounding slam, the ball shot over the net at tremendous speed and despite his jump, Jay took it right in the face. He hit the floor, blood spurting from his nose. He wiped it away with the back of his hand, then sprung up, charged the net and belly-dived beneath it. Scrambling to his feet, he came at Tan with a shout.

Tan caught Jay's body with his arm. Twisting, he tried to bring him down, but Jay was too wiry to maneuver. They crashed onto the hard wooden floor together, Jay atop Tan until he twisted out of his grasp. They struggled up, slipping on wet wood as they moved apart, then charged each other. Tan grabbed Jay by the waist, another attempt to pin him, but he did not see Jay's fist until it was too late. The medical student caught him to the right of his nose, just beneath the eye. Tan saw stars, but it did not stop him. Blood spurted out, covering them both with sticky red fluid. Tan managed to hold on, pulling Jay to the side until he slid one leg behind his adversary's and finally brought him down.

They battled on the floor until countless pairs of hands pulled them apart. Tan fought his captors, shouting Quechua epithets at Jay; Jay hurled similar barbs in English.

"You're both disqualified from play!" yelled the ref, looking with disgust at his own blood stained shirt. "And you're both outta here until next quarter. If I see either of you in this building, I'll permanently bar you!"

Luís kept his arms around Tan until he felt muscles slacken. "What the hell are you doing?" he shouted into his ear. "Are you crazy?"

"Ask him, he started it," Tan snarled.

"And you finished it. Ai, mama! Look at you! You are a bloody mess!" He released his hold, shoving Tan aside. He walked over to Jay. "I don't know what this is about, Weiss, but this is foolishness!" Turning around, he headed for the locker room.

In the locker room, someone brought Tan an ice pack that he gratefully applied to his aching face. Luís examined the damaged area, muttering but refusing to speak to Tan directly. One of the Medics, a resident in trauma, stopped by to give him the once over and declared the nose unbroken, but that one hell of a shiner should be visible by morning. Tan managed to thank him and then asked about Jay.

"Oh, about the same. You guys must really hate each other," he said dryly, taking a last poke at the swelling just beginning to throb. "You might want to see someone if that eye swells shut. Just stop over at student health in the morning."

In silence, Luís drove Tan home. As he struggled to get painlessly out of the car, Luís finally said something. "It's the woman, isn't it?"

"Yes."

"Let it go, Tan. No matter how much she loves the people, women like her will not give up life in America to live in an ayllu."

Tan fell heavily against the seat. "I am a divided man, my friend. A part of me wants to go home, the other part never wants to see the mountains again. My heart is torn."

"All of us are torn," sighed Luís, "we know we are needed at home, yet the lure of Ruti-Suyu is powerful. You have the advantage, Tan, you have strong ties to Mamaquilla and She will help you to decide what is right. The rest of us.... we must rely only on our heads. She does not speak to those who have not served Her well." There was a twinge of remorse in his last words.

Getting out of the car, Tan wished he could say something of comfort to his friend, but there was nothing to be said. His words, from the deepest part of his heart, were truth, and Tan knew it as well as Luís. He could only pray to Mamaquilla in hopes She would answer him as She did in the forest.

Tan had not taken two steps inside the house when he heard Ingrid's gasp. "My God!" she cried, "what happened to you?" Without waiting for a reply, she called to her husband. "Arne, go get washcloths from the linen closet and bring them down to me. Tan's been hurt!" She hurried him into the kitchen and pulled a stool over to the sink. "Sit here," she ordered.

He did not have the strength to argue. Instead, he obediently perched himself on the stool and watched through swollen eyes as she took a raw steak from the refrigerator. His eyes widened as much as they could when she gently pressed the cold meat against his cheek. He yelped, just a little, then grimaced as she applied even pressure.

"Shhhh! This is will help take down the swelling, dear. Just close your eyes and try to relax."

Dr. Halstaad walked in, his gasp almost as loud as his wife's. "Who did this to you?" he demanded, his voice about as angry as Tan had ever heard it.

"You should see the other guy." said Tan, managing a weak smile.

"A fight? You've been in a fight?" Dr. Halstaad was amazed. "You, of all people, from a people who do not fight! What the hell happened?"

Moving his mouth as little as possible, Tan explained as best he could without mentioning Leah.

Arne Halstaad was not fooled. "It's the girl, isn't it? The one we met at the reception." His anger gave way to booming laughter. "Do you tell Hector...or do I?" Tan only groaned.

Ingrid peeled back the meat for another look at the battered face. "If you were my son, Tan Villac-Quilla, you'd be grounded for the rest of your natural life!"

ео ⊖ ое

Jay met with similar response from Leah when he stopped by her office the next afternoon. "Good God, Jay!" she cried, her green eyes opening wide, "were you mugged?" It was a typical New York assumption.

Sheepishly, he told her about the game and the ensuing fistfight. "He's okay, or so I've been told. But he's not as pretty as he used to be." There was certain smugness in his voice that irked Leah.

"What kind of crack is that?" she nearly shouted. "You mean you're glad you beat him up?"

"No, not exactly."

Leah flopped back in her chair, her head in her hands. When she finally spoke, it was with deliberate patience in an attempt to mask the anger welling up inside. "If this was the Middle Ages, I might actually be flattered, but this is not the twelfth century. Both of you are acting like children."

"I'm sorry, Lee, really."

"Sorry my foot, Jay." Leah picked up the book on her desk and, turning her back to him, resumed reading.

When he was gone, Leah resisted the urge to find the Halstaad's number in the phone book. A part of her wanted to rip that damn aclla up one side and down the other, but the other side wanted to make sure he was not hurt too badly. Digging into her pocket, she pulled out her little golden conopa and squeezed it until her hand hurt. Shutting her eyes tightly, she tried to send him a message.

CHAPTER 18

Tan's head snapped up. For the first time he heard Leah's voice, clear as if she were standing in the room beside him. *This is not the way.* Then the voice was gone. A painful smile stretched his face, making him wince. With a new sense of tranquility, Tan resumed his reading.

The last day of exams coincided with the equinox. Acutely aware that in Ruti-Suyu it was the vernal equinox while at home it was the autumnal, he could sense the gathering at Janajpachallacta. He had an undeniable need to be in a high place, somewhere away from the lights of the city where he could make his offering to Mamaquilla.

It was Ingrid who, after listening carefully to his explanation of the festival, suggested that perhaps Luís would like to go with him to celebrate the holy day. "There aren't any real mountains here," she said, "but there are a couple of places I can think of which would give you an unobstructed view of the night sky."

Though they hadn't really spoken since the night of the fight, Luís jumped at the chance to go with Tan. He even refused Tan's offer to pay for the gas it would take to get them to Taylor's Falls and back.

While he completely abstained from food and drink on the day of the ceremony, Tan gathered the things he would need to make an offering. Out into the Halstaad's garden, he searched for a sprig or a branch with buds already swollen in preparation for the arrival of spring. From the kitchen window, Ingrid watched him trudge through stubborn snowdrifts, determined to find the most perfect specimen.

Luís picked him up right after rounds. "I feel like an altar boy chosen to carry the Host," he told Tan, grinning ear from ear. Tan gave him a puzzled look and Luís laughed. "Sorry, my Catholic upbringing again. Never mind, let's get on the road."

Following the directions Dr. Halstaad had written out, they headed north. It was dark when they reached the section of the Saint Croix River that he had described, but they easily found the turnoff to a place where they could park the car.

Tan tied his old carry pouch around the outside of his coat while Luís got the flashlights they would need to find their way. With Tan in the lead, they followed a narrow path through winter bare woods until they came to the edge of the rock cliff overlooking the river. Building a huaca would not be easy, but they managed to stumble across a boulder poking its craggy face through the white blanket.

"This will do," announced Tan. Kicking at the snow with his boot, he cleared a space around the boulder and was rewarded for his efforts when he located several other large stones, big enough to use but small enough to pick up. Together, they placed the smaller ones in a circle atop the boulder. Tan removed a carefully folded leaf from his pouch and emptied the contents into the center of the small circle. Along side it, he set three sprigs from Mrs. Halstaad's forsythia bush.

Whispering quick thanks for the mild weather, Tan stripped off his coat, then his shirt. Bare-chested, he stood before the little huaca, his eyes closed, his mind's eye focused on how it would be at home in the circle of Rimoc. In a low voice, he began the first chant, a hymn of praise to the Goddess who gave fertility to Her beloved people.

The words, slow and sonorous, hung in the air, making Luís shiver with the intensity of the moment. As a child, he had never been permitted to attend the festival when it was celebrated by the old ones, yet he had heard them chanting the same verse Tan now sang. The chant ended, the words drifted away until the silence of the woods filled their ears.

Overhead, the thin sliver of a waxing moon shed pale light in a cloudless sky dotted with an infinite number of stars. Slowly, Tan raised his arms, then opened them to the sides to embrace the moon. With his face turned toward Mamaquilla, he closed his eyes and recited the sacred formula asking the Goddess for the renewal of Her blessings. A gentle breeze ruffled his hair, but instead of being chilled, Tan was warmed by Mamaquilla's soft caress. The breeze subsided and he opened his eyes once more.

Tan removed the striking stones from his pouch and hit them sharply together. A spark flew out to ignite the sacred *uchapa*. A single column of smoke, a perfect *jonchi*, rose from the center of the stone and floated straight upward until a slight movement in the air bent it southward. Relieved, Tan smiled; it was the one sign he had dared to hope for. The top of the jonchi spread outward before it dissipated into the night air. Tan bowed deeply to the south, remaining low for a moment. *You are safe, you are still in our hearts*, spoke a voice from within his own heart. He righted himself and opened his arms again to Mamaquilla, while closing his eyes to receive the vision he knew would come. The green eyes fringed with long, dark lashes loomed before him. The voice spoke again. *Your hearts are bound as one; you will seek each other in another forest. Be patient, my beloved churi and you will know what She has put in your heart.* Tan recognized the voice and he was at peace. The words of the closing hymn came forth, unbidden, from his own mouth; he let the sweet melody carry his soul to Janajpachallacta where, he was certain, Mamacuna was sitting on her stone chair, smiling to herself.

Tan was shivering when Luís dropped his coat over his shoulders. Never before had he been so moved by the power of absolute belief in God. The glow that had bathed his friend's face in the moonlight had been holy, if such a simple word could describe what he had witnessed. If he had ever harbored any doubt about what Tan said he was, it was gone now, fled in the face of sacred experience. Luís wondered why his own people had abandoned the old ways, which, after observing Tan in prayer, seemed so much more pleasing to God...or Goddess, depending on one's point of view. But there was something else he had seen in Tan's face at the moment the jonchi disappeared; he could only describe it as yearning, a profound loneliness from deep within Tan's soul. Perhaps it was the ancient link they shared which made the sharp sensation slice through Luís's own breast.

Through the night they stayed at the little huaca; Tan, in hushed tones, told the stories of Mamaquilla, Illi-Intip and Viracocha he had been told as a child. Together they watched as the moon set in the west, until the crescent disappeared beyond the horizon. Only when the steel edge of dawn became visible in the east did they go back to the car to begin the drive homeward.

Tan slept through most of the next day, awaking mid afternoon to find a tray with a note and a glass of orange juice left beside his bed. The note read: "To break your fast. You'll need a little sugar to make it down the stairs in time for dinner." He could imagine Mrs. Halstaad's smile when she must have tiptoed in to find him sprawled on the bed wearing nothing but his trousers. Admittedly, his head ached from lack of food; he sipped the juice slowly so that the cold liquid did nothing to add to the pounding in his brain.

For the week of spring break, Tan did little more than eat, sleep and read interesting books culled from the Halstaad's library. A much-subdued India came home and transformed herself into a far more pleasant companion than she had been before. She spent quiet evenings teaching him to play chess and backgammon. When she asked him about his life at home, Tan told her bits and pieces and surprised himself when he told her that he had gotten his name, Villac-Quilla, because he spent the last years in service to Mamaquilla, although he did not tell her the specifics. In turn, India began to tell him about her life and started taking him to all the places she thought he should know as a resident of the Twin Cities. Much to his surprise, Tan found he enjoyed her company. And much to her surprise, she found herself liking his friendship.

On one foray, this one to the James J. Hill Library in Saint Paul, India discovered Tan had come to America with only a winter wardrobe. They were strolling across Rice Park when Tan asked her about the short, light jacket she was wearing. He wanted one like that. "My parka is too heavy," he complained uncharacteristically, "in truth, *all* my clothes are too heavy now that the weather is warmer."

India grinned from ear to ear. "I have just the solution, sweetie," she laughed. "Forget the library; we can do that later. Let's go to Dayton's!"

Although Tan knew the name of the department store, he had never been in one. "Is it far?" he asked.

"Nope, just down the block." She linked her arm through his. "Got your AmEx with you?"

"Never leave home without it!" he grinned.

India's taste in men's wear was almost as conservative as Hector's, but with a keener eye toward fashion. Patiently, she picked out clothes for him, instructing him on what could be worn when, and how the colors changed with the seasons. "You'll be wonderful in whites," she told him with sisterly affection, "but not until after Memorial Day."

"Is this a rule or a tradition?"

"Both. No, neither; it's social convention," she giggled.

"Your will is my wardrobe," he teased as he followed her through the maze of departments with his eyes still wide at the available selection, not to mention what he thought were steep prices.

Laden down with packages, they were laughing at the outrageous outfit on a mannequin when Tan spied Leah standing across the aisle. All traces of humor drained from his face as he met her gaze with his. India turned, wondering why Tan had stopped laughing, and she, too, saw Leah. This time, she made no move to slip her arm through his; rather, she took a small step backward. The gesture was not lost on Leah who suddenly averted her eyes and dipped her head downward disappearing around a rack of colorful shirts.

The lighthearted afternoon was shattered. Feeling very sad for him, India whispered, "Let's go home."

Only when they were in the car did India bring up the subject of Leah. "If you are in love with her, Tan, why don't you go after her?" The question was gently asked and required an equally gentle answer.

Tan sighed and his voice was soft. "If it was that simple, India." There was no easy way to explain to her the complexities of the situation. He had unexpectedly discovered a good friend in India, but he was not ready to confide something so intimate to her.

She, however, would not be put off. "It's none of my business, I'm sure, but judging from the look in her eyes, she is more...ummmm... afraid of you than anything else. Don't ask me how I know, just chalk it up to a woman's intuition."

He was unfamiliar with the term. "And what is a woman's *intuition?*"

India's small laugh was disarming. "Oh, I don't know quite how to explain that," she admitted, "but it's sorta like a hunch, a specific kind of feeling that women are known to have when they get a particular insight into something they would normally have no reason to know." She paused, unsure as to whether or not she had made herself clear. "It's not empirical," she added brightly, "it's speculative!" Tan's sudden grin was enough reward for India; she had made him understand by using the kind of language he liked best: scientific. Furrowing her brows thoughtfully, India decided to take the opportunity to ask a more personal question, but she asked his permission first.

"You may ask anything you'd like, India," he told her honestly, "and if I am able, I will give you an answer."

"I noticed it again today, when we saw her, two things, actually. One is why, and I saw her do this to you before, does she look away and nods before she walks away from you? She just doesn't strike me as the shy, retiring type."

"And two?"

India sucked in her breath and raced through the question. "Is there some reason you wear matching birds? Is that like a Peruvian thing?" Her woman's intuition told her it wasn't.

Tan allowed himself another small smile in India's direction. He considered his answers carefully, at the same time thinking how much younger she seemed now that she had stopped trying to seduce him at every turn. A month ago, he would have growled at two such personal questions, believing her to want the information to use against him. Now, he had no qualms about answering her. "The first is difficult to explain, so I will begin with the second," he told her, catching her look of utter amazement from the corner of his eye. "The bird is not, as you called it, a Peruvian thing. Both pins are hers; she left one as an offering to Mamaquilla at a shrine near to where I lived."

"And you took it?" she interrupted with some horror in her voice.

Tan chuckled at her indignation. "You already know a little about who I was in the forest, India. Any offering left at that shrine was left for me."

"And she left it for you?"

"She did not yet understand that was how it would be interpreted. I kept the bird for it was the first sign I received that my *unachai*, my destiny I think you would call it, was not to be in the forest."

India whistled softly at the implication. "And the dipping of her head?" she asked.

"Leah," he said, carefully pronouncing her name correctly aloud for the first time, "was a participant in the ceremony held at the winter solstice. The way she turns her eyes away, and the bow of her head are proper signs of modesty amongst young women of my people. In that way, she respects who I am or rather, I suppose, what I was."

"But you are no longer serving Mamaquilla; you said so yourself."

"That is correct, but were I to return to my people now, the young women, at least until I was bound to one woman, would not speak to me as they would any other man." The thought of it made him wince; it was a part of being aclla he never liked.

India's next question took him completely by surprise. "How old are you?"

Tan had to think about it for a moment. He knew Americans put great importance on age, but he had given it little consideration. "I entered my twenty-seventh cycle of the sun on the day of your vernal equinox, our autumnal one," he said. He knew he was born on that day because it was viewed as a powerful omen, a sign that his mita would be to the Goddess Herself. "That makes me twenty-six just last week," he added with a laugh.

"We missed your birthday! How terrible!"

"I've never had a birthday so it is not something I would miss."

With a secret smile, India decided *that* would be remedied as soon as she got home.

෨ ⊖ ෨

A quick word in her mother's ear was all it took to get the ball rolling. Mrs. Halstaad checked the pantry for a cake mix and found a box of devil's food on the shelf. She had already planned on making spinach lasagna, Tan's favorite, so there was no need to alter the menu for such a special occasion. "Keep him out of the kitchen," she warned India when the layers were cooling on the rack. "I don't want him to see the cake once it is decorated."

It was easy to keep him away. Tan was stretched out on the couch in the library, **A Tale of Two Cities** face down on his chest, sound asleep. Closing the door, India reported this to her mother and then dashed out of the house. It wouldn't take more than a few minutes to run into Dinkytown and still be back in time to challenge him to a pre-dinner game of chess.

For her parents' gift, India found two exquisite photographic journals on Minnesota. But for her own gift to Tan, she bought a leather bound set of the complete works of F. Scott Fitzgerald and quickly inscribed each one. While the clerk gift-wrapped the books, she ran next door for a dozen helium balloons.

He was still snoring softly when India cracked the door to check on him. Closing it again, she went out to the car and returned with her purchases. Her mother hid the beribboned packages while India tied several balloons to Tan's chair in the dining room, and then attached the rest around the rim of a basket her mother filled to overflowing with jelly beans from her secret candy stash. Moving quickly, India set the table with the good china, silver and crystal, and was pleased by the festive appearance.

Her work finished, India went back to the study. Standing over him, she noticed again how truly handsome he was: his thick black lashes resting against the dark, burnished bronze of his skin, the strong, straight line of his nose, the faint discoloration remaining on his right cheek just below his eye, from the fist fight at the volleyball game. Even his hands exuded strength, with long fingers ending in carefully trimmed nails. His hair, usually brushed back, fell to one side of his forehead, giving him a boyish innocence. There was something so erotic about him, so arousing to India that she almost ran out of the room. Warmth flooded her face as she remembered what it was like to kiss his full, sculpted lips. For a brief moment, she hated Leah Fine for not knowing what kind of man she was spurning when she, India, would give anything to be the one in his arms. With a feather light touch, India reached down and brushed the errant lock of hair from Tan's face.

When his hand shot out and nabbed hers, she jumped back. "Ouch!" she cried, pulling her hand away.

Tan yawned. "Sorry, India, you startled me." He grinned sleepily at her, at the same time noticing the high color of her cheeks. "Is dinner ready?"

"No, but I'm up for a game of chess. What about it?"

꙳ ⊖ ꙳

They played until Dr. Halstaad came in the front door. Tan went to wash up, India hot on his trail going up the stairs. When Tan said he was going down to offer to set the table, India grabbed his hand, claiming she needed help to move her dresser because she had dropped a book down the back. The ploy worked; no sooner had she fished out the errant book than Ingrid called them to the table. Ever the gentleman, Tan allowed India to precede him down the stairs, and she took advantage of it in order to be in the dining room when he entered.

"Surprise!" the Halstaads shouted in unison, loving the look of absolute puzzlement on Tan's face when he saw the balloons.

Ingrid enlightened him, but not before giving him a peck on the cheek. "Happy birthday, Tan," she laughed. "India tells us you've never had a birthday party so we thought better late than never."

Speechless, Tan was touched by the gesture. At India's prompting, he took his place at the table and the celebrations commenced. After the main course, instead of just coffee, Ingrid brought out the chocolate frosted devil's food cake, decorated with "Happy Birthday Tan," and the appropriate number of candles proclaiming Tan's twenty-sixth birthday. "Speech, speech," they demanded when he had blown out the candles in a single breath.

The words came hard for a lump had formed in his throat. "I cannot tell you how welcome you have made me feel," he said, choosing his words with care. "I came to your home a stranger, and you have made me a part of your family. I have never before had a home such as this," he laughed at the small joke, "with brick walls. I have never been treated in such a warm, open manner, not even in my own ayllu." The long years alone in the jungle had kept him from having a family to call his own. Instead of finding the constant presence of people oppressive, Tan had found it quite the opposite; it was freeing to have someone around whenever he wished company, privacy when he needed to be apart. "Thank you for making a birthday party, my first, and I hope I can, in return, bring you only happiness and pride."

"Bravo, Tan!" applauded Dr. Halstaad. "A fine speech for a first birthday! Now, bring on the presents!"

Later, alone in his room, Tan closely examined the books, carefully turning the pages as not to leave finger prints on the beautiful pictures of Minnesota's changing seasons. But it was the set of Fitzgerald he knew he would cherish most. Somehow India had managed to pull all this off while he slept, including an inscription in each volume with a word about its contents. Tan had never paid any attention to his own sister, Rahua, a sweet little girl born shortly before he was called to serve Mamaquilla; India was becoming the little sister he never knew.

∾ ⊖ ∾

Anxious to begin the next academic quarter, Tan bought his books as soon as he could, so he could scan them all. Pre-calculus was by far the most fascinating, if the book was any way to judge. He wanted, more than anything else, to unlock the secret of numbers. Rather than register for another philosophy class, he opted for physics, another gateway into the world he found so fascinating. He was advised to take Advanced Composition for his English requirement and because he wanted to know more about the world he left behind, he signed up for a survey course in Latin American history.

On Monday, Tan was up early. He fairly ran to campus; he wanted to stop at the bookstore to pick up a couple of extra notebooks. Jogging along at a comfortable pace, yet deep in thought, he carelessly brushed past a woman coming up the stairs from Williamson Hall, knocking her into the wall. Realizing what he had done, he turned to call "Sorry" over his shoulder, and missed the next stair. He lurched for the handrail, then tumbled, only to land in a heap at bottom of the staircase.

Leah stood at the top of the stairs, halfway between shouting and laughing at the crumpled figure on the cement. "*Imaynallam kashianki?*" she choked, trying not to laugh.

He felt like a fool, more so for the redness he knew was staining his cheeks. "*Allin*...I'm fine," he answered, switching into English.

Slowly, she walked down the steps and squatted, so her eyes were level with his. Her hand touched his right cheek as she clucked disapprovingly, "Nice bruise; old but impressive." The fingers traveled over the area, sending chills up and down his spine. She had noticed the shiner the day she saw him at Dayton's, but now it was almost gone. "A foolish wound for a foolish man. I hope you learned your lesson, Aclla." The last words were barely a whisper. She left him on the ground as she trotted back up the stairway.

Tan watched her small behind, neatly outlined in a pair of tight jeans, move provocatively up the stairs. The sight of it caused his blood to pound violently in his veins; it took every ounce of control not to run after her, to grab her and hold her close. A wave of students coming down the stairs made him scramble to his feet. Reluctantly, he went into the building.

Leah laughed all the way to her office. It wasn't the act of his falling down the last two steps which she found so humorous, it was the incredulous look on his face, the one which said *I can't believe I fell over my own feet*, that tickled her innards. For the first time, she wasn't frightened at the sight of him; that he was lying in a heap at the bottom of the stairs made her think of him as human, rather than the ghost of her dreams. *Perhaps this was Mamaquilla's doing*, she thought as she neared her building; *maybe this is how I'm supposed to see him*. With a shrug, Leah went about her daily business.

CHAPTER 19

From the moment she moved back into her old apartment, Leah felt considerably better; she credited the improvement on having her own things around, not to mention being able to cook for herself again. It felt good to be sitting in her own overstuffed chair, her feet on her own overstuffed ottoman, eating her own kind of food. Her furniture had survived storage intact and with Jay's help, everything was back in its proper place.

Leah spent most spring break with her head in her books, getting ready for her preliminary oral examination. The one outing she allowed herself ended abruptly when she saw Tan with the Halstaad girl, heads together, laughing. Leah hadn't expected the knife sharp stab she experienced when she saw them there. Jealousy, anger, frustration; none of the words adequately described what she felt as she fled down the escalator. Just a few nights before, on her last night in the dorm, she'd had strong visions in her dreams, visions of Tan at the huaca, his arms open to her, calling her name, drawing her into his world with his dark, dark eyes. She could hear the voices of the Rimoc chanting hymns to Mamaquilla, the Aclla's voice raised in song with theirs. When she awoke, she realized that it was the twenty-first of March, the night of the equinox.

So on the first day of classes, it seemed to Leah to be *unachai* that she had literally run into Tan. Nor could she have resisted touching the bruised cheek, letting her fingers feel the hard planes of his face *on her terms*, as tenuous as they were. Instinctively, she knew the very touch of her hand heated his blood; she could see that in his eyes. And the feel of his skin against hers rendered in her a similar response, a warmth that stayed with her long after she walked away.

Up in the office, Leah reviewed her list of appointments for the week, trying to decide what was necessary preparation for each. Dr. Muñoz was expecting a member of the Peruvian consulate from Washington, D. C. and wanted her at the meeting, but before that, he wanted to see the latest proposal draft. Swamped, but not quite buried, Leah set to work.

In the middle of the mess, Mary poked her head in the door. "Mail call, Ms. Fine," she called.

Leah slid back in the wheeled desk chair. "So, where is it?"

"You were expecting special delivery?" countered Mary with a grin. She produced an envelope from behind her back. "I suppose you don't want to read this right now."

"Give it to me, Cavanaugh...or die!"

Mary handed her the large, creamy envelope.

A smile danced across Leah's face when she saw the return address. Carefully opening it, she slid out a large ivory card and read it aloud. "You are cordially invited to the Twenty-Second Annual Hispanic Conference to be held May 17th though 19th at Black Heron Lodge, Black Heron Lake, Minnesota." A smaller card slipped from the envelope. Leah's eyes opened wide when she scanned it. "Oh my God!" she cried. "Listen to this: 'Ms. Leah Fine is graciously invited to attend the Conference as lecturer in Mythology and Religion of the Andes.' I can't believe it!"

"Believe it, Lee. Dr. Ruíz called Muñoz that weekend you were at the cabin and he had me check your calendar. The old boy has already accepted on your behalf, so unless you have something really major, like your own funeral, you are going to Black Heron Lake."

❧ ⊖ ❧

Leah's preparation for the conference began as soon as Mary walked out the door. When she spied Sarah Perkal in the hallway, Leah grabbed the unsuspecting student and dragged her into the office. "Here's your big chance to prove how much you're really worth, Perkal," said Leah, thrusting a stack of books into her outstretched hands. "My thesis is on the top. Go through the footnotes and the bibliography and get the page number references for Bellamy, Baumann, Bushnell and Molina. Then, go to the library and pull these books." She handed the girl a sheaf of paper. "Don't worry, it isn't all that much and there's tons of repetition of reference. Shouldn't take you more than two hours, tops."

"Yes, ma'am!" Sarah replied crisply, a twinkle in her eye.

"Any questions, soldier?"

"Only one. Why?"

"Because I am doing the Latino conference, that's why! Can you handle it?"

"You bet!" Struggling to adjust the load, Sarah stumbled toward the door, then stopped. "Did you ever do anything about that guy in the back of Intro?"

"Was I supposed to?" asked Leah.

"I don't know; you're the one who asked about him." Sarah leaned against the doorframe trying to balance herself and the books. "I haven't seen him much since the start of the quarter. Oh well, it was just a thought." With a bright "Catch you later," Sarah was gone.

Leah's forehead hit the desk with a clunk and an "aaaaaaaarrgh!"

∞ ⊖ ∞

The weather turned unexpectedly warm on Monday and it was evident from the antsy-ness of her students that spring fever was in the air. Leah raced through her lecture; she wanted to be outside just as much as they did. As soon as her one o'clock class was over, she strolled home.

There was far too much work to be done to justify sitting on the chaise in the little back yard. Instead, she settled for stretching out on the couch with all the windows open and a warm breeze floating through the curtains. She was holding a textbook upright, but instead of reading, she let her eyes wander over the living room, taking a moment to appreciate the simple fact that she was in her own home. Her favorite posters hung side by side on one wall. The first, from the Metropolitan in New York heralding an exhibit of Inca art, was a photograph of a golden conopa, not unlike hers, although the poster was bought long before she ever dreamed of going to Peru. A similar poster from the Minneapolis Art Institute showed a single Fabergé Easter egg. Leah liked the contrast between the two golden objects, both with religious connections, yet strikingly different in appearance. One was a study of simplicity, yet elegantly beautiful, while the other was a marvel of craftsmanship, a delicate but ornate tribute to another kind of belief. In some ways, the juxtaposition of the posters mirrored her own life.

With an exaggerated sigh Leah tried to concentrate on the book. It was hard; the room was growing uncomfortably warm. Unwinding herself from the couch, she stood at the window and watched people strolling along the street. "Sorry," she announced to the empty room, "it's too nice to stay here!" She gathered up the books she would need and stuffed them into her backpack.

The outside was almost as warm as the apartment, but Leah was glad she had taken a sweatshirt. It was hard not to skip down the street, luxuriating in the spring sunshine. As she reached the corner, she heard her name called out.

"Li-ah! Wait!"

She stopped dead in her tracks, then turned to see Tan jogging toward her. He looked like any other guy in sweatpants and a polo shirt. The banded sleeves of the shirt stretched taut over his biceps and the arms of a grey sweatshirt dangled casually over his shoulders. Standing beside him, Leah found it hard to believe this was the same man who dove off the cliff and into the pool at the huaca. Gone was the naked spirit of the jungle, replaced by a flesh and blood regular guy. Unable to resist, Leah asked, "Do I detect India's fine hand in your choice of clothing?" She flashed a pixy's grin. She knew he would blush.

He did, changing his bronze coloring to burnished red. "No....I mean yes, she has helped me find clothing for warm weather. Do you disapprove?" His question was boyishly nervous.

Leah slid her sunglasses down the bridge of her nose to give him the once over. With his collar turned up, she nearly missed the tiny silver bird fastened to one side. The shirt was tucked neatly into the tied waist, outlining the tapered expanse of his chest. But the baggy pants did not mask his powerful legs. The final touch, however, was the screaming white sneakers. "You look good," she admitted.

A smile grew across his lips, extending, were it possible, from ear to ear. "I'm glad you approve." There was a momentary pause before he spoke again. "Where are you going on such a beautiful day, Leah?"

His pronunciation of her name surprised her; she was unaccustomed to hearing it pronounced as a single word with a Quechua accent. "Wilson Library. You?"

"The same." Shyly, he asked if he might walk with her and relaxed visibly when she said yes.

They strolled along in companionable silence, each acutely aware of the importance of this unexpected moment. Leah stole a glance at her escort, smiling to herself at the odd twist that landed her beside the aclla, walking along in plain sight of anyone who might see them, something that would have been so unthinkable in Peru. She also noticed the less than surreptitious looks he got from women they passed; Leah found those more than just a little amusing. But the overwhelming sensation at the core of her very being was that this felt *right*.

Tan's thoughts were similar; at least as far as Leah was concerned. How marvelous it was to walk beside the Qewa Ñawi in broad daylight! The simplicity of the act had far greater implications for him, for it gave Tan a new sense of normalcy that had been lacking since he left home. He dared not touch her, although he ached to have her fingers entwined in his. Instead, he settled for ambling close beside her, his arm almost touching hers. There were so many things he wanted to say, so many stories he knew would bring a sparkle to her grass green eyes, yet, he held his tongue; to be near her was enough.

As they approached the bridge over the Mississippi, Leah finally broke the shared silence. "How are you enjoying your studies," she asked, still speaking English.

The answer exploded rapidly from his mouth. "Ai! There is so much to learn! There are days I think there are not enough hours to master everything I want to learn."

"I noticed you have stopped coming to my class."

His laughter was soft. "Not by my own choice, Leah," he said, her name a caress on his lips. "It would seem I must be in the library more and more these days."

Leah smiled and touched his arm, launching shivers up his spine. "As well it should be, mulkan," she said, lapsing into Quechua. "*He who chooses the path of knowledge becomes, at least for a time, its slave.* Isn't that what Mamacuna always says to those in training to become collahuaya?"

"That is true!" he answered with a grin. "Another example of how wise she is, even in Ruti-Suyu."

Stopping midway across the river, Leah turned to face him. "Tell me, do you ever get homesick?"

The question caught Tan off guard, but it was the kind of question he expected her to ask. "Yes, late at night, when the moon is at the highest point in the sky I think of the Rimoc. I can almost hear their voices..." his voice trailed wistfully off.

She wanted to tell him she could hear their voices in the wind, but Leah said nothing. Her eyes wandered over the planes of his face, so different with his short haircut. Without the long hair and his llautu, he looked far less wild, if that was the word, than he did then. Also gone was the haunting loneliness she had once seen in his eyes, replaced with the easy comfort that came with the companionship of others.

He did not want the conversation to end. "Mindy tells me you have returned to your old apartment," he said, switching back to English, trying to sound casual.

Leah's eyes widened slightly. "As a matter of fact, I have."

"Was that the house you came from when I saw you?" When she nodded, he said, "it looks like a nice house. You are happy to be there?"

"It's nice to have my own things around me," confessed Leah. She was tempted to invite him over, but resisted the urge. It would serve no purpose to be alone with him in her home, where her good sense might flee in the face of his dark, probing eyes. "Are you still living with the Halstaads?"

"Yes, for now." He flashed a broad smile. "Now that I have my license," he told her proudly, "I will be able to find a place for myself. Once I have my own wheels, I shall be more... mobile."

She laughed despite her utter amazement. Somehow, she could not envision Tan behind the wheel of a car. It seemed more incongruous than his even being in Minnesota.

His brows knit together and Tan frowned. "Do you not think this is a good thing, my having a license?" he asked, puzzled by her reaction.

"Oh, no; it's a wonderful thing! It's just that I never thought of you and cars in the same sentence." She tried to reign in the mirth.

"If one is to survive in this place, one must drive," he said seriously. "It allows me greater freedom."

"Just don't let it divert you from your studies."

This time, Tan laughed, surprising Leah. "Nothing could divert me from my studies! They bring me the greatest joy of all." He paused and studied her face for a moment. "Almost the greatest joy of all," he added soberly.

The old, shaky feeling ran right though Leah's heart. She turned away from him, afraid to meet his gaze and began walking again.

Tan's hand stopped her. "Don't go," he commanded softly and she stopped, her face still averted. He had so much to say to her at that moment, and he realized if he remained silent now, he might never have the opportunity again. "When you sat vigil at the huaca in the wall," he blurted, his words rushing from his mouth, "I was above you. I could hear your songs, songs from the heart. I think it is called *Hallel*."

All blood drained from her face, leaving Leah with eyes wide open in perfect shock. "Yes, it was. How did you know?"

"I heard it again at Mark's. The melodies remained in my heart for they were ones I heard before. I could not forget; they were windows!"

Despite the sunshine, Leah was suddenly cold. "What else do you know about it?" she demanded. "And *why* do you know about it?"

"I learned that your God has a female side, like Mamaquilla. She is called the *Shechinah*." Tan sighed; he had said too much and now he could see fear in her eyes grown stormy. "As you came to Peru to learn about our ways, and came to understand us in a way no other had, I am learning to understand your ways. As Mamaquilla forms the center of my soul, so God does for you. Mamaquilla has bound us together, but the Shechinah shall seal that bond. Is this not truth as you know it? As I know it?"

Leah's teeth chattered and her body shook. "I do not know; I do not have the same connection to God that I think you do."

"Have you no *kavanah*?" he asked, using the Hebrew word that described the moment when one experienced the complete inwardness of prayer that renders it worthy to ascend to Heaven itself. His voice was curious.

She winced at the word. "I strive for *kavanah* when you seem to have it all the time," cried Leah, pulling her arm from his grasp. "You are Aclla; for good or for bad, you are the chosen of Mamaquilla. In any religion, what you have would be considered sacred."

"What I have, Leah, is empty without someone to share it." His voice was soft, without accusation or complaint; Tan was simply stating one more truth for her consideration.

There was a deafening silence between them. Leah looked up into his dark brown eyes then quickly averted them again. "I have to get to the library," she murmured as she started to walk.

Tan let her go, watching the way she kept her head down, certain she was silently weeping. Even without hearing it, the sound broke his heart. He wanted to sweep her into his arms, to wipe away the tears, to reassure her that everything would work out for them in the end. His long legs crossed the short distance to her, and he walked wordlessly a pace behind, allowing her privacy while letting her know he was still with her.

ϧ ⊖ ϧ

In front of the glass library doors, Leah stopped, allowing Tan to come along side. Instead of going inside, Leah went to an empty bench nearby and sat down, waiting for him to join her. "There are things about me you cannot even begin to know," she told him. "This is not the same as my coming to your world. I studied your culture on a broad scale for years. I came to the district knowing about Viracocha and Mamaquilla. I already had knowledge of your language. You cannot expect to master everything western in a matter of weeks!"

"Why? Why not? Is there a law in nature which says it cannot be done?" he demanded, challenging her words. "I eat learning for breakfast, lunch and dinner. I consume everything put before me. It is as though my head is an empty pot waiting to be filled." He raised his head proudly. "Have you never been so thirsty that you drink constantly to fill yourself? I think you have! I think that is how it was for you in my home."

Leah stood her ground. "To some degree. But it was not with the burning intensity you have. My search was methodical and well planned. Structured. And you! You wander into my life, my world, and completely turn it upside down!"

Tan gently laughed, at the same time daring touch her face with his palm. "I did not mean to turn your world upside down, Qewa Ñawi. I think you worry too much."

Her hands went up in mock surrender. "You're right, you're right. I worry too much." Without warning, she jumped to her feet. "In fact, I worry so much, I'm going to worry myself right into that library where nobody cares if I worry too much unless my books are overdue." She blasted through the doors, leaving Tan alone on the bench with a silly grin.

After a respectable wait, Tan went into the library and headed to the second floor. Despite the unseasonably warm weather, the tables were occupied. He was about to give up, when a yawning woman vacated a carrel. Tan quickly tossed his pack on the empty chair, pulled out a notebook and went in search of a particular volume.

Leah saw him disappear into the stacks as she came around the corner. "Nuts," she muttered as she took her seat a scant few feet from where Tan's backpack was hooked on the back of his chair. She glanced around hoping to spy another open table, but realized she was lucky to even have a chair.

When Tan returned, he pretended not to see Leah with her nose buried in a thick, musty-looking book. He envied the way she could read and write at the same time, her eyes never seeming to come away from the book as the page beside her filled with writing. *Practice*, he told himself, *this will come with practice*. But now, there was work to be done and Tan wanted to finish as much as he could before he had to go home for dinner.

That single, little thought stopped him cold. He hadn't given it much consideration before, but there were people in that house who would welcome him when he came *home* for dinner. Not since he was a boy had there been a mother awaiting his return at the end of the day. The feeling warmed him unexpectedly and he imagined what it might have been like to grow up in a household such as the Halstaads'. Surely, it was not so different from his own, if one discounted the house itself. *Would it be like that for my own children if I stay in America*, he wondered, stealing a glance at Leah. Pushing the musings from his mind, Tan opened his book.

More than an hour passed before Leah put her text on the table and stretched her tired neck. She could see Tan hunched over the small desk, obviously deep into his work. It gave her a chance to study him without his eyes meeting hers. When his chair slid back, Leah popped her face back into her own volume. He seemed to ignore her as he headed toward the center of the floor where the Xerox machine stood awaiting the next dime.

Impulsively, Leah left the table and strolled toward the stacks, intentionally passing Tan's carrel. Pausing to shift her load of books, she stole a glance at the notebook. The two visible pages were almost completely covered with small, precisely formed letters, as if the minuteness would increase the amount of knowledge that could be retained in a single sitting. Atop the textbooks on the shelf above the desk, sat another open notebook, this one filled with one equation after another, a mathematical wonderland of precise graphs and diagrams with notes written up one side and down the other. There was no question in her mind that he understood exactly what he was doing. Afraid that he might see her staring at his work, Leah scurried away.

Tan did see her as he rounded the corner. Stopping, he waited until she left before he returned to his seat. He was glad she saw his work; it was proof that he was there for an education and he was, indeed, getting one. With a smug, self-satisfied grin, he went back to work on his Hispanic studies assignment.

CHAPTER 20

Leah sailed through her oral exams with relative ease. The questions posed by the committee were tough, but she was prepared for the worst. For two and a half hours, she expounded on the experience of her fieldwork and explained how she would translate that work into a dissertation. Muñoz was present and every so often, Leah would see him nod slightly, the most approval he could give her under the circumstances. When it was over, she felt her next two years at the University were secured.

There was no time to rest on her laurels, however; the morning after the exam, Muñoz summoned her into his office. He was not alone; another man was sitting there. Muñoz introduced Leah to Vincente Lubrano.

"We understand, Señorita Fine," began Lubrano, "that you have had great success in your dealings with mountain people. We are very interested in reading the results of your field work. Your assessment of possible threats from those less than… environmentally concerned… is also of interest to us." He had come a long way to meet her face to face and now he wondered if the trip had been worth the effort. He was not impressed with the diminutive Leah Fine; she seemed bland in contrast to the stories he heard about the Qewa Ñawi.

"My field report was filed with your government last November, Señor Lubrano," Leah replied, shifting slightly in the chair. There was something about him which made her think of a snake and she was uneasy about providing him with additional information without consulting Hector first. Still, Lubrano was here and there was always the possibility she could manipulate him into providing more information she could relay back to Hector. Leah decided to probe the issue directly. "What, if I may be so curious, do you hope to learn from my work that you don't already know from your own sources?"

"We are most interested in the migratory patterns of the upper Andean peoples." The smile stretched even tighter beneath his mustache.

"But they are stationary, Señor Lubrano. The ayllus of that area are permanent structures."

"That much is obvious, señorita, but you and I both know that they do, on occasion, move their locations. We would like to learn what you have learned about the selection process."

Warning bells went off in her head. Hector had written that not long ago people had again been in the district surveying portions of the plateau, ostensibly for new geographic surveys, but he was disturbed by the surreptitious way they were collecting specimen samples. He was worried that the government was about to allow extensive, invasive land use in the district. "I wish I could help you, Señor Lubrano, but I'm afraid my work was mainly with myth and religion as it influenced cultural development, not agricultural patterns." She laughed lightly, as to dismiss the topic. "I never paid much attention to the selection of *chacras*; I was far more interested in how they were blessed by the collahuaya once chosen."

"Ah, so you did see them choose a new location."

He was trying to trap her and Leah knew it. "No," she replied, "I saw a rotation of fields. One left fallow the year before I came was about to be planted. It was already marked off and had been used before." She did not add that she had been on two scouting expeditions with Mayta and his men to choose new cultivation sites. She was not present when the actual selection had been made, therefore she was not lying. Technically.

℘ ⊖ ℘

From his chair in the corner, Dr. Muñoz watched the exchange with great interest. He knew Leah was withholding information and he suspected he knew why. It amused him to see the student become the master in a game of such delicate diplomacy and he silently congratulated himself on having taught her the technique she now employed; he would get nothing from her. When Lubrano arrived, he had spent an hour trying to get the professor to release Leah's field notes to him, but Muñoz had refused, insisting they were not his to release. Finally, he had agreed to this meeting with Leah, certain his pupil would be savvy enough to see through the Peruvian's smooth attempts to gain access to intelligence which the people had been savvy enough to hide from the government. More than once he had told Leah governments often used anthropological research to manipulate native populations.

❧ ⊖ ☙

"If you would like to see my notebooks, Señor Lubrano, I certainly would have no objections, but I warn you, they are written in my own shorthand and are not easy to decipher." Leah saw Muñoz give her a small nod. She had handled herself well and his approval was clearly evident.

Lubrano stood. "I would like that very much. Shall we go get them?"

"I'm dreadfully sorry, Señor Lubrano," said Leah mustering all the sincerity she could, "but they are at my apartment. It's not far from here. Why don't I go get them while you and Dr. Muñoz have lunch? I can meet you back here in an hour."

This was not what he wanted; he wanted to be there when she retrieved the notebooks so she would have no time to remove key pages, if there were indeed key pages to remove. But it would have to do, he decided; the girl did not seem clever enough to know what exactly he was looking for. "That would be acceptable, señorita."

Leah dashed down the hall to her office and quickly dialed Muñoz's number. "Call me Joe," she told him as soon as he answered.

"I'm glad you caught me before I left, Joe," said Muñoz. "I was expecting you to call."

"I want to call Hector, but I'm going to have to do it from home. Before I give that guy anything, I think we should check with him."

"That's an excellent idea, Joe." He moved the mouthpiece and spoke to

Lubrano so that Leah could still hear. "*Un momento, mi amigo.* A student is doing me a favor." He spoke into the phone again, "Do whatever is necessary, and get back to me as soon as you can. And thank you."

಄ ⊖ ಄

By the grace of Mamaquilla, the call went right through, but when someone picked up at the clinic, it was not Hector. "*¿A quién es ?* " she asked.

"*Es Mico,*" said the tentative voice.

"¡Ai, Mico!" Leah was relieved; Mico was the grandson of Hector's sometime housekeeper, a woman who lived in the modern hamlet near the clinic. "*Eso es Li-ah. Es muy importante: ¿donde está el medico?* "

"*Momentito, Li-ah,*" said the boy. She could hear him call to the doctor who must have been standing outside.

The first words out of his mouth asked her if everything was all right. "Everything is fine here. Is everything *in order* there?" she asked cautiously.

Hector's laugh was brief, but hearty. "I am now the proud owner of a scrambler, Leah. For the moment, at least, we can talk."

Leah breathed a sigh of relief. "There's a guy here... Vincente Lubrano. He wants to see my original field notes. You know who he is?"

"Yes, unfortunately. He was here the last time you called. Did he say what he was looking for, niña?"

"He claims he's looking at migratory patterns for our ayllus. What's the bottom line, Hector? Why does he really want to know?"

When Hector sighed, Leah could imagine how he was sagging against his chair. "They want to know how far back they can push the outer ayllus. They view this as the precursor to...ah... development." The hesitation, however slight, spoke volumes. "So far, they've sent three expeditions into the district, but they've met with little success in finding the outer boundaries. They don't know how far the ayllus go back and they don't know exactly where they are. The people have convinced them they do not go beyond the little river to the east. Mamacuna and the Rimoc are doing their best to keep everyone calm. But I don't know how long they can do it."

"What are the choices, Hector?"

"Very few, niña. They can bulldoze them east, unless we can get legislation enacted to protect the area. The environmentalists are working hard in that direction. They're working on the theory the land has to be preserved, not the people, in the hopes that they'll can keep the mining and lumber companies out of the district all together. They figure that if you keep them out, the people are safe. The grant you and Muñoz are negotiating is important to that end." There was a sense of great urgency in his words. "The only thing Paolo has seen from the air are a couple of burned out areas way to the south of me, but I think surveyors are moving north. If they come over the ridge immediately to our south, our ayllus could be in serious trouble."

"What about drugs, Hector?"

"You mean the growers?"

"Yes."

"Ah, that's another story. Up at the Ecuadorian border there have been several arrests made, but they were mostly Colombians. For the moment, our little corner is too remote even for them, but once lumber companies are in, the drug cartels will follow. The leñadors will improve the roads and probably add landing strips at strategic locations. Once the leñadors are finished cutting, there's suddenly a lot of land which is cleared enough to grow coca in quantity. The cartels will pay off whomever they have to so they can use those facilities; one will front for the other. I would bet Lubrano is tied into them as well."

"That's the greatest danger, isn't it?"

"Yes, niña, it is." There was another transcontinental sigh. "You'll have to give Lubrano something, Leah. Can you do that without adding to our troubles?"

"I'm going to give him three notebooks, Hector. There is nothing in them that can jeopardize the people; no maps, no diagrams."

"Leah, they know the people are there somewhere, but they don't know exactly where. They'd have to find them."

"It isn't hard, Hector. There are an awful lot of people living in the ayllus. But I don't understand why he's bugging you."

"Ah, there's a great deal to gain by bugging me." He told her about the conflict over the deed. "Lubrano thinks if he gets me off my land it will leave the people without a civilized champion to plead their cause."

"Would it?"

"Actually, no; it would not. I've got some contacts down in Lima who are pushing hard for the legislation we need, but those things take time and time is what we don't have much of."

"Hector, have you told this slimeball anything about me?"

"Not much, but Leah, you should know that tales of the Qewa Ñawi are filtering out of the jungle."

"Huh?"

"Apparently, a couple of surveyors had some contact with an ayllu. No one here is talking, but suddenly, there are rumors about a green eyed messenger from Mamaquilla who came to warn the people they were in danger and to arm themselves."

"Are you kidding?"

"I wouldn't kid about something like that, niña."

"Arm themselves with what? Sticks and rocks?"

"No," Hector laughed, "with magic. I don't get it either, but the Coya says that's okay. Let them think what they want, so long as it makes 'em stop and think before they come into the district. She worries about you, niña....and about her beloved churi in Ruti-Suyu. Speaking of which, how is our mutual friend doing?"

"He walked me to the library the other day," she reported, knowing Hector's eyes would open as wide as saucers. "He's just fine."

"You actually talked to him? That should make him happy," he laughed.

"I don't know about happy, but at least I know he's human."

"That he is, niña; that he is! Did he tell you he got a driver's license?"

"Yes. Somehow, I find that amazing."

"He *is* amazing. You should've seen his grades last quarter. Very impressive."

Leah didn't want to keep talking about Tan; he was still a difficult subject for her. "I'll keep you posted on Lubrano," she promised.

Hector got the message loud and clear. "I trust your judgment, but you know you're going to have to tell Tan."

"I know."

"And you'll know when to tell him." He paused, then added, "Be careful, Leah."

"The same goes for you, Hector; you be careful...and tell the Mamacuna that we'll do everything we can."

∾ ⊖ ∾

She took all eight notebooks; it occurred to her she didn't want them either at her apartment or in her office. As she jogged back to campus, she thought about trying to find Tan at the student union until she spotted a familiar face coming towards her. "Sarah!" she called and the girl hurried over. Leah handed her five notebooks. "I need you to do me a favor, if you can," she said. "Take these over to the student union and see if you can find Tan. Give him these and tell him I'll call him at home tonight."

"We *are* talking about the guy from the back of the lecture, aren't we? The one you don't know." Sarah was puzzled by the request.

"Yes."

"Aren't these your field notes?"

Leah nodded. "If you can't find Tan, take them over to the School of Public Health and find Dr. Halstaad. If he's available, hand them *only* to him and say they're from Hector...that it's important for him to hang onto them; he shouldn't leave them in his office. And if you can't find Halstaad, take them home with you and leave a message on my machine that you still have them."

"Gee, I feel like a secret agent. Is this stuff classified or something?"

"Something like that."

"Okay. I was on my way to Coffman Union anyhow. See you later."

Leah watched her go, then ran upstairs to Muñoz's office where he and Lubrano were waiting for her. "Sorry I'm late in getting back, but I grabbed something to eat at my place. I hope you don't mind," she said brightly, handing three notebooks to Lubrano.

"Who was the attractive young lady you were speaking with outside?" asked the Peruvian. He was less than discreet about letting her know he had seen her hand off the books.

"Oh," she replied airily, "that was one of my undergrads." Leah turned to Muñoz. "I lent her your copy of Carnival and Coca Leaf. I thought she might find it interesting to see how a native records his own culture."

Muñoz raised an eyebrow, then smiled. "I hope she finds it enlightening."

"So do I," responded Leah, hoping he understood what she had done. She turned back to Lubrano. "These are the notebooks you wanted. You will find most of the agricultural information in the blue one, about halfway through. It isn't very complete, I'm afraid, but like I said, it really wasn't important to my fieldwork. I would ask, Señor Lubrano, that you read the notebooks here and not remove them from the building." She smiled sweetly, "My life depends on those books."

"I think that's a fair request," agreed Muñoz, before Lubrano could protest. "There's a vacant office just down the hall. You may sit in there and read without being disturbed."

Lubrano accepted the offer and left Leah alone with Muñoz.

"Did you reach Morales?" asked the professor as soon as he could close his door.

Leah repeated her conversation with Hector, adding that the books she had given Sarah were the five other notebooks. "They'll be safe with her; I've told her what to do with them. But I'm going to have to tell Dr. Halstaad what's going on."

"A wise move," confirmed Dr. Muñoz. "You handled yourself magnificently with Lubrano. Now you are seeing first hand how important an anthropologist's work can be in the political arena."

"I already knew, Dr. Muñoz. I just hope we can hold off their efforts to move the people farther east. It wouldn't be a good idea to put them in too close range of the Caribs. This may be the twentieth century, but down there, in the deepest part of the jungle basin, it's business as usual. Very little has changed in five hundred years."

ප ⊖ ෙ

A machine answered Leah's call to the Halstaad residence. Disappointed, she left a brief message asking the doctor call her at home. With nothing to do but wait, Leah fixed herself an early dinner and went to work grading papers. When the phone finally did ring, Ingrid Halstaad was returning her call.

"I remember meeting you at the reception for Dr. García, Leah. I'm sorry my husband's not returning your call personally, but he's at a dinner this evening and I don't expect him back until ten. Is there some message I can relay?" asked Mrs. Halstaad, successfully masking her surprise at Leah's call.

Quickly considering her options, Leah asked if it would be possible for her to come by around ten and, if necessary, wait until Dr. Halstaad returned. "I have some information for him from Hector," she told her.

If she was surprised by the request, Ingrid did not admit to it. "That should be just fine but why don't you come around nine-thirty, that way you'll catch him as soon as he comes in."

⇛ ◯ ⇝

Ingrid Halstaad answered the door wearing a blue, flour-dusted sweat suit with her hair tied back in a bandanna. "Please come in, Leah," she said, stepping aside. "And excuse my appearance; I'm baking bread," she laughed. "Can I offer you a cup of coffee while you wait?"

Leah accepted and followed her into the warm kitchen, redolent with the smell of yeast and fresh bread. She set her pack on the chair her hostess indicated, then perched on a stool beside the counter.

Ingrid poured two cups of coffee, handed one to Leah, and went back to her kneading. "As long as I have you to myself, Leah, tell me how Hector is doing. I'm not ashamed to admit I absolutely adore that man!"

"As a matter of fact, I talked to him this afternoon. He sounds great, as usual, and very busy."

"He's quite devoted to the district, but I suppose I don't have to tell you that," she said with a smile. "I envy the time you were able to spend down there."

Leah found herself liking Ingrid Halstaad. In response, she began to tell her about her time in the rain forest, sharing some of the funnier things

Hector did to service his patients. She began to tell her the story of Cusi, a little boy with a broken leg. "...So he sets the leg again and tells Cusi not to go swimming with the cast on his leg. Two days go by, and again a runner shows up asking Hector to come back to the ayllu. This time, Cusi had wedged a stick so far down the cast that he could not get it out."

"I suppose Hector was hard pressed to keep a straight face," interjected Mrs. Halstaad with a grin. "He's always the worst when it comes to children."

"Then you know him well, because he couldn't stop laughing as he removed the cast and replaced it with a fresh one. Two more days and the runner is back. Cusi has wriggled his leg halfway out of the cast and it's stuck. The cast comes off, another goes on, but this time, Hector carries the child back to the clinic, a four hour hike, on his shoulders, and puts him in the infirmary where he can keep an eye on him."

"More to have someone to play checkers with than to keep the Cusi monkey quiet," said a voice from behind Leah. When she spun around, he smiled at her. "*Yau allinllanchu*, Li-Ah."

"*Yau*, Tan." She dipped her head, mostly out of habit, but partly to hide her blush. It was the first time she called him by name to his face.

Ingrid looked from Tan to Leah, then Leah to Tan. Again, she had noticed the bird each wore. Seeing them together in one room without others to distract them, she could feel the tension between them. "Did you need something, Tan?" she asked.

"I smelled coffee," he grinned.

"Help yourself, dear."

Leah watched with amazement as Tan padded barefoot across the kitchen to take a mug from the cabinet. *Obviously, he knows his way around,* she chided herself, *he lives here.* He raised a questioning brow at her as he poured, and Leah extended her cup. "It's just as well you're here. I need to talk to you and Dr. Halstaad as soon as he arrives."

"Is Hector all right?"

"Everything is fine at home." The eyebrow went up again when she said *home.* "But there are things happening you need to know about."

Just then, the door opened and Dr. Halstaad came into the kitchen.

"Well, what do we have here?" he asked as he gave his wife a peck on the cheek. "Would it have anything to do with these?" He held up the notebooks Leah had handed off to Sarah that afternoon.

Leah nodded. "It has a great deal to do with those. They're my field notes."

"So I gathered when I looked at them, but other than following the young lady's instructions not to leave them in the office, I have no idea what this is all about."

"Why don't you three go on into the study," suggested Mrs. Halstaad. "You'll be more comfortable in there."

In the study, Leah began explaining about the grant and the visit from Lubrano. "Have you had any contact with him, Dr. Halstaad?"

"As a matter of fact; he called me this afternoon. Wanted to set up a time to meet with me, but I put him off until tomorrow afternoon. He's been around before, about a year ago, asking a lot of questions about Hector's connection with our people in environmental health. Didn't tell him very much though, only that I knew Hector. Said he was from the consulate in Washington, but there's something about him I couldn't put my finger on."

"Hector thinks he's somehow connected to the drug cartels," Leah said. "In any event, I think what he wants is to get the government to let them push the ayllus eastward so they can get into the mountains and upper end of the forest."

"What does Hector have to do with this?" snapped Tan. "Hector's a doctor, not a politician."

"That may be so, Tan," Dr. Halstaad replied, "but Hector has a good many friends in high places who would not want to see the jungle disturbed. Still, economically speaking, the district is rich in natural resources and anyone who can gain lumber and mining rights would stand to make a fortune." He turned to Leah. "Not to mention coca production. So I take it you sent me the notebooks to prevent him from seeing your data on agricultural development. Why?"

Leah allowed herself a small chuckle. "Paranoia, I suppose; too many spy movies. Take your choice. I was worried that he might arrange to search my office or my apartment. I couldn't leave the notebooks anywhere he might find them."

"Not a stupid thought, if perhaps far-fetched. I certainly understand your concern," concurred Dr. Halstaad. "What would you like me to do when I see him tomorrow?"

"Tell him the truth...that you do know me, if only slightly, and confirm that the bulk of my work is in strictly cultural matters. But do not, under any circumstances, tell him anything you know about him," she shot a thumb in Tan's direction, but refused to call him by name, "other than he is a student of Hector's...if he asks. We can assume that if he knows about me," she said, turning to face Tan, "he knows something about you. But we don't know what he knows. In any case, if he thinks he can frighten you, he'll do it."

Tan was puzzled. "Why would he want to frighten me? I'm sorry, I do not understand."

"Didn't Hector tell you anything about this stuff?" sighed Leah, more than a little surprised at Tan's apparent naiveté.

He shook his head. "We never really discussed it, other than he said there were people who would like to use the mountains for mining and the trees for lumber. He never said anything about drugs as a threat to my people."

"I think Hector was wise in that," said Halstaad to Leah. "To tell him more would make him a potential pawn in their game. Let them think he is a simple Indio for the time being."

Tan was angered by the comment and his jaw clenched. "I am many things, sir, but a simple Indio is not one of them."

"Be reasonable, Tan. No one is accusing you of being simple. It's just that what they don't know can't hurt you. If Lubrano thinks you are just a student, and to have found out more he would have had to go through me...or Hector, then you're not in danger. But, if they think you are Hector's representative here, then they will try to get to Hector through you."

"I think what Dr. Halstaad is trying to say is that Hector has been quiet about you because he does not want you involved in this fight. I am barely involved. What Hector wants for you is an education and all the benefits which go with it, not to put you in the middle of some sort of economic war. You see, if they win, life as we know it in the jungle will disappear. The ayllus, if the people remain, will become regular towns, and the ways of the people will be swept away. The grant we are trying to get is really a rather sad one: its purpose is to completely record a culture which is dying."

Tan sat quietly in his chair, trying to comprehend the full impact of their words. "Tell me about the grant." His voice was as cold as Leah had ever heard it.

Slowly, choosing her words carefully, Leah outlined the proposal she and Muñoz were writing. "The end result will be a complete ethnography of the people, something that will stand as a marker that such a people existed as long as they did without the outside world changing their ways."

"It is too late for that; the Spanish changed our ways when they came in the days of the Inca," Tan told her. "My people fled from their homes in order to preserve their ways, and even those ways changed because there was no *Villac-Umo* to guide us. We are not so primitive that we do not remember how it once was." His voice trailed off; the words of the Mama-cuna were coming back to him. When she took her leave, she told him to go in peace. Unlike every other time he had left her, she had not bid him return in peace. Tan got up and went to the window. Mamaquilla showed only Her profile; even then, She seemed to be looking away from him, toward the people he had left behind, as if She longed to protect them from what would come.

CHAPTER 21

There wasn't much else to say. Leah could not tell if Tan was weeping, but she could feel his pain. Never had she considered the possibility Hector did not tell Tan about the brewing battle for the land, yet she was fairly certain his visits to Janajpachallacta were spent discussing just that with the Mamacuna. Her own short time with old woman led her to believe the old woman knew the score; it had to have been the reason she was invited to participate. Mamacuna had only one purpose, and that was to protect her people.

Dr. Halstaad broke the silence. "Are you in any physical danger, Leah?" he asked quietly.

"I don't think so. When Lubrano returned my notebooks, he seemed satisfied with the information he got, but then again, I can't be sure." She did not add that she feared more for Hector.

"Still, I would prefer if Tan took you home."

"That won't be necessary, Dr. Halstaad, but I appreciate the offer."

"I won't take no for an answer, Leah. Tan can drive you." Leah explained she lived only a couple of blocks away. "Then he will walk you home; won't you, Tan?"

Tan turned from the window. "It would be my pleasure," he replied, his voice flat. "If you would excuse me for a moment, I will get my sneakers." Just as quietly, he slipped from the room.

"He's in great pain, Leah," said Halstaad, his face grim. "Perhaps you will be able to talk to him about this at greater length."

"Only if he chooses to talk about it, Dr. Halstaad," she answered. "You must understand that even though we are here, I respect the rules which govern a relationship with him. To do otherwise would be disrespectful of who he was....is, and right now, that's very important. It may well be that he is the last....... someone must always remember that, even he if chooses to put it aside." Leah felt conflict within herself. Part of her believed she was foolish for her reservations with him; the other part recognized the ingrained need to cherish a dying culture. *Even if he chooses to put it aside*: the very words were anathema, she wanted him to be what he was always, never to push his sacred mita completely away. Inwardly, she wondered if it was a shared belief in what he was that gave her that feeling.....or the anthropologist who wanted only to preserve an ancient ritual.

Dr. Halstaad studied Leah closely. He could understand why Hector was so fond the slight woman with the great, green eyes. She did more than just see what was around her; she had a keen analytical sense which she used to calmly assess a difficult situation. Idly, he wondered if Tan knew just how unusual she was. He imagined Tan's arrival must have affected her greatly, more than he might have thought, now that he had seen them together. "I will leave this to your discretion. I have no doubts that you'll handle this as Hector would wish."

"Thank you, Dr. Halstaad, I appreciate your confidence. I just wish I shared it."

They walked back into the kitchen together. Leah thanked Ingrid for the coffee and wished her good night just as Tan appeared at the door. Leah noticed the Minnesota sweatshirt and thought how odd it was to see him wearing one.

ೲ ⊖ ∾

Outside, the lunar crescent was visible above the treetops, casting thin light on the sidewalk. The air was comfortably warm, yet Leah was chilled. Noticing the way she walked with her arms folded, hands tucked beneath her sleeve, Tan broke the rules and gently slid his arm around her. Leah did not protest, finding his warmth enough to stop the shivering. In silence they walked the short distance to her apartment. When they stood outside the white clapboard house, Leah stepped away from him.

"Thanks for walking me home," she said. "I'm okay from here."

"I will take you inside, Qewa Ñawi. I do not want you to go inside alone." He held her eyes in his steady gaze.

"Really, I'm okay." Leah's protest fell on deaf ears.

Ignoring her, he took her by the elbow and guided her up the steps. He waited while she fumbled with the lock, then followed her up the stairs. When she unlocked her own door, Leah turned to face him. On the tip of her tongue was another *thanks*, but instead, she asked him in. She knew she needed to talk to him, to hear his voice.

"Allow me to make us some of Mama Saba's tea," she murmured in Quechua, feeling vaguely awkward in her own home. Leaving him in the living room, she fled into the kitchen to put up the water. When she came back, Tan was standing at the fireplace, near her collection of conopas. His eyes took in everything on the mantle and the shelves nearby.

Tan pointed to a framed photograph. "Mama Sophie?" he asked gently.

"Yes. How did you know?"

"I recognize her." Tan did not elaborate on how he recognized someone he had never met, but he did not have to; Leah already knew. "Your heart misses her very much," he said.

Leah nodded. She watched as he moved around the room, looking at all her things, suddenly worried that he would think her frivolous for the number of odd mementos scattered about. She saw him touch the brim of her red chinan's hat, and the simple act made her shiver anew.

When his eyes found the posters, Tan smiled. "I like your taste in art," he told her. "This place is much like you, Qewa Ñawi. It is warm and comfortable." He paused to watch her face blush, a habit he found delightful. "You carry my conopa with you, like the bird on my collar." It was not a question, but a statement of fact.

Her cheeks grew even redder. "This is true, I carry it in my pocket." She stuffed her hand into her jeans and withdrew the little gold aclla, holding it in her open palm as proof. "How did you know?" she asked although she knew the answer.

Tan shrugged, "When your heart is in the heart of another, you know these things."

The shrill whistle of the teakettle startled them both. "Come sit down," commanded Leah, pulling herself back together.

Obediently, Tan took the seat at the table she indicated and silently observed her as she moved gracefully in the small kitchen. With nimble fingers, Leah opened one of the packets of crushed leaves Saba had insisted she take from the jungle and slid them carefully into an infuser. She opened a cabinet and took down an old china teapot, a legacy from Grandma Sophie, along with two cups and saucers. She set them on the table, then piled cookies on a small china plate.

Before she sat down, Leah disappeared into the bedroom and returned with a shoebox which she placed on the table between them. "While the tea steeps," she told Tan, "I thought you might like to see these." She lifted the lid to reveal photographs separated by file dividers. Leah thought for a moment, then pulled out a section and slid the pictures across the table.

"Ai!" cried Tan, "these are wonderful!" He began to examine the pictures one by one. "Hector looks as though he is ready to kill!" laughed Tan, sliding a photo to Leah. "What was the problem?"

Leah began to narrate her collection as her guest laughed with delight. "Here, look at this one again," she said, making him go back to a picture of the pool near the second huaca. "Look at the very top of the ridge and tell me what you see." She pulled a magnifying glass from the box and slid it across the table.

He studied the photo carefully and then laughed aloud. "It is me!"

"I did not notice you in the picture when I took it," admitted Leah with a grin. "Only when I was looking at it one night, when I was already back here, did I spot you standing on the edge of the cliff. What were you doing up there?"

"Watching you," he said. "I had followed you from the first huaca to the second; I already knew you were the one called Qewa Ñawi, but I had not seen you up close. And you never would have seen me had the woman not come to the huaca." The last sentence was uttered with his face turned away from Leah.

"You knew I was there, yet you accepted her offering," said Leah softly.

"No, I accepted her offering because you were there. I cannot explain..." his voice trailed off.

But Leah would not let it go. "Did it fulfill a vision?" she asked.

Tan nodded slowly. "Mamacuna once told me someone would come into the jungle for me and I would know that person by their eyes. I never thought it would be a woman."

"Oh." Busying herself with the teapot, Leah filled the two cups and passed one to Tan.

Slowly, he lifted the steaming brew to his lips and tasted the flavor of the jungle, something he missed terribly. It was only right he would share this moment with the woman in the grass. "When I was born," began Tan slowly, "there were omens. When I was summoned to Janajpachallacta, the Coya told me I would become Aclla. I did not believe her, but she was right. She knew before I even faced the tests."

"Were you frightened?"

Tan gave her a wry smile. "Is this the anthropologist asking?"

"No, this is the...." she hesitated, "the friend asking."

"Then the answer is yes, I was terrified. Every child hears stories of one aclla or another. And to be a candidate is a great honor. But a boy knows few who try, succeed." He took another sip of his tea, but his eyes were far away. "I went to Janajpachallacta, but I wanted to run away, back to my grandmother and parents. Yet to do so would bring shame on them. So I went, a boy, hardly the man an aclla must be, and I stood before the Rimoc with my knees shaking so badly I thought they would hear the rattle. But the Mamacuna was kind and explained what I was to do."

"And you became a great aclla in your own right. You know that, don't you?"

Tan nodded. "It was not by design, but by the will of Mamaquilla. I was only Her instrument." He picked out a picture of the last huaca. "When a baby is born, the woman brings the child to this place and leaves it inside the stone hut. She then she goes to the huaca itself and bows down to Mamaquilla. While her face is averted, I go into the stone house and hold the baby in my arms to give it Mamaquilla's blessing. Sometimes, when I held the child against my skin, I would weep. This child of my soul would never know me as its spirit father, for it is forbidden. The child belongs only to the husband of the woman. I felt great emptiness that I had no woman or child of my own to protect."

"But you would have been expected to declare for a woman at some point. Why didn't you?"

"Because of the prophecy, I think. No eyes ever met mine until you looked into my face when I asked if you wanted a baby to fill your arms." He reached across the table to touch her cheek. "When your eyes flew open, Qewa Ñawi, I understood at last the words Mamacuna had said to me at my first solstice as Aclla."

Her face warmed where he stroked her cheek. "When I saw your eyes, Aclla, my heart stopped and I could not breathe."

"You were frightened."

"No, it wasn't fright; it was ...something else." She paused, then grinned to break the tension. "Sheer panic, maybe."

Tan matched her grin with one of his own. "Do you still feel panic when you look at me?" he asked.

"Sort of. But it's not the same; I'm dressed now."

He chuckled at the memory. "We have much to learn from each other, Qewa Ñawi."

The tea finished, they moved to the living room where Tan continued to pour over her photographs of his home. Sitting on the floor, the pictures spread on the low coffee table, he asked her questions, then told her things about the district she had not known. Leah curled up on the couch directly behind him, so she could follow his progress. The world they left behind was a world they both longed to see again, yet Leah had the funny feeling when she finally returned, it would be a much different place. Try as she might, Leah could not keep her eyes open .

She had no memory of going to bed, but when she awoke in the morning, Leah was alone in the bedroom, still dressed, covered by her alpaca blanket. "Tan?" she called his name aloud, but there was no answer. She stumbled, still half-asleep, into the living room where she found her pictures neatly stacked on the table, but no Aclla in sight. Too late to worry about it, Leah went to shower and dress. As she undressed, her fingers went to her shirt pocket to retrieve the pin, then stopped. Leah looked in the mirror and smiled: Tan had switched birds once again. Somehow, this came as no surprise. Had he not done it, Leah would have thought it strange.

꘏ ⊖ ꘏

Two campus policemen were standing in the hallway outside her office when Leah arrived at Ford Hall. Brushing past them with a polite "hello," she was about to put her key in the lock when she noticed the splintered wood at the latch.

"Is this your office, miss?" asked the older of the two.

"Yes. Is there a problem?" She wondered why she said that; it was obvious the door had been forced.

The second guard rested his hand casually on the knob, preventing her from going in. "They're waiting for you down the hall. They'll tell you more."

Leah frowned, but thanked them anyway. The door to the conference room was closed, so she knocked and waited for a response.

"Come in, Leah" said Muñoz when he saw who it was. He allowed her to precede him into the room where four men sat around the table. "Allow me to introduce Captain Wilson of campus security, Detective Johnson of the Minneapolis Police, and Miguel Gutiérrez, attaché to the Peruvian ambassador in Washington. I believe you already know Dr. Halstaad."

She managed a thin "Good morning, gentlemen," before taking the chair Muñoz held out for her.

Captain Wilson spoke first. "It would seem someone wanted something in your office late last night or very early this morning, after the custodian was gone, Miss Fine. Whoever it was got into the building by breaking a window, then went only to your office. We are ruling out vandals because there was no other damage to the building other than the broken window and your door. And of course, the mess in your office. Dr. Muñoz seems to think you are in possession of papers which might be of some importance."

"Not really," said Leah, turning to her advisor. "Could Lubrano be so stupid as to break in the same day he was here?" she asked, not quite believing it herself.

"Lubrano is not that stupid, as you say, Miss Fine," replied the attaché. "But he is under a great deal of pressure from certain elements to prove the people of your district are not tied to specific locales and can therefore be moved elsewhere."

"That's not true at all! They are very much tied to one small area of the district and my research supports that." Leah took a deep breath and willed herself to stay calm. "They can't move Janajpachallacta!"

Gutiérrez shook his head. "Janajpachallacta is of relatively no importance to them, Señorita Fine. What lies below that little piece of antiquity, at the edge of the jungle, is the key."

"What I gave Lubrano should have been enough to convince him the people will not leave without a fight," said Leah. "Oh, who am I kidding? If they want the jungle, they'll take the jungle and the mountains and any other damn thing they want."

Gutiérrez laughed grimly. "I'm afraid you're right, but what they want is documented proof that the Indios of the district are already seeking out new fields further to the east; their rationale being if the people move, the sacred site will be more inclined to move, thereby opening a vacated area to... development."

"You mean exploitation," Leah shot back, suddenly feeling very hostile toward him. "And what exactly is your position, if I might ask?"

"The government is split. There are those who fear the cartels far more than they fear for their immortal souls."

"The Colombians?" asked Leah, rising from her seat. She caught Muñoz raise a single finger in the direction of his lips and she sat back down with a thump. "Never mind; I don't want to know."

Detective Johnson cleared his throat. "This is all very interesting, I'm sure, but we still have a burglary on our hands."

The word burglary made Leah sit upright again. "My apartment!" she whispered.

"We already have a man watching your house, Miss Fine," said Johnson.

"I have what Lubrano's looking for," Dr. Halstaad interjected. "I told you it's in a safe place."

"That may be, doctor, but they don't know that and if this Lubrano fellow is anxious enough, he will try to get into Miss Fine's place or arrange for someone else to get in."

Leah slumped in her chair, the implications of the conversation swimming wildly in her head. Never had she considered her work to be of a political nature, but now it seemed others thought it was so. In fact, at first thought, the whole affair seemed rather ridiculous, but everyone else was taking it quite seriously. Hector's face popped into the middle of the churning stream of thought and suddenly Leah was afraid for him. The dreams at Muñoz's cabin were beginning to make sense now; it was not natural disaster she had seen, but the coming threat to her friends. She waited for a break in the discussion around her. "Señor Gutiérrez, is Dr. Morales in danger?"

"Unfortunately, your friend has made a few powerful enemies. We are not in a position to protect him."

Dr. Halstaad almost jumped out of his chair. "What the hell is that supposed to mean, Gutiérrez? That he's a sitting duck?"

"Basically, yes. He refused to cooperate with Lubrano and that makes him most unpopular. I know they've offered him a great deal of money to use his influence with the holy ones to convince them to move, but..."

"He cannot be bought!" snapped Leah

"That," Gutiérrez commented dryly, "is most obvious. They're trying to get him out of the clinic by introducing a deed which questions his ownership of the land."

"That's absurd!" cried Halstaad. "Hector owns the land outright."

"We've gotten an injunction against the eviction, but there will have to be a court hearing on the matter in Piura. There's no guarantee the judge isn't already bought and paid for."

"You haven't answered the question, Señor, is Dr. Morales in any physical danger?" Leah barely spoke above a whisper, but her anger was evident.

The Peruvian sucked in his breath, weighing what he would tell them next. "Sincerely," he said slowly, "I hope not. In truth, I do not know."

∽ ⊖ ∾

The remainder of the meeting floated by Leah in a haze. She barely heard what was being said, instead she concentrated her thoughts on Hector, trying to decide how to warn him. Somehow, she managed to promise the policemen she would take extra precautions, and would tell them anything that seemed odd or unusual. As soon as she could, she escaped the close confines of the room.

The two policemen were still standing in the hall when Leah returned. This time, they allowed her entry, but asked her to keep the door ajar until a locksmith arrived to repair the damage. The office had been ransacked, but in a methodical, almost neat way. She was certain nothing was missing; the notebooks in question were not in the office, and the rest of her field-work was still at home. If they took a copy of the paper, it was no big deal; it had already been published. Hector's letters were at home, not in the office, so she didn't have to worry about those...for the moment. A sharp rap on the door brought her head up. "Yes?"

"I hope I'm not disturbing you," said Miguel Gutiérrez, poking his head in the door.

"No, not really. I was just cleaning up."

Without being asked, he took the spare chair and drew it close to the desk where Leah sat. "I wanted to speak with you alone," he said, switching to Spanish.

"Aren't you afraid my office is bugged?" she countered sarcastically.

"We've already checked. It is not."

Leah sighed, shoving the papers into a pile in the center of the desk. For the first time, she took a good look at the Peruvian attaché. A lean man elegantly dressed in well cut suit, definitely Savile Row, he had the classical face of a Spaniard: finely arched brows above dark Latin eyes, a long, chiseled nose, and artfully sculpted lips. All put together, he was quite a piece of work, and would one day, when his hair had streaks of silver, be considered distinguished looking. Even his tapered hands bespoke wealth, with carefully manicured nails and a Rolex watch tucked discreetly beneath the monogrammed cuff of his shirt. "What can I do for you, Señor Gutiérrez?"

He leaned forward, bringing his face closer to hers. "It is more a case of what can I do for you, Señorita Fine. I can tell you not to telephone Hector." He saw her green eyes flare. "Those who want access to the mountains are ruthless; they view him as a threat to their ambitions. As long as our friend encourages the people to resist a forced migration, they will continue to do so."

Leah was startled when he called Hector *our* friend. "Have you ever been to the clinic, Señor Gutiérrez, or are you relying on some report you've read?"

"I've done more than just visited the district," he said in smooth, un-accented Quechua. "During my rebellious youth, I served the janpeq as a chasqui."

"I don't believe you."

"Ask me anything you want. Chances are, I will know the answer." His smile widened. "Let me answer even before you ask. In your paper, you wrote Saba liked to have you translate articles sent by Hector. You did not write, however, that she has an uncanny knowledge of internal medicine.... courtesy of Gray's Anatomy which she keeps hidden in her hut." Leah's mouth dropped open. "Or didn't you know that?" he grinned. "I brought it from Lima for her.

"I still don't believe you." Her mouth clamped shut into a tight line.

"I know that Hector is paying for Tan Villac-Quilla's education."

"Anyone could know that."

"Not just anyone could know that you are the reason the aclla left his mita, Qewa Ñawi."

It was as though he dropped a bomb on Leah. Her faced turned bright red and she sputtered, trying to deny the allegation. "You have no right!" she snapped in English, "Do not draw conclusions with your misinformation, Señor Gutiérrez!"

He sat quietly for a moment. "I apologize, Ms. Fine; that was unfair."

"You're damn straight it was," she said.

"What more can I do?"

"Try getting out of my office."

The attaché stood. "I will, but only under one... no, two conditions."

"I'm not promising anything, Señor Gutiérrez, but let's hear it."

"First, promise me you won't try to call the clinic. If he is being tapped, it could be physically dangerous for Hector." He paused for her response.

She didn't want to, but Leah agreed to the first condition. "And the second?"

"Have dinner with me tonight."

"Yeah, right; I don't think so."

Surprisingly, he laughed. "Hector said you could be difficult, but I'm afraid he understated the case. I cannot offer you omelets à la Hector, but I hear the food at the Quail is quite good."

It was the mention of Hector's omelets that convinced her Miguel Gutiérrez just might actually be on the level.

CHAPTER 22

Mico huddled on the bench beside the clinic door waiting for the janpeq to return. He was cold and hungry and upset that the sun was already low in the sky and his friend had not come home when he promised. "Stay here and wait for me," Hector had told the boy after lunch. "I will be back before supper...even before your grandmother returns!" But it was long past supper time and still, Hector had not yet returned. There was nothing to do but wait for someone to come back.

Darkness had already fallen when Líuta, Hector's unofficial housekeeper, found the boy curled in a little ball, fast asleep on the bench. "Ai, churi!" she clucked, shaking him gently, "it is so late! What are you doing outside? Why aren't you in your bed?"

Mico rubbed his eyes and yawned. "The janpeq has not come back from the ayllu by the stream. I was waiting for him."

Líuta took off her shawl and wrapped it around the little boy. "I should have taken you with me to the market today, Mico. I should know better than to trust the janpeq to come back on time." Though she made it out to be her mistake, Líuta was worried. Hector had gone only to check on a baby born at the ayllu the night before; it wasn't that long a walk and he should have been back hours ago. Taking the boy inside, she made him sit at the table while she fixed a tortilla for him. "Eat this," she said as she kissed the top of his tousled head, "I will be right back."

Scurrying as fast as she could, Líuta went to the small hut tucked behind the guesthouse where Hector's chasqui was sleeping. "Wake up,

Anco," she said, sticking her head into the tiny room. "Hector is not back. Go see if you can find him." She handed him a flashlight.

Without a word, Anco took the cylinder and sprinted into the jungle.

⌒ ⊖ ⌒

Halfway between the clinic and the ayllu by the stream, Anco heard a strange sound. His knife unsheathed, he scanned the path with the thin beam of light, trying to locate the source of the sound. "Janpeq?" he called again and again until he heard the moaning increase. Cautiously wading into the underbrush, he caught sight of a body slumped against a thick tree trunk. Anco had been around the doctor long enough to know how to check out an injury. He decided Hector was better moved than left where he was. As gently as he could, Anco lifted him and carried him back to the clinic.

Under the bright lights of the infirmary, Líuta gasped at the sight. "No animal did this, Anco," she whispered, "this is the work of man." Hector's face was already swollen beyond recognition, his nose all but invisible in his face. His arm was clearly broken and his leg bloody where it had been slashed. What scared Líuta most were the three holes she found in his shirt: one in the shoulder, and two on the side. Peeling off the shirt, she cleansed the wounds as best she could. One bullet seemed to have passed through Hector's body, but she could find no exit wounds for the other two. "It's a miracle he has not bled to death," she told the chasqui. Afraid her own rudimentary medical knowledge would not be enough, she ordered Anco to run to Janajpachallacta to summon help.

Outside, the sky was beginning to lighten. Working as fast as she thought wise, Líuta continued to bathe Hector, applying antibiotic salves to the wounds and cool towels to his face. Occasionally, the swollen eyes would struggle open, only to close again when the pain became unbearable. Throughout the day, Líuta kept talking to Hector, ordering him to hold on to life until help could come. When Mico awoke, she pressed him into service fetching clean water and washing out bloody compresses.

At dusk, Hector opened his eyes. Through swollen lips, he instructed

Líuta to inject him with an antibiotic and again with tetanus vaccine. Líuta found the medications in the cabinet and did as she was told with shaking hands. "Good," he told her, managing a lopsided smile, only to wince with pain. "What day is this?" he croaked out.

"Tuesday."

He smiled again and pointed a finger upward. "Mañana," he murmured.

At first, Líuta panicked, thinking that he meant he would die. But Mico understood. "He means the airplane will come tomorrow." And when Paolo came in the courier plane, they would be able to get help from the outside.

Mico and Líuta took turns at Hector's bedside, watching the doctor sleep fitfully. Constantly counting the beads of her rosary, the woman prayed the Mamacuna would send someone and the plane would arrive in time to save this life.

The sun was inching its way into the sky when Anco burst into the clinic. "She is coming!" he cried, collapsing in a chair.

Líuta brought him a drink and waited for the chasqui to finish before she asked who was coming.

"Mamacuna herself, and her own collahuaya. They should be here soon. We have traveled all night."

꙰ ⊖ ꙰

As majestically as any queen, the Mamacuna walked out of the jungle with Saba at her side. Although Líuta had never seen her before, she knew this was the great lady of the jungle. She bowed low and touched her fingers repeatedly to her lips as the old woman approached. "He is in here, Coya," she murmured, stepping aside to let them enter the clinic.

The Mamacuna stood beside the bed, looking down on the battered janpeq. "Open your eyes, my friend," she commanded and his eyes opened. "Now you will hear me, janpeq." She touched his forehead with her hand. "There is no heat, so you have the power to heal yourself. You will live and you will tell us who did this to you. Now you will sleep." The eyes closed but not before Hector managed to curve his lips slightly upward.

The Mamacuna faced the others. "When the silver bird arrives," she said, "we will take the janpeq to the hospital in Piura."

"Yes, Coya," said Líuta as the Mamacuna sat down on the chair beside the bed. She was not about to ask the old woman what she knew about Piura, let alone hospitals.

⤢ ⊖ ⤣

Before too long, the dull whine of an airplane floated into the clinic. As soon as Paolo set down, Anco ran to the plane and told the pilot the news. Paolo picked up his radio and immediately signaled the air traffic controller in Piura. "We need a medical evac team *now*," he told them. He gave them his location and waited for a reply.

Inside the clinic, Hector opened his eyes when he heard Paolo speaking softly to the Mamacuna. "We're going to airlift you out, old friend, so hang on. They'll be here within a couple of hours." Hector grunted and closed his eyes.

"I will go with you," announced the Mamacuna. "And Saba, you will stay here." There was a no nonsense edge to her words which brooked no dissent.

"The evac plane may not be able to carry an extra passenger," Paolo explained.

"Then you will fly me to Piura."

⤢ ⊖ ⤣

The evac team arrived and the paramedics went to work on Hector, complimenting Líuta on her quick thinking and ability to follow Hector's instructions for the injections. Gently, they lifted him onto the gurney and the little procession marched out to the airstrip behind the moving bed. As soon as Hector was aboard, the paramedics assisted the Mamacuna into the small jet and helped her to buckle her seat belt. Líuta passed a bundle containing Hector's wallet and other things she thought he might need to the Mamacuna before the door was pulled shut. That accomplished, they took off, leaving Saba on the ground, her hand shielding her eyes as she watched them soar into the glaring sun.

Stoically, the Mamacuna sat beside Hector with one eye on the paramedics. It wasn't that she didn't trust them; it was just the way they looked at her, as though she had dropped from the sky instead of the other way around. When they finally stopped staring at her, she dared to glance out the window, only to turn away. She was not at all certain she liked sailing above the clouds like a condor, although it was something she had secretly wanted to do for years.

In the jet, the flight to Piura was quite short. Soon they were descending from the clouds and the Mamacuna gripped her armrest until her knuckles turned white. They taxied to a corner of the airport where an ambulance was waiting for them. Hector was taken off first, and then, when the Mamacuna emerged, there were gasps from those standing on the ground. With her head held perfectly erect, the Mamacuna allowed the pilot to help her down the short flight of stairs and over to the ambulance. The driver, an Indian from the mountains, knew by her robes that she was a rimac of great importance and insisted she take the front passenger seat, relegating his assistant to the rear with the paramedics. Lights flashing, siren wailing, the ambulance made its way through the streets of Piura to the hospital.

Sisters in flowing white habits took charge of the gurney as soon as it touched the pavement outside the emergency entrance, ignoring the great lady who followed them inside. Silently guarding her janpeq, the Mamacuna stood at the edge of the cubicle watching as the women stripped away the bandages and attached strange looking things to the prone body. Hector's eyes were open, and he reached out to grab a sleeve. Pulling the nun close, he spoke in raspy phrases, explaining what had already been done as far as he knew.

"Do not worry, doctor," reassured the sister, "we will take good care of you. Dr. Segura will be here any moment." She proceeded to insert a needle into his arm and withdrew several vials of blood under the horrified stare of the Mamacuna.

Hector relaxed, relieved the surgeon was someone he knew. About to close his eyes, he spotted the Mamacuna standing in the corner. He blinked, unsure whether or not to believe his eyes, but her brief nod reassured Hector he was not hallucinating.

Two young men and a woman in white lab coats came into the cubicle where Hector lay. They noticed the old woman and did little to conceal their amusement at her attire. "What's she here for?" asked one of the men in Spanish, not bothering to whisper.

"Maybe to shake her beads over him," laughed the other. The woman blushed and giggled.

With fire in her eyes, Mamacuna stepped towards them. "Young fools!" she spat in her heavily accented Spanish. "Have you no respect? I am here to make sure you make no mistakes with one who is beloved of the Faceless One."

Shamed into silence, they busied themselves with looking at the machines and reading the notes the nun had written on her clipboard. Only when the surgeon entered did they stop what they were doing and step aside.

Dr. Segura gave the Mamacuna a short bow, acknowledging her status even in the city. "I welcome you to my hospital, Coya," he said in Quechua. "I am sorry only because of the reason you have paid us this visit."

"Your words are kind, friend to our friend, but it is good to see a familiar face." Segura had, on occasion, visited the mountain clinic and once Hector wrangled an invitation to Janajpachallacta so he could see first hand how the Mamacuna trained her collahuayas. The Mamacuna had liked the short, pudgy doctor with glass covers over his eyes. "The wounds are beyond my abilities to heal. He is strong, but he has lost much blood. They have even taken more blood from him."

Segura nodded solemnly; he admired the Mamacuna for her courage in coming to Piura with Hector. A lesser woman might have insisted on treating him herself, thereby sealing the doctor's death warrant. As it was, the surgery was already being prepped and as soon as he checked the patient over, he would send him to pre-op. "We will do all that we can do, Coya," he said. Turning his attention to Hector, he carefully examined the bullet wounds while asking the attending sister pertinent questions.

The battered eyes opened when Segura paused in his examination. "Hey, Felipe, *como 'stás?*" He tried to smile.

Segura laughed grimly. "Never mind me, amigo, you're the one on the gurney. You know who did this?" Hector's head moved slowly from side to side, but Segura suspected he knew more than he would say right now. "We're going to go in, Hector, to remove the bullets."

"More than bullets," croaked Hector, "internals. Bad. Brain's okay, I think."

"What? You admit you're not the man of steel?" He tried to sound light, but he knew Hector understood the seriousness of his own injuries despite his weak, lopsided grin. "Try to relax, amigo, I'm going to examine the torso now." As softly as he could, he poked around the abdomen. When he was finished, he instructed one of the sisters to take the Mamacuna to a waiting room.

"I would observe your work, Janpeq Segura," she announced.

"That," stated the sister with a disapproving frown, "is not permitted."

Segura looked from one woman to the other; one would have to be thwarted, and he had to decide which one. He opted for the sister; she could be handled more easily than an annoyed Mamacuna. He took the sister aside. "What would be wrong if the lady was permitted to scrub and observe through the window in recovery?"

The nun was speechless; her mouth opened and closed in rapid succession until she sputtered, "It's against hospital rules, doctor!"

"We would afford the privilege to a visiting physician and she is, if nothing else, a powerful healer." The look he gave her closed the argument and he turned back to the Mamacuna. "Go with sister, Coya, and do exactly as she says and you may watch through the window. When the operation is over, you may stay with Hector."

She did not thank him; she merely nodded as befitting her status.

"Come with me," ordered the nun and she briskly led the old woman down the hall.

∾ ⊝ ∾

The sister showed the Mamacuna a surgery gown designed especially to cover the nuns' habits. She instructed the older woman to remove her shawl, then demonstrated how to use the faucets and soap, scrubbing up and down her arms until they were white with lather. She helped the Mamacuna to rinse, then handed her a sterile towel. She dropped the voluminous white garment over her head. When shown the surgical cap, the Mamacuna allowed the nun to help her get all her hair inside. A second scrubbing was in order, and the High Priestess complied without comment. Another gown, this one green, went over the first. Since she was not going into the operating theater itself, no facemask was necessary, but the sister showed her one so she would understand its use.

Their small conversation was stiff, but the nun came away with a healthy respect for the lady. Her probing questions were not asked with skepticism, but a real desire to understand what was going to be done to her friend. A commotion outside the recovery room where they waited announced the arrival of Hector and the others. The sister was about to leave when she stopped, brought over a tall stool, and placed it beside the plate window. "Here, sit on this," she said in Quechua, then pointed to a bed near the wall. "I don't know how long the surgery will last, but should you grow tired, you may lay down on this bed. I will be in and out to let you know what is happening."

The Mamacuna allowed a small smile. "I thank you for your kindness, acllacuna." She used the ancient word for those women who served with honor in the times of the Inca.

The reference was not lost on the nun. "Let us pray Dr. Morales recovers quickly."

ↁ ⊖ ↁ

With great fascination, the Mamacuna watched as her friend, now on a strange looking table, was cut open by the masked janpeqs in the other room. Because of the way the table was placed, she could see some of the progress of the operation, although she wished she could have been closer to see inside the man. Hector had, when she deigned to visit the clinic, shown her pictures of the internal workings of people, but pictures could hardly do justice to the real event. Perched on her stool, she sat perfectly still, craning her neck to see as much as possible. She saw the bags of blood and other liquids being dripped into his arm to replace that which was lost; the other strings running from his body, the nun had told her, caused flashes of green light on a screen nearby. His face was covered by a mask, and she assumed it was for air.

Dr. Segura first removed the bullets from deep inside Hector's chest and shoulder where, by the grace of Mamaquilla, they had lodged without doing more damage than they might have. As he removed the first bullet, he turned to the window and held it up for the Mamacuna's inspection. She nodded her approval and soon, the second bullet came out. They continued to work in the area; she wondered what they were doing that took so long. When the sister returned, it was with good news.

"The shoulder wound is not great," she explained to the Mamacuna. "The bullet shattered some bone, but the muscle and the nerves appear to be without great damage." She hoped the old lady understood her rough Quechua, and was relieved when she was told this was indeed good news. "The other bullet bounced off the breastbone," she pointed to a place on her own chest, "and pierced the left lung. That should have killed him, but it didn't. Now Dr. Segura is working in the areas that were hurt when Dr. Morales was beaten." She pointed to the x-rays hanging on a light-box. "Have you seen x-rays before?" she asked.

"Yes. The janpeq has shown me such pictures," confirmed the Mamacuna. "The cutting man studies them to guide his hand, yes?"

"Yes, but they don't tell everything. There is stomach damage as well, and Dr. Segura will try to repair it." When the Mamacuna's eyebrow shot up, the sister tried to explain a partial colostomy. "He will need another operation in several months so that the intestine can be reattached."

When the sister left, the Mamacuna stretched her legs, allowing her eyes to look about the room. There were so many things she did not understand, yet she had no choice but to trust the strangely dressed people who held the janpeq's heart, literally, in their hands. Minutes turned into hours, yet the Mamacuna kept vigil from her place behind the glass. Someone brought her some food, which she ate cautiously.

Limb by limb, the doctors worked their way over Hector's body, cleansing and stitching the deeper wounds, until they were satisfied all were tended. His broken arm was set; Segura seemed to relax as he watched other hands apply the plaster cast. Once that was finished, the sister returned to take the Mamacuna to Dr. Segura's office.

She sat on the edge of a wide chair, patiently awaiting the surgeon. When he arrived, his face was haggard, but grinning. "He's a tough man, Coya, and he will be sore, but Hector will recover. The best news is that there appears to be no harm done to his head, other than a fractured nose and the swelling. There is no evidence of damage to the brain."

"He will need more cutting for the *co-los-to-my*," she said, carefully pronouncing the foreign words she had learned that day.

He was more than a little amazed. "Sister explained all that?"

"Yes. The acllacuna said his stomach needs to rest in order to heal. The *co-los-to-my* will allow this."

Dr. Segura took a plastic model off his shelf. With great patience, he showed Mamacuna exactly what he had done and why the second surgery would be needed. "Other than that, he's a perfect example of a healthy male." His light manner did not hide the concern the Mamacuna could see in his heart through his eyes.

She stood and nodded regally at the doctor. "I will go to him now. My people thank you for your good works and know that whatever comes of this, we are forever in your debt."

Mamacuna found Hector wrapped in white blankets, unnaturally pale, in the recovery room. His plastered arm rested atop the blankets, still damp and smelling of hospital disinfectant. Mamacuna took the chair beside the bed. Singing softly the chants for quick healing, she held his good hand in hers and waited patiently for him to awaken.

∾ ⊝ ∾

Hector opened his eyes and blinked at the bright light. For a moment, he tried to remember where he was, for certainly this was not his clinic. The light was strong, yet unlike home, the room was very cool. Slowly moving his head, grimacing at the pain, he managed to turn enough to see the Mamacuna sitting beside him, asleep. With a sigh, he drifted back into the netherworld of anesthesia.

A nun was bending over him taking his blood pressure when he opened his eyes again. "*Hola,*" he croaked.

"*Buenos días, señor doctor,*" She studied his eyes, then asked "Do you know who you are?"

"Felipe Segura."

She scowled at him. "Do you know where you are?"

Somehow, a laugh rasped from his sore throat. "Hotel Simon Bolivar."

"Good enough, Dr. Morales. Welcome back to the land of the living, also known as Hospital Santa María. Sound familiar?" She gave him a re-assuring pat. "You're in the recovery room and Dr. Segura is waiting to see you. I'll fetch him." With a swish of skirts, she was gone.

The next voice he heard was the last one he thought he'd hear in this place. "So, you have decided to come back to us, eh, janpeq?"

The voice was familiar, but the clothing exceedingly strange. He managed another raspy laugh. "Did I have a choice, Coya?" he asked, trying to focus on her face.

The Mamacuna chuckled. "No, my old friend, you did not."

ↄ ⊖ ↄ

Segura had given the go ahead to move Hector to a private room. When the nurses were finished fussing with him, Hector beckoned to the Mama-cuna; he had a favor to ask. "You must call Leah in Ruti-Suyu," he whis-pered. "And not in your head. On a telephone."

Without a word, the Mamacuna dug into the parcel she carried with her and held up his wallet. "These are your travel things, janpeq. Tell me how to use them to call to the Qewa-Ñawi and I will do so."

Hector fumbled single handedly with the wallet and finally pulled out a slip of paper. "Give this to Segura. He'll call. Do it at midnight." Hector fought hard to stay awake a few seconds more. "Tell her to beware of Lubrano."

"Is he the one?" she asked, her face close to his.

"No, but this will do for now." Unable to fight any longer Hector drifted back to a place where the pain was not so bad.

A sister was assigned to stay with Hector. A middle aged Indian, she both feared and respected the presence of a mamacuna. Although she had grown up in town, the legends were popular, especially when one knew people like this still existed on the other side of the mountains. No sooner had she sat down, then the old woman rose majestically and wordlessly swept out of the room.

Mamacuna remembered the way to Segura's office; it was no more difficult than finding her way from one ayllu to another. Without knocking, she opened the door to find Dr. Segura at his desk, startled by her entry. She handed him the small piece of paper Hector had taken from his wallet. "You use the talking box to call this woman at midnight," she commanded.

He looked at the paper, recognizing the sequence as a telephone number in the United States. "Who's number is this?"

"The woman Li-Ah. She is to know what has happened."

"Did Hector tell you what to say?"

"Yes."

"And?"

"I will give the message to her alone. Will you use the machine?"

Dr. Segura agreed, but only if the Mamacuna would agree to have dinner at his home. "It would be a great honor for both my wife and myself if you would take a meal at our table," he told her gravely.

❧ ⊖ ☙

María Segura was waiting at the front door of their modest stone house with three freshly scrubbed children at her side when her husband arrived with the Mamacuna in tow. "Welcome to our house, Coya," she said, touching her fingers to her lips. "You bring honor to our humble home."

The Mamacuna returned the greeting with an appropriate nod of the head. "Your hospitality is kind in this time of sadness, *huahuan*." As was the custom, she entered the house ahead of her hosts.

The table was set with the simplest of Señora Segura's dishes; to do otherwise would have been considered ostentatious since this was not a joyous occasion. In keeping with that tradition, she had prepared a meal of various potatoes and salads; she knew the Mamacuna would eat no meat. The Mamacuna tasted everything, complimenting the hostess of her choices and ability at the stove. María longed to ask a thousand questions, but held her tongue; it would be impolite to speak to the old woman while she ate. Forewarned, even the children remained uncharacteristically quiet during the meal.

In the hour between the end of dinner and midnight, Felipe and María Segura sat with their honored guest on the patio. The children were already in bed and the housekeeper had taken care of the dishes, leaving the three to speak earnestly about conditions in the mountains and the jungle.

"You should bring your children to see Janajpachallacta before it is no more, Segura," instructed the Mamacuna. "Our janpeq is a bad liar; the land robbers are coming and he can do nothing to stop them."

The Seguras exchanged worried glances. From reading the newspapers, they knew the district was ripe for development and worse, members of Shining Path, the Communist guerrillas, were known in the mountains to the south. Still, like their friend lying in the hospital, they hoped the government would be able to do something to prevent ruination before it was too late. And like many of their peers, they were all too familiar with the dire conditions in which most of the indigenous population lived. The rich heritage of the Inca Empire was systematically destroyed by the Spanish and the thought of this last remnant of the old civilization being bulldozed under was terribly sad. María tried to explain that there were many like Hector who would fight for them, but the Mamacuna just waved her hand.

"It will do no good," she said, "our days at Janajpachallacta are few in number. We have seen this coming and there is little to do to stop it. The jonchi has already risen and we see the end of our ways."

"Is there any place you can go? Perhaps deeper into the jungle or higher into the mountains?" asked Segura.

The Mamacuna shook her head. "When we leave the home of our ancestors, we will disappear like the others before us."

In the house, the telephone rang shrilly. Segura excused himself and went inside, leaving his wife and guest on the patio. "My grandmother was from the mountains," said María. "She used to tell me of the old ways, but she, like the others of her ayllu, was Catholic. Sometimes, I think, her stories were a mixture of both."

"Better to have something than nothing," replied the Mamacuna with a knowing smile. "Did she tell you of the ways of Mamaquilla?"

"A little. Mostly she made Her sound like a version of the Blessed Virgin." She blushed a little at the comparison.

"Ah, the mother of your god on the piece of wood. I have heard of her. I will tell you something, if you promise to tell your children when they are old enough to understand."

"Please, Coya; I would be honored to tell your words."

"I have heard of the Father, the Son and the Holy Spirit, although I do not understand it. But I will tell you the Faceless God, the one you call the Father, is the same as Viracocha. Truth is truth, no matter what name you give to it. Devotion to Mamaquilla is devotion to Viracocha; it is merely a matter of how you pray to God. In this way, we are still of one people."

Felipe Segura appeared at the door. "That was the international operator, Coya. The call is going through now."

CHAPTER 23

They did not eat at The Quail; Leah convinced the attaché that Sammy D's would be more comfortable for her. "Sorry," she told him, "but the thought of dressing for dinner is not appealing."

"Then I shall have to put on jeans."

Leah met him at the restaurant; she wanted neither to be in his hotel, nor have him come to her apartment. Sammy D's was a place she felt safe and the food was reasonably good if you knew what to order. When he asked her to do the honors, she did so, choosing veal piccata for him and a plain baked rigatoni, no meat, for herself.

"Are you vegetarian?" he asked, seeing it as a conversational opener.

"No, but a proper chinan would never eat meat."

"Forgive me, Coya," he teased, "I had forgotten."

"Tell me, Señor Gutiérrez," said Leah, changing the subject, "are you in the military? I thought most of the Peruvians on the embassy staff were all majors and colonels and that sort of thing."

"Not all, and please, call me Miguel. If Hector heard you calling me *Señor Gutiérrez*, he would think I've grown pompous in my old age." He liked the way her green eyes sparkled when she smiled. He could see why the doctor was so enamored with the American student. "Hector spent a lot of time reminding me I was just a dumb city kid."

"I'm curious to know how you ended up as a chasqui for him."

"It's a long story which began when I purposefully flunked out of Yale in order to disgrace my father. I had long hair, no socks, and an attitude, none of the attributes a father wants in a son. I heard about Hector's clinic from a friend in Cajabamba, so when I ran away from home, I went there." Over dinner, he wove a comic tale of misadventure and lessons learned at the feet of the master of understatement. "How much do you know about Hector?" he asked, his story finished. "About his past? His history?"

"A great deal about his life now, but he rarely talked of things outside the jungle," admitted Leah, her curiosity piqued. Her guts told her to trust the Peruvian; his respect for Hector and the people bordered on the devotional. "Will you tell me what you know?"

"Hector's family was strictly middle class," began Miguel, "though he is loath to admit it. He was a brilliant student at the university in Lima, and when he decided to study medicine, it was arranged for him to go to Johns Hopkins in Baltimore."

"But he returned to Peru."

"As soon as he could. As much as he loved America, his wife loved Peru more." He noticed her quizzical expression. "Did you know he was married?"

She shook her head.

"He married a Trujillo girl, just as bourgeois as himself," smiled Miguel. "According to Líuta, she was very beautiful.... Apparently, Hector has shown her photographs."

"I had no idea."

"They had one child, a son. Antonio."

He paused, seeming to debate how much to tell her, but Leah prompted him. "And?"

"And they were killed in the great earthquake twenty years ago." He paused again. "Hector was in Piura when the quake hit. By the time he could get to Trujillo, they were pulling Barbara and Antonio from the rubble that had been their house. Barbara was already dead, but Antonio managed to stay alive long enough to die in his father's arms. Hector stayed in Trujillo, working to rebuild the city, but after a while, he couldn't stand being there anymore. One day, he went into the mountains and, basically, never came back."

"He never said a word to me."

"In the highlands, he found he could help save lives after the ones he wanted to save were lost to him. Villac-Quilla is about the same age Antonio would be had he lived."

That explains a great deal, thought Leah. The father-son relationship was so obvious in the way he protected yet pushed Tan to achieve in the outside world. And there was the question of whether or not Hector realized this on a conscious level. *Surely he must,* she told herself. "What about this Lubrano guy from the consulate?" asked Leah, purposely steering the subject away from Tan. "Isn't the consulate tied to the embassy, at least in purpose?"

"Yes and no. We all represent Peru, but the consulate represents the economic interests whereas the embassy is more concerned with matters of state. Unfortunately, Lubrano is tied to the mining interests through his family, but that's not where his interest lies."

"Oh? And where do they lie, Miguel."

"In Colombia. Lubrano has, on more than one occasion, been linked to drug trafficking. It's only the power of the father that keeps the son out of prison."

"Is that how the Peruvian government works? If you can't arrest a criminal, give him a high level post in a foreign country?"

"Well, it certainly works to keep him out of our hair," replied Miguel smoothly. "Look, we both know the people grow coca up there. And while we know how coca is used, we also know the conditions for growing coca are ideal. The pueblo where Hector lives is dying; the rest of the area is virtually inaccessible except by air. Who would be any the wiser if a small, but profitable coca plantation began operation up there? Who would care? If the people are gone, who would notice two or three men living reclusive lives on the edge of the jungle?"

Leah still had trouble believing anyone would find her field notes important enough to risk getting arrested for burglary. "I was around the ayllu long enough to hear them talk about the strangers coming into the district, but no one seemed overly concerned about it, Miguel. Is it possible they do not realize what is going on?"

"Possible, but not probable. The Mamacuna is not as isolated as you might think. She knows what is happening in Lima because Hector keeps her informed. In turn, the Rimoc know and, to some extent, the local sinchis and curacas are told. There was a major council held while you were there, was there not?" Leah nodded and Miguel continued. "The Mamacuna told them there were men in the mountains who would see the people moved to another location and ordered them to seek out chacras on the other side of the Marañon."

"I remember the first expedition; it was all rather secretive and Saba wouldn't say much about it. But I did go out on two others. They were looking for ancient markers for areas that had been cultivated in the past. I never associated the forays with any external pressure to move the ayllus."

"That may be because at that time the Mamacuna may not have told them just how threatened they were. She tends not to be an alarmist. She knows about the conditions in the south; the virtual slavery in the mines down there. The Coya believes she can protect her people from a similar fate by moving them away if necessary. But that does not answer your question about why they would want information from you, so let me try to explain," said Miguel, pushing away his empty cup. "In your field report to the government, you mentioned the rotation of the fields was becoming somewhat problematic; that the land was not supporting crops as well as it had. You also said there were other sites being considered for chacras. That, to Lubrano and his men, is good news. It means when they propose to the local government that the indigenous population be moved, they can use this as evidence that it would be a good thing since the people are already seeking greener pastures, as it were. They would appear to be concerned for the well being of the people. And if there turns out to be gold, or bauxite or even emeralds in the hills, so much the better....for Lubrano."

"Well, that's bullshit," snapped Leah.

"You know it and I know it; but it's convenient bullshit. Leah, we are a democracy, but a fragile one at best and the country is still run, in essence, by a powerful upper class...."

She cut him off. "Of which you are part?"

"Of which my family is part, but not as you might think. My family is descended from the conquistadors, but we strongly believe in the rights of the indigenous population. Not only does this mean we want to see improved economic conditions for the Indios, it also means we believe people like those in our beloved ayllus have the right to remain as they are where they are if that's what they want. I am sure you have seen the horrendous conditions in the shanty towns around Piura and the other cities."

"I have."

"And you also know the condition of the people is wealthy by comparison. They are not poor by anyone's standards; they eat well, have plenty of clean water, and, by the grace of Hector Morales, they have modern medicine to some extent. Basically, they live their own lives in their own way without interference. They don't want cars and air conditioners; they want to be left alone. If Lubrano has his way and they mine the district, they will need cheap labor........" his voice trailed off.

There was nothing to argue; Leah understood exactly what he meant. The bulk of the native populations had been basically enslaved by the conquistadors and had never recovered; they lived in squalor and disease without hope. Her people, on the other hand, had fled the Empire before the coming of the white man, when the infighting between the Incas and the rest of the population had become a state of constant civil war. When the Spanish arrived, they were already hiding in the mountains, and far enough away from the turmoil to be left out of the fray. Small, peaceful, and firm believers in minding their own business, the community flourished. It was only with the coming of modern exploration of the other side of the northern mountains that anyone ever found them. Even the Catholic Church found them unrelentingly uninterested in what they had to offer and eventually stopped sending missionaries to salvage their heathen souls. Hector was the first white man to move to the edge of the jungle and actually stay. This much about him she did know: it had taken him years to be truly accepted by the people and once that was accomplished, he became, for all practical purposes, one of them. And because of that honored status, they allowed the strange woman, her, to come into their midst and become part of their life.

As if he could read her thoughts, Miguel reached out and touched her hand. "You see, Qewa Ñawi, it was no accident he permitted you to come.

Others had asked and had been rejected. But Hector saw the need for them to see another white person who was not interested in changing who they are. I have long suspected he chose you *because* you are a Jew, and not one of those who worship the man on the wood. He had to be certain there was no hidden agenda."

Leah had never given it any thought, but Miguel might very well be right about that. She had wondered why no one had ever surveyed the culture and it might have been because Hector would not support a field expedition into the area; his support was crucial to the success of any anthropologist who wanted to even find the ayllus. And she had done more than just survey, she had been a participant in rituals never before witnessed by an outsider.

The hour had grown late. Leah glanced at her watch and realized it was already ten thirty and she should be getting home. "I appreciate your candor, Miguel," she told him, "and you have given me a great deal to think about."

"I hope I haven't frightened you, Leah, but you needed to know more about the machinations than you already knew." He pulled a small card from his pocket, wrote something on the back, and slid it across the table to her. "This is my number in Washington. On the flip side, is my pager. Understand, we are all in this together and if we help each other, we may be able to help Hector before it's too late."

Miguel insisted on paying the tab since he had invited her to dinner. Outside the restaurant, Leah tried to say goodnight, but the Peruvian insisted on driving her the few blocks to her apartment. "It would serve no purpose to have you abducted after dinner with me, for I would be the first one they'd arrest," he joked, but behind the levity, he was deadly serious.

Parking the car in front of the house, Miguel walked her to the steps. "I had a wonderful time, Leah, and if I did not live in Washington, I would ask to see you again," he said seriously.

Leah smiled, glad the night made it difficult for him to see her pink cheeks. "I'm flattered, Miguel."

Gallantly, the Peruvian took her hand and raised it to his lips. "Perhaps we will meet again, Qewa Ñawi, in less stressful times."

His lips were warm against her skin, sending an unexpected shiver up Leah's spine. "Thank you again, Miguel," she murmured before she hurried up the stairs to the front door.

He watched her go in, then waited for her lights to go on before he returned to his car. The unmarked police car parked discreetly at the corner did not escape his notice.

∽ ⊖ ∾

Coming from the other direction, Tan was jogging toward Leah's when he saw her get out of the car with the tall stranger. He stopped, leaned casually against a tree, and watched as the man raised her hand to his lips, while his own lips stretched tight in anger. Something about the man with her was vaguely familiar, but he couldn't quite think what. Jealousy burned hot in the pit of his stomach. Spinning around, he jogged back to the Halstaads.

∽ ⊖ ∾

The message light on the machine was blinking furiously. Plopping down on the couch, Leah listened to Jay asking her to call, Mindy wondering if she was alive, her mother asking the same thing, Dr. Muñoz telling her to come by his office before her first class, and Captain Wilson reassuring her there was an officer posted outside her apartment. It was too late to return any of the calls, so Leah jotted down a list for the morning and went to bed.

No sooner than she crawled between the sheets, the telephone rang. "Damn it," she swore softly as she padded barefoot back to the living room. "Hello?" she nearly shouted into the receiver.

"Person-to-person call for Leah Fine," said the operator with a Spanish accent.

"Speaking." Panic gripped her as she clutched the telephone. No one called person-to-person anymore, she thought as the connection was completed. "Hello? This is Leah Fine," she said into the mouthpiece when no one came on the line.

A frighteningly familiar voice asked "Qewa Ñawi?"

"Who is this?" she asked in Quechua, although in her heart she already knew.

"You know who this is, huahuan. Your heart speaks to your mind," was the answer.

Leah began to shake. "Coya, is the janpeq alive?"

"Yes, he lives, but he is in great pain."

"Where are you, Coya?"

"We are in Piura. The janpeq is among friends in the healing house."

Hospital. Hector was in the hospital in Piura! "What happened, Coya?" she cried.

"Three bullets, many wounds. The silver bird came and carried us to the town. Another janpeq has cut him open and sewn him closed. He will live." The Mamacuna took a deep breath. "Before he went to sleep, he sends a message to you, Qewa Ñawi. He says to beware of Lubrano. Do you understand this?"

Leah felt tears dripping down her face. She wiped them away with the back of her hand. "Yes, I understand." Suddenly a thought came to her. "Coya, do you remember a chasqui from the big city? He stayed with Hector for a time. His name was Miguel."

"Here, he is called Ayar Monsonsoré. He is a good man. His step, like that of his brother jaguar, is swift and silent. He can be trusted."

"You must tell Hector that Ayar Monsonsoré is with me. Here, in Ruti-Suyu. We know about Lubrano. Coya, you are in danger in the mountains. You must tell the people to watch out for the strangers. They wish you harm!"

"We have waited many years for their coming, huahuan. Mamaquilla has told us they will come." There was a resignation in her voice that frightened Leah all the more. "Mamaquilla will provide for us as She has done in the past."

The words were not in the least convincing. Leah managed to sit down, trying desperately to collect her thoughts. "Ayar Monsonsoré is in the government now, Coya, perhaps he can help us."

"Perhaps." The word held no real hope. "Tell me, Qewa Ñawi, is my beloved churi well?"

"He is well and flourishing, Coya. He studies hard and makes you proud of your faith in him." A thousand questions popped into Leah's head, yet she could not find the words to ask a single one.

But Mamacuna knew. "You must permit your heart to be proud as well, huahuan. Treasure my treasure, for he will bring you understanding of things you do not yet understand."

All she could reply was "Yes, Coya."

"I know this is hard for you, Li-ah, but you must not tell him of Hector's battle. He will want to come home and this he *must not do*! He must remain in Ruti-Suyu to finish what he has begun."

"But..."

"Do not go against my wishes, huahuan. It would serve no good purpose."

"Yes, Coya."

"And do not weep. I can feel your tears in my heart and my heart weeps with you, but you must be strong. Stronger than you think you are."

It was as though a floodgate opened; Leah could barely catch her breath. She felt alone and abandoned, yet she could feel the Mamacuna's courage flowing through the wires and into her. Pulling herself as together as she could, Leah promised the Mamacuna she would tell those who needed to be told, and would seek help from Miguel Gutiérrez.

The Mamacuna broke the connection, leaving Leah calling for her over the dead telephone. Recovering herself, she called the hotel. When he answered the phone, she said only two words: "Ayar Monsonsoré."

Although he had not told her his name in the ayllus, he was certain it was she on the other end. "Leah! What is wrong?"

"It's Hector, Miguel. He's been shot."

"Stay where you are; I'm on my way over. Don't open the door to anyone but me!"

ঌ ⊖ ঌ

He was there in a matter of minutes. When he pulled up, Leah, wearing her robe, ran down the staircase to open the door, then let him wrap his arms around her as she started, once again, to cry. He helped her to the apartment, sat her down on the couch, and listened to her as she repeated her conversation with the Mamacuna, her fingers busily winding and unwinding the quipu in her hand.

"Did she say where she was?" he asked.

"In Piura."

"Where in Piura? Was she at the hospital?"

"I don't know; she didn't say and I wasn't thinking clearly enough to ask." She accepted his handkerchief and noisily blew her nose. "Thank you," she said, trying weakly to smile.

Miguel went and stared out the window. The police car was still across the street. Suddenly, he slammed his hand against the wall. "Felipe!" he shouted. "She must have called fromFelipe's house." Without asking, he picked up the phone and dialed. "*Piura, por favor... Por favor, dígame el Número del Doctor Felipe Segura. Vive en la calle de Los Lirios.*" He scribbled a number on the pad beside the phone. "*Muchas gracias.*" He quickly punched another, longer series of numbers and waited, tapping his fingers anxiously on the table. He brightened when someone answered. "¿Hola, Felipe?........This is Miguel Gutiérrez. I am calling you from Leah Fine's apartment. Is the Mamacuna with you?"

Leah looked at him hopefully and was vastly relieved when he nodded. The questions he asked were far more sensible than the ones she had asked, but then, he was not in shock from hearing the Mamacuna's voice on the telephone.

"Hector was severely beaten by parties unknown, and shot three times at close range: twice in the chest, once in the shoulder," explained Miguel once he had hung up the phone. "One of the bullets went clean through him, doing minor damage; the one in the chest bounced off the sternum and hit the lung, but lodged in such a way that it appears to have kept him from bleeding to death. A third, in the shoulder, shattered a small section of bone, but nothing that cannot heal. Felipe thinks he'll make it, but Hector's going to be in the hospital for quite a while; his assailants did a pretty good job of beating him up. Felipe had to give him a temporary colostomy because of a rupture in the upper intestine. Here, I've written the number down for you."

"Oh, God," groaned Leah, wiping her nose again. "Does he think it was Lubrano's people?"

"Probably, which is probably why Hector had the Mamacuna call you."

"Can you do anything, Miguel? Is there some way to find out if that's what happened?"

"Not without putting everyone in even greater danger. I will go back to Washington tomorrow and talk to the ambassador. Chances are, he will make some discreet inquiries which should produce greater results than were I to make them." He gathered Leah into his arms and held her until she breathed more regularly and the sobbing had diminished. "There is little to be done tonight, Leah, but if you'd like, I stay with you."

She gently broke away from him and managed a weak smile. "Thanks, but I'll be okay." She blew her nose again. "You're right, though, there is nothing to be done tonight." She looked at the wet, crumpled handkerchief. "I really don't want to give this back to you like this," she said. "I guess I'll wash it and send it to you, if that's okay."

He laughed, an oddly pleasant and reassuring sound amidst the chaos. "How about if you promise to give it to me when you meet with the ambassador to present the grant?"

"Deal," she sniffled, wiping the reddened tip yet again. "But you'll call and tell me if you find out anything?"

"Deal. I'll do even better than that, Leah, I'll call you tomorrow night after I have dinner with His Excellency."

Leah walked him back down the stairs. On impulse, she reached up and gave him a quick kiss on the cheek. "Thank you, Ayar Monsonsoré, for coming to my rescue."

Taking her hand in his, Miguel lifted it to his lips, holding it there for a lingering moment. "I would spring to your rescue any time, any place, Qewa Ñawi."

CHAPTER 24

In his room, Tan stared at his computer, not seeing the lines of text . He wasn't in the mood to work; the green fire of jealousy at seeing the stranger with Leah still burned in his belly. There was something odd about the man; Tan wished he could have seen him up close. He wasn't a local, that much he knew from the way the stranger moved in the night, with discernible grace, something that Tan thought Americans, as a whole, lacked. If that was not enough, when the stranger turned, he experienced a glimmer of recognition, as though he had seen the man before, but not in this place. Racking his brains did no good; he could not attach a face to the body, yet he was certain if he saw him in the light, he would know him.

Then suddenly, as if a voice had called his name, Tan's head snapped up. Something had changed, not for the good, and someone was calling to him from afar. There was no clear message, no word which, when the Mamacuna would call for him, sprang to mind, only a vague sensation of need. His first impulse was to return to Leah's, but he disregarded that immediately. He did not want to find her in another's arms as he was sure she was. Closing his eyes, he tried to listen to the sound from within his heart, but it was muffled, indistinct, and faded the harder he concentrated. Angrily, he shut down the computer, flicked off the lamp, and practically hurled himself on the bed.

A breeze was blowing into the room, carrying on it the sweet scent of spring. He turned to the wall, trying to ignore the craving to be outside; the outside he desired was one far from Dinkytown where he now lay.

Willing himself to sleep, he clamped his eyes shut, regulated his breathing, and waited for sleep take him.

His rest was uneasy; his dreams were filled with unhappy pictures of those he left behind. The Mamacuna's seat at the sacred circle was empty although the Rimoc stood in place chanting hymns to Mamaquilla. The songs increased in intensity, and he could hear his name over and over again. He floated above the circle, peering down, a soul without a body, unable to hear clearly what prayers were being offered. He cried out, yet no one heard him.

He continued to cry out to them until he felt his body being pulled apart. Flying from his bed, he knocked Arne Halstaad to the floor.

"Tan!" shouted the older man, scrambling to his feet. "Are you all right?" He saw Tan flat against the wall, his breathing ragged, his eyes wide open in terror. Halstaad slowly walked toward him and grabbed his arms. "Wake up, Tan! It's all right. You're safe here!"

Slowly, Tan's heart ceased its wild rhythm and his eyes focused once more. He slumped against Dr. Halstaad. "I'm all right," he whispered, barely able to speak.

Halstaad led him back to the bed and pushed him until he sat down. "What happened, Tan? Did you have a nightmare?"

His voice was low, almost inaudible. "There is trouble at home."

"How do you know?" he asked, trying to keep his voice even, without letting on he was withholding information.

Tan shook his head, then snorted sarcastically, "A dream, a vision....I do not know what you would call it. The Mamacuna is away from the people and they sing prayers to avert danger, but the danger is already close to them."

Dr. Halstaad knew about the visions; Tan had, once before, spoken of them and Hector had written extensively about his own strange ability to hear the Mamacuna's call long before a chasqui arrived. It was just one more mystical element that defied common explanation. This time, however, it was a little bit different. There was a danger to the people and he knew what it was while Tan did not. He had been tempted to tell him about it, but when he had the opportunity after dinner, something inside prevented him from carrying through with his intention. When Halstaad remained silent, Tan looked him straight in the eye and asked "You know about this, don't you?"

"What I know may or may not be of importance, Tan. It may be totally unrelated to your vision."

"You will tell me, Dr. Halstaad, so I may decide."

Heavily, the older man sat on the edge of the bed beside the younger one. "Last night, Leah's office was burglarized."

"What does that mean?"

"The lock was broken and her office was ransacked."

"Is she all right? Was she hurt?" The urgency in his voice was not lost on Dr. Halstaad.

"She wasn't there." Dr. Halstaad described the extent of the damage and the meeting with the officers and the attaché. "Gutiérrez believes the people will resist any attempts to remove them from the area. He is worried that Hector may be caught in the middle."

Tan left the bed and stood before the open window, staring out onto the street below. Now the muted voice was more important than before. "Who is this Gutiérrez, Dr. Halstaad?"

"He's an attaché to the Peruvian ambassador. My understanding is that he has been at the clinic and knows Hector fairly well."

Then Tan knew the man he had seen was the Ayar Monsonsoré, the pale chasqui Hector had used when he had first become Aclla. They had never met; it was before the time Hector had become his friend, but like everyone else who moved along the jungle paths, he had been carefully observed. Hector liked the Ayar Monsonsoré, making references to him on several occasions, usually when encouraging Tan to go to Lima rather than the United States. Now he was here and he would know more about what was going on in the jungle than either Dr. Halstaad or Leah. "Where is he?" Tan asked as he slipped a shirt over his head.

"At the hotel on Washington Avenue. Why?"

"I will go to see him."

"Now? In the middle of the night?"

"There is no time to waste."

Dr. Halstaad knew there was no way to convince Tan otherwise. "Take my car. The keys are on the kitchen table."

☙ ⊖ ❧

Tan drove the short distance to the hotel. At the front desk, he maintained his outward calm long enough to have the clerk ring the Peruvian's room. There was no answer. The clerk reassured him Mr. Gutiérrez had not checked out and offered to take a message. In a tight voice, Tan thanked him and left.

He drove to Leah's. The light in the living room was off, but the car that had been there earlier was gone. He drove slowly down the block and was about to turn the corner when he noticed the silver car parked at the curb. Pulling in behind it, Tan got out and walked over.

Miguel got out of his car. He waited until the tall Indian stood directly before him before he spoke softly in Quechua. "Find your bed, Aclla," he said without malice. "There is a police car behind you and I am here. No harm will come to the Qewa Ñawi."

Oddly, Tan was relieved, partly because the man was here and not in her apartment, partly because he knew she was safe. "I will trust you, Ayar Monsonsoré, because Hector trusts you. That is the only reason. If harm comes to the Qewa Ñawi, you will not live to regret it."

In the darkness, Miguel's white smile seemed to glow. "She is safe here, Aclla." The smile faded. "Listen to your heart and go back to your bed. You cannot be caught in this. *It will not be permitted.*"

The strange words hung between them; a bond had been forged in a place far from where they stood. Instinctively, Tan knew the command came from Mamacuna and he was powerless to contradict it; he bristled at the restrictions being placed upon him. "I will go, Ayar Monsonsoré, but I will not be far away. I will entrust you with her safety for I believe you have been given that trust instead of me. I do not know why, but I will abide by this." He paused, then he added "For now." Turning on his heel, he returned to the car and drove off.

☙ ⊖ ❧

For the time being, Tan avoided all contact with Leah. To see her would anger him, causing him greater pain than he wished to experience at the moment. The Ayar Masonsoré's words echoed in his memory; each time, he searched their content for a hint of the meaning he knew lay behind them. Whatever was happening, he had been forbidden the knowledge he was certain others had gained. In the quiet moments, when he listened for the comfort from home, he felt deserted, unable to hear the voices he needed to hear, to feel the lifeline between Ruti-Suyu and home. Tan threw himself into his classes with a vengeance, spending long hours at the library and longer hours at his desk.

The Halstaads were concerned. Night after night, Tan sat at the dinner table, saying little, appearing distracted and unable to respond to the simplest question without having it repeated. Since the night of the vision, Tan had avoided sleep until he sagged against his desk. More than once, Mrs. Halstaad found him asleep in his chair, waking him gently to shoo him toward the bed. He would slide beneath the covers she pushed aside for him, and let her tuck him in as any mother would her son. As his eyes closed again, he would feel her cool hand on his forehead, and for a brief moment, he wondered if he were indeed back in the house of his grandmother who would do much the same thing when he was not well.

Although she never confronted Tan directly, Mrs. Halstaad put the question to her husband. "I'm worried about him, Arne," she said over breakfast one morning. "He's not sleeping well, he's barely eating, and even though his grades are good now, how long can this go on?"

"He already knows everything I know, Ingrid, but you must remember, he is far from home. He is committed to staying here, but I think he's suffering from an acute case of homesickness."

"He was homesick in February; this is different. He looks gaunt."

"I agree. What would you like me to do?"

"Have you tried to call Hector?"

Arne nodded. "Every night this week. There's been no answer at the clinic. Hector must be off somewhere in the jungle."

Ingrid sipped her coffee and thought for a moment. "Maybe you should do something to take his mind off his country. Something productive, but fun."

"Did you have something specific in mind, dear?" asked her husband, suspecting that she already did.

She raised an elegant eyebrow and smiled. "How much pull do you have in other departments, Arne?"

"It depends what it's for," he replied, his curiosity piqued.

"The Hispanic Studies annual retreat is next weekend. He mentioned it a couple of weeks ago, but said it was only for upper classmen. I think he was hoping I would know of way to get him invited. What do you think?"

Halstaad leaned over and gave his wife a loud, smacking kiss. "A brilliant idea and just the thing to get our boy back on track. Let me call María Ruíz and see what I can do."

The invitation was not difficult to arrange; Dr. Ruíz was more than delighted to learn the Peruvian special student would be interested in coming to the weekend since he was more than well acquainted with Andean mountain society: he was a product of it.

❧ ⊖ ❧

Over dinner, Tan listened with half an ear as Dr. Halstaad described a particularly important meeting he had attended that afternoon. Then, when there was a break in the conversation, Tan cleared his throat.

"Is there something you wanted to say, Tan?" asked Mrs. Halstaad a little anxiously.

"I would like to buy a car." There, he said it; it was easier than he had anticipated, but he was surprised by Dr. Halstaad's sudden laughter. "Is this not a good thing to do, sir?"

"It's about time! I was beginning to think you'd never get around to even looking!" He was more than pleased with this development. "And just in time, I might add," he added with a wink to his wife.

Tan was puzzled by the response. "Sir?"

"Well, if you want to drive yourself to the Hispanic conference next weekend, you'll need wheels and I wasn't about to lend you mine for the weekend."

"The Hispanic conference? That's only for uppers. I did not qualify to go."

"And specials if they just happen to be card carrying members of the culture subject to discussion." Tan's confused look did not dissipate, so Dr. Halstaad continued. "I talked to Dr. Ruíz this morning and suggested you might be a good addition. She was delighted to hear it. Would you like to go?"

"How can you ask?" cried Tan. "I have wanted to go since I heard about it!"

Mrs. Halstaad reached over and patted his hand. "Then why didn't you ask? You knew the topic and could have said something yourself."

"I understood it was by invitation only. I would not have presumed to make such a request."

Folding his napkin, Dr. Halstaad stood and looked at Tan. "Well, what are we waiting for? Let's go buy a car!" He tossed him the car keys.

ॐ ⊖ ॐ

The money, Dr. Halstaad explained as they drove toward dealership row in White Bear Lake, had been wired to Tan's account as soon as Hector heard Tan had a license. "I figured I'd mention it as soon as you were ready," he said merrily. "Have you given any thought to what you want?"

"A Porsche?"

"I don't think so, fella," laughed the older man. "How 'bout something more in line with a student's budget?"

"Actually, I thought I would like to look at Mazdas. Luís has one and their repair record is good."

Dr. Halstaad shot him a curious glance. "Are you thinking of any particular model?"

"Oh, I shall look at them all, I think."

They arrived at the dealership and started by wandering around the showroom. A salesman introduced himself and Tan immediately began listing the features he wanted in a car. "A good stereo, air conditioning, and a sunroof are most important," he said casually, trying not to seem as excited as he felt.

"Color preference?" asked the salesman.

There was only one answer. "Red."

The other two men laughed, and then the salesman led Tan outside. "I have something you might be interested in," he said walking along a row of brightly colored cars of varying models and years. At the end of the line stood a cherry red 323, brand new, with everything Tan wanted.

Almost too afraid to look, Tan stole a glance at the sticker price. It was well within the budget Hector had recommended for the purchase of a used car and this one was new! He opened the door and peered inside, experiencing for the first time that alluring new car fragrance. He looked at Dr. Halstaad who nodded, and Tan slipped behind the wheel.

"Wanna to take it for a test drive?" asked the salesman.

"Very much, thank you."

"Make yourself comfortable, and I'll be back in a flash with the keys."

Carefully, Tan adjusted the seat. Dr. Halstaad got into the passenger seat and smiled as he watched the young man's elegant hands finesse the position of the rear-view mirror, making sure it was in just the right spot. The salesman reappeared with the keys, hopped into the back. "Any time you're ready."

Tan eased the car forward, then out toward the highway. Sailing down the road, he tried out the wipers and the radio, asked questions about mileage and warrantees, while at the same time impressing Dr. Halstaad with how much thought he had actually given to the prospect of car ownership. Like any guy who had grown up in America, he seemed to have psyched out the philosophy of wheels. It was hard for him to believe that up until a scant five months ago, Tan had never even seen a car.

After a while, Tan seemed satisfied with his test drive and returned to the showroom. He pulled alongside the building and handed the keys to the salesman. "I would ask for a few minutes to speak in private," he said, politely dismissing the other man. When he was gone, Tan turned to Dr. Halstaad. "I do not know how to negotiate to purchase such a large thing. I understand from my reading, it is customary to make an offer and then haggle over the price. Would you be able to do that for me?"

"Absolutely," agreed Halstaad, relieved Tan had asked for his help. "Are you sure this is what you want? You do not want to try anything else?"

Tan shook his head. "A sports car would be nice, but Hector would be angry, I think. This is a nice size and I do not feel cramped behind the wheel as I thought I might. No," he said seriously, "this is a good car, with a good rating in the consumer magazines."

Somehow, Dr. Halstaad managed not to laugh; it should not have surprised him that Tan had researched his choice of car in the same methodical way he evaluated everything else. "If this is what you want, I think we should go in and cut a deal."

∾ ⊖ ∾

Tan watched in amazement as his easygoing friend successfully negotiated a price well below the one on the sticker. When at last they reached an agreement that satisfied both customer and dealer, there was what he thought must be a ritual handshake, followed by the salesman disappearing to have the paperwork completed.

"Things change remarkably when you say you are dealing in cash, Tan," said Dr. Halstaad. "Most people would prefer a loan since it is unusual for one to have that much cash readily available."

"And I do." The sentence teetered between statement and question.

"Yes, Tan, you do. You have more than enough in the bank account to cover the car and a full year's insurance. We can call the after-hours line at the bank and transfer the money into checking as soon as we get home." He smiled at Tan and added, "Since I had a feeling this was coming, I've already spoken with my agent and have arranged for insurance in your name."

Tan knew a little about insurance; he learned about the necessity of having auto insurance when he studied the learner's manual. "How long will it take before I can get insurance?" he asked.

"Tomorrow morning, we'll go over to Pete's office and get the paperwork taken care of, then we can pick up the car tomorrow after dinner," said Halstaad, "unless of course, you've got other plans."

Any plans he might have had, Tan would have canceled for such an auspicious occasion. "Tomorrow will be good!"

The salesman returned with the documents and while he waited, Tan wrote out a check for the exact amount. It seemed no more real than the shell beads he and his friends used to trade on the banks of the Marañon River, when they played fishmonger with the girls. Unlike the beads, this flimsy piece of colored paper had power: the power to obtain for Tan the things he wanted. Every month, he carefully entered the amount of five hundred dollars in the credit column of his checkbook, while he kept close tabs on the checks he would occasionally write. At the start of the month, he would withdraw two hundred and fifty dollars for pocket money, keeping little in his wallet and most of it in the dresser drawer, taking more only when he needed it. His out of pocket expenses were few, although he knew he could certainly spend a great deal more if he desired. But as for how much was actually kept in the account Hector had opened which supplied his checking account, he had no idea. Nor, in actuality, did he want to know. Modesty in spending was, in Tan's way of thinking, as important as modesty of self.

As they rode home, Dr. Halstaad brought up the subject of Tan's spending habits. "A car costs money to maintain," he reminded the new owner. "Should you find you need a bit more in your monthly allowance, let me know and I will arrange it with the bank." He paused, considering whether or not to tell Tan about Hector's last letter. In it, the doctor had detailed the evaluation of the emeralds Tan had given him; they were worth far more than Hector had first suspected. Hector had left the decision to tell Tan to Arne's discretion. But the young man had proven himself cautious and not in the least bit frivolous when it came to money; he saw no reason not to inform Tan of his actual financial status. He mentioned the emeralds and saw one winged brow slide upward in surprise. "The value of the gems sold exceeds two hundred and fifty thousand dollars, Tan. That's quite a bit of capital."

A soft whistle slipped between Tan's pursed lips. "I did not realize they were that valuable, sir."

"You are a wealthy young man in your own right, Tan. How you choose to use that money is your decision alone."

Tan laughed suddenly. "Then I'm worth a hell of a lot more than that, sir! Those stones were only a few of many that I have hidden at home."

Hidden in the stone house beside the last huaca was a cache of rough gems he had found during his long, lonely years haunting the mountains and the jungle. He had given Hector only a few medium-sized stones. Repaying the Healer was the first order of business, but it would have to be done quietly, without Hector knowing. "How much money has our friend sent to the American bank?"

"About fifty thousand in American dollars. The rest remains in Banco Popular de Peru."

"How much of my money here comes from Hector's accounts?"

"A thousand a month."

"Of which I take five hundred. That leaves a cushion of five hundred for emergencies. Correct?"

"Correct." Halstaad wondered what he was getting at.

"Can I open another account at the bank here, by myself?"

"Yes, but why?"

"I would take eight hundred of the thousand each month and put it in an interest bearing account for Hector. I would then transfer two hundred thousand from Lima to here and live off of that. My tuition is paid and I would insult him if I refused that gift, but I can and must learn to live on my own funds."

"It is not easy to transfer that much capital out of Peru, Tan."

"Gutiérrez will help. He will know how to move the money." He grinned at the prospect of asking the Ayar Monsonsoré for this favor.

Arne Halstaad admired Tan greatly for the way he was beginning to take charge of his own life. If what Gutiérrez feared came to pass, Tan would never be able to return to the jungle and resume life as he had known it. But, after all, wasn't that exactly what Hector had written: that Tan would never return there to live. "In the morning, Tan, if you are free, we will go to the insurance agency and then to the bank downtown. The international division is there and they have everything you need to complete the transfer. You can call Gutiérrez if need be. It will be up to you, however, to figure out what excuse you will give Hector for the sudden transfer of funds."

That would not be hard. "Political instability, Dr. Halstaad. You know it, I know it, and certainly Hector knows the political climate of Peru is unstable at best." He gave his passenger a wry grin. "Having the money in America protects us all."

CHAPTER 25

At Miguel's insistence, an alarm was installed at Leah's apartment. With the Hispanic conference just a week away, everyone agreed that the vacant apartment might be an attractive enough nuisance to warrant the purchase of the small security system. He also insisted on covering the cost, despite Leah's protests that she could pay for it herself.

Feeling somewhat safer, Leah set to work on preparations for the weekend. Diligently, she sorted through her notes, putting together enough material for two sessions; one to be held on Saturday afternoon, the other on Sunday morning. Sarah Perkal helped, running back and forth with material to be copied and collated for the retreat.

Two days after he had gone back to Washington, Miguel called Leah. He had spoken with the ambassador who, in turn, promised to make a few inquiries regarding Lubrano's current assignment. "Have you called Felipe?" he asked her.

"No, not yet. I thought I'd wait until I heard from you. Now that I have, I'll try to get through tonight."

"Good. I will be anxious to hear what he has to say."

She wondered why he didn't call Dr. Segura himself, then decided it was to avoid a rash of traceable calls from the United States to Piura. If, on the chance there was someone in the embassy on Lubrano's side, it could cause unnecessary problems at the hospital. "Should I call you after I get through?" she asked.

"Yes, but call my pager. I will call you back."

꩜ ⊖ ꩜

It took a couple of tries, but finally Leah heard the phone ringing in Piura. When a woman answered, she asked for the doctor and waited for what seemed an eternity until a man's voice came on the line. "This is Leah, Dr. Segura. I'm calling to check on Dr. Morales."

"The old bird is tougher than he looks, Señorita Fine. He is already complaining about his treatment at the hospital." His genial laughter was reassuring. "He is still under pretty heavy sedation, but his waking time grows less painful with every hour. I imagine he'll be wheeling about the hospital sticking his nose into everyone's business by Monday or Tuesday the latest."

Leah was definitely relieved. "What about the Mamacuna? Is she still there?"

"No, Paolo flew her back this morning. She decided Hector was in adequate, if not good hands. You would have enjoyed the scene; she worked her magic ways on Paolo and charmed him into being her personal chasqui. He promised to check frequently on Hector's progress and report to Líuta at the clinic. But before I forget, the Mamacuna wanted me to give you a message."

"Oh?"

"She said to tell you that you will know when the time is right to tell her churi of what has happened. I trust you know better than I what she meant."

Leah said nothing. She did not like having the responsibility laid on her, yet she understood why the Mamacuna had done it. Eventually, Tan would have to be told, if he did not already sense something was wrong.

"Are you there?" he asked into the silence.

"Yes. Yes, I'm here."

"Is Miguel still with you in Minnesota?" asked Segura.

"No, he went back to Washington, but I'll talk to him tonight."

"Tell him I am certain Hector's assault was not leftist motivated as some might like us to think; there is no confirmed guerrilla activity on the eastern side of the mountains. Hector did not know his assailants, but he suspects they were Lubrano's men because of where they were in the forest: right at the edge of the foothills." Segura paused to consider his next words. "You know, Señorita Fine, two weeks ago, I would have disagreed with him, but not now. Paolo said when he flew over the southern most ridge of the district he spotted two separate camps, one on each side of the gorge. Do you know where I mean?"

"The place they call the eyebrow?"

"That's the one. He said the camps were small, three tents each, but they did not look like tourists. Too much heavy equipment and each had a couple of jeeps. Tourists up there do not cut roads, however rough, into the terrain."

She wondered if Miguel knew about the camps; she would have to ask him. "Dr. Segura, you have my number. Please call me if you come up with anything else, or, when Hector is feeling up to it, have him give me a call, collect."

He promised he would. "And you call here if you learn anything we should know. Please remember, señorita, Hector is not the only one who is worried about what will happen to those people."

ల⊖ల

Leah sat for a few moments thinking about her conversation with Segura before she placed a call to Miguel. It would have almost been a relief to learn the assailants were members of Shining Path or one of the other radical guerrilla groups instead of goons for a mining company. At least, if it was politically motivated in the classical sense, the government could be pressed into providing some protection. But in Peru, the economy was faltering and if opening the mountains to mining would increase the gross national product, they would be hard put to do anything more than simply shrug their shoulders. In either case, Miguel needed to know and she dialed the number he had given her. He called her back in minutes.

Miguel was not surprised by Segura's report. He also agreed with Leah's assessment that economics would hinder any serious help the government might be able to provide. "If the Mamacuna has indeed envisioned this day," he concluded, "then she has already started work on a plan to save her people. The Mamacuna is a most thorough woman, the kind of leader I wish we had down in Lima. God knows, Leah, we could use her savvy in our congress."

"What are the odds Dr. Segura is wrong and there really are drug people in the mountains?" she asked Miguel. Drug trafficking would bring the Federales almost as fast as Shining Path would.

He thought for a moment before he admitted fifty-fifty. "If Lubrano is involved with trafficking, and frankly, we're reasonably sure he is, then I think the heavy equipment is a ruse. These are not stupid people," he reminded her, "and they often pose as respectable operators. I'm sorry I can't be more encouraging."

With another promise to call if anything happened, Leah rang off and went back to her work. The conference was a scant week away and she felt miles from being fully prepared. Settling herself at her desk in the living room, she switched on her computer and began to compile her notes for the retreat.

❧ ⊝ ☙

In the morning, Leah awoke with the dawn, unable to sleep any longer. She showered and dressed, grabbed her bag and headed over to Al's Breakfast in Dinkytown. The counter was crowded despite the early hour and Leah had to wait for a space of her own. With a cup of steaming coffee in her hand, she stood looking out the window onto the street, the trickle of traffic seeming to grow thicker with each passing minute. Someone vacated a place at the counter; she was about to take it when she noticed a bright red car go by and she could have sworn it was Tan at the wheel. Shaking her head, she chided herself for being ridiculous.

❧ ⊝ ☙

Leah didn't get home until dinnertime, having spent the afternoon in the stacks up to her eyeballs in books on southern Andean mythology. Tossing her bag on the table, she caught the steady blink of her answering machine from the corner of her eye. There were several unimportant messages, but the last one was at least interesting.

"Hi, Lee," played back the tape, "Consi Ruíz, here. Look, I just had this incredible thought. My mother said you were planning on driving up to the lodge with her next week, but how 'bout you ditch the old folks and go up with me on Thursday morning early? You were leaving Thursday anyway, so it wouldn't interfere with classes or anything like that. Whaddya say, Lee? Give me a call back, I'm at my apartment."

It sounded great to Leah. Consuela Ruíz, much to her mother's chagrin, was a French lit grad student and a good friend of Leah's. Consi had been in Paris during fall and winter quarters, returning barely in time for spring classes. Since they hadn't seen each other since her return, this sounded like a great chance to catch up. Leah dialed her number, got her machine, and left a brief, but positive answer.

Glad to be home with nowhere to go, Leah stripped off her clothes in favor of an old caftan. Her first order of business once dinner was in the oven was to call her parents and tell them about the fellowship. She chatted with her mother for a while, then called Jay and left a message for him on his machine. It seemed to her no one was ever home these days, and that her life was filled with leaving and receiving messages. Leah worked for a time, putting the finishing touches on her notes for her first session, then opted to watch the news and turn in early.

She crawled between the sheets and quickly drifted off, snuggled against her pillow. At first she slept soundly, then the dreams began. She hadn't been bothered for what seemed like a long time, but tonight the visions were crystal clear and frightening.

She was standing in the sacred circle at Janajpachallacta, alone. The wind whistled mournfully through the trees, echoing off the deserted buildings. She heard her own voice calling for the Mamacuna, but there was no answer. Leah wandered across the bridge, from house to house in search of someone to tell her what had happened, but no one was there. She went back over the bridge to follow the path to the huaca where she had held her vigil. It was overgrown and unkempt; weeds sprouted from the stone walls, nearly covering the little grotto.

Leah stood at the edge of the sheer cliff, her hand shielding her eyes from the bright sun. As though she had wished him to appear, a lone condor circled overhead, each ring bringing him nearer to where she stood until she could see he carried something in his mouth. Closer and closer he came, until his last circle took him immediately over her head. With a screech, he dropped what was in his beak and a single, perfect tail feather floated down, landing softly in her open palm. As soon as the feather touched flesh, the condor screeched again and soared over the ridge.

Magically, Leah found herself transported to the edge of the pool near the second huaca. She ran to the huaca itself, only to find it bare of all offerings, naked in its emptiness. Racing back to the pool, she scanned the top of the ridge in search of the Aclla, but he was not there. Only the condor reappeared, again sailing in decreasing circles until he dropped a second feather in her outstretched hand.

She carried the two feathers like a torch as she hurried down the fading path toward her own ayllu. Underbrush had already begun to reclaim the well-worn track and she stumbled as she moved faster and faster. The sun disappeared and a full moon rose, casting light enough to find her way. At last, she came to the carved markers that meant she had entered the territory of the village. But the village was gone. Where the huts once stood was nothing but the crumbled remains of a people long gone. Even Saba's house, with its stone foundation, had fallen in on itself, as though no one had lived there in years; it was an eerie relic bathed in moonlight. Leah checked every hearth for some sign of the people; not a trace remained except for the ruins and the blackened earth where cooking fires once burned. Returning to where the central fire had been, she raised her arms above her head, calling to Mamaquilla for help. Her cry, which should have caused birds to rise screeching from the trees, did nothing more than dissipate into the oppressive silence. Without warning, the moon darkened. Fat raindrops started to fall, drenching her through, until water ran down her upraised arms and pummeled her face.

She was rooted to the spot, unable to move. A slash of lightning split the sky, followed by a low, rolling rumble of thunder that seemed to go on forever. Leah, finding her voice again, cried out to Mamaquilla for Her help; she was answered with more lightening and thunder. Instead of being frightened, Leah was comforted by the display. Clearly Viracocha was angered by what had happened to the people and the rain was Mamaquilla's tears of anger and despair. Suddenly, Leah felt herself not alone. Still frozen in the rain, she turned her head to see the Aclla, as wet as she, standing at the edge of the jungle, his arms open to her. She ran to him, letting him wrap his powerful arms around her trembling body. He murmured something in her ear, something she could not understand, yet the sound was comforting. The Aclla guided her along the path deeper into the jungle for what felt like miles. Her tired muscles ached, but they pressed on until the sweet strains of a reed flute could be heard floating through the trees. A pinpoint of light was visible in the distance as they made their way through the underbrush, growing larger and more defined with each step.

At long last the trees gave way to a clearing where a fire burned brightly, the people gathered around it. Happily, Leah turned to face the Aclla, only to find he was gone, nothing but darkness behind her. It did not matter, for the Mamacuna was beckoning to her from the edge of the fire and Leah ran to her waiting arms.

She awoke. Sitting upright in her bed, Leah noticed a thin shaft of moonlight coming in her window and this, too, she found to be a comfort. Clearly she remembered the dream: the destruction of the ayllu, the abandonment of Janajpachallacta. But the people were safe. Instead of being frightened, a wave of relief washed over her, as though she were sure the dream had been sent by the Mamacuna to prepare her for what was to come. There was still the matter of the Aclla. He had been there, but disappeared. Leah was uncertain as to make of this, but she had to believe that he, too, was safe. She longed to call him up and tell him, but something inside her, a little voice that sounded too much like the Mamacuna's, told her it was not the time to tell him and she would know when the time was right.

Sleepily, Leah hunkered down beneath the covers and concentrated on hearing the haunting melodies of a reed flute until she drifted back to unconsciousness.

෭ ⊖ ෬

The rest of the week was spent quietly, with Leah concentrating on getting everything done before the conference. There were times she amazed herself at how much she could accomplish when she set her mind to it, even allowing herself time off for dinner at the Steinbergs on Friday as well as attendance at Sabbath services with Jay on Saturday morning, after which she made him lunch. It was a balmy spring day, warm without being hot, sweet smelling and fresh, just the kind of day they both loved. To celebrate the warm weather, they went to Como Park Zoo.

They hadn't been together very much of late, and Leah found herself catching him up on all the events of recent weeks, stopping just short of telling him about the dream the night before. She assiduously avoided all mention of Tan; Leah felt there was no reason to provoke him. But it was Jay who mentioned him first, asking Leah if she had seen him at all.

"Here and there," she shrugged, "but not lately. Why do you ask?"

"I thought he might be getting in your way or something."

The comment annoyed her. "And what if he was? What are you going to do....go beat him up again? That's real useful."

"Lee..."

"Jay, I'm a big girl who can, in most instances, take care of herself. I am not currently in the market for a white knight."

"That's not what I meant."

"Then what did you mean?"

Jay sighed and looked at his toe scuffing pebbles in the dirt. "What I mean was I was concerned he might be hassling you, that's all. Sometimes guys can talk to guys without getting in a fight, y' know."

Leah reached over and gave his hand a squeeze. "I know you are concerned and I appreciate that. But there are things about him," she paused thoughtfully, then added, "which you do not understand. It has more to do with his position, religiously speaking, at home, than it does about whatever happens here. He's a like a priest, with ties to their spiritual well being. While I was there, I was, to some extent, a part of that. There are things I know because I was there; I know them, but don't always understand them. Mystical kinds of things, Jay."

He gave her an odd look, then began walking, expecting her to keep up. In his silence, he tried to put words to what he was feeling, but it was difficult to name the hodgepodge of emotions running through him. With Leah at his side, he felt complete; he loved her and to him that was simple fact. Obviously, it was not that simple for her. He had carefully bided his time, hoping she would come back to his waiting embrace, as content to be with him as he was with her. Yet even now, when she said she did not see the Peruvian jungle man, he could feel her slipping away at the very mention of his name. "Do you love him, Lee?"

The questions stopped her dead in her tracks. There was no answer she could give him that would satisfy them both. She had never thought of Tan in those terms. True, there was something so deep, so unfathomable about their relationship, but did she love him? Leah was not sure if that was the word to attach to that condition.

When she didn't answer, Jay answered for her. "I guess you do," he said quietly.

Her reply was just as quiet. "Please don't put words in my mouth, Jay. It's just that I really don't have an answer because I don't see this in terms of yes or no."

The rest of the afternoon was awkward, neither able to move past the specter of Tan's presence. They meandered through the zoo, each in private thought, unwilling to discuss the inevitable parting of their paths.

Jay drove her home and walked her to the front door. "I'm not coming up," he said, a twinge of sadness in his voice. He put his arms around Leah, holding her close for a moment. "I've told you I love you. I love you enough to marry you tomorrow if that's what you want, Lee. But I can't stand by and watch you torn apart by this guy and all the mystical mumbo-jumbo that goes with him. If you need me, you know where to find me." With a last tender kiss brushed against her lips, he was gone, leaving her standing on the steps alone.

Tears burned in Leah's green eyes, turning them red and painful. She stayed on the steps long enough to see him drive away, then sluggishly walked upstairs. This was not how she wanted their day together to end, but she had to admit, she did not know how it should have ended. "A bang, not a whimper, would have been better," she said to the empty apartment.

The light on the message machine was blinking. Miguel's voice sounded tired, but concerned as he asked her to call him at home as soon as she got the message. She wasn't in the mood to talk to anyone, but she dialed the number anyway.

He answered on the first ring. "I'm glad you got the message so soon, Leah," he said. "I have news from Piura."

"I hope it's good news, because I don't think I could handle anything depressing right now," she replied surprising herself with her candor.

"Hector is back in the land of the living, according to Felipe. He was able to identify a picture of one of the assailants, a fellow name Pedro Ortega. The Federales are looking for him now, but they won't find him. He's a Colombian working for Lubrano's less than reputable uncle."

"I don't get it, Miguel. Why is a Colombian involved in this?"

"Why do Colombians do anything, Leah?"

"Cocaine?"

"Bingo. A cocaine road." Miguel sounded exhausted as he explained. "On the surface, this Ortega fellow is supposed to be surveying and assaying for the mining companies, but he has a long list of drug connections behind him. I think what they are doing is trying to set up a system so coca can travel out of Peru and into Colombia under the guise of mining exports. The ambassador thinks this might be the grand scheme. Peru has stayed pretty much out of the drug trade, but it's there, just like it's everywhere. Damn near every tribe grows coca. Even ours."

"Yes, but very limited amounts. And unlike some of the other groups, the people don't chew coca leaves, only the Rimoc and then it's pretty rare."

"But it means the conditions are right for production. Look, Ortega is a geologist by trade and it's possible, albeit remotely, he's on the level. Have you heard from Lubrano?"

"No, not at all."

"You will. Count on it. He's most likely going to ask you about the Rimoc. Tell him what you want; it's common knowledge they chew coca. Under the guise of controlling substance abuse, he'll probably ask you about where they get it from. You can tell him the truth, that they grow small quantities. He's looking for two things: confirmation of what he already knows, and whether or not the people could be supplying outsiders with the leaves."

The latter was laughable; there were no outsiders to supply. "But what about the mining business, Miguel? Are they going to try to push the people further into the jungle?"

"Probably, like I told you last time. The Mamacuna is well aware of what's going on and we have to assume she knows what she's going to do about it. How would you feel about a trip to the district in July? Our treat."

She had not expected that at all. Of course, she wanted to go back. "If you want me to go, I will."

"Good. I'll let you know as soon as I know."

Leah told him she would be away the following weekend, and gave him the name of the lodge. "You can reach me there if necessary." Tan's face popped into her mind. "What about *him*? Do I tell him anything?" she asked Miguel.

Miguel wondered why Leah never called Tan by name. "That is for you to decide, Qewa Ñawi."

The use of her jungle name caused shivers up and down her spine, yet somehow she knew that was what he would say.

CHAPTER 26

The ever-ebullient Consi Ruíz appeared at the curb at precisely seven-fifteen as promised. Waving to her from the window, Leah made a last pass through the apartment, checking the faucets and the stove as she went, a habit she was certain she inherited from Grandma Sophie. She opened her purse just to make sure she had her wallet and other necessities of life. With a final push on the alarm button, she was out the door.

Consi stood by the open trunk waiting for Leah to toss in her bags. "Good to see you, sweetie!" she cried, giving her friend a quick hug. "Now let's get on the road. We can eat breakfast later at some greasy spoon somewhere."

"God, look at you! You've all but disappeared!" Chubby Consi had been replaced by a svelte person with a radically short haircut.

"Never again tell me the French know how to cook. I starved in Paris!" Her eyes twinkled with the little lie. "Get in and I'll regale you with all the gory details."

Belted into the front seat, Leah prepared for rapier sharp wit and fast paced chatter. If nothing else, Consi was one of the most intriguing people Leah knew. "Start with your first day in Paris, chère dame, and I promise not to interrupt unless I can't understand a word you're saying," laughed Leah.

Consi launched into the tale, beginning with the customs agent at Charles De Gaulle Airport. Obviously, her sojourn in Paris had agreed with her, giving her the boost she needed to emerge from her chunky post adolescent cocoon as a brash and beautiful intellectual. Skillfully, she wove a tale of mishap and happenstance, punctuating the story with frequent references to her parents' constant worrying. "But here I am," she announced as they finally left the highway for the back roads leading to the lodge, "alive, and, despite my mother's dire predictions, well. In fact, better than alive and well. I am deliriously happy with myself."

"I just can't believe you even came back."

"Neither can I. But I figured the degree was almost as important as stuffing myself at life's never ending banquet. The banquet will still be there after I hold that sheepskin in my hot little hands. So, what about you? I got your rather bizarre letter in March, but I figured you had about as much time to write to me as I had to write to you..."

"So you didn't write back. Your mother said you were never home when she called and that I shouldn't worry if I didn't hear from you. In fact, she said if I did hear from you, would I please let her know since she never heard from you either." Leah gave her an edited version of her year, leaving out the weirder parts and carefully omitting any mention of Tan. "I take it you heard about the break-in at my office."

"Everyone heard about it, Lee. Mother says, there I go again, quoting the old lady," she stopped long enough to giggle, "mother says you should avoid South American politics at all costs. She says they're crazy down there. And wouldn't she be one to talk!"

Dr. Ruíz's distaste for politics was legendary, as were her opinions on what students should and should not do. Waving the comment aside, Leah went on. "Well, I'm in good hands. I've got an alarm at the house, and a safe in the office. It's crazy, Consi, but it makes me feel better." Leah felt the need to change the subject. "So tell me, why are we going up at this obscene hour of the morning?"

"More for your benefit than mine, *ma chéri*. Had you driven up with my mother and father, you would have been forced to share the back seat with Eduardo Gúzman. The old fart has decided to bore us all with his stupid Chilean folktales."

Leah groaned in agreement. Dr. Gúzman was brilliant, but an incredibly boring speaker. "Well, I know which sessions I'm cutting."

"Ha! You're an honored guest at this shindig, maestra. You don't *have* to attend anything but your own."

"And just why, may I ask, are you coming this year? I thought you hate the conference."

"Oh, I usually do, but this one promises to be most interesting."

"Oh?"

"Oh, yes. On the advice of one of my *other* friends, I decided to humor my mother and attend."

"Hmmm, humor your mother? How very unlike you, Consuela. What's the hitch?"

Consi's lips curved upward into an angelic smile. "This friend of mine, the one who suggested that I go, well, she told me there was an incredibly cute guy who was also going and she said it just might be worth my while to go."

"So? Who is this paragon of masculinity?"

"Well," she drawled, "maybe I shouldn't tell you or you'll want to go after him yourself!"

"Thank you, I'm not shopping."

"All I know about him is that he's about six-two, built like a god, has incredible brown eyes, and his name is Tan."

"Huh?" Leah's open mouth snapped shut.

"You know him?"

Leah had little choice. She could tell Consi the truth, thereby having to explain how she knew him, or she could lie. If she lied, it would be only a matter of hours before Consi knew she was lying. She decided in favor of truth with reservations. "Yes, I know him, but no, I have no desire whatsoever to discuss him." It came out harsher than she wanted.

Consi was definitely taken aback by the answer. "I didn't realize....I'm sorry, Lee," she sputtered.

"Don't be sorry. I didn't know he was coming." Silently, she wondered if had she known, would she have declined the invitation. Forcing herself to smile, Leah suggested they change the subject to something less stressful like global warming.

"I get the message, but I'm warning you, Lee, I'm going make a serious pass at this guy."

"Do what you want, Consuela; just be careful."

∽ ⊖ ∾

Black Heron Lodge was a beautiful setting for the conference. Tucked deep in the woods at the edge of a lake, the lodge had a reputation for casual, yet complete conference facilities with good food and excellent service. The main building was a rustic log manor; the rough hewn exterior gave no hint to the creature comforts behind its oak plank door. A young man welcomed them as he pulled their bags from the trunk of Consi's car. "You can check in at the desk and then someone'll carry your bags to your room."

Leah signed in first. When the gentleman behind the desk looked at her card, he gave her a puzzled glance. Leah asked if there was a problem. "No, Ms. Fine, I am just a little surprised. Forgive me for asking, but aren't you a little young to be a professor?"

"I'm not a professor... yet; just a grad student with some expertise in the field," she answered with a grin.

"Well, in any event, you are in Loon Lodge with the other professors." He turned to Consi. "Are you an instructor as well, miss?"

"No, I'm merely a daughter." She laughed aloud at the shocked look on his face. "Not her daughter, Dr. Ruíz's daughter."

He chuckled politely. "Well then, Ms. Ruíz, you are in Egret House." The deskman rang for a bellhop. "Egret House is the first building on your left when you walk out the door. Loon Lodge is a little further, but you'll see why when you get there."

Consi and Leah followed the bellhop outside. They stopped at Egret House where Consi and her bags were deposited in a spacious room with two beds, each covered with Hudson Bay blankets. "Meet me in the lobby in an hour, Lee, and we'll go exploring," she called as the bellhop led her friend out the door.

Loon Lodge was perched on the side of a hill, smaller than Egret House, but definitely more elegant. Leah allowed the bellhop to precede her into the hallway where he stopped at a door and opened it. "I hope you'll be comfortable, miss," he said as he put her suitcase on a bentwood rack. "If you need anything, just press 'O' on the telephone." Leah tipped him and stood back to admire the room.

A small sitting area opened onto a deck with a lounge chair and a wrought iron table, overlooking Black Heron Lake. It was not quite the end of May, but the trees were already dressed in pale green lace. Inside, the sitting room was decorated in shades of deep claret, forest green and midnight blue offset by buckskin colored walls and a deep forest green carpet. The overall effect was that of the outside brought indoors. Leah unpacked her bags, refusing to live out of a suitcase when there was a perfectly good closet and bureau available. Humming to herself as she worked, Leah felt totally free of stress for the first time in weeks, despite knowing Tan would be there.

She changed into a pair of baggy old jeans and her Columbia U. sweatshirt before she strolled back to the lobby.

Consi was waiting for her near the desk. "Here's a schedule, Lee," she said, handing Leah a piece of paper. "Faculty cocktails at six, dinner at seven. Informal gathering at nine. Most of the student types are coming up tonight, a few in the morning. Your session is at eleven. That means we can party tonight and sleep in tomorrow."

"Aren't you going to any of the sessions?" she asked.

"Probably. Yours for sure, but maybe I'll go to Costanzo's on classical literature. He's pretty interesting," replied Consi as they strolled leisurely out the door. "I'm definitely not going to Gúzman's, that's a for sure. No way am I going to sit and listen to that old fart ramble on and on!"

They walked along the narrow, sandy strip which ran along the edge of Black Heron Lake. The water lapped gently against the shore, crystal clear and teeming with tiny marine life. The nature of the conversation changed as they strolled along the beach, centering more on their recent travels and the impact the time abroad had made.

"There were times I thought I could never come back here at all," she told Consi, "I felt as though I was part of the jungle and the mountains, especially toward the end after I'd been to the solstice ceremony. I was at home there."

"But you just said things are changing so fast down there, that there is no guarantee the ayllu will even be there when you do go back."

Leah sighed. "It's part of the problem; the people aren't really aware they're in real danger. I mean, the Mamacuna knows, and probably the Rimoc....."

"How mystical are the Rimoc, really?"

Leah laughed, understanding the real nature of the question. "Not like voodoo or any of that stuff; they just seem to have a very intense relationship with God. The Mamacuna reads the sacred smoke, then tells the Rimoc what she sees. Most of the time, someone else has seen basically the same thing, so it's sort of a confirmation."

"But you wrote about strange dreams in your letter. Are those in the same class as visions?"

"Yes, but dreams are in a different category. Dreams are important to the people, they're harbingers... omens might be a good word. In any event, each time I have one of those dreams, I feel like someone is trying to tell me something."

Consi was fascinated. Leah was never one to speak of very personal matters with anyone, so when she had written about the dreams, Consi guessed they were a bigger problem than she readily admitted. Still, she wanted Leah to have the chance to talk about them if that was what she wanted. Gently, she prodded her to continue.

"Sometimes they're a little scary," Leah admitted. "There are things I cannot understand, symbols which I'm positive should be clear, but just aren't."

"Lee, you are talking in riddles! Cut to the chase." There was only so much tact Consi could muster.

"Condor feathers dropping into my hand must mean something, but I don't know what. I see the Aclla," whom she had not named to her friend, "dancing taqui, beckoning me to join him, but when I do, he disappears. All these things are supposed to be telling me something, I'm sure of that, but I haven't the foggiest notion what. Okay?"

"Okay! I think the best thing you can do is just let nature take its course. Eventually, you'll figure all this stuff out, but there's no point in losing sleep over it, Lee. Besides, how much of the dreams do you think you're manufacturing yourself?"

This was one question Leah had asked herself over and over again. "I don't know. Some, I'm sure, but most of it comes uninvited, truly. I go to sleep thinking of a book or a lecture, and I wake up sweating. I worry constantly about the people in the ayllus and I feel powerless to help them."

"And what exactly do you think you're supposed to be doing?"

"The Mamacuna said I was to write about the way it is, so when it's all gone, there would be a record. She seriously believes their days are numbered and without me, no one will ever know they existed as they have for hundreds of years."

"Do you believe all this, Lee?"

"Honestly, Consi, I just don't know. Wish I did, but I don't." Leah stopped on the rise above the water and stared down at Black Heron Lake sparkling in the sunlight. She thought about what she had told Consi, a little surprised at her own ease in speaking of the dreams. She had told Mary a little about them, Jay, too, but not in the detail she wanted to share with Consi. Perhaps it was because Consi had grown up with her mother's interest in the mystical aspects of religion in South and Central America, or perhaps it was because Consi herself had a healthy respect for the inexplicable. In either case, telling her seemed like the right thing to do, so long as she kept his *name* out of it.

Consi knew Leah well enough to know there was more to this than the sketchy details she had mentioned thus far. "Look," she began quietly, "if you don't want to talk about it, I'll understand, sort of, but I think you need to tell someone what you're feeling and it might as well be me."

Tears filled Leah's green eyes. "There are so many confusing things, Consi, I can't begin to put names to them all." Sitting down on a large rock, she told her about encountering the Aclla at the pool, the strange nocturnal visits, and finally, the events at the solstice ceremony. "I am tied to someone through bonds I can only sense, not define. I think, sometimes, I've been set up, conned, yet I know the work the Mamacuna has given me is very real. In Peru, in the jungle, there were no questions I could not find answers to; here, everything is a question. And there isn't anyone to ask."

"You know, my mother believes in the power of mystics," said Consi with gravity, "she always has. When I was little and she would sing me songs from the hill country in Costa Rica, I used to think she was nuts because there were some words she would always whisper, never say aloud because they were sacred words. I used to try to get her to say them, but she never would, telling me they were not for my ears. I think that for all her academic degrees, she still believes in evil spirits and the ghosts she knew in the old country. And what's worse, the older I get, the more I'm beginning to believe in them, too."

Oddly, her words were reassuring; they made her feel a little less crazy. Still, she had not told Consi about Tan, nor did she want to, at least not yet. Digging into her pocket, Leah pulled out the little gold conopa. "I carry this with me all the time now," she said, handing it to Consi. "Whenever I feel unsure, I wrap my fingers around it and the jungle comes back to me. I remember all this really happened: I did wear a red felt hat, I did dance taqui in the sacred circle, I did belong to another people, at least for a little while."

"It's very beautiful, Lee," murmured Consi as she turned it over and over in her hand, studying the minute yet graceful lines of the little Aclla. "He gave it to you?"

Leah nodded. "It's weird, but when I have it with me, I don't feel so isolated."

"Then keep it; it's now a part of who you are." She laughed lightly. "I am definitely a firm believer in talismans, anyway."

The little laugh broke the tension and they headed back to the lodge.

ᐁ ⊖ ᐁ

Leah stood beneath the stinging needles of the shower for a long time. Wrapped in a thick towel, she brushed out the tangles and patiently worked the wet mass of hair into a tidy French braid, then tied it off with a simple black silk ribbon. Rather than wear pants, she took her black dress from the closet and hung it in the bathroom. She turned the shower back on hot at full blast, hoping the steam would ease the packing wrinkles.

By six-fifteen, she was ready to go. With a last touch of mascara, she slipped on her shoes and took a quick glance in the mirror. Somehow, she did not think she looked any different than she had last year at the conference, only this time, she was faculty. That was, she decided, a little hard to believe.

Dr. Ruíz was holding court in the lobby. Her diminutive form seemed even smaller sheathed in a tailored blue dress; she looked more like the perfect corporate wife than the author of endless books on mythology and ancient history. Taking Leah's hand in her own, she pulled her close for a traditional European peck on both cheeks. "You look lovely, Leah; very professional," she whispered with a wink. "I am glad you are able to join us."

"Thank you, Dr. Ruíz, I'm excited to be here."

"I heard you and Consuela had a non-adventurous day, thank God. When you two get together, I worry." Dr. Ruíz gave Leah's hand a squeeze. "Now, go inside and mingle. The others are anxious to meet you."

∎ ♾ ∎

After dinner, everyone gathered in the lodge's great room. A fire blazed in the hearth, making the room cozy and informal, giving those already present the chance to meet the faculty and guests, thereby setting the tone for the weekend. Small groups clustered around the teachers, anxious to discuss some aspect of the conference topic. Leah sat in a wing chair beside the fire, Consi to her left, chatting comfortably as she enjoyed her new position.

Unexpectedly, Dr. Gúzman interrupted the patter. "Did you bring your guitar so we may sing tonight, Consuela?"

Consi sighed, but smiled anyway. "My mother brought my guitar, not me."

There were numerous calls for Consi to sing, and with a blush and a flourish, she disappeared momentarily to retrieve the instrument. Someone moved another wing chair close to where Leah sat, in preparation for Consi's return.

It took a moment to adjust the strings before Consi launched into a soft, but humorous Bolivian song about a girl who has two boys chasing her. Some of the students joined in the chorus, filling the air with merry music. There was laughter and applause with each new song, whether romantic or bawdy, much to Dr. Ruíz's chagrin. Still, Consi continued singing the tunes popular in rural Central and South America.

Her repertoire was quite extensive. Several of the songs she had learned from Leah in years past, others she had picked up from some of the South American students her mother had befriended at the University. Only when her fingers grew tired, did she look to Leah for relief. "Tell me you haven't brought anything new back from the jungle, Lee," she teased, handing the guitar to her friend.

Those who knew Leah urged her to take up the slack. Finally, she accepted the proffered guitar and settled it in her lap, letting her fingers wander over the strings for a moment or two. "It's been a while since I've played," she announced, "so bear with me." Tossing her long braid over her shoulder, Leah began to pick out a simple tune, hesitating at first, then with more confidence. "Okay," she said at last, "this is a Chimu song about a young chinan, that's a girl who serves Mamaquilla. She loves a man who does not know she exists; the most tragic of tragedies," she added with an exaggerated sigh.

Nimbly, Leah began the introduction to the song, usually played on a reed flute, but a guitar would have to do for the moment. In a comfortable contralto, she began to weave the tale of the girl Tocto and the boy she loved from afar.

She was soon lost in the melody; she closed her eyes and saw Rina sitting at the door of her hut singing the melancholy verses the way she often did as she turned clumps of wool into fine thread for weaving. Gone was the room filled with expectant faces, replaced instead by the sweet smell of the jungle and its comforting warmth. The Quechua words came easily, old friends not shared in recent memory. Verse after verse she sang, each more haunting than the last, until at the very end, Tocto expired from a broken heart.

If few understood the lyric, no one could miss the sadness tempered with hope, the fading to resignation, and the final, tragic loss of the innocent Tocto. As the last notes drifted over the crackling of the fire, no one moved. All were silent, touched deeply by the simple elegance of the elegy. Leah slowly opened her eyes, taking time to allow the room to return to focus. When she did, she saw Tan leaning in the doorway. His eyes met hers, and she could hear his voice though his lips did not move: *Your heart is in my heart.*

CHAPTER 27

Drained, Leah put down the guitar. Ordinarily, she might have done another number, but knowing Tan heard the song rattled her. As if on cue, the manager announced a midnight snack was awaiting the company.

The crowd slowly started to move toward the dining room, leaving Consi and Leah at the fireplace. "That song was incredible, Lee," gushed Consi, replacing the guitar in its battered case. "I'll teach you a couple of French bawds if you teach me that one."

"Deal." Leah leaned back and sighed, allowing the warmth of the fireplace to replace the heat she had felt from Tan's gaze. She could not see him from where she sat, and was glad. She did not want to meet his eyes again at that moment, while the notes still lingered in her mind. The decision to sing that particular song had been a calculated one; one to remind herself she was still a chinan even if she no longer stood at the edge of the sacred circle. A part of her would remain forever in Janajpachallacta no matter what happened.

Consi tugged at her sleeve. "Come on, you look like you need a cup of tea to calm your nerves," she said in an attempt to bring Leah back to the present.

Docilely, Leah followed her into the dining room. She waited her turn at the buffet, keeping her eyes on the urn instead of letting them wander about the room in search of Tan. She took a steaming mug of tea and placed a couple of cookies on a plate; Consi lead her to the table where her parents sat.

"That song was exquisite," said Dr. Ruíz when Leah arrived. "You sing so beautifully, you should do it more often." She looked to her oft-silent husband and smiled. "Arturo thinks your talent is wasted; you should be studying music instead." Those at the table laughed good-naturedly when Leah blushed.

"Thank you, Maestro," said Leah, addressing the other Dr. Ruíz, a musicologist at another college. "But my ability is severely limited by my lack of range."

The conversation turned to traditional folk music, giving Arturo Ruíz an opportunity to share his own vast knowledge. Usually quite reserved at his wife's events, he was pleased to expound on his own area. "I hope you will do me the honor of singing into my recorder," requested the specialist, "it is rare to hear such a sample of such purely Quechua music away from the mountains."

"And she knows many more songs," said Tan, coming to stand beside Leah. "The area of my country which she visited is rich in music."

Dr. Ruíz took the opportunity to introduce Tan to the others at the table. "Although Señor Villac-Quilla is attending the University as a special student, I believe he will add a dimension to our studies which only he could provide," she said warmly.

"Won't you join us, señor," invited Dr. Gúzman, anxious to learn about this newcomer to the conference.

Surreptitiously glancing in her direction, Leah caught Consi giving Tan the once over and stifled a laugh. For his part, Tan was enjoying the attentions of the cute Consuela, flashing his gorgeous white smile in response to something she whispered to him.

Leah lasted a little while longer at table until exhaustion began to overtake her. Excusing herself, she returned to the buffet, hoping to refill her mug with tea before sneaking off to her room. She had almost made it to the front door when she was intercepted by a couple wanting to know more about Andean folk music. Patiently, she answered a couple of questions about the folksongs.

Tan came through the dining room doors. Spotting her, he strolled toward them. "I hope she's been telling you the truth about our songs," he said as soon as Leah stopped talking.

Leah stiffened slightly, but managed a brittle smile. "I was explaining songs are often used as teaching tools for the children."

"And for the adults as well," he smiled back at her. He turned to the students. "A woman might sing a particular song to tell her lover how to arouse her."

"Really?" giggled the woman. "Will you sing some of those later? I could use a few communication tools." She glanced up at her boyfriend who reddened ever so slightly.

Leah noticed Consi was now standing beside Tan. "I don't really know those," she shrugged.

"Oh, I know you know at least one or two! I've heard you sing them before."

"Then sign me up for that class!" laughed Consi.

Leah shook her head. "I'll think about it and let you know."

The two students said goodnight, leaving Leah with Consi, but it was to Tan she turned. "Why, in the name of Mamaquilla, did you do that?" demanded Leah in Quechua, furious with the display she had just witnessed.

Tan grinned as he replied "Did I say something wrong? Do you not know those songs?"

With a snarl of disgust, Leah left Consi alone with Tan.

"My, my!" chuckled Consi, switching to English. "That was definitely worth hanging around for!" Slipping her arm through Tan's, she turned her face upward toward him. "Are you going to sing me these songs, or are you just going to leave me guessing?"

Extracting his arm from hers, he replied, "I am afraid, Miss Ruíz, you must ask Leah."

 споре ⊖ слово

In her room, Leah vented her anger on her clothing, nearly tearing it off as she changed into a nightgown. With the same vehemence, she yanked back the bed covers and dropped face down on the pillow.

It was no use; she couldn't sleep. After a while, she got up. The night air was pleasant as she opened the sliding door to the little deck and stepped outside. The sounds of the woods beyond were soothing, and she could hear the water lapping on the nearby shore. Impulsively, she went back into the room, grabbed her alpaca cloak from the closet, and went out again, this time taking the steps down to the lawn.

The grass was cool and damp beneath her bare feet, but Leah did not notice. She walked toward the sound of the water, desperate to see if she could find the peace she felt in the jungle at the edge of Black Heron Lake. Surely, with Mamaquilla to light the way, she could calm herself enough to eventually go to sleep.

ↄ ⊖ ᴏↄ

From his window, Tan watched the pale specter gliding along the lawn, her soft cloak billowing in the gentle breeze. He knew it was Leah; she moved with the assurance of one used to walking in the forest alone and unafraid. Although he wore nothing but sweat shorts, the air was not cool enough to keep him from following her down to the lake.

Leah walked swiftly along the beach, going farther and farther away from the ambient light of the resort. As she rounded one curve of the shore, she quickened her pace as though she had a destination in mind, and soon she was running, her small feet leaving smaller footprints in the damp sand. Tan ran on higher ground, keeping her in view without revealing himself. Once, he stepped on a branch and immediately crouched down when she paused to determine the direction of the sudden noise. Certain it was nothing, she continued, unaware of Tan in the undergrowth.

A large bolder protruded from the sand at the edge of the water, and there, Leah stopped running. Nimbly, she climbed atop it to sit down with her cloak drawn around her to keep out the chill. The moon, at its zenith, shone down upon the still surface of the lake, a pale disk reflected golden on the water. Her knees drawn up, she remained perfectly still, a statue on the rock, her eyes intent on the mirrored moon.

Slowly, silently, Tan moved closer, one step at a time, until he stood directly behind Leah. He yearned to reach out and touch her; he longed to take her in his arms and hold her forever but he could not. Keeping his breath even and silent, he remained as close as he dared.

Leah spotted his movement in the glossy surface of the lake and watched as Tan drew near. Like a deer caught in the headlights, she didn't dare move a single muscle, lest she give herself away. She could feel his stare on her back as acutely as if it were his hand. His breath was warm on the nape of her neck where her cloak fell away. Her own breathing was becoming ragged from the intensity of watching him, and when she could stand it no longer, she dropped her head onto her folded arms.

Thus Leah remained for what seemed like an eternity, until a strange, muffled sound caused her to raise her head again. In the reflection, she could still see Tan, but his arms were stretched out and he moved slowly behind her. The motion was not random; he was dancing taqui in the sand.

The small, shuffling steps he took went from one side to the other, while his arms were spread wide to receive Mamaquilla in his heart. Leah could tell his eyes were closed, his face uplifted, glowing in the moonlight. She slipped from her perch, her back still to him, and stood in the sand. She slowly raised her arms out from her sides, her palms turned upward. He moved behind her now, his arms near, yet not touching. As he danced to one side, she mirrored him, swaying to the other. They needed no music; the breeze and the gentle slap of tiny waves provided the necessary accompaniment.

Tan came closer, until the bare skin of his chest brushed against the soft wool of Leah's cloak. A barrier between them, she let the cloak drop to the sand; she could feel the heat of him through the thin fabric of her gown, the night air no longer of consequence. When his hands grasped her wrists, she gasped; his flesh was fire against her flesh. She willed herself to be calm, yet she trembled. Now they danced as one, his hands and his body guiding her slightest movement in praise of Mamaquilla's bounty.

Letting his hand slide up her bare arm, Tan circled Leah, turning her at the same time to face him. His brown eyes caught her green ones and held them fast as they continued their dance in the moonlight. It was Leah's hands that broke away to remove the last barrier between them, unfastening the tiny pearl buttons of her nightgown, only to let the garment slip from her shoulders onto the sand.

Tan's breath came sharply now. Coming to her, he continued to dance taqui with no space between them. Without touching her with his hands, he bent to touch her lips. She tilted her head so that his lips brushed only her cheek. Tan could not help but smile; she was as modest any Chimu girl would be: modest in her movement, sweet scented, yet alluringly seductive. The taut tips of her breasts touched his own skin, further igniting his passion. Again, he allowed himself to take her wrists, this time, pulling her against him. When his mouth came down upon hers, their dance ceased.

Tenderly, he tasted her, neither pressuring nor demanding a response. Her lips were warm and open to him, letting him discover the building fire he aroused. His hands caressed her hands; he reveled in the feel of Leah's satin skin beneath his fingers. Leah moaned when his tongue touched hers; she longed to wrap her arms about him, to feel his warmth, yet they remained captive in his grasp. Together, they sank to their knees upon the soft alpaca cloak.

Inch by inch, Tan made her body his own, touching her with his hands and his mouth. Wave upon wave of passion swept through her until her skin tingled with every breath. Her breasts swelled beneath his fingers, and when his mouth closed over one rose tipped nipple, Leah moaned and fell back against the cloak. She did not notice when his shorts slid from his body; she felt only the searing heat of his flesh against her own.

Tan spoke to her in the words she could not understand, but it did not matter. The soft, slurring sound was enough to enflame her, and she gave herself over to his ministry. He found places in her she did not know were there, places which, when touched, caused her to arch against him. His fingers moved though her hair then over her face, touching her eyes, her nose, her mouth. When he reached her ears, he leaned close. "I have coupled, I have joined, I have served," he whispered in words she could understand, his breath hot against the shell of her ear. "I have never loved before now." With a single, fluid, motion, he entered her.

He lingered for a moment, letting the sweet sensation burn into his heart. Slowly but with raw, hungry need, he began to move within her. Leah answered him motion for motion, thrust for thrust, rising to meet him, letting Tan fill her completely. His mouth covered hers, sucking the core of her being into him.

Leah's hands kneaded his back, thrilled by the way his muscles moved as he moved. She opened both her body and her heart to receive him, giving to him from the deepest part of her soul. It was as if she were complete only now that he thrust inside her, driving her to the brink of some great abyss, only to be saved by the sheer strength of his hold. Every nerve was stretched taut, every cell cried out to have and be had. Her mind yielded to the passionate demands of her body, and she cleaved to Tan until she was at once one with him.

The light of Mamaquilla was enough for Leah to see herself lost in the depth of Tan's dark eyes, open and holding hers fast with his. She could see the fire of his soul as clearly as if it burned outside, matched by her own. Again and again she quivered against him, moaning with abandon at each plateau, only to be drawn higher along the shared path. Only at the final moment, when Tan's head was thrown back, his own release poised within her, did he cry out before covering her face with a thousand kisses.

Lying quietly beneath him, Leah savored the pressure of Tan's body still covering hers. He remained deep within her, their union unbroken as they shared the afterglow of lovemaking. His eyes still held hers captive; the green centers dancing with golden lights from behind half-closed lids. Leah smiled as she stroked the smooth skin of his cheek, the palm of her hand soft and warming as the lake breeze cooled their damp bodies. Leah shivered just a little, and Tan reached out to pull the alpaca cloak over them both. Beneath the soft grey wool, they continued to touch and find each other, neither willing to separate.

"Your heart is in my heart," Tan murmured in her ear.

"As your heart is in mine." Her answer, barely more than a whisper, sent renewed flames through them both. This time, it was Leah who took command, exploring his secret places with her slim fingers. He let her love him, tumbling so that she was atop. No woman had ever touched him so, giving of herself instead of taking from him what Mamaquilla's mita demanded he give. He moaned when her tongue outlined the edge of his ear, trailing down along the sinewy cord of his throat. She paused to devour that little hollow at the center of his collarbone where two golden stars hung together, sending hot waves over him. Her mouth sought out and found his nipples; her tongue teased them until they became pebble hard on his smooth chest. Leah laughed at his gasp, then licked the place again until Tan cried out. He grew within her, and began slowly thrusting again deep into the silken depths until he touched the center of her soul.

It was Leah's turn to gasp when Tan shifted so it was his mouth capturing her breast. Growling sensually against the pale skin, the vibrations both tickled and teased Leah, and she arched her back to allow him to continue his progress. Engulfed in her flame, Tan quickened the pace, a new savagery adding fuel to the brightly burning fire. Still straddling his hips, Leah drove herself against his shaft, swallowing it, riding him with abandon.

Wrapping his arms around her, Tan pulled her down to him, devouring her mouth; his tongue thrusting as wildly as his loins. Leah answered his every move with one of her own, undulating against him until he cried out, unable to hold himself back any longer. He erupted, spilling himself into her as he consumed her with desire as her own climax slaked his thirst for her.

Spent, Tan cradled Leah in his arms, stroking her hair, brushing soft kisses against her face until her breathing slowed. The dewy sheen of perspiration made her face shimmer in the moonlight, giving her an ethereal glow. Tan smiled at her and she laughed, quickly nipping at his lower lip. He returned the favor, but let his own lips linger, tasting her sweetness again.

"We are bound together in the eyes of Mamaquilla," he said softly, touching her cheek with his hand.

"We are bound," echoed Leah, her eyes gazing into his. "Will I bear your son?" she asked.

The question hung delicately between them, his answer would have to be truthful. "Only when you choose to bear our son," replied Tan. "Mamaquilla will not permit that until we are bound at an altar." Then he added gently, "Either yours or mine."

For a while they lay together, Leah nestled against the broad expanse of his chest, her face toward the reflection of moon now shining low on the water. The birdsong had changed from the lone hoot of the owl to the haunting call of the loon, an eerie trill echoing through the still night. To the east, the barest hint of grey smudged the black sky. Leah let her eyes close and slept, safely tucked within his arms.

Tan dozed lightly, the scent of her filling his nostrils, giving him a peace he had never known before, not even in the jungle. He had serviced many women while he served Mamaquilla, but never had he made love to any of them; they were faceless beings who sought him out to ease their pain. But the woman he now held in his arms held his heart in hers, a sensation he had longed to experience but had never dared to believe would one day come. She gave herself to him, but the giving was shared, the way the Mamacuna had promised it would be when he allowed himself to love. A heady, freeing feeling, Tan thought if he spread his arms, he would fly with sheer joy. There was no question that the woman loved him for himself, not for what he could give her. And in the end, he was certain she would bear the sons he would hold in his arms, the children they would raise as their own. Drifting between wakefulness and sleep, he wished the night to never end.

But the dawn was creeping over the edges of the trees. Leah stirred, turning so when her eyes fluttered open, she felt his hand caressing her face. Tan loved her slowly, taking his time to arouse her. Gone, for the moment, was the burning need to possess and be possessed, replaced by a quieter, simpler giving and taking of pleasure. When it was over, Tan helped Leah to her feet and together they walked to the water's edge. Cupping his hands, he poured cool water over Leah, then allowed her to do the same for him. Cleansed, they turned together to face the fading moon, raising their arms to bid farewell to Mamaquilla.

Tan shook out the alpaca cloak and draped it over Leah's bare shoulders. Slipping on his shorts, he picked up her nightgown, carried it to the water, and, in the way of his people, set it adrift, watching until it disappeared from view. "Mamaquilla has joined us; there are no barriers between us now," he said, reciting the ancient formula for betrothal. Had they been in the jungle, it would have been her skirt he had offered to the Goddess. With his arm around her, Tan walked Leah back to her room.

CHAPTER 28

Tan left Leah alone in her room; there were only a few short hours before she would teach her first session and she needed to rest. Warm and spent from their lovemaking, she slept deeply, dreamlessly.

When she awoke at nine, bright sunshine flooded the room. Still feeling a bit light-headed, Leah waltzed into the bathroom to start the shower. She caught her own reflection in the mirror and wondered why she looked the same as she had yesterday when inside, everything was different. There was a hesitation before she stepped in, almost a reluctance to wash Tan's scent from her skin. But the time for her lecture was coming quickly and she wanted to review her notes beforehand.

By nine-forty five, Leah was ready to go. She grabbed her briefcase and hurried up the sunny path to the main lodge where she hoped there would still be a cup of coffee available; she had long missed breakfast. The desk clerk directed her to the dining room where the buffet still held the remains of a continental breakfast. Helping herself to coffee and a roll, she went in search of the meeting.

Dr. Gúzman was holding forth on the modernization of ancient culture in the mestizo community in Chile. Finding an empty seat in the back, Leah settled in to listen to the professor while she sipped her coffee and nibbled her roll. The content of Gúzman's speech was not boring, but he was sonorous as he waxed eloquent about the disappearance of aboriginal culture. Although his arena had little relation to her own, Leah had a sinking feeling the lessons taught there were ones her own people would soon be forced to learn.

Leah let her eyes wander about the room. She knew most of the students, and spotted Dr. Costanzo sitting beside the Drs. Ruíz off to one side. Finally, she saw Tan in the second row and wondered if he was as pleasurably exhausted as she. Concentrating was difficult, but Leah forced herself to focus on Gúzman.

Gúzman talked until a quarter past ten, before opening the floor to questions. Most of the students had opinions rather than questions, and several of them centered on the methodology used by the missionaries and early European settlers to eradicate the native culture. Gúzman, long used to this, made no apology for the injustices of history; instead he took the position that what remained intact needed to be protected. Leah agreed with him completely. Long a champion of the preservation of culture, Gúzman had not been popular with the Chilean government and until recently, had been living in exile. Listening to his assessment of Araucana cultural remnants, Leah felt herself mourning for those southern natives who had withstood westernization until the nineteenth century.

When Dr. Gúzman pointed to Tan's raised hand, Leah's ears pricked up. "In your opinion," Tan asked, "do you think it is possible for any small group to resist being swallowed up?" He went on to speak briefly, if not specifically, about the plight of his own people.

Gúzman was touched. He had met the Peruvian the night before, but Dr. Ruíz had already told him about the man who had come out of the jungle only a few months before. By reputation, the professor had heard about Morales and his clinic, his work with this last independent Chimu community and to meet one of them was, in his estimation, a phenomenal stroke of luck. That the man turned out to be eloquent enhanced the fortunate event. "Your people," began Dr. Gúzman, "are in great danger, as you already know. Personally, I know little about them, except what I have read, most recently the paper by Señorita Fine who is here with us this weekend." Leah felt herself blush when he pointed to her sitting in the back of the room. "Unless the people are able to move deeper into the eastern jungles or further into the high Andes, I have no doubt that they will indeed disappear as an independent people. And even then, they risk their physical safety." He went on to describe the brutal ways the industrial developers assured themselves of a constant supply of workers. "Although slavery is technically illegal, I think we all need to admit it does, under the thin veneer of day labor, still exist. This is the greater danger, for abuse of the work force is the major factor in the destruction of the community. It robs the people of self-esteem and makes them prey to the worst western civilization has to offer. As you know, the attempt on Dr. Morales' life has not gone unnoticed amongst those who would see that small community left alone and intact. We are all thankful that he is recovering."

The attempt on Dr. Morales' life. The words rang out and Leah cringed. She could feel Tan's confusion spark into anger, but there was no way to reach him now, to explain what should have been explained. With shaking hands, she lifted her cup to her lips, but the coffee could not wash away the suddenly dry feeling in her mouth. There was nothing she could do but wait until the session was over.

ઌ ⊝ ૭

Tan walked woodenly toward the exit as soon as Dr. Gúzman ended his talk. His jaw was clenched, the small muscles twitching as he made his way toward where Leah sat frozen in her chair. Anger burned in the brown eyes, turning them dark, almost black. Without a word, he grabbed Leah's arm and hauled her to her feet. She did not fight him, instead she allowed him to push her through the door and to a corner of the lobby where he stood her against a wall. His face was an inch away from hers when he finally spoke. "You knew," he growled in Quechua, his voice dangerously low. "You knew and you have told me nothing. You will tell me now!"

Leah was trembling, grateful the wall was holding her upright. "I could not tell you," she whispered. "Mamacuna forbade it."

"How could you know what Mamacuna forbids and permits? Does she send you telegrams in your sleep?" There was a snide, cynical edge to his words that frightened her.

She shook her head. "I know what Mamacuna permits because I spoke to her on the telephone."

Tan's eyes widened, then narrowed. "I do not believe you," he spat.

"Hector is in the hospital in Piura. When they flew him out, the Mamacuna went with him.... Yes, Tan, she flew in a jet, the air ambulance Paolo called in because he was afraid to move Hector himself. Felipe Segura, Hector's friend, placed the call." Leah sighed as she reached back to make sure the wall was still supporting her. "Mamacuna forbade me to tell you. She was afraid you would try to come home and this was not what she wanted." Leah averted her eyes and tilted her head downward. "I could not contradict her."

Tan willed himself to regain control. Slowing his breathing, he studied Leah's face, and realized she was telling the truth. It did nothing to assuage his anger, but he knew she had done exactly what he would have done had their positions been reversed. "Later, you will tell me everything." Spinning on his heel, Tan strode away, leaving Leah to pull herself together before her lecture.

ೞ ⊖ ೞ

Somehow, she found comfort in talking about the religious and cultural life of the people even though Tan sat dead square in the middle of the room, his eyes intent on her. With liberal use of Quechua expressions, Leah spoke of the Mamacuna and her Rimoc, and of the hours spent with Saba and Rina learning the ways of the people. In precise but loving language, she described the devotion to Mamaquilla. She could see Tan's impassive face soften as she spoke of the soul of the people; her own devotion to their ways was evident. The only time she stumbled was when she mentioned the nine huacas of fertility. As she spoke, she knew her heart was reaching for Tan's, and she could feel his warmth as close as if his hands held hers.

Leah blushed faintly when she told her audience of the rites of courtship and marriage, the open sexuality so natural to the people. When she described how a young man in love would secretly leave gifts for the girl who had captured his heart, she was warmed by the memory of the gifts he had left on her bed while she slept. "When a girl realizes she is being seriously courted," said Leah, looking directly at Tan before she dipped her head ever so slightly, "she attains new status in the eyes of her ayllu. No longer does she worry about being *huasipascuna*, a forgotten girl; she walks a little taller, but should she meet her beloved on the path, she averts her eyes, tipping her head to the side, a recognizable sign of modesty and good upbringing. To do otherwise would imply she was brazen. A courtship may be stopped if the boy or his family suspects the girl of immodest behavior." Leah paused and smiled before she added, "the bawdy humor characteristic of the womenfolk is reserved for older ladies with grown families."

Listening to her words, Tan was warmed by the love with which she spoke of the people, yet he kept his face bland; anger still burned in a corner his belly. He was hurt that Leah had not told him, even if the Mamacuna had forbidden it. They were far from Janajpachallacta, and as wise as the old woman was, she did not have the right to decide what he should and should not be told. *I am not a child to be protected from the world,* he told himself. Surely the Mamacuna had enough faith in him to know he would not go running back to Peru! Or would he? Having been denied the opportunity to choose, Tan felt robbed. Dismissing the thought, he turned his attention to Leah at the podium. Undeniably, she was an enthralling lecturer and if he hadn't known for a fact she was an outsider, he'd have thought she was one of the people. When she spoke of the rituals and ceremonies, there was tenderness in her voice; clearly she loved the ways of his people and was intimately involved in the life of that community. He was torn between the anguish he felt at learning of Hector's troubles and the love he felt for the Qewa Ñawi.

❧ ⊖ ☙

Leah easily fielded the questions posed at the end of her talk. At the end of the session, Dr. Ruíz took the podium to announce a brief recess before lunch. As the room emptied, she congratulated Leah on a fine speech, squeezing her hand as a sign of congratulations. "Do sit at our table, dear," she whispered conspiratorially, "I'm sure there will be lots of questions for you."

Leah had hoped to sit with Tan, but there was no way to refuse the invitation. Perhaps, she thought, he would join her. Every few feet, however, someone would stop her to make some comment or ask another question. Both flattered and frustrated by those who would prevent her progress, Leah patiently answered each question, defining terms or adding an extra bit of information. She encouraged those with more complex concerns to come to her afternoon study group, when they could sit outside beneath the trees to discuss Chimu culture in greater depth.

By the time she reached the dining room, Tan was seated at a table with students. There was no vacant seat, but it didn't matter, Leah was already committed to Dr. Ruíz. The saving grace was Consi beside an empty chair, a bright, but definitely sarcastic smile plastered on her face. Greeting the others, Leah sat and waited for the pleasantries to cease before asking Consi why she looked as she did.

"Gúzman is driving me nuts. He keeps asking me if I would mind letting him tape me singing those damn Guatemalan love songs! I think it's weird."

How Consi managed to keep the smile and keep talking was a mystery to Leah. "Don't let it bug you; just be flattered."

Throughout lunch, Leah kept one eye on Tan who seemed to be having a wonderful time. She choked down her salad, picked at her fish, and refused dessert completely. If Consi noticed, she graciously refrained from comment. As soon as she could excuse herself, Leah left the table and hurried to her room. She wanted a few moments to change into comfortable clothing and compose herself before teaching the next session.

ຂ ⊖ ຂ

Tan did not attend her study group. Disappointed, Leah put the feeling aside when she saw the eager faces of her students. There were ten all together, two of whom she had had in seminar during fall quarter; the other six were familiar faces from around both departments. Consi showed up, too; she wanted to watch Leah operate in Spanish. Leading them outside, Leah took them to an area near the beach she had spotted the when she first arrived, where several Adirondack chairs had been arranged in a circle.

She took the one that faced the water and waited while everyone else got settled. "Ready?" she asked when they were seated. "Bueno, then let's talk about customs and traditions which relate to the worship of Mamaquilla."

Leah hardly glanced at the folder lying open in her lap; the subject had become second nature to her, easy to discuss even while explaining the complex system of taboos which underpinned life in the ayllus. She opened her talk with a more complete description of the nine huacas, then moved on to the rites of passage in childhood, adolescence and finally adulthood, each stage of maturity linked to approved and forbidden activities. What seemed to surprise her listeners most was the lack of taboo associated with sexual expression. "Virginity is useful only to a point," explained Leah, "after a girl is no longer a candidate for chinan, her maidenhood is no longer an issue. It is rare for a girl to take multiple lovers, although it happens on occasion; more likely, once a girl and boy become sexually intimate, marriage follows."

"Why?" asked one of the young men. "If there is a laxity of morals, one would think sexual variety would be commonplace."

"Ah," grinned Leah, "you have applied a western standard against non western values. The moral code is quite stringent by their standards; they just have a different sense of what is permissible from what we have. One should never judge by our standards. Fidelity after marriage is a far more important issue than fidelity before."

He was not convinced. "What about the Aclla? You said an infertile woman would seek out the Aclla. How does that stack up in the fidelity department?" He crossed his arms in a way that said he believed he had stumped the prof.

"In a shrinking community, such as the one I observed, reproduction is crucial to survival. When a woman is unable to conceive, it is incumbent upon her to try every method available to change that status...much like a woman might try artificial insemination or fertility drugs here. Only a woman who has never experienced a pregnancy is permitted to seek out the Aclla, and then, if a child is born, he or she is marked in such a way to remind others he or she is such a child. When the time comes for the selection of a spouse; specific taboos prevent the inadvertent marriage to a half-sibling. For three generations, offspring of that child carry quipu that designates their shared status. Again, this prevents inbreeding, a definite danger in a small population." Mentioning the Aclla's role was not as difficult as Leah anticipated, so long as she spoke impersonally about the man who served Mamaquilla. But when asked if she had ever seen the Aclla in the flesh, Leah almost choked.

It was tempting to tell them he walked amongst them, thereby letting the students accost Tan, but she resisted the urge, chalking it up to the mixed emotions she felt at lunch. "Yes," she admitted, hoping she would not blush, "I have seen him." Recklessly, she added, "He is very handsome, taller than almost anyone else in the jungle." She wondered why, in the next second, she felt compelled to say anything at all.

For a while she answered questions about the Aclla, mostly from the women, although the men in the group seemed equally fascinated. One asked how a man managed to live alone in the jungle, serve endless numbers of women, yet remain untouched by his acquired status. "Wouldn't he have some sort of inflated ego problem?" she asked curiously.

Leah shook her head. "Quite the opposite; the Aclla views his role as a duty to Mamaquilla; a holy order. I think he is somewhat in awe of his ability."

"Obviously, you had opportunity to speak with him," said a voice from behind her chair.

Leah did not turn; she did not have to look to know who had spoken. "Yes, but we never engaged in a discussion of his mita. The knowledge I have has been gained from other sources."

Tan strolled around to sit on the grass at the edge of the circle of chairs. "If the Aclla lives alone in the jungle, who could possibly know what he thinks?" The question was without rancor; only a sense of idle curiosity pervaded his words.

"Oh, there are those who know him well," replied Leah meeting his gaze dead on, "who say he is as modest as a chinan when it comes to his unusual talent. There is, of course, the possibility I am wrong."

Tan snorted, but said nothing.

"Aren't you from the same area, Tan?" asked one of the women. "Have you ever seen him?"

It was Leah's turn to snort, but she resisted; instead, she awaited his answer patiently, anxious to see how he would get out of this one.

"Men have little time for this kind of thing," he said airily. "I give it no thought whatsoever." In Leah's eyes, he saw the word *liar*, but he refused to acknowledge it. "I would be interested in hearing about your views on the power of the Mamacuna and the Rimoc, Lee."

He called her *Lee* and it made the little hairs on the nape of her neck tingle. The word slipped from his mouth like a caress and she was not prepared for the power of her own reaction to it. Taking a deep breath, Leah dissected the concepts of ascribed and implied power, linking the role of the mystical Rimoc to life cycle of the population. As dispassionately as she could, Leah spoke about the role the Mamacuna played in daily life, even though she was essentially isolated in Janajpachallacta. "In much the same way the ancient Inca ruled from Cuzco, the Mamacuna has a network of runners and assistants scattered throughout the district who tie the people together. No ayllu is more than five days walk from Janajpachallacta," she explained, "so news can and does travel relatively quickly. But more importantly, the Mamacuna seems to be able to...to..." she found it hard to say the Mamacuna was capable of sending visions although she knew for a fact the old woman did it with great regularity.

"Able to do what, Lee?" drawled Tan, a small smile playing on his lips.

Leah sighed and silently prepared herself for the onslaught she knew would follow her next statement. "The Mamacuna is, to some degree, able to utilize telepathic methods to get her point across." There was a collective gasp from the students, followed by the anticipated rush of questions. Leah held up her hands to halt the chatter and attempted to explain. "I am aware that telepathy is usually construed as mumbo-jumbo, but there are those, especially amongst this tribe, who would debate the issue. Successfully." She allowed herself a stern glance at Tan, dismayed when he flashed a skeptic's smile. Leah wished he would leave.

The session lasted only another few minutes. Several students lingered to chat with the teacher, and Leah was more than relieved when Tan drifted off toward the lodge with a couple of guys. She definitely was not in the mood to fence words with him.

"Y'know, Lee, if I was a student, after listening to you I'd go tripping off to the Andes as fast as my feet could carry me," said Consi as they strolled back to Leah's room.

"Yeah, well, right about now, I would like to run off to the Andes as fast as my feet could carry me," sighed Leah as the reached the steps to her little balcony.

Inside, Consi threw herself across Leah's bed with a groan. "That Tan has the sexiest, come-hither eyes I have ever seen in my life! And what a bod! I would love to run my hands up and down that stomach for a while." When Leah didn't respond, Consi sat up, her back against the headboard. "He's pretty tall for an Indian, isn't he?"

"Yeah, I guess so." Leah busied herself with putting her notes in her briefcase.

"Tall as the Aclla?"

Leah froze, then slowly closed the flap and set the bag beside the desk. "I never noticed," she replied as casually as she could.

"You've seen them together?"

"Consi, what's this sudden interest in the Aclla?" snapped Leah. "If you are so curious, why don't you go off to Peru yourself?"

"Hey, settle down, Lee," protested Consi, her eyes wide open in utter amazement. "Honestly, I didn't mean to tread on sensitive toes. You want to tell me what the hell is wrong? Or do I have to play twenty annoying questions?"

"There is nothing wrong and please don't start with questions. I was up late last night; I'm tired, I guess." She flopped down beside Consi on the bed. "Maybe I'll take a nap. Okay?"

"I'll wake you at four and we'll take a nice walk before dinner."

"Sounds like a plan to me," answered Leah as she closed her eyes. "Go out through the balcony, please, and leave the door part way open. The breeze feels good."

As soon as Consi was gone, Leah fell asleep

She was standing at the end of the path through the jungle, that little rise where the dense foliage abruptly ceased and the grassy field began its upward slope. Leah could see Hector's clinic, the tin roof shimmering in the sunlight. Children's voices were coming from across the field where they played whenever Hector had a free moment. Surely, Hector was throwing a ball to the boys while their mother was working in either the house or the clinic. As was her habit, Leah let loose a shrill, two-fingered whistle to let Hector know she had arrived.

Instead of running towards her as they usually did, the three little boys came as far as the crest of the hill and stood there, staring at her as though she were a stranger. Leah waved, but they did not move. A taller figure joined them, but the sun was behind and Leah could see only the silhouette of the man. When he waved and began to walk down the hill, she could see he leaned heavily on a cane, one arm missing completely, his head wrapped in tattered bandages. He came close enough for her to see his shirt, or what was left of it. Strips of fabric fluttered as he moved, yet they were covered in fresh blood. Leah began to cry "No! No!" as the figure moved closer, the stump of the missing arm outstretched as if to embrace her. "No!" she wailed, unable to either run toward him or flee.

Suddenly, someone grabbed her from behind, pinning her arms, whispering unintelligible words in the ancient dialect used by the Rimoc in only the most secret of ceremonies. Leah thrashed against her captor, flailing her arms, struggling to break free, but his powerful arms were like steel bands around her chest. When his hand covered her mouth, Leah awoke, a scream caught in her throat.

Tan was holding her close against his chest, his mouth beside her ear whispering words of comfort. The struggle ceased and she sagged against him sobbing, her breath coming in short, painful bursts. "Shhh, shhh, Qewa Ñawi, you are safe. Shhhh." Like a father soothing a frightened child, he stroked her hair until she calmed. "Tell me what you dreamed, little chinan," he murmured, loosening his hold.

Slowly, haltingly, Leah told him the truth.

Right at four, Consi headed back to Leah's, rather than call to see if she was awake. Walking around the back, she noticed the door was still open.

Consi went up the steps and was about to go in when she heard soft voices speaking what she assumed was Quechua. On the bed, Tan was holding Leah in his arms as he stroked her long hair. Leah was obviously upset, judging by the way she kept wiping her nose with a tissue. Their heads were bent together, Tan listening to whatever she was saying, replying in short, soothing sounds each time she sobbed. Consi felt she had stopped just shy of intruding on something so intimate that she hurried back down the stairs.

Consi had no desire to return to her own room and settled into an Adirondack chair at the edge of the lawn. Sitting herself down, she made a conscientious effort to put the pieces of the puzzle together. As early as last night, she was certain Leah knew Tan. This morning, around dawn, Consi had gotten out of bed to go to the bathroom and had looked out the window. Coming out of the mists she had seen two people walking; they were too far away to really distinguish and she had assumed they were two of the students, but on second thought, the man was tall, the woman was very short and they could easily have been Tan and Leah. Add to that the element of bearbaiting which occurred at the end of Leah's study session and suddenly they seemed to be far more than casual acquaintances. And the way he held Leah in his arms made Consi dangerously curious. Never one for walking away from a mystery, Consi marched back to Leah's balcony.

CHAPTER 29

This time, when she went up the steps, Consi made enough noise to interrupt anything that might be going on inside the room. She rapped sharply on the doorframe and waited until Leah called to her before she entered. Leah was still sitting on the bed, Tan beside her, a respectable distance between them. "Hi, Lee, ready to go?"

Leah nodded, then looked at Tan. "I think we made the right decision," she said in Quechua, not caring whether or not speaking a foreign language might be considered rude.

"Good," he replied, giving her a warm, reassuring smile. "We will do it after dinner." He rose, then flashed a wide grin at Consi. "Don't let her run you into the ground the way she runs herself," he said in English as he strolled out the back door.

"Well, he seems to know you pretty well," frowned Consi when he was gone. "Now the question remains, how well do you know him?"

Leah shrugged and said nothing.

"Oh, come on, Lee. This is me you're not talking to."

"I know him, okay?"

"I think you know him a lot better than okay. What is going on, Lee?"

"Nothing is going on, Consuela. There's nothing to tell."

"Y'know, Lee, if I didn't happen to know that you have this big thing about honesty, I'd think you weren't being honest at all. I'd think you're lying...if not to me, then to yourself."

"No one is lying to anyone," snapped Leah, suddenly very angry. "Who I know and how well I know them is really my business, isn't it?"

"Yes, it is. But it becomes other people's business when you start acting weird...and you're acting weird now."

"I am not acting weird."

"Oh, yes you are." Consi narrowed her eyes and pursed her lips before she blurted out, "He *is* your lover, isn't he?" And as soon as the words were out of her mouth, she regretted saying them.

Without a word, Leah stalked into the bathroom and slammed the door.

သာ ⊖ ော

Leah stood beneath the shower letting the water pour over her. Afterward, wrapped in a towel, she called the desk and left a wake-up call for five-thirty that would leave her enough time to dress for dinner. Curling up beneath the covers, Leah tried to sleep but could not. She got up and turned on the television, found an old movie, and went back to bed. The drone of the dialogue finally lulled her to sleep.

သာ ⊖ ော

The bar was crowded when Leah arrived at the lodge. Nudging her way to the bar, she ordered a drink and stood chatting with Dr. Gúzman. When the dining room doors opened, she allowed the old gent to escort her to the faculty table where Dr. Ruíz was busily assigning places for the sake of interesting conversation. Consi was nowhere to be seen, but Leah did not care; she had no desire to be with her now.

"I want to congratulate you on an outstanding lecture this morning," said Dr. Muñoz with obvious pleasure as he joined her at the table. "And I heard your study session was equally exceptional." He fairly beamed at Leah.

Señora Muñoz leaned over her husband to add her own congratulations. "I wanted to come to the session, but my little one fell asleep after lunch and I was confined to quarters. Such is the life of a mother," she laughed. "Eduardito said he would be quiet if I took him to your class, Lee," said the señora, "but the baby-sitter we had last night let him stay up too late."

"Tell him that I missed him today."

Dr. Muñoz chuckled, knowing well his youngest son harbored a crush on the pretty student. "He will be delighted to hear that."

That settled, the talk turned to more timely topics. Leah relaxed, relieved to be with people she liked, discussing things about which she was passionate. The dinner was another delicious example of local cuisine, although Leah again chose fish over the meat entrée. Her teachers were well aware of her preference to observe Jewish dietary laws; indeed, she had earned a great deal of respect because of it. Toward the middle of dinner, Dr. Muñoz brought up the subject.

"How *did* you manage in the ayllu?" he asked with a good-natured grin. "Surely there was no kosher butcher nearby!"

Leah returned his smile with one of her own, explaining that due to the abundance of crops and the high value of the llama herd, meat was rarely served. "And, once I became a chinan, there was no question of my eating meat; it was not permitted. When I first arrived, the women of the ayllu thought I was a little strange because I declined meat at a festival, and some whispered I might even be a spy from the Mamacuna. Saba, our local collahuaya, thought *that* was outrageously funny."

There was a lull in the conversation and Dr. Gúzman took the opening to address Leah. "I am afraid I might have said something untoward this morning when I mentioned your friend, Dr. Morales."

"Why would you think so, Doctor Gúzman?" asked Leah, curious.

"Because that Peruvian fellow approached me this afternoon and questioned me rather carefully about it. I told him I knew very little, but that you would certainly know more. Hasn't he spoken to you about it?"

"As a matter of fact, he has." Leah looked up and caught Tan looking at her from a table across the room. He picked up his wrist and discreetly touched his watch. She nodded imperceptibly and was relieved to see him turn away. A moment later, he left his seat and walked toward the lobby.

Dr. Gúzman did not notice the exchange. "He seemed greatly agitated; I take it he knows Morales."

Leah felt compelled to explain at least some of her actions. "I was instructed not to tell him because Dr. Morales thought he might leave

campus and rush home. The danger of that is past, so no harm was done."
She gave him a warm smile and hoped he believed her.

Judging by the slight squirm, Dr. Muñoz decided this was not a subject
his prized pupil cared to discuss. With the seamless agility for which he was
justly noted, he drew Dr. Gúzman into a conversation about symbols in
Chilean folk tales. When he was convinced he had sufficiently stimulated
a new topic of conversation, he leaned over to Leah and whispered, "Tan
just went out; I saw his sign to you before, when he touched his watch. Go
on, I'll cover for you." He gave her a quick grin.

"Thanks," murmured Leah, grateful for his sharp eye. She waited for an
appropriate moment and then excused herself.

ᴥ ⊖ ᴥ

Tan was waiting on the deck, stretched out on the lounge, his eyes closed.
Leah was tempted to kiss him, but resisted, instead she told him to wait
while she went through the front door of the room. A moment later, she
slid open the glass door and beckoned him inside.

"We'll call Miguel first then I'll call to Peru," she said, digging his card
out of her purse. When Miguel answered on the second ring, Leah motioned to Tan to come sit beside her on the bed. "Tan would like to talk to
you," she told the attaché before she handed Tan the phone.

In rapid Quechua, Tan fired questions at Miguel, hardly pausing to
wait for the answers. As best she could, Leah followed the conversation,
leaning close to Tan as he held the receiver at an angle so she could hear.
Tan concentrated on what action was being taken to protect the people
and Janajpachallacta, offering information about how the Rimoc might be
approached should it be necessary. Miguel seemed grateful, asked several
questions of his own, and was relieved by Tan's willingness to answer them.

"I will go home after the end of the quarter if you believe it will help,"
said Tan. "My concern is only to protect them, not to bring more outsiders
into our world. Do you understand this, Ayar Monsonsoré?"

"It may be necessary, but I cannot give you an answer at this time. I will
be in touch." He asked to talk to Leah. "You are doing the right thing, Lee,"

he reassured her. "Tan is a valuable asset; his influence with the Mamacuna cannot be discounted. But if he goes, we want you to go with him."

Leah looked at Tan who stood at the window staring out over the lawn. "If that's what it takes, Miguel, that's what we'll do."

"Call me if you need me," he told her before hanging up.

As soon as there was dial tone, Leah pressed the long series of numbers required to reach Felipe Segura in Piura. The phone rang repeatedly and Leah was about to give up when a breathless voice answered. "*El médico, por favor*," she said and then waited for the doctor to take the call. "How is Hector?" was the first question she asked.

"Mean as ever!" was the laughing response. "He is doing very well, if his irascibility is any indication. He has no patience for being a patient."

Relieved, Leah explained Tan was with her and wanted to talk to him. Dr. Segura assured her he would answer any questions Tan might have. Again, Leah handed over the phone.

"How serious are his wounds?" asked Tan in Spanish. He listened intently as Dr. Segura explained the nature of the damage and the prognosis for recovery. He seemed accepting of what the doctor told him and then asked about the duration of the Mamacuna's visit. "Did she say anything to you about what she might do?"

"Only that she was prepared to move the people away from the danger. She said there were places they could go, where the outsiders could not touch them."

Tan knew immediately what she meant. There were places to the north and east of where they were now which could support the ayllus should they leave the place where they had lived for hundreds of years. It would be, Tan knew, a long, arduous trek but it could be done. "How long do you think they are safe?" he asked, his voice tight.

"We don't know. Paolo has been back and forth three times this week, circling over the area looking for evidence of any exploration, but other than the camp he saw on the ridge to the south of Janajpachallacta, he has seen nothing unusual," explained Segura. "There is, however, a reliable source in Sullana who says a representative of Terra Nueva Mining was outfitting an expedition to head southeast toward Jaén."

"What were they doing in Sullana?" asked Tan. Jaén was the closest town to Janajpachallacta, though not a place the people usually went.

"He said the expedition was originating in Chiclayo, but would actually depart from Sullana. They were looking for a native guide."

"Did they find one?"

"No. The area is not one the locals wish to travel; I think they are afraid of what's up there." Dr. Segura laughed, a short, harsh sound. "Your people are the most peaceful on the face of the earth, but they are, in common understanding, fiercely protective of their own. Everyone north of Trujillo knows this and no one wants to take *los destructores* into the jungle or the highlands. No one knows what to expect up there."

The news pleased Tan immensely. "Good, let them think what they want, Doctor. In fact, tell your contact in Sullana to pass the word that the people are on to them and will permit no one to travel past Huacachimu unless they have a desire to die, for the mountain spirits will not let them pass. They might not know exactly where it is, but they will not venture out to find it, especially the people of Jaén. They want nothing to do with us and that is for the best. Tell Paolo what I have said and he will know what to do with the information. I expect by week's end, the Mamacuna will be plotting with the Rimoc."

"I will do what you ask, but I will tell Hector the orders come from you."

"Hector will understand." Tan paused to take a breath. "And tell Hector for me, my respect is his." Then he added, "and my grades are good."

Dr. Segura laughed heartily. "That will make him feel much better. He has been worried that if you knew all this, you would forget to study."

Tan did not tell him he had just learned the news, but he did reassure this janpeq that his hard work would continue. Satisfied with the conversation, he handed the phone to Leah.

"Give Hector my love," she instructed the doctor, "and tell him that everything here is all right. The Ayar Monsonsoré is a good friend and a strong support."

As soon as the connection was broken, Tan told Leah to call Miguel. "He must know what I have told the doctor; it would not serve to have him surprised by this information."

ℰ ⊖ ℱ

They returned to the main lodge in time to hear Dr. Muñoz speak on the importance of folk tales and myths in the development of modern cultural mores. Tan and Leah sat together at the back of the room where he clasped her hand in his. Leah did not object; as long as his flesh was against hers, she felt safe.

CHAPTER 30

The hospital in Piura was small, clean and very busy. Ensconced in a private room overlooking the hospital's courtyard garden, Hector was sitting up in bed arguing with the Mother Superior about the diet she prescribed. "I may have a colostomy, Sister, but I am a hungry man with a great need for food that tastes like something other than boiled quinoa!" he shouted, waving his good arm in her face. "Get me something reasonable to eat!"

The nun was unmoved; her clear, smooth face remained impassive against his demands. "Are you finished?" she asked with measured patience.

"Food, Sister; I need food. I will not improve if I do not eat!"

"Nor will you improve if you remain in this state of constant agitation, Hector Morales. Now get a grip on yourself and stop making trouble in my hospital." She allowed herself a small, triumphant smile when he thumped against the pillows. "There, that is so much better. When Dr. Segura arrives, I will relay your message and allow him to decide what is best for you." She removed her hands from beneath the folds of her flowing habit. "If you promise to behave yourself, I will give you these." She splayed open a fan of magazines.

Hector laughed and held up his hand in mock surrender. "I promise to be good. May I please have the journals, dear Sister María Ynez?"

She dropped them in his lap and turned to leave. At the door, she paused and shot back "Sister gives and sister can just as easily take away if sister thinks the patient is being uncooperative." She chuckled as she disappeared down the highly polished hallway.

Felipe Segura found Hector, glasses perched on his nose, studying the New England Journal of Medicine. "Ah, I see the good sister finally coughed up the journals I gave her yesterday. What did she make you promise in order to get them?"

"To behave myself: a difficult, if not impossible feat. But I shall try." Hector removed his specs and placed them on the table. "So, how am I, amigo?"

"Doing quite well, considering your blood pressure goes up and down like an elevator. Hector, if you want to come to my house, you have got to keep yourself calm. I won't take you out of here unless you stabilize."

"I am as stable as ever," protested Hector.

"Not good enough. I'm talking about normal people. I will not subject my housekeeper to a raging maniac, not to mention the children or my wife." Felipe sat on the edge of the bed and began checking his handiwork. "You will have some very sexy scars, Hector. Líuta won't be able to keep her delicate little hands off you when you get home."

"Bah! Líuta had better keep her delicate little hands off me. I am not in the market for a wife."

"God knows you need one, old man. She says you need the 'loving guidance of a good woman to straighten you around,' and that's a direct quote."

"Since when do you talk to Líuta, Filo?"

"Since she made Paolo call me on your telephone two days ago. Actually, she makes Paolo call me every time he lands."

"How are things up there?"

"Fine. Your lady friend is holding down the fort admirably, dispensing antibiotic creams and the occasional acetaminophen tablet with great aplomb... according to Paolo. I've now got two residents rotating up there."

Hector grunted his approval. "What about the Mamacuna? Anyone see her?"

"She came down to the clinic with a couple of her buddies two days ago. She wanted to hear from Paolo's own mouth that you were still alive. Paolo is planning on coming over this evening, if you are up to it."

Hector nodded. "I'll try to stay awake."

"I spoke to Leah and Tan last night."

Hector's head snapped up. "Tan knows?"

"Tan knows." Felipe repeated gist of his conversation with Tan.

"He is amazing!" whispered Hector when he heard Tan's message about the Huacachimu. "Tan's understanding of human nature is far beyond anything I might have ever hoped. He's right, you know. If the people withstood the Incas and survived, our little band will survive this. They may be a peaceful people, but it is not beyond them to fight back."

"But they will lose against modern warfare if it comes to that, Hector," said Felipe with sadness. "All they can hope for is delay."

"And delay may be all they need to move further into the mountains. They are not as attached to that little district as one might think."

"I hope you're right."

Hector smiled, but it was not a happy look. "Can you be here when Paolo comes? I would like you to tell him exactly what Tan told you."

"Fair enough. I'll be here." Digging into the pocket of his coat, Segura pulled out a pack of envelopes. "Are you up to a little mail today, Hector?"

"Sure, why not." He accepted the packet and began sorting through them, separating the envelopes into neat little piles.

The two men continued to talk for a few minutes and the conversation ended with the doctor promising to tell the nuns to vary Hector's diet, providing it remained bland. When he finally left, Segura felt Hector was in infinitely better spirits.

ം ⊖ ം

The thick envelope from the bank was the first piece of mail Hector tackled. Ripping it open, he studied the documents carefully, not at all surprised that Tan had transferred a significant sum of money to the United States. The accompanying letter explained in detail the reasons for the transfer, all logical and certainly understandable. Hector had wondered how long it would be before Tan figured out he could earn a better rate on his money in the States than he could in Peru.

The second piece he opened was from Arne Halstaad. In his precise writing, Arne told of how Tan had bought a car and how the decision to move the funds had been reached. *Politically speaking*, wrote Arne, *it is better to have the money here and invested than to leave it in Peru. As to any question you might have about Tan's suddenly becoming a spendthrift, forget it; he's as tight as you are.* The remainder of the letter was the usual banter between good friends, ranging from Tan's academic progress to other, assorted observations.

There were two other letters from Tan, both newsy and obviously blissfully unaware of what was going on. He never mentioned Leah, which did not surprise Hector, but he did write at great length about the options being presented to him by his advisor and asked Hector for his thoughts.

Satisfied with the news from the north, Hector refolded his letters, put them in the drawer, and went to sleep. There was only so much excitement he could handle in one sitting.

❧ ⊖ ❧

The Mamacuna sat on her stone seat and listened to the reports of chasquis who had come from all over the district bearing news. The people had been frightened by the attack on their healer, angry and seeking revenge for what they considered an act of open warfare. The Mamacuna was not willing to either agree or disagree, instead she asked that each ayllu send representation to a council to be held at Janajpachallacta. The chasquis had been sent, and now returned with the word that all ayllus would comply and the council would be convened on the night of the half-moon. Already, delegates were beginning to arrive.

Some questioned the delay in beginning the meetings, but the Mamacuna only held up her hands to silence them. She was waiting for the last chasqui, the one who now sat at the clinic awaiting the arrival of the flying man. Mamacuna wanted him at the council, the first time this outsider would be welcomed to speak amongst them. She knew the flying man had been carefully watching the district from the eye of his silver bird and she wanted the others to hear what he had to say.

Saba stood beside the Mamacuna, her thin shoulders covered with a thick, woolen cloak. Ever since the last equinox, she had been attending the High Priestess as her first assistant, learning her ways, practicing the art of visions and prophecy. At first, she was surprised by her own ability, although Saba had used the ways of the mind to communicate before. She was not in the habit of using coca, but the Mamacuna had carefully selected leaves for her to chew before going into deep meditation. Her senses heightened, Saba could hear clearly the sounds of the animals in the mountains when before she could only hear faint noise. Each trance taught her something new. When she watched the jonchi, she saw nuance when before she saw only the column of smoke. The Mamacuna wanted her to rely more on her own interpretations than on what she thought the Rimoc wanted to hear. The first time the Mamacuna ordered her to read the jonchi to the assembled mystics, Saba had done so nervously. When it was over and the Mamacuna accepted her prophecy, Saba was so relieved she nearly fainted. Now she was more comfortable in her new role, but she worried that there would not be enough time to learn everything the Mamacuna had to teach. Every night, Saba would lie on her pallet of vicuña skins and whisper prayers to Mamaquilla to protect her Coya; so far, Mamaquilla seemed to heed her words. Despite all the hardship and strain she suffered in these last weeks, the Mamacuna seemed stronger than ever, but she tired more quickly, cutting her meetings with the Rimoc short so she could have time to lie down.

The Mamacuna motioned to Saba to come closer. "They are almost here," she whispered. "I want you to listen closely to what the flying man has to say; he will be our link to safe haven."

Saba shuddered. Without being told in words, she knew their time in this place was at an end. "Will he lead us to safety?" she asked.

"No," answered the Mamacuna, "but he will help us to find it."

ം ⊖ ം

The sun was almost at its zenith when the chasqui arrived with Paolo. He approached the Mamacuna and dropped to his knees, his head bowed, his fingers touching his lips repeatedly. "I have done as you asked, Coya," he said loud enough for everyone present to hear. "I have flown above the jungles and the mountains and I have seen many things."

"What have you seen, my son?" asked the Mamacuna, certain she already knew.

"Little has changed, but there are six more tents at the edge of the mountain. No more equipment, just tents. I have had word from a friend from afar and he gives good counsel."

"What is his counsel?" asked the Mamacuna.

The pilot took a deep breath and recited exactly what Hector had told him to say. "A friend has sent a message to those in the towns who would dare to travel this road. He has warned them not to pass the Huacachimu lest they be destroyed by the mountain spirits. The history of the people is known to them; we survived the Incas, we resisted the conquistadors, we can resist them."

The use of *we* was not lost on the Mamacuna. She cackled with glee as she patted his dark head. "Our friend has spoken well," she told the gathering. "The message he brings from Ruti-Suyu is a wise one. It will make them hesitate, giving us time to make plans." With great effort, the Mamacuna rose. "Come, my son, walk with me. I would speak to you without listening ears." She led him a short distance away from the circle. "Our Aclla continues to serve us," she said, grinning broadly.

"You know who sent the message?"

"There is much your mother has not taught you, son of Camica." She saw his eyes widen. "There is little I do not already know about you, Paolo. Despite your upbringing, you are to be trusted." She stopped walking when she reached the brink of a cliff. The moon was just visible in the twilight, a pale disc in the fading daylight. "Hector has told me you have good, accurate maps of the mountains and pictures taken from the sky. Is this so?"

"Yes, Coya, this is so."

"Bring to me whatever you have. I have a plan."

Paolo was amazed and curious. "Have you seen maps before, Coya?" he asked as politely as possible.

The Mamacuna arched a gray eyebrow at him. "I have seen maps, churi, and what I do not know, you will teach me." She extended a long, bony finger northward. "There is a place one full moon cycle from here, where the people once lived long ago. My chasqui tells me it is still there, uninhabited and difficult to reach. The water is clean, the land suitable for planting our crops, and there are places in the mountains where we can graze our herds. It will be a difficult journey. We will be able to take only the strongest animals with us, and I worry about leading my people away from here. If you help us, it will be easier on them."

This is a set-up, thought Paolo. She wanted him to do something and he knew he would agree to whatever terms she laid out. "What would you have me do, Coya?"

"Follow us. Each night, before the sun disappears, look for us from the air. On your maps, we will mark out the route we shall take, and each evening, we will camp and listen for sound. Then I will send a sign."

"What sign, Coya, would penetrate the canopy of the jungle?"

"A fire stick." She paused, knitting her brows together for a thoughtful moment, then smiled. "*Una pistola llamarada*," she said in Spanish, "like the one Hector sometimes uses."

"A flare gun?" repeated Paolo.

"Yes, exactly. You will bring it to me and teach me to use it. When we hear your noise, I will shoot one flare if everything is fine, two if we are in trouble. Just like Hector."

"When do you want to do this, Coya?"

"After the solstice. We will celebrate Intip Raimi at Janajpachallacta and make our final preparations at that time." Obviously, the decision had already been made and the Mamacuna needed only confirmation from the unsuspecting Paolo. "Well?"

"I will do as you ask, Coya."

"Good. Let us return to the council."

The Rimoc were standing exactly as they had left them, faces drawn, all eyes on the odd couple as they returned to the circle. Patiently, they waited while the Mamacuna allowed Paolo to escort her to her seat, then step back and drop to his knees again. She raised her hands, spreading them wide as if to embrace the people. When she spoke, her voice was clear and strong. "We have grown comfortable living on this land. But it is the will of Viracocha that we leave this place to preserve the ways of our ancestors." A murmur arose from the assembly, and the Mamacuna stilled it with a wave of her hand. "We will leave this place, under the eye of Mamaquilla after the night of Intip Raimi, but we will not go alone. The silver bird will watch us from the sky and keep us safe from those who would harm us." She paused, then gently placed her hands atop Paolo's head. "You will be known in your mita to Mamaquilla as *Ayar Kuntar*. As we have watched the progress of the condor from the ground, we will now watch for you."

∾ ⊖ ∾

Paolo returned to Piura in the morning and went immediately to the hospital. Hector listened to his report and supported the Mamacuna's request for maps and flares. "She's not stupid, Paolo," said Hector, his face grim. "She knows what she's asking and it's to their advantage that we do as she asks." He did not mention that ultimately he would follow them into the jungle; that would be saved for another time. "Take two sets of everything with you, Paolo, then keep one set for us. Let no one know what you are doing."

"It's a damn good thing I don't work for anyone, Hector. This is going to take a lot of fuel."

"Don't worry about the money, Paolo. Mamaquilla will provide." Hector leaned back against his pillows and closed his eyes. He was stuck in the hospital, unable to help, and angry about it. At least he had Paolo to represent him. He opened his eyes again and looked at the pilot. "Keep me informed, and I will, in turn, send the word to the north. If you see or hear anything unusual, let me know. And thank you, Paolo. What you are doing will, in the end, save a people who otherwise would be swallowed up."

The pilot smiled grimly. "No thanks are necessary, Hector. I will do whatever has to be done."

When Paolo had gone, Hector rang for the nurse. "Sister, would you know of someone who could write a letter for me?" he asked in his sweetest voice.

The nun looked at him dubiously. "I am sure I can find someone, Dr. Morales. Are you sure you are up to it?"

"Undoubtedly, sister. And I shall rest more comfortably once the letter is written."

"If you promise you will sleep until lunch, I will promise to send you a scribe this afternoon. Deal?"

"Deal."

CHAPTER 31

Throughout the night, whenever Leah would open her eyes, she would reach out to assure herself Tan still lay beside her in the large bed. There was so much to learn about each other; they took their time exploring. Between lovemaking, they lay face to face, talking about little things they had never spoken of before.

Tan was standing at the sliding glass door looking out over Black Heron Lake when Leah awoke in the morning. "Inti-Illa has come to greet the people," she said, the traditional first words of the morning.

"And Mamaquilla has gone to tend to the children of the night," replied Tan, crossing to the bed in a few long strides. He knelt down so his face was at the same level as hers. "You are so beautiful in the morning, Qewa Ñawi, that my breath leaves my body."

Propped up on her elbow, Leah giggled and brushed a light kiss against his lips. "And you, Aclla, are a restless sleeper and a bed hog." She liked the way he reddened all the way to his ears. "I won't mind, so long as it is only my bed you hog."

Tan deftly caught her arm, toppling Leah to the mattress and leapt on top of her. His mouth took possession of hers while his hands pinned her down; she was not an unwilling victim. Answering each of his kisses with one of her own, Leah yielded to him, giving as much as she was taking from him. Their coupling was quick, fired by their thirst for each other, a need fulfilled only by joining as one, two parts of a single whole. Leah pressed against him, and Tan answered with deep, penetrating thrusts reaching to the end of her soul. Rhythmically, they moved together, each finding in the other the part missing in the one. Lying together in the damp afterglow, they laughed into each other's eyes, reveling in the miracle that they were, at last, together.

The telephone startled them. She picked it up, only to be relieved by the smooth tone of the desk clerk's reminder that this was a wake-up call. Languorously, Leah stretched against Tan's lean body. "We have to shower and go to breakfast," she said gravely. "Not that I want to get out of bed…"

"But you have to," he finished for her. With a swat on her backside, he untangled the sheets. "Come, let us stand beneath the water and imagine we are at the huaca."

ᴇᴧ ⊖ ᴧᴇ

When they walked into the dining room together, several pairs of eyebrows shot up, not the smallest of which belonged to Dr. Muñoz. The wife poked her husband, and the professor grinned. "Somehow," she whispered, "they look right together."

Little Eduardo left his place at his mother's side and went bounding up to Leah. "Come sit with me, Lee," he demanded indignantly, "I haven't heard one good story all weekend and it's almost over!"

"Let's see……there's a nice table set for two, so shall we go?" She gave Tan a quick glance and saw him nod.

Like the gentleman his father expected him to be, Eduardo extended his arm for the lady. "May I escort you to our table, señorita?"

"Why certainly, señor; I'd be delighted." Linking her arm through his, Leah and Eduardo strolled over to the table set for two beside the window overlooking the lake.

ᴇᴧ ⊖ ᴧᴇ

Leah attended the morning lecture, sitting between Tan and Eduardo, who promptly fell asleep with his head in her lap. "You look wonderful with a child beside you," murmured Tan into her ear. "You will look even better with our child in your arms."

She turned bright red, but Leah didn't care. She liked the feel of his words against her skin as well as the implication. A few days ago, if someone had asked if she would like to be a mother, she may have demurred; now she would scream *yes* a thousand times over. And there was no question in her mind that when she bore a child, that child would be Tan's. It was as if she suddenly had answers to all the questions in the world.

From his place at the podium, Dr. Muñoz could see Leah with Tan and little Eduardo. His wife, he decided, was right. There was an aura around them, the connection between them visible to anyone who bothered to look. As he spoke on the changing roles of courtship, marriage and kinship in Latin American societies, the words became even more meaningful when he noticed the way Tan spoke to and looked at the woman beside him. In the same moment, he realized the relationship had not just begun, but had been forged long before that, while Leah was in Peru.

❧ ⊖ ❧

Muñoz was not the only one to notice. Consi Ruíz spied them the moment they entered the dining room at breakfast; the intimate way they touched hands before Leah went off to sit with Eduardo. A twinge of jealousy nagged at her, but Consi dismissed it as the lack of man in her own life. Still, something had clearly changed in the last twenty-four hours and she made up her mind to discover what exactly it was.

As soon as the last question was asked and her mother recessed the conference for lunch, Consi made a beeline for Leah. Standing before them, the words to her questions froze in her mouth. Tan's face gave nothing away; his eyes looked down at her impassively, while Leah, dwarfed by his size, merely smiled. Clearing her throat, she finally was able to speak. "We need to talk, Lee," she said quickly before her courage deserted her, grabbing Leah's arm. "I promise to have her back to you before the end of salad."

"I'm not mad at you," whispered Leah as Consi dragged her into the bar, "even though I probably should be."

"I wanted to apologize for what happened yesterday. I feel really bad about what I said. It was crass, stupid and...and....."

"Yeah, but there's no need to apologize, Consi. I was upset, that's all. Not at you. Just so much is happening so fast that I can't process it. What you said just made me realize this was all going to be very public very soon. But how did you know?"

Consi was relieved Leah was not angry with her. "I saw Tan holding you in your room yesterday," she confessed, her eyes on her hands. "I'd come to get you, and when I went up the back way, I saw you with him. I guess I assumed."

"It doesn't matter. I was less than honest with you about him. I'm the one who should be apologizing."

"Do you want to talk about it?"

"Yes, but not now. Later....when we can sit down and have an uninterrupted stretch of time."

A great sigh came from Consi, and a smile finally appeared. "Okay, Lee, so long as you promise to tell me the truth, the whole truth, and nothing but the truth, so help you Mamaquilla."

Leah agreed. *I might as well get used to talking about it*, she thought; there were going to be a lot of questions from a lot of people who deserved honest answers.

ɘ⊝ɞ

"Is everything all right?" asked Tan as soon as she joined him in the dining room.

"Yes, Consi wanted to apologize for something she said yesterday." Leah did not say what, nor did Tan ask; privacy was sacrosanct. "I told her we'd have a chance to talk later, when we drive back down to the cities."

"Are you going with her?" asked Tan, sounding rather disappointed. "I hoped you would drive with me."

"With you?"

Tan grinned like a child with a new toy. "In my car."

"You didn't tell me you bought a car."

"You didn't ask." He put his lips close to her ear, nibbling as he spoke. "There are a great many things I haven't told you yet."

Leah giggled at the chills running up and down her spine. "Like what?"

"Like my car is red and has a sunroof and a great stereo. It's very...." he paused to find just the right word in English, "sexy....like you."

"Beast!" she growled, only to be rewarded by tiny kisses on her earlobe.

"You have yet to see, to feel the beast in me," he whispered.

Leah looked up to see several familiar faces staring at her. "I think people are watching," she said in Quechua.

"Let them watch. They are jealous."

A sigh escaped Leah's lips as she turned toward him. "One of us has a reputation to maintain."

"With thanks to Mamaquilla, it's not me this time." Tan let a slow, lazy smile beam in her direction.

She rolled her eyes, then patted him on the cheek. "Then don't destroy mine. I've worked too hard to have you turn me into a wanton before all these people." She smiled sweetly and added, "Besides, I am still a self-respecting chinan who should not be shamed in public."

∼ ⊖ ∾

After lunch, Dr. Ruíz spoke briefly, her remarks serving as the conclusion for the conference. As the participants left the dining room, a sort of reception line formed in the lobby. Leah took her place between Dr. Muñoz and Dr. Costanzo even though she would see most of the students around campus in the coming weeks. Shaking an endless line of hands, Leah answered a few last questions, complimented the more active participants, and generally felt, for the first time, like a real professor.

When the line dwindled, Dr. Muñoz shook her hand and congratulated her. "You have made me very proud, Leah. I admit I was a bit nervous at having a new doctoral candidate serving on this faculty, but the fear was misplaced. Your sessions were excellent. You have once again confirmed the respect you have earned."

"Thank you," replied Leah, feeling as though her head was in the clouds. "I enjoyed myself immensely and learned a lot as well. And I'll admit I was probably as nervous about this as you were."

"I hope you and Tan will come to the house for dinner in the very near future."

His words served as a sort of seal of approval on what Leah knew he had seen in the last few hours. "We would be delighted, Dr. Muñoz."

"And I think, Ms. Fine," he added with a twinkle, "that it is high time you called me Diego."

Consi was standing outside Egret House, her bags beside her. As soon as Leah appeared, she waved her over. "We can leave as soon as you're ready," she said brightly.

"Would you be very hurt if I didn't go back with you?" Leah asked as gently as she could.

"No," replied Consi, still smiling, although not as broadly. "I kinda expected that. Not to worry, my mother asked if she could come with me, anyway."

"And you said yes?"

"We haven't had much time together since I got home. One of those mother/daughter things. You know...."

Leah grinned at Consi. "Yeah, I know. I have a mother, too."

"Maybe you and Tan could come over to my place for dinner one night. I'd like to get to know him....as your squeeze."

With a promise she would try, Leah trotted down the path to Loon House to collect her things. Tan said he would meet her in fifteen minutes at the lobby and she did not want to keep him waiting.

&ebdc; ⊖ ⊙

"What a car!" whistled Leah when she saw Tan leaning against his cherry red Mazda. "Whew! I hope you took a picture to send to Hector."

He tossed her luggage in the trunk, then opened the door for Leah. "I'm not sure Hector would approve," he said with a small frown.

"Approve? He would love it! It's just the kind of car Hector would adore."

Tan slid behind the wheel and carefully fastened his seat belt. He methodically checked his mirrors, and gently turned the key. He smiled at the smooth hum of the engine and slowly eased the car down the gravel road leading to the highway.

"Do you like music in the car?" asked Tan with a silly grin. Leah nodded, and he offered to play her his favorite song. "It is a good song for walking in the yunka."

Leah sat up a little straighter in her seat. "Is it a traditional song?" she asked. "Maybe it's one I know."

His grin widened as he pushed the tape into the stereo. A moment passed before the unmistakable strains of The Police filled the small space. Leah's hands flew to her cheeks; she could feel them grow hot and red. Tan chuckled at her discomfort.

"Every breath you take, every move you make, every bond you break, every step you take, I'll be watching you.........." He sang along with the tape.

Leah was frozen in her seat. He had heard her as she walked in the jungle. Had she known, would she have sung so loudly? At the same time, she marveled that he remembered it well enough to find it. Surely he had no idea what the words were, what they meant, even the tune itself must have been strange to him. But he was singing it now; he obviously knew the words well, and he reached for her hand to pull it from her face.

"It's not a nice song," she admitted. "It's about someone spying on you and not in a nice way." She saw his face fall. "I used to sing it because I knew everyone was always watching me. It was...kinda....funny, at least to me."

"Do not be ashamed, Qewa Ñawi," he chided, "this was the song I carried in my heart in months we were separated. You did not sing it only in the yunka, you sang it when you walked on the campus. I heard you. Over and over I would hear this song in my dreams. It was not hard to find it once I came here. It was my....my...," he searched for the proper word, found it and smiled broadly when he said, "anthem."

Leah found it curious that he spoke English; it was something she found almost odd, yet endearing. His accent had the gentle slur of the jungle, making his pronunciation almost erotic when he spoke. "You never cease to surprise me," she said softly.

"I told you before, there are many things you do not know about me, but you'll learn."

Kicking off her sneakers, Leah tucked her legs beneath her. "Why don't you tell me something I don't know, then I will tell you something you don't know."

"Okay," he drawled, his brows knitting a straight line over his dark eyes. "You do not know my name."

"Of course I know your name. Tan Villac-Quilla."

"Wrong."

"Wrong?"

"My name is Na-Tan Manco. It was the name given to me by my grandfather when I was born. My father is Manco."

"Like the first Inca?"

Tan smiled at the reference to the history of his people. "It was given to my father because my grandfather was a mulkan who brought new blood to our people. The collahuaya said the name Manco was a powerful one, belonging to a man of great strength. She was certain my father would be a man of great strength because his father, my grandfather, was so powerful." His voice grew soft at the memory of Iztak.

"And is he?"

"Without me around, my father is the tallest man in the yunka. And," he grinned, "I like to believe the strongest."

"And your mother? You told me a little about her last night, but not enough."

"My mother is a flower, the kind woman who loves her husband and her children more than her own life. Her name is Cura, and she is little, but strong, with kind eyes and gentle smile. She will like you, Qewa Ñawi, because you love her son in spite of who he is."

Leah understood he meant in spite of his place amongst the people. "Do you write to her?"

"I send messages through Hector. He tells me she worries."

"Like any other mother."

"Like any other mother," he echoed. "Sometimes my head tells me I will not see her again, but I do not believe that in my heart."

Leah reached over and touched his warm cheek. "Are you homesick, Na-Tan Manco?"

The way she said his name touched his heart. "Yes and no. The day I became Aclla, I was set apart from my people. I knew this would be and did not want to go when the chasqui tapped my shoulder. I went knowing I would never return to my ayllu to live as a man should live."

"Will you go back to live there?"

"How? Why? I can no more go back there to live than you could go back to live at your mother's house." He did not tell her of the visions he had had, the ones that told him there would be nothing to go back to.

Her lips suddenly dry, Leah chewed at them thoughtfully. She sensed he was not being completely honest, yet she did not want to challenge him. "What about during the summer, like Miguel suggested?"

"I will return if it will help, but I will not stay. That would dishonor Hector's wishes and I will not do that. What about you?"

Leah sat silently for a moment. "Yes, I will go with you."

For the longest time, neither spoke. Finally, Tan said, "Tell me something about you that I do not know."

"Like you," she said slowly, "I have visions. I had them long before I ever went to the yunka, but until I began to have them here... after I came back, I did not know what they meant."

"Tell me, what have you seen?"

"I used to dream of walking in a jungle and I just assumed it meant that one day I would. I never gave it a lot of thought. "

"Is that all?"

Leah shook her head. "I sometimes saw eyes watching me. Dark eyes," she whispered, looking away from him, out the windshield.

"My eyes." It was not a question.

"Your eyes," she said, "but I didn't know they were your eyes." Leah leaned back against the headrest and closed her eyes. "I used to think, when I was little, that I would marry a man with dark eyes. Maybe that's why I never said yes when Jay asks. His eyes are blue."

"Does he ask often?"

"He used to."

"But he no longer asks. Have you turned him away?"

Leah smiled at the way he put it. "Yes, I suppose I have."

Tan reached for her hand and held it tight in his. "That is good. I do not wish to share you with him."

"Do I share you with India?"

"No, you do not. You have never shared me with anyone."

His tone told Leah the subject was closed, but she did not mind. Warmth flowed from him into her, giving her a peace she had never known before. It was enough just to be in the car with him; words were unnecessary as long as Tan held her hand.

Driving down the highway, Leah listened to Tan as he sang some of the songs of his childhood, the same ones she had heard in her ayllu. Through half-closed eyes, she studied the profile beside her. His nose was a straight line, almost arrogant in the way it sloped to the narrow nostrils above full, dark lips. The skin of his cheeks was smooth, almost untouched by the bristles most western men scraped away daily. His eyes, set on the road, were almond shaped, but not narrow, as if they were designed to take in the world. His lashes were very long, dark and thick, providing a curtain between his eyes and the sky. When he was at ease, the high cheekbones were less prominent. He no longer used a llautu to keep his hair from his face, but Leah could almost see the line it left after years of wear. Gently, she brushed a stray lock back from when it had fallen in front of his ear. Tan tilted his head, capturing her hand against his neck.

"When you touch me, my heart soars," he told her.

"Your heart is in my heart, Na-Tan Manco," said Leah, initiating the pledge for the very first time. "You are bound to me forever."

❧ ◉ ☙

It was twilight when Tan pulled up in front of Leah's house. Leaning over, he kissed her sleeping face until she awakened with a smile. "We are home, Qewa Ñawi."

"Hmmmmm."

He kissed her again, this time letting his tongue tease her lips. "Open your eyes, my heart."

One eye opened. "Do I hafta?"

"Yes. I have no key to your house or I would carry you in."

"The neighbors would talk," she murmured, snuggling into the seat.

"Neighbors talk in neighborhoods all over the world," muttered Tan as he opened his door He went around to her side, then slid her out of the car and hoisted her up onto his shoulder. His nimble fingers dug the keys from her back pocket. When he reached the front door, he felt her giggling against his shoulder.

"This is like what grooms do to their brides when they go into their house for the first time. Put me down."

He ignored her, instead concentrating on working the key in the lock. The heavy oak and stained glass door swung open. Shifting her, he bounded up the stairs to her apartment. This door he opened with ease, but froze when he heard a strange beeping noise.

"Stop!" commanded Leah. "Turn, two steps left." Tan did as he was told. "I'm shutting off the alarm," she said, starting to giggle again. "Okay, now proceed."

He marched into the bedroom and dumped her unceremoniously on the bed. It was his turn to give the orders. "Do not move. I'll be back."

"Like Schwarzenegger!" she called after him, realizing too late he probably had no idea who Arnold Schwarzenegger was.

Tan was back in a minute, her bags in hand. Closing the door behind him, he joined her in the bedroom. "Do you have to be anywhere tonight?"

"No. Do you?"

"No." Stretching out beside her, Tan slipped his arm around her, drawing her close. "I cannot get enough of you, Qewa Ñawi," he whispered as his free hand began to undo the buttons on her shirt.

Leah moaned softly when his flesh touched the tender flesh of her breast. His mouth found her nipple, teasing it erect with the tip of his tongue, savoring the sweet taste of her skin. Her own hands undressed him until he lay naked beside her. Running her hands along the hard planes of his chest, Leah stopped when she found the tiny, masculine points, taut against his skin. She slid down to kiss them, taking delight in the way he shuddered when her tongue circled his nipples. Leah pushed against Tan, forcing him to lie on his back.

Legs apart, she straddled him, her hair, now loose, falling in waves brushing tantalizingly over his torso. "Let me love you," she whispered as she began kissing him at the top of his face. "You who have always given, it is your turn to take." One inch at a time, Leah feasted on him, her lips burning an indelible brand on him, making Tan as much hers as she was his. When she allowed him to enter her, she was ready, wet and hot, hungry for Tan to fill her with his love. Her hips moved against his, drawing him into the deepest part of her body until his hands reached for her. Grabbing her shoulders to pull Leah down to meet him face to face, Tan's tongue probed her mouth as his shaft explored her from within. Nothing in his world had prepared Tan for the all-consuming fire she could ignite.

Leah's breath came in short gasps as every nerve in her body strained for release. Tan thrust into her until he could feel her tighten around him, driving him to a new level of consciousness. He could delay no longer. With a muffled cry, burying his face in her hair, Tan exploded, pouring his seed into her as she met his release with her own.

For a moment, Leah rested on Tan, then slowly sat up. In the ambient light of the street lamp outside her window, she saw a tear trickle from his eye to slide slowly down his smooth face. She wiped it away with her finger, then kissed the source of the errant wetness.

"*Aht motzei chain b'eineini,*" he said slowly, carefully pronouncing each word.

Leah looked at him with disbelief. "What?"

He repeated the words. "Did I say it wrong?" he asked, the dark brows coming together to form a single line across his forehead.

She shook her head. "Do you know what it means?"

Tan's smile lit his face and Leah's. "You find favor in my eyes. It is a beautiful way to say I love you."

"You never cease to amaze me!" cried Leah as she fell on him, covering his face with kisses.

With jaguar grace, he flipped her over and covered her with his body. "And you, Qewa Ñawi, you never cease to arouse me!" He was inside her again, this time moving slowly, teasingly, daring her to demand more. Measuring his strokes, Tan kept himself propped on his elbows, enabling him to watch her face reflect her desire. Building gradually, he allowed only their hips to touch, leaving the rest of her exposed to his view. He watched her breasts rise and fall rhythmically with every thrust, thoroughly enjoying the way the tender skin moved when he did. Her scent filled his nostrils, a soft, human smell which belonged only to his woman and no other. Her eyes were closed, but Tan did not mind, he was too busy memorizing each minute detail of the moment to lose himself in the luminous green pools. He felt her heat growing around him as he quickened his movement, and only at the very last moment, when he knew he would again pour himself into her, did he close his own eyes, relishing the waves of pleasure washing over him and through Leah.

They slept for a while, nestled together, their hearts beating in one rhythm. When Tan awoke, Leah was lazily stroking his broad back. He found her mouth with his, letting the sweet taste of her fill him again.

The telephone rang, the sharp, intrusive bell shattering the silence of the room. "Let it ring," murmured Leah, nibbling his lower lip.

The machine kicked in and after a moment, Leah heard her mother's voice. "Just checking in, dear. I thought you'd be back from the conference and I wanted to know how it went. Call me when you get home." Click.

Leah erupted into a fit of giggles. "What a great way to end an evening of incredible passion," she laughed when Tan rolled off her.

"What is so funny? Who was that?"

"My mother. Get used to the voice; I suspect you will hear it a great deal in the future." Leah sat up and surveyed the mess. "We should have pulled back the blanket," she said, looking at Tan.

"You should call her back," replied Tan, concern in his voice. "She will worry, will she not?"

"Oh, I suppose." Leah left the bed with a sigh and took a t-shirt from the hook beside her closet door. Pulling it on, she padded into the living room to call her parents.

☙ ⊖ ❧

She was talking to her mother when Tan emerged from the bedroom wearing only his jeans. Leah smiled at him, liking the way he looked when he lacked a shirt; it reminded her of the way she saw him at the huaca, all hard muscle in its natural, most attractive state. She took his hand and held it while she finished up the call. "What I want to know," she sighed as she replaced the receiver, "is how I am going to explain you to them."

"Mark has already warned me about Jewish parents," commented Tan dryly.

"And what exactly has the good rabbi told you, Aclla?"

"That nice Jewish girls marry nice Jewish boys, or at least that is what is supposed to happen."

"And you are not a nice Jewish boy. He's right, you know."

"It is a difficult position for you, but you will know what is best for your family, as I will know what is best for mine." He leaned over and kissed the top of her head. "I want to stay with you, I do not want to leave, but I must go to my home. They are not my parents, but they will worry if I am too late in coming back."

Leah stood and wrapped her arms about Tan. "And how will you explain me?"

"Easily," he shrugged. "But do not worry; we will work out the details." Tan went back to the bedroom to get his shirt.

Arms around each other, they walked to the door. "Sleep well, my Aclla, and when you dream, dream of us at the pool beside the huaca," murmured Leah, her head against his chest.

With a last, sweet, lingering kiss, he was gone.

⥲ ⊖ ⥮

Sarah Perkal yawned as she gathered up her books. It was only eleven o'clock, but she had had enough of the library for one night. Usually, she used Wilson Library on the west bank, but the music collection was in Walter and that's what she needed. For two and a half hours, Sarah had been listening to tapes of Andean folk songs, compiling a list of titles and copying lyrics appropriate to the topic Leah had given her. The music was haunting, wispy reed flutes and high voices singing in a language she did not understand, yet the sounds spoke eloquently of love and devotion even if the words remained a mystery. Satisfied that she had enough information for Leah, Sarah dropped the tapes off at the desk and headed out of the building.

As she passed Ford Hall, Sarah noticed a bit of light coming from Leah's second floor window. "Great," she said aloud, "Lee's back." Quickening her pace, she went to the side door and found it unlocked. She ran up the stairs and down the dim hall until she came Leah's office. "Hey, Lee!" called Sarah as she pushed the door open. "How was the conference?"

The lamp was on, but there was no one at the desk. "Lee?" called the student. She did not see the dark figure behind the door, she only felt the single, glancing blow to the back of her head as she sprawled onto the cold, linoleum floor.

CHAPTER 32

The telephone was ringing. Leah opened her eyes and tried to focus on the clock; the green digits glowed one a.m. She struggled out of the bed and went into the living room, catching the phone just as the answering machine clicked on. "Hold, please" she yelled into the receiver as she switched the machine off. "Hello?"

"Leah, this is Captain Wilson. I am sorry to wake you, but we have... um...a problem over at Ford Hall."

"My office?" asked Leah, suddenly wide-awake.

"Uh, yes. Could you come down here?"

"On my way."

Squad cars with flashing lights and an ambulance were parked outside Ford Hall when Leah pulled up. She gave her name to the nearest officer; he waved her through after he told her to park behind the last police car. Grabbing her bag, she bounded up the stairs to the door and then up to her office two steps at a time where Captain Wilson stood with several men, including Dr. Muñoz. In her office, she saw Sarah Perkal sitting at the desk, a paramedic bending over her, holding an ice-pack to the back of the frizzy, blonde head. "What happened?" demanded Leah, catching her breath.

"It seems Sarah walked in on someone in your office about eleven o'clock this evening. Whoever it was gave her a pretty good knock. When she came to, she called 911."

"Whoever it was?" Leah demanded. "What's that supposed to mean?"

Captain Wilson looked beseechingly at Dr. Muñoz. "She didn't see who hit her, Lee," said the professor, his face grim. "But I think we can draw our own conclusions."

Leah brushed past them and into her office. "Are you okay?" she asked Sarah, squatting beside the girl.

"Yeah, but my head hurts." Tears welled up in her eyes. "I'm really sorry, Lee. I saw a light on in the office and I thought you were here, but there was no one at the desk and I didn't see the guy, I mean I think it was a guy, it had to have been a guy, wouldn't it.... I mean..." She ran out of steam and just sobbed.

"Hey, slow down, Sarah," said Leah, stroking the girl's arm. "You didn't do anything wrong. Just take a deep breath and here..." She opened her desk drawer and pulled out a box of tissues. "Blow your nose."

The girl dutifully did as she was told. "I didn't see him, Lee. I don't know who it was or anything. I just thought you were back."

Captain Wilson stepped into the room. "We're going to let the paramedics take her over to the hospital now."

"I don't need a hospital," protested Sarah, clutching Leah's hand.

"Yes, you do, Sarah." Leah helped her up. "You need to be checked over by a doctor."

Pain flooded though her head, and Sarah fell back into the chair. The paramedic signaled his partner in the hall and a gurney slid into the office. "We're gonna help you lie down, Sarah, so you don't have to walk. Okay?"

The girl nodded. It hurt too damn much to stand up.

❧ ⊖ ☙

"Do you think Lubrano is back?" asked Leah as she perched herself on the windowsill in Muñoz's office.

Captain Wilson shook his head. "Not personally, but my guess would be it's one of his people; probably the same one who raided your office the first time. Whoever it was knew how to pick a lock..."

"Last time, the door was splintered," Leah countered. "Why didn't he pick the lock last time?"

"Because that dead bolt stuck. You said so, yourself, Ms. Fine. If he couldn't get it to turn, he had to force it another way," explained the captain. "Now you have a new, rather smooth working lock and it probably turned quite easily with the right tool."

"Great security we've got." Leah was muttering to herself, but she did see the quick, sardonic frown cross the professor's face.

"Was there anything in the office this time that Lubrano would find interesting?" Wilson asked.

"No, the infamous notebooks are at home." She added, "And I set the alarm before I left the apartment. Or won't that do any good either?"

As if on cue, an officer poked his head in the door. "The alarm at the apartment just went off. Our guys got him."

The three in the office jumped up. "You'll ride with me," said Wilson as he sprinted out.

∾ ⊖ ∾

There were no flashing lights on the block, but Leah saw the squad car as soon as they turned the corner. Jumping out of the car, she ran over to the car where a man was sitting in the back seat. She looked inside, but the face was not familiar. "I don't know him," she told Wilson when he stepped up beside her.

"Pull him out," barked the Captain.

The officer none too gently helped the stranger out of the car. "What's your name?" The man did not reply. "He's got no identification, not a thing on him and he's not talking."

"Did you read him his rights?"

"Yep, but he seems not to understand."

"Give me the Miranda card," said Leah. The officer was about to refuse, but Wilson nodded and he handed over the little card. Leah quickly translated the words into Spanish, but the man remained impassive. "He speaks Spanish, I'm sure," she said to Wilson and Muñoz, "but let's give it one more try." Making sure his face was clearly visible in the streetlight, Leah began again, this time in Quechua. When his eyes widened, then quickly narrowed, Leah allowed herself a triumphant smile. "You understand now?" she asked, still in the ancient language.

"What's there not to understand," he answered in heavily accented English. "This is a futile exercise. I am a diplomat."

"Shit." Captain Wilson walked away, then came back and took Leah's arm. "That could be a real pain in the ass. You can't even get a rape charged if the bastards are dips."

Leah went back to the stranger. Speaking in Quechua, she addressed him directly. "They can't understand me, so you may as well listen. I want to know who you are and why you're here, or I will appeal directly to the Mamacuna and you will never know another quiet day in your life. Do you understand me?" Underlying her voice was an edge of steel, calculated to disarm.

"So you *are* the Qewa Ñawi," he whispered, definitely impressed. "They say you have the power of visions and are beloved of Mamaquilla."

"Did you doubt it?"

"He told me you would not be here."

"He is Lubrano." It was not a question.

The eyes flared, then narrowed again. "He said you would not be here," he repeated.

"But I am. Mamaquilla protects those who serve Her."

The man leaned casually against the car. His lips curved into a thin, unfriendly smile. "The power of Mamaquilla will not be able to stop what will happen, Qewa Ñawi. It is too late."

Leah drew herself up, hoping the flint in her voice would more than compensate for her lack of height. "You will be plagued all the days of your life with the undying knowledge that you have desecrated huacas. Your prayers to whatever god you hold sacred will go unanswered for you have shamed your people by your actions. Your name is unimportant, but your face will be remembered and despised. And in the end, not even Lubrano will be able to help you." She spun on her heel and returned to where Captain Wilson and Muñoz were waiting.

"What did you say to him?" asked Wilson, noticing the blanched look on the prisoner's face.

"Oh, nothing much. I merely reminded him of his roots." Leah's airiness belied the intensity of what they had witnessed.

Dr. Muñoz chuckled. "Conjuring up the spirits, are you?"

"More or less." Leah turned to Wilson. "What's next?"

"If he doesn't want to give us his name, we'll simply fax his picture and prints to Washington and they'll give it to us. As to what we can do with him? We'll book him as a John Doe and wait until we hear from Washington. Right now, however, I'd like to go back to campus and have you go through your office."

ɞ ⊖ ◦ɔ

Nothing had been taken. Her files had obviously been rifled, but, as far as she could tell, they were intact. They went back to Muñoz's office where they could all sit down. "I just don't know what they were hoping to find," she said, accepting a cup of coffee from her advisor.

"Assuming they don't know about the other notebooks, they have to be looking for something which they think you have and you don't know you have." Muñoz frowned. "Have you gotten anything in the mail lately, anything from Morales?"

"No, he's still in the hospital. I spoke to his doctor from the lodge on Saturday night, but he didn't mention anything being sent out."

"Maybe it hasn't arrived," offered Wilson, not at all sure he understood what was going on.

Leah stared out the window. The sky was already turning from black to grey, signaling the coming dawn. She racked her brains, trying to think of what, if anything, could be of such value that Lubrano would risk another break-in. He couldn't be that stupid, she decided, unless there was something worth the effort. Going to the desk, Leah reached for the phone.

Miguel answered on the first ring. He waited for a moment while she switched on the speaker so Muñoz and Wilson could listen in. Quickly, Leah told him what happened, but the attaché did not seem to be surprised by the turn of events. "What does he look like?"

"Definitely mestizo. Medium height, about five nine, dark hair, dark eyes, mustache and a jaw-line beard. I think he had a scar on one cheek, but it was very faint. He really freaked when I mentioned the Mamacuna."

"My guess is that the fellow they're holding is Mañuel Barrantes...one of Lubrano's buddies from Chiclayo. He's rural enough to be superstitious when it comes to Indio things. You probably scared him thoroughly. You said he knew you were the Qewa Ñawi?"

"Yeah...and that surprised me a little. What's the story?"

"The local grapevine is buzzing with rumors about the Qewa Ñawi who has taken the Aclla from his home. Up in your end of the world, no one is particularly upset, because the Mamacuna seems to be pleased with her boy. In fact, after the attack on Hector, the people believe the Aclla has gone away in an effort to protect them."

"But who else knows about him...or me, for that matter?"

"People talk. Everyone likes a good mystery, you know that." His laughter was short, rather sarcastic.

"Mr. Gutiérrez, this is Captain Wilson," interrupted the officer. "Is this Barrantes attached to your embassy?"

"No, ostensibly he's with the consulate. But if you're asking about immunity, the answer is probably yes, he qualifies. However, it would be to our advantage to hold him as long as you can. That way, if Lubrano ships him back to Peru, we can intercept him when he gets there. I'm sure we can find something to charge him with." There was another short, bitter laugh.

"But do you know what he's looking for?" asked Dr. Muñoz.

"No, not really, but I can guess he's looking for one of two things. Either it's some sort of conopa given to you, Lee, by the Mamacuna, or it's the notebooks with the maps you drew, outlining the field rotation."

"What's a conopa?" asked Wilson.

"A small figurine. They are sometimes given as a sign of favor by the high priestess," answered Leah just as quietly.

"Did the Mamacuna give you anything like that?" asked Miguel.

Leah thought for a moment, then said, "Yes, but not a conopa. When she accepted me, she gave me a string of shell beads like the other girls had."

"Where is the string?"

"At the apartment. Do you think that's it? They're of no value to anyone but me."

"Ah," sighed Miguel, "that's where you're wrong. If someone shows up with your shells and, say, something ceremonially important which is clearly yours, then throws them on the ground at the feet of the Mamacuna...."

"It would mean I've betrayed them."

"Exactly. I don't know why we didn't think of this before. But if Lubrano did something like that, the Rimoc would have no choice but to believe you have broken with the people and have stolen their Aclla for purposes unholy."

"Oh, God."

"We need a recommendation from you, Mr. Gutiérrez," said the captain.

"First off, make sure you still have your shells. If you do, put them in a safe deposit box somewhere and don't take them out until...."

Leah jumped up. "Wait. Keep talking. There's something else." She dashed down the hall to her office. From the doorway, she looked at the wall near her desk. The bulletin board was covered with papers, but something was out of place, or rather, missing. Her *paicha*, the thick vicuña tassel Saba had sent, was gone. She raced back to Muñoz's office. "Miguel, he took my paicha!"

"That would be enough, Lee."

"What's a paicha?" asked Wilson, needing to know what he was looking for now.

"A tassel. Mine is multi-colored wool, the kind a girl gets when she begins training to be a collahuaya, a...a...a sort of local healer." Leah flopped into the nearest chair. "We have to get it back."

"The hell with getting it back, Leah. How soon do you finish school?"

She glanced at the calendar on Muñoz's desk. "Three weeks, Miguel. Classes end in two, then exams. Tan can't miss his exams; they're too important."

"Exams can be rearranged," said Miguel.

"Make that two, then. There are some things which have to be done before I can go."

"Two weeks should be fine. Dr. Muñoz?"

"Yes?"

"Will you pull the necessary strings for Villac-Quilla so he can go with her?"

"That should present no problem."

"Good. I'll make the travel arrangements. And we'll pick up the tab. In the meanwhile, say nothing to anyone who doesn't absolutely have to know. And if asked, just say you are going to finish some left over research. Captain Wilson?"

"Yes, Mr. Gutiérrez?"

"Can you arrange some sort of protection, discreetly of course, for Leah?"

"I'm sure I can."

"Good. And Leah, have the police check your phone at home and in the office for a tap. If it is tapped, leave it alone; just don't use it for anything important, just everyday conversations. And keep all office phone work related only. We don't want to tip our hand to Lubrano."

◦ ⊖ ◦

Mañuel Barrantes denied knowing anything about the paicha, but his ever-present thin smile told Leah otherwise. Disgusted, she joined Captain Wilson in office where he sat reading the document Miguel had faxed him later that morning.

"I'm sure he took it, but what do you think he did with it?" asked Leah.

"He could have taken it any time over the weekend. We don't know whether or not this was his first foray into your office, Ms. Fine. For all we know, he's been in there on and off since Thursday night."

Leah picked up her book bag. "I'm off. I've got two classes to teach and then I'm going over to the hospital to see Sarah. After that, I'll be in my office until four, then in class at Ford Hall until five thirty. I'll call you from some other phone or something."

With a smile, Captain Wilson watched the woman leave. *She's one tough cookie*, he decided, *that's what she is, all right.... one tough cookie.*

◦ ⊖ ◦

Tan had spent a restless night. Tossing and turning in his bed, he regretted not staying the night with Leah. At dawn, he had been awakened by his dreams, images of a strange woman in danger, and he was unable to go back to sleep. It was too early to call Leah, so he settled for a shower before he went downstairs to make coffee.

He was in the kitchen reading the newspaper when Mrs. Halstaad came in, wrapped in her robe. "You're up early, Tan," she said, pouring a cup of coffee. "Anything wrong?"

"I could not sleep, ma'am."

"Too much weekend." As soon as he had come in the night before, Ingrid knew there had been a change in the young man. "Tell me about it."

Tan reddened. "Is it so obvious?"

"Yes." She smiled and patted his hand. "A mother knows these things, Tan, even when it's not her own son."

"My mother," he laughed, the color deepening, "would not dare to ask."

"Well, this one does. Tell me what happened between you and, if I am guessing right, Leah Fine."

"She is in my heart," he said softly, "and our hearts are bound together."

"And she has been in your heart since before you came, hasn't she?" They had had bits and pieces of this discussion before.

Tan nodded. "There were obstacles..."

"And they have been overcome?"

"Yes."

Mrs. Halstaad took the chair beside Tan's. "Don't feel obliged to tell us your every move, Tan. I am a realistic person and know how people in love behave. All I would ask is that you occasionally have dinner at home and let us know you are alive."

❧ ⊖ ❧

Tan was sitting on the front steps when Leah got home at six. Wearing a pair of shorts and a t-shirt, he hardly looked like the aclla, but Leah would have known those legs anywhere. When she slammed the car door, his eyes came up and he smiled, sending shivers, as he always did, right down her spine. Leah joined him on the step and let his mouth taste hers before she pulled away.

"There was another incident at my office last night," said Leah, resting her hand on his bare thigh.

"Someone was hurt, but it was not you. It was a curly head. And something was taken"

"Yes! How did...never mind. Did Dr. Muñoz or Captain Wilson get a hold of you?"

He shook his head. "I saw it in my sleep, but I did not know what it meant."

Leah told him the story, adding that Sarah, with a slight concussion, was feeling better and would be released from the hospital in the morning. "But we can't find my paicha, Tan. Barrantes didn't have it on him. That worries me."

"It is on its way to the mountains. This, too, I saw. But I think the Mamacuna will know it was stolen, just as I know."

"I hope you're right." She leaned against him, her head on his chest. "We leave in two weeks. You'll take your exams ahead of schedule; it's being arranged."

Tan drew her face upward and studied the grass green eyes. "I will declare for you before the Mamacuna," he said. "This, too, I have seen."

Leah nodded gravely. "I have seen it, too."

"This pleases you?"

"Yes, my heart, this pleases me."

His mouth covered hers, savoring the sweetness, renewing the fire he felt each time he touched her. "I am yours, body and heart," he murmured, "There is room for no one else, save our children."

"May there be many," replied Leah against his ear.

❧ ⊖ ❧

There was a great deal to accomplish before the day of departure. Leah rammed through her work, grading papers ferociously as she hurried to tally grades so that all Mary would have to do was add in the final exams. At Muñoz's suggestion, she filed for incompletes in two classes, giving her more time to finish papers due in the remaining two. At night, Tan came to the apartment after the library, and usually stayed over. He did not want her to be alone, afraid that Lubrano might send someone else to discourage her from going back to Peru.

Miguel arrived at the end of the first week. He met with Tan and Leah, along with Captain Wilson and Dr. Muñoz, and told them of Barrantes' arrest as soon as he stepped off the plane in Lima. "Trumped up charges, to be sure, but he is out of action. Lubrano's mouth is shut; he knows we're on to him."

"What about Hector?" asked Tan. "Is he safe where he is?"

"For the moment, he's furious at being kept in the hospital. We've got a guard on him round the clock. However, we're letting him go to Felipe's at the end of the week. The house has a walled garden and will be easy to keep under surveillance. Hector doesn't know you're coming, though." Miguel allowed himself a chuckle. "He'd be absolutely impossible if he knew you were coming back, Tan."

"Then don't tell him," he snorted. He still had his reservations about the Ayar Monsonsoré, especially when he turned his eyes on the Qewa Ñawi.

The way Tan held her hand, almost too tightly, amused Leah. She understood what he was doing and was, admittedly, flattered by the little pitchforks in his eyes. "And where will you be during all this sneaking about, Miguel?" she asked pleasantly.

"Probably at the capital. There is legislation set to be debated in our congress which requires my attention, but I will try to join you in Piura as soon as possible."

After the meeting, Tan went off to class while Leah returned to her office. The empty space on her bulletin board still bothered her, though Tan kept reassuring her the Mamacuna would not believe such evidence, especially after he had meditated and come away knowing in his heart this was so. She was about to start reading when there was a sharp knock on the door.

"May I come in?" Miguel was standing in the doorway.

"Sure." Leah swept her books off the extra chair. "Thanks for coming, Miguel," she said with a smile.

He took the proffered seat, and stared at Leah for a moment. "I can see in your eyes that it's true," he said in Quechua.

"What's true?"

"Tan will declare for you."

"Yes, it's true."

"I knew he would." Miguel switched back into English. "Are you prepared for life with him?"

Leah sighed. "If this was the yunka, I might say no, but it isn't. I am fully aware of the intricacies of life with him, but it is because of those very things that I am bound to him."

"Then you believe all the mumbo-jumbo that goes along with it."

"Miguel, the mumbo-jumbo, as you call it, is over. Tan is no longer aclla; he is simply a regular kinda guy, one whom I happen to love very much. We will have our problems, just like any other couple, but we'll manage."

"And that your bonding is tied up with a lot of mystical strings doesn't make you even a little nervous?"

Leah shook her head. "Any time a person agrees to spend the rest of their life with another person there are mystical strings, unless, of course, you are heading into an arranged marriage. You cannot honestly tell me that attraction between two people is quantitative."

"No, I suppose not," admitted the attaché, "but I don't discount the necessity of getting to know someone rather well before running to the altar with them."

Her grin was enigmatic. "And, of course, you are an expert on matrimonial affairs."

He merely shrugged. "I've had my share of experience in these matters..."

"But you're not married, are you?"

"Well, no....but I've had a couple of close calls.

Leah's laughter filled the room. "What you need, *boychik* is a good, old fashioned quiverful of Cupid's arrows. Haven't you ever been madly, passionately in love?"

One elegant eyebrow soared over Miguel's dark eyes. "Up until recently, I never gave it much thought. And when I did," he stood, towering over Leah, his dark eyes holding hers tight, "the lady was already taken."

❧ ⊖ ☙

In the busy lobby of Hillel House, Tan stood out from the other students, a few of whom gave him an odd look as he sat quietly waiting for the rabbi's door to open. When it finally did, he jumped up.

"Sorry to have kept you waiting. Come on in."

He followed Mark into the book-lined office and tossed his backpack on the floor beside an empty chair. "We are going back to Peru in ten days, Mark. While we are there, I will declare for Leah before the Mamacuna."

"Have you asked Lee?" asked Mark, thoughtfully rubbing his chin.

"Yes and she agrees. But to marry her, according to your laws and customs, will have to come next."

"You've been studying with me for what, four months now? You know what's involved. Conversion is not something we encourage."

Tan looked into the Rabbi's eyes. "The way of my people is dying. I will not go back there to live, for that is impossible. If we are to have a life here, our children must have the faith of their mother. Your ways are not so different from mine. Better your ways..." His voice trailed off.

"Have you talked to Lee about any of this?" He suspected the answer would be no.

"The time has not been right."

"You're asking a lot, Tan," said the rabbi, his voice serious. "I don't think Lee would jump for joy if you suddenly announced you were converting to Judaism." In truth, he didn't know what Leah would do.

"It's not so sudden, is it?" Tan smiled slowly. "Leave Leah to me. I will tell her when the time is right."

Mark whistled, "I hope you know what you're doing. In the meanwhile, I think you'd better plan on coming over for dinner on Friday. Mindy's gonna want a lot more information than I'm willing to give her."

"In other words," laughed Tan, "you think we should be near when the ladies talk amongst themselves."

"Only if you don't want long distance calls in Peru!"

༄ ⊖ ༄

The night before they were to leave, the Halstaads asked Tan to bring Leah over for dinner. Mrs. Halstaad had prepared Tan's favorite spinach lasagna, and was delighted when Leah asked for the recipe. "I suppose I'm going to have to figure out what he likes to eat," she said with an impish smile, "if

I'm going to be the one cooking for him."

"So far, you make very good toast," he teased, giving her hand a squeeze under the table.

Dr. Halstaad chuckled at the exchange, at the same time wondering how they would ever manage to close the cultural gap between them. Even though Leah was well versed in the traditional ways, he knew how difficult it could be over a long period of time. Still, they were so obviously in love that it was a pleasure to watch them.

Leah automatically began to help Mrs. Halstaad clear the table as soon as everyone was finished with the main course. In the kitchen, the two women worked companionably side-by-side, Mrs. Halstaad rinsing and Leah loading the dishwasher. They chatted comfortably, discussing things of mutual interest, like the ballet and chamber music, until Ingrid reached over to stay Leah's hand.

"I don't mean to pry, dear, but I feel I have to say something about to-morrow."

"It's okay, Mrs. Halstaad, I understand," replied Leah in a reassuring tone.

"I think what you and Tan are trying to do is as noble as it is right, but Arne says there is terrible danger in the area and that Tan's presence might draw, if you will, fire."

At first, Leah thought she was going to object to their relationship but it was the act of going back to Peru that had her worried. The statement that there was danger in the jungle somewhat surprised Leah. Tan said he hadn't told Dr. Halstaad much about it, only that going back might be reassuring to the people. "I'm not sure what you mean."

Ingrid Halstaad leaned close to Leah. "He's had two phone calls in the last week, both of which were basically threats to Tan, I think. He's tried to talk him out of going, but Tan's mind is made up."

Arne Halstaad was not the only one to get phone calls; both she and Muñoz had gotten them as well. One was from Lubrano himself, who, in a less than veiled tone, told her that there would be no guarantees that, if she were to walk into the jungle, she would walk out. The other was from a deep voiced man who left a nameless message on her machine. He told her white skinned women who slept with her chosen ones were considered an affront to Mamaquilla and would be sacrificed to appease Her divine anger. If it was meant to frighten her, it did not. Still, she did not tell Tan about either call. "I don't think these are important, Mrs. Halstaad; I think they are scare tactics. The only danger in the district right now is to the people themselves. This is the reason we are going back. We want them to fight if necessary, not only for themselves, but for the safety of the land. It's more than a cultural issue; it's an environmental one as well, and that will be the most efficient way to go after the bad guys. Everyone loves to cheer for saving the planet," said Leah with a smile, " and, if in the process, we just happen to secure the land for the people, well, so be it."

"I wish I had your optimism, Leah," sighed Mrs. Halstaad, "not to mention your strength! I would love to go with you."

Leah laughed and gave her hostess a quick hug. "Maybe if you bug your husband enough, he'll take you to see Hector."

SUMMER IN THE STATES
WINTER IN PERU
1989

CHAPTER 33

Dr. Halstaad drove them to the airport. In the front seat, Tan went over last minute requests, mostly concerning his mail and his registration for fall quarter. Always one to worry about the practical side of living, he had given his host a wad of cash, asking him to deposit it in his own account so when the American Express bill arrived, there would be money to cover it. Dr. Halstaad shook his head and chuckled; this was so characteristic of Tan he could've predicted it. At the airport, when the redcap at the curb had taken the bags, he opened his arms to the young man and hugged him.

"Take care of yourself and this woman," he instructed, "and come back to us soon. Call if you need anything, and we'll be in touch with Felipe Segura if anything happens here. Watch your step, Tan, and...." He ran out of words.

"I will be careful, my friend," replied Tan.

Leah hugged Dr. Halstaad, too, and gave him a kiss on the cheek. "Thank you so much for everything, Dr. Halstaad. And not to worry, *I'll take* care of *him*." She shot a thumb at Tan.

Dr. Halstaad watched them disappear thought the sliding doors and for a moment, he wished he was going with them.

જ ⊖ ৎ૭

The flight to Miami was crowded, making Leah doubly appreciative of the first class tickets Miguel provided. Seated beside Tan, his nose buried in a book, Leah thought it wondrously strange to be sailing throughout the sky with him. Somehow, she could not believe they were on their way back to Peru together. She could feel the tension in Tan as his hand idly rubbed hers, an intimate gesture, yet one almost as much for his benefit as was it for hers.

In Miami, they had four hours to kill until the flight to Lima boarded. The terminal was hot and sticky, the air-conditioning barely enough to keep the air moving through the humidity. Leah was glad she had worn a loose denim skirt, rather than jeans; at least her bare legs were not dripping with sweat like the rest of her. Tan, however, in a pair of khaki trousers and a polo shirt, seemed perfectly comfortable. As always, and Leah was getting used to this, he drew the surreptitious stares of women whenever they caught a glimpse of liquid brown eyes set in a chiseled bronze face.

"Can I get you something cold to drink?" asked Tan, catching the far away look in Leah's eye.

She laughed, then brushed an impulsive kiss on his full lips. "Yes, my heart, a Coke would be wonderful." Again, the very normalcy of the act tickled her soul. She watched Tan saunter toward the bar crowded with waiting passengers. Going back to her magazine, she hardly noticed the man approaching her.

"Well," drawled a too familiar voice in Spanish, "if it isn't the intrepid Señorita Fine. And where, may I be so bold as to ask, is your Indio lover?"

Leah looked up and her mouth set into a tight line. "What do you want, Señor Lubrano?"

"I see we are both headed in the same direction. Do you need a traveling companion?"

"Are you on this flight?" she asked, trying to keep the bile from rising in her throat.

"As a matter of fact, I am. Does this please you?"

Leah smiled a thin, unfriendly smile. "Yes, it does. Now I won't worry about the plane blowing up mid-air."

His laughter had a cruel, taunting edge. "It would hardly serve to have you and your lover killed. You are not worth the effort."

Tan returned with two Cokes. He saw the man talking to Leah and instinctively knew him. He moved menacingly toward him. "Why are you here?"

"Going home, same as you, Aclla." He watched Tan bristle at the mocking sound of the word.

"Have a nice flight," growled Tan in English, "and stay the hell away from us." He watched Lubrano stroll away.

The gate agent materialized beside them. "Señor Villac-Quilla?" he asked, looking directly at Tan. "There is a telephone call for you."

Tan handed the cups to Leah and followed the uniform to the desk. "Yes?" he said into the white phone.

"Tan, it's Miguel. I'm standing about thirty feet from you, behind and to the right of Leah. Don't worry about Lubrano. He's on the flight, but he's not an issue. Sitting in the row behind you will be two of our men."

"I feel as safe as a baby in a sling, Ayar Monsonsoré. Thanks; I'll tell Leah." He ambled back to Leah, hands in his pockets, looking perfectly at ease. "Nothing to worry about, my heart," he said with a grin and a glance behind her. "Don't look now, but your friend the jaguar is a few yards away."

Leah reached up for his hand. "Then I shall not worry, Na-Tan Manco."

⤳ ⊖ ⤶

Finally, the flight was called. Settled into her seat, Leah adjusted the small pillow Tan had pulled out for her from the overhead bin. His arm, draped around her, felt warm and secure, a protective shield as they flew south in the belly of a great silver bird. Leah snuggled against him, letting the familiar scent lull her to sleep. Tan stared out the window at the waters of the Caribbean below. An endless stretch of blue, it seemed to be the perfect separation between the drab, concrete world of the cities in which he now lived and the sea of variegated green he called home. Still, a part of him was apprehensive about his return to Peru. He had only been gone six months, but in the way of living, it was a lifetime. His mind drifted back over last year, to the moment he was first aware of the presence of the Qewa Ñawi in his world. He knew of her presence the moment she set foot out of Hector's doorway on her way to the ayllu, or perhaps even before that. He had watched her tramping through the jungle; he heard the songs she sang, strange at first but now so very familiar. Each trip she made between the ayllu and the compound became another reason to observe the small, fearless woman with the startling green eyes shaded beneath the brim of her cap.

How ecstatic he had been when she left the little silver bird at the huaca! It was a sign: a sign from the Qewa Ñawi, and Mamaquilla Herself, that she was ready to greet him. And how amused he had been at the startled expression in her grass eyes; the way her lips moved wordlessly at first, tantalizing him and it took every ounce of his self-control, so carefully honed in the years apart, not to sweep her into his arms and kiss that mouth. She was unlike the girls he had known, those girl children of the ayllus who giggled at the boys while keeping their eyes modestly lowered. Before he had been summoned to Janajpachallacta, when he would walk on the paths by the river with his friends, discussing who was pretty and who would make a good wife, Tan was left with the unsettled feeling that there was more to picking a wife than a pretty smile. His mother was clever, as was his grandmother; his father had often told Tan that his love for Cura grew fat with the endless questions she asked during their courtship. And whomever Tan finally chose for a mate would have to have the key not only to his heart, but his head as well.

Tan let his eyes wander over the sleeping woman whose head nestled against him, fitting neatly into the crook of his arm, seemingly unaware of the real danger they would face when they reached the jungle. Shifting slightly, he drew her a little closer, as though the tightness of his grasp could protect her from the evil he felt in the marrow of his bones. Tan drew strength from her; he believed that with Leah at his side, he would be able to reach his people in time to prepare them for what was inevitable. Closing his own eyes, Tan allowed himself to concentrate on the images that were beginning to dance in his head, certain that these were messages from the Mamacuna.

ตา ⊖ ตา

When he opened his eyes again, the sun was barely visible in the west even though Tan's watch said seven o'clock. He chuckled as he thought about how, at this same time in Minneapolis, the sky would be bright blue; despite the change in hemispheres, they were flying in the same time zone. This was something that, a year ago, Tan would not have considered, yet now he was as bound to the hands on his watch as he had once been to the position of the sun. Leah was still asleep, but when Tan moved, she shifted slightly, a tiny smile on her lips. Gently, he stroked her hair and murmured her name.

"Mmmmm," she hummed, burrowing deeper into the crook of his arm.

"Open your eyes, Qewa Ñawi," he answered, kissing the top of her head. "They are bringing dinner. Are you hungry?"

"Mmmmm, sleeping," was all she said, her eyes fluttering for a brief moment.

Tan laughed and kissed her again. "You can sleep some more after you eat, skinny woman."

"Who you callin' skinny?" Leah murmured, opening her eyes at last.

Tan helped her to sit up. "You, my beloved, are skinny. My mother will think you do not eat enough and will try to feed you great quantities of *sara mot'i* and *quinoa*, so do not say I didn't warn you!"

"Warning duly noted and filed," sighed Leah as she stretched her cramped legs.

"And duly ignored, if I know anything at all."

ℰ ⊖ ℰ

Leah went back to sleep after dinner despite Tan's desire to talk. It was just as well; once they got to Lima, it would be hours before they passed through customs and got to their hotel. There would be no connecting flight to Piura until morning, and then they would be in for another long and arduous day.

Only when the captain announced their descent into Lima's Chaves Airport did Leah finally open her eyes. "Are we there yet?" she asked sleepily.

"Almost, my heart." He leaned over and brushed a kiss on her lips. "Are you ready for what is to come?"

Leah nodded, but she could feel her heart pounding a little quicker in her chest. "Have you seen Lubrano?"

"No, but he is back there. Do not let him worry you. When we get to Lima, we will make sure he does not see where we go."

The flight attendant walked down the aisle and stopped in front of Tan. "Señor Villac-Quilla?" she asked.

"Yes."

"May I have your passport, please?"

"Is there a problem?" asked Tan as he pulled the booklet from his jacket pocket.

The attendant smiled pleasantly. "I'll return this to you in a moment."

"What was that about?" asked Leah, her voice full of worry, her hand clutching Tan's arm.

He patted her hand calmly. "I'm sure it is nothing," he replied casually, hoping his own concern was successfully masked.

"Thank you for your patience, Mr. Villac-Quilla," smiled the attendant when she returned a moment later with his passport. "We received a message for you in the cockpit and the pilot would not release it until he had verified your identity." She handed Tan a small, folded piece of paper and walked away.

Tan opened the note and laughed out loud as he handed it to Leah. "I see we now have friends in high places."

Leah sighed with relief when she read the note from Miguel's father. "At least we won't have to find a taxi into Lima at this late hour, but the Hotel Bolivar? Isn't that a little much?"

"I wouldn't know. I've never been there. Have you?"

Leah shook her head. "Too rich for this student. But," she grinned, "I hear it's very romantic."

∽ ⊖ ∾

The plane landed at ten fifteen, only forty minutes late. Despite the hour, customs was bustling with incoming passengers. Hand in hand, Tan and Leah went to the baggage carousel to await their luggage; Lubrano was standing a few feet away.

The Peruvian approached them. "I hope you had a pleasant flight," he said with a thin smile. "Do you need a ride into the capital?"

"No, that will not be necessary," replied Tan, his own mouth taut with displeasure.

"There is no flight to Piura this evening. Do you have accommodations?"

Tan narrowed his eyes dangerously at Lubrano. "What we do here is of no concern to you, Señor Lubrano, so if you will excuse us?"

A guard approached them. "Señor Villac-Quilla, Señorita Fine? Welcome to Lima. If you would follow me, please."

"But our luggage!" protested Leah.

The official waved his hand. "Your luggage has already been taken off the plane. If you would come with me please."

Tan and Leah looked at each other and then at Lubrano, whose smug smile sent chills up their spine. Tan took her hand as they followed the uniform past the other passengers and through a small, unmarked door. "Your passports, please." The man took the passports and checked the pictures against the people. Satisfied they were the right ones, he said, "You can wait in here, please." He closed the door behind them.

"What now?" asked Leah as soon as they were alone in the drab little room with only a table and three uncomfortable looking chairs.

Tan put his finger to his lip, then shrugged. He pointed to the chairs and then stood behind Leah, his hands protectively on her shoulders, when she sat.

They waited for what seemed like an eternity before a portly, red-faced gentleman came huffing through the door. "Forgive me, Señor Villac-Quilla, but the traffic, even at this time of night, can be terrible! Just terrible. Stop and go, go and stop. I hope you had an easy flight?"

"Thank you, we did," said Tan, keeping his voice as even as possible. "Excuse me, but might I ask what this is all about?"

The chubby man looked positively surprised at the question. "You do not know about this?" Tan shook his head. "Well, then, the apologies are indeed all mine! I am so sorry; I thought you knew who I am! Allow me to introduce myself, then. I am Antonio de Leon, personal assistant to Don Francisco Gutiérrez! I hope you didn't think you were being detained." He chuckled aloud as he extended his hand to Tan. "We are so pleased you were able to get here so soon, Señor Villac-Quilla. And of course, this lovely lady must be Señorita Fine! Miguelito said I would know you because you would be the most beautiful woman on the flight. And of course, Miguelito was right! Miguelito is never wrong about these things."

"Thank you," she stammered, noticing the odd look Tan was giving her.

"My pleasure, señorita, my pleasure. Now, if you will come with me, the car is waiting outside." He opened the door and held it for Tan and Leah, then barreled along beside them. "I'm certain you will find the accommodations most satisfactory. Don Francisco thought you would be more comfortable there than at his home which is quite a distance from the airport, in Miraflores," rattled de Leon as they walked toward the exit, "which is far too far to drive at this late hour, especially when Don Francisco is already in the city. Since the connection to Piura is early tomorrow, he felt this would be better and besides, he is at the opera tonight and will stop at the hotel to speak with you himself. Which means we should hurry. I am certain you are hungry and want to refresh yourselves before meeting with Don Francisco."

A black Rolls Royce stood waiting at the curb. As soon as the little party pushed through the glass doors, the driver tipped his hat and opened the rear door. If the car surprised Leah, she said nothing as she slid onto the seat.

The ride into the city was made shorter by de Leon's constant chatter; his explanations of recent events in the northern jungles answered many of their questions before they could be asked. "The news, I'm afraid, is not as good as we would like, Señor Villac-Quilla," said de Leon shaking his head. "It would seem that when the native guides out of Sullana refused to take the so-called geologists into the mountains for one superstitious reason or another, they were able to find two rather disreputable fellows from Chiclayo who would. At the moment, there are three expeditions in the mountains near Dr. Morales' clinic despite our best efforts to prevent their going."

"What does Dr. Morales say about this?" asked Tan.

"Oh, he is very angry, of course, but there is precious little he can do at the moment. Dr. Segura has refused to let him leave Piura, what with the colostomy still in place. Don Francisco has stationed five of his own men at the clinic, strong men who usually work on his rancho in the south. So far, they have reported several confrontations between your people, Señor Villac-Quilla, and the intruders, but there has not been bloodshed, only a great deal of shouting. Your Mamacuna, God bless her strength, has sent two of her own men to join the others at the clinic. They have been largely responsible for confounding the expeditions by obliterating paths through the jungle. Very clever, those fellows."

Leaning back against the plush seat of the car, Tan relaxed for the first time since he learned he would be coming home.

℮ ⊝ ℮

A suite awaited the travelers and when they arrived, the opulence of the accommodations took them aback. Tan had, understandably, never seen anything quite like the Hotel Bolivar. With a low whistle, he took in the decor. Señor de Leon was too busy issuing orders to the bellhop to pay much attention to Tan and Leah, but when the young man finally departed with a generous tip clutched in his hand, he stopped running long enough to tell them what was to come next. "I've taken the liberty of ordering a late supper for you," he told them with a wide smile, "vegetarian, as Miguelito instructed. I shall leave you for now, but will return shortly with Don Francisco. Until then, you might want to freshen up, but of course, you will do as you please." With a wave of his pudgy hand, he was gone.

"Interesting fellow," commented Tan dryly when the door closed behind de Leon.

"A very efficient fellow, I imagine," Leah laughed, flopping onto the sofa as she kicked off her shoes. "Why don't you take a quick shower before Don Francisco comes?"

"Why don't you join me?" Tan countered with a sly grin. "It would certainly make me feel better."

Leah ignored his leer. "If you go first, you will be dressed and ready when they come back. If I am a few minutes late, it doesn't matter; it's you they want to talk to."

"I suppose you are right, my heart, but I would rather you came with me."

An elegant finger was raised and pointed in the direction of the bedroom. "Go take a nice *cold* shower and I'll feel better."

Laughing, Tan disappeared into the bedroom.

ଚ⊖ଚ

Leah, refreshed from her own shower, joined Tan as he stood at the window overlooking Plaza San Martin where pedestrians were strolling after an evening on the town. "One day, Qewa Ñawi, I hope we will be strolling in the plaza, " he murmured into her ear.

"You've never been in Lima, have you?"

"No; only at the airport. It's strange; this is the capital of my country and I have never seen it before. I should like to be a tourist here."

Leah turned to face him. "I was here only briefly; it would be nice to see more of the city." She reached up and touched his hand. "But just wait 'til I take you to New York!"

A rap on the door caught their attention. Crossing the room quickly, Tan opened the door for a slim, impeccably dressed gentleman with a mane of thick silver hair. "You must be Señor Gutiérrez," said Tan, extending his hand.

"And this will be your first lesson in Lima etiquette, Señor Villac-Quilla. Never open a door unless you know who is standing on the other side." Only then did he accept the proffered hand. "I am delighted to meet you at last."

ଚ⊖ଚ

Over supper, Don Francisco filled in the gaps de Leon had left in his explanation of the situation. He brought along several maps, as well as reconnaissance photographs of the region, most of which had been taken by Paolo.

Tan was amazed to see his home from the sky; there were things visible from several thousand feet that he could not have imagined from the ground. Still, he was able to make several observations missed by the experts.

"Here, on this ridge," said Tan, pointing to one photograph taken of an area several miles south of Janajpachallacta, "there has always been a wall of stone along the outer edge; now, follow my finger and you can see where it has been removed."

Leah immediately saw the point to which he was referring. "I see it, but over here, where the wall seems to stop, isn't that a ñan? Wouldn't the wall have stopped there any way?"

"Yes," agreed Tan, his brows knitted together, "if the path had been there before the wall was built; but there has never been one there before. The ñan we use is over here." Tan pointed to another spot where the wall bulged out, but no path seemed to come from it. "My guess would be that someone has deliberately closed it off."

"Perhaps an effort to make access to Janajpachallacta more difficult?" asked Don Francisco.

Tan nodded. "Exactly. The way the wall is curved would tell one of us that the path is no good, but I think it was done to ward off the strangers. That ñan happens to be a particularly easy one to follow. I would also guess that a huaca has been placed beside the bulge to scare anyone who would dare to breach the wall."

Don Francisco stroked his long chin and studied the photographs laid out on the table. "Assuming you are right, do you think it was enough to delay the expedition up to the next elevation?"

"Possibly." Tan pulled another picture from the stack; it showed the area directly to the south of Janajpachallacta. "Look at this one. Here is another break in the wall, but this one not nearly as neat as the other. Who ever made it seems to have cut a new ñan along the edge of the forest. But it stops here. Another huaca would be my guess, but probably one with more prohibitive signs. Leah, look at the end of the path. When you went to the Raimi, did you walk up this side of the mountain?"

"Yes, but there were no paths leading from the upper ridge. To get to where we went, you had to walk all the way down the side and then back up on the other side of this gorge. The new ñan seems to stop far short of the gorge, don't you think?"

"As though something prevented them from going farther?" asked the Don.

"Exactly. Here, at this point," Tan traced a finger along the edge of the forest, "there was a ñan into forest, but it was a false path, a *panta ñan*; it dead-ended at an *apacheta*. From the look of this, it would seem someone tried to go beyond the apacheta, but could not. That tells me the Mamacuna has fortified the apacheta with forbidden markers."

"And no Indio guide would cross that, would they?" asked the Don, impressed by the astuteness of the young man.

Tan nodded. "It would seem that it has worked." He dug through the photographs until he found what he was looking for. "Here is a picture of the Huacachimu. There is obvious activity here, but again, it stops abruptly." He gave Leah a triumphant smile. "This would have been the most expedient way in, Don Francisco, but something, again, has stopped the expedition. This is a good sign. See? There is no evidence they have reached Janajpachallacta."

"At least not as late as last week. A great deal can change in seven days, Señor Villac-Quilla," admitted Don Francisco with a grim smile. "When we get to Piura, Paolo should have a more recent pictures for us."

Tan raised an eyebrow. "We? Us?"

"Yes, I will go with you in the morning; I have government business in that city which will serve, as you can see, as a most convenient excuse to accompany you."

"Are you certain you will be safe, Don Francisco?" asked Leah.

"Nothing is ever certain, señorita, but I believe my presence will, for the moment, insure *your* safety." The silver haired Peruvian stood and extended his hand. "I am glad we had this opportunity to speak privately before our departure. I shall send a car for you in the morning, about seven. Until tomorrow, then."

Tan walked him to the door. "Until tomorrow, Don Francisco."

⤳ ⊖ ⤶

At the blackest hour of the night, while Leah slept restlessly beside him, Tan awoke drenched in sweat. He'd had frightening dreams before, but the return to Peru intensified the images flashing across his sleep, making him both hot and chilled, as if a fever gripped his body. Slipping from the bed, he went to the window to look out over the city, now dark and empty, forbidding in its silence. Although he was in the place he called home, Tan saw no resemblance to his beloved mountains in the shadows of this city; nothing which made him feel any closer to his people than he had been the night before when he slept in his bed in Minneapolis. Tan closed his eyes, willing himself to listen for the voice of the Mamacuna, a sound he was certain he had heard in his dreams, yet he could not make out what she had said. In his bones, he felt something had radically changed and the silence that enveloped him was more frightening than the dreams. He had not expected to experience the intensity he felt at that moment, the awful feeling of isolation increased since he set foot on Peruvian soil. "This is not my home," he said to the moon barely visible in the sky, "I am apart, Mamaquilla, and I am alone." The last word echoed in the darkness.

The Rolls was waiting when Tan and Leah stepped outside at exactly seven the next morning. The driver stowed their bags in the trunk, then whisked them out of the city toward Chaves Airport. Instead of going to the terminal, the driver turned off the main road and toward a security gate where the guard waved them through and onto the tarmac. At the far end of the terminal, a Lear jet sat gleaming in the early morning sun, a staircase nestled against its side. Don Francisco stood at the bottom of the stairs, deep in conversation with Antonio de Leon.

"¡Buenos días!" he called as Tan and Leah emerged from the back seat. "Let's get on board and we can be off. The commuter flight was full," he said as he led them to the cabin, "so I thought it would be more comfortable to take my plane. I wish I could fly you all the way to the clinic, but I am afraid the landing strip is inadequate for this craft."

"Thank you for the offer, anyway, Don Francisco," replied Leah, "but we still need to stop in Piura to see Dr. Morales."

As soon as they were airborne, an attractive woman in a navy business suit emerged from the cockpit. "Would you like breakfast served now?"

"Yes, that would be fine, Raquela." He did not introduce her to the others.

But Leah noticed her accent; it was definitely not Peruvian, nor was it really Castilian Spanish either, judging by the way she spoke the language. Leah did not feel comfortable enough with the senior Gutiérrez to ask about her, yet she was curious.

As if he could read her thoughts, Don Francisco suddenly laughed. "How rude of me!" he exclaimed good-naturedly, "I did not introduce Raquela. When she returns, I shall have to apologize to her. She often complains of my mistreatment in social situations, but I am afraid I am so used to having her about me, I merely assume everyone knows her."

She was back in a moment, carrying a tray with coffee, sweet rolls and the appropriate accouterments, setting the tray on the table in the center of the ring of seats. Skillfully, she poured the coffee into sturdy china mugs, handing them to each of the passengers before taking one for herself. Satisfied everything was as it should be, Raquela took the empty seat between Don Francisco and de Leon.

"Forgive me, Raquela, for my lack of social graces," said Don Francisco with a twinkle, "and allow me to present Señorita Leah Fine of the University of Minnesota and Señor Tan Villac-Quilla of that same august institution."

"And of Janajpachallacta," added the woman, gracefully extending her hand to Tan. "I am so pleased to meet you both. Miguel has spoken highly of your work, Señorita Fine."

"Are you also involved in government work?" she asked.

Raquela's laughter was light with genuine amusement. "If you consider being a bodyguard government work, I suppose so."

Antonio de Leon jumped into the conversation with a hasty explanation. "We found Raquela in London three years ago when she was working for the...ah.... the.... ah...." he stammered when he realized he was about to reveal something he should not, but Don Francisco rescued him.

"A security agency," he said, filling in the blank. "Not only does she speak a dozen languages fluently," he added with obvious pride in his discovery, "but La Mendoza, as we sometimes call Raquela, is an expert in anti-terrorist activity; she is an invaluable addition to my staff."

"And I make an excellent cup of coffee which is more than we can say for Antonio, here." She flashed a smile at the portly little man turning pink beside her. "Don Francisco would have been reduced to American tea-bags had I not come along when I did."

"Literally or figuratively?" quipped Tan with a grin.

"Both," Raquela and Don Francisco said in unison.

There was still something about Raquela that set off bells in Leah's brain. She could not put her finger on it, but there was definitely something about the woman and Leah could not decide what exactly it was. Curious, Leah asked a more obvious question. "How does one go about becoming an expert in anti-terrorism?"

She did not answer at once; instead, Raquela glanced at Don Francisco long enough to see an almost imperceptible nod before answering. "Working for the Mossad," she said, switching into Hebrew, "is the most expedient method I know."

Leah almost dropped her cup. "You're Israeli!" she cried in the same language.

"And you sound like a native," Raquela laughed, "how refreshing. I expected you to have a more American accent." The two women launched into a rapid-fire conversation, leaving the men to watch with amused grins.

After a while, Don Francisco held up his hand in an effort to bring them back to the present. "I appreciate your desire to communicate in your own language, but I am afraid we have to discuss our immediate future."

Raquela apologized. Opening the briefcase beside her seat, she pulled out a sheaf of papers and handed them to Tan. "These came in late last night by courier. We thought you would like to see them before meeting with Dr. Morales."

The papers were a record of new movement in the mountains as reported by several sources close to Janajpachallacta. Another expedition had departed for the interior from Chulucanas, a town on the western slopes of the Andes, less than two hundred miles from Janajpachallacta. While the terrain was rough, Chulucanas could be easily reached by roads and could easily serve as a launching point for an excursion via helicopter. A party of six men had been in the town, asking questions about the availability of

guides familiar with the other side of the mountains and had been successful in locating two Indians who agreed to take them at least as far as the
Chimuhuaca. "Our sources tell us that the guides said they would not go
past the huaca because rumors coming off the slopes say anyone who passes
without the permission of the Mamacuna will not return," said Raquela,
looking directly at Tan. "I suppose you know something about that, Señor
Villac-Quilla."

"Yes. I thought it would buy us some time."

"You're right; it has. The local population is very superstitious and any
mention of the mystics on the other side of the mountains tends to rattle
them. They may be devout members of the Church, but they are extremely
superstitious." She turned to Don Francisco. "Were you able to discover
anything about Lubrano's return?"

De Leon jumped in again, pulling a sheet of paper from his jacket.
"The senior Lubrano is meeting with His Excellency, the Minister of
Energy and Mines, and high level representatives of Minero-Peru. Lubrano
the younger, the one who visited you in Minnesota and was on your flight
from Miami, will be in attendance at the meetings today, but beyond that,
we don't know." He pointed to the paper and frowned. "Bauxite. They say
they want bauxite, of all things, but there are significant lodes of copper
and possibly silver in the area. Specific, they are not; whatever it is they
are planning to take from the mountains, they are being very secretive
about it."

"But why do they keep coming back to my field notes?" asked Leah
in exasperation. "I know they are looking for new migratory patterns, but
I'm sorry, I just don't get it. What's the ultimate significance of my work
to them?"

Don Francisco allowed himself a sad smile before beginning his explanation. "About two years ago, shortly before you arrived, a new geologic
survey of the area had been conducted and what was once thought to be
marginal mineral deposits were, due to advances in technology, reevaluat-
ed. Instead of small, unimportant lodes running through the mountains,
there appear to be mineable quantities of bauxite and silver, along with a
rather significant vein of copper. To work these areas would endanger the

small population that we knew existed up there. Our laws prohibit land robbing, if you will permit the implication, so there had to be evidence that the people had other locations to which they migrated with some regularity." He handed the basket of sweet rolls to de Leon and spread a map on the table. "In your field report filed with the Ministry of Culture, you made mention of chacras across the Marañon, chacras which had been cultivated in the past and would be cultivated again when the present fields were exhausted. That was exactly what Lubrano and his people wanted to hear. So long as the people would follow a natural path of migration, they could move into the area and begin prospecting in earnest. Legally. But the information in your report was inconclusive, according to the Ministry; therefore, Lubrano was forced to seek you out in order to determine how extensive the migration might be."

"And when I did not provide that information, he assumed I had withheld it," finished Leah.

"Did you?" Don Francisco asked.

Leah shook her head. "Not really. I had a little bit more, but it was not as extensive as he obviously needs to move them off the mountain."

"Nor did he anticipate the permanent nature of Janajpachallacta. He had wrongly assumed it was as mobile as the ayllus," said Don Francisco, "and once that was established, any hope he had of moving them was crushed by the Ministry of Culture."

"Where do you and Miguel fit into all of this?" asked Tan.

"My son is officially an attaché to the embassy in Washington, but his interests, like mine, lie with the protection of our heritage. I have been working on an unofficial basis with the Ministry of Culture as well as the Inca Institute in an effort to protect those who cannot protect themselves. By the grace of God, I am in a financial position to support this activity." Don Francisco leaned back and studied his guests for a moment. "You must understand that my only desire is to see your people left alone to live as they wish, without the interference of the government...or multinational corporations. That the people live along the edge of the jungle and the mountains was not unknown. But who they are and what they are remains a mystery to most. No one wanted to go exploring in such an inhospitable and inaccessible region. Your people, Tan, were simply another isolated tribe doing nothing. Until the reevaluation of the mineral lodes in your district, you were all but invisible."

"And we would prefer to stay that way," said Tan dryly. "In all of Leah's writings, she has been careful not to reveal the precise locations of the ayllus..."

"It was intentional, Don Francisco. I never wanted to jeopardize the people."

"Nor did you," reassured Don Francisco, "if anything, you have done the people a great service for had you not come, had the field report not been published, it is highly unlikely they would have had anyone to fight for them except a lone physician. You have made their plight public knowledge, at least in the proper places, and the people will find they have more friends in Lima than they might have suspected."

"But," warned Raquela, "do not discount the danger to you when you go up to the highlands. Lubrano is cunning; he has surrounded himself with men skilled in the ways of the mountains and the jungles, using cash to buy loyalty. Those running around the district are not the scientific types; they are would-be guerrillas checking out ways to make the mountains an even less than hospitable place." She paused before continuing. "You may not be aware, Tan, that in the southern Andes gold is being mined under the most inhuman of conditions. The Indios are virtual slaves, especially the children who are trucked in and made to work in the mineshafts. The government does little to stop this and we are afraid if the northern mountains are mined, the same thing will happen there." She paused before she added, "There is also the matter of coca. Whatever the mining interests are, the ability to grow high quality coca on the land is more important for men like Lubrano and his Colombian friends. For Lubrano, it does not matter where the money comes from, so long as it lines his pocket. And you cannot ignore the presence of left-wing guerrillas either. Too many rural people have come to support them because they believe the government does not listen. Something like Shining Path comes in, tells them whatever they want to hear, and suddenly, there is another stronghold."

"Are you saying those people are foolish?" asked Tan.

"No, Tan; they are innocents. They are looking for a great leader who will restore them to some former glory. They believe the rhetoric because that is all they have left."

Tan sat quietly, absorbing the full impact of her words. Although she was a stranger to him, this woman seemed to have a great understanding of the plight of his people. She was experienced in things he knew little about, and her advice, he was certain, would be important. "Tell me, please, what you believe to be the best way to proceed once we reach the clinic?" he asked, his eyes boring into hers.

"Since Lubrano knows you are here, we must assume that his people know. If they believe you have come to lead the people to some sort of victory over them, they will do everything possible to stop you. Therefore, extreme caution must be taken in order to insure your safe arrival at Janajpachallacta."

"That should not be hard; there are ways to reach the mountain without being seen," Tan told her. "There are many paths through the jungle which are not paths."

Raquela nodded in agreement. "And you must use those paths wisely, without inadvertently exposing their location."

"Will you be going with us?" asked Leah.

Don Francisco answered for the Israeli. "I would like Raquela to accompany you at least as far as the clinic. She has been there several times and has trekked through the jungle as far as your sacred waterfall. Her eyes can be a valuable asset; she sees things others easily miss."

"I would be pleased if you would come," Tan said, his face grim, "your expertise will be helpful in understanding the reports at the clinic itself."

A soft chime sounded in the cabin. Raquela excused herself and returned a moment later to announce their imminent arrival in Piura. For the remainder of the flight, the passengers sat in silence, each wrapped in private thought.

∽ ⊖ ∾

The little jet taxied to the far end of the terminal where Paolo stood on the tarmac, one hand shading his eyes as he watched them approach. As soon as the door opened and Tan emerged, his hand shot up with a wide wave. He called out the traditional greeting! "*Ama sua, ama llulla, ama quella!*"

"*Quampas hinallantaq!*" shouted Tan over the whine of the engine. "It is good to be home!" He thrust out his hand.

A little surprised, Paolo shook the extended hand. "They've made a city man of you," he laughed, "I hardly recognize you."

"And you look as though you haven't slept in a week. How is Hector?"

Paolo waited until Leah joined them to answer the question. "Either he will be much better when he sees you or he will have a fit. Take your choice; he does not know you are coming."

"Let's hope he is happy to see our pale faces," laughed Leah, hugging the pilot. "Can we go directly to the hospital?"

"As a matter of fact, we are going to Felipe's house. The nuns threw the grumpy janpeq out yesterday; said he was becoming a disrupting influence in the hospital." Paolo turned to Don Francisco and the others. "Señora Segura has invited you all for lunch."

ↄ ⊖ ℃

Although it was a tight squeeze, they managed to wedge themselves into Paolo's old Ford. A second car took Don Francisco and de Leon to their meeting at the Ministry of Culture with the promise they would be along in an hour or so, giving Tan and Leah a chance to visit with Hector before they arrived for lunch.

At the house, Señora Segura assured them Hector was completely unaware of their impending visit. She led them to the courtyard where the doctor sat, his nose buried in a magazine. His right arm, still cast in plaster, rested on the arm of the chair. He did not hear them approach.

Leah stayed back while Tan snuck up as close as he dared. He whispered loudly "What a scoundrel to be sitting in the sun doing nothing useful!"

Hector almost flew out of his seat. "Tan!" he cried, dropping his magazine as he struggled to regain his balance.

"Ha! They told me you were sick and look at you! You are the picture of good health! Is this why I have been brought back? To tend to an imaginary invalid?" He opened his arms wide to embrace his teacher.

Hector pushed Tan to arms' length and looked at him, his eyebrows knit in concern. "Is this Miguel's doing?" he demanded.

Leah stepped out from her hiding place. "Don't blame him, Hector; you, of all people, know how difficult Tan can be when his mind is made up."

CHAPTER 34

In the pleasant little garden, Hector quizzed Tan about his life in academia. His face glowed with pride as the young man detailed his progress, recounting the successes and the challenges he had faced in his first term away from the jungle. "Grades are important, janpeq," said Tan seriously, "but they are not everything; I have learned to weigh the mark against what I have accumulated in knowledge."

Hector clapped his hands with delight, pleased that his protégé had learned so quickly the secret of academic happiness. Still, a quipu full of "A's" did much to encourage that particular outlook and he said as much. Hector asked after the Halstaads, equally pleased that Tan's experience in their home had been a good one, giving the newcomer a sense of stability, not to mention love. The way Tan lit up when he spoke of Arne and Ingrid, and even India, confirmed that his choice had been a wise one. That Leah sat quietly beside him, her fingers often entwined with his, could not possibly escape his notice; the unspoken closeness spoke volumes. Finally, the doctor turned his attention to the Qewa Ñawi. "And what about you, niña? You are so quiet, but I am sure you have something to add to all this."

"Your friend is as intense in civilization as he is in the jungle," admitted Leah with a grin. "He works too hard, I think, and doesn't take time to enjoy himself."

"How would you know?" Tan shot back with a chuckle, "we have not been together long enough to make an assessment like that!"

"Ah, that's where you are wrong, bud; Mark Steinberg has a big mouth."

Leah patted his smooth cheek, delighting in the way he flushed beneath the copper of his skin. "Our mutual friend says you spend your nights either in the library or at your desk, and that you haven't seen a movie in weeks despite your professed love for big explosions."

"Explosions?" roared Hector, holding his still tender stomach. "You like explosions?"

"He is loath to admit it, Hector, but he just loves special effects movies like BATMAN and BEETLEJUICE."

He could hardly believe his ears. "Is this true, Tan?"

Tan nodded, a little embarrassed by it all. "I also like the ballet," he muttered in self-defense, "and Mozart."

"You've created a renaissance man, Hector, so you may as well admit it."

Hector was about to say something else, but Tan cut him off. "Enough of this foolishness, Hector; it is now time for you to do the talking. Tell us what happened that night in the jungle. I have heard everyone else's version of the story and now I would hear it from your lips."

Hector leaned back in his chair to consider his words carefully. He had not, until this point, told anyone the complete truth about his last night in the jungle, but he knew it would be pointless to lie; Tan would instinctively know what was fact and what was fiction. "After you left, my friend, there were great rumors floating about the district as to the reasons you had left your mita. Some said it was an omen of evil things to come, and that, because of the sudden appearance of small groups of outsiders, was given a certain amount of credence. Leah, even you were implicated, with some of the more foolish people saying you had told others of the riches to be found near Janajpachallacta. Hector noticed the way Tan's grip on Leah's hand tightened. "And there are those who said that the Aclla had left to follow the Qewa Ñawi and this was a portent of evil as well."

"Will we be shunned when we return?" asked Tan, well acquainted with the ways the people showed their displeasure to those who transgressed.

"The Mamacuna had a difficult choice to make, my children, and she chose to tell her people that the Aclla had followed the ñan of the Qewa Ñawi in order to learn the ways of the outside world so that those ways would benefit the people, not harm them. She sent the Rimoc out to the ayllus to personally dispel the rumors as best they could; she declared you, Leah, to be one of her own, saying you had left the people with her blessings to return, much the same way their Aclla had left. But I am getting ahead of my story." He told them of the night he had gone to an ayllu, summoned by their collahuaya, to tend to a difficult birth. It had been a long day, but Hector thought he could make it back to the clinic safely. A chasqui walked with him as far as the big stream. About five kilometers from the clinic, three men ambushed him. "They came out of nowhere; there was no camp, no smell of fire; it was as if they were waiting for me," said Hector, remembering the surprise of meeting strangers in the forest. "I asked them if they were lost, but they laughed. The biggest of them pushed me up against a tree and began to threaten me, saying that if I continued to send reports of their activities to the *ecologistas*, I wouldn't live to see the next solstice."

"Were they Indio, Hector?" asked Leah.

He shook his head slowly. "It was dusk, almost too dark to really see clearly, niña, but I think not. One was much taller than the other two and heavy-set, with a big mustache; the leader, I think. I did not handle myself well," he frowned; "I should have said '*bueno*' and gone on my way, but instead, I told them I would do whatever I felt was right for the people. That's when the big one punched me in the face. Again, I did the wrong thing; I should have fallen to the ground and played unconscious, but I fought back instead." Hector smiled, adding "and I did a certain amount of damage because it took all three of them to beat me up."

"But they shot you," Leah insisted. "Didn't you see they had guns?"

"The first shot was fired to get me off the smallest of the three; I had him pinned on the ground. The leader picked me up and threw me into the brush, but I came at them again. That's when the other two shots were fired. I stayed conscious long enough to listen to their conversation. The little one said 'He's as good as dead, José," and the leader agreed and said to leave me to the big cats. That way, when they found me, no one would suspect what really happened."

"How did you survive the night?" asked Leah.

"With difficulty," replied Hector, "and the grace of Mamaquilla. I managed to drag myself to a tree and get into a position I thought would best staunch the bleeding. I don't know how I did it, but I did, and then passed out for a while. When I awoke, I heard something moving in the brush and it was a very big cat. I prepared myself for death as soon as I saw the yellow eyes moving toward me, but instead of attacking a downed creature, the jaguar sniffed at me for what seemed an eternity, and then he licked my arm. I thought he was tasting me. I think I talked to it, but I'm not sure if that is truth or my subconscious trying to protect me from the memory. Whatever it was, it walked about three meters from where I sat and lay down across the trail. I could still see its eyes glowing in the darkness. For the longest time, it lay there, constantly making a strange growling sound, almost a purr, until as suddenly as it arrived, it got up and left."

Tan looked at Leah. "It was Inka, the Mamacuna's cat. He is wild, but he has a uncanny way of looking out for those favored by the Coya."

"I thought of that, but I'm not certain. Perhaps. Probably. It was dark and I was not in a condition to check for the Coya's collar around his neck. Still, it might have indeed been Inka; the cat did nothing but protect me in the night. At dawn, he got up and disappeared."

Leah pressed Hector to continue his tale. "What happened when the jaguar left?"

"I heard Anco was calling my name. I tried to call back, but I did not have the strength. The next thing I remember, I was in my own clinic, Liuta's face hovering over me." Hector gave an amused snort and confessed "I never thought she was beautiful until that very moment."

Both Tan and Leah laughed, but the sound was not very merry. "Did you hear any other names when they spoke amongst themselves?" asked Tan.

"Just one other, 'Cente.' And who do you think that could be?" Hector grimly asked.

"Lubrano," replied Leah and Tan in unison.

"Exactly. The leader, José, said Cente would not be pleased to hear I was dead, but would be relieved to know I was eaten by a jaguar while coming home from a house call."

"Why didn't you tell this to anyone, Hector?" asked Leah, her mouth set in a frown. "Surely Miguel could have used this information effectively."

Hector sighed and closed his eyes for a moment. "As long as Lubrano did not know I knew the truth, he could not tie you two to any efforts to stop their movements. If he thought I did not know who did this, or at least did not have proof positive, you would be safe. Obviously I was mistaken."

"I feel safer here than in Minnesota," snorted Tan; "Here, I know my enemies."

"And what is that supposed to mean?" Leah demanded.

"Here, our enemies will be strangers in a place I know well; I will see them long before they see me."

"Don't be so sure, Tan," said Paolo. "They're cunning and most determined to see you displaced. They've been in the mountains far longer than we thought."

Tan grumbled something inaudible and sulked. He did not like being told he might have missed something so obvious.

The arrival of Don Francisco, Raquela Mendoza, and Antonio de Leon cut the conversation short. When they were settled, Señora Segura brought refreshments before disappearing once again into the house. She was well aware of the nature of the visit; her husband would expect her to be an invisible, yet gracious hostess. From her seat in the salon, she could see them through the window, her only concern being that Hector neither excite nor overtire himself. That, in her opinion, would be far more dangerous to the tranquility of her home.

The talk centered on the aerial shots Paolo had taken the day before. Once again, Tan pointed out place after place where long established paths had been obliterated in ways common to the people, but unknown to outsiders. Walls had been moved literally overnight, obscuring the easy way into the foothills and finally, the mountains. In several places, Paolo pointed out what he thought to be evidence of three expeditions, one on each of the three major routes along the ridge leading south to Janajpachallacta. "If you look at this photo taken last week, you can see the ñan Quilla is clearly marked." Paolo pulled out a more recent picture and laid that one on top. "This is the same shot five days later. Now, where's the ñan Quilla?"

There was no evidence whatsoever that a path had ever existed. It was an incredible piece of work, eradicating any indication of a major foot track, one that had been in use for hundreds of years. The men Gutiérrez had stationed at the clinic confirmed what was shown in the pictures; their last radio message had emphatically stated something was going on beyond their range, something which the local chasqui refused to discuss. But no importance had been assigned to the activity until the day before yesterday, when the chasqui had been sent to Janajpachallacta. He returned to the clinic, but after delivering a message from the Mamacuna, had taken his leave, saying he would not be coming back.

"Which chasqui?" asked Hector.

"Tocay," replied Don Francisco.

An unsettling silence fell over the little gathering. Instinctively, Tan knew the farewell meant Tocay, a man he knew well from his childhood, had not gone back to his ayllu. *But why?* The question remained unanswered. Tan glanced at Paolo. There was something he was not telling them.

Very quietly, Leah picked up several of the photographs and studied them; something was not quite right. She picked up earlier ones and compared the two sets, looking for a clue she believed should be obvious, yet was not. She saw the changes in the walls, the alterations of the paths just as Paolo described them. Still, something was missing. Leah could not decide what it was.

Don Francisco spoke first, breaking the silence. "What do you think needs to be done, Tan?" he asked. It was the first time anyone had asked about the future.

"We must prevent anyone from reaching Janajpachallacta!" he nearly shouted. "Isn't that obvious?"

"Not necessarily, Tan," said Hector, reaching out to restrain Tan from jumping up. "I am concerned more about the physical safety of the people and, if we challenge the expeditions, what measures they will take to stop us."

"This is not foolish thought, Tan," agreed Don Francisco, his voice grave, "you cannot discount their ability to make war in a way which the government cannot halt. They can cut off water supplies, paths to the chacras, things like that; they can lay siege to the ayllus, endangering the people beyond simple attack."

"But surely you cannot expect us to do nothing? There are ways to halt their progress, Don Francisco," Raquela insisted, her eyes bright with anger, "you cannot let them be pushed off their land!"

"It's too late." Leah's words were soft, almost inaudible.

Her words caught everyone off guard. "What did you say?" asked Hector.

Leah thought she was going to cry. "It's too late. They're gone."

Tan exploded. "Don't be ridiculous, Leah! "

She shook her head. "They have already gone. The ayllus are deserted and so is Janajpachallacta."

"How can you say such a thing?" Tan demanded.

It was Hector who quieted him with a restraining hand. "Sit down, Tan, and listen to what she has to say." He turned back to Leah. "What makes you think they are gone, niña?"

Spreading the two sets of photographs on the table, Leah pointed to the oldest ones in the pile. "Here, and here, you can see smoke. This one," she said, pointing to the eastern most cloud, "is the Ayllu Mayu, the one closest to the river and the clinic. And over here, this is my ayllu.... I can tell by the location of the chacras. There is definitely smoke coming from the central fires of both ayllus. There should always be smoke coming from them; the fire burns all day and all night. And here," she pulled one of Janajpachallacta, "here's the Mamacuna's fire. Now, look at the ones taken yesterday. There's no smoke."

She was right; there was no evidence of any fire in the last pictures. But she did not tell them everything and Hector suspected this when he looked into her brimming eyes. There was something else in their depths, a frightened kind of look he had never seen there before. Softly, he spoke directly to her. "You wrote to me that you had had dreams you believe were sent by the Mamacuna, niña. Have you had more dreams?" He watched as Leah nodded. "What were those dreams, niña?"

Leah took a deep breath; she had not slept well at the hotel, her rest had been punctuated with dreams of nightmarish proportions. Even now, in broad daylight, the memory of the dreams was hauntingly real. "I was standing at the bottom of the path leading to Janajpachallacta," she said slowly; "I started up the path, expecting someone to come down to meet me. Saba, maybe, I'm not sure. But no one came so I began walking. The streets were empty; the houses were deserted as though no one had lived there for a thousand years. It was, I guess, a ruin, like Macchu Pichu: intact, but empty. I called for the Mamacuna, but there was no answer. Then I saw the condor circling over my head; it was very close and kept coming closer." She paused and reached for Tan's hand, tears running down her cheek. "Then, the condor landed and transformed into the Mamacuna. She smiled at me and said '*Ama sua, ama llulla, ama quella,*' and then she turned back into the condor and flew away."

"Don't steal, don't lie, don't be lazy?" asked Raquela, familiar with the ancient greeting. "Isn't that a proper way to greet a visitor?

"Yes, but it's not the usual way she would greet a chinan. She would've said *Yau, chinan albado....* welcome and praise God."

"Then why would she say *ama sua* to you?"

Leah shrugged. "I don't know."

"I do," said Tan. "She would have said it if she never expected to see you again." He rose from his chair and went to stand alone at the far end of the garden. Closing his eyes, he concentrated on the image of the Mamacuna. He could not form her face in his mind; he kept seeing Paolo. Tan turned and stared at the pilot.

Wordlessly, Paolo crossed the patio to join Tan. "I had no choice. I could not tell you or anyone else. Not even Hector."

"She forbade it?"

"Yes."

"Do you know where they are?"

Paolo nodded. "I have tracked them from the air. She asked me to."

"Am I to go to them?"

"I believe she expects you to come. She said you would demand to be taken to the clinic, and once you were there, you would know what to do."

Tan clapped his hand on Paolo's shoulder. "Then we shall fly to the clinic as soon as you are ready. Once I am there, I will know what to do."

☙ ⊖ ❧

The little airplane was crammed with supplies and passengers. Despite Felipe Segura's categorical refusal, Hector was strapped into the co-pilot's seat. In the rear, Leah, Tan, and Raquela were wedged between the mounds of luggage and crates. No one spoke; no one dared make a noise while Tan sat perfectly still, his eyes closed, desperately trying to hear the Mamacuna and the Rimoc. But it was not Tan who heard them; it was Leah.

Into her mind flashed the image of the Mamacuna as she stood on the edge of a great canyon, her hands outstretched toward the sun. *Go back, Qewa Ñawi! Fly away in the belly of the silver bird, but do not come here! You are in danger!* The image faded leaving Leah shaking uncontrollably as she clutched Tan's arm.

"What is it, my heart?" he asked, rubbing her arms to heat them. "What have you seen?"

"They're gone, Tan; they're gone." She repeated the Quechua words slowly, as if the weight of them was too much to bear. "We are too late, my heart, they are gone. She says not to come. She says I should go back."

"This is one time I will ignore her warning," said Tan softly. "We will go to her together."

Paolo announced he could see the clinic and they should prepare for a rough landing on the unpaved field. Within minutes, they were taxiing toward the shack where Don Francisco's men stood waiting.

ళ ⊖ ఁ

The clinic looked strangely deserted even though several men had been living there while Hector was recovering in Piura. The plane stopped in front of three lanky men whom Raquela identified as Pepito, Diego and Raoul. The fourth man, the one Raquela said would be most helpful, was Altahualpa, a local who had left his ayllu years ago and wandered south until he found himself on the Gutiérrez ranch looking for work. At first, according to Raquela, he refused to go back to the mountains, fearing the anger of the Mamacuna who did not look kindly upon those who strayed from the people, but when Don Francisco told him the gravity of the situation, he agreed to return. As soon as Raquela stepped off the plane, Pepito told her Altahualpa was in the mountains looking for some sort of trail.

"Every ayllu is deserted?" she asked hurriedly.

"To the last child. Not a scrap of anything remains. One minute they were there, the next, they were gone. We can't figure out how they did it."

Tan did not wait for any more explanations. Sprinting across the field, he reached the house and disappeared inside. Other than a few dishes scattered on the table, Hector's house looked exactly as he had left it months earlier, even if the absence of Hector screamed from every wall. Ignoring the overwhelming fear deep within, Tan went to the closet and pulled out the box in which he had carefully placed his belongings. Quickly, the trappings of western civilization were removed and replaced with those things in which he still felt most comfortable: a breechclout and his old carry pouch. The soft wool of his sash was comfortingly familiar against his skin. He pulled a rough alpaca tunic from the box and slipped it over his head. Although his hair was short, he tied the llautu around his head anyway; he did not bother to look in the mirror, he did not need to see himself.

Leah was walking slowly with Hector when Tan came out again. He met her eyes and smiled as best he could. "Meet me at the second huaca, but not at the pool," he whispered as he brushed a kiss against her open mouth, "take the ñan beside the waterfall and go up... up to the ridge from where I first saw you. I will join you there." With a last kiss, he sprinted toward the jungle and disappeared into the dense brush.

Paolo watched him go, then turned to Hector. "I must go, my friend," he said, shielding his eyes against the sun. "I have several other deliveries to make before dark."

Hector thought Paolo looked nervous, but he said nothing. Leah, however, took his arm and walked with him toward the plane. "You will do as you were told, this I know," she said quietly. "I just hope you know what it is you are doing."

He lowered his mouth close to her ear, although there was no one around to hear him. "I am bound, Qewa Ñawi, just as you are. I will do as I was told." He bowed his head toward her and touched his lips several times. "You are in her heart, coya."

Leah blanched, but said nothing. She merely stood and watched as Paolo got back into the cockpit and taxied away from her.

ঔ ⊖ ঔ

Tan followed the path he had always followed between the clinic and his makeshift home deep in the jungle; he could see more subtle changes had been inflicted along the way. Part of the ñan had been covered over with dead growth, obviously, at least to him, put there by skilled human hands. The deeper he went, the greater the changes, as if someone purposefully had hidden the way until the path disappeared completely and it was simply his knowledge of the jungle which kept him heading in the right direction. Marker after marker had been obliterated by carefully placed vines until they were invisible to the uninitiated; two huacas had been completely dismantled, nothing but scattered stones in their place. For a fleeting moment, Tan wondered if the fertility huacas had met the same fate, but a sudden flood of warmth told they remained intact. He hoped that the ñan Leah would take would be in better condition.

At the end of the first trail, Tan agreed with Leah: there was no one left in the district. Where chacras should have been under cultivation, there was nothing but empty fields already being reclaimed by the jungle: overgrown plots stripped of carefully planted rows of potatoes and corn. Whatever had taken them away, it had not been a hurried exodus; time had been taken to remove all vestiges of communal life, including the scarecrows and the thatched shacks that served as shelter from the frequent storms. Tan walked through what had once been the chacra from which he had taken his own food. Where the shelter stood, there was barely more than a couple of indentations where the posts had been in the ground. During the years of his mita, an old, ornately carved box stood beside the shack, inside of which the women of the ayllu would leave delicacies for their Aclla. Now the box was gone and Tan hoped it was traveling with the people so that in the future it might serve another who had been called into the service of Mamaquilla.

When he finally reached his old home, he was not surprised to see it untouched, since it was already considered abandoned and looked that way. He stood before the doorway, then knelt to offer a prayer thanking Mamaquilla for his safe return while at the same time asking Her for guidance.

As he rose to his feet, he heard a noise in the brush. Freezing, Tan held his breath as he waited for whomever it was to make himself known as he tried to determine from what direction the visitor traveled. The crunch grew louder and Tan slowly positioned himself between the doorpost, drawing his knife from his sash as he moved. Then he heard the low, menacing growl. He was about to spring when a large cat strolled out of the brush.

"Inka!" he called, returning the knife to its sheath. The jaguar growled again, but without menace, as he ambled toward the man to rub his thick fur against Tan's leg. Squatting, Tan put his arms around the animal and let Inka curl himself up in a ball, his large head resting comfortably on Tan's knees. "Where have you been?" asked Tan, continuing to stroke the cat. "And why aren't you with your Coya? Has she released you from your mita, too?" Inka answered with a long purr. "Ai! I wish you could talk to me, Monsonsoré, for then I would know what has happened to our Coya and our people.

As if he could understand, Inka stretched and stood, allowing himself a last rub against Tan before heading back into the brush. When Tan did not follow, Inka stopped, turned, and roared. Suddenly, it was Tan's turn to understand and he followed Inka's lead.

Through the jungle, along paths barely visible beneath the overgrown brush, Inka ran, occasionally turning his head to make sure his friend still followed. He avoided the better-worn path along the river, taking instead the first ledge of the valley. Deeper and deeper into the jungle they went, the gradual rising of the land not apparent until the rain forest began to give way to the rockier paths leading up into the highlands. Soon the brush had thinned out and the jaguar changed course, hugging the cliffs of the foothills; they darted along the edge, hidden from view by the scrub and tall grass. Tan kept as low as he could; from his vantage point he could see evidence of human occupation on the valley floor below. He did not know who they were, but he was not about to stick around to find out.

ल ⊖ ल

Leah stayed just long enough to see Hector settled in his favorite chair to await the villagers who were now coming across the field in small groups. She took her bags into the bedroom and pulled out only the barest necessities: her carry pouch, a knife, a flashlight, her woolen tunic and her cape. Quickly, she changed her clothes. Her cloak over her shoulders, she was about to put her baseball cap on her head, but changed her mind. Instead, she took her red felt chinan's hat from her bag; somehow, it seemed more appropriate. Joining the others in the living room, she smiled at their stares. If it weren't for the bush pants and boots sticking out from the bottom of the tunic, she might have passed as a fair skinned Indio.

"Now that's the Qewa Ñawi I know!" murmured Hector.

Raquela seemed quite impressed with the outfit, especially the cape. She fingered the material lovingly, obviously a connoisseur of the finer things in life. "How did you come by such a beautiful cloak?" she asked.

"A gift from Mayta, our ayllu capac."

"And the hat? Surely you did not buy that in the market!"

Leah reddened when she said "A gift from my Mama'amuata Saba when I became a chinan to the Mamacuna."

Raquela looked from Hector to Leah and back to Hector. "You understated her importance, Hector," she commented dryly. "You might have told us she was more than a casual visitor to Janajpachallacta."

"It was not for me to tell," shrugged Hector as he struggled to his feet. "Niña, there is something I would tell you in private." He led her back to the bedroom, closing the door behind them, then went to his bureau. Opening the top drawer, he removed a snub nose Smith and Wesson .38 and a box of bullets. "Do you know how to use this, niña?"

"Yes, but..."

"No buts, Leah, you will take this with you into the jungle; it is not the safe place it was a year ago. We do not know who is wandering about in the brush and I will not have you unarmed." He checked the chamber, then handed her the weapon. "Now, show me how to load it."

Before she had come to Peru the first time, Leah had, on the advice of Dr. Muñoz, undergone small arms training at the University. She wasn't a marksman by any means, but she was a pretty good shot. Deftly, she loaded five bullets, leaving an empty chamber beneath the hammer. Clicking the chamber into place, she handed the gun back to Hector.

"*Bueno, niña, bueno,*" He handed her the box of bullets and instructed her to fill her carry pouch with ammunition. "Put the gun in your belt, like this, " he slipped the gun so that it caught on her snugly wrapped sash. "You should be able to pull it easily, from beneath your cape, without being seen. Show me." Leah did as she was told, then tucked the gun back in place. "I pray you will never have to use it, niña, but if you do, shoot to kill."

Leah swallowed hard and nodded; Hector would never give her the gun if he did not think it was absolutely necessary. She also knew she could, if necessary, use it. "I am going to meet Tan at the second huaca," she told Hector, "do not tell the others unless you must. I will be back as soon as possible."

e⁓ ⊖ ⁓e

The changes in the jungle damped her natural joy of being back in the yunka. Familiar landmarks were all but gone; the further she walked the more difficult it became to follow the overgrown track. Instead of taking the path she would have used to go back to her own ayllu, the one that ran along the river, she veered to the west where the shadow of the foothills would serve as her guide.

Of all the things she noticed, the worst seemed to be the oppressive silence all around her. Where once there were endless birdcalls and the footfall of animals, it seemed that the jungle was completely deserted. She heard the occasional chatter of monkeys, the screech of a lone parrot, but without the frequency to which she had become accustomed during her stay. When she passed the location of where an ayllu had once stood, the hamlet was eerily invisible; only the barest remnants of their central fire remained. It was as if the people had systematically dismantled the tiny village; not even the footprints of the little houses could be seen in the dirt. Leah did not linger; there were too many miles to cover if she was to reach the huaca before darkness fell.

CHAPTER 35

Raquela paced the length of the living room, her silence respected by the men seated around her. She listened carefully to the reports, asking for certain details to be repeated again and again until she was sure she had a complete picture of the events of the last week. Raoul insisted the last time they had had contact with the Mamacuna's chasqui, everything was, according to him, quiet in the mountains and apparently normal. There had been a meeting of the collahuayas at the full moon, nothing which might have been construed as abnormal, but it was shortly thereafter that the ñans between the ayllus had started to disappear. Altahualpa told them it was a defensive method often used when an enemy threatened, but no one had made any mention of an exodus from the land. But there was one facet that kept coming back to Raquela: the meeting at the full moon. "How was it that we had no representative at that conclave?" she asked, directing the question to no one in particular.

"But we did; Altahualpa was there."

"And he insisted nothing important was said?"

Pepito slammed his hand down on the arm of the couch. "We have told you a dozen times, Mendoza, he said nothing changed."

"And Paolo confirmed this from the air?" she pressed.

"Paolo did not say a thing."

Raquela sat on the low table opposite Pepito, her face as close to his as she dared. She could see the anger building in his dark eyes and the last thing she wanted was to get him upset. Using a quiet voice, she asked him to think about the exact words Altahualpa had used when he came back, and how he behaved. Raquela believed there was a clue the others had missed; something the chasqui said or did which would be the key into what took place on the mountain a few days earlier. "Close your eyes, Pepito, and try to imagine how Altahualpa looked when he came out of the jungle."

Pepito did as he was told, leaning back against the couch as he searched his memory once more. "Altahualpa walked out of the forest about two o'clock in the afternoon. He was tired."

"How could you tell?"

"He wasn't running, or even jogging; he was walking slowly. I saw him first and waved to him. He did not wave back, he just kept walking toward me."

"Was he breathing hard, as if he had been running?"

"No."

"What did he say when you reached him?"

"He said the meeting was very long, and he had not been permitted to cross the bridge, even though the Mamacuna met with him when he first got to Janajpachallacta."

"So he was not at the meeting itself."

"No."

Raquela kept her voice soft and even. "Was this the first time he saw the Mamacuna since he came back; since he left his ayllu?"

"Yes. He said he asked her forgiveness and she gave it, but not without recrimination. She said he was welcome to stay on the mountain, but he was no longer permitted to go across the bridge to the meeting place. This would be his punishment for leaving the people. She said she understood he had returned with a good heart, but he had broken trust with the people."

"But would she accept his help?"

"Yes."

"Good," sighed Raquela. "Did she speak with him again after the first night?"

"I told you, he could not cross the bridge. She sent one of her guys to tell him the people were willing to do whatever it took to protect themselves from the invaders. He told Altahualpa they knew about the gold mines in the south."

This was a new piece of information, not something Pepito had mentioned before. "What did they know about the gold mines? Think hard."

Pepito shook his head. "Only that they exist and Indios are enslaved there. Especially the children."

"How would they know that, Hector?" Raquela asked the doctor. "Had you ever discussed this with the Mamacuna?"

"Of course, I told her about the mines."

"Raoul, what exactly did Altahualpa tell her?"

"He said he told the great lady that there were three expeditions in the mountains and more getting ready to leave from Cajamarca and Trujillo. He told her exactly what Don Francisco told him to say."

"And what was her response? Does anyone know exactly what she said?" demanded Hector, suddenly frustrated by the circular nature of the conversation.

"She said *I will protect the children of my people as a mother jaguar protects her young*," said Diego, reading from a small note pad, "*as a mother condor protects her nestlings.*' Those are the words of the Mamacuna."

"As a mother jaguar....a mother condor," repeated Raquela. Suddenly, her head snapped around and she stared at Hector. They both knew exactly what she had done.

"That's the answer, you idiots!" cried the doctor, "As a jaguar who hides her young in a den and a condor who builds her nest on the most inaccessible pinnacles of the mountains. She told Altahualpa she was taking the people away. He knew it and you all missed it! And he's gone to join them!"

Raquela ran to the dining table and spread out the map with the aerial photographs above it. "Damn Paolo! He knew," she growled, studying the pictures with a magnifying glass as the others gathered around her, trying to follow her finger as Raquela traced the lines on the map. "Here!" she suddenly shouted. "Here they are as of three days ago. Look, right here," she jabbed the photograph repeatedly. "See this? This isn't a natural formation, this is tenting. Camouflage tenting. Here...and here....and here..." her finger moved along a straight line about fifty miles away from where the most outlying ayllu would have been. "They are moving at a tremendous pace, heading north-northeast, but staying along the ridge of the Cordillera. Hector, how far do you think they will go?"

"They won't go into the basin;" said Hector, "they'll stay at the edge of the mountains, maybe even going into Ecuador; it's hard to say. But the area up there is uninhabited and definitely remote, much more so than where we are right now." Instinctively, he understood why the Mamacuna would do this, but he worried about what would become of the people as they struggled to create a new home for themselves in an area so far from their traditional home. Would there be a place for a landing strip? How would he get medicine for them? Would he be able to transport everything he would need? It never occurred to Hector that he would be left behind. But his concern for the moment was for Tan and Leah. They had gone into the jungle separately.

As if she could read his mind, Raquela came to stand behind Hector and rested her hands on his tired shoulders. "I think I should go after Leah. Do you know where she was heading, Hector?"

He showed her the huaca with the pool, finding it on the map and then on one of the aerial photographs. "It will be difficult to find, especially with the paths obscured."

"I've been there," said Raquela.

"But you haven't gone in the dark," said Diego, "I have." He turned to Pepito and Raoul. "Wait here for Altahualpa. If he returns, come find us. If he's not back by morning, come anyway. We won't make the huaca tonight, but...."

Hector cut him off. "Then why not wait until morning? Do you really want to travel the jungle after dark?"

"We can find a place to camp," said Raquela as she gathered up her gear, "it's better to make progress now; if we wait to leave until morning, we may miss her completely."

❧ ⊖ ☙

The constant sound of falling water reassured Leah she was near the huaca. Keeping close to the jungle undergrowth, she reached the second huaca and was relieved to see the little shrine still standing, even if it had been stripped bare to nothing but the pile of stones. She paused for a moment at the pool, but there was no time to recollect the first moment she looked into Tan's dark eyes. She shaded her eyes with her hand and looked up; the ledge was exactly as she remembered. Leah walked passed the place where she had camped a year ago and instead, went to the end of the pool. There, behind the never-ending wall of water, were two stones covered over with vines. Tan had described the place carefully that night she had shown him the pictures and she knew the vines were hiding the entrance to the path which would lead to the ridge. Carefully, she pushed aside the foliage and stepped through before replacing it with equal care. Satisfied that it looked undisturbed, she pulled out her flashlight and made her way along the slippery rocks leading into the mountain.

The path leading to the ledge was difficult, taking her higher onto the cliff than she had ever been on the outside. Keeping her body flush against the sheer wall, she moved slowly, her hands groping for any sort of hold until the path turned to go into a narrow passage. She could see dim light at the other end and when she stepped out of the tunnel, she gasped. She was in the center of what could only be described as a roofless room; the sides towered at least thirty feet above her head. At eye level, the walls were filled with intricate drawings, some very ancient, others definitely more recently inscribed. Using her flashlight, she examined the pictures, most of which centered on the worship of Mamaquilla. The anthropologist in Leah wished she had a camera, or at least a notebook, but the light was fading and she had to find the path Tan told her would lead to the ledge. Picking up her pace, she left the chamber through a passage on the western side. At the end of this tunnel was a carefully constructed screen of brush thick enough to hide the entrance from the outside while allowing enough light through the brambles to signal the end of the second tunnel. She pushed the brush aside, then replaced it.

The top of the ridge was a flat, dusty mesa that stretched for miles. Estimating how far north she had traveled within the cliff, she estimated the path to the ledge would be at least a kilometer south from where she stood. There was a well-worn ñan, a sort of shallow depression which seemed to serve as a guide to those who would brave the climb up the cliff. The steep peaks of the central Andes shadowed the mesa. Taking a deep breath of the thin, crisp air, Leah hiked along the path. Finally, as the ñan skirted the edge, she looked over and realized she was above the place where Tan had been in the photograph of the pool. The ledge was directly below, the pool beneath that. She continued until she found a narrow path off the main ñan, one that led downward as it snaked around the ridge though dense scrub and past several small grottos. Finally, she stood on the same ledge on which Tan stood when she accidentally caught him in the eye of the camera.

A cave opened at the center of the ledge. Tossing her pack inside, Leah explored the ledge, checking out the point where it dead-ended into the cliff. The only access seemed to be from the path which she had followed; she understood why Tan had insisted she stay there instead of down below at the pool. At its widest point, the ledge was almost fifteen feet. A blackened ring of stones told her someone had spent the night up there before and she hoped it was Tan and not one of Lubrano's goons. The sun was disappearing as she returned to the cave. Taking out her flashlight again, she went in.

There was no evidence of wild animal habitation inside, no telltale signs of feces or bones that would have warned her to stay out. Instead, she found a couple of pencil stubs and an eraser tucked into a little hole in the wall. Examining them carefully, Leah laughed softly; they were obviously Tan's. In another hole, she found a small basket with a slip of paper tucked in the top. "May this keep hunger from you, my heart," read the note in Tan's small, neat hand. Inside, there was a bunch of tiny wild bananas and several handfuls of peanuts. That an aclla had, in essence, left an offering for her was not lost on Leah.

She slept wrapped in her cape, her head on her pack. Her dreams were comforting dreams of Tan dancing taqui at the edge of the pool as she stood in the sand. His arms reached for her yet never touched her skin as he moved slowly around her, the scent of him filling her nostrils until he stepped away, transformed into a condor, and flew straight up, over the ridge, disappearing into the bright disc of the moon hanging in the black, star studded sky. His departure did not frighten Leah; it seemed to reassure her of his place in his world. Twice during the night she awoke, each time hoping it was because he now joined her on the ledge, but it was not so; she was still alone.

The sun was not visible when Leah opened her eyes. Instead of a vivid azure sky, the canopy was thick with cotton wool clouds, all but obscuring the face of Illi-Inti. Cold, Leah drew the alpaca cloak around her in an effort to ward off the uncommon chill in the air; she wished she could build a small fire but that was out of the question. Any evidence of fire in this part of the jungle would bring unwanted attention. She settled for parking herself at the entrance to the cave, flush against the wall from where she could see yet remain unseen.

Leah stayed there as long as she could. Her mouth was dry and her stomach rumbling so loudly she thought she could hear it echoing against the stone walls. From her pack, she pulled the bread she had taken from the clinic and slowly ate it, along with two bananas. Had she been on the valley floor, Leah would have found plenty to eat growing around the pool, but she dared not go down; she would have to carefully measure out what she ate and when she ate it since it might be a long time before Tan could reach her. Leaning against her pack, she closed her eyes and dozed; it was hard to stay awake with nothing to do but wait.

℮ ⊖ ℮

At Kimsa Chayankuna, the place where three mountain streams joined to form a single, fast flowing arroyo, Tan found what he sought: the Mamacuna's marker. An outsider would have missed the configuration of stone and wood, deliberately hidden on a mound of land at the point of juncture. Tan had successfully navigated the long trail the people had traveled, although their passage had been carefully obliterated by the young men who closed their ranks. They had been taught to do this as children, the older men instructing the boys on ways to become invisible to the enemy. But completely invisible they had not been; there was no known way to obliterate the tracks of scores of men, women, children and herd animals. But unless one knew what to look for, the trail would not be seen.

The current was fast and the water cold when Tan left Inka on the bank and swam across to the alluvial island where he hoped to find some sign from the Mamacuna. It was the perfect place to make an offering of good faith, a sacrifice of something representative of the people, but not something necessary to survival. Emerging on the steep bank of the island, Tan shivered beneath the threatening clouds. He offered up a prayer to Mamaquilla, repeating the same words he had spoken each time he felt himself close to something that might guide his way. He closed his eyes, opened his arms to the sky above, and called to the Goddess, asking for Her help in his quest. And, as had happened the other times he called to Her, Tan felt a flood of warmth in his veins and a sense of calm before he opened his eyes to scan the little isle.

He almost missed the hand-made mound atop the rise of the island. Covered by a nest, it was the perfection of its placement that caught Tan's eye. Not quite round and built of sticks and grasses, it lacked the touch of a bird. Tan approached it slowly in the event it was actually inhabited, but, as he expected, it was not. The interior of the nest formed a neat triangle, the two longest sides forming an angle which pointed precisely to the narrowest crossing place to the other side of the stream; a fording place. Dropping to his knees, Tan gently lifted the nest and placed it to the side, revealing a layer of blue powder, a sure sign the Mamacuna had been there. Tan used a leaf to sweep the powder aside without scattering it. A hand cut, five-angled slab appeared. With another quick prayer to ask Mamaquilla's forgiveness for disturbing this huaca, Tan lifted the slab and stared into the cache below.

A tightly tied llama skin pouch was neatly stuffed in the clay-lined hole. Tan worked the knot without removing the pouch; to take it unnecessarily from its place would have been an even greater transgression. He gently parted the skin and studied the objects inside one by one without touching them. A great smile began to grow across his face; the Mamacuna knew he would come and she had left a clear map which only one of her own could interpret. With the same exacting care, Tan retied the skin, replaced the slab and the powder, and finally the nest. Keeping his hands away from his body lest the sacred powder touch any other part of him, Tan returned to the water and washed, offering up a prayer of thanksgiving to Mamaquilla before he swam back the way he had come. If he was going to find his Qewa Ñawi at the pool before a second night had fallen, he had to run as swiftly as his jaguar companion. Already he was away from her longer than he had planned and he worried for her safety.

e⁓ ⊖ ᴑ⊝

The sun was directly overhead, yet there was no sign of Tan. Leah was still huddled beneath her cloak at the mouth of the cave, but she was seriously considering coming down from her perch to find something to eat. She had no foreboding of danger; what she felt was closer to restlessness. She did not feel abandoned, yet she was anxious to see Tan's face. In the same way, Leah was certain when he arrived, he would bring good news with him.

The sky was still thick with the promise of rain, but the air was warmer than it had been in the morning. Every so often, the sun would peep through the clouds, revealing a brief moment of blue sky: a reassuring sign in an otherwise foreboding day. The few animals who appeared at the pool below seemed only to come at those scattered bright moments. From her perch on the ledge, Leah saw a female jaguar and her cubs cautiously approach the pool and drink. She was familiar enough with the big cats to notice the way the mother secreted her cubs in the tall grass while she explored the area instead of allowing the cubs immediate access to the pool. It was as if the cat knew someone was watching and Leah could not help but wonder if the jaguar had seen her, or if there were other humans in the vicinity.

She could sit no longer. Leah stood and stretched, easing the cramps from her shoulders, arms and legs as quickly as she dared. For a moment, she debated whether or not to wear her cloak; a chilly breeze convinced her it was warranted. She left her pack in the cave, but took her flashlight and the small pot for boiling water she always carried with her. The gun was still tucked in her sash and she left it there, drawing a certain amount of comfort from its presence. Hector, she grudgingly admitted, was right; the gun was a safety measure.

Retracing her steps, Leah found the entrance to the tunnel. She moved the brush covering the entryway, stepped inside, then pulled it back into the mouth of the tunnel. She did not linger in the stone room, nor on the path leading down to the huaca. She passed behind the waterfall, pausing only long enough to quickly wash her face; she resisted the temptation to drink. Last year, she wouldn't have thought twice about drinking from the pool, but she had not been in the area long enough to re-acclimate herself to local water. Leah was cautious as she moved into the clearing, staying away from the open area. As close to the waterfall as she could be, Leah gathered a little bit of dried grass and twigs in order to build a sheltered fire. The spray of the waterfall would keep the smoke from rising. Leah filled her pot and set it on a stone, leaving it to boil while she went in search of something to eat.

Leah hadn't gone very far when she heard the coarse sound of men's voices rasping nearby in the brush. They were speaking Spanish, but a guttural version, the kind spoken in the slums and barrios. Silently, Leah backtracked; she had to reach the waterfall and path hidden behind it before they did. There would be no time to douse the flames, but if she could manage to slip behind the water, they would not be able to find her. Crouching, she crept along taking care to avoid dead foliage that would crunch beneath her feet. Leah counted the number of distinct voices; there were five men in the party, none particularly skilled at jungle maneuvers. They made too much noise as they hacked and slashed at the dense growth. She took advantage of their constant conversation, running while they shouted to each other, her own footsteps drowned out by the noise.

The roar of the waterfall was closer to Leah than the sound of the men. She reached the edge of the clearing and crouched in the brush as she tried to determine their position. Deciding they were still well in the jungle, Leah sprinted across the grassy strip between the jungle and the pool, stopping at the fire long enough to grab her pan and dump the contents. It was a mistake.

"Over there!" shouted one of the men emerging from the jungle at the far side of the pool.

Leah froze, a deer caught in headlights, rooted to the spot. Swinging the pan over her head, she hurled it with all her might in their direction, not waiting to see where it landed before she scampered behind the water-fall, quickly pulling the covering after her.

Their shouts gave Leah the few seconds she needed to reach the other side and disappear into the first of the canyons leading to the ledge. She forced herself to remember the route without stopping; there was no time to make a wrong turn. Only when she reached the stone room, did Leah stop long enough to catch her breath. There were choices she had to make and they had to be the right ones. Leah knew if she went up onto the ledge, it would afford her a good view of the valley below, but it would also make her visible. In addition, the ledge was a dead end; if the men found their way up there, she would be trapped, with nowhere to go but down. True, Tan dove off the ledge, but she was not Tan and was afraid of hitting the water from that height. On the other hand, considered Leah, the odds of them finding the way to the ledge were not very good. Taking all possibilities into consideration, Leah opted for the ledge.

When Leah exited the western tunnel, she blocked the exit with a denser covering of brush than had been there originally, knowing that the tiny pinpoint of light she had been able to see from the stone room would now be obliterated. If they made it as far as the room, they would be forced to explore several tunnels before they would discover which one led out. Satisfied, she scurried along the rocky path, keeping low to the ground, until she was again above the ridge. Laying flat on her belly, she crept as close to the edge as she dared. Three of the men were still in at the pool, guns drawn, scouring the area for evidence of her presence. She could see her little pot sitting primly beside the pool as if someone had picked it up and casually placed it there. Pulling Hector's gun from her belt, she checked the chamber and took careful aim at the pot. It never occurred to her that she might miss. Narrowing one eye and bracing her arm, she waited until the three men were each at a different spot away from the kettle and, sucking in her breath, she fired a single shot.

The little pot flew up into the air as the three men hit the dirt simultaneously. The echo ricocheted off the cliff, making it impossible to determine the direction. Leah allowed herself a little giggle as she watched them crawling on their bellies, trying to determine from whence the bullet had come. Successfully having diverted their attention, Leah slid back until she touched the wall and then scooted toward the downward path, keeping close to the ground, dragging a large piece of scrub behind her to obliterate her tracks.

When she reached the mouth of the ñan, Leah used her knife to dig out several dead bushes and placed them over the entrance to the path. Not completely satisfied, she managed to drag and push a couple of small boulders to the edge and followed that by beating the ground with a large piece of scrub. The effect was exactly what she wanted: it looked as though no one had walked there in ages. Moving slowly, she scattered whatever she could behind her until the little ñan was strewn with ancient looking debris.

Safely ensconced on the ledge, Leah wrapped herself in her cloak as much for the warmth as the camouflage it provided as she positioned herself in such a way to afford an unobstructed view. She could see the three men more clearly now; they were sitting at the far end of the pool, their backs to the waterfall in an effort to protect themselves from any further attack. Leah did not recognize them; they looked like three ordinary men in hunting garb, a sort of khaki and green camouflage like that worn by hunters in Minnesota, but without the orange safety vests. All three were scruffy, two with droopy mustaches and one with a beard. Leah decided the one with the beard was the most alert of the three, his head moved constantly as he scanned the walls of the pool; a rifle rested on his lap. The other two seemed content to sit, or rather stretch out in the grass, waiting for something to happen. Idly, she wondered where the other two had gone.

Night was falling fast and still there was no sign of Tan, nor of the other two men. Only when the last rays of light had disappeared and she was sitting in complete darkness, did Leah crawl back into the little cave to go to sleep. She was tired and once her head rested on her pack, her .38 still curled in her fingers, Leah fell quickly asleep.

Tan danced taqui in her dreams. Like so many other nights, she could see his graceful body move in the slow, measured steps of the dance, near to her yet not touching, translating into the raw desire she always felt when she was with him. Nude but for the small breechclout he wore, Leah could see the sinewy muscles of his body ripple as he danced, his arms outstretched as though to engulf her. In her dream, his eyes held hers, his lips moved in words she did not need to hear to understand. Leah could see herself standing still as he circled her, each tour bringing him closer and closer. She reached for him, but at the last moment, Tan transformed into a condor and with a harsh shriek, soared into the sky.

Leah awoke with a start. The screech had been a warning, of that she was certain. Feeling for the gun with her fingers, she sat up and pointed the snub nosed revolver at the entrance to the cave where the first light of day was easing the blackness outside. On her belly, Leah crawled out of her hiding place until she could see the valley below. It was still too dark to see anything, but she was patient; daylight would soon reveal what was below and she had nothing to do but wait.

There were three bodies in sleeping bags beside the waterfall while a fourth sat watch on a flat rock nearer to the water. When the fourth had arrived, Leah did not know, but it had to have been after dark. She could not tell, in the thin morning light, which of the four was the newcomer, but it really didn't matter; what mattered more was that there were only four accounted for on the ground and that meant the fifth, or more, were still on the mountain.

A rumble in her stomach interrupted Leah's train of thought. "Damn," she swore softly, wrapping the cloak even more tightly around her. There was no denying hunger, it was still gnawing at her. She allowed herself a single banana, but it only made her thirsty. Rummaging through her pack, she found out a forgotten roll of Lifesavers tucked into the pocket back in Minnesota. Popping one into her mouth, she slowly sucked the little candy, hoping it would stave off the need to forage for food. With nothing to do but wait, Leah crawled back into the cave and tried to sleep.

∽ ⊖ ∾

Human voices awakened her. Someone was on the ridge above her ledge, shouting to the others in the valley. There was only one voice, giving credence to her theory that the fourth man had been one of the two who had gone after her. That this one had made it to the ridge frightened Leah at first, but she stayed deep in the cave, trusting her own skill at obliterating her path. So long as she did not move, thought Leah, she would be safe.

"Can you get to the ledge below?" called the bearded man to the one on top of the ridge.

"Maybe. There's a path, but it looks blocked," called the one above Leah. "¡Mierda! It's starting to rain." The voice echoed off the canyon walls and faded. The sound of rain grew louder.

Leah sat listening to the back and forth conversation between the man on the mountain and his four friends below. The danger was closer than she expected and just as she feared, she would be trapped. Yet, the steady rain would delay any attempt to try the path and, better than that, would obscure any footprints she had missed. Pressed against the farthest wall, Leah yearned to use her flashlight to see if any exit existed in the cave, but resisted; a simple misdirection of the beam would reveal her location. Instead, she inched along the rock, her fingers at the joint of the wall and the floor, searching for a break that would indicate another passage might exist.

Leah found it hidden in a grotto on the southeastern wall. A bulge in the wall, she discovered, was not solid, but rather a small boulder slid into place. Using her knife, she dug around the rock until she could get her fingertips around the sides. With a deep intake of breath, she pushed against the rock and moved it an inch. She dug some more, and again, the rock moved. Dig and push, push and dig, she worked until her fingers bled, but in the end, she had opened another passage in the small cave. Leah grabbed her pack and shimmied through the tiny opening. Once inside, she found smaller rocks and used them to cover the entrance. As she crawled along the narrow passage, her heart pounding wildly in her chest, she could still hear the voices growing fainter as she made her way through the tunnel.

In the blackness, Leah could feel cool air coming from someplace. There were no other tunnels leading off the one she traveled, so she was sure she was heading in the right direction. When the tunnel became too narrow to accommodate both Leah and her pack, she hooked her flashlight to her belt, along with her knife, loaded extra ammunition into her pockets, stuffed her cloak inside and left the backpack behind. The scent of fresh air grew stronger, but she could not see the end of the tunnel. Risking it, she pointed her light ahead of her body and briefly switched it on. A few yards away, the tunnel widened. Quickly, she crawled toward the place and once there, stood up. She was in a chamber barely wider than she, definitely higher. Standing, she used the flashlight again and when she saw the chamber, she gasped. Thick grey-black veins streaked the walls. Chunks had been hewn out, obviously by human hand, and the remains of their work littered the floor. Picking up a small rock, Leah examined it carefully and laughed silently to herself as she put it in her pocket.

There was only one passage out of the chamber beside the one through which she had come. It was higher and wider than the one from the ledge, but she still had to crouch. Switching off the beam, Leah used her nose and her hands to follow the path until a pinpoint of light appeared in the distance. As she neared the end of the passage, Leah slowed her progress, finally stopping at the mouth of the cave, behind a thick covering of dead brush. There she rested, dozing for an hour or so before retracing her way in the blackness. Now that she knew she had a way out, she felt secure hidden inside the mountain.

ॐ ⊖ ॐ

Inka still at his side, Tan crouched at the top of the waterfall and watched the scene below. He could see the four men at the pool and the fifth standing on the ledge where Leah should have been. He was wild with worry until he heard the one on the ledge shout that no one was there and that he had wasted the better part of a day tracking a ghost. Relief flooded Tan's heart and he offered a quick prayer to Mamaquilla, thanking Her for making Leah quick of mind and resourceful. He was certain she had found the tunnel, was deep within the cliff and, for the moment, safe. Hidden in the tall grass beside the river, the rain pounding heavily now, Tan watched as the stranger started back up the path, away from the ledge.

Short of going over the waterfall, there was no quick or easy way down to the pool or across to the ledge. The stream above was not wide, but the current was strong enough to be treacherous. And even if he could cross, the other side was laced with sheer wall canyons with no footholds to enable Tan to scale down to the next level. Still crouched in the grass, Tan considered the alternatives: he could either go down to the pool and take the path behind the fall itself, or backtrack until he could ford and take the canyon route. Either way, it would be hours before he could reach Leah. Checking the position of the sun, Tan opted for the canyon; it afforded better shelter in the event he ran into the scouting party.

CHAPTER 36

Hunger and thirst drove Leah back into the cave on the ledge. The basket holding the last banana was still secreted in a niche, undiscovered by the man who had been on the ridge. Footprints in the dust told her he had indeed followed the path down to the ledge, but nothing had been disturbed; either he did not go into the cave or decided it was not in use. Rather than take a chance, Leah carried the basket into the tunnel and rebuilt the little rock barrier, believing it was safer to eat in the darkness than to risk being seen.

The air was cooler now. Leah pulled her cloak from the pack and wrapped herself in its soft warmth. Sitting as close to the barrier as she dared, Leah listened for voices drifting up from the valley floor. Occasionally she heard a shout or a sharp laugh, but mostly she heard nothing. And *nothing* did not calm her frayed nerves; no amount of wishing could make them go away and for the time being, there was nothing to do but sit and wait. Muscles cramped, she stretched out as far as the small tunnel allowed and began singing quiet songs to herself to ward off the dreadful combination of fear and claustrophobia. Despite efforts to keep herself mentally occupied, the minutes dragged into infinity until she thought she could bear it no longer.

᙮ ⊖ ᙮

The search for the huaca at the pool had taken much longer than Raquela estimated. The rain halted their progress, forcing them to make camp for a second night. Diego swore constantly as he built a crude shelter against the storm while Raquela silently cut branches for the structure, ignoring Diego as best she could. She did not like this helpless, lost feeling; this was not what she was trained to do. In other situations, she would have insisted they continue, but the mud and the lack of paths had made movement in the jungle foolish at best. But now they were near the huaca; the rush of the waterfall was impossible to miss and twice she caught the sound of shouting. Keeping well hidden in the dense brush, she and Diego moved slowly toward the sound, their only communication through hand signals.

Raquela saw the men first. Motioning to Diego to join her, they watched as five men went about the business of breaking camp. They could hear their voices, but they were too far to make out what was being said. From their vantage point, they could not see the ledge above the pool. Deciding it was safe to talk, Raquela whispered "How do we get up there?"

"We'd have to go all the way around the back, then up."

"How long will it take?"

"Three, maybe four hours."

Raquela sighed and rested her head on her arms for a moment. "Can we make it by nightfall?"

Diego shrugged. "Who knows? Maybe...maybe not. It depends on the trails."

"Well, sitting here isn't going to help. Let's go."

The tunnel walls pressed against Leah until she could no longer breathe. With her ear against the opening, she could still hear voices coming from the valley. Muttering, she pushed her back into a crevice and shucked her cloak, folding it as compactly as possible before tying it to her waist with her belt. She let her felt hat hang by its woolen thread down her back. There was no point in going out onto the ledge, the voices decided that for her, so the only other choice was through the tunnel and out the other end. Leah checked the gun, hooked her flashlight onto her belt, and ate the last banana before she began the cramped journey to the other exit.

The area was deserted when Leah emerged from the tunnel. Carefully, she covered the entrance to the shaft before she walked northward. The sky was still mottled, the threat of rain lessened but not completely gone and the air was comfortably cool. Setting her hat squarely on her head, Leah stayed close to the wall, beneath the stone overhang, hoping if anyone saw her, she would be dismissed as a local. The path, while not steep, moved definitely along an upward incline; Leah believed that if she stayed on it, she would come to a place from where she'd be able to see the waterfall and the valley.

The path twisted its way up the cliff until it disappeared between two large rock formations resembling a gate. As she passed between them, Leah noticed the carvings drawn up the smooth walls, indications that this had been, at some time, used as an entry to a crypt. Involuntarily, she shivered, but it was not enough to keep her from continuing along the trail. Once the walls were behind her, Leah breathed easily when she realized up ahead was the entrance to the other tunnel that led to the ridge. Feeling more confident than she had when she set out, Leah quickened her pace. She was certain now she knew why Lubrano had set his sights on owning this particular corner: he wanted that little vein of emerald for himself and she had the proof in her pouch.

The end of the walled path was in sight; Leah could see the opening straight ahead and she knew instinctively she would find herself on the wide, flat mesa above the ledge. Up there, she would not only be able to watch everything from a sheltered spot, she would have room to maneuver if necessary.

No sooner had she stepped out into the open, than a screech caught Leah's ear. Looking upward, she saw a large condor swoop down directly at her, coming with such speed that she hit the ground. Taking it as a warning, she remained in the dust, crawling along on her belly until she reached the edge of the ridge. Four men were in the valley and she knew, in that moment, that the fifth was somewhere nearby. Moving as quickly as she could, Leah headed to where the opening to other the tunnel was hidden. She found it just in time; the fifth man was coming down the path from the other direction. Ducking inside, Leah ran along the passage.

∽ ⊖ ∾

Barrantes saw a flash of red disappear into the wall and smiled to himself. He was right after all; the little *bruja* had been on the cliff all along and now he would find her. Breaking into a jog, he closed the distance between them and followed the flash into the mountain.

It took a moment for his eyes to adjust to the darkness, but Mañuel Barrantes did not allow that to slow him down. Keeping his head low, he ran as fast as he could along the path while he listened to the echo of Leah's footsteps. As he came around another corner, he could see a pinpoint of light flashing ahead of him and Barrantes decided it was Leah's movement that caused it. Suddenly the flickering stopped. There was no way Leah could have reached the opening; she must have either turned off the trail or....there was no other conclusion he could reach. Barrantes slowed when he estimated he had reached the place where she had disappeared.

∽ ⊖ ∾

Leah realized she was blocking the light and because of it, must be more visible to whoever was behind. Falling to the ground, she began crawling furiously toward the high walled chamber, hoping against hope there was either a foothold she could climb, or a second passage she had missed. As soon as she reached the room, Leah scrambled to her feet and hastily searched the wall.

There were footholds notched into the wall, leading to a ledge and another cave opening. Sucking in her breath, Leah placed her foot in the first notch and began to scale the wall straight up. Her fingers bled as she climbed, grabbing at the notches with all her might. Leah was halfway to the ledge when her foot slipped and a hand grabbed her ankle, pulling her down from the wall. Leah screamed as loud as she could.

"Asshole," snarled Leah as she scrambled away from Barrantes after she had tumbled him when she landed.

Barrantes was more nimble than she anticipated as he grabbed her cloak, pulling her away from the opening to the tunnel and back into his arms. "Stop struggling, niña," he laughed mirthlessly, pinning her arms behind her back, "there is no place to go."

Leah stomped her heel into his foot but his grasp on her remained firm as she was lifted into the air, her legs kicking, her body twisting with as much force as she could muster. "Let go of me, you mother's abortion!" she shouted in street Spanish. She twisted again and this time, as her head came around, he pushed her away, sending her crashing into the stone wall. Pain ripped through Leah and she crumbled. Deathly still, she lay on the ground.

Barrantes, hands on his knees, caught his breath as he watched the inert woman. Straightening, he prodded her with the toe of his boot. When her eyes opened, he allowed a small, cold grin. "Where are your spirits now, Qewa Ñawi? Have they deserted you like the people have deserted their jungle?" Her eyes slid closed and he thought she had passed out.

Leah said nothing, but she watched him cautiously through half-closed eyes. Her head was throbbing and her left arm hurt more than anything she had ever known, but her hand, still pinned behind her back, closed over the handle of her gun. Barrantes, she knew from their last meeting, was arrogant and a fool. Keeping herself still, she waited for him to do something, anything, which would allow her to draw her gun and catch him off guard.

Tan heard the scream and knew it was Leah. With Inka beside him, he ran the twisted path until he came to the opening over the stone room. Looking down, he could see one figure, a man, but he could not see Leah. He had to get in closer. Scrambling along the top of the canyon, he reached a scrub-covered spot and without waiting, pulled back the brush. Sliding down into the tunnel, he was amazed when Inka followed him. Into the blackness they went, although Tan knew exactly where he was and where he would end up when he reached the end of the tunnel. He could feel the hot breath of the cat behind him and the occasional growl as the animal put his faith completely in the man.

The narrow slide turned into a path and Tan followed it until it opened onto the ledge above where Leah lay still on the ground. Lying on his belly, he could see Barrantes clearly now and tried to determine which was the best way to take him out. Suddenly, a slight movement caught his eye, and he realized Leah was, behind her closed eyes, obviously awake. He prayed to Mamaquilla that Barrantes had not noticed the same thing. Sucking in his breath, Tan lay motionless on the ledge with his arm around the cat, signaling the animal to stay quiet. Inka stretched out beside Tan, his powerful muscles taut, ready to spring.

At the bottom of the chamber, Barrantes eyed his captive. She was far better looking than he thought that night he saw her in the lamplight. Whatever it was she had, it was enough to take the Aclla, the man who fucked untold numbers of women at will, away from that savory task. If he was ever going to find out what it was, it was going to be now. Kicking Leah's legs apart, he grunted when she made no move. He leaned over and pushed her cloak open and groped her breasts. Still, the Qewa Ñawi did not move.

From his perch, Tan thought he would explode. The sight of those filthy hands touching Leah made the blood pound in his ears. Clenching his fists, he willed himself to be still. Leah had to know what she was doing.

It took all of her energy not to move when Barrantes squeezed her breasts. Leah sensed he would give her the opening she needed, but only if he was convinced she was unconscious. Moving her eyes so she could see through the curtain of her lashes, Leah thought she saw someone on the ledge above her. She kept her breathing steady when she saw Tan's face in a blur. *Please, Mamaquilla, keep him still,* she prayed silently.

Barrantes, hot for her now, stood up and began to unbuckle his belt. "Too bad you are not awake to enjoy this, Qewa Ñawi,"

Leah waited until both his hands were busy with his trousers. Slowly, so that the movement was masked by the folds of her cloak, she slipped the gun out of her belt and brought her hand forward until the muzzle was pointed directly at his head. "Too bad you won't live long enough to enjoy it, Señor Barrantes."

His laughter was mocking. "I am flattered you remembered my name, Qewa Ñawi." His eyes narrowed and Barrantes clucked his tongue. "Put that thing down, niña, before you get hurt. Didn't anyone ever tell you never to pull a gun unless you plan to use it?" he drawled.

"I didn't miss the bucket so I doubt if I will miss you point blank." Slowly, Leah rose to her feet, keeping her wounded arm close beneath the cape. If he tried to take the gun, she was afraid she would be unable to defend herself. But Tan was above her. "Put your hands over your head and turn around, and I promise not to put a bullet in your brain."

His hands rose slowly until they were shoulder high, then Barrantes whirled around, his arm extended to take the gun. Leah jumped, but he caught her hand, sending pistol into the air. Before she could hit the ground, there was a flash of dark fur and Inka, claws extended, was on Barrantes. He screamed as the cat's mouth clamped on his arm.

"*Inka, tiaikui!*" commanded Tan and the jaguar sat, his fangs bared dangerously; a constant steady growl coming from deep within him was just enough to hold Barrantes at bay. "Are you all right?" he called to Leah, her back flat against the wall.

"Yes." She was shaking but saw no reason to share that information. "Can I move?"

Tan laughed, a reassuring sound to Leah's ears. "Yes, my heart, Inka knows you and will let you pass. Take his gun and go to that place at which we agreed to meet and I will come to you there." For safety's sake, he would say no more.

But Leah understood and said so. Retrieving her pistol, Leah stuck it in her belt and then relieved Barrantes of his weapons: a long bladed knife as well as a pistol. With a last look upward, Leah disappeared through the opening in the western wall of the chamber.

When she was gone, Tan ordered the cat to back off and Inka obliged him, but not before positioning himself in such a way which prevented Barrantes from moving so much as an inch. Tan swung his body over the edge of his perch, his feet finding the familiar toeholds as he lithely climbed down the wall to face Barrantes. The man was bleeding, but not too badly; he would be able to walk out the way he came in. With a snap of his wrist, Tan removed Barrantes' belt, then ordered him to stand. "You are lucky I do not tell Inka to kill you, for he would on my command," commented

Tan dryly as he bound Barrantes' hands behind his back with his own belt. "Now, move." The cat leading the way, Tan walked behind the Peruvian, prodding him when he moved too slowly, forcing himself not to make short work of a man who would harm his woman.

❧ ⊖ ☙

Leah's arm throbbed mercilessly, each step causing new waves of pain searing through the offending limb. As she walked, she opened and closed her left hand slowly as she tried to determine whether or not she had broken her arm. Joint by joint, she found she was able to move it, even the elbow, although it hurt enough to bring tears to her eyes. Finally, Leah reached the end of the tunnel and immediately noticed the brush that covered the entry the last time was missing, which meant Barrantes and his friends had already used that path. Pausing to look around, Leah saw nothing else out of the ordinary and she allowed herself an extra moment to stretch out her arm and try to bend it a couple of times at the elbow. Yes, it hurt to beat the band, but no, she was convinced it was not broken, only bruised and wrenched; annoying perhaps, but certainly not enough to impede her progress.

Leah reached the ledge without seeing anyone else. The valley floor was deserted, with nothing to show for its recent inhabitation. She found her pack in the cave and brought it back out. Settling herself in her favorite spot, Leah sucked on the last of her Lifesavers, secure in her belief that she would soon be on her way back to the clinic with Tan.

❧ ⊖ ☙

"What do you mean you lost Barrantes?" demanded Lubrano, his dark eyes glittering dangerously at the four men standing before him.

"He went up onto the cliff to look for the girl and we haven't heard from him since," muttered one of them, pulling uncomfortably at his mustache.

"He said not to wait for him; if he found her trail, he was going to follow it," said the shortest of the group. He did not like the way Lubrano's hand was clenching and releasing the stock of his gun.

Lubrano shot a stream of spittle so that it landed on the ground beside the short man's boot. "Your assignment was not to follow the girl, you fools; it was to secure the top of the ridge and the route to the Janajpachallacta. Are you so stupid as to think the people have left their mineshafts intact? Or that the Mamacuna has left no one behind to guard what she believes is hers?"

"But Vincente, there is no one there. *Nadie. Ninguno.* We have not seen a single soul, other than the girl and," the short one stopped to take a breath, "Barrantes says if she is here, the man will be here, too."

"The man?" repeated Lubrano.

"You know...him." The last word was whispered.

Lubrano's laughter was short and cruel. "Don't tell me you are becoming a believer in legends, Paco! I gave you more credit than that!"

"It's not the legends which are frightening, Vincente, it's this place." Paco shivered involuntarily. "It is too quiet and there are condors...too many condors to count and eyes which stare in the night. I have seen them, we all have!" The other four nodded, unwilling to agree aloud, yet willing to support Paco silently.

"Bah! A bunch of clucking women!" Lubrano stalked away from the rag tag group, toward the helicopter that brought him to this clearing. He pulled open the door and yanked a high-powered rifle from the rack behind the passenger seat. Ordering the pilot to stay put, he rejoined the others. "Now you will take me down to the valley and we shall all wait for Barrantes, together."

ᘒ ⊖ ᘒ

Raquela and Diego moved cautiously around the perimeter of the pool, keeping well hidden in the grass, out of sight of anyone who might be up on the ridge. They had heard what sounded like a muffled scream coming from above, but there was no way to tell, because of the echoing, from which direction it had come. Still, Raquela had to admit it sounded like a woman, although she could not be certain. The helicopter, however, had been unmistakable. They caught only a brief glimpse of the whirly-bird before it disappeared over the top of the cliff, but it was enough of a sighting to keep them both in the thick stand of grass. Suddenly, a flash of red appeared on the ledge above the pool and vanished as quickly as it had come. "Diego, did you see it?" whispered Raquela.

Her companion nodded. "It's her, I'm sure of it," he answered, crawling toward her. "I hope she has enough brains to stay up there."

"Yeah, I hope so. But where the hell is Tan?" Another movement, this one on the ridge above the ledge, caught Raquela's eye. "Uh-oh, it looks like we have company." She scooted backward on her belly, motioning to Diego to do the same. Pulling a pair of compact field glasses from her pack, Raquela focused on the ridge. "I see five, no six men, five in fatigues, but not military...no insignia." She passed the binoculars to Diego. "Look at the one on the far right...the one in the black pants and tell me if that's Lubrano."

Diego let a thin whistle escape his pursed lips. "I can't be sure; I've only seen the bastard once. They're heavily armed and moving to the south. I think that's where the path is."

"Shit," swore Raquela softly. "There is no way to warn Leah from here, and even if we found the path behind the waterfall, it would take too long to reach the ledge."

Not waiting for the order, Diego checked his rifle and aimed it at the top of the ridge. Raquela snorted and did the same. "Shoot to kill; we have no time for games."

Eerie silence hung over the valley, oppressive in its calm, making Raquela even more nervous as she watched for movement on the ledge and the ridge above it. Suddenly, the figure appeared, but it was flush against the wall, hidden from the men above her.

& ⊖ &

Leah heard the chopper and she heard distinctly male voices coming from above. Stepping out of the cave, she kept well back as she scanned the valley floor below. She would have missed the movement in the grass completely had the sun not bounced, if only for a split second, off of one of the figures hiding there. Squatting, she trained her eyes on where she had seen the sharp ray of light, holding her breath as slipped the cloak off her shoulders and pushed the hat from her head.

"Good woman," muttered Raquela when she saw the hat come off, making it harder to see Leah against the rocks. She hoped Leah had enough sense to stay back.

But Leah had other ideas. Flat on her stomach, Leah inched forward to get a better view of the valley floor. Her gun was drawn, but something inside told her not to fire; she knew there were men above her, but she did not know how many. And it was possible that those hidden in the grasses had been sent by Hector.

"Over there!" shouted one of the voices from the ridge.

Leah almost jumped out of her skin then quickly moved back into the cave. Her heart was pounding in her chest, filling her ears with her own noise. Breathing deeply, she willed it to slow down so she could hear what was happening. There were several more shouts, and then the unmistakable sound of running feet.

"This way!" cried one of the voices.

Raquela caught sight of two men tearing down the path that led to the ledge. Pointing her rifle toward the waterfall, she fired a shot and watched as the men both on the path and on the ridge hit the ground. She could not see Leah, but she hoped the woman had done the same thing. Creeping forward, she came as close as she dared to the edge of the grass, waiting for the echo of the shot to fade. Raquela could see the two men on the path begin moving in a crouched position down toward the ledge, guns drawn. There was no way to warn Leah who now stood, her own gun drawn.

Leah was trapped. When she had gone back into the cave, planning to make her escape through the tunnel, she had gotten only as far as the first turn when she heard two other voices coming from within the mountain. Racing back to the ledge, she planned to make her stand from there. She heard the first shot and hit the dirt, then realized it must be someone from the clinic, for otherwise she would most likely be dead. The only way out was down, but she would take out whoever set foot on the ledge before she went over. Suddenly, she heard her own name being called from the valley floor.

"Leah! *Takshivi-li!*shouted Raquela at the top of her lungs in Hebrew, "*Kafatzi!*"

Leah did as she was told and without waiting an instant, she jammed the gun in her pocket as she ran three steps and flew off the ledge. All around her bullets were flying, but she landed, feet first, in the water. Turning quickly, she stayed beneath the surface and swam under the waterfall to where she knew she would be safely hidden.

Once she was off the ledge, the two men on the path changed directions and went back the way they had come, continuing to fire in the direction of Raquela and Diego. A bullet grazed Diego's shoulder, but he did not stop to examine the wound; he followed Raquela's lead back into the jungle, continuing to fire as he went. From behind a tree, Raquela lined up her shot carefully and fired at the only man on the ridge not wearing fatigues. All firing ceased when Lubrano fell.

"Did you kill him?" Diego asked as he checked the tear in his shirt.

Raquela shook her head. "No, I hit his right leg. What about you?"

"Hardly a scratch worth mentioning," he laughed grimly. "It won't even leave a decent scar."

A strange sound filled the air and when she looked up, Raquela saw not one, but three choppers swoop down over the ridge. "Well, either we are in a shitload of trouble, my good friend, or the cavalry has arrived." Leaving Diego to tend to his arm, Raquela sprinted though the bush to the waterfall. "Leah?" she called.

"*Kol b'seder,*" came the response. A wet, but much relieved Leah emerged from behind the waterfall. "*V'at?*"

"*B'seder.* Where's your friend?"

"Somewhere inside the cliff. Barrantes caught up with me, and Tan caught up with us. It's an ugly story, but Tan has a jaguar with him and I don't think Barrantes is going to try anything."

Raquela raised an eyebrow but did not ask for clarification. "Did you hear the helicopters?"

"Yes. Whose are they?"

"I have no idea, so we're going to wait for a while until we find out. Either we are safe or we are dead."

Something in the last statement struck Leah as very odd and she gave Raquela a puzzled look. "There is something I don't understand and maybe you can explain it to me, Raquela. What exactly does Lubrano think he'll accomplish by killing me and Tan? I mean, these guys were shooting at me and I don't know why. The people have left the land, Janajpachallacta has been deserted, and they have what they want. What conceivable threat do we pose?"

"That's a good question and I don't think there's an easy answer, but the way I see it," she looked over to her compadre who just joined them, "and Diego, feel free to jump in at any time... I suspect they think that if Tan is eliminated, and Hector as well, there will be no one left to press the claim that one: the land and all its mineral rights belong to the people, and two: the people were moved off the land illegally. The Mamacuna and the Rimoc are not about to start lobbying the Peruvian congress for land rights, but if it turns out there is a major advocate, the mining rights could be tied up in court for years."

"Believe it or not," offered Diego with a modest shrug, "we are a democracy. And Indios do vote. And their voices are getting stronger. It's a slow process, but it's happening. You know about the gold mines in the south, don't you?"

"Of course!"

"Well, Don Francisco doesn't want to see the same thing happen in the north and he fights to prevent it." Diego smiled gently at Leah. "If the minerals are to be mined, it must be done in such a way that neither the land nor the people are exploited. It is a dream, of course, but a good one."

Leah opened her pouch and withdrew the stone she had picked up in the tunnel behind the cave on the ledge. "Does this have anything to do with it?" she asked, handing him a rough emerald.

Diego whistled when he saw the stone, but shook his head "No, not really. Gemstones are always nice if you have them, Leah, but there isn't enough up there to make it profitable on a large scale. I'd guess Lubrano's already seen stones like this one. Perhaps he was hoping to have a private mine to add to his personal collection." He returned the gem.

Replacing it in the pouch, Leah sighed. "What do we do next? We can't just stand around waiting for something to happen."

Raquela noticed the way Leah was holding her arm. "Obviously, you are hurt," she said.

"Sprained, not broken. I'll live."

"Are you up for another trek up the cliff? We may as well see what's happening up there."

Leah laughed, but it was a tired, joyless sound. "Sure, why not. It beats waiting for them to find us." She stood quietly while Raquela fashioned a sling out of her sweatshirt. "Thanks," said Leah, feeling infinitely better once the arm was nested in the fleecy material. "Shall we go?"

ၕ ⊖ ၜ

They stopped at the end of the passage atop the ridge. Raquela went first, poking her head as far out of the brush cover as she dared to prevent being spotted. The flat expanse of rocky terrain was deserted; there were no helicopters in sight, nor was there any sign of anyone or anything else which might mean danger to the little party. "How far to the path?" asked Diego, wiping the dust from his face.

"About a kilometer to the path, but there's a tunnel which goes into the cave from a path about halfway on the other side of the mesa."

"Please," moaned Diego, rolling his eyes for sympathy, "no more caves."

"There, there, amigo, we'll go along the mesa as far as we can," replied Raquela as she patted his hand.

They walked at a brisk pace, their eyes trained on the horizon looking for any sign of approaching danger. They kept their conversation to a minimum, any sound might drift on the wind and reveal their position. Suddenly, Raquela spotted what looked to be a lone runner moving in their direction. "Quick, get down," she commanded as she hit the ground.

Leah was about to follow suit when she realized the runner was not alone, there was an animal with him. With a cry of delight, she broke into a run.

"Must be the boyfriend," commented Diego dryly.

Raquela shot him a warning look and got up, briskly slapping the dust from her clothes.

ഏ ⊖ ൦

Tan led Leah, Diego and Raquela to the government helicopters at the south end of the mesa. Inka, annoyed when Tan slung his arm about the woman, tried to wedge himself between them then settled for trotting beside Leah. "I heard shots inside the cliff," he told her, a trace of worry still in his voice, "and by the time I came out and could see into the valley, you had disappeared. I wanted to kill Barrantes right then, but I saw the helicopters and knew they had come from Hector."

"They have Barrantes now?" asked Raquela.

"Yes, the Federales have him and the other four with him, also Lubrano and his pilot. It seems they have finally broken enough laws to be arrested." His grin said more than his words and Leah could not resist reaching up to kiss his dusty cheek. "Had they not been there to arrest him, my heart, I would have sliced open his chest and fed his heart to Inka."

"I don't doubt it for a minute," Raquela snorted. "He's lucky the government decided to step in."

"What happens next?" asked Diego.

"Will your people return?" asked Raquela.

Tan shook his head sadly. "No, I do not think so. Their sacred places have been desecrated and our law demands a new home must be found." He did not tell them he knew in which direction they had gone; the fewer who knew, the safer they were, but a quick glance into Leah's eyes told her what she needed to know.

In the distance, they could see the helicopters and hear the cacophony of voices. It seemed strange to Leah to hear that much noise in the area after being so used to the silence. Still, they sounded like the most welcome voices in the world and it was Leah who quickened the pace.

A dozen uniformed men guarded the prisoners who sat in the dust, their hands cuffed behind their backs, while several others stood to the side engaged in conversation. Only when the party approached did they turn and Leah recognize three of them.

Hector raised his cane and waved it at the hikers. Leah returned the wave and hurried toward him. "What are you doing here?" she demanded as she hugged him as best she could with one arm. "Couldn't you keep him at the clinic?" she chided Miguel.

"Niña, what happened to your arm?"

Leah told him quickly, noticing the way he scowled at the very mention of Barrantes. "And I would have shot him had I not seen Tan above me on the ledge," she informed him. "But as it happened, I saw him and Inka sitting up there and I didn't fire. I should've though, because then he knocked the gun out of my hand."

"Could you have fired, niña?" Miguel asked in a quiet voice.

Leah's eyes narrowed as she stared at him. "Without a second thought." She raised an eyebrow and added, "Does that surprise you?" Tan's hand touched her shoulder.

"No," admitted Miguel with a wry smile, "I think not." There was something different about this Leah, a change from the woman he had seen in Minnesota and this one could be dangerous. Again, he found himself more than a little jealous of Tan. He was about to say something inane when his father joined the group.

Don Francisco motioned for Raquela and Diego to join them. "I am pleased with the way it has ended," he said, "but I am sorry we were too late to prevent the people from leaving."

"It is not the first time my people have been forced to move, Don Francisco, but it is the first time outsiders have come to their defense. On behalf of the Mamacuna, I thank you for your efforts." Tan extended his hand to the older man. "It will be good to have friends in the capital."

Leah, however, was not completely satisfied. "What will happen to the land now?" she asked.

"Eventually, it may be mined and the natural resources of the jungle utilized, but not right away. There will be environmental studies made beforehand, and with God's help, the land will be used wisely. There are no guarantees, of course," Miguel shrugged, "but we shall try to do the right thing." He was about to turn away, when he pulled something from his pocket and handed it to Leah. "I believe this is yours."

"My paicha!" cried Leah, delighted to see the tassel that had been taken from her office bulletin board. "How did you get it back?"

"Your buddy Lubrano had it hanging from his belt."

Tan scowled, his anger yet to abate. "He's lucky I didn't find him; I'd have cut him in half to get it."

"And what will you do now?" politely inquired Don Francisco, changing the subject. "Will you go back to the United States to continue your studies?"

"He'd better," growled Hector, glaring menacingly at Tan.

He was rewarded with good-natured laughter and Tan reassured him that he would be back at school by fall. "But now, Leah and I are going to take a walk."

"A walk?" Hector cried, "she's not going anywhere until I've had a chance to look at that arm!"

Leah leaned forward and kissed his stubbly cheek. "Look all you want, janpeq, and then we'll go for our walk."

CHAPTER 37

Beneath a grand canopy of stars, Tan and Leah spent the night beside the pool. They refused the generous offer of supplies from Miguel, so while Tan gathered the wild delicacies he yearned to taste again, Leah bathed in the pool to wash away the dirt and dust, relishing the sweet cascade of the waterfall. They dined on succulent fruits and traditional herbs, the familiar flavors suffusing them both with a sense of well-being. Afterwards, when the black sky shimmered with a million diamonds, and the face of Mamaquilla shone down upon them, Leah sat gazing out across the water, giving Tan the time alone he needed to pray at the huaca. Although he was now simply a man, not the Aclla, he retained the right to visit the shrines sacred to women. It was not an obligation, but rather a desire to make his peace with Mamaquilla.

Leah did not hear him approach yet she knew he was near. Rising to her knees, Leah remained perfectly still, her long hair unbound, flowing down her back, her only clothing her cloak to keep her warm in the cool night air. She closed her eyes and waited and when she opened them again, she caught the reflection of Tan standing behind her, his arms outstretched. Slowly Leah rose to her feet.

Just as slowly, Tan began to dance taqui, coming close to the Qewa Ñawi, yet never touching. His arms encircled her and when he raised them, Leah's arms rose, too. She lifted her face to the moon as he caressed her without caressing. The cloak slipped from her shoulders and she felt his heat on her bare flesh. As if tied to him with invisible strings, Leah matched him move for move. When he finally allowed his fingertips to touch her, his warmth surged into her and she thought she would burn up in a single, shooting flame.

In the soft sand, Tan devoured Leah, tasting, sucking, licking every inch of her supple body. The tips of her breast hardened into points thrusting upward, demanding attention that he willingly gave. Leah arched her back, yearning to become part of him in this sacred place, offering herself with abandon. Her skin tingled with every touch; she stroked the contours of his body to reassure herself this was real and not another dream from which she would awaken in Ruti-Suyu.

"Open your eyes to me, Qewa Ñawi," commanded Tan as though he could read her thoughts, his voice ragged with passion. "Let me see the grass eyes so I might know you are real!"

"I am real, my heart," murmured Leah. "I come to you with no barrier between us." The words caused his soul to rejoice.

"Your heart is in my heart," he whispered looking into the depths of her soul.

"As your heart is in mine. You are bound to me forever."

Joyously, Tan entered her, sliding deep into her as her slender legs wrapped around his hips. They moved together, a single being; lips, legs, hips and tongues fused together. As he touched her with the tip of his tongue, she returned the favor, letting the sweet taste and masculine scent of him fill her to overflowing. Leah could feel his heart match the rhythm of hers, beat for beat, as though in their union their bodies had melted together.

Tan's passion enflamed them both; Leah kept pace with him, meeting each thrust with one of her own. She could not get enough, feel enough of him on her, in her, around her. She savored the satiny texture of his skin against her own, the slipperiness which came with their exertion, enhanced by the contrast of the evening chill. They were warm against each other, their passion a blanket on the soft sand. When Tan whispered strange words in her ear, Leah did not need to understand them to tell they were the words of his heart. The gentle caress of his breath against her ear aroused her beyond anything she had ever experienced. It drove them into each other, and then, at the moment when they thought their hearts would burst, their souls came together in a singular explosion only to linger together until their breath returned to their bodies and they descended from the zenith of their love.

When they lay beside each other, their legs still entwined, their loins still touching, Leah let her fingertips trace the rugged outline of his face. Tan nipped the inquisitive digits when they reached his lips, laughing softly at the look of quick surprise in Leah's grass eyes. "You are as beautiful by the light of Mamaquilla as you are in the light of Illi-Inti," he whispered; "I see your face before me and I cannot believe Mamaquilla has allowed me such happiness."

Leah nestled closer against him and let Tan pull her cloak over them. "You are the dancer in my dreams, Na-Tan Manco; my heart dances taqui when I see you in the day. I am afraid to sleep now, for I worry you will be gone with the face of Mamaquilla, as you were on my last night here."

"I never left you," replied Tan, kissing her lightly, "my heart went with you. Without the Qewa Ñawi, I was incomplete." With his arms wrapped around her, Tan listened until Leah's breathing grew evenly deep before he allowed himself to close his own eyes.

ഔ ⊝ ഔ

At first light, they took only their clothes and their carry pouches, leaving everything else secreted in a niche behind the waterfall. The trek to where Tan believed the people now camped would be long and best made with as little extra baggage as possible. Still, Leah insisted on taking her little spiral notebook and several pencils that Tan tucked into his own pouch. He helped Leah to organize her sling; although her arm felt better, it still throbbed and needed to be kept as quiet as possible while they walked. With a final tug on the brim of her red felt hat, they started walking.

"How long will it take us?" she asked him, munching on a wild banana as they hiked northward.

"Eight, perhaps ten days; it's hard to tell. But we are in no hurry, are we, Qewa Ñawi?" he teased.

"No, I suppose not. But, as long as we're heading northeast, can we stop at the outer huacas?"

Tan threw his head back and laughed. "Ai! Always the mulkan!" He tugged at the strings of her red felt hat.

"Would you have it any other way?"

❧ ⊖ ☙

They slept in places Tan knew, visiting huacas as they trekked through portions of the district Leah had not seen during her stay. At each little landmark, Tan told stories about the people and their ancestors. In return, during the long hours between markers, he asked that Leah recount tales of her people, explaining that their friend, the rabbi, had only told him so much and there were so many questions to ask.

Through it all, Leah was struck by the uncommon silence of the rain forest, devoid of any human laughter and chatter as they passed places where once ayllus had thrived. Even Inka seemed unsettled by the silence. When they reached what had once been Tan's own village, she saw tears in his eyes, tears as silent as the jungle around them. But Tan would not let his sadness linger, choosing instead to show her the places where he had played as a boy. He stood at the spot where his grandfather's hut had been and spoke lovingly of the tall old man who taught him how to fashion a boat from reeds and how to catch fish with his bare hands. "All things a man needs to know," he told Leah proudly. "They used to say he was from far to the north; now I think it must have been Mexico, the Yucatan, perhaps. On the long winter nights, he could carve little figures from wood. I have seen carvings from the Yucatan at the Art Institute," he said wistfully, "and they were much like his." He wondered if he had learned enough from Iztak to carve them for the sons he was certain they would have.

Leah touched the chain around Tan's neck, separating the two stars hanging there. "This one is mine," she said as she slid it to the side. "But I think, when I touch this one, it is from the hand of your grandfather."

"Yes, this is true. When I was ready for my manhood ceremony, my grandmother gave it to me. She said my grandfather had made it when I was born in preparation for that day."

"Odd that it's a six pointed star," said Leah. "I have never seen one like it in the drawings or the carvings. Do you think it had a special meaning to him?"

Tan nodded. "He used to draw stars like this in the sand when I was small. He said it was the sign of his tribe."

"I like his taste in symbols," Leah grinned, patting his chest. "Perhaps it was an omen that you would love a woman whose own tribe uses this symbol."

"Perhaps," echoed Tan. He was staring off into the distance as though he were struggling to remember something. Shaking the memories from his head, he led Leah away from the last vestiges of the ayllu and up a steep path toward the foothills. They walked in silence until they reached a ñan cut into sheer rock. "I would visit my ancestors one last time before I leave this place forever," he quietly said, squeezing Leah's hand. He commanded Inka to stay and left them both while he disappeared through a narrow passage.

The sun was almost hot and Leah stretched out in the shade of an ancient tree with the cat beside her. It was easy to sleep in the midday heat, and Leah drifted off to Inka's constant purring. In the dream that overtook her, Leah saw the Mamacuna standing on a rise, the whole of the people on the grassy plain before her.

She raised her arms to the sky, chanting prayers to Viracocha, asking His protection on their journey to the north. In the purple rays of the setting sun, the Mamacuna seemed to be aflame. Her supplications concluded, she called for Na-Tan Manco, son of Manco, grandson of Iztak to step forward. Slowly, he approached the priestess and knelt, bowing his head in respect, touching his fingers to his lips again and again. Then Leah heard her own name called and she watched herself join Tan before the Mamacuna. High above them, a single condor made lazy circles in the sky before calling to its mate and soaring off to the south.

ᘒ ⊖ ᙣ

Leah's eyes fluttered open and she realized Tan was sitting beside her, his hand gently stroking Inka's fur. The cat purred contentedly, happy for the attention he received. "So you are awake, lazy woman!" he teased gently.

"Mmmm...barely. Are you ready to leave?"

Tan let an uncommon sigh pass his lips before he spoke. "My grand-mother is beside my grandfather," he said, the sadness so evident in his voice. "I had not known, but I think this must have just happened. The offerings around her are fresh."

"I am so sorry, my heart. I had looked forward to meeting her." Leah looked up to see tears shimmering unshed in his eyes. "But she was a happy woman and we would have made her happy as well."

Tan merely nodded, then stood and helped Leah to her feet. "When the time comes, my heart, there will be many stories to tell of the woman I called Baibai."

"Not awila?" asked Leah

Tan shook his head. "My grandfather always referred to her as *your Baibai*, so I called her Baibai. I think it was my baby name for her."

Side by side, Tan and Leah walked through the dense jungle, the jaguar still beside them. Leah, out of respect for Tan's loss, remained silent, letting him think his own thoughts without intrusion. She thought about all the things she didn't know about him, all the questions she would ask when he was ready to talk. As well as she knew the people and their customs, Leah could only imagine what it was like to grow up in a world so different from her own. She hid a smile when she considered how she would explain her own world to a man who spent his childhood in a place without Captain Kangaroo and Sesame Street, without Good Humor ice cream bars and Fourth of July parades. Oh, he now knew of some of those things, but just as he would try to explain the games and the stories of his childhood to her, she would have to do just as much explaining.

Tan's thoughts were not so different. As they walked, he remembered the long winter nights in his grandparents' hut; the familiar smell of his grand-mother's hands as she carded wool while her husband filled the little boy's head with endless tales of adventure. *Will you understand these stories?* wondered Tan, stealing a glance at the woman beside him. *Yes*, he decided, *you will understand*.

~ ⊖ ~

They camped at Kimsa Chayankuna. Leah made a fire while Tan foraged for food nearby. Inka remained with her, a clear sign that Tan, although believing they were safe, was not comfortable leaving her alone. The night air was cool and Leah wished they had at least brought blankets, but they had not. Grinning just a little, she thought of how they would have to sleep, entwined together for warmth.

Tan returned with more fruit and wild potatoes than they could possibly eat. "It will save time in the morning," he told Leah, dropping his collection at her feet. Turning to the cat, he ordered Inka to go and the jaguar bounded into the jungle. "He must find his own dinner," explained Tan, "but he will be back before dawn."

After they ate, Tan and Leah snuggled together on a bed of moss and dried leaves and made slow, languorous love. And when it was over, as they lay entangled, he began to talk about some of the things he loved about his home and compared them to things he had come to love in Minnesota. "I never gave snow any thought, except as the white blanket on top of the highest mountains. I had gone up into the mountains as a boy, we all did, to play in the cold and I can even remember a time or two when it grew so cold that it snowed in the foothills, but in Minnesota! Ai! The snow became the world!" His eyes were bright, even in the darkness, reflecting the sparks of the fire.

"Did it frighten you?" asked Leah.

"Yes, a little. I was not prepared for streets of ice. Everywhere I walked, I slipped."

"I'm sorry I missed that," she laughed softly. Leah snuggled against him, savoring the feel of his flesh against hers. She reached up and touched his cheek. "What will you do when this is over?"

An eyebrow shot up; Tan was amazed at the question. "Go back to school, of course; I promised Hector I would do so."

"And after that?"

Tan did not answer; he stared into the fire and said nothing.

❧ ⊖ ❧

For five days they continued northward, following the obscure trail the Mamacuna left for her beloved churi. Sometimes the path was easy, other times it was almost impossibly hidden by artfully constructed obstructions. But Tan had the advantage; the markers left on the isle at Kimsa Chayankuna had given him clear sense of where the people had gone and what route they had used. In the bag had been several items, each significant in their simplicity yet unless one knew the Mamacuna well, their meaning would have easily been missed. As each one came into play, Tan explained it to Leah.

They had reached a place at the edge of the jungle where four distinct paths diverged in four directions: west, northwest, northeast and due east. Tan laughed aloud as he stood at the center of the circle where all four met. "Look down, Qewa Ñawi, and learn the ancient ways of the travelers."

Leah did as she was told. In what appeared to be dust, there were actually patterns, intricate designs that seemed to have been carved into a manmade paving stone. The outer edge consisted of two concentric circles with parallel lines between them. A series of geometric shapes made up the design of the central portion of the stone, each one unique, but with unifying elements linking one to another. At the very center was a perfectly formed pentagon. "The point at the top," said Leah as she puzzled over the message, "points between the second and third path, yet the figures are equally divided between the four."

"And what does that tell you?"

Squatting to get closer, Leah brushed the stone with her hand. "I think the path of choice would lead to the west, over the mountains to the Inca road running along the coast. These figures," she pointed to several crude, arm-like designs, "seem to point in that direction." She looked up at Tan whose face remained impassive. "The stone is old, so I think there are several layers of information here. The chasquis would take the road to the west, because that is where the next enclave of civilization would be. But the hunters would go east. See these? They look more like animal limbs than human limbs."

Tan was pleased with her astute observation, but continued to question her. "What about the other two paths? Where do they go?"

"Nowhere important," grinned Leah, certain she was right. "They are local markers. To huacas, perhaps, or maybe even to meeting places." She waved her hand toward the northwestern and northeastern paths. "The roads are clearly marked, but they are narrow."

"So which road do we take?"

Leah stood and looked around, chewing her lip as she took everything into consideration. "None of the above. We go straight north, between the center two roads."

"And how do you know that?"

"You told me, my heart," replied Leah, patting his face. "You said in the llama skin bag, the Mamacuna left markers, one of which was a string from a quipu with five knots, the largest of which was the knot in the middle of the strand. If the strand represents the crossroads, then the Mamacuna was telling us there is a fifth road to be traveled." She gave Tan a smug, self-congratulatory smile.

And Tan gave her a frown in return. "You know too much, Qewa Ñawi." Only when her face crumpled did he dare kiss her. "I am impressed." Grabbing her hand, they ran between the center two paths and into the tall grass.

The path was there, hidden in the grass and they made good progress, Inka loping along side. For several days they traversed the gentle hills, stopping only when the sun disappeared behind the mountains. Finally, evidence of a mass migration became more and more apparent; the grass had not yet recovered from being crushed by hundreds of feet. Tan and Leah picked up their pace, knowing they were closer than ever to the people. The wide plain seemed to go on forever and it soon became evident they would not reach them as soon as they hoped. As they jogged closer to another series of sharp cliffs and rougher terrain near the end of the broad plain, made camp where, judging by the blackened fire rings they found scattered in the area, the people had camped no more than forty-eight hours earlier.

With first light, Tan and Leah broke camp and continued northward, following the path of crushed grass. Tan estimated there were almost a thousand people with the Mamacuna but it seemed, to the practiced eye, to be a carefully constructed move consisting of several columns over about a mile swath. Equally evident was that they were using the older boys to trail behind, raking up the grass in order to obliterate the most obvious of tracks. The trampled grasses, explained Tan, would take only a couple of days to spring back and then that, too, would mask their progress.

By midday, Leah was flagging. The trail was leading them back up into the hills. The air was thinner, but they kept going and stopped only after crossing a deep gorge via the *chaca,* a rope footbridge suspended precipitously over white water rapids rushing far below. Tan went over the bridge first, then called Leah and Inka to follow. As much as she feared crossing, Leah closed her eyes, took a deep breath and stepped onto the span; it was not the first such bridge she had crossed, but it was by far the longest. The span rocked gently and Leah gripped the hand rope until her knuckles turned white. Her arm was no longer in a sling, but it throbbed with the sudden, violent movement. From behind, Inka nudged her gently and Leah, placing one foot in front of the other, began to move. Halfway across, a sudden movement caught her eye. Swooping toward her was an enormous condor. Instinctively, she ducked and nearly tumbled from the bridge.

"Are you all right?" called Tan, afraid to meet her where she sat frozen.

Leah weakly raised her injured arm. "Just give me a minute to catch my breath." Inka licked her cheek and gave her a friendly purr. "Come on, cat, let's go," she said softly as she righted herself and stood up. With the jaguar close behind her, she walked slowly, steadily toward Tan's open arms. "Did you see the condor?" she asked as soon as her feet touched solid ground.

"I saw him, but I think he did not mean to frighten you. I believe he was a good omen."

Looking into Tan's eyes, Leah believed it was a good omen as well, but something puzzled her. "Why is it that the condor is always with us? Where ever we go, it seems we are followed by the birds."

"It is not me who the kuntar follows, Qewa Ñawi. It is you."

"Me?"

He nodded slowly. "The kuntar, I think, is your spirit brother. Did he not warn you on the ledge? Are not your dreams touched with his presence?"

"Yes, but..."

"Here is a single mystery not meant to be questioned; only to be accepted as truth." Tan touched her face with her hand. "Accept it, Qewa Ñawi; it is the way it is." He slipped his arm about Leah's shoulder and walked her up a narrow, rocky path. It wasn't a difficult ñan, nor was it long, but once it passed though three pairs of stone pillars, an entire valley was laid out at their feet. In the distance, barely visible against the brown landscape, were five distinct lines, all in motion like a military maneuver. "We are close to the end of our journey, my heart, for there are my people. Now, look out over the valley and into the sky."

Leah shaded her eyes with her good hand and looked to the north. There was the condor, sailing and soaring directly toward the front of the columns. "Does the condor belong to the Mamacuna, too, like Inka?"

"She will tell you tonight," replied Tan simply.

𝄔 ⊝ 𝄓

Tan insisted that Leah eat something before they began the long climb down into the valley. They sat on the edge of cliff munching on fruit they had collected before they left the jungle that morning, their eyes focused on the columns of people moving northward. Leah wished she had brought field glasses; she longed to be able to see actual bodies in motion instead of billows of dust made by marching feet; it reminded her of the exodus of the Hebrews from Egypt. Then she thought about individuals below them, moving northward, about Pia and Hua, Saba and Rina and how they were managing. What had been all speculation was now suddenly real and she wondered how they had all crossed the bridge, whether or not anyone was lost, and who had been buried along the route. These were not questions to ask Tan, for Leah could see that he was lost in his own thoughts. Finally, the last wild banana was gone and it was time to continue.

The path down the steep cliff was treacherous. At several points, Tan showed Leah where the road had been deliberately obliterated to discourage those who would follow. Tan gripped her strong hand as he gingerly picked his way through the scattered boulders, letting Inka take the lead whenever the cat deemed it necessary. When they reached the valley floor, Inka bellowed loudly and took off in the direction of his true mistress.

"I think he is in a hurry to reach the Mamacuna," laughed Tan as they watched the jaguar bound away in a cloud of dust.

"I think you are in a hurry to reach the Mamacuna, if you ask me," Leah countered with a squeeze of her hand in his. "Come on, Tan, let's get moving.

The distance, as judged from the top of the cliff was deceiving; once in the valley, it appeared to be endless. Jogging along, Leah managed to keep up with Tan, all the while thinking that had he been alone, he would already be greeting his family. But having seen the columns from above, Leah found the strength to go on at the pace Tan set. Over the barren, flat expanse, over the occasional hill they ran; through tall grass and prickly scrub they jogged. Racing against the sun, Leah thought her lungs would burst if they did not stop soon.

The face of Mamaquilla was rising, pale in the eastern sky, as the face of Inti touched the top of the mountains to the west. Even were the darkness to fall, they knew they would not stop. And then, just as Leah was about to cry out from fatigue, they heard a strange sound. Tan froze in his tracks with Leah almost crashing against him, as he listened to the noise coming closer and closer even as they stood still, hidden by shoulder high grass.

"What is it?" Leah whispered, more than a little frightened by the sudden change in Tan.

Just as suddenly, Tan gave a short, shrill whistle and his whistle was answered. A second, then a third whistle followed, each a receiving an answering call, each call a little different from the last.

There was a great rustling and Leah would have hit the ground had Tan not held her up. Almost dragging her, Tan pulled Leah toward a break in the grass and released her, just as three fierce looking men appeared, running through the grass, waving long shafts with sharpened stone tips.

Their eyes opened wide when they found the two dusty travelers and then, one threw his spear to the ground. Without a sound, he charged at

Tan, who sprang at his attacker. Only the raucous laughter of the others prevented Leah from doing anything to stop the two men wrestling in the dirt.

Tan pinned his adversary, but not without some difficulty, his knee digging into the other man's chest. "So, Tupac," rasped Tan, "I see our father allows his son to run wild."

"No wilder than my brothers," came the quick retort.

Laughing, Tan released the youth and brushed himself off. "Has our father grown foolish in his old age, or is it the journey which had made you reckless, little brother?" He noticed his brother was not listening.

Tupac stared openly at Leah while his friends were a little more discreet. "She is the Qewa Ñawi. I have seen her before, when she walked in our forest." He raised an eyebrow at his brother. "She is the reason you were released from your mita?"

Taller than his brother, Tan stared down at Tupac and shrugged. "There are things you do not understand, *wawqesitu.*"

"Like why you have cut off your hair like a stranger?"

One of Tupac's friends poked his toe nervously in the dust; this was not a conversation for others to hear. "We should be on our way if we will be on time for the situa."

"You are in time, Na-Tan Manco," said Tupac, slapping his brother on the back. "Our mother will be pleased to have all of her children together for the first time in eight cycles of Illi-Intap. She will dance without an eye turned toward Mamaquilla tonight!"

∽ ◡ ∾

Scattered fires were already burning brightly when the scouting party returned. Leah was a little surprised at the way everyone acknowledged Tan as he passed, opening a wide path for them, yet saying nothing. The former aclla nodded greetings to those he knew, but remained silent as they made their way through the basket weave of campsites. Only when they reached the fire at which Leah's ayllu had gathered did shouts of welcome envelope her.

Rina was squatting at the fire busily tending a pot of quinoa when she looked up to see Leah walking towards her. Her hands flew to her mouth and then she sprang up, running with open arms to greet her friend; Pia and Hua raced ahead of their mother. Soon all the women of the ayllu were clutching at Leah, hugging and asking questions as fast as Leah could answer. The barrage ceased when Saba approached.

"You have come back to us, Li-ah," said the old woman, wiping tears from her eyes. "I am pleased to see you walk amongst us again."

Leah embraced the collahuaya, hugging her tightly as her own eyes overflowed with tears. "I came because the Mamacuna has summoned me with her jonchi, Mama'amuata." She stepped back and saw that Tan and his brother had kept what would be considered a respectful distance from the little community. "I have come with Na-Tan Manco."

"I would have been disappointed to have seen you alone," replied Saba, returning Tan's silent nod. "The ceremonies will be starting soon, huahuan, and you may not attend until the Coya has invited you to come to her." Turning to the other women, Saba clucked her disapproval at their inhospitality. "Are you all chattering monkeys?" she demanded sternly. "These are hungry people!"

The women averted their eyes and scattered when Tan drew near. "We thank you for your offer of food, but my brother and I will eat at the fire of our mother."

Saba nodded and grinned at the two sons of Manco. "Then take yourselves away now, little boys, for soon he," she pointed at finger at Tan, "will be summoned with my daughter and it would be foolish to have him faint from hunger at the feet of the Coya!"

With his eyes, Tan told Leah he would come for her at the appointed time and disappeared with Tupac and his friends into the gathering crowd.

"Pia! Hua!" shouted Rina as soon as the men were gone, "fetch water for Li-ah; she must wash before eating and bathe before going to the Mamacuna." She took Leah's hand and was about to lead her away when Saba held up her hand.

"You have been hurt, my daughter," she said, gently touching her arm.

"It's a sprain, Mama Saba, nothing serious."

Probing the injury, Saba grunted then smiled. "I can feel Hector's fingers have been here. He was with you?"

"No, but he was there afterward." She was not sure how to explain a helicopter so she opted not to mention it. Besides, there would be plenty of time to tell stories later, after the ceremonies were over. Docilely, she allowed Saba to take her to a secluded place where she could clean up and prepare for the night to come.

ھ ⊖ ھ

The face of Mamaquilla loomed enormous over the people gathered at the base of a hill, atop which the Mamacuna stood, her arms outstretched, her own face bathed in the moonlight. At her side, Inka sat erect, his head tilted slightly as though he was listening to the chanting of the Rimoc. Neat rows of chinan lined the bottom of the little hill, all in cloaks and red felt hats. And over them all, circled a single condor.

Leah walked to the gathering with her ayllu family, with Saba leading the way. When they reached their appointed place, the old woman waited for Leah to step forward, then escorted her to where Tan was waiting. Silently, Saba indicated they were to remain there until summoned by the Mamacuna.

From her vantage point, Leah watched the slow procession of chinan as they carried the sacred objects to the Mamacuna. Accompanied by the song of the quena and the sonorous chanting of the Rimoc, the line of red hats slowly moved up the hill. Leah felt a little twinge of jealousy when she saw the last chinan deliver the golden basin to the Coya, performing the same ritual she had performed a year ago. All eyes were on the Mamacuna as she lit the uchapa; the sacred jonchi rose into the night. Straight upward went the thin column of smoke, bending northward only at the last minute. But never once did a puff or a billow leave the main body of the jonchi.

"Mamaquilla has been our guide," pronounced the Mamacuna in a strong, clear voice, "and our path has been the true path, a ñan to safety away from those who would see the sacred ways destroyed and the people vanquished." She looked out over the hundreds of faces staring intently at her. "Sacred ways are not the same as old ways," she continued, "and we will honor the ways of our ancestors when we build a new home for ourselves. Once again, we will have homes and fields, chacras and huacas. At the time of the next situa, we will bring the first fruits of our labors to Mamaquilla."

The Rimoc began chanting again and the people joined in the song of thanksgiving. The air was filled with ancient harmonies, making Leah shiver with emotion beneath her cloak. Unexpectedly, a dark figure emerged from the crowd and approached Leah. She recognized the woman as one of the other collahuayas and when she touched Leah's hand, the Qewa Ñawi knew she had been summoned. With a last look at Tan, she followed the collahuaya through the mass of people until she came to the long line of chinan. Dozens of familiar hands touched Leah's as she took her place, and then, as the music changed, the chinan started to move in the slow, shuffling steps of their *wai-yaya*, the taqui to honor Mamacuna.

They danced for what seemed to be hours, until the face of Mamaquilla was low in the sky. At last, the chinan returned to their places and the Mamacuna raised her arms to the moon. "We were blessed by Mamaquilla with an aclla of great power, but when his time was over, this aclla left the people and we were saddened. But the ways of the Mother are mysterious; She has taken him from us, yet has called him to serve Her in a way we could not have foreseen. Through him, the greatest danger has passed. Through him, the fate of our journey has been sealed with good fortune. He has completed his mita to Mamaquilla, yet he continues to serve Her with his heart. Once again, he will take his leave from us, but this time, he will leave as a whole man."

The crowd parted as Tan approached toward the base of the hill. When he reached the line of chinan, he walked before them, seeing only the bowed red hats, until he stopped directly in front of Leah. Offering her his hand, he escorted her to the Mamacuna. As they neared the place where she stood, they both repeatedly touched their fingers to their lips in sacred greeting. Then Tan spoke. "I ask for your permission and we ask for your blessing, Coya," said Tan, his voice ringing through the night, as they knelt before the Mamacuna.

"Have you have sought permission and blessings from your mother and father, Na-Tan Manco?"

"Yes, Coya."

"Have you sought permission and blessings from your mother and father, Li-ah?"

Leah panicked; she had not even mentioned Tan to her parents, let alone asked for their blessings. She glanced at Tan, hoping he would come up with an answer.

But it was Saba who came forward. "I am her mama'amuata, Coya. There has been no time for the woman Li-ah to seek permission from her parents, so I shall grant it."

"This is acceptable to you, Li-ah?"

"Yes, Coya," breathed a relieved Leah.

The Mamacuna took the right hand of each and tied them together with a thin plait of vicuña wool. "As their hearts are bound, so are their hands." She leaned forward and whispered in Leah's ear, "Within the space of nine moons, on the night of the equinox, you will bear a son. Name him for my friend Iztak Arro Ba Na-Tan."

∽ ⊖ ∾

The remainder of the night passed in a haze for Leah as they danced an endless taqui until the face of Mamaquilla disappeared and the first rays of Inti appeared over the eastern horizon. When the festival had ended and the people started back to their campsites, the members of both their ayllus gathered around the couple to escort them to a place where they could spend a few hours in privacy. In a little grove of trees, buried beneath hastily borrowed alpaca blankets, Tan and Leah came together again and again until exhaustion took them both.

"What did the Mamacuna tell you?" asked Tan, just as Leah was about to fall asleep.

"Oh, nothing much," Leah sighed, snuggling against his warm body, "just a little prophecy."

"Ai! The Twins *will* go to the World Series!"

Leah gave him a playful jab with her elbow and promptly fell asleep.

ভ ⊖ ৵

The ground was still damp with morning dew and the sky barely light when Tan left Leah, still asleep, to join the Mamacuna. As he had so many times before, he approached the place where she sat, stopping at prede-termined intervals to await her command to draw near. At last, he knelt before her, his head bowed in respect, his heart beating as fast as it had the day she declared him Aclla.

"Come, churi, and sit by an old woman," she said, patting a spot beside her. "The quinoa is fresh and the tea is hot, just as you like it."

Graciously accepting the proffered bowl, Tan joined her, relishing the warmth of her little fire. The taste of the tea, something he had dreamt of in Minnesota, felt friendly and refreshing and he drank it slowly, savoring every swallow. As was the custom, he waited for the Mamacuna to speak first.

"My heart is happy to see you beside me, Na-Tan Manco; I was begin-ning to think you would not come."

"But you summoned me, Coya. I heard your call and I came, just as I have always come."

"And you brought the Qewa Ñawi even though I wished not to put her in danger." Her voice gently admonished him and he bowed his head, his cheeks reddened by her words. "Do not feel shamed, churi; she is a head-strong woman who came of her own accord as she did when she came the first time. I had only hoped you would have discouraged her."

Tan laughed at the thought. "As a mountain cannot be moved, neither can the Qewa Ñawi once her mind is made up."

"Then she is a good match for you, churi, for you are two of one kind." She allowed a chuckle at her own joke, for she knew this was true. "Tell me, do you like your new life?"

He told her about school, about the things he was learning, about the people he met and the places he saw. "It is all so different, so overwhelming at times, yet my heart tells me it is the right path. I live with a foot in each world and my heart is divided, but I know I have made the right choice."

"You have made many right choices, churi," she told him; "and you will make many more. And some wrong ones, too. That is the way of life."

"Was it a right choice to leave Janajpachallacta, Coya, now that it is safe to be there?" asked Tan, daring to question her wisdom.

The Mamacuna sighed and sipped her tea slowly. It was not an easy question. "In the end, Na-Tan Manco, we would never be safe there again. The outsiders are too close, they know too much and we would spend our days fighting a winless battle." She spread her arms wide, "This place, this land to the north, this is where we shall stay. The soil is good, there is a high point on which we will build a new gathering place; there is plenty of grass for our herds. And it is far enough away from the roads of the city people."

"What about Hector?" asked Tan, suddenly worried more about what the healer would do without the people more than the people without him.

The Mamacuna smiled warmly at Tan and took his hand. "He will join us when he is well. The Ayar Kuntar knows how to find us and," waving her hand to the north, "I am not so old and foolish as to find a place where a silver bird cannot land. We will build him a house and he will be happy. This is a truth, my son."

Much relieved, Tan did not doubt her for a moment. Still, he wanted to ask about his own future, whether or not he would come back to the place his family would learn to call home. As much as he loved what he was doing, as much as he loved the woman Li-ah, would she be willing to return to the mountains and the jungle with him when his studies were over? Once before the Mamacuna had told him he would not come back, but after everything that happened, he wondered if that truth had changed. Would his son one day be called to serve the people?

She could read his mind as well as his heart, and the Mamacuna was reluctant to tell him what she already knew. She would not, she had decided, tell him that the Qewa Ñawi already carried his son; that was something only the woman could tell him at the right time. But the question was in his heart; since time was short, it had to be addressed immediately. "You have questions you hesitate to ask, so I will answer them without waiting for your words." The Mamacuna took his hand in hers and held it fast. "You will always have a foot in each world, Na-Tan Manco, and this is not a bad thing. We will always be in your heart, as you are in ours. The gifts you have given will be remembered and in them, we will always see you;

you will not be forgotten. But your place, as I have told you before, is in the outer world, in the land of Ruti-Suyu where man builds the mountains you have seen and we can only imagine. It is there you shall build a house of stone and wood and it will be filled with the laughter of your children. You will come and go, but you shall never live among us."

"I will be a man without a people, Coya."

"No, my son, you will always be of the people, but you will find a new family in the people of the Qewa Ñawi. But I will ask you one thing, churi."

"Whatever it is, I shall honor your command."

"When you build your house, make the place where you sleep open to the face of Mamaquilla. When we look to Her, our hearts will still be joined."

The words of the Mamacuna tore at his heart, yet he knew she spoke only truth to him. He let the old woman put her arms about him, as a mother would comfort an injured child. She felt his tears mingle with her own and wept with him, sharing his pain but gaining strength from his inner strength until he was ready to face her again.

The rest of their time together was spent speaking of practical matters. There were messages to be sent to Hector and to their unknown friends battling for them in the government. The Mamacuna believed in the ability of those friends to keep the outsiders from their new home. She told him Hector and Paolo would be welcome whenever they came, and should the Ayar Monsonsoré decide to pay a visit to his old friends, he, too, would be welcomed. Tan knew that would please Miguel no end and he promised to deliver the Coya's words as she had spoken them.

"You said I will come and go," said Tan as he prepared to take his leave of the Mamacuna, "but Coya, will I ever see you again?"

"Are you asking me to predict my longevity, churi?" she replied with a chuckle. When he began to protest, she stilled him with her fingers on his lips. "I cannot give you an answer, Na-Tan Manco. You must not worry nor plan your journeys on a wish. You must live a full life in Ruti-Suyu and when your heart tells you to come home for renewal, you will come." She pulled out a parcel from deep within the folds of her tunic. "If times were as they once had been, your grandmother would have given you this. But times are not, so it has fallen to me to give you this thing which your grandmother held for you for many years." She handed him the leaf wrapped package. "This comes to you from the hand of Iztak Arro Ba Na-Tan, your grandfather. Take it with you when you leave us, but do not look at it until you are far from here. My old friend was a man of many mysteries; he had visions and dreams as strong as your own. He knew one day you would need this and, like the spirit brother he left for your manhood ceremony, he left this for the time when you would take a wife." The Mamacuna paused to look deep into Tan's soul through his eyes. "Iztak was the one to clear my vision when I first spoke to him of the Ñawi. Iztak told me this was a good thing, a thing meant to be and it would help heal a great hurt. I do not understand that which he left you, but I believe you will." She took Tan's hand in hers and squeezed him with great, loving strength. "Had I not been called to serve Mamaquilla, I might have spent my days learning with Iztak. He was a man of powerful wisdom." Leaning on Tan for support, she rose and walked to where she could see the valley spread majestically beneath them. "Go to your wife, Na-Tan Manco, and tell her I will speak with her and Saba before you leave us."

⁀ ⊖ ⌒

Leah was not where he left her, but Tan didn't worry; she was as much at home with the people as he was, if not a little more so, and he was sure to find her at one fire or another. In their secluded bower, Tan stretched out on the pile of alpaca skins on which they had spent the night. He needed the time alone to sort through the emotion running haphazardly through his heart and mind, so when he faced his family, he would know what to say. Eyes closed, he was lost in thought when a voice invaded his privacy.

"Get up, lazy boy, and find your wife, lest she find a more attentive man to care for her!"

Tan grinned at his father as he jumped to his feet. "Is my mother waiting for us?"

"My wife is hopping up and down waiting for you, Na-Tan! You are an inconsiderate child!" The rebuke was gentle, belied by the smile in Manco's eyes. He looked his son over critically, then reached out and touched his hair. "You look like a stranger, but your face is the face of my father," said Manco gruffly with a paternal sigh. "Come, let us wash before finding your woman, lest she discover that, amongst your other faults, you are slovenly."

With a laugh, Tan joined his father in search of a place to bathe in private. Although the ceremonies had gone long into the night, already the children were running about while the adults prepared for the day. At the stream, women were washing clothing, their chatter filling the air with friendly noise; the men steered away from them, walking further upstream to where a bend in the little river afforded them shelter. Stripping off their clothes, they waded into the water.

It was an intimate, personal moment for Tan, something he had not had with his father in many years. They spoke of many things, of Tan's new home, the people he met, the things he saw. The father listened as the son tried to explain about his car. Manco knitted his brows as he tried to imagine this red thing with wheels that went of its own accord. He was certain if Tan said it was so then, indeed, it must be so, yet he found it as difficult to believe as the stories of the Mamacuna in the belly of the silver bird.

"Tell me more about the people with which you live, churi," instructed Manco, more interested in the company his son kept than in the toys he had acquired. After all, that was the measure of a man.

Omitting the early days of India's infatuation, Tan described in great detail his life with the Halstaads. This seemed to satisfy his father; the older man was reassured that his son was warm and safe in the place of terrible cold where he chose to live. When Manco ran out of questions, Tan was, at last, able to ask his. "Your mother, my Baibai, is beside my grandfather and I saw that this is new. When did she leave us?" asked Tan as gently as he could. Speaking of the recent dead was a delicate issue and one that needed to be handled carefully, even with his father.

Manco strode out of the water, sat down on a boulder on the bank, and waited for his son to join him there. "My mother was very old, churi. Your departure from the people saddened her greatly, yet she knew this was a right decision. When the strangers came into our land and began to threaten our ways, it was decided we would leave that place to seek safety. My mother, your grandmother was not faring well and was afraid she would not be strong enough to make the trip, yet she believed strongly she would see you once more. When the time came to leave, the Mamacuna herself came to see my mother. They spoke long into the night and we could hear the sound of weeping. The face of Mamaquilla had disappeared from the sky when their talk ended and the Mamacuna left my mother's side. She summoned my brother and me to her and we sat with her as she spoke of her grandchildren. But it was you, Na-Tan Manco, whom she loved best and it was your name on her lips when she slipped away from us before the face of Inti rose in the sky."

Tan looked out over the water both saddened and glad that his beloved grandmother had not been forced to leave her home. She had died with grace and dignity, the way she had lived, with her sons at her side. "She was a woman of great happiness and I am honored to be her grandson," said Tan.

"The Coya assured her you were with the Qewa Ñawi and you were happy. She wished us to tell you that she carries you in her heart to my father and wishes you should carry her with you always."

"I shall honor her request, for she is always in my heart." He did not tell his father of the package the Mamacuna had given him. There were some things better left unsaid and his heart told him this was one of them. His father might be hurt at the thought his mother had not entrusted him to pass the parcel to his son.

At their camp, Tan found his mother and the rest of the family busy with routine tasks. His brothers were tending to their flock of llamas and alpacas while his mother was preparing a stew for the evening meal. Sitting beneath a lashed shelter was a pretty young girl spinning wool into thread. Amidst all the confusion of reunion the night before, Tan had not seen his sister for more than a moment and even then, there had not been time to sit with her. After greeting his mother, he crawled beneath the lean-to and began carding wool with his fingers.

It had been too long since Tan had felt the soft lanolin of raw alpaca and he found the sensation pleasurably familiar. Rahua glanced at him from beneath lowered lashes and smiled at her brother, the one she did not remember as anything more than a shadow in the night. Rahua had grown up knowing her brother was aclla, yet never permitted to speak about him in public. Her parents told her he was very handsome and kind, no one in her memory had ever said a bad word about him, even when he left the people to go to Ruti-Suyu. Now he sat beside her, the handsomest man she had ever seen, and she found it hard to believe this was her eldest brother.

Grinning silently, Tan began feeding the carded wool to Rahua. He could almost read her mind as her nimble fingers became clumsy while questions raced around her head. He caught his mother's approving nod and, after a few more silent moments, started to speak to the girl. "You were a silly baby when I left our parents to serve my mita," he began casually, "but you have grown into a beautiful young lady. Tupac has told me you are sensible."

This was high praise from Tupac who usually chased her away from where ever he was. "He is a good brother, but Cachi and Roca are nicer to me and my friends," she mumbled, almost afraid to have conversation with this stranger.

"They are closer to your age than Tupac," replied Tan in what he realized was a rather avuncular voice. "I am sure I would have been a terrible older brother to have around; just ask Tupac. He will tell you this is so."

"Oh,no! Tupac says you were great fun! You led all the games and you were the strongest!" gushed Rahua, suddenly finding her tongue. No one, not even Na-Tan Manco himself, could say a bad thing about her eldest brother.

Impulsively, Tan put an arm about her and hugged her. "I remember when you were born, little Rahua. Our mother was so happy to have a daughter at last that we all thought she would never look at us boys again! How hard she prayed to Mamaquilla for a girl to dress like a little doll and you were certainly the fanciest baby in the ayllu." He liked the way her cheeks turned pink at the compliment. "I see you spin well and you dress modestly yet with style," he continued with a grin, "I should think you will have many boys teasing you soon."

"Oh, no, I hope not!" giggled the girl, "I want to be a chinan when I am old enough and they never take girls who have too many boys hanging around." Her eyes flashed and Tan saw himself in them. She had Iztak's eyes, all light brown with that strange rim of golden amber that made their grandfather's gaze so compelling. "I am good with my quipu and already our mother lets me keep count of the baby llamas by myself. Our collahua-ya says if I learn the names of all the herbs she will let me learn with her after my ceremony."

"Are you good at learning, little sister?"

She puffed with pride. "Our father says I am almost as good as you were, better than our brothers."

For a moment, Tan wished that was not so, for it was that unquench-able thirst for learning which had taken him so far from his home. It was better, he thought, for a girl like Rahua to learn the things she needed to know to have a home than to yearn for greater knowledge. Still, he under-stood exactly how she felt.

Cura approached the lean-to and beckoned to her children to join her outside. "My heart is happy to see you together, my children, but Na-Tan, you have a wife to consider now," she admonished gently, taking his large hand in her small one. Looking up at him, she wondered how she had given birth to a tiny baby who had grown to his incredible height and for a moment, she caught herself remembering her first-born son in his cradle. She touched his smooth cheek and smiled at her son. "You look well, churi; the happiness of your soul shines brightly in your eyes and this makes me happy." She swiped at an errant tear. "Go now and find your wife and bring her to us, for she is a member of this household and should be here to help."

Tan knew his mother was more interested in instructing Leah in the care and feeding of her first born son than in having an extra pair of hands; he smiled, bent over to peck at her cheek and promised to return with his bride.

CHAPTER 38

Leah was nowhere to be found. Tan returned to their bower, but there was no sign of her there. Strolling from campsite to campsite, he stopped to visit with those he knew before his mita while surreptitiously glancing about for Leah. Finally, when he reached her ayllu, he spotted Pia and Hua giggling together before they dashed toward the place where the women had been washing clothes. He followed them but was stopped by Saba who stood, arms akimbo, at a bend in the path. "It's about time you came for your wife," she scolded, her eyes ablaze. "We thought you had gone off to the fire of your parents to eat, leaving your woman to starve."

His mouth dropped open, words of self-defense frozen on his tongue until he heard more giggling from behind a clump of bushes. Hanging his head in mock shame, he turned his palms upward, asking forgiveness from his wife's spirit mother. "I am sorry, Mama Saba, and I humbly beg your pardon for my thoughtlessness." There were more giggles and when Tan dared to look up, he noticed Saba struggling to maintain her stern countenance. Still playing the part, he dropped to one knee. "What must I do to reclaim my wife?"

"You must bring her a gift of great value, careless one. Then I will consider allowing my daughter to go with you."

Tan thought for a moment, then rose to his feet. "I shall be back in a moment." He dashed off to find Tupac. In a few minutes he was back, a young, snowy white alpaca draped across his broad shoulders. "Will this do, Mama Saba?" he asked with all the seriousness he could muster.

Saba examined the lamb carefully, checking its color for the slightest imperfection. With a grunt, Saba accepted the animal on Leah's behalf. "I suppose this is what he considers a thing of value," she announced airily to the women gathered to see the offering. "Pia! Take this puny beast to our flock and tie a green thread about its neck. Hua! You go to Li-ah and bring her to me." Saba watched the little girls run off in opposite directions, then turned to face Tan. "I hope you learn consideration now that you are a husband, little boy, for if you do not, my daughter will leave you faster than Monsonsoré can run. Remember, you have not bonded with a simpleton, you have chosen a chinan of high rank!" The ladies murmured their approval of Saba's stern warning, but Tan could sense the mirth behind their eyes. Saba, not one to let up on a joke, folded her arms across her chest and stood her ground. "For a man with so many years behind him, let's hope he is a better lover than he is a protector." The women, a little shocked at Saba's blatant reference, hid more giggles behind their hands as Tan's face reddened.

It wasn't so much the mention of his mita that made Tan blush, but rather his being unused to such public displays. During his years as Aclla, he was forbidden from such contact with his own people; he never really experienced the normal teasing and joking to which a young man in love was subjected. Of course, he remembered such ribald barbs, but they had never been directed at him. Now, a new groom, he was the butt of their jokes and unsure of himself.

"He is of strong body and pleasant to look at, but who can see in the dark?" called one woman in the crowd.

"If a husband is as good as his word, looking is not necessary," answered another lady and her compatriots laughed wholeheartedly at the joke.

Shuffling uneasily, he kept his face down as the ladies of Leah's ayllu inspected him. He could feel their eyes on his body and was afraid if he looked up he might recognize one or two of the women as ones he had served; still, he kept himself in check, knowing that to run away would shame his bride.

The ladies were only encouraged by his apparent modesty. "He owns large hands," announced one, "but can he play beautifully with them?"

"And such large arms! Let's hope for Li-Ah's sake the rest of his muscles are as big!"

The laughter grew louder as the jests continued for several minutes, each comment turning Tan's face redder and redder until at last, Saba held up her hands to stop. "The bride comes," she announced, "and she must not know we are on to her poor excuse for a husband." Stifling the giggles, the ladies formed a line between Tan and the direction from which Leah came. When Hua stepped through the line, the gap closed again preventing Leah from joining Tan. Saba cleared her throat and waited for the ladies to settle down. "The bride is reluctant to go with a groom who has neglected her so thoughtlessly on their first day of bonding," said the collahuaya with great seriousness. "We will make her go with you now, but should she return to us with complaints, we will keep her from you. Do you understand, Na-Tan Manco, son of Cura?"

"Yes, Mama Saba, I understand. I promise to be more considerate," replied Tan, matching the gravity of her tone. The women of the ayllu stepped aside and Tan caught the first glimpse of his wife in the sunlight. She was the perfect image of a bride, dressed in a long tunic of finely woven alpaca wool and decorated with delicate lines of beads and colored embroidery. Hanging from her narrow waist, Leah's quipu had been replaced with one befitting her new status as wife, one with colored threads, each denoting a different line of accounting for her household possessions. Her long hair was carefully braided into twin plaits and tied off with leather strips into which parrot feathers had been entwined. On her head, squarely set, was her chinan's red felt hat. Tan noticed her paicha, the one stolen from her office and returned to her by Miguel, now dangled from the brim. Saba and Rina took Leah's arms and, with her eyes downcast, escorted the bride to her groom. The collahuaya linked their arms together and, with a little push, sent them on their way.

Word of the return of the bride to the groom spread quickly through the encampment and soon all the women were in position to make a path to Tan's family. As was the custom, Tan and Leah walked silently through each camp, accepting gifts of flowers and herbs at each one. Soon, their arms were full and the pungent scent of jungle flora wafted around them, but pervading it all was the scent of Leah, herself. The ladies of her ayllu had rubbed *c'coto-c'coto* into her skin and the scent was heady and enticing, an aroma designed to arouse even the most diffident of lovers. Her face glowed with happiness as she dipped her head to all around her.

At last, the end of the double line of women was near an end. Looking up, Tan saw his mother waiting for them, her eyes shining, her arms outstretched to welcome them. As soon as they reached Cura, both Tan and Leah dropped to their knees and touched their fingers to their lips. "I would ask my mother's permission to allow this woman to live in our ayllu," said Tan, keeping his head bowed.

"You are bound to this woman with our permission, so it is only fitting that she live amongst our clan, churi," she replied, her voice choked with emotion. She had not dared to dream that Tan would perform this ceremony; she had assumed they would take their leave without ever having officially come to live with them, even if for a brief time. The Mamacuna herself had warned Cura that Tan might not feel it was proper and that his wishes in this matter were to be respected. But now, as the couple knelt before her, Cura felt at peace with her eldest son. Whatever this Qewa Ñawi was, it was evident to her that she was reared to respect tradition and would make a fine wife for her Na-Tan.

As if on cue, Rahua relieved Leah of her bouquet, allowing her mother to embrace the bride, welcoming the woman Li-Ah into the family. "You will be a good daughter," said Cura as she hugged Leah, a little surprised that her new daughter-in-law was not much taller than herself. The women of the ayllu murmured their approval and dispersed, leaving the family to continue their welcome of the bride and groom in private.

The column continued its move north along the puna. The days were long and the nights too short, but until they reached the place the Mamacuna had envisioned, they would continue at that same arduous pace. They crossed several rope chacas, each more rickety than the last, and it took two full days for the entire company to cross over each one, slowing their progress to a crawl. They shifted the path to the east until they skirted the edge of the jungle once more. Finally, the Coya called a halt to the march and announced temporary camps could be built. She picked a place similar to the one they had left: yunka to the east and foothills to the west. A fast moving arroyo flowed nearby. There was a flurry of activity as the makeshift shelters were constructed at the edge, but beneath the canopy of the jungle.

During the days, Leah learned the customs and traditions of their ayllu while Tan, his father and his brothers went on scouting expeditions for the Mamacuna. The strongest men left each morning to search the area for the places that would eventually been assigned to each ayllu and, more importantly, to discover where the Mamacuna's own compound would be built. While they were gone, the women set to work gathering what food they could find in the area to sustain them for the months before a crop could be planted and harvested. The older children tended the flocks and life went on as it had for hundreds of years.

Instead of taking notes for an ethnography as she had the last time, Leah recorded the things she would need to tell the children she would bear. There were a thousand stories if there was one, and each had a purpose. In the daylight, she listened carefully to Cura's instructions on how to weave the clan designs, what foods were traditional at family celebrations, who had lived and who had died. It was the custom for a new bride to learn these things so when she sat with her young children, she would have endless stories to tell and crafts to transmit to the next generation. Rather than be overwhelmed by the amount of information given the shortness of her time with Cura, Leah made up her mind to record everything possible.

Although Cura took up most of her time, whenever she could slip away, Leah sought out Saba. The old woman, aware that she would be joining the Mamacuna at her new village, was busy teaching her craft to Rina and Pia. The little girl had expressed an honest desire to become a chinan and then collahuaya, but she was too young to begin her formal training. On the advice of the Mamacuna, Saba chose the youngster on the condition that Rina, already well skilled in healing and herbs, would train with her daughter and together they would fill the role of collahuaya until Pia was old enough to undergo her formal initiation. Sitting along side them, Leah sorted leaves and roots, surprised with how much she already knew about the medicinal qualities of each tender plant. After a particularly difficult lesson, when Leah was helping Saba to carry her baskets back to her shelter, the old woman muttered "It is you who should be my pupil, Qewa Ñawi; you should be the one to follow me in the ayllu. Not some silly little girl with clumsy fingers."

Leah was flattered and hugged her mentor. "Would that I were able, mama'amuata, and it is nice to know you feel that way, but give Pia time. She loves you and will learn her lessons, for you are a patient teacher." She knew that eventually Pia would make a fine collahuaya.

At night, when the fires burned low, Leah spent her time sitting with her father-in-law and his sons, hearing from them the stories Cura could not recount. They were amazed when Tan, too, began writing things down, then repeat what they said by staring at little marks drawn with silly yellow sticks onto flimsy white sheets. Cachi and Tupac demanded to try the pencils and laughed at the scratch marks they made in imitation of their older brother. Tan, with deliberate patience, showed them how their names were written and watched with amusement as they repeatedly copied the letters in the dust with sticks.

Leah enjoyed the sight of Tan and his brothers: the flash of a grin, the easy way he laughed. Seeing him with his family gave her new insight into the man to whom she was bound, a different man from the one who wandered through the rain forest or walked the campus in solitude. There was airiness in his manner she had never seen before, a sense of peace that had been lacking in Minnesota. It frightened her a little and she worried that perhaps returning to the United States would be a mistake for him. She wondered, one night as she listened to him trading barbs with his brothers, how she could ask him to leave here again. Suddenly feeling uncomfortable, Leah slipped away from the fire and walked off toward the arroyo to think.

The river shimmed in the moonlight, the face of Mamaquilla rippling in the moving waters. Leah stood at the bank, her mind racing with confusion. In her heart, there was no question about her love for Tan, yet she feared their love would grow as cold as the winter in Minnesota if he lived forever in exile. The words of the Mamacuna echoed inside her head; the Coya said she already carried Tan's son within her womb. If she were to leave the encampment, she would always have a part of Tan with her, but could she deny this child the right to know his father? Her eyes filled painfully with unshed tears and Leah thought her heart would break.

A sudden sharp noise caught Leah off guard and she stepped back to hide in the shadow of a gnarled tree. She strained her eyes to see who approached, but the figure, obviously a woman, was cloaked.

"I told you once that you brought bad luck to the people," said the shadowy figure with a knife edged voice. "You took our aclla from us and now you return to watch us suffer the hardship of exile from our land."

Leah recognized the voice immediately. "I did not take him away, Micay."

"You lied when you said he looked at me with favor; you knew his eyes were on you at the situa." Micay came closer to Leah and blocked the way back to the encampment.

It was unclear to Leah whether or not Micay meant her physical harm, but all the same, she wished she had a weapon. "I can no more control who he looks at any more than you can control who looks at you. But I will tell you this, Micay, you are no longer wagging your serpent's tongue about a stranger, you are talking about my husband."

Micay spat on the ground in front of Leah. "He had betrayed us with you. Take him away again and we shall perish!"

"Oh, for God's sake!" Leah muttered in English. *This*, she thought silently, *is bordering on the ridiculous*, but Leah didn't quite know how to stop the verbal assault. Switching back into Quechua, she tried to reason with Micay. "Na-Tan served his mita and like every aclla before him, he voluntarily left his mita. If it hadn't been me, it would have been someone else. Would you blame her...or yourself had you been the one he chose?"

"I am of the people and would not have spirited him off to Ruti-Suyu. I am not the possessor of green eyes like a witch. I would honor Mamaquilla by giving him strong-blooded sons, something you cannot do, Qewa Ñawi. You bring a curse to the people, but I will tell you this, the curse will be far worse for you, for he cannot stay away from the people forever. Eventually, he will leave you and return to us." Micay took another step toward Leah. "If you are as wise as the Mamacuna says you are, you will leave us...alone." Micay disappeared down the path, her final word echoing in the night.

☙ ⊖ ❧

"Where did you wander off to?" whispered Tan when Leah returned to the fire.

"You were so engrossed in your sibling rivalry, I thought I'd leave you all alone to mock each other in private." She sat down beside him and listened to Manco tell of Iztak's arrival and his courtship of Aima, the most beautiful girl in the ayllu.

"I'm sorry I missed the beginning of the story, Tan," apologized Leah.

"Do not worry;" replied Tan, "I will tell it to you and our children so often that you will grow tired of the tale."

As the story wound to a close, Leah yawned sleepily and was teased for it by the brothers.

"We bore your new wife, Tan," chuckled Tupac.

"Or perhaps," Cachi said with a sly wink, "she is really looking for an excuse to go to bed; his skill is quite famous." He laughed when Leah's face turned as red as the glow of the fire.

Manco glowered at his sons, but they did not relent. Poking at Tan, Tupac asked whether or not his brother had grown too soft in Ruti-Suyu to enjoy his new status as husband. "Enough!" roared Manco despite the twinkle in his eye. He had waited a long time to hear his elder son taunted by his brothers on such a delicate subject, but Leah's growing discomfort was becoming obvious.

"Would it be rude if I went to bed?" Leah asked softly. "You can stay if you like."

Reaching up for her hand, Tan kissed her palm. "Go on, my heart, and I will be along in a moment."

Leah left the little group and scurried to the shelter Tan had built for them not far from his parents' fire. She had no wish to be present while the brothers made light of Tan's prowess; her heart was breaking and if she stayed, she might not have been able to keep from crying. Crawling under the blankets, Leah forced her fears from her mind while she waited for Tan to join her. Soon enough he was there, his hands seeking out the familiar curves of her body. Leah thrilled to his touch, responding to him in kind, but with urgency even he could not ignore. When he entered her, Leah pressed hard against him, as though the act would capture him forever within her memory.

Afterwards, Tan held her tightly against him. "Share with me what eats at your heart, Qewa Ñawi," he murmured in her ear. When she did not answer, he probed a little deeper. "I can feel you are unsettled. Won't you tell me what you are thinking?"

Leah fought back her tears; she could not tell him anything. "Only women's thoughts, my heart."

Tan was silent for a moment; he had his own thoughts to consider. Sleepily, he murmured, "It will be difficult to leave my people again, but we will do what we must do.

Clinging a little tighter, Leah pushed her pain from her mind and drifted off to sleep, knowing Tan was still beside her.

∽ ⊖ ∾

At first light, Tan rolled over to take Leah in his arms and instead, he awoke with a start: the place beside him was empty. Bolting upright, Tan rubbed his eyes and looked about the campsite. Her cloak was gone and her carry pouch was no longer hanging on the little peg he had fastened to the lashed shelter. Only Leah's hat remained, but her paicha was missing from the brim. Tan leapt from the bed and ran through the still sleeping camp toward Saba's ayllu.

The old woman was sitting at her fire preparing herbs for her morning tea. "No," she told him, "Li-ah is not here. Perhaps she has gone to bathe in the stream."

Nor was she at the stream. Tan searched the bank for any sign of his wife, but there was nothing except the occasional animal track. Returning to the lean-to, he opened the skin bag Leah had borrowed from Rina the first day after their bonding. Instead of finding her khakis and hiking boots, Tan found the soft tunic she had been wearing since they joined his family. His cry brought his brothers and father immediately to his side.

Quickly, Tan told them Leah was missing, that during the night, he had felt something wrong, but she had not answered his questions. Just as swiftly, the alarm was sounded and men gathered to join in the search. As they were about to head south, the direction Tan was certain she would have gone, the Mamacuna appeared in the crowd, Inka at her side.

Falling to one knee, Tan asked for her help in finding Leah. She put her hand on his head and stood silent for a moment before her voice rang out. "Someone has poured the poison of falsehood in the ear of the Qewa Ñawi. She is frightened but she will be safe. You may search with Na-Tan Manco until you reach the first bridge, but if by then she is not found, he must cross over alone. I will seek out the cause of this evil and I will deal with it myself." She told Tan to rise. "In seeking the Qewa Ñawi, you must begin by searching your heart, my son."

Tan ran at the front of the phalanx as they set off toward the puna to the south. They moved quickly, fanning out until they stretched the entire width of the plateau. Inka ran beside Tan for a while, then, for whatever reasons the cat had, left them until all they could see was the dust rising behind him. Tan prayed for the cat to reach her before she crossed the bridge.

❧ ⊖ ☙

With the face of Mamaquilla still high enough to light her way, Leah made good progress along the puna. Privy to the ways of the people, she was careful to conceal her tracks by keeping off the dusty road and staying in the matted grasses along the side. By late afternoon, she could see the cut in the hill that led up to the last bridge they crossed. Despite the fading light, Leah started the climb upward, knowing it would be too dark to cross the chaca. She remembered seeing a grotto near the bridge and decided that would be the safest place to wait for morning.

The trek upward seemed neither as difficult nor as long as the trip down. She was able to scale the ñan with relative ease until she stood at the top of the ridge, the puna behind her. Staring northward, she checked for any sign of movement; Leah was relieved when she saw nothing but stillness below. She found the grotto empty, tucked herself beneath the overhang, and ate some of the fruit she had taken from Cura's basket as she left the camp. Feeling less afraid here than in the cave at the huaca, she dozed intermittently through the night.

Dawn was barely cracking in the east when Leah awoke. She ate another banana before she felt strong enough to cross the swaying chaca. Gathering up her gear, Leah took a last look at the puna stretching northward. There was no movement in the grass, nothing to indicate she was being followed. Part of her was relieved; part of her wanted Tan to come running to stop her. She felt her eyes filling with tears again and she wiped them away with her arm. "Don't stop now," she commanded herself aloud. Her voice echoed off the stone walls. She turned her back on the puna and headed toward the bridge.

The chaca hung precipitously between two sheer cliffs. To cross it would mean she would never return, never see Tan again. Until now, Leah had been resolute in her decision, but her courage fled, leaving her breathing hard as she willed herself to take the first step. She closed her eyes, reaching out with her hands to take hold of the fibrous span, then put one foot onto the first tread. Steeling herself against her fear, she reached the middle of the span before a sudden, ferocious roar filled the air around her.

The largest, darkest jaguar she had ever seen stood at the opposite end of the bridge, his ears pinned back, his mouth opened wide as he bellowed his objection to her intrusion. Moving her hand as calmly as possible, Leah withdrew her pocketknife from her carry pouch and tucked it into her palm. The cat started toward her, shaking the span with every fluid step. Leah glanced behind her, but there was no way to return to the other side without causing the cat to charge. Clutching the ropes with one hand, she crouched as low as she dared, at the same time adjusting her grip on the knife. Overhead, a condor screamed, but it did nothing to distract the beast from his quarry. Leah willed her heart to a steady beat and waited for the cat.

A second roar broke the silence of the ravine. From the corner of her eye, Leah spotted a second jaguar poised on the ledge from whence she had come. "*Sh'ma Yisroel*," she whispered as she prepared to die, "the Lord is our God, the Lord is One." As if he could hear her, the second cat roared again and Leah realized it was Inka standing at the end of the bridge. There was not enough room to allow Inka to pass; she would be caught between the cats and would surely fall. Still crouching, Leah waited for something to happen.

ↄ ⊖ ↄ

Tan heard the battle roar of the jaguar and ran at full speed, leaping over rocks and roots as he tore up the side of the mountain, his father and brothers close behind. He reached the plateau and froze when he saw where Leah was trapped. To call her name would do more harm than good and he bit back the cry in his throat. His own knife unsheathed, he approached the bridge slowly, crawling in the dust to prevent being seen by the strange cat moving closer to Leah.

In the sky above the bridge, the condor appeared and circled over the heads of the combatants. Twice, three times the bird passed over Leah, but she dared not raise her eyes to him. The jaguar was no more than ten feet away, easy springing distance, and Leah prepared herself for the attack, her body coiled, ready to take on the cat with all her might. The jaguar stopped moving; the outline of his bunched muscles was clear in the thin morning light. His yellow eyes locked with hers, and his mouth opened, baring his fangs. A long, hideous growl erupted from deep within his belly and was immediately answered by Inka.

Leah gripped the handle of her knife until her knuckles ached; beads of sweat pooled at her hairline and dribbled into her eyes. She kept her breathing even as she waited for what seemed an eternity. The cat, with a low, intimidating growl, sprang at Leah. Suddenly, the condor screamed from above and came tearing out of the sky, claws extended, heading directly for the bridge. The cat, startled by the noise, twisted in the air, giving Leah the advantage. The span swayed dangerously, throwing Leah off balance, but as the jaguar came down, she shot straight up, ripping her knife into the soft underside of its belly.

A blood-curdling scream tore through the air, then silence; a deathly, horrible silence broken only by Tan's voice screaming her name as Leah collapsed beneath the weight of the animal. Again, there was silence as the bridge rocked back and forth, two figures now prone on the foot bed.

Manco and Tupac ran past Tan and grabbed the fiber span in an attempt to steady it before Leah tumbled into the ravine below. Without waiting for the motion to cease, Tan stumbled onto the bridge but was pulled back by his father. "There is no honor in joining Li-ah in death," said Manco softly, his iron grip still restraining his son.

From the bottom of Tan's soul came Leah's name, reverberating ceaselessly through the ravine.

And then, when the echo had faded, from the center of the bridge came a small, less than pleased sound, unmistakably English. "Give me a minute, puh-lease!" Slowly, Leah pulled herself out from under the carcass and faced the men standing on the ledge. As steadily as she could, she walked toward them, her clothing red and wet with blood.

Tan went out as far as he dared, opening his arms to gather her in. Pulling her onto land, he held her against his chest, tears of relief washing over her, his mouth covering her with kisses.

Leah pushed against him, separating herself from his grip. "I'm okay, I'm okay," she repeated several times. Standing erect, she faced Manco and the others. "What do we do with the cat?" she asked with perfect pragmatism.

Tupac's broad grin and brotherly slap on the back took Leah by surprise. "If you were a man, you would skin the beast and give the pelt to your bride!" he laughed, the others joining him. "Now, you'll have to skin it and give it to your husband!"

The faces swam around Leah; the laughter seemed to be drifting farther and farther away. "I don't think I know how to do that," mumbled Leah, reaching out to grab someone, anyone for support. With a last glance at Tan's face, Leah promptly fainted in Tupac's arms.

ꙮ ⊖ ꙮ

She had no recollection of coming down from the mountain, nor did she remember anyone removing her stained clothing, bathing her or wrapping her in a blanket. Vaguely, through the deep haze of exhaustion, she heard voices, some strange, others hauntingly familiar, yet she hadn't the energy to respond, let alone move. When she finally managed to open her eyes, she saw blue sky through the lashed branches of the shelter. The aroma of vegetable stew filled her nostrils, letting her realize how hungry she was.

"At last you have come back," said Tan gently as he squatted beside her. He brushed a strand of hair from her eyes and studied the green depths. "I was afraid you would never look at me again."

There were many things Leah wanted to say, but she kept her mouth clamped shut. No matter what had happened on the bridge, it would not alter her decision to leave Tan where he was happiest; if she spoke, she would betray herself and, in the end, him. Instead of answering, Leah rolled over and waited for Tan to leave.

"She was badly frightened, churi," said the Mamacuna when Tan told her of Leah's silence. "She is battling a great war within herself and you are at the center. Do not press Li-Ah lest you lose her forever." The Mamacuna looked past Tan into the shelter where Leah lay. She did not need to talk to the woman to know what had happened. "Go away, Na-Tan Manco and leave me alone with her."

With a touch of his fingers to his lips, Tan did as he was told. He did not want to sit at his mother's fire, nor was he particularly interested in watching his father skin the enormous jaguar Leah had slain. Skirting the edge of the encampment, he headed toward where the flocks of llamas and alpacas were grazing contentedly in the sun. Somewhere in the distance, a shepherd played lonely tunes on a quena. Sitting down on a rock overlooking the herd, Tan let the face of Illi-Inti warm him while his mind wandered over the events of the last cycle of the sun. Unconsciously, his fingers counted the lines of knots on his quipu, each knot marking another event in his life. He felt a large beaded knot at the end of a strand and he remembered the last winter solstice, when he stood before the Mama-cuna knowing his time as aclla was drawing to a close. The next beaded knot marked the night he asked to be released from his mita and between those two were six smaller, unadorned knots, one which Tan had put there himself to mark the number of moons until he flew in the belly of the silver bird. He laughed bitterly at how the mysterious silver bird was now as commonplace in his life as the condor had been. His fingers touched another strand and another stream of knots. He did not have to look at it to know these were the nights he had spent close to the Qewa Ñawi while she slept unaware of his presence. Strand after strand he counted, each marking a different chain of events, all of which led to the place he now sat, in love, torn, and confused. Leah had retreated into herself, not telling him the truth behind her actions, and her sudden withdrawal weighed heavily against his heart. When he saw her on the bridge with no way to escape certain death, he thought his heart had split in two; it was as though the jaguar had sliced him open, and in that moment, when the animal at-tacked, Tan believed he would die with Leah. In all the years he had spent alone in the forest, Tan had never felt this kind of pain and now he won-dered if perhaps solitude was not better. He had no experience with which to bolster himself, no youthful sweetheart to have taught him the hardships of loving another. Always apart, even before he took the mantle of Aclla, Tan had kept his heart in check, as if he could protect some treasure that he would not or perhaps could not share. But the Qewa Ñawi, with her melodious voice and her grass green eyes, walked uninvited into his jungle and changed everything he ever knew.

His fingers moved along the quipu and the next strand he touched seemed empty compared with the others: only two knots marred its smoothness. Tan allowed a half-hearted snort as he caught himself think-ing Leah would be amused by how he counted the number of Twins games he had attended. It was an odd thing to include on his quipu, yet it was representative of the way he viewed his life.

∽ ⊖ ∾

The Mamacuna shooed Saba away and took her place beside the sleeping Qewa Ñawi. Curious eyes peered from behind tall grasses and large shrubs, anxious to see what the Coya was doing sitting on a blanket in a make-shift hut, so unusual the sight. Rarely, if ever, did she personally tend to those outside her own mystical community. She ignored the prying eyes as she chanted, her hands busily preparing an herbal concoction to re-store the woman's strength. Soon the steam from her little pot, set close to Leah, filled the lean-to with a sweet, tangy smell. Leah stirred beneath the blankets when a hand touched her cheek. Shifting slightly, the Mamacuna raised Leah's head so it was supported on her knees and continued singing a hymn for healing.

Slowly, Leah's eyes opened and she managed a weak smile. "I feel like a newborn lamb," she whispered through dry lips.

With one hand, the Mamacuna ladled tea into a clay cup and held it to Leah's lips. "Drink, little chinan," she urged, "and the dark specters of the mountains shall vanish." The cup was emptied and refilled twice before the old woman put it down. "Now, close your eyes and listen as I tell you the legend of the colored eyes." She made sure Leah was comfortable in her lap and, while she stroked the woman's face, she began her tale.

"In the days before Topa Inca's rule over the people, there was a woman who chewed on coca leaves and deciphered the spittle. She was a wise old woman, yet feared by many for when she spoke, she spoke of things they did not want to know. Because of this, she lived alone, outside Cajamarca, deep in the cloud forest. The old woman was privy to many things and soon she learned of Topa Inca's desire to conquer the people and take them into his empire as servants. Our men gathered to defend the city, but the old woman came to the gates of Cajamarca to tell them this would cost too many lives and the city would be lost.

"The people were angry at the old woman and they chased her away. Just before she disappeared forever into the cloud forest, she held up her hands and stopped the shouting crowd. 'I will tell you this last thing,' she cried over their voices and the shouting ceased and the people listened. 'Topa Inca will conquer those who stay here. But those who want to live as we have always lived must come with me now and I will share with them the secrets that I know!' Only ten young men, all known for their devotion to the ancient ways, followed her into the cloud forest. For three days and three nights, they fasted and prayed to Mamaquilla for help. The old woman told them many things; some of the youths were frightened and ran away. But those who were strong of heart pledged to follow the old woman into the mountains.

"The six young men returned to the city. Six gathered their wives and their children, their tools and their household goods and prepared to join the old woman. But first, they had a message for the people who would stay behind." The Mamacuna stopped and looked deep into Leah's eyes. "Do you know about the prophecy, my daughter?"

"No, Coya," Leah whispered as she clutched the old woman's hand.

"Of course not," chortled the Mamacuna, "for no one dares speak of the prophecy, especially in these times." She stoked Leah's brow and sighed before going on with the story. "The prophecy was one of faith in the face of destruction. 'Topa Inca shall defeat you,' she told them, 'and many shall perish. Those who survive will live honorable lives and become one with them. But there is a price to be paid. When the ones with sickly faces and sky eyes come to the land, the Inca will pay with his own blood and Mamaquilla will be avenged for the death of Her children. The Chimu who remain Chimu will escape the destruction that will come to the Inca and they will flourish, apart and happy, away from the disease and death that comes with the sky eyes. When the one with cat's eyes comes, he will herald a great danger to those who cling to our ways, yet he will not bring the disaster. Through him will come a great gift, a treasure to be treasured, but one to be sacrificed to the winds of change. The winds of change will come when the grass-eyed one comes into the land but do not fear; the one with grass eyes will travel swiftly, taking that which is to be taken, but leaving in its place the grace of Mamaquilla."

"Iztak was the one with cat's eyes, wasn't he, Coya?"

"This is so."

"And Tan is the gift," asked Leah.

"This, too, is so, huahuan."

"And...."

"And you are the herald of the winds of change. I saw you in the jonchi at the Inti Raimi long before you came. I saw your eyes and I heard your voice." She smiled at Leah. "You sat on steps of stone with your face turned to the sun. You wore strange leggings the color of dusk and a gray tunic with strange blue markings."

"Sweatshirt," Leah murmured.

"And your feet! I thought there was something wrong with your feet because they were as white as the most sacred vicuña."

"Sneakers," she managed to say.

"When the Hector asked my permission for a woman to live with the people, I knew the strange woman I saw in the jonchi would be the one to come. Even in the vision, I saw your grass eyes."

Leah looked up into the heavy lidded eyes of the Mamacuna. "You said the gift would be sacrificed. Does this mean Tan will die?"

"No, Qewa Ñawi, this is not so. A sacrifice can be made in many ways; I do not think Mamaquilla means to take Her beloved churi to Her home. It means we had him with us for a time and now we do not. He is here for the moment, but his place is away from here, with you...in Ruti-Suyu." She smiled, the wrinkles deepening in her leathery face. "Your son will need his father if he is to learn the history of his people."

"I do not think so, Coya," said Leah, shaking her head; "Tan needs to be here, not in a land of man-built mountains. I will tell our son of his father."

"Do you doubt my wisdom?" the Mamacuna chided gently, but the rebuke was clear nonetheless. Leah turned her head away, but the Mamacuna was not fooled. "Hush, huahuan, and sleep now. The world will seem less confounding when you awaken." With a feather soft touch, she stroked Leah's brow until the tears ceased and she slept.

೦ ⊖ ೦

Cura replaced the Mamacuna; Rina replaced Cura, and Saba, Rina. Throughout the remainder of the day and long into the night, the women sat beside Leah, all the while singing soft songs of comfort. Her wounds were not all on the surface; other than a few scratches and bruises, Saba and the Mamacuna concurred that the most painful injury was the one in her heart, the one which had driven her away from the people during the night.

When she was certain the medicines would help her chinan to sleep deeply, the Mamacuna returned to her own fire to seek the counsel of her Rimoc. Someone had indeed told lies to the Qewa Ñawi, however noble the intention, and the source must be discovered. The legend of the colored eyes was ever a guarded story, not a simple tale to be bandied about with children, but a sacred prophecy only to be shared at important moments in the life of the community. Most everyone knew something of the prophecy, if only because the legend was recounted at ceremonies when other prophetic tales were told. But at no time had the Mamacuna revealed her belief that Iztak had been the one with cat's eyes and through him, the gift had been Na-Tan Manco, the most powerful aclla anyone could remember. When the woman came, some of the Rimoc had wondered aloud if the one called Qewa Ñawi was the one foretold, but the Mamacuna neither confirmed nor denied rumors. She was more interested in waiting to see what came with the grass-eyed woman. The prophecy made no distinction between male and female, only the color of the eyes was of importance. Now, however, there was no doubt in her mind.

"The truth is the truth," the Mamacuna told her council when they had gathered at her fire. "The Qewa Ñawi is merely the herald; beyond that, she has no importance. Her presence is the fulfillment of the prophecy; she influences neither what we do nor how we accomplish it."

"A sign, not a voice?" asked one of the older mystics.

"Exactly. Her presence is not necessary to our survival; we have no wish to prevent her from leaving."

"And him?" another asked.

The Mamacuna shook her head. "Na-Tan Manco's mita is complete. He is a man; no more, no less. His departure will not change anything." Slowly, her eyes searched the circle until she found the face she sought. "The chinan Micay is of your ayllu, is she not, Tocto?"

"I am her mama'amuata, Coya," admitted the collahuaya with some shame in her voice. She suspected her hua'amuata, who had spoken against Li-Ah before, was involved.

The Coya saw her discomfort. "We will talk of your part in this later, Tocto," she said sternly. "Go now; bring Micay to me." The order was swiftly obeyed. When the woman was gone, the Mamacuna turned to Saba, who sat stone-faced beside her. "When the chinan Micay arrives, my friend, you will hold your tongue and say nothing."

"Yes, Coya," promised Saba, wondering what Micay had to do with any of this.

Tocto returned with the chinan in tow, her head modestly bowed beneath her red hat, touching her fingers to her lips repeatedly as she knelt. "I have been summoned and I have come," she murmured respectfully.

The Mamacuna lifted the hat, exposing the pretty face for all to see. "You have studied hard with your mama'amuata, Micay?"

"Yes, Coya."

"Have you learned the laws and customs in proper order?"

"Yes, Coya."

"Tell me, Micay, what is the first law of healing?"

Micay dared to look up; she could not see anything but kindness in the ancient face. Sucking in her breath, she recited the sacred words. "The first law of healing is to seek the nature of the illness."

"That is correct. And what is the second?"

"To find the truth in the illness and to separate it from the fear."

"That, too, is correct, Micay. Now, tell us how one determines this truth."

"By watching with eyes, hearing with ears, but listening with the heart." The girl's palms grew damp and it became difficult to keep her fingers from clutching the strands of her quipu in nervousness.

"As a chinan, are you permitted to make statements of truth without the presence of your collahuaya?"

"No, Coya; I have not yet been given permission."

"That is what I have heard, Micay, but my heart tells me you have presumed to speak that which was not a truth to another chinan."

Micay's face blanched, then reddened and her hands flew to her face as if they could hide her shame. "But it was a truth, Coya; she has brought nothing but bad fortune to us since she came!"

The Mamacuna's hand touched Saba, a reminder of her promise to remain silent. "Your words were not truth, Micay, and they may have cost my beloved churi that which he holds most dear in his heart. Once you lay beside the aclla as his consort. Is it possible your words were colored by your desire to be the chosen woman of the man Na-Tan Manco?"

Micay bit her lip, unwilling to answer the question.

Her silence was enough for the Mamacuna. "Causing death to the woman you see as your rival would not have made you the chosen woman of Na-Tan Manco; his heart was bound to hers long before he chose you to be his consort for a single night. She is favored by Mamaquilla, for otherwise she would not have come. You cannot possibly know what pain we would feel had the Qewa Ñawi been harmed. It is because of her we are safe now and will be safe in the future. For the same reason we do not harm the condor, we protect those who are favored by Mamaquilla." She paused to let her words sink in. "Would you jeopardize the safety of your own people?"

"No, Coya," hiccupped Micay.

"Then we have reached an understanding between us. Now it is for me to decide how you will make amends for this most serious transgression of our faith in you."

Saba cleared her throat and the Mamacuna nodded, giving her permission to speak at last. "I am angered by the actions of Micay, yet this chinan has, in the past, shown good judgment and skill in healing. Part of my heart would take her hat and throw it in the river, but another part of my heart believes she spoke the words of a child who is in need of instruction. Do we banish a child for foolish talk? No, we teach the child to think wisely before speaking." Saba thought she saw a glimmer of a smile cross the Coya's lips. "It would be a fitting lesson for this chinan to spend her days teaching children the ways of Mamaquilla."

The suggestion was not without peril; Saba was the mistress to the chinan assigned to the teaching of children and this would put Micay directly under Saba's sharp eye. Still, there was justice in the punishment and the Mamacuna silently congratulated herself on her wise choice of a successor. "Is this agreeable to you, Tocto?" she asked the Micay's mama'amuata.

"This is agreeable to me," replied the collahuaya, relieved her spirit daughter was not to be removed from the ranks of the chinan.

"Then it is done." The Mamacuna rose and held out her hand to Micay. "You will take your belongings and live within hearing of Mama Saba's voice. You will also seek out Na-Tan Manco and ask his forgiveness. When the Qewa Ñawi awakens, you will go to her and apologize for your foolish words. And you, Tocto, you will make a special offering to Mamaquilla to ask Her forgiveness for your lack of attention to Micay's inner heart."

Dismissed, Micay scurried off in the direction of her shelter, her face still burning with humiliation even though she was more than relieved at the sentence passed on her by the Mamacuna. Life with Saba would not be so bad; the collahuaya was known for her patience and willingness to teach a young chinan the ways of healing. The thought of having to face Tan and Leah, however, chilled Micay to the bone.

CHAPTER 39

Pale sunlight filtered through the boughs of the little lean-to when Leah opened her eyes. Saba was nearby, snoring softly. Slipping from the pallet, Leah found her pouch hanging on its peg; her laundered but bloodstained clothing folded neatly underneath. She dressed silently and laced up her boots. Moving quickly, she made her way to the stream to wash.

The events of the last hours left little impression on Leah. She could not recall being bathed after they brought her back to the encampment, yet she was clean now; what she did remember was the vague sound of never-ending chants and the voice of the Mamacuna traveling through space with stories she could not remember. As she knelt at the edge of the rushing water, Leah wished she was anywhere else, then caught herself; this place was so central to her being now, how could she possibly want to be elsewhere? The water was icy cold, stinging her face and eyes where she splashed herself. It did nothing to make her feel better; it only crystallized her need to be away from the people. Walking back to the shelter, Leah decided she would ask Tupac's help in finding a chasqui who would take her back to the old place from which she could easily reach the clinic unharmed.

Saba was awake when Leah returned. "I am glad to see you are walking amongst the living, my daughter," she said with a concerned smile.

"I am fine, Saba."

Her brittle voice belied the words, but the collahuaya did not challenge her. Instead, Saba stood up and stretched. "I will leave you for only a few moments, Li-ah, while I find something hearty for you to eat. You must be hungry after such a long rest."

"Thank you, Saba." Leah watched the woman disappear toward the main body of the ayllu. Once she was gone, Leah began to roll up her blanket.

"May I speak?" Micay was standing outside the lean-to.

"Can I stop you?" was the curt reply.

Micay would not be put off. She knelt at the opening of the lean-to and bowed her head. "I have come to beg your forgiveness for my foolish tongue. I have done great harm in speaking words which were not truth and I would be at fault if I did not apologize."

Sitting back on her haunches, Leah stopped rolling and looked over her shoulder at the chinan. "That's where you are wrong, Micay; you spoke perfect truth and I had not been willing to believe what my heart already knew."

"But...."

"You are forgiven, Micay." She turned her back on Micay and resumed her work. She heard the hurried footsteps running away. Gritting her teeth, Leah stuffed her pack with a vengeance, glad to be alone with her pain.

A new voice interrupted her work, this one hard, angry and speaking English. "What the hell do you think you are doing, Leah?" demanded Tan, his body blocking the light from the doorway.

She answered him as he had spoken; the sound seemed strange and discordant to her ears. "I am leaving. Please do not follow me."

"You cannot," he roared. "You are my wife; I do not permit you to leave!"

"You?" shouted Leah. "Permit me? We may be in Peru, buster, but don't think for one New York minute you control what I do!"

Tan's fists clenched as tightly as his jaw, the muscles in his cheek twitching as his came toward Leah, towering over her. "You are my wife, Leah; I won't stand aside to let you do foolishness. You are not speaking as an educated person; you are raving like a madwoman!"

"Blow it out your ear, buddy." Spinning on her heel, she picked her bedroll and slung it over her shoulder, then pushed past him and out of the shelter. His hand shot out and grabbed the strap, pulling her off balance. Leah bounced into him, regained her footing and struggled to break his iron grip. She used her elbow to jab him in the ribs, but it had little effect. Tan reached around her waist and hauled her upward until her feet left the ground. She writhed, trying to escape. "Put me down, you sonofabitch!" she screamed.

"No way." He stormed from the shelter, taking enormous strides that jostled Leah's still sore arm. The more she struggled, the tighter his grip became.

She was still screaming epithets when Saba came scuttling down the path, waving her arms and shouting, "What are you doing? What are you doing?"

A crowd was beginning to gather; sleepy faces awakened by the tumult came to see what caused the ear-splitting commotion coming from the shelter of the newlyweds. They could not understand the words, but it was obvious the Qewa Ñawi had angered her husband and he had wrested control of the situation.

"Put me down!" yelled Leah as Tan kept walking.

"I'll put you down when I'm ready, woman, and not a moment before." Past the curious eyes of his neighbors, past his parents and his brothers, Tan kept going up the path toward the Mamacuna's camp. Leah continued to rail, but he ignored her; he kept his mouth clamped shut and his eyes forward. By the time he reached the Mamacuna's fire, with Manco and Cura in hot pursuit, the old woman was waiting for them, her hands on her hips, her mouth set in a tight line. He did not release Leah nor did he kneel. Instead, he stood tall while his captive flailed her arms and kicked her legs; assorted epithets in several languages spewed from her lips.

"Forgive me for breaking the peace of your morning, Coya, but my wife has taken it into her head that she should leave the people without me." Unceremoniously, he dumped Leah on the ground.

The Mamacuna snorted as she willed herself not to laugh; this was not a humorous situation and required great delicacy. Tan could not be condoned for bringing the Qewa Ñawi to her in so undignified manner. "I can understand why, Na-Tan Manco," she said in a calm voice, "if this is the way you treat your wife."

Struggling to stand up, Leah took a step away from Tan, but his hand locked onto her arm, preventing her from moving. She tried unsuccessfully to jerk free. "Coya, I ask that our bond be annulled. I cannot divide my heart in two any more than I can divide my body. Na-Tan Manco belongs here with you, not with me in Ruti-Suyu. His heart will always be here."

"Do not presume to tell me where my heart will be, Qewa Ñawi," growled Tan in his native tongue.

"Then don't presume to tell me what I think!" Leah snapped.

He slipped back into English. "I already know what you think, woman."

"The hell you do! But I know enough to know you will never be happy in the States and you know it, too. You said...."

"I said it would be *difficult* to leave my home, but I never said I did not want to leave." Tan's shouts carried over the tops of the trees causing birds to take flight.

"Like you're gonna be satisfied driving to work, living in a house, paying a mortgage? Give me a break!" She narrowed her eyes at him. "And let go of my arm," she growled.

The Mamacuna held up her hands. "Children! Children! Cease this monkey chatter and speak in a civilized way!" She saw two mouths shut, four eyes blaze, and two spines posture defiance. "Good, you have both shut up," said the Mamacuna.

"Na-Tan Manco!" His father stepped forward, "release Li-ah." The offending hand immediately dropped from her arm.

"Thank you, Manco," said the Mamacuna. She turned a stern eye to Tan and Leah. "I do not usually interfere in household disputes, children, but you are forcing my hand on this day. Li-ah, you are afraid Na-Tan Manco will not be happy in Ruti-Suyu; this you have said already. But have you asked Na-Tan Manco what it is he wants to do?"

"He will not speak truth to me, Coya, for he does not know the truth in his heart," Leah explained unhappily.

"I know my heart will be split in two when I leave here, but I cannot stay. I am of the people, yet no longer of the people. I will not be satisfied living this life any longer. There are things I want to know, things I must learn, and I cannot learn them here." Tan glanced at Leah and thought he saw her lower lip tremble. "More than my heart is bound to the Qewa Ñawi, my soul is bound to hers." Very gently, he took her hand in his. "A life without her would be slow death for me."

Cura stepped forward to stand beside her son. "On the night Na-Tan was born, Coya, I knew there would come a time my son would leave our ayllu; he was a gift only lent, not given, to me. The whole of his days has been spent walking along a line that led away from us. No mother wants her child to go so far from home, but I am prepared to see him leave." She smiled at Tan, then looked to her husband who silently signaled for her to continue. "We are pleased with his choice of wife and have no wish to lose the woman Li-ah as our daughter."

The Mamacuna looked from one to the other, searching for some sign of reconciliation between them. It was a surreptitious little glance at Tan by Leah that made her breathe a bit easier. "Li-Ah, do you love Na-Tan Manco?" asked the High Priestess.

"Yes, Coya," she admitted grumpily.

"And do you," she asked Leah, "believe his welfare would be best served if you offer to leave the people without him?" She saw Leah's tiny nod. "But Na-Tan Manco says he would perish without you. Do you love him enough to live with him in Ruti-Suyu on the cold days he longs for the warmth of his old home?"

"If I believed his heart would be happy in Ruti-Suyu, yes. But of this, I am not certain."

A tense silence settled over the little group, but the Mamacuna waited patiently for the right words to be spoken by someone other than herself. Finally, Tan touched Leah's chin, turning her face toward him. "I cannot promise that every day in Ruti-Suyu will be a happy day just as I cannot promise I will not sometimes long for my parents' fire. But I can promise you that my heart will only be at home with you. Your heart is in my heart, as my heart is in yours. Separate them and we will both perish. We are bound to each other. This is the final truth, Leah, one to which we are both committed."

Two tears dribbled down Leah's cheek. "Your heart is in my heart, as mine is in yours. We are bound to each other."

Leaning over, Tan grazed Leah's lips with his own, then flicked away the offending tears with his finger. There were clucks of approval from Tan's family. But the Mamacuna was not finished with them yet.

"It is custom for a young couple to seek solitude so that the bond between them is strengthened without the meddling of others. It would be a good thing if you spent time away from all others to mend the hurt which has been done, lest it fester into a greater hurt." She stepped toward Tan and Leah, taking their hands in hers and joining them together. "Your time here is to be short, my children; use it wisely."

\~ ⊖ ~

The time was shorter than anyone anticipated. As the people gathered to hear the Mamacuna late in the afternoon, when she would detail how the ayllus would choose their new sites, the stillness of the air was broken by a strange thup-thup-thup coming closer with every minute. The men, grabbing their knives and spears, quickly formed a battle square while the women took the children into the cover of the jungle. Leah refused to go with the other women; instead, she joined the Mamacuna and the Rimoc as they walked behind the army toward the open plateau. Neither she nor Tan were surprised to see a helicopter circle above them several times before it slowly descended to earth, stirring up a great cloud of dust as it landed. From their vantage point on the little rise, Leah and the Mamacuna watched the blades slowly stop.

Paolo hopped out first. "Anyone here call a cab?" he shouted to where Tan stood with his father and brothers. He then turned to assist another passenger, who waved vigorously in the direction of the Mamacuna. "It's Hector!" cried Leah, squeezing the old woman's hand excitedly.

With great dignity and grace, the Mamacuna descended from her hill and walked slowly toward the chopper, her face stern, her bearing regal. "So, you have finally managed to pull yourself together, janpeq, to rejoin your family," she said, her voice slightly reproving.

Hector bowed his head and touched his fingers to his lips several times. "I have come to beg your forgiveness for my absence, Coya, and ask your permission to settle once again amongst the people."

"Not until you are completely well, and your stomach has been set to rights," she countered sternly. "You need to have your innards attached, do you not?"

"This is so, but I needed to gain your permission while we could still find you."

The Mamacuna extended her hand and the doctor took it in his. "You are always welcome, Hector Morales. I shall look forward to your coming. But since you are here, there are those who need your keen eye."

Hector grinned a silly grin. His clinic was back in business.

∾ ⊖ ∾

Over the evening meal at the Mamacuna's fire, Hector and Paolo outlined what was needed for a new clinic, taking into account where the people would live, what water supply could be tapped, and where a small plane could land and take off without making an airstrip easily visible to strangers in the sky. Leah sat beside the Mamacuna, and Tan beside her. At the Coya's insistence, Manco sat beside his son, listening carefully to the way he spoke; impressed by the weight his words were given by the others. It was clear to him that his son had gained much wisdom from his experiences outside their world, and, at the same time, he saw Tan would never fully be a part of this community again. Long into the night they talked, and when at last the fire had burned into a pile of glowing embers, the Mamacuna called an end to the conversation.

"We have talked enough for one day," she said, "and I am pleased with our decisions." She looked over at Leah, who leaned sleepily against Tan's shoulder. "Tomorrow, you will return to the other world with the Ayar Kuntar and the janpeq."

Tan looked up, not wanting to argue although he felt he was not ready to leave his home quite yet.

As if she could read his mind, the Mamacuna raised her hand. "The time is right for you to leave us, churi. You must go back to Ruti-Suyu and make your peace with the Qewa Ñawi's people. You have been bound by me, but until you have her parents' permission, you are not fully bound." She stood and pointed at Hector. "Come my friend, we have things to talk about before the face of Inti shines in the morning." Together, they strolled toward Mamacuna's shelter.

Tan and Leah returned to their own shelter to find the blankets strewn with flowers. Surrounded by the sweet fragrance, they made love through the night as if with each possession, they joined body and soul, heart and mind, until they were completely one, bound flesh and spirit.

"It will pain me to leave my home," said Tan as they lay together beneath the skins, "but already I am thinking about what classes I shall take in the fall."

Leah laughed softly. "Math, math and more math, if I know my husband." The last word lingered in the still night air.

That she called him her husband made him shiver with pleasure. "Will my wife mind being bound to an undergrad?" teased Tan before he brushed a kiss on her lips.

Closing her eyes, Leah spooned her body against his, savoring the warmth of his bare flesh. She played with his fingers, outlining each one with her own. "I suppose I'll have to put up with it, Na-Tan Manco."

"I like when you call me by name, Leah. You never said my name in Minnesota."

"I couldn't. I don't know why, but I couldn't. It would have been like," she paused to think, "...hmmmm, I don't know, disrespectful."

"Foolish chinan," he murmured, kissing her again. "Go to sleep."

"I can't. I'm all wound up." Leah noticed Tan was speaking English again.

"Then I shall teach you a sleeping chant." Tan tightened his arms around her.

"I never heard of a sleeping chant."

"It was one my grandfather taught me when I was very small. He said they were secret, sacred words. If I said them seven times, I would fall asleep and Mamaquilla would keep me safe." In the darkness, he smiled at the memory of his grandfather.

"Okay, I'll bite; teach me the sleeping chant."

"Ready?"

"Ready."

"Listen closely, then say what I say. *Sha mah, ish rah....*"

Leah started to repeat the words slowly. "Sha...ma...ish.... rah..."

"*Ah dah, ay lo, ah dah, eh-kat.*"

"Ah...da...ay...lo...ah..................." She stopped and suddenly flipped over so she was facing Tan. Her brows were furrowed. "Say it again, Tan. Say it faster."

He propped himself up on his elbow and looked at her oddly before he repeated the chant.

This time, Leah sat upright and stared at Tan. "What is your name?"

"What?"

"What is your name?"

"You know my name, Leah!"

"Say it!" she ordered.

Tan shrugged. "Na-Tan Manco."

"And your grandfather's name?"

Tan sat up and faced her. "Iztak Mulkan."

Leah shook her head. "No, not that...his full name, the one the Mama-cuna called him."

"Iztak Arro Ba Na-Tan."

Leah's open palm smacked against her forehead. "Yitzchak! Yitzchak Aaron. God, am I dense! Your grandfather's name was Yitzchak Aaron ben Natan! My God, Tan, your name is Natan," she cried. "What a name! It means *to give* in Hebrew. Iztak must have been a Jew! What the hell was a Jew doing in the Andes? How did he get here? Why was he here? When did he come? I mean, I know we're wanderers, but this! This is...this is...."

The words were so fast Tan could barely understand them. "Slow down, Qewa Ñawi, you are talking too fast. Explain!"

"How come you're circumcised, Tan?" When he looked at her blankly, she explained the word.

"My father and brothers are.... circumcised; this was decided by our father and his," he answered, looking down at himself. "It is done in my family when we are too young to protest. Others do it, too."

"Could it be Iztak decided this was one way he could bind his own sons to the Covenant of Abraham? Was he the first to do this?"

Tan shook his head. "I don't think so. This is not unknown amongst the people, but not everyone does this to their sons. But how do you know all this?"

"The sleeping chant, Tan. It's the prayer we say before we go to bed. The *Shema*. Mark must've told you about it, if he told you about the *Hallel* and the others. Surely, you've been to services at Hillel...you must've heard it a dozen times. *Shema Yisrael Adonay elohainu, Adonay echad.* Hear, O Israel, the Lord is our God, the Lord is One. It's the core prayer! I said it on the bridge, when I thought I was going to die. My God, how did I miss this?"

Tan was silent; he tried to understand what she was saying, but it was difficult. He didn't remember enough about his grandfather to know if what she said was the truth. His grandfather, he knew, came to the people not speaking their language but he learned quickly, according to the stories he had been told. And the stories Iztak told him were always of people and places so far removed from the people he would sometimes wave Tan's questions away with a laugh and *maybe one day you will know.* Now he knew. "Does this mean I am a Jew?" he asked Leah.

"No," she answered bluntly. "We count our descent through the mother, not the father. But that doesn't matter, Tan. It only means this is.... *b'shert,* " she laughed. "Meant to be. Prescribed by heaven." She grabbed his hand and held it against her breast. "Grandma Sophie used to tell me that one day, I would find the person who would fill the special place in my heart the way only one person would be able to fill it. When those two people come together, it's because God made them to join as one. Two parts of one soul! It is *b'shert,* destined to be."

"We are *b'shert,*" said Tan, repeating the new word. He drew her to him and pressed his lips against her hair. "I told you at the huaca, the first time I saw you, our unachai was as one. We have always been *b'shert.* "

"I have to see the Mamacuna before we leave," sighed Leah, leaning against Tan.

When Leah was asleep at last, Tan reached behind him and felt for the parcel the Mamacuna had given him. Assured it was still there, he let himself drift off.

CHAPTER 40

The Mamacuna was sitting at her fire with Hector when Leah approached late in the morning. She was wearing her tunic and her hat was squarely on her head, her paicha dangling from the side. Touching her fingers to her lips, she waited for the Mamacuna to wave her closer. "Forgive my intrusion, Coya," she said, her head still bowed, "but I would speak with you."

Hector glanced from Leah to the Mamacuna and slowly stood up. "I shall leave you with your chinan, Mama Qimpu. There are medicines which need to be given before I leave." With a small bow and a touch of fingers to lips, he left them alone.

"I think," sighed the Mamacuna when he had gone, "he is the last person alive who would call me by my name." She looked up at Leah. "No one else would dare." Her laughter took Leah by surprise. The Mamacuna patted the place Hector had vacated. "Are you so surprised that I have a name, Li-Ah?"

"I never would have asked, Coya; it would have been improper."

"But there is a question you would ask, is there not? About my old friend, Iztak Arro."

It never ceased to amaze Leah how the old woman knew ahead of time what the question would be. "Yes, Coya. I would ask about my husband's grandfather."

A chinan appeared with two cups of tea and handed one to the Mamacuna, the other to Leah. Alone again, the Mamacuna sipped her tea. "You wish to know what I know about Iztak's history. I will tell you this: he came from far away in order to heal a great hurt. I never knew what this hurt was, but I do know in the years he lived with us, the pain was slowly replaced with the joy of living. Iztak had eyes ringed with the color of amber, like a cat's, but they were kind eyes. I grew to trust and love those eyes, although he was already bound to another." The Mamacuna laughed lightly and it was a girlish, uncommon sound. "And I will tell you something no one else knows, huahuan; I was terribly jealous of Aima. I thought Iztak the most handsome man I ever saw, more handsome than his grandson, although in some ways they are much alike. I wanted to be the one he courted. I was already a chinan preparing to become a collahuaya when he came, but that would not have stopped me from going to him had he asked. But Iztak saw only Aima and they became one, just as you have become one with Na-Tan Manco." She stopped to sip her tea and let the memories wash over her. "Iztak, when he first came to us, had hair on his face. We thought that very strange and for a long time he refused to scrape away his beard, but he finally did. He was far more handsome without it." She paused, her eyes closed, as if summoning Iztak's image into her mind. "Like you, my daughter, he was pale and sickly looking, but after many cycles beneath the eye of Inti, he grew dark and healthy like us."

"Did he ever tell you how he came to be here, Coya?" asked Leah

The Mamacuna raised an eyebrow at Leah. "You do not know?"

Leah shook her head. "Should I?"

"No, I think not. When the time is right, Tan will know more, but for now, I will tell you part of the tale." She put down her cup and took Leah's hand in hers. "I was hardly more than a girl when Iztak Arro stumbled into our ayllu, the one in which your husband's family... and mine... lived for many generations. He was a young man made old from suffering, terribly thin, and the pain in his eyes was so great that my mama'amuata feared for his life. He was not well, although the stories they tell now speak of him as a robust mulkan; he was not. The men carried him to the house of Paucar, the sinchi of our ayllu, where he lingered between life and death, speaking strange words, calling strange, unpronounceable names. The people were afraid of his cat eyes, but when our Mamacuna came to see the stranger, she instructed my mama'amuata to step aside and let her heal him. When Iztak awoke from his illness, he asked our Mamacuna for permission to stay with the people and this she granted. Rahua, Paucar's wife, and his daughter Aima tended Iztak until he grew strong enough to begin his life anew. As was natural, he fell in love with Aima, but only after our Coya herself gave permission, did they bind themselves in the eyes of Mamaquilla."

"Do you recall any of the words he spoke?" asked Leah.

"Yes. He called for *Sor-ka* again and again, but when he was well, he never again said the word."

"You came to be his friend, Coya. Did you never ask him what it meant?"

The Mamacuna nodded. "Once, when we were already old, I asked about this *Sor-ka*. Great pain came into Iztak's eyes and he told me never to say that word again. I never did." She looked at Leah questioningly. "Does this Sor-ka mean anything in your language, my daughter?"

"Sorke," replied Leah slowly, "is a woman's name. Perhaps his mother's."

"No. He once said his mother's name was Ruti... like the land. I have often wondered if the reason his grandson has been called to Ruti-Suyu was to return to the land of his ancestors."

Leah smiled, but shook her head. "Ruti must have been Ruth. It is a name of great meaning to my people. She was, in our history, a woman who left her home to follow her husband's mother to a new home after her own husband and husband's father had died. She is considered to be a woman of great strength and honor."

"If this is the ancestor of your husband, then he follows her ways."

Leah laughed gently at the thought. "Ruth lived so many sun cycles past that we can hardly count her children, but I will tell you this, the god on the piece of wood, the ones the strangers talk about.... he is considered to be of her blood."

The Mamacuna looked strangely at Leah. "Are you of his blood, too?" she asked cautiously.

"Ai! What difficult questions you ask!" laughed Leah, now sorry she had mentioned it. "The man on the wood is.... is.... one of my people, but he is not our god. He lived long before the time of even Pachacuti Inca. It is very complex and I'm afraid I couldn't explain it very well in so short a time."

"No matter," said the Mamacuna with a wave of her hand, "you do not strike me as the kind of woman who believes suffering is the way to please Viracocha." There was an underlying tone of relief in her voice. "Keep your knowledge to yourself, huahuan; you will know when it is time to share it. Go now, Qewa Ñawi, and find your husband. The face of Inti is already high and you must prepare for your journey. There are many who would bid you farewell."

Leah rose and bowed to the Mamacuna, touching her lips several times as she backed away from the old woman. "I thank you, Coya, for your words."

"Ai! Do not thank me, huahuan. I wish only that I could tell you more."

ᘒ ⊖ ᘐ

Tan was waiting for Leah when she returned from her visit to the Mamacuna. "What did you discover, little mulkan?" he asked after he kissed her. "Your eyes are bright with discovery."

"Never mind that, Na-Tan Manco. Help me gather our belongings. Paolo wants to leave before it gets too late."

Tan furrowed his brow, but resisted the urge to press Leah for details of her conversation with the Mamacuna. "Are you in such a hurry to leave?"

Leah stopped rolling their blankets and looked up at him. "No, I am not in a hurry to leave, but I want to get everything done so we might spend our last minutes with our families."

Duly chastised, Tan knelt beside Leah and helped her with the bundling. He watched her work and marveled at how she performed the mundane tasks with grace and agility uncommon to the other women he encountered in Ruti-Suyu. He laughed to himself as he imagined India trying to roll a bed in the traditional manner.

"What's so funny?" Leah asked with a frown. When he shared his thought, she scolded with him. "Not everyone is able to turn their world upside down and do as I have done, Tan. Do I laugh at you when you confront the toaster?"

"I know how to use a toaster!" he protested.

"Oh, yes. By sticking a knife in it to get out a bagel while it's still plugged in." She raised a dubious eyebrow at him, "You're lucky you haven't electrocuted yourself, oh wise one."

Tan raised his hands in mock surrender. "You are right; I'm sorry I said anything at all."

"Is she henpecking you already, Tan?" Hector poked his head into the lean-to and laughed.

"You, señor medico, neglected to teach your protégé about the dangers of electricity, knives and toasters." Leah wagged a finger at him. "Are there any other gaps in his education I should know about?"

"Yes." From over Tan's shoulder, Hector mouthed a single word. "Contraception."

Leah sat down with a thump. "Tan, would you go find Mama Saba and ask her for the tea she promised?"

"Hrrmph," snorted Tan with mock annoyance. "I know when my company is not desired."

When he was gone, Hector slowly lowered himself onto the pile of folded alpaca skins. "How are you feeling after your encounter on the bridge?" he asked in English. He did not want anyone who might be in listening distance to understand their conversation.

"I'm okay." Leah eyed him warily. "What's on your mind, Hector?"

"No spotting? No bleeding?"

Defensively, her hands came to rest across her flat belly. "He is safe within. How did you know?"

"I just did. You are not the only one who has dreams, Leah." He grinned broadly at her.

"What about you, Hector? Can you come to this place and leave the old clinic behind? What about the others who depend on you there?"

Hector shrugged and held out his hands, palms open. "I am, I'm afraid, more one of the people than not. Felipe will find some young doctor to take over the old clinic; there will soon be a real town there. As for me, I am bound to this little band in a way I never thought could happen. I could no more let them live up here without me than I could cut off my right hand. My place is wherever they finally settle...with Paolo's help, of course."

"Of course," smiled Leah. "Will you now become a rimac and finally take your rightful place at the side of the Mamacuna?"

Hector laughed long and loud. "There are no secrets from you, are there, Qewa Ñawi?"

"None."

"I don't know if I will accept her offer quite yet, but in time, I suppose I will have to, especially if Saba has her way." His voice grew more serious. "She will succeed the Mamacuna, you know."

"I've known since before I left the last time. She's a good choice. Saba has the heart and the head to follow in this one's footsteps, but not for a long while, Mamaquilla willing."

"The old lady is in good health, if that's any consolation. She'll live a good while longer *if* she takes care of herself."

"And you'll see that she does?"

Hector shrugged, "It's the least I can do."

"How long until you can establish a clinic here?" asked Leah.

"A couple of months at least. I'm going to have to do a little scrounging for equipment; I can't very well strip the old clinic."

"Talk to Francisco Gutiérrez, Hector. I'm sure he'll get you whatever you need. You're going to have to learn to rely on him...and his son as your voice in Lima. They will serve the people well."

Hector held her hand in his. "May Mamaquilla hear your words, Qewa Ñawi."

⁃ ⊖ ⁃

Manco, Cura and Saba stood together on the flat mesa not far from where the helicopter sat in silence awaiting its passengers. Tan and Leah approached them, then knelt together to ask their blessings on the journey back to Ruti-Suyu.

"I will care for your daughter, my wife, with my heart and my soul," Tan told Saba when the collahuaya put her hands on his bowed head. "She will not want for food or for shelter."

"See that you feed her from your heart as well as your hand, Na-Tan Manco. She is precious to me." Saba stepped back and Cura took her place.

"I will care for your son, my husband, with my heart and my soul," said Leah when her mother-in-law touched her head. "He will not know disharmony in his home."

"See that you feed him from your heart as well as your hand, Li-Ah. Raise his children to respect our ways."

Manco joined his wife. "You leave with our blessings. We shall count the cycles of the moon until you return once more."

Tan and Leah stood and embraced the parents one last time. The slow thup-thup-thup of the helicopter's rotors broke the silence on the mesa. "It is time," Tan whispered to Leah as she continued to cling to Saba.

Reluctantly, Leah let go of her mama'amuata and let Tan take her arm. She could see Hector standing nearer the chopper with the Mamacuna and Inka and she braced herself for yet another farewell.

"Go on, my children!" called the Coya over the noise, "go on your journey, but return to us when you are in need of renewal!" She waved her hands as if pushing them toward the helicopter.

⤛ ⊖ ⤜

They reached the clinic just before sundown. Paolo needed to return the helicopter to his friend in Piura, and took off with a promise to be back as soon as he could. "Probably not tomorrow," he said, "but the day after."

They watched the helicopter disappear over the ridge from Hector's front door. When Hector asked Leah if they would rather spend the night in the guesthouse, she readily accepted, but Tan was, for a moment silent.

"Would you mind if I did not spend the night here, Leah?" asked Tan.

"You're going to the huaca?" she countered with surprise.

Tan's hands held her cheeks. "If my wife was more thoughtful, she would remember that we left our belongings behind the waterfall." He laughed when Leah's mouth dropped open. "Not to worry, little chinan, I will be safe in the jungle. There are no women left to seek me out."

Leah did not dare object. Besides, she had the feeling he needed to make a second peace with Mamaquilla before they left for Minnesota.

Inside the house, Hector was rattling pots and pans as he tried, with his one good arm, to put his kitchen back to the order in which he liked it best. "The problem with house guests," he muttered, rearranging the stacks in his little cupboards, "is that they never put anything back."

"Tell me something, amigo," said Leah as she carried a dirty plate from the table to the makeshift sink, "what happened to Barrantes and Lubrano? In all the time we were up with the people, you never said anything about them."

Hector stopped moving and leaned against the sink. "Barrantes was in pretty bad shape when they brought him in; he's in the hospital in Piura. Lubrano, however, is the Teflon man...nothing sticks to him. Don Francisco's beautiful bodyguard was disappointed her bullet did little more than knock the bastard over. They treated him at the hospital and he was released."

"Wasn't he arrested?"

Hector shook his head. "The local prefect claimed he could not press charges based on hearsay."

"What? Are you kidding?" Leah was incensed.

"No."

"Where is he now?"

"Lima, I'd guess. No doubt he's down there lobbying for mining rights."

∾ ⊖ ∾

Tan used the old paths to get to the huaca beside the pool. Even though he knew Barrantes and the others were long gone, he could still sense the presence of strangers. Instead of the comforting safety of the jungle, Tan felt new dangers and he kept his eyes sharp for any unusual movement or markings along the trail. He jogged easily through the place he had called home, although where once he would skirt the occasional ayllu, he saw nothing but jungle. The sun was long gone when he reached the second huaca.

A noise caught Tan's ear and he dropped to a crouch behind a fallen log. For the moment there was silence, then Tan heard the noise again. Someone was walking in the brush nearby. Closing his eyes, he concentrated on the sound until he was sure it was only one human's footfall and not the sound of an animal. Creeping silently past the huaca, Tan held his breath as he counted the steps made by the stranger. The footsteps drew near to Tan's hiding place, then away, stopped briefly, then began again. Whoever it was, he was pacing the area restlessly. Unevenly. Whoever it was, he...or she limped.

The pacing eventually stopped, but not before Tan's muscles ached from crouching. He waited a while longer, then slowly crept forward, keeping himself concealed in the brush. He was on the verge of scooting wide around the perimeter of the pool when he heard a good deal of crashing coming from the opposite direction. Taking advantage of the noise, he threw himself on the ground, not worrying about his own noise. Through the brush, Tan saw a man carrying a flashlight. He scanned the area; the beam passed harmlessly over Tan's head. The man whistled shrilly, three short bursts which were answered by two longer ones.

"What took you so long?" called the limping man as he made his way toward the newcomer.

"It's dark; the trails are hard to follow."

"Stop whining and build the fire, Nardo. I'm not in the mood for listening to your complaints."

There was more stomping about and then the unmistakable scent of burning leaves. Soon, the two men sat themselves down beside the fire. Their voices carried through the night air but Tan was unable to make out clearly what they were saying. Daring to crawl closer, he inched around until he was in a better position to listen to their words.

"The mistake was not to kill the woman when you had the chance, Vincente," said one of the men. "Had you eliminated her in the States, we wouldn't be running around the jungle."

"Had I eliminated her in the States, Nardo, I would most likely be rotting in a prison there. No. Better to get rid of her here, with a well planned accident...all three of them in the plane. No one will be any the wiser."

Tan recognized the lazy drawl belonging to Vincente Lubrano and he knew the three meant him, Leah and Hector. Cold anger coursed through his veins, making Tan grit his teeth until his jaw twitched.

The man called Nardo spoke again, his harsh, guttural accent wounding the softness of the night. "Shame to waste her on a plane crash, Cente. It would be better to have her first, then slit her throat."

"Would you ram your cock where that Indio stuck his? Shame on you, Nardo." Lubrano's laughter was rough and grating.

Tan felt bitter bile rise in his throat and he forced himself to swallow. He pulled his knife from his belt and placed the blade between his teeth. He began creeping forward again and would have made it to the far side of the waterfall had he not disturbed a nest of guinea pigs. The animals yelped and scurried away, their panicked flight over dry leaves screaming another presence nearby.

Lubrano and his friend jumped, guns drawn. "Over there!" shouted Nardo as he fired his weapon.

The bullet slammed into the tree beside Tan. Rolling, he moved quickly into a crouch and began running. He could hear the one called Nardo in pursuit. He used his knowledge of the place to his advantage; even in the dark, he knew how far he was from the waterfall and where he could slip beneath the pounding curtain without being seen. Rounding the last curve in the trees at the edge of the sandy strip, Tan dove headlong into the waters.

Lubrano turned in time to catch sight of Tan midair. He fired a single shot as he hobbled toward the waterfall. A grunt of pain rang out before the water closed over Tan. "Nardo!" he shouted, "he's hit! He's gone behind the waterfall!"

The other man tore out of the jungle and stopped short beside Lubrano. "You're certain?"

"Yes. Look." He shone his beam on the water where a red splotch spread across the quieting waters.

Without being asked, Nardo jogged toward the end of the pool. Using the flashlight, he scanned the area until he found what seemed to be a path leading behind waterfall. "I'm going after him, Cente."

॰॰ ⊖ ॰॰

Tan climbed out of the water on the side of the pool opposite Lubrano. The bullet had done nothing more than strafe Tan's buttock, but he was bleeding profusely. Quietly ripping a broad leaf from plant growing near the edge of the water, Tan pressed it against the wound in hopes of staunching the flow. Had the stinging not been so bad, he would have thought it comical, but there was no denying the sharp pang of raw fear he felt as he hit the water. A narrow beam of light pierced the blackness and Tan knew he was being stalked. Swearing softly, he tossed the leaf into the water before he ducked into the cave hidden behind the waterfall.

Nardo found the spot where Tan had come out of the pool; in the beam of light, droplets of blood sparkled like rubies on the black rock. It was easy to follow the crimson trail leading into the cave, but just to be sure, Nardo pulled his gun from his belt and held it in his free hand. Moving slowly, he followed the trail into darkness so profound that he stopped long enough to shudder before he ducked to prevent hitting his head on the low ceiling.

Deep within the cave, Tan found the footholds he used before to scale the inner wall to a niche no more than six feet above the rock floor. He crouched in the space, his knife ready, waiting for the man to appear. Flashes of light bounced off the damp walls, making them glow eerily in the blackness. The light moved closer and the sounds of labored breathing filled the narrow passage. At last the man entered the space directly below Tan. Pressed back against the wall, he watched Nardo straighten up, but before he had a chance to scan the walls with his light, Tan leapt from the ledge and crashed into him.

The gun flew from Nardo's hand and clattered to a stop somewhere away from where the two men struggled on slippery rock. Nardo's bare hands closed around Tan's throat, intending to squeeze the life out of him, but the younger man was too agile and, using his elbows, Tan broke the hold. Slamming hard into Nardo's chest, he shoved him into the wall as he brought his fist up into the man's nose. His head snapped back and hit the wall with a resounding crack before he slipped to the ground.

Tan slid to the floor; his buttocks burned when they made contact with the cold, hard stone. Gingerly, he touched the wound and groaned when he felt the warmth of his own blood. Tan swore as he pulled himself up; he could not just sit there while Lubrano waited outside with a gun. Groping in the darkness, Tan's hand found Nardo's weapon. Although he had never held a gun, he knew enough from movies to know a pistol should hold no more than six bullets. He let his hand explore the gun, careful not to touch the trigger. Unsure of how it worked, he carried it to where he had hidden Leah's pack and left it there.

⊂⦾ ⊖ ⦾⊃

Leah awoke with a start. Sitting upright on Hector's couch, she realized her breathing was rapid, too rapid, and she willed herself to calm down. Her shirt was soaked with sweat and she was chilled despite the heavy blanket wrapped around her. Closing her eyes, she moderated her breathing and tried to recall what exactly she had seen in the dream that awakened her from such a deep sleep. She concentrated as hard as she could and listened to the stillness around her. Hector's gentle snoring from the bedroom faded into the background and just as she thought it was hopeless, she heard her name whispered. Her eyes flew open, but the room was still empty. A sweet, cloying scent filled her nostrils. Leah closed her eyes again, this time keeping them closed until the voice returned. Springing from the couch, she hurried into Hector's bedroom.

"Wake up, Hector," she said as she shook him gently. "Come on, amigo, open your eyes."

Hector's eyes fluttered and it took him a moment to understand it was Leah at his side. "What is wrong?" he asked, letting her help him to sit up.

"It's Tan. He's hurt."

"Did you have a dream?"

"More than a dream, Hector, more than a vision. He is calling me."

Hector saw the fear in her eyes; he knew, whatever it was that she saw, it was clearly a vision. "Where is he, Leah? Do you know?"

"Yes. He's behind the waterfall, in the cave where we hid our packs."

"Is he hurt badly?" asked Hector.

"No, but he is bleeding. I can smell his blood."

Hector did not question her last statement; there were some things he knew better than to doubt. "What do you want to do?"

Her mouth knew before her head. "I'm going to the huaca."

"Now? It's the middle of the night, Leah!" he protested.

She shook her head. "It's closer to morning than to midnight but the moon is still up. I can find my way."

Hector wanted to argue the point, but instead, he took her hands in his. "Take the gun from the drawer. Make sure it is loaded and take extra bullets. And wear regular clothes. And boots. ¿*Comprende*?" Leah nodded and hurried into the other room to dress. By the time she was finished, Hector was standing beside his bed in a bathrobe. "Take this," he said, handing her a thick wool sweater.

Leah slipped the garment on and let the hood settle over her hastily braided hair. "I'll be back as soon as I can." Grabbing the flashlight from Hector's nightstand, she ran out the door.

The moon was high enough to keep Leah from switching on the flashlight. She ran along the path as quickly as she dared; the sound of her own footfall seemed deafeningly loud in the night. The adrenaline rush kept her from tiring and she easily maintained a steady pace. Even though much of the path had been obliterated, she trusted her instinct to keep her headed in the right direction. Tan's voice seemed to stay with her, a soft whisper in her ear to guide her steps.

∿ ⎌ ∾

Tan knew he was weak from the loss of blood, yet he did not slow his progress. From behind the waterfall, he could see Lubrano's fire, but he could not see the man. Quietly, he moved to the place where the waterfall met the dry land and dropped to his knees. Crawling into the brush, Tan positioned himself so he could see Lubrano sitting at the fire. He waited for a few moments, until he could steel himself against the pain, and then slowly he walked toward the fire.

Lubrano heard the rustle of the grass. "Nardo?" he called out.

Tan sucked in his breath. "You are alone, Lubrano," Tan answered.

Lubrano struggled to his feet, the gun in his hand glinted in the fire.

"You are a dead man, Indio." He fired in what he thought was the direction of the voice, but the only sound to come back was the echo of the ricochet off the rock walls of the pool. "You will not live to see the moon rise again!" shouted Lubrano, trying to draw him out.

"Neither will your friend Nardo. He's dead."

"You do not frighten me, Indio. You will not win this battle." He fired a second shot into the darkness.

Tan's voice came from a new direction. "You must find me to kill me, Lubrano," he drawled, mocking him.

"I know about the emeralds, Indio. We all know about your private little mine."

"Are they worth your life, Vincente Lubrano?"

The voice was very close. Lubrano spun around in the sand. "Face me like a man, not a boy. Are you too afraid to show your face?"

"And have you blow it off with your toy?" taunted Tan from a new location. A third shot rang out. "You missed again, Lubrano."

Lubrano's sweat trickled down his forehead and into his eyes. Moving away from the fire, he tried to hear Tan's footfall in the grass. "You are noisy for a jungle boy, Indio." He fired toward the huaca itself.

Tan's harsh laughter seemed closer, but still he could not be seen. "And you are getting careless, little man. Keep playing with your toy; it will not save you." The fifth shot whizzed too close to Tan for comfort and he moved quickly in another direction. He let Lubrano stew in the silence for a few moments while he secreted himself in the brush.

His hand was beginning to shake; Lubrano stared down at the trembling gun. He wondered if he had hit his target a second time. There had been no shout of pain, no sound of a body falling in the brush. Tightening his grip, he tried to move in a crouch, but the injured leg buckled and he fell clumsily to the sand. Something whistled past his ear and splashed in the water. Lubrano rolled and fired in the direction from which the rock had come.

Tan did not waste a precious second. Stepping out of the brush, he stood over Lubrano, his knife glinting in the firelight. "Your toy is useless, Lubrano. Stand and meet your enemy like a man."

With a roar, Lubrano charged across the sand, arms extended, and launched himself at Tan. They tumbled to the ground, intent on destroying each other. Tan's knife sliced through the fabric of Lubrano's shirt; blood spurted from the wound, covering them both with sticky ooze. Lubrano's western clothing was easy to grab and Tan made use of that, hauling the man up by the shirt before slamming him into the sand. But the blood made his hands slippery and he lost his hold, giving Lubrano a moment of advantage.

The wiry Peruvian grabbed hold of Tan's hair and twisted as Tan flipped over. Jabbing his bare elbows back into Lubrano's chest, Tan forced the unwanted hands to loose their grasp. Lubrano grabbed Tan's sash to pull him back before he could turn over again. He threw himself on Tan's back, his nails raking across naked flesh causing welts to rise and weep blood. Tan grunted in pain at the same time he rose up to throw his attacker off his back. This time, he was able to turn and he lunged at Lubrano, his hands open and ready to close around the man's throat.

Wet with blood, Lubrano's arms shot up through Tan's and broke the hold. Sand flew as he twisted himself away from Tan and onto his feet. Despite the pain, he leapt at Tan, but again, Tan was ready for him. Springing up as Lubrano came down, Tan grabbed his face, twisted, and snapped the Peruvian's neck. Lubrano's eyes opened wide, but did not close again.

He was holding Lubrano in his hands; Tan did not dump him on the sand. Gently, he laid his enemy so that his face was away from the fading face of Mamaquilla. Tan took a step away from the body and dropped to his knees, his arms extended. He saw the blood covering his hands and arms and he did not care whether it was his or Lubrano's. With a piercing wail, he called to Mamaquilla. "I have desecrated your sacred place, *Mamatai!*" he cried. When he said, "Forgive me," it was barely a murmur before he crumpled face down on the sand beside the water.

∽ ⊖ ∾

The most painful, terrible sound Leah had ever heard shattered the stillness of the night. Quickening her pace, she drove herself as hard as she could, no longer caring if her steps made a sound. Time seemed to stand still as she traversed the last miles to the huaca, but she was unaware of the distance. When she finally heard the familiar rushing of the water, the face of Mamaquilla had gone and the night sky had already started to lighten.

She saw, in that thin light, two bodies on the sand. She cried out as she ran past the clothed figure of Lubrano to throw herself beside her husband. The sickening, sweet smell of blood hovered over Tan and when she saw how it covered his back, she clamped her hand over her mouth. Swallowing back the bitter taste that rose in her throat, she reached out to touch Tan. She felt the steady rise and fall of his breathing beneath her fingers and only then did she dare whisper his name.

"I am alive, Qewa Ñawi," rasped Tan; his eyes remained closed.

"Lubrano?" she whispered, afraid to look at the other body.

"Dead."

"Shhh, my heart. Lie still." Leah pulled her handkerchief from her pocket and wet it in the pool. Gently, she lifted Tan's head and let the water dribble into his mouth. Without getting up, she began to slowly wash the blood from his body.

෨ ⊖ ෬

She sat with his head in her lap until the face of Inti lit the jungle. Finally, Tan's eyes opened and she helped him to sit.

"I am not hurt badly," he told her, although his eyes said he was in pain. Struggling, Tan rose to his feet and faced the water. He opened his arms slowly before he walked into the water. Tan did not swim, but remained in the pool long enough to let the water cleanse his body completely. When he emerged, he silently walked to the waterfall and disappeared behind the curtain. He came out cradling Nardo in his arms. As gently as he had with Lubrano, he laid the second body on the sand. "Find peace in your final rest," he murmured as if they would understand. "May your god forgive you for what you have done to the people."

෨ ⊖ ෬

The steady whir of a helicopter broke the morning silence. Tan and Leah stood at the pool and waited until someone appeared on the top of the cliff. Both were relieved when Paolo's voice rang out over the water. "I'm with the Federales," he called. "We're coming down."

It took a while, but at last, Paolo arrived with three men in military garb. "Hector telephoned as soon as you left, Leah," he explained. "I figured it best to bring these guys along."

"A wise move," agreed Tan. He watched the soldiers examine the bodies still lying in the sand.

Paolo introduced the leader of the group as Colonel Suarez. The man seemed almost relieved to find Lubrano dead and was satisfied with Tan's explanation of self-defense. He took a statement from Tan, then returned to where his men were preparing to remove the corpses.

"There's room in there for you," said Paolo when the soldiers started back with the bodies.

"No, thank you. We will meet you at the clinic."

"Are you strong enough to walk?" Leah asked him.

Tan nodded. Limping slightly, he left her standing in the sand while he disappeared behind the waterfall one last time. When he emerged, he was carrying her pack. Tan handed Leah hers, waited for her to slip the straps over her shoulder, then began walking.

No words passed between them as they made their way through the jungle toward Hector's clinic. Leah kept a pace behind him, giving Tan the space he needed to sort through the tumult of emotion raging within. Without being told, she could palpably feel his struggle and although she yearned to comfort him, she dared not. Only when he was ready would he tell her what had happened at the place he considered most sacred.

Rain began to fall as they walked. At first, it was a friendly rain, shrouding the jungle in a fine mist, enveloping Tan and Leah in its gentle embrace, but after a while, the droplets grew fat, drenching them to the skin. Tan's bare feet made slapping sounds in the mud; Leah's shod ones were soon squishing uncomfortably in her boots. When she saw a fallen log, she stopped to remove the offending footwear.

Suddenly, Tan realized he no longer heard the steady, second footfall that had been unconsciously pacing his speed. He halted and turned, but he could not see Leah through the rain. With desperate anguish, he cried out her name.

"I'm right here," she answered from not far behind him.

Tan ran to her, his broad feet splashing mud up his legs. Reaching her, he gathered her into his arms and crushed her against his chest. "Do not disappear like the spirits of the winds," he murmured, "I thought I had lost you."

Leah's soft laugh caressed his ear; she kissed the tender spot at the base of his throat. "You cannot lose me so easily, my husband." She turned her face up to his and the rain made little rivers along the contours.

His mouth crashed down on hers, possessing it with ferocity and tenderness mingled together with the rain. His tongue sought hers and he sucked strength from inner source. As if the rain could wash away the pain as it washed their bodies, they melted into each other, a single being to be washed clean of the horror of the night.

⚬ ⊖ ⚬

The skies were still thick with clouds and gray mist when Tan and Leah walked out of the jungle. Hector, sitting outside his house in the shelter of his little wooden porch, saw them and waved before he slowly got to his feet. "Are you hurt?" he called when he noticed the way Tan supported himself against Leah's small frame, his limp having worsened during the trek through the jungle.

"It is nothing but a flesh wound, janpeq," answered Tan.

Once inside the clinic, Hector examined the line across Tan's buttock where the bullet had torn flesh. Fresh blood still oozed from the wound. "You could use a couple of stitches, my friend," said Hector. "Lie on your belly on the table. Good thing I can sew with my left hand."

Tan scowled, but did as he was told. "This is a most undignified position, Hector."

Leah hid a giggle behind her hand; she could see the hard line of Tan's jaw grow harder as he awaited the sharp stab of Hector's needle. "Hold my hand," she offered.

"I'd prefer you not watch my humiliation," he grumbled although he knew she would stay no matter what he said.

"Close your mouth and lie still, Tan," ordered Hector. "This will sting for just a moment." As gently as he could, he washed the dirt from around the wound, then sprayed it with a topical anesthetic. He muffled a laugh when Tan clenched his buttocks at the sudden cold. He barely felt it when the janpeq injected him with a second anesthetic. Deftly, Hector plied his needle and closed the gash into a neat, thin line. "I'd almost prefer you stayed out of western clothing for a while, but unfortunately, that will not be possible. You can't go walking through Lima's airport in a breechclout."

"Actually," teased Leah, "he's one of the few people I know who could probably get away with it." She rested her hand on the uninjured side of his rump.

Tan growled again, but let his head fall onto his arms. Hector motioned to Leah, and after she covered him with a blanket, she left him to sleep.

"He's lost a fair amount of blood," said Hector as they stepped outside the clinic, "but he'll be fine. You, on the other hand, should get out of those wet clothes before you catch a chill."

Leah did not argue with him. When Hector was right, he was right.

CHAPTER 41

The district authorities arrived at the clinic, demanding to see the Indio killer. Leah stood at a short distance away while Hector explained he was asleep, but they were in no mood to wait for him to awaken. Despite Hector's protests, they ordered him to bring Tan out.

Tan emerged from the clinic wrapped in the same blanket Leah had put over him. His face was still pale, but his eyes were clear and alert. "You have the bodies?" he asked in a strong voice.

"Yes. The Federales brought them out in the helicopter. What happened to them?" asked the inspector general.

"I killed them."

"Just like that?"

Tan snorted; he did not like the way the inspector general was eyeing him. "They tried to kill me. They also planned to blow up Paolo's plane with the doctor and my wife aboard."

As if noticing her for the first time, the inspector general stared at Leah. "This is *your* wife?"

"Yes."

"You are not...Peruvian." It was not a question.

"*Soy una Americana*," Leah replied. She moved to stand beside Tan.

"Your passport please, señora."

Leah looked suspiciously at him, then ambled slowly toward the house to retrieve her passport from her bag. She knew she had been, if only momentarily, dismissed.

When she was out of earshot, the inspector general turned to Hector. "Is this the grass-eyed woman?" he asked, "the one the locals are in an uproar about?"

"Yes," replied Hector.

The inspector general let out a thin whistle. "Barrantes called her the green-eyed bruja. She doesn't look like a witch to me." He studied Tan for a moment, stroking his chin as he stared at the tall Indian. "You, then, are the one who left." Again, it was not a question.

For a long moment, neither Tan nor Hector relented in their hard glare at the inspector general. The three men with him shifted uncomfortably from one foot to another. Finally, when the inspector general spoke again, it was with greater deference. "My apologies to you and your wife, Señor Villac-Quilla. We were not told you were the ...ah...Indio... in the jungle."

"I was the *only* Indio in the yunka," spat Tan in Quechua. He drew himself up to the fullest measure of his height and looked down at the Peruvian official. "My people have gone far from this place of blood and destruction. You will not see them again."

Leah returned, the passport in her hand. She stood beside Tan and was reassured when his arm encircled her shoulder. When she held out the document for the inspector general, he waved it away.

"That will not be necessary, Señora Villac-Quilla. I already know what I need to know." He ordered his men back to the Land Rover. "Again, Señor Villac-Quilla, my sincerest apologies." He bowed briefly, but courteously toward Tan.

"What was that all about?" asked Leah when the inspector general drove off.

"It would seem, my dear Señora Villac-Quilla," mused Hector with a wry grin, "that someone desired to arrest your groom."

Tan was puzzled. "Then why didn't he arrest me?"

"My best guess, Tan," Hector said after a moment, "is that Francisco Gutiérrez is your protector. That man has more connections than the telephone company."

❧ ◎ ❧

Inside the house, Hector's old radio was crackling away. Hurrying to the table, he picked up the microphone and answered the call. "On my way in. Over," said Paolo's voice through the static.

"We're ready when you are. Over." Hector flipped the switch. "He'll be here soon, *mis hijos*. It's time to pull ourselves together." Hector went to the table and sat down. He watched Tan lower himself gingerly in the chair. When they were seated, he pulled a wad of paper from his shirt pocket and set it in the middle of the table. "Now that you are married, there are some details which must be handled." He pulled off a single sheaf and slid it toward Leah. "This, Mrs. Villac-Quilla, is a letter of introduction for Banco Popular de Peru. I would strongly advise that while you are in Lima, you go to the bank and become a signer on these accounts." He handed her a second sheet. "It's not that I don't trust your husband's most astute judgment in all matters financial, but his relatively new knowledge has gaps. As for you, Na-Tan Manco, am I correct in assuming you are carrying another, somewhat larger cache of emeralds in your pack?"

Tan shrugged his broad shoulders. "Is this a problem?"

"Only if you want to sell them in the United States," replied Hector dryly. He handed Tan a square, folded document. "This is yours, courtesy of Francisco Gutiérrez." He waited while Tan flattened the paper. "You are the sole owner of the land and waters of the second huaca. Don Francisco felt it was in the best interest of all concerned if the huaca was in private hands. If you read the document carefully, you will find the matter of the small emerald vein settled quite legally. You will need this when you pass through customs in Miami. When you are ready to sell the gems, make certain you carry the document. At any other time, keep it in the safe at your bank in Minnesota...with the stones."

Tan remained speechless for a long moment. "I don't know what to say. This is more than I ever expected...or wanted, Hector."

"Then don't say anything. It's best if few people know," replied Hector seriously. "I told you long ago you were a wealthy man in your own right. Now it is up to you how you use that wealth."

☙ ⊖ ☙

After a grueling week of testimony in Lima, they were more than ready to head home. Don Francisco made certain Tan spoke to everyone who had any connection to the situation; by week's end, Tan felt somewhat assured that his people would be, for the time being, safe in their new home. Before they left, Leah suggested that two of the emeralds be sold in order to provide Hector with more than enough funds to move the clinic to the new location. Don Francisco handled the sale, with Tan and Leah present so they would know how it was to be done properly; the cash was put into an account that could be drawn upon from Piura. Satisfied he had done all he could, Tan announced it was time to leave Peru.

∞ ⊖ ∞

On the plane, Leah tried to sleep, but could not. She knew something was bothering Tan, judging by his uncommon silence as he stared out the window at the contours of South America. Finally, Leah sat up and took his hand. "Can you tell me what's on your mind?"

Without answering, Tan leaned forward and pulled a package from his bag. "The Coya gave this to me. It comes to me from my grandfather."

"What is it?"

"I do not know. She said I was not to look at it until I was away from my home." He smiled sadly. "I am afraid to open it."

Instinctively, she knew what lay within the broad leaf wrapper. "There is nothing to be afraid of, Tan."

He looked at her quizzically, but did not respond. With a gentle tug, he released the knot and removed the wrapper. "A book? My people do not have such things." The cover was crafted of hard leather, the type the people used for sandals. Carefully, Tan opened the cover. The pages, grayish yellow and rough in texture, were obviously handmade. "How did he do this?" Tan asked Leah.

Fingering the top, blank sheet, Leah told him she thought it was made with bits of wool and soaked leaves. "Like felt for hats, but thinner. He must have worked hard to find a combination that worked. Turn the page," she urged softly. When he did, they both gasped.

"Hebrew?" he asked, staring at the precise letters.

Leah took the book from him and studied the first page. "It's Yiddish, Tan, the language they spoke in the ghettos in Europe. It's really a form of German."

"Can you read it?"

Leah sucked in her breath. She could speak Yiddish better than she could read it, and this was written in cursive, not block print as she was used to. The letters were the same as Hebrew, but the language was so completely different. Slowly, awkwardly, she began to translate the text.

> *My name is Yitzchak Aaron Rabinowitz, son of Nathan and Ruth, husband of Sarah Rivke, father of Moshe Yacov and Shmuel Chaim, all of us from Lodz. They are all dead yet I am alive. I escaped, I fled, I crossed the ocean, I began to walk. To walk away from the madness. I do not know how long I walked. I did not keep count of the days nor the weeks nor the months. The longer I walked, the more determined I became to start a new life somewhere where no one ever heard of Jews and Nazis, death camps and ovens. It is enough that I remember...*

Leah looked at Tan. "Your name would be Nathan Rabinowitz in the world your grandfather left behind. It's funny, my mother's family was from a place not far from Lodz."

"Where is this place?"

"Poland." She pulled the airline magazine from the pouch before her and flipped through it until she found a world map. "Here," she said, pointing to a spot in Eastern Europe. "This is Poland and Lodz is here."

Tan stared at the map, then at Leah's hand, so pale beside his own. "I do not look like you, nor do my brothers nor my sister, my father nor my uncle."

"For whatever reasons She had, Mamaquilla made you all to favor your grandmother's side." She smiled at him. "It's not so bad; we'll have beautiful children."

He raised her fingers to his lips and kissed each one, then placed his hand over hers atop her flat belly. "This son will have your eyes, Qewa Ñawi."

"You know?" she asked quietly.

"Did you think I did not know?" A slow grin crossed his face. "Foolish chinan! Have you learned nothing in the jungle?"

GLOSSARY

Quechua	English
aclla	chosen one
acllacuna	"chosen women" who served in the ancient temples
Ama sua, ama llulla, ama quella!	Don't steal, don't lie, don't be lazy (traditional greeting)
Apu-Rimac	chief sage
apacheta	sacred place
ari	Yes
awila	grandmother
Ayar Masonsoré	brother of the jaguar
Ayar Kuntar	brother of the condor
ayllu	village
capac	chieftans
c'coto-c'coto	attar of flowers ground into a paste
chaca	rope footbridge
chacra	planting field
chasqui	messenger or runner
chicha	a drink similar to beer.
chinan	acolyte, student of the collahuaya
collahuaya	village healer
conopa	small statue, usually one that fits in the palm of the hand

Quechua	English
Coya	"great lady," a title of respect when addressing the Mamacuna
hua'amuata	protégé, literally spirit daughter
huaca	shrine usually a pile of carefully placed stones
huahuan	daughter (formal)
huasipascuna	unmarried or "forgotten" girl
Illapa-Illi	Thunder god
illaq	traveler
Imaynallam kashianki?	Are you all right?
Inti	Sun god
Intip Raimi.	Solstice ceremony
Janajpachallacta	Village in the Sky
janpeq	healer; the doctor
jonchi	smoke from the sacred fire
kuntar	condor
llautu	fillet, headband
machai	burial marker
Mama'amuata	spirit mother
Mamacuna	High Priestess
Mamaquilla	Moon goddess
mamatai	my mother
mana	no
monsonsoré	jaguar
mita	sacred duty
mulkan	a wanderer in search of knowledge
ñan	foot path
Pachamama	Mother Earth
paicha	a tassel; usually attached to a hat
panta ñan	false path
puna	flat, grassland plateau
Qewa Ñawi	Grass eyed woman
Quampas hinallantaq	"same to you!" (traditional response)

Quechua	English
quena	wood flute
quipu	Knots; multi colored strings used to keep counting records
rimoc (rimac)	male elder council (plural)
sara mot'i	cooked ground corn, not unlike polenta
sinchi	first order capac
situa	gathering
taitai	father
taqui	the shufflng line dance
unachai	destiny
uchapa	sacred powders mixed for an offering
ususi	daughter (personal)
Villac-Umo	high priest
Viracocha	Great Creator God
wai-yaya	special dance for Mamaquilla
wawqesitu	little brother
yau	Hey!
Yau! Allinllanchu	Hey! How's it going?
yunka	rain forest

Made in the USA
Charleston, SC
01 February 2017